THE BOOK OF
AMERICAN TRADITIONS

THE BOOK

~ *of* ~

AMERICAN
TRADITIONS

Stories, Customs, and Rites of Passage to Celebrate Our Cultural Heritage

edited, with original selections and commentary, by Emyl Jenkins

CROWN PUBLISHERS, INC.
New York

Editor's Note: Those stories marked with an asterisk are original to this book.

Published by Crown Publishers, Inc., 201 East 50th Street, New York, New York 10022. Member of the Crown Publishing Group.

Random House, Inc. New York, Toronto, London, Sydney, Auckland
http://www.randomhouse.com/

CROWN is a trademark of Crown Publishers, Inc.

Printed in the United States of America
Book design by Susan Hood

Library of Congress Cataloging-in-Publication Data
The book of American traditions: stories, customs, and rites of passage to celebrate our cultural heritage/ edited, with original selections and commentary, by Emyl Jenkins.—1st ed.
p.   cm.
1. Holidays—United States.   2. Rites and ceremonies—
United States.   3. United States—Social life and customs.
I. Jenkins, Emyl.
GT4803.A2B66 1996
391'.0973—dc20   96-25590
CIP

ISBN 0-517-70312-2

10   9   8   7   6   5   4   3   2   1

FIRST EDITION

For Bob, with love as we
embark on a new life
enriched by old traditions.

And Langdon, who lent
his youthful voice and
enthusiasm to these pages.

In memory of
Ken Sansone
and
Gay Crutchfield Birdsong

Contents

The Writer's Apology and Appeal to the Readers

IN ALL THINGS I YEARN FOR THE PAST.

Kenko, 1283–1350

"Dear Reader," wrote many eighteenth-century authors. Then they proceeded to apologize for omissions, shortcomings, and inadequacies in their books.

In today's politically correct world, I, who have spent years gathering the material in this book, yearn to begin: "Dear Reader," and apologize for all the omissions, shortcomings, and inadequacies of this book.

Readers I've never met and friends alike may reproach me: "But why didn't you include. . ." followed by that person's favorite tradition.

Some critics may chastise me for not writing a serious or scholarly enough book and for being too nostalgic and sentimental.

To the first group I say this: Everyone knows it is impossible to include each bit of material I have found. In the interest of space I have left out many of my own favorite traditions. And needless to say, there are thousands of wonderful traditions that I do not even know about.

To the second group I say: This is not a book about social history, nor is it intended to reflect our current political scene or demographics. This book is a collection of first-person recollections of traditions that capture the flavor of long-ago days and present times. For those who think traditions are fluff, like it or not, it is the good times, the sweet times, the happy times, that make us smile. Who among us wants to impose unhappiness, hardship, and tribulation on others?

To all who read this book I say, I hope you will take the time to share your traditions with me. I welcome receiving your stories and traditions.

OLD CUSTOMS! O! I LOVE THE SOUND,
HOWEVER SIMPLE THEY MAY BE;
WHATE'ER WITH TIME HATH SANCTION FOUND,
IS WELCOME, AND IS DEAR TO ME.
Old English poem

TRADITION! WE SCARCELY KNOW THE WORD
ANYMORE. WE ARE AFRAID TO BE EITHER PROUD OF
OUR ANCESTORS OR ASHAMED OF THEM.
Dorothy Day

THE BOOK OF
AMERICAN TRADITIONS

Introduction

— —

Why Traditions?

RING OUT THE OLD, RING IN THE NEW,
RING, HAPPY BELLS, ACROSS THE SNOW!

Alfred, Lord Tennyson,
In Memoriam

Were someone to ask me, I'd say I'm a thoroughly modern American woman.

I'm a divorced career woman who has worked hard to get where I am today. I love jetting from town to town. I don't mind being alone in hotel rooms. Before I remarried, not only did I pay for my own dinner but many times I paid for my date's. Furthermore, I know how to access the Internet!

Yes. I'd say I'm a thoroughly modern woman. Well, almost.

Many are the times when I call my grown kids on the telephone just to hear them say, "Hi, Mom." And I love old things. Family pieces are my most prized possessions. Most of all, if I ever *could* steal a day and not have it count, my dream would be to spend it taking a quiet walk in the woods with my husband of just a few months.

In other words, the life I lead and the life in my head are often at odds with each other.

That's the state I was in the day I found myself seated next to an unusually talkative gentleman on the flight from wherever I was to wherever I was going. That day I wanted to be where I wasn't: at home.

The stranger and I went through the usual niceties: name, current address, occupation, marital status, kids, previous residences.

We were ready to start in on the weather when suddenly, out

1

of nowhere, I heard myself asking, "Tell me. What's your favorite tradition?"

He sighed. Sat back in his seat. Closed his eyes for a moment.

"Picnics." He smiled. "I love picnics. We don't seem to have time for them much anymore, but when I was a little boy I thought going on a picnic with my family was the most fun in the world."

That's the thing about people. No matter where life takes us, we cherish the good times. We hold dear those traditions that bring back memories of carefree, heartwarming moments we shared with family, friends, neighbors, and sometimes people brought together just for that one occasion.

Oh, learned men poke fun at the sentimental and nostalgic. "Custom does often reason overrule," wrote the seventeenth-century satirist John Wilmot, the second earl of Rochester. Two hundred years later, Nietzsche hated tradition. "Every tradition grows ever more venerable —the more remote is its origin, the more confused that origin is," he said. In the twentieth century, the social critic Lewis Mumford described our nineteenth-century ancestors' lives as "the jolly and comfortable bourgeois tradition of the Victorian age, a state of mind composed of felt slipper and warm bellywash."

Nonetheless, colleges and universities give fellowships and grants to students to document and study our traditions. As the pages of this book testify, writers spin volumes reminiscing about their family traditions.

Why? Because traditions bind us together for a common good, especially in America.

"It's a family tradition," we say, regardless of our ethnic, religious, political, and national background or our family's makeup in these days of new and changing lifestyles.

What *difference* does it make that we have forgotten the specific origins of many of our traditions? What is *important* is that we have kept our traditions alive and that in America it is possible to do so, for time-honored traditions unite generations, one after the other, regardless of family origins.

Traditions are living things. They are part of all the people. They are the thoughts and the memories of the past. They are filled with the spirit of everyone who celebrated them in the past. As long as traditions live, so will the laughter and joy of those who cherished them and passed them on.

But could we be in danger of losing these cherished bonds?

Look around.

Our children often spend more time sitting alone in front of a computer or TV screen than they do playing and chatting with one another.

In the workplace we are told to send abbreviated e-mail messages instead of talking over the phone or, heaven forbid, meeting face to face.

Gone are many of the casual, friendly conversations once carried on in neighborhood post offices and banks. Automated machines spit out stamps and cash these days. A computer-generated voice, perfunctory and without feeling or caring commands us, "Have a good day."

Could our traditions be the next to go? Never.

People instinctively remember the past. As long as human beings cherish and long to share their richest remembrances and happiest times, traditions will endure.

Think how often you sprinkle your conversation with mentions of the past. "I remember," "When I was young," "Years ago," "I'll never forget," you begin. Occasionally the romantics among us even say "Once upon a time" or "Lo ͜ ago."

As we search for a sense of direction and permanence in our hurried lives today, traditions provide an anchor, a guidepost. Traditions, like wisdom, spring from history and people, not from the machines that rule our lives today. They are, as one person told me, replays of life.

Traditions nourish our spirit. They soothe that vague sense of unfulfillment that nags at each one of us. The memory of those times can be as refreshing as a whiff of springtime, as restorative as a good night's sleep.

To that end, I have gathered in these pages stories, quotes, poems, memories, and activities past and present. These selections are not meant to be read all in one sitting. As with all anthologies, the pieces will be most enjoyed if you browse through them according to your mood, the time of year (since many traditions are seasonal), and your needs at the moment. Some of the stories will enrich your present life. Others will fuel your dreams for the future. Just remember: our hopes for tomorrow are rooted in the past.

When reading these pages remember also that the selections span the life of our country—from Anne Bradford's seventeenth-century love poem to the childrens' pieces written only a short time ago. In these last years of the twentieth century, some of our ancestors' writings have references and mentions which we, today, call "politically incorrect." We cannot rewrite history or change words, nor is it our place to. Each essay, poem, or book is written within the historical context of the time. Soon, we, too, will be history.

Simply put, if our brave ancestors could survive the unknown future, so can we. To make the unknown easier to face, we should glean the best from the past and carry it forward, just as they did.

What better proof of this heartfelt longing could there be than these words of one child of change, Diane Wilson, who writes: "How can I give my children traditions to carry on into their adulthood? There is no Grandma in their life to welcome them at the front door with smiles and warm embraces; there won't be homemade noodles or savory desserts, much less anyone swaying with a spoon and any cousins to chase or swap stories with. But there will be a smile on Grandpa's face as we pile out of our subcompact Mazda after that 750-mile trip in 14 hours. There will be a turkey dinner with all the trimmings. There will be an assortment of semi-related family and friends. There will be plenty of love and caring, hugging and sharing, and thankfulness. And of course, there will be that 750-mile dash back to North Carolina—how much more tradition can I hope for?"

Like the tolling bells that ring out the old and ring in the new and celebrate the rites of life, traditions unite our memories of the past with our hope for the future.

Why traditions? Because children and adults, the poorest and the richest of us alike, yearn to make life better, not just for ourselves but for future generations as well. Traditions do that. Traditions link the past with the future. They give us pleasant memories, and they give us hope.

I learned this each time I asked the simple question, "What is your favorite tradition?" I asked everyone—friends, neighbors, writers, children, people I met on airplanes or waiting in line at the post office. (Yes, I start up conversations with complete strangers.) Almost always the answers were recounted by smiling lips and dreamy eyes. Almost always I was told a tradition that not only had been handed down in that person's family but was being continued and that would be carried into the future. Just read what today's young people of all experiences cherish and hope to pass on to their own children.

―‿―

It was hard for me to think of a family tradition, mostly because I didn't know what it meant. I'm only seven, so I had to ask my dad what family traditions we have. He said that my great-grandfather gave them to my grandfather, then he gave them to my father, and now I have them. Dad said they are called the three H's: honesty, hard work, and happiness. He says I have all of them already.

I am honest with him.

I work hard in school.

I laugh a lot.

Dad says the three *H*'s will help me when I get bigger, too.

You can have a family tradition and not even know it, like me. I am glad my dad gave me three. I hope I can keep them.

Brent F. Butterworth, elementary school

Ever since I can remember, my family has had the tradition of "Kiss and Tuck." "Kiss and Tuck" is what my brother and I call my mom and dad giving us a good-night kiss and tucking us in our beds at night.

My dad would go into my brother's room, and my mom would go in my room. They would kiss us good night and cross the hall. My dad would then come in my room, and my mom would go in my brother's room. Then and only then could we feel like we could go to sleep.

Now that my parents are divorced, my brother and I argue about who gets kissed first. When we finally get it straight, we are restless and wide awake. As long as we get kissed good night, though, we can go to sleep.

Without getting kissed good night, I cannot go to sleep. I feel like something is missing. I'll toss and turn in my bed till I finally fall asleep. Even my morning is off-track.

I think I'll look back on "Kiss and Tuck" when I'm older and I'll see how special it was to me.

Kelli Triplett, middle school

Today I shared our family tradition with my second grade class. We have a large coffee can and we cut a hole in the lid. We leave it in a place where everyone can reach. All year, each time something good happens, we put a note in the can. When we have Thanksgiving dinner we open the can to see the many reasons for us to give thanks.

Ella Richardson, elementary school

The tradition started a long time ago. I think it was my great-great-grandmother who started the tradition.

She went to an antique store and bought a black box. The lady at the store told her that the box was used by another family. The mother of the family got her children to write a letter to themselves and then put it in the box. They did this when they were eleven years old. The children were not allowed to read their letters until they were eighteen.

My great-great-grandmother thought that was a good idea. She started this tradition with her children. She told her children to write a letter to themselves explaining what they did for fun, what they liked to eat, what they thought of their parents, and pretty much anything that was important to them at the time.

A few years passed and the children had totally forgotten about the letters and the box.

Before you knew it, the children were eighteen and my great-great-grandmother got the box and let the children open it and read the letters they wrote to themselves.

The tradition has been passed down, and now I am about to read the letter I wrote to myself when I was eleven.

Sam Brewer, high school

The Christmas holidays are very special at our house. The family tradition of helping others is now in the third generation.

My great-grandfather started his tradition years ago. He was a coal miner and a farmer. He worked long hard hours to support a family of eleven. He always had enough food to share with families who had none.

The winters were cold with lots of snow. On Christmas Eve, my great-grandfather and great-grandmother would spend hours preparing the boxes of food they delivered to the families.

This act of kindness made their Christmas very special. This tradition was passed down to my grandmother. She starts baking breads, cookies, fudge, and cakes early in December. On Christmas Eve she delivers baskets of her baked goods plus fruit to the families she has picked to help.

The children in the families get gloves and socks to keep their hands and feet warm. My grandmother still carries on this tradition. Now my mother has started to help with this tradition. Now the tradition is passed down to me. Our family believes you should always help the less fortunate.

Chris Newton, elementary school

I have many traditions, but the one that I think is the best, and my favorite, is I Got You Day. I know when I say "I Got You Day," you probably wonder what in the world is I Got You Day. Well, I am going to tell you. . . .

My tradition is special to me. I Got You Day is when my parents adopted me. It's like having two birthdays; I have I Got You Day on March 6, and I also have my real birthday. The reason I have my traditions then is because that is when the adoption was final. My first tradition was March 6, 1984, and we have celebrated every year since. The way we celebrate this day is to buy a cake and ice cream. We eat it, of course. Then I open my present that my parents give me.

I am grateful to have parents like mine, most of the time. I think it is wonderful for them to start a tradition like ours. I would have never known that I was adopted, because I look just like my mom. Having I Got You Day makes my adoption extra special.

Carrie L. Eury, middle school

Today my family and I observed Desert Storm–Desert Shield Day. The reason we celebrated this day is we are lucky our mother came home safely two years ago. We put up banners, had a big dinner, and played family games. My mother received special treatment. We told jokes. My family also took a minute to remember those who died.

My mom told us stories. We told her of how we felt that time when she was on the front lines. We all sat on the couch and drank hot cocoa. I got a warm feeling inside today. My whole body had a touch of love.

My brothers and I tried our best not to fight today. We all played a game where someone sits in a chair and everyone else said something nice about the person in the chair. That was my favorite game. Another game was where we had an object. Someone hid the object and they gave us all these clues. We had to try to find the object.

My favorite part was the big dinner.

My mom loves the tradition. So do I. I'm going to keep this tradition.

Kathy Wells, middle school

Every year my grandparents from my father's side fly down to our house for Thanksgiving. I don't get to see them much because they live in New York, so the week they are here is very special to me!

Six years ago, after my parents' divorce, I didn't expect to be sharing Thanksgiving with my grandparents anymore, but I found out that wasn't going to be the case.

The next Thanksgiving, after the divorce, my grandparents came to our house for Thanksgiving. They even wanted to stay with us—my mother, brother, and me—instead of my dad. I thought this was a little weird, but it didn't matter. I had everything I wanted.

My grandparents still fly down every year. I get to see them, so it means a lot to me. Even though I was younger when my parents divorced, I should have realized that a divorce would never come between my grandparents and me.

Nothing can destroy that tradition and the love it brings to me and my grandparents!

Robert Rice, high school

＊＊

Traditions begun in childhood are more than just experiences that we fondly remember. They can shape our character and become chapters in our personal and family histories. They are worth passing on as we learn from these two closing reminiscences that were written by teachers and shared with their students and us.

I can remember in elementary school we always made things. One year around the Christmas holiday my class made ornaments out of salt dough. I was so excited. I decided I was going to make my mamma a Santa Claus ornament. We made those ornaments, then we painted them.

I painted his suit red and white and his skin was painted brown, just like mine. I can remember being so proud of it. I took the Santa home and gave it to my mother to hang on the tree. She hung it right in the front where it could be seen.

It has become a tradition for my mother to hang that "little black Santa" right in the front of the tree. When our family gathers for Christmas at my mother's, we are reminded of the story of the ornament I made for my mother. Even after twenty years, that ornament brings joy to our family.

Martha J. Moody

＊＊

My brother, sister, and I grew up on a small farm. We knew the reasons and merits of hard work in tobacco to earn money for school clothes and college funds. Also we raised large vegetables—canning, freezing, selling, and giving away vegetables. This meant being in the fields early and often working until dark. This hard work was required. We children understood why. It was our livelihood.

What we kids did not understand was Mama's choosing to have another garden—one-half acre of *Hemerocallis,* or day lilies. We hated the extra work that cut into our free time. We had to weed, fertilize, hoe, and then plant new varieties each year. This went on throughout childhood and didn't make sense to us.

We are grown now. We purchase our children's clothing. Nobody does farm labor. But we have large vegetable gardens. My brother, sister, and I all have beautiful *Hemerocallis* gardens.

We weed, fertilize, hoe, and take trips with our mother each spring to purchase new *Hemerocallis* to increase our gardens.

We know joy now. It's a beautiful tradition. Mama's love of life and plants and God blooms for us daily in our day lilies.

Thank you, Mama.

Carolyn Hudson

LET TODAY EMBRACE THE PAST WITH REMEMBRANCE
AND THE FUTURE WITH LONGING.

Kahlil Gibran

PART ONE

HOLIDAYS AND CELEBRATIONS

CHAPTER 1

Thanksgiving

WE GATHER TOGETHER

~ *Raise the Song of Harvest Home* ~

*EMYL JENKINS

For most of us Thanksgiving holds the sweetest, most pleasant memories of all our holidays. Its history is rich, its meaning poignant. Its selfless spirit asks nothing in return. Indeed, in the olden days Thanksgiving far eclipsed Christmas. Yet Thanksgiving, too, is changing. It took my young adult son, Langdon, to show me just how much.

The Thanksgivings of my grade school years were nippy, wintry days. All fall, from my desk near the second-story window at Forest Hills Elementary School in Danville, Virginia, I would watch nature's rich gold and tawny red colors slowly fade away until only late November's brown leaves dotted the trees outside.

After school I didn't dawdle much on my walk home, the way I had in September and October. Each day grew a little shorter and colder, and soon it became dark before five. At night as I lay toasty warm under a thick down quilt (we didn't call them comforters in those days), the roar of the coal furnace was a reminder that if Jack Frost had yet to spread his white blanket across the ground, he soon would. And many mornings I walked to school in a gray mist.

Back then there were no teachers' workdays or other breaks, so Thanksgiving vacation was special indeed. Our spirits were always high when we returned to our fourth grade classroom after lunch on Wednesday, the last day of school. We knew what would happen next.

Standing tall before us, Miss Stone would announce there would be no more lessons. She would tell us to pack up our books. Then she would say the same words that we had heard the year before and the year before that. "Now, children, you may take out your crayon boxes."

Every year we created a traditional Thanksgiving scene. With great gusto we drew Pilgrims dressed in tall, pitch-black hats and greatcoats and Indians wearing bright feathers and colorful blankets. In the foreground we added plump turkeys and orange pumpkins. By the time the bell rang we each had a masterpiece to take home for our parents to enjoy.

But that year something *different* happened after lunch. Miss Stone stood at the front of the room, book in hand. "Class, take out your history books and follow along as I read to you," she began. . . .

I could hardly wait until dinnertime came to tell my parents what I had learned that afternoon. Over supper, in my best grade school manner, I chirped, "Did you know that America's first Thanksgiving was in 1619 on the shores of the James River when the good ship *Margaret* landed?" I babbled on and on.

I will never forget my Massachusetts-born father's reply.

"Now listen here," he said in his crisp Boston accent, putting down his knife and fork. "Virginia has enough to be proud of. She doesn't need to claim the first Thanksgiving. Let's leave something for the rest of the country."

I recalled that 1950s day a couple of years ago.

A friend and I were enjoying a balmy, late fall day on the beautiful beaches of Saint Augustine, Florida, when she told me, "You *do* know that America's first Thanksgiving can be traced back to 1565 when Pedro Menéndez and his men disembarked right here and were welcomed by friendly Indians. The explorers gave the Indians clothing and beads from Europe, and then they feasted together."

"No, I didn't know," I replied.

My reaction was like my father's. Thanksgiving in 1565? Conquistadores? What happened to 1621 and the Pilgrims? I wondered.

And I remembered that fourth grade day again this year when the first wintry winds began whistling around my windowsills and the autumn leaves began rustling under my feet on my daily walk.

In my nostalgic mood, I thought to myself, When it comes down to it, what difference does it make *who* had the first Thanksgiving in America? Or where? Thanksgiving may be a wintry time, but it's also a time of warm feelings, a time of sharing. Thanksgiving is a time for giving thanks.

What *is* important, I told myself, is that in those three very distant and very different colonies there *was* a Thanksgiving, for it is hard to imagine three groups of people less alike than the Pilgrims, the Cavaliers, and the conquistadores.

The Pilgrims came to America seeking religious freedom. They were weary of the elaborate services and great ceremony of the Catholic and Episcopal churches in Europe and England. These people wanted a simple life free of frills and frivolity. They wanted to keep their religion and their lives pure.

The adventuresome and spirited Cavaliers were a different sort. They braved the seas to come to Virginia to make money for England and for themselves. They brought their Anglican religion with them, ceremony and all.

So did the sword-bearing, crusading conquistadores who came to Florida looking for cities paved with streets of gold to claim for Spain and the pope. Priests as well as soldiers were members of Menéndez's conquering army.

But all three groups had one thing in common.

Despite their differences, after crossing the vast ocean in little boats that were nowhere near as large as today's jets, they gave thanks. And in this foreign land, each group received a helping hand from the American Indians.

In no way did the native Indians and the European explorers resemble one another—not in their language, skin color, religion, or ways. Yet in each the human spirit came through. They each shared what they had.

To the Thanksgiving feast in Saint Augustine the conquistadores brought provisions left over from their long ocean journey—cheese, wine, salt, flour, bacon, dried figs and raisins, garlic, marmalade, even oil, vinegar, honey, and confections. The Indians contributed fresh food—raw, boiled, and roasted fish and oysters, and, of course, maize.

The Cavaliers could not have known about that celebration in 1619, nor could the Pilgrims in 1621.

My heart was so full with these thoughts that later, when preparing supper in the warmth of my cheerful yellow kitchen, outfitted with modern appliances and decorated with old things, I began humming, then singing, "Come, ye thankful people, come. Raise the song of harvest home. All is safely gathered in, ere the winter storms begin. . . ."

Suddenly my grown son, who had dropped by for a visit, poked his head into the kitchen.

"Talking to somebody?" Langdon asked.

"No, just singing a Thanksgiving song, 'Come, Ye Thankful People, Come.' "

"Don't remember that one." He shrugged. "The only Thanksgiving song I know is 'Alice's Restaurant.' "

What could I say? You see, my kids grew up in Raleigh, and every Thanksgiving Day since I can remember, WRDU 106 FM has played "Alice's Restaurant," Arlo Guthrie's song about peace, written in a turbulent time. That is how the station raises money to feed the hungry. Listening to "Alice's Restaurant" and pledging our contribution was a tradition as much a part of my family's Thanksgiving as eating turkey and dressing.

I smiled to myself.

What difference does it make whether the first Thanksgiving was in Florida or Virginia or Massachusetts?

What difference does it make if you hum "Come, Ye Thankful People, Come" or whistle along with "Alice's Restaurant"?

Sharing, like all of life's most important values, cannot be traced to one time, one event, one country, or one culture. What is essential is that the tradition be continued.

~ *Come, Ye Thankful People, Come* ~

H. ALFORD

Come, ye thankful people, come,
Raise the song of Harvest-home:
All is safely gathered in,
Ere the winter storms begin;
God, our Maker, doth provide
For our wants to be supplied;
Come to God's own temple, come,
Raise the song of Harvest-home.

All the world is God's own field,
Fruit unto His praise to yield;
Wheat and tares together sown,
Unto joy or sorrow grown:
First the blade, and then the ear,
Then the full corn shall appear:
Grant, O harvest Lord, that we
Wholesome grain and pure may be.

For the Lord our God shall come,
And shall take His harvest home;
From His field shall in that day
All offenses purge away;
Give His angels charge at last
In the fire the tares to cast,
But the fruitful ears to store
In His garner evermore.

Even so, Lord, quickly come
To Thy final Harvest-home;
Gather Thou Thy people in,
Free from sorrow, free from sin;
There, forever purified,
In Thy presence to abide:
Come, with all Thine angels, come,
Raise the glorious Harvest-home.

⁓ To Serve Turkey and Cranberry Sauce ⁓

EDWIN MITCHELL

Edwin Mitchell takes us back to the days of colonial New England where wild turkeys were abundant and cranberries grew wild. Sound familiar? And, according to him, the women did most of the work. Sound familiar? Do you know where the phrase "talk turkey" originated? And how did cranberries become part of our traditional Thanksgiving fare?

This sketch recalls firsthand accounts of the early Thanksgivings, which scholars will enjoy, and it brings high points of this revered celebration down through the years to the twentieth century for the rest of us to learn about. Most of all, Mitchell reminds us that no matter who celebrated the first Thanksgiving, we owe a debt of gratitude to New England for the tradition of giving thanks for our sustenance.

Thanksgiving has, of course, always been the time *par excellence* for food in New England, with roast turkey the traditional *pièce de résistance* of the feast. Even the Puritans forgot their fear of sensualism at Thanksgiving, abandoning themselves with gusto to the pleasures of the table, though there were times when the country was a desert island for food, and the colonists, like castaways, were in no danger of overeating.

There seems, however, to have been an abundance of provender at the first Pilgrim Thanksgiving at Plymouth in 1621, which was not an affair of a single day, but lasted a whole week and, contrary to what many persons think, was without any religious significance. It was simply a period of relaxation and recreation following the gathering of the first harvest.

Yet it could hardly have been a time of rest for the four women of the colony upon whom fell the burden of preparing the food for the week's festivities. There were only fifty-five English left in Plymouth at the time, but Chief Massasoit stalked in at the head of ninety braves, and these friendly redskins were entertained by the whites for three days. The Indians for their part contributed venison to the communal larder. As the quartet of colonial dames, assisted by a servant and some young Puritan maids, slaved to feed the six score men, the smell of the meat roasting over the open fires must have been good.

It is safe to say that enormous quantities of food were consumed, because the Indians were born gluttons capable of tumbling more victuals into themselves than anyone would think humanly possible; and the colonial men present, if one may judge by the inherited capacity of some of their descendants, likewise gave a satisfactory account of themselves. Anyhow, the shooting was good around Plymouth that fall, so there was plenty of food for all. This we know from a letter which Edward Winslow wrote to a friend in England on December 11, 1621, in which he said:

"Our harvest being gotten in, our governor sent four men on fowling that so we might after a special manner rejoice together after we had gathered the fruits of our labors. They four killed as much fowl as with a little help beside served the company about a week. At which time among other recreations we exercised our arms, many of the Indians coming amongst us, and among the rest their greatest king Massasoyt with some ninety men, whom for three days we entertained and feasted, and they went out and killed five deer which they brought and bestow'd on our governor, and upon the captains and others."

It is a pleasant picture which Winslow sketches of the Pilgrims at play after a year of unspeakable trials and hardships on the edge of the wilderness. Here is no group of long-faced men and women taking their pleasures sadly, but a lively band of people in holiday mood, indulging in feasting and in their favorite sports and pastimes.

Since Governor Bradford mentioned that "beside waterfoule there was great store of wild turkies" that fall, we may be certain that the men he sent out to make provision for the feast succeeded in bagging enough unsuspecting turkeys to make the tables groan.

Other writers of the period have told of the great flocks of wild turkeys that inhabited the oak and chestnut forests of New England. So common were they that in the 1730s dressed wild turkeys sold for only a penny and a half a pound in western Massachusetts. The price, of course, increased as the wild turkey population decreased, and by the close of the eighteenth century they were bringing fourpence per pound. In 1820, when these great game birds were rapidly vanishing, the price had risen to twelve and a half cents a pound and it became less common to see wild turkey wings used as hearth brushes in New England homes.

There is a delightful chapter in Brillat-Savarin's classic work on dining, *Physiologie du Gout,* in which the famous French gastronomist tells how he shot a wild turkey near Hartford, Connecticut, in the autumn of 1794. A refugee from the French Revolution, Brillat-Savarin while staying at Hartford was invited by an old farmer who lived in the backwoods to come and have some shooting. The farmer promised partridges, gray squirrels, and wild turkeys. Accordingly, one fine day in October the Frenchman and a friend, mounted on two hacks, rode out some five leagues from Hartford. Reaching their journey's end toward evening, they sat down in the farmhouse to an abundantly supplied supper table. "There was a superb piece of corned beef, a stewed goose, and a magnificent leg of mutton, with vegetables of every description, and at each end of the table two large jugs of cider."

The next day they went shooting, killing some plump partridges first, then knocking over six or seven gray squirrels, and finally their lucky star brought them into the middle of a flock of wild turkeys, which rose one after the other at short intervals, flying noisily and screaming loudly. The last and laziest bird rose only ten paces from Brillat-Savarin, who promptly brought it down. He and his friend took the partridges, the squirrels, and the turkey back to Hartford, where the celebrated gourmet arranged a little dinner for some of his American friends, at which the wings of the partridges were served *en papillottes* and the gray squirrels stewed in Madeira.

"As for the turkey, which was the only roast we had, it was charming to look upon, delightful to smell, and delicious to taste; and so, until the last morsel was eaten, you could hear all around the table, 'Very good! Exceedingly good,' 'Oh, my dear Sir, what a glorious bit!' "

It is not known where in the vicinity of Hartford Brillat-Savarin shot his wild turkey, but it may have been among the Turkey Hills of East Granby, which are the same distance from Hartford that Brillat-Savarin says he traveled, and, as the name indicates, were once a haunt of the noble bird. A few years later there were no wild turkeys left in Connecticut, for the last specimen was recorded shot there in 1813.

By the end of the eighteenth century the wild turkeys of New England, which had been retreating steadily westward, reached the line of the Connecticut River, where they made their last stand. There were flocks of them in the Berkshires and the mountainous regions of Vermont and among the hills of the Connecticut Valley. In the lifetime of the writer's grandparents there were still wild turkeys around Mount Holyoke and Mount Tom. During the winter of 1850–51 the last one was shot on Mount Tom. A turkey killed on Mount Holyoke in 1863 is thought to have been a fugitive from a barnyard.

Before the wild species was exterminated they sometimes visited their civilized relatives of the barnyard. In the mating season a wild turkey cock would fly in and strut and gobble and fight the domestic cock for the favors of the females. The wild gobbler always won, and in this way the domestic species was invigorated and kept up to scratch.

The old New England expression "to talk turkey" was coined in New Hampshire some time before 1846, when an Indian and a white man who had been hunting together came to divide the spoils, which consisted of a crow and a turkey. The white man, who was anxious to have the turkey, but wished to appear to make a fair division, said, "You take the crow and I'll take the turkey, or I'll take the turkey and you take the crow." The Indian grunted and replied, "Why you no talk turkey to me?"

In the olden times the New England housewife never had to worry about the Thanksgiving turkey being too large to fit her oven because she cooked it over an open fire. Families were larger then, and big birds favored. But the oven problem brought about an unusual Thanksgiving innovation just before the festival of 1945. This was the sale of split turkeys occasioned by the great number of extraordinarily large birds coming into the market. Raised to meet the requirements of the armed forces, these birds were released for civilian consumption as a result of the sudden end of the war. Marketmen, knowing that many housewives had ovens too small to accommodate such whopping birds, split the oversize turkeys in two, and the housewives, agreeing that half a turkey was better than none, bought the bisected birds, although they were uncertain how to prepare half a bird for the table and were apprehensive that it might dry unduly while cooking. All apparently turned out well, but in the future smaller turkeys will probably be the rule.

It is quite fitting that most of the cranberries which are made into sauce and eaten with turkey on Thanksgiving Day should come from New England, where the custom of serving cranberry sauce originated. The berry had existed in a wild state along New England shores since long before the coming of the Pilgrims, who, because the white blossom and stem bore a fancied resemblance to the head and neck of a crane, called it the cranberry. It still grows wild along the coast, not only on the mainland, but on the coastal islands as well. The Cranberry Islands off the Maine coast near Mount Desert were named from the abundance of wild cranberries found growing there.

The cultivated berry as we know it today is largely a product of Cape Cod. It was not until the days of sail were on the wane that the inhabitants of the Cape became interested in growing anything in the wastes of sand which reminded travelers of the deserts of Arabia. Obliged to cast about for a new means of livelihood, they began to cultivate the cranberry. A Cape resident had noticed that the vines around and over which the sand had drifted bore the best berries, and from this simple observation the modern cranberry industry was developed. The old salts of Cape Cod financed many of their cranberry bogs in the same way they financed the building of their ships, by splitting the cost into sixty-four parts and selling interests in a bog as they had sold shares in a vessel. These cranberry shares have often been held in the same family for generations. Today the cranberry bogs of Cape Cod produce three-fourths of the world's supply of the red berry with the tart taste.

Pie, especially pumpkin pie, was considered as essential to the old-fashioned New England Thanksgiving dinner as turkey and cranberry sauce. A want of molasses with which to make pies was more than once the cause of a New England town postponing its observance of the day. Once at Newbury, Vermont, when the minister read the Thanksgiving proclamation, a worthy deacon, who was not unmindful of the earthly pleasure to be derived from a good dinner, rose and said that as there was no molasses in town and his boys had gone to Charlestown, New Hampshire, to get some, he would move that Thanksgiving be postponed a week. When the boys did not return, the day was put off again, until finally the people of Newbury had to go without their molasses, and, since there was no "sweetning," presumably also without the customary pumpkin pies. One can only guess what happened to the boys. Similarly, at Colchester, Connecticut, the celebration of Thanksgiving was delayed a week beyond the appointed day because a sloop from New York with a hogshead of molasses for pies failed to arrive.

The New England governors in colonial times were not above using their annual Thanksgiving Day proclamations for purposes of political propaganda. Not only did they bid the people give thanks for the bounties of nature but also for wise and beneficent laws effectively administered and for other blessings of good government. People who considered such political statements gross exaggerations or inventive reporting were thrown into a trampling rage, and ministers delivering Thanksgiving sermons in unheated meetinghouses would sometimes give an offending governor a thorough raking over the coals.

An amusing account of a public dinner given in 1714, at which bear meat and venison were eaten, has come down to us from the pen of the Rev. Lawrence Conant of Danvers, Massachusetts, who was evidently not averse to eating game that had been killed on the Sabbath:

> "When ye services at ye meeting house were ended," he wrote, "ye council and other dignitaries were entertained at ye house of Mr. Epes, on ye hill near by, and we had a bountiful Thanksgiving dinner with bear's meat and venison, the last of which was a fine buck, shot in ye woods near by. Ye bear was killed in Lynn woods near Reading.
>
> "After ye blessing was craved by Mr. Garrick of Wrentham, word came that ye buck was shot on ye Lord's day by Pequot, an Indian, who came to Mr. Epes with a lye in his mouth like Ananias of old.
>
> "Ye council therefore refused to eat ye venison, but it was afterward decided that Pequot should receive 40 stripes save one, for lying and profaning ye Lord's day, restore Mr. Epes ye cost of ye deer, and considering this a just and righteous sentence on ye sinful heathen, and that a blessing had been craved on ye meat, ye council all partook of it but Mr. Shepard, whose conscious was tender on ye point of ye venison."

At Norwich, Connecticut, it was once the practice to celebrate Thanksgiving not only by eating turkey and cranberry sauce, but by lighting bonfires. In 1792 a young man was killed during the celebration.

> "On Thursday evening last," says a newspaper account, "a young man by the name of Cook, aged 19 was instantly killed

in this town by the discharge of a swivel. The circumstances, as near as we can recollect, were as follows:—In celebration of the day, (being Thanksgiving), a large number of boys had assembled, and by pillaging dry casks from the stores, wharves, etc. had erected a bonfire on the hill back of the Landing, and to make their rejoicings more sonorious, fired a swivel several times; at last a foolish fondness for a loud report, induced them to be pretty lavish of their powder—the explosion burst the swivel into a multitude of pieces, the largest of which, weighing about seven pounds, passed through the body of the deceased, carrying with it his heart, and was afterwards found in the street 3o or 4o rods from the place where it was fired. —While the serious lament the accident, they entertain a hope that good may come of evil, that the savage practice of making bonfires on the evening of Thanksgiving, may be exchanged for some other mode of rejoicing, more consistent with the genuine spirit of Christianity."

But this local custom of lighting bonfires on Thanksgiving Day continued in Norwich throughout the era of wooden barrels, or down to about the year 1925.

"They were touched off Thanksgiving morning," a man from Norwich told me, who as a boy had participated in these celebrations. "There were bonfires on all the seven hills of Norwich on Thanksgiving Day."

Thanksgiving did not immediately become a fixed annual festival in New England after the first Pilgrim observance, but it made headway steadily. It proved popular because it was a substitute for the festival of Christmas, which the Puritans had banished. It was as if they said, "If we can't have Christmas, we'll have our own feast." The idea of a Thanksgiving Day for the Lord's bounties gradually spread throughout the country until this old New England custom became a national one.

~ *Thanksgiving Day* ~

We think of Thanksgiving as America's most typical, most distinctively national holiday. But other cultures have long celebrated the bounty of the earth. The Hebrew Feast of Tabernacles (Sukkoth) is a thanksgiving festival, as is the ancient Greek Feast of Demeter (in honor of the goddess of agriculture) and the corresponding Roman holiday, Cerealia. Our English settlers were accustomed to celebrating the Anglican church holiday of "harvest home," an event followed by secular feasting and sporting events. In 1624, the General

Assembly of Virginia proclaimed March 22 as Thanksgiving Day in an act of thankfulness to commemorate the colony's survival of the 1622 Indian massacre and war. By the mid-eighteenth century, Thanksgiving was now being celebrated throughout Massachusetts. President George Washington proclaimed the first national Thanksgiving Day in 1789 following America's victorious Revolution. Later, in 1846, Mrs. Sarah Josepha Hale, editor of Godey's Lady's Book, began a campaign to make Thanksgiving Day an annual celebration held the last Thursday in November. One by one, the states began adopting the day and the date when the Civil War interrupted the process. Then, in 1863, President Abraham Lincoln proclaimed Thanksgiving Day a national day. In 1939, President Franklin D. Roosevelt tried to set the day back to the third Thursday in November in order to lengthen the time between Thanksgiving and Christmas—but tradition ruled.

~ Thanksgiving Memories ~

As I remember, it must have been just after World War II when gasoline rationing was lifted. Once again families could travel to see one another over the holidays. My aunt Mary, who was living in New York, rode the train to our Virginia home for the long Thanksgiving weekend. (Danville, Virginia, the scene of the famed wreck of the Old '97, was on the direct New York–to-Miami Seaboard Railroad line.) The next morning we piled into our new Studebaker and headed south to North Carolina for a family gathering at my aunt and uncle's home. Only thing is, my aunt didn't cook much in those days. When they swung open the door to welcome us, Aunt Mary made a comment I've always remembered. "Where are the cooking smells?" she asked. "When you go into a house at Thanksgiving you're supposed to be overcome by the smell of food."

~ Thanksgiving Kitchens ~

DOROTHY BROWN THOMPSON

Thanksgiving kitchens
    Are gay with color—
Pumpkins are yellow,
    Apples are red;
And though the puddings
    Are somewhat duller,
A richer fragrance
    Is theirs instead.

And what a fragrance!
  Spices and sweetness
Wreathing stem-clouds
  Round eager faces;
The turkey stuffed to
  Luscious repleteness;
Thanksgiving kitchens—
  Promising places!

⌐ *Poem 814* ⌐

EMILY DICKINSON

One Day is there of the Series
Termed Thanksgiving Day.
Celebrated part at Table
Part in Memory.

⌐ *Thanksgiving in the City* ⌐ *Pennies and Parades*

* RAY RHEINHART

Few people think of Thanksgiving as a kids' day. That's Christmas or Hal-
loween. But my good friend Ray Rheinhart recounts how, in Hoboken, New
Jersey, during the 1940s a unique Thanksgiving tradition centered around
the children—but it had to be over with before the neighborhood parade began.
  By the way, the world-famous Macy's Thanksgiving Day Parade has been
a tradition since 1924—the same year Hudson's of Detroit held its first
Santa's Thanksgiving Day Parade. Philadelphia's Gimbel's Thanksgiving
Day "Circus" and Parade was the granddaddy of them all. It began in 1920
when Ellis Gimbel gathered together fifteen cars and fifty people, added a fireman
dressed as Santa, and called it a parade. It caught on, and a tradition was born.

The fate of Thanksgiving was tied to that of Halloween because of a
curious tradition that I have come to learn was unique to New York
City and the urban areas of northern New Jersey.

  On Thanksgiving morning it was the custom of children to dress
up as ragamuffins. This could be accomplished with your father's or
your mother's old clothes. Inadvertent precursors of Madonna, our goal
was not fashion but a kind of heaped-up raffishness.

Once costumed, we would roam the streets that morning in packs of four to a dozen ragamuffins, going from one apartment door to the other (there were no security guards to ask us for our names and the purpose of our business). "Anything for Thanksgiving?" was the common refrain. Typically, the response was candy, fruit, and if we were really lucky, a plate piled high with shiny pennies.

Word got out quickly as to the relative degree of generosity. At the thresholds of the most bounteous households there was something that I have since come to know as a feeding frenzy.

However, the frenzied darting up and down the flights of tenement stairs was not driven solely by the prospect of riches and the fear that we would arrive too late, only to find a picked-over selection or, worse, an empty plate. It was also fueled by the short time in which we children had room to operate, for at noon there was an unspoken consensus that the time for begging had passed.

Also, it was at noon that a parade assembled and marched down Hoboken's main thoroughfare, Washington Street. There were bands and floats from which some of the city's manufacturers—Tootsie Rolls and Tootsie Pops, among others—threw candy to the spectators lining the parade route. And there were the ragamuffins running along on all sides, gathering a few last pieces of loot before they returned home to count their good fortune and clean up for Thanksgiving dinner.

I'm told that this tradition has an Italian origin, brought over to this country by the waves of immigrants who gave America pasta, opera, and Frank Sinatra—also from Hoboken. I don't know for sure.

But I do know that once we started to dress up in costumes to go trick-or-treating at Halloween, the life quickly ebbed out of the band of ragamuffins. What point was there to go around in costume asking for handouts twice in the space of less than a month?

More has been lost, I think, than a quirky regionalism. Before we learned from television about the rest of the world, we had neatly separated generosity from fear. The crisp McIntosh apples and the chocolate peanuts handed out to us in the pale sunlight of Thanksgiving morning were freely given. Halloween dispenses its treasures to hold back the terrors of the night.

~ Horn and Hardart Pumpkin Pie ~

*Gerry Davis

Those of us who think "over the river and through the woods" is the essence of Thanksgiving never give thought to the city dwellers' holiday. We just assume they leave town and go to the countryside. For Gerry Davis, the memories of wonderful Thanksgiving Days when everyone was together and happy in New York City continue to provide comfort amid sorrowful times, no matter what the season.

My mother and father were traditionalists—especially my mother. There were lots of family traditions that I took for granted, and it was not until I was instilling them in my own children that I realized how wonderful traditions truly are.

Thanksgiving is the one that I can sense, smell, and savor, even in July, if I think about that November day.

When I was little, I knew it was Thanksgiving time because there would be one day when my mother and I would spend longer than usual in the grocery store. The groceryman would diligently list all the items Mother stated, the butcher would display several gray-white turkeys for her to choose from, and before I knew it, all the items were filling the kitchen of our twelfth-floor apartment.

On Thanksgiving morning, breakfast was consumed more rapidly than usual—if at all—because a job was pending for my brother and me. The long loaves of white Bond bread had to be toasted, then torn into pieces. They would be mounded up over the top of the roasting pan, which was the receptacle for the stuffing-in-progress. Eggs were beaten, onions and celery chopped, and Bell's seasoning added to the mound. (Is Bell's seasoning used at any other time of the year?)

"What's this?" one of us would ask Mother as the "parts" were removed and the turkey was washed and propped up in the sink to drain.

"That's the gizzard" or "that's . . ." whatever part we were pointing to, and if time permitted, Mother would give more details as to its function.

Periodically we heard her say: "I've got to get this bird in the oven." Somehow that big mound we had created would fit into the turkey, and the turkey was finally put in the oven. It seemed that when the turkey was in the oven, it was time to bundle up and go to the parade.

Going to the Macy's Parade with my father and brother while mother saw to the dinner preparations was also a part of our Thanksgiving Day. Originally we would view the parade from Daddy's shoulders, but as we got older it was "push and peek" as best we could to see the parade.

(Little did I think then that it would not be an eternity before I would be making the same statements to my sons when the process was being repeated years later.)

While we were gone, Mother worked miracles. By the time we returned, the brilliant white tablecloth was on the dining room table, the silver place settings were in place and sparkling, the tall white tapered candles were ready to be lit, and the aroma of all the "cookings" was saturating the air.

Excitement was all around and throughout our being. When we returned from the parade, we would bathe and dress up before guests arrived. Mother and Daddy invited family and friends who didn't have a reason to cook a turkey. It was so festive and friendly.

As people arrived, my brother and I would run to and from the door with enthusiastic greetings. It didn't take long to fill our sunny living room with happy talk. I enjoyed it so very much.

Although Mother did all the preliminary cooking, we did have someone to help serve the meal. Every so often Mother would check the cooking and then finally we heard the meal being brought out of the kitchen. The next thing, we were all at the table saying the blessing: "God is great, God is good, and we thank Him for our food. . . ."

I am not certain if we had an appetizer, but if we did it would have been a small shrimp cocktail or a very fresh fruit cup. The rest of the meal I know for certain. The turkey was golden brown, the mashed potatoes creamy, the corn pudding crunchy, the peas and carrots colorful, the sweet potatoes orangy, the cranberry sauce bright crimson, the rolls warm and soft, and of course, the gravy piping hot. The salad was cool and colorful. My mother thought the Horn & Hardart pumpkin pie was outstanding, and I remember it was served warm and with fresh whipped cream and vanilla ice cream. It was delicious.

My brother and I were excused from the table while the adults talked and enjoyed their coffee. We would go into the living room, our small forms so full we could hardly move. We'd flop on the sofa or into a chair and wait until we heard people coming, and then we would sit up straight. When everyone was back in the living room, often someone would play the piano, and sometimes my brother and I would be asked to play the piano, recite a poem, or tell of a school event.

The excitement of the day, the cold air that had stung our faces at the parade, the foods that filled our bodies, made my brother and me sleepy, and often the living room became our nap place.

This New York Thanksgiving scenario was repeated yearly for the better part of fifty years. There were times when a pregnancy, bad weather, or distance caused a change. When these disruptions did occur, I tried to duplicate the ritual wherever I was living. After my father passed away, there were a few Thanksgivings away from New York, but the tradition was maintained as faithfully as possible.

Oftentimes things do come full circle. For the last eight years my brother and I and our families all went back to the original: Thanksgiving in New York City.

Although the routine of grocery shopping had changed, we did have the same menu—except that the stuffing was not made from scratch, the pumpkin pie was not Horn & Hardart, and I had taken over most of the kitchen duties. Those who went to the parade did freeze, but returned as always with red cheeks and enthusiasm. My brother now sat in my father's chair and our families and friends still gathered, and it was a day my mother cherished.

Sadly, a year ago our New York Thanksgiving tradition ended. I was now sitting in my mother's chair as we all held hands: "God is great, God is good, and we thank Him for our food. Amen."

~ Turkey Bowl ~

*CAROLYN SCHWARTZ

Oftentimes traditions are born of necessity. A suggestion for those of you who are frustrated by the inevitable Thanksgiving weekend TV football games that draw the men and boys in front of the screen and away from the kitchen and dining room: try creating your own "Turkey Bowl" to bring everyone together.

That's what our family did when the children were young and full of unharnessed energy. What began as a pickup game became a full-fledged tradition. Sometime around Halloween, when the younger children began excitedly chattering about the upcoming Turkey Bowl, the older family men began talking about their well-intended but seldom carried-out pre-game training. After the first year or two, one of the fathers was assigned the duty of designing and ordering Turkey Bowl jerseys for the ragtag football squad—even for the girls in the family. When they were young, these members of the fairer sex joined in the game. Later they opted to be cheerleaders. Eventually they joined their mothers as onlookers content to enjoy the macho shenanigans.

Last year, for the first time, there was no Granddaddy Jenkins for the game. But this year the family's first son-in-law will join the squad. Pretty soon one of the dads will become the first granddaddy. The tradition continues.

We thought our family's Turkey Bowl was original with us. But Carolyn Schwartz's family had one, too—bigger and better. And so do countless other families across the country. It's a great tradition.

For my family, football has always taken precedence over turkey on Thanksgiving. For years, my husband and young sons gobbled their dinner and rushed to the TV for an orgy of games, one following another. Often it was past dark and some of the group was dozing when the final quarter wound to a finish.

About a dozen years ago, as my young sons grew into young bucks, a former pro football player moved into our neighborhood. For old times' sake he often joined the boys and their friends in a scrimmage at a local playing field. Soon some of the other neighborhood dads were jumping into the free-for-all. It was a chance to show off their enduring jockhood.

Surprisingly, the elders held their own. Soon they were proposing a challenge: the old goats against the young bucks. Snickering and puffing up their chests, the bucks agreed.

So began our annual neighborhood Turkey Bowl.

At first, the tournaments were played at the Rec Club field. After each game, I invited everyone—players and spectators—to a post-tournament "wind-down" at our house. Most years we packed the kitchen body to body, pungent football odors blending with delectable turkey aromas coming from the oven.

As the size of the teams grew, so did the groupies who came out to watch and then party: kid brothers and sisters, grandparents, wives, sweethearts, babies, and a beauteous array of neighborhood teenyboppers. Often the decibel level made our ears ring long after the gang had dispersed.

When my family moved to the country, it seemed as if the six-year tradition might die.

But no one would hear of it.

Every year since, the bowl game diehards have made the forty-mile trek to our house. My husband even clears a special playing field for them. Rain, shine, sleet, or snow, the tournament must go on.

Even personal injury doesn't fell these modern gladiators. One time it was a badly sprained ankle. Once it was a dislocated shoulder. Twice it was broken fingers. All four trips to the emergency room meant that the victims and I returned to dry turkey and warmed-over dressing.

Often the guys arrive for warm-ups before I'm out of my night-gown. So what if they skip church or incur the wrath of spouses left at home to baste turkeys and cater to mothers-in-law? We wives have learned to gauge the turkey's cooking time to include a few moments at the sidelines and a few more for the ubiquitous team photo at the end of the game. We've also learned to put the dinner on hold while team members down one more cold beer and rehash the game's most brilliant plays.

The team roster changes every year, but never stops growing. Now there are two, eleven-man teams and scores of eager benchwarmers. In some cases, the players represent three generations in the same family. And some of the babies, instead of nursing at the sidelines, are now the team's best ballplayers.

This year, at halftime, I watched my husband and his cronies stagger to the kitchen. I watched my grown sons limp in, massaging elbows, shoulders, and sunburned necks.

Ah, but the younger generation. There they were, hale, hearty, and rarin' to play the final two quarters.

And, thank goodness, to carry on the tradition.

~ It's Thanksgiving Because ~ It's Homecoming

HENRY BEETLE HOUGH

These days the lights of Christmas cast long shadows. They begin to fall in mid-October, even before Halloween. Thanksgiving is sandwiched in between. Still, of all our traditions Thanksgiving is the one time when we put commercialism aside. No presents are needed. No treats are required. It is the time when, in its largest and most loving sense, the word "family" reigns. People are all that we need on this day that binds the past to the present the way no other holiday can. Its central theme is the simple giving of thanks.

Year in, year out, the advent of Thanksgiving brings sentimental references to the Pilgrims and the first celebration of the feast day in the New England wilderness. Thanksgiving remains peculiarly the product of the New England tradition, but you won't be able to catch or define the holiday's spirit by talking about the first Thanksgiving.

The first Thanksgiving is memorable only as an instinctive birth, a spiritual preparation and, perhaps, a faint, warming fragrance of family repasts to come. It was much too early then for the Pilgrims to have grandchildren, though naturally they invited the neighbors, who happened to be Red Men. But many a threshold had to be worn deeply into the grain of the wood, many a winter's snow had to drift the fields and the path from the kitchen to the barn before there could be a real Thanksgiving.

Great-great-grandchildren were needed, as well as uncles, aunts and nephews, with long memories and golden tales to go with the rush of young anticipation. The fullness of the day never stemmed from colonial times but from that later period when family and community life had accumulated like wild honey and thriven with the sun, the wind and the soil.

Thanksgiving needed family, although lacking guests with blood ties (as the Pilgrims felt), neighbors could be made to do. It also needed room and scope. A year ahead, at least, Uncle Jared and Aunt Clarissa claimed their turn to entertain. Uncle Jared planted and harvested accordingly, and Aunt Clarissa made the necessary calculations in putting up her preserves. From the first of November she cleaned, scoured and fixed up the spare bedrooms and the cots and patchwork quilts for children in the chilly, aromatic attic.

The winds of Thanksgiving always blew toward home, and so the course lay from city to town, or from town to village, or from village to country. Even on ordinary days New England dinners were served at noon, and dinner guests were polite if they arrived around 10 for a 12 o'clock meal. For Thanksgiving, early arrival was of the essence, and members of the clan who did not come the day before were expected immediately after breakfast. The men walked around in their good clothes for the sake of better appetites, the women helped in the kitchen, which was large enough to hold them all, with elbow room. The children, hollered at frequently, kept in touch with important matters through a grapevine system of their own.

Then, when the moment came, the extra chairs were lugged into the dining room and every piece of choice china and silverware which Aunt Clarissa owned was displayed on the table. Nothing was held back. Yet the effect was not at all finicky. It was both simple and fine. The generations came to be seated, men first, women next, as they hurried from the kitchen with bright faces, discarding their aprons hastily. Uncle Jared might ask the blessing himself or he might defer to Cousin Luella's husband, who was a deacon, or this might be the year they were having the minister, the minister's wife and their four children.

As grace was spoken, the repose of the Lord and the surcease of labor settled upon the room, and all the New England past seemed to be there also. Then, THEN the company took up its spoons for the preliminary soup, a trial run of the bounty which was already pressing in from the kitchen as from a great horn of plenty. And the bounty was Uncle Jared's and Aunt Clarissa's own.

If there were turkeys, Uncle Jared had raised them and Aunt Clarissa had roasted them until their skin was golden crisp and shiny. If there were rabbits, Uncle Jared had shot them at the copse over the hill, or if they were canvas-back ducks, he had brought them down at the border of the great pond on a gusty morning. But Aunt Clarissa might have stuffed a brace of barnyard geese, long fed for the occasion, or a young pig, or prepared an enormous eel stifle.

Tradition did not dictate too narrowly. She might have used stuffing of bread, onion and summer savory or sage, or she might have tried a new chestnut dressing or sent Uncle Jared to the cove for oysters. Cranberry sauce might be made from the whole cranberries or strained into the form of jelly. The parsnips might appear in fritters. Each departure would arouse exclamations of enthusiasm, but it was not certain that Uncle Canton's wife would adopt any of them when she entertained next year. She probably had a few of her own in mind, such as whipping quarts of cream for a gigantic charlotte russe.

The one indispensable of the dinner was its roll-call, in plenty, of all the New England vegetables. There could not be one missing, and the heartiest were most important. Begin with the classic white turnip. It had the pungent flavor of something wrung from nature, produced by toil and ordeal through drought, frost and scorching sun. Not everyone liked turnip, but everyone ate it, knowing what was good for him. Then there were the winter squashes buttered and spiced, onions boiled and creamed, great heaps of potatoes, carrots, parsnips, celery and a flanking of watermelon preserves, pickles and wild grape jelly and beach plum jam.

There was a running supply of Uncle Jared's cider and the ultimate of mince, squash, apple and pumpkin pies and maybe Indian pudding or plum pudding. Except for raisins, sugar and spices, everything of the dinner would have been grown, caught or garnered in the countryside or on the farm itself, and in maritime New England even the spices would have been obtained by barter from some passing vessel or brought in person by Cousin Hosea, just back from the Orient as mate of the clipper *Good Return.*

Immediately after the main course the younger generation would go outdoors and run around the house in a vain hope of shaking things down and making more room. But there would be room, miraculously, for pocketsful of nuts at the very end as well as for some of Uncle Jared's pears and apples. Then the legendary peace of Thanksgiving became complete, the Lord was praised with distended stomachs and repletion was somehow near to holiness.

While the women were clearing up in the kitchen the men went outdoors again and leaned over the barnyard fence with Uncle Jared to admire the farm animals and the improvements he had made in the place. They had looked around before, but this was official. This was ceremonial.

Then, in due course, the church bells. The women were eager to show themselves in their new dresses, bonnets, ribbons and shawls, and the young men were proud of their homespun and home-dyed coats, wool hats and cowhide boots. No less strongly, the generations of Grandpa and Uncle Jared were drawn to church, too.

Bass viol and fiddle were taken to the singing gallery, and hymns and anthems were never sung with more power and feeling. The minister read out the lesson: "The Lord reigneth; let the earth rejoice, let the multitude of the isles be glad thereof." But when he came to the sermon he was not averse to letting his opinions on the tariff and other timely matters appear. That, too, was New England, and his flock, deeply aware of a superintending Providence and of eternal gratitude for life, safety and the freedom they and their children breathed, sat contentedly and filtered the minister's words.

After church had ended with little sociable talks at the vestry door, and greetings to friends and neighbors driving home, Aunt Clarissa mentioned that she wanted to run over to Josie Hammett's for a minute, and a bevy of relatives went along. So, with calling back and forth, the renewal of friendships, and the sound of voices and laughter in the aisles of browned oak trees along the dirt roads, Thanksgiving drifted gently to a temporary end, an adjournment of a year during which Uncle Jared's hair would turn a little frostier, the youngest scion would grow a couple of inches, and a new crop of white turnips would mature.

So the tradition of Thanksgiving, and in essence the observance, has never changed. It has only contracted, partly because of smaller families and the increasing dominance of town life, and partly because of the pressure of an industrial civilization which tends to pool the bounty of the entire world.

Uncle Lemuel, who as a small boy sat at Uncle Jared's Thanksgiving board, likes to tell the assembled company that he raised the turkey on the place. But these are new times, and everyone knows the turkeys at the bargain store are just as good. Aunt Bertha did not make the watermelon pickle by the almanac, but took them out of a store bottle. Only the cranberry sauce, wild grape jelly and beach plum jam are hers. Soon only the white turnip and other vegetables will be Uncle Lemuel's, the last regional accents of what was once a regional feast.

There is still no day of homecoming in New England equal to Thanksgiving, but with automobiles, and, one must say it, with airplanes, the cousins, aunts, brothers, and even the grandchildren, may swish over just an hour before dinnertime. There's no helping to be done in the kitchen and no room for outsiders, either. Aunt Bertha has her electric mixer and range, and so many things come practically ready for the oven or the table.

Yet no stranger could ever mistake the Thanksgiving dinner for any other dinner of the year, not with that array of vegetables, the heirloom china, the representation of all ages, the communing of past and present. Dinner over, the family listens to the football game on the radio, though Aunt Bertha may mention that she wants to run over to Lizzie Hammett's for a minute and won't someone come with her? Long before dark most of the dinner guests are homeward bound in car or plane, and only one or two miscellaneous offspring remain to sleep under ancestral spreads.

Once in a while nowadays one hears of country people going to the city for Thanksgiving, but they are not New Englanders. No matter where their homes, as soon as their cityward journeys start they become members only of that indistinguishable race—moderns. Thanksgiving will never be transplanted. Though diminished, it remains now and forever what it was and what it has to be.

⏤ *Reflections on Thanksgiving* ⏤

GLADYS TABER

Isn't it wonderful to sit down at Thanksgiving dinner, look across the feast at your grown-up children, and think that it was not long ago when they were just big enough to sit at the table? Though we may remember those times past only when we are repeating them, still the memories give even more meaning to each new occurrence.

Gladys Taber wrote lovingly and insightfully of her family in her journals, newspaper and magazine articles, and beloved books. Here, she and her lifelong friend, Jill, both widowed, are joined by their daughters' families and the next generation for that day of days. Have things changed for the better? she wonders. Does it matter? There are always things to be thankful for, regardless of the changing world.

Thanksgiving is gay with massed greens in the big copper bowl, with harvest vegetables piled in the old wooden dough tray, with red corn hanging against the mellow pine by the fireplace. Apples and raisins and nuts brim the bowls on the coffee table by the fire, the cheese board is decked forth with pale Swiss, bright Cheddar and creamy Port Salut.

Jill blisters her fingers on the chestnuts for the dressing for the plump turkey, but decides chestnut stuffing is worth it. When the turkey roasts, the savory smell of sage and chestnuts drifts from the kitchen and the onions glazing in honey and catsup add their fragrance.

The children are all at home for the week end, plus Jill's exquisite granddaughter, rosy and sweet as a young apple blossom. She is now over a year old, and busily absorbing every detail of this strange and wonderful world. We naturally see signs of very surprising genius in her every gesture, and I am reminded of that doting mamma who kept saying "look at my baby breathe!"

Well, it is pretty wonderful to breathe, at that.

The children sit quietly while I talk over with God what blessings we have, but I note they lift knife and fork the instant I raise my head. They are, I reflect comfortably, just as hungry now as they were when they were very little, and went out after dinner in bunny suits.

A family holiday, such as this, gives one a chance to estimate the changes in the children. As we pass the plates heaped with the crisply crackling turkey, mellow and delicate under the skin and golden brown on top—the conversation seems like a montage of their lives.

That serious young intern, surely only yesterday he was asking, "who is the leader of the stars?" The gay young mother, yes, she was the very one who fell off her bicycle and flew through the air a mile a minute. And Connie, as she relates some riotous happenings in her class at Columbia, must be the same little girl that came home from kindergarten and said, "Mama, T. J. kissed me. You know he's the one with the lavender up-top."

Sometimes one wishes they were little again, yet on the whole I think it is so rewarding to know them as equals that I would not really wish the romper days back. Every mother must feel that occasional ache for her child's baby days and in retrospect even pushing spinach through a sieve seems fun. Nowadays, I think a baby would be no bother at all. Everything is pureed before you get it and what bliss! Disposable diapers or diaper services, nylon, dacron, orlon and what-not to wear that irons itself as you shake it out, whole meals from soup to nuts in little sterile jars—what a change.

As I was pondering this, however, it came to me that Jill's daughter spends all the time there is on the baby, and Papa's time is added to it when he is at home. This is a mystery. For all that timesaving seems to have gotten them exactly nowhere!

When the baby naps, they wash things, mix things, collect and wash toys, shake blankets. Get the medicine dropper ready for those miracle drops. And run up and down stairs every five minutes just to *be sure* she is not too warm or too cold.

So I finally decide things haven't really changed so much. A baby is a time-consuming affair even now.

I think on the whole I am glad I brought Connie up just as things went along. Now there are so many experts to consult, so many books to look things up in, it is dizzying. Parents watch like hawks to be sure the baby begins to crawl when he or she should, grasps things at the right moment, speaks in the right time, shows timidity at the correct age, shows stubbornness at the certain period he should. It keeps them on edge all the time, lest their own particular piece of heaven should fail Dr. Spock or some other great authority. I was spared this, for I never even knew at what age my child was supposed to be standing erect and saying Da Da. I wasn't alarmed that she first said "Abach," which translated into zwiebach which she really adored. I just kept on taking things as they came, and confining all my worries to blankets and mittens and socks and bonnets, and at that, I worried enough.

After Thanksgiving dinner, the house simmers down to quiet. It seems cosy and natural to hear muted voices from all over—the baby upstairs waking up, Connie and Don talking, Don's wife tuning the guitar and humming. With all the food around, I reflect comfortably, we won't need to get another sit-down meal, they can raid.

Naturally in a very few hours, there is a kind of stir.

"When are we going to eat?"

"Is it almost supper time?"

"Mind if I eat a little more chestnut stuffing?"

It is very much as it was on Christmas when I said to Jill, "we can have the leftover turkey tomorrow," and she said, "what turkey?"

It turns out there is just enough to slice thin and have cold, plus extra dressing, and reinforced with a casserole of homebaked beans nobody perishes of starvation.

"And all of them as thin as pencils," I mourn afterward, "it just isn't fair! They can just eat alarmingly and never gain an ounce. Whereas I—no, no justice at all."

Thanksgiving is far more than the family dinner and national festival. I know all people have always had harvest celebrations of one kind or another, so there is nothing distinctive about a feast time after the crops are in. But our Thanksgiving seems very close to our relation with God. It has a deep religious significance not always spoken of, but, I think, felt.

I like to slip away for a brief time and sit by the pond on the one bench left out all winter. If it is a warm hazy day, the sun is slanting over the hill with a gentle glow. If it is cold, the wind walks in the woods. I think of everything I have to be thankful for, and it is a long list by the time it is added up. I am thankful for love, and friends, and the family gathering together. For starlight over the old apple orchard. For the chilly sweetness of peepers in April. For my winter birds, so brave, so hungry, particularly for my little chickadee with the bent wing that bangs away at the suet cake right while I type. He cocks a shining eye at me and seems to say, "life is really what you make of it, eh?"

I am thankful for music and books. And for the dogs barking at the gate. Well, there are so many things to be thankful for that the list is infinitely long.

And it is good to take time to be thankful, for it is all too easy to let the world's trouble sweep over one in a dark flood and to fall into despair.

— The Clean Plate Club —

* NONNA DON WOODS

Speaking of the children's place at the table, Thanksgiving is the one meal at which everyone is expected to clean his plate. To make sure, Nonna Don Woods keeps a pair of scissors close by when preparing the family's traditional applesauce cake.

It has always been a tradition in our family for the Thanksgiving holidays to have our famous homemade-from-scratch applesauce cake that my mother-in-law made. A few days before each holiday my children's grandmother would harvest the walnuts from the backyard, hull them, pick them from the shells. The raisins she would cut into tiny bits with scissors so those children who didn't like the raisins wouldn't recognize them and try to pick them out. She stayed up late into the night to complete the process.

The ride to Grandma's house would always be a quiet one, the children as well as the grown-ups with pictures floating around in their heads of all the goodies that would be waiting. Upon arrival, all of the cousins, aunts, and uncles would greet everyone, all talking at the same time.

Dinnertime would arrive with the huge golden turkey on the table. About that time one of the kids would ask, "Where's that big old turkey that was out in the barnyard?" Some quick grown-up would always say, "Come on, now. Let's fill your plate."

Now I make the applesauce cake and most of the other fixings and off we go over the Missouri River and through the woods to my kids' house for the holidays. I will always have stayed up late the night before, cutting the raisins into tiny pieces.

~ An All-American Thanksgiving ~

MARGARET LOUISE ARNOTT

Thanksgiving may be the most American of our holidays, but past influences from many corners of the world enrich the traditional meal in many homes. Here, from The Folklore of American Holidays, *is an international smorgasbord of Thanksgiving dishes served up with the usual roast turkey as taken from a paper by Margaret Louise Arnott, "Thanksgiving Dinner: A Study in Cultural Heritage."*

The Puerto Rican will serve turkey, rice and beans, with *Arroz con Dulce,* a pudding made of rice, sugar, coconut milk, and milk spiced with cinnamon and ginger in place of pumpkin pie. Among the Armenians the old country people serve the traditional Armenian foods but do use turkey because it is similar to chicken and will feed a large number of people. Those born in the United States vary in custom but most have turkey with pilaf and the Armenian bread, *Cheorig,* while all the food is seasoned with oriental spices. Pumpkin pie is not generally served by the old country people but the new generation does use it, though there is no hard and fast rule. On the other hand, the Greek community tends to serve the traditional American menu, even in those families which adhere regularly to the Greek cuisine. However, the salad and condiments, namely feta cheese, are Greek, and sweet sauces or candied yams are avoided. Families from India usually depend upon being invited by an American family, but when they are not, since most of them are vegetarians, they tend to keep to their own cuisine. The Italians mix the menu, serving soup, roast turkey, ravioli, macaroni, pumpkin pie, wine and coffee. They cannot tolerate the sweet potato. The Poles use turkey with various vegetables, but serve apple pie and lots of beer and whiskey.

~ The Tradition Continues ~

Interestingly, there are few really new Thanksgiving traditions. This holiday is the one when the same old same-old is more than good enough. Unlike Christmas and Halloween, when new products and gimmicks flood the stores and are touted in all the magazines, Thanksgiving remains a reflective, prayer-

ful, and comforting time. Thanksgiving is its own tradition. It continues year in and year out, self-propelled and self-contained. Still, it is always interesting and fun to learn how others celebrate this day.

A neighborhood Thanksgiving bonfire. Family prayers. A Thanksgiving tablecloth. Secret mementos intended to be shared. The videotaping of each person's special blessing for a true Thankful turkey. The hiding of a cherry in the turkey dressing. Simple traditions truly are best for this day. These Thanksgiving narratives by the younger generation capture the essence of the day down through the years while providing ample ideas to enrich your Thanksgiving celebration. And don't forget the Thanksgiving play!

November 23. The traditional bonfire my family has every year on Thanksgiving Eve is tomorrow. I can't wait! They're always so much fun. While we were setting up, my dad told me about the first bonfire. I was only about one year old at the time. My aunt and uncle were visiting from South Carolina. We decided to have a bonfire. It was a small fire in the backyard. We had some popcorn and Coke to drink. We put it out at about 8:00 P.M.

The next year we had another bonfire. We invited some of our friends and had more food and drinks. We kept on having more bonfires every year on the same day. They have gotten a lot better and bigger! We have tons of food and lots of drinks. That's a good thing, because we invite a lot of people. Last year we had up to a hundred! We had such a big crowd of people, we had to move into a huge open field. We set up our tent for kids to play in. We also gave pony rides on our pony. We stayed up really late! Last year people didn't start leaving until 4:00 A.M.! We roasted marshmallows and ate them. They're always delicious.

We sleep in late the next day. When we finally wake up, we go outside and clean up. That's the only part that's not fun.

I think I'm very lucky! Not many people get to do what I get to do. I can't wait one more minute. I have to go and gather sticks and twigs. I hope it goes okay!

Kristin Walls, elementary school

My family tradition is going to Maryland every year for Thanksgiving. First we pray and then all of my family gets into my grandma's van. Then we begin to ride and almost everyone goes to sleep. When we get up, we're almost there. We continue to ride, tell jokes, sing songs, and play games. When we get there, my aunt Sharon has some food fixed for us because she knows we will be hungry from a long trip.

After eating, the grown-ups get together and fix Thanksgiving dinner while the children are playing video games.

It's Thanksgiving morning and the house is smelling good. There is a long line to get in the bathroom to take a bath and get a change of clothes. After everyone gets on their clothes, we go out on the balcony to sit and look down. A couple of hours later, we sit down and have Thanksgiving dinner. We all stand around the table and hold hands while someone says a prayer over our Thanksgiving meal.

After Thanksgiving dinner, my grandma gets the video camera, goes around, and asks everyone what they are thankful for. Then we get ready for the long ride back home.

Tequan K. Chalmers, elementary school

In my family we have a special tradition where we draw on a tablecloth with markers every Thanksgiving. We do this as a way to keep track of us growing. We can tell by our handwriting, plus we always sign our name and date.

We usually draw some turkeys and other holiday scenes. Last year my brother drew a maze, which took up the whole cloth.

We're not really sure how this tradition started. My mom just decided to have a unique way to tell how we've grown from year to year. My family thinks this is special.

Jenny Flaherty, elementary school

In my family we make a "thankful turkey." A thankful turkey is just some sort of jar made to look like a turkey. You can make it by washing out a jar (peanut butter jars are best). Then cut construction paper into turkey parts like a head, waddle, legs, and feathers to put on the jar. We get anybody who stops by to write what they are thankful for. During Thanksgiving dinner we read the little pieces of paper. We like to hear what everyone else is thankful for. We like the tradition and intend not to forget to make a thankful turkey. It helps us to be thankful for what we have.

Danielle Marie Lee, elementary school

Today I awoke to the smell of fresh turkey roasting. I hurriedly got dressed and ran toward the kitchen.

"Time to make the dressing," Mother said. She took out all the ingredients and then skillfully mixed them up. After it all was finally mixed, she asked me to get her the cherries. I pulled out the crystal bowl from my refrigerator which held the ripe, red fruit and placed them next to the mixing bowl. "Leave!" my mother commanded. I smiled, "No, not this year. You leave." Either she was tired or just had too much to do, but at any rate, she left.

I poured half of the dressing into the glass baking dish, then carefully picked the prettiest and juiciest cherry I could find. I then spread the rest of the batter over my little surprise and slipped it in the oven.

That day we had lots to do, but finally everything was done. I greeted the guests at the door while the others finished. Finally when everyone had arrived, we sat down to our feast and humbly bowed our heads in prayer. We had tons of food, too numerous to mention. We were peacefully eating when my brother jumped up and said, "Yes!"

He had found the cherry, which allowed him to be "king of the day"—our family's Thanksgiving tradition. Now we all had to obey him, so he ordered us to watch football for the rest of the day.

Mary Claire Graham, middle school

As my family gathers from far and wide for a Thanksgiving celebration, trinkets and mementos are quietly unpacked and slipped upon the dining room table. Each person must bring a small item symbolizing a thankful moment of the past year. No one may explain the article until we come to the table, and there is often much guessing and puzzlement over each object. As the meal begins, the mysteries unravel for the rest of the family, and we laugh and delight in each new story. A college acceptance letter, cordless telephone, antique school bell, and even a mixing beater are examples of items that have had a secret story behind them. In this way we can all share in those special moments and remain close in spite of the miles between us. I wonder what I will be taking next year?

Lynn Paterson, elementary school

One of my most exciting family traditions is celebrating Thanksgiving together with my relatives. They are from my mom's side of the family. They come from four different states, which are California, Colorado, North Carolina, and Maryland. I have one relative that lives in Australia. My relatives' ages are from three to sixty-one.

The celebration is held at a different family member's house each year. It lasts for three days.

One thing we always do is eat. We have different foods such as turkey, fruit salad, homemade breads, and sweets. Each family volunteers to make or bring something each year. I really like the sweets and bread.

We have different kinds of entertainment. We do things like playing games, videotaping, and making animal noises. When we finish making animal noises, we listen to them on tape and laugh. The younger children, mostly girls, do things like plays and skits. The boys go skateboarding and play basketball games. The men watch football games and talk sports.

The day after Thanksgiving, we go somewhere special, like the zoo, shopping, swimming, movies, or take nature walks.

We learn about our family's history. The older people tell about their life in the past. They talk about things when they were kids. The younger ones talk about what they do that might compare and contrast life now and life long ago.

I think it is important to carry on this tradition. Why do I think it is important? I am learning a part of my family's history to pass on to my children someday.

Lauren E. Lowry, elementary school

I can't wait until tomorrow, the day we will carry on our Thanksgiving tradition. Early tomorrow morning my family will go to a big field behind our house. There we will start to set up for our unusual celebration. My dad and I will build three teepees made with tree limbs and burlap.

Everyone dresses as Pilgrims and Indians. The Indian girls wear colorful clothes and a lot of bead necklaces. The Indian boys wear jeans, T-shirts, and something leather. The only person who dresses as a Pilgrim is my aunt. She wears a long blue dress. Every year my grandparents have the best costumes. My grandmother dresses as an old Indian woman wearing a long flowered skirt and a headband with yarn braids. She has one lone feather in the back. My grandfather dresses as a warrior with war paint and a headband with fake raccoon tails and feathers.

We have a great feast, but that's a small part of our Thanksgiving. This tradition is very special to me because it is the one time when our whole family is at my house for a holiday. I hope we carry on this tradition for a long time.

Amy Boyer, elementary school

Thanksgiving is fast approaching, and I am eagerly anticipating the big day. Of the many traditions in our family, I think the most enjoyable one is Thanksgiving.

On the night before Thanksgiving Day, my mother reads to us the Thanksgiving story of the Pilgrims as we fall asleep. The next day we all go to our grandmother's house.

Upon our arrival, we put on our Pilgrim and Indian hats to bring alive the very first Thanksgiving. My father wears a hat to resemble Governor William Bradford. My mother wears a black-and-white Pilgrim costume as Mrs. Dorothy Bradford. My grandfather portrays Wampanoag Indian chief Massasoit. Wearing a white Pilgrim bonnet, my grandmother is Priscilla Mullins. My uncle James wears Indian feathers to remind us of Squanto who taught the Pilgrims how to grow corn and other vegetables. My uncle A.C. is Captain Miles Standish, the military leader; and I am Oceanus, the Hopkins baby born on the ocean.

After we all sit down at the table laden with scrumptious food, we bow our heads, pray, and then recite the One Hundredth Psalm.

This is a meaningful family tradition that I cherish. I hope to pass it on to my children.

Laura Smith, elementary school

~ Psalm 100 ~

Make a joyful noise unto the Lord, all ye lands.
Serve the Lord with gladness:
Come before his presence with singing.

Know ye that the Lord he is God:
It is he that hath made us, and not we ourselves;
We are his people, and the sheep of his pasture.

Enter into his gates with thanksgiving, and into his courts with praise:
Be thankful unto him, and bless his name.

For the Lord is good;
His mercy is everlasting;
And his truth endureth to all generations.

～ *Iroquois Prayer* ～

This nineteenth-century Iroquois prayer would add a lovely, meaningful touch to any reenactment of Thanksgiving Day, or to the dinner table.

We return thanks to our mother, the earth, which sustains us.

We return thanks to the rivers and streams, which supply us with water.

We return thanks to all herbs, which furnish medicines for the cure of our diseases.

We return thanks to the corn, and to her sisters, the beans and squash, which give us life.

We return thanks to the bushes and trees, which provide us with fruit.

We return thanks to the wind, which, moving the air, has banished diseases.

We return thanks to the moon and stars, which have given to us their light when the sun was gone.

We return thanks to our grandfather *He-no,* that he has protected his grandchildren from witches and reptiles, and has given to us his rain.

We return thanks to the sun, that he has looked upon the earth with a beneficent eye.

Lastly, we return thanks to the Great Spirit, in whom is embodied all goodness, and who directs all things for the good of his children.

HERE'S TO THANKSGIVING, THE RELIGIOUS AND SOCIAL FESTIVAL THAT CONVERTS EVERY FAMILY MANSION INTO A FAMILY MEETINGHOUSE!

CHAPTER 2

The December Celebrations

❧ ❧

Christmas

A MERRY TIME OF YEAR

⌁ *Gifts and Remembrances* ⌁
Family Tradition

*LIBBIE JOHNSON

Traditions go back to time immemorial. I'd wager that more than once Adam and Eve told their sons, "It's a family tradition!" Many people, feeling a deep-seated and very human need to belong, search out their past. Who were our ancestors? we wonder. So it was only natural that Libbie Johnson's relatives sought to trace their roots in the past. They spent hours documenting family heirlooms and researching their relatives. Little did they know that a simple spiral notebook could hold more family history than any eighteenth-century secretary-bookcase or leather-bound volume.

Our family has a long tradition of documenting everything. We've documented our family tree back to the Stuart's royal line in England. We've documented the origin of family antique furniture. We've documented that great-grandfather Phillip Meekins was *not* a Civil War deserter (and obtained amnesty 110 years after the fact). Even with that tradition of tradition, my favorite family tradition was the documentation of our family's Christmas gifts from year to year.

In a spiral notebook that after years of use started to resemble the Magna Carta, my mother would record every year's gifts we each received and the source. The reasoning was to ensure that all gifts were accounted for and the giver would receive a timely thank-you note after the holidays. Good thinking.

Years after the notebook recordings ended in 1980, my mother's last Christmas, I looked back and saw not just entries for thank-you notes but a history of our family.

Beginning in 1953, my first Christmas, a yearly record gives a glimpse of not only our family but of culture and even pop culture. Scanning the spiral notebook record I see:

1956, blocks, doll, doll cradle—I was three. My parents divorced, Mom and I living with my grandmother. Mimi. Uncle Bill. Aunt Tootsie. Lots of toys under the tree for the house's only grandchild, me.

1960, spring horse from Santa—Mom remarried. Christmas morning finds us in our newly built house. Baby sister Kay is not yet two.

1963, rickshaw—Yes, a rickshaw. The best Christmas toy I ever received. Loved it. Wish I could find one for my children.

1965, Monkees album, stretch pants—Enough said.

1968, stockings, makeup, angora sweater—High school, trying to fit in.

1970, Uriah Heep hard rock album from me to Mom—She smirked a thank-you, then returned it to me with a "Maybe you could use this in your record collection." That's okay. My son, sixteen, replayed the whole scenario twenty-four Christmases later when he gave me a gift bought for me with him in mind.

1973, original (contemporary and abstract, of course) art from friend Lynn, blender (for daiquiris) from boyfriend, Our Bodies, Our Selves *from sister*—First year away at college, I returned home quite the sophisticate . . . or so I thought. My gifts that year reflected a move from small town to Grownupsville.

1974, new coat from Mom, extra stocking hanging—The year I eloped and told the family two days before Christmas. Mother, determined to offer her new son-in-law a warm and welcoming family Christmas, whipped up a stocking to add to the family lineup and did extra newlywed shopping—the day before Christmas.

1978, photo album, family artifacts—This was the year we were expecting our first child and the family's first grandchild. Family had become more important than ever. I had asked for and received selected family heirlooms.

1980, money—The last entry in the notebook, an especially heart-tugging year, since Mother would die suddenly less than a month later. But that Christmas, a gift of money in my stocking helped us buy a new station wagon for my growing family. It was a good Christmas filled with lots of toys for the only grandchild, not yet two.

The Christmas gift register was one of the best gifts ever, in and of itself. It taught us initially that a gift, no matter how big or small, is worth a thank-you. The list, with its check marks by each entry, ensured that proper thank-you protocol prevailed. More important, it was a history of our family. Its contents remind us of the Christmases that were perfect and not so perfect. Gifts that still have a place in our lives remind us of the giver, in many cases long since gone. Our Christmas tree, adorned with ornaments that were gifts from friends and neighbors, are yearly reminders of those who played a role in our lives.

Today I have my own Christmas gift register. It's filled with jewelry from my husband during especially sentimental years, computer equipment, electronic gadgets, and the latest toys. It's a great encapsulated history of technology (first microwave, Texas Instrument computer, VCR, and CD player) and the history of leisure (in-line skates, scuba equipment, etc.).

Last Christmas? Listings hint we're getting older, more settled: binoculars for watching birds, gardening tools, classical music, season tickets for local theater, books.

A grand tradition. Ingredients: spiral notebook, pencil, love and passion and family and friends.

~ Christmas Angels, Out of the Blue ~

* JAN KARON

Everyone loves the tradition of gift-giving, especially when the presents come in beautifully wrapped packages topped with the sort of exquisite bow that we ourselves can never tie just right. Yet the gifts that mean the most often are those that come unwrapped. They just drop down upon us, out of the blue, so to speak, says Jan Karon, author of the charming Mitford books. That doesn't mean they can't become one of your Christmas traditions.

My family never observed many of the usual traditions of Christmas, although the heart and spirit of these holy days were always at the core of what we did.

One year we might have a floppy little white pine from the woods of our foothills farm, decorated with strings of popcorn and cranberries.

Another year a cedar would find its way home to us, which my sister and I would smear with "snow" made from Lux flakes mixed with water. This, by the way, is an ingenious recipe, resulting in something that mysteriously resembles the real thing.

Gifts in those years, in the forties, were often simple. I shall never forget the paperback book of poetry I received when I was ten years old. It was Robert Frost's poems, and it cost fifteen cents. For a little girl living in the country, it was the grandest gift imaginable. The dolls, the mirrored music box, the blue Schwinn bicycle—none of these presents ever measured up to a bookful of words that stirred the heart to wonder.

So, while it never quite occurred to me to see many of the "traditional" traditions, a tradition at last sought me.

Several years ago at Christmas a total stranger did something wonderful for me, quite out of the blue.

"You're my Christmas angel!" I exclaimed with wonder. It was true; I believed it! My angel thought it over and, with some wonder, believed it also!

Now each year I look for my Christmas angel to appear. It is always someone different, of course, who does something simple and even extraordinary, quite out of the blue—from hauling my car out of a snowbank to giving me a stray puppy that has endeared herself to me forever.

(I suspect that Christmas angels work year-round, like the rest of us, but gain increasing enthusiasm for their jobs as the season ripens.)

Fitting nicely as it does into the random-acts-of-kindness category, a further tradition has developed from all this. I, too, try to be someone's Christmas angel, a total stranger who, by Providence alone, is led to do something simple and even extraordinary.

Quite out of the blue, of course.

❧ A Moveable Feast ❧

Christmas. December 25. The date never changes. But does it matter on what calendar date you celebrate the day, or where? Not to Carolyn Schwartz or to navy brat Suzy Barile who learned early on that you must seize the moment —especially these days, when change is all around us. Change is part of our lives these days. We move from town to town. Even our family structure changes through death and divorce. A tradition can give us a guidepost of past years and provide a much-needed reminder of life's joys and purpose.

Don't Forget the Muffin Tins

*Carolyn Schwartz

I never thought my family would notice. But one year, instead of fixing our standard Christmas breakfast, I whipped up a batch of blueberry pancakes.

You'd have thought I'd committed a sacrilege.

"Mom," they gasped in disbelief. "Aren't you going to make popovers?"

It was then I realized my popover breakfast had become a Schwartz family *tradition.*

Actually, my own mom had first rights to the idea of popovers on Christmas morning. Where she got the recipe for those puffed-up, light-as-a-feather muffins is anybody's guess. She told us that they originated in England and that when they're soaked in roast beef drippings they're known as Yorkshire pudding.

As a teenager, I watched Mom get out the ingredients: eggs, milk, a dab of butter, flour, and a pinch of salt. Before she put the mixture together, Mom turned the oven up high, then poured a glop of oil in each muffin cup. When the oven was ready, she slid in the muffin pans.

"The only way you'll fail is if you put the batter in too soon," Mom said. "Wait 'til you see the oil start to smoke."

When it did, Mom poured batter into the sizzling oil, then popped the pans back in the oven. Szzzzzzz! You could actually hear the first stirrings of the magic transformation.

Forty-five minutes later, out came the golden beauties, billowing above their muffin-cup boundaries, crusty on the outside, almost hollow on the inside. Without waiting another minute, we filled their cavities with butter and strawberry jam and chomped into them. Often the aftereffects included bloated bellies and burned tongues.

I started making popovers when my kids were barely out of diapers. Poor little guinea pigs! They didn't care when the batter baked into little knots of leathery dough. All they cared about was what I slathered on top of them. My butter and jam camouflage trick worked wonders.

I owe my first popover success to the genius who invented Teflon. There's been steady progress ever since. Except for the time the electricity went out and we had to eat our popovers with our spoons.

And the time I fell for the new recipe that said: "Forget what you've read elsewhere. The secret in making good popovers is to start them in a cold oven."

And the time I used self-rising flour by mistake and watched the batter bubble over into a lake at the bottom of the oven.

Through all the popover goof-ups, my kids have kept their sense of humor.

Each year they've posed for the requisite photos to mark each milestone meal. We have an album full. There are the ones of the popovers coming out of the oven, the ones of me serving up a heaping plateful, others of the boys, opening their mouths wide to take the first bite.

As the kids have grown into adults, my husband and I have started another annual Christmas tradition. We take them on a trip: to Acapulco, the Cayman Islands, or the Bahamas.

"But what about our popovers?" someone always asks.

Leave home at Christmas without my muffin pans?

I wouldn't dare!

The Moravian Love Feast
*Suzy Barile

During my last year of college, a friend invited me to Winston-Salem, North Carolina, for the annual Moravian Candle Tea held at Old Salem. What an afternoon it was! Singing carols to the strains of an old organ in a room lighted only by candles, sipping sweet coffee, and munching on warm coffee cake was just what I needed to get into the Christmas spirit. Years later when by chance I moved to Winston-Salem, I invited my family to come for the Candle Tea and unwittingly started a tradition that continues today.

This story, however, isn't just about enjoying the Candle Tea year after year, for the Moravians have many lovely Christmas traditions. One of those, the Christmas Eve Moravian Love Feast, has come to have deep meaning within our family. There was the Christmas I dipped my one-month-old daughter's pacifier into the coffee so she would be a part of the feast. Then there was the first Love Feast after my mom died, when it was all we could do to hold back the tears as we lifted our candles high and sang "Morning Star, O Cheering Sight."

But the Christmas Eve service I remember the most fondly was the Love Feast we ourselves held at home.

Growing up a navy brat, I was accustomed to celebrating Christmas at such unusual times as Thanksgiving or the week after New Year's. So the year I realized my husband would have to work on Christmas Eve only meant a little more planning was necessary to celebrate our annual Love Feast.

I flipped through the Winston-Salem cookbook until I found the recipe for the famed sweet buns and began preparing them. (It's a long, time-consuming process.) I had found a program from an earlier Love Feast service. From it I copied into handmade songbooks the words to "Morning Star" and other Christmas hymns. When my mom and brothers and sisters arrived late Christmas Eve afternoon, we busied ourselves with preparing Christmas dinner and doing the last-minute gift wrapping. After dinner, we gathered in the living room, built a fire, and began our Love Feast.

Mom brought all the Love Feast candles she had collected over the years so everyone would have one. We read Saint Matthew's account of the first Christmas, sang carols, and lighted the candles before sharing the sweet buns and coffee we had prepared. It was the most beautiful Christmas Eve Love Feast ever.

Families change. I divorced and remarried. Each year whoever is home on Christmas Eve attends the Love Feast at Raleigh Moravian Church, and each year we listen as the minister tells the same story over again—of how the Christmas Eve Love Feast was designed especially for children. Yet I never tire of hearing him tell the story.

My daughter, now nearly fourteen, has attended the Love Feast every year since that first Christmas. Even now, in the years when she is with her dad for Christmas, we attend the Love Feast before she must leave. Instead of the service being the beginning of our Christmas celebration, however, it becomes the ending. We change Christmas Eve to December 23, open all our presents on the morning of the twenty-fourth, welcome friends and family throughout the day, then end the day with our annual Christmas Eve Love Feast celebration.

~ *Too Dear to Forget* ~

Scholars are quick to tell those who love Christmas and think of it as having solely Christian origins, that historically this combination holiday and holy day is a continuation of pagan celebrations. It was during the fifth century that December 25 was established by the Western church as the day to celebrate Christ's birth. That was the day on which the pagans offered thanks to Apollo, the sun god. Indeed, many of the pagan customs used to celebrate this day at the end of Saturnalia (the festival honoring Saturn, the god of agriculture)— feasting, gift-giving, and the use of candles and evergreens—were readily embraced by the Christians.

So today we take our family, ethnic, and national Christmas customs with us, no matter where chance, fate, and circumstances lead us. Ironically, many of these time-tested traditions have found a new life, and even been kept alive, in new surroundings.

That is what happened to many cherished Lithuanian traditions that were snuffed out in the military and political wars that ravished Eastern Europe in recent years. Those customs were kept alive by Gene and Lil Bezgela, both first-generation Americans born of Lithuanian parents, living in Raleigh, North Carolina. As the Bezgelas explained, "After visiting with relatives in Lithuania in 1991, we learned that many of their traditions were no longer observed, as it was not permitted under the Russian regime. Then, in 1992, a Lithuanian biochemistry post-doctoral student at North Carolina State University located us through the International Program Directory. We reintroduced the customs and traditions her grandmother used to tell them. Now that she is back in Lithuania we are learning that they are not only rebuilding a country but also reestablishing many of the forgotten traditions."

How much this one experience tells us about our deep love and need for memories that bridge the years, the miles, and the generations. As Vincent Boris points out, Christmas truly is amenable to cross-cultural exchange. The traditions lend themselves to the celebration of unity and the brotherhood of all people.

A Tradition Transplanted

VINCENT B. BORIS

Among my earliest childhood memories are those of *Kucios* (Christmas Eve dinner) at my paternal grandmother's home. My first remembered *Kucios* was circa 1936, and, by that time my father's family had been in the States some thirty-five years. Yet Lithuanian traditions were very strong. (My grandmother throughout her life—and she died in her seventies—never learned to speak English. The common language at home was that strange patois developed by the early Lithuanian immigrants who settled in the coal mining areas of Pennsylvania and the industrial cities like Detroit, Pittsburgh and Chicago.) Being of hearty peasant stock, Grandma would not be satisfied with commercially produced foods. Everything had to be prepared by hand from scratch. In her advanced years, when arthritis made it difficult for her to manipulate all the kitchen utensils, the daughters and daughters-in-law were pressed into service, but Grandma's eagle eye and iron will demanded perfect performance.

Preparation began days earlier. *Plotkeles,* the thin communionlike wafers, were acquired weeks earlier from the parish organist, who dispensed them for a stipend to augment his meager salary. The *silkai,* or salted herring, were purchased days earlier so that they could be adequately soaked to remove the salt, cleaned and put into a spiced marinade for at least a week. The Christmas Eve biscuits, which were to be served with poppyseed milk were also made days earlier so that they could be dried to a nut-like hardness. Today, we call them *slizikai;* but then we called them "klatskies." (Note the probable Polish-derived name with the English plural ending.) One other *Kucios* essential was also made days earlier. We called it "Kimmel" (based on the German name for caraway seed which was one of the main ingredients along with honey and citrus peel. It was a semipotent home-concocted liqueur and is now referred to in Lithuanian as *Krupnikas*).

On Christmas Eve, itself, the family gathered early—the women to help out in the kitchen; the men to smoke and sip "Kimmel" in the parlor. The house was redolent with intriguing smells from the numerous dishes being prepared in the kitchen. There would be no tree or other decorations yet to signify the event; just a family gathering with a lot of hustle and bustle in the kitchen. It became customary for aunts and uncles to use this gathering as the occasion to introduce their intended spouse to the entire family. So there was frequently no lack of opportunity for good humored earthy banter, most of which we children were not supposed to understand. This was especially so if the situation had changed during the previous year and a new "intended" was brought forth.

At sunset we would all gather around the table for the ritualized dinner called *Kucios.* First, there was grace, pronounced by Grandma, as was her right as matriarch. This was followed by the breaking and sharing of the "plotkelies." Dinner began with marinated herring and rye bread followed by a specially prepared mushroom-barley soup known as *Rasele* (Little Dew), which was made only for *Kucios.* I should note that these first two courses were usually passed over by the non-Lithuanian fiancés or fiancées, partly because the concept of eating fish separated from its natural state only by salting and marination was beyond the ken of "typical Americans," and partly because of the highly pungent taste of *baravykai,* that truly unique Lithuanian mushroom, was enhanced with a liberal dash of pepper and vinegar. This was usually more than an uninitiated palate could take. The family knew that, once the non-Lithuanian guest could savor and enjoy the *Rasele,* the relationship was serious and had a future.

The rest of the meal consisted of more or less routine dishes— baked fish, a meatless kugelis, cottage-cheese blintzes, a buckwheat porridge, sauerkraut, and cucumber salad. There were supposed to be twelve courses (one for each of the apostles), but as a kid I looked forward to the klatskies and poppy seed milk, which were served as dessert, along with other pastries.

Soon after dinner we youngsters were put to bed and most of the adults would be off to Midnight Mass. A few adults would remain to baby-sit but, more importantly, to put up and decorate the Christmas tree and arrange all the gifts on the floor around the tree. It was indeed the middle of the night when, after returning from church, the adults would loudly announce that "Santa had come." I shall never forget the awe and joy I felt upon seeing that majestic and brilliantly lit tree. Christmas had indeed come.

Nor will I ever cease to hold *Kucios* as an integral part of Christmas. There could be no Christmas for me without also a *Kucios.* Even when living far from home with nary a Lithuanian within sight, I have found a way to celebrate *Kucios.* In Texas, it was with a group from the parish choir; in Germany, it was with fellow residents of the bachelor officers' quarters. Two things, fortunately, changed over the years: the church abolished mandatory abstinence on Christmas Eve, and American tastes (at least the palates of those with whom I was associated) developed a much higher sophistication. After all, if you are in the military, you probably have had a tour in Europe and were well acquainted with the marinated herring widely available in German restaurants. If assigned to the Far East, you undoubtedly would have tried sushi in Japan. Then, living in south Texas in San Antonio, the home of Tex-Mex dishes, one would become accustomed to foods that far outrivaled the *Rasele* for spiciness.

Somehow I always managed to get *Plotkeles* from home, find commercially prepared herring, and a reasonable facsimile of *baravykai.* The Germans have a close cousin called *Steinpilzen* (stone mushrooms). Adequate help and sometimes food contributions from choir members or fellow officers were always available, particularly if the participants were fortified with *Krupnikas.* It was no problem to organize a *Kucios* that started traditionally with *Plotkeles,* herring and *Rasele* and ended traditionally at Midnight Mass, even if there were non-Catholics at dinner. In between, we have had a venison roast with *bulvine desrele* (potato sausage), roast pork with sautéed sauerkraut, and charcoal-grilled London broil.

After Grandma died, Mom assumed the responsibilities for the extended family *Kucios.* Growing up, it had been one of my duties to help prepare for *Kucios,* so I gradually learned all the tasks, and Mom had written out the recipes to help me prepare the *Kucios* in Texas. After Mom died and most of the food preparation was left to my brother and me, I suggested that roast turkey and ham were infinitely easier to prepare and their leftovers much more palatable. So our meatless tradition at home was also adapted to modern times. In time I came to realize that the significance of *Kucios* was not in the traditional foods but in the coming together of friends and family to share in that most human of joint endeavors—the breaking of bread together.

I found my non-Lithuanian friends so taken with and impressed by the event that they would eagerly anticipate the next *Kucios.* A couple of friends in San Antonio continue the tradition of a Christmas Eve sit-down dinner with their own family and friends. They even refer to it as *Kucios*—a Lithuanian-derived custom.

It may be a unique facet of Christmas that it is so amenable to cross-cultural exchange. As we celebrate the feast in this country, we might observe that the Christmas tree tradition comes from Germany, the carols from France and Germany, caroling from England; and the Creche from Italy. From our Lithuanian heritage comes *Kucios.* I realize that others, namely the Poles and Slovaks, share a similar custom. The more the merrier. Revel in it. Share it with your non-Lithuanian friends. God took on human form and validated the fact that all humankind shares a common nature. Celebrate the coming of Christ by celebrating the unity and brotherhood of humankind.

"Let us break bread together."

~ The Centuries-Old Tradition of Christmas ~

DOROTHY CANFIELD FISHER

Who among us does not complain about the commercialism of the season—the shopping, the expensive gifts, the time it takes to put up and take down the decorations? Take the time to read Dorothy Canfield Fisher's essay. Oh, you may still complain, but with a new insight into how these traditions have evolved you will see the rich link these multicultural traditions have with the past. Even more importantly, as Fisher says, these traditions are good for children and adults alike. They create a common bond among all people, and they give us greater understanding of ourselves.

Do you know anyone who is really satisfied with Christmas as we observe it now? I don't. I could not count the people I have heard speak mournfully of the way Christmas has been "spoiled," nor the number of guesses I have heard as to the reason why, against our wills, we have allowed it to be so spoiled. My guess is that we have been helpless to defend Christmas because of our muddle-headedness. Certainly not from lack of good intentions. Perhaps if we took the trouble to do some thinking about what Christmas is, and to use our imaginations a little about what it might be, we could direct with more effectiveness our efforts to keep it from being an orgy of "give and grab" as someone has sadly dubbed the day that should be hallowed.

Look with me for a moment at the history of the festival, which is of all the greatest antiquity. From the dawn of time, before history, all peoples have celebrated the winter solstice with thanksgiving. North, south, east, west—the Jewish Feast of Lights, the Druid Mother-night, the Roman Feast of Saturn, the Scandinavian Yule ceremonies—everywhere there have been ceremonies to express the emotional relief felt by humanity over the day which marks the turn of the year, the day when the sun, giver of life, after having for months grown steadily weaker and feebler, turns back from death and begins to grow stronger and warmer. From this primitive rejoicing over the annual rebirth of the sun come all those of our Christmas usages that have to do with fire—lighted candles and lamps, the Yule log, the cheerfully illuminated home and street. After about four hundred years, the Christian Church, trying to simplify the tradition from paganism to Christianity, wisely decreed that the celebration of the birthday of its Founder should coincide with the date on which this older and universal folk festival was held, thus uniting into one, two mighty currents of human feeling.

Our Christmas customs come from the strangely varied ways in which men have celebrated this old feast. The bountiful Christmas dinner is a reminiscence of the Roman banquets at this time, in honor of ancient gods and goddesses, in whose name cheerful hymns, the originals of our carols, were sung in the streets. In ancient Rome also, people exchanging presents along with the lighted tapers which symbolized the relighted sun. Our decorations of holly and mistletoe come from an entirely different direction, straight down from our pre-Christian Druid ancestors, to whom these were sacred leaves. The Christmas tree is infinitely more modern, starting in a corner of Germany (probably from dim memories of the Scandinavian sacred tree) only three centuries ago, taking two hundred years to spread over all of Germany, and another century to reach England and America. The Christmas card is the most recent of all, not starting till 1862. So you see that of all our Christmas program, the crèche and going to church are the only ones to express our joy in celebrating the birthday of the Founder of the religion we profess.

Now, examine the variegated items in this old, old folk-festival from another standpoint, that of the person who is looking for chances to make money, and in an instant you will see why the giving of presents, and the exchange of Christmas cards have received such an enormous amount of skilled, commercial publicity as practically to make us forget all the many other beautiful and significant aspects of the day. And isn't it considerably easier to resist commercial propaganda when you see clearly where and how you are being exploited?

The festival of Christmas is a part of the universal history of our race, unimaginably rich with old meanings. There is something awe-inspiring in the thought that, as with our children we light the candles on the tree, we are one with our prehistoric ancestors, poetically and symbolically, rejoicing over the rebirth of the sun. A usage as old as that, as beautiful, based on such a fundamental human instinct should not be hurriedly passed over as a mere preliminary to getting something for nothing. It should be explained to the children whose naturally fresh and poetic imaginations are always apt to understand and appreciate folk-ways; it should be considered a dignified part of one of our finest old traditions. And the Christmas greens—! Give its true, strange, thought-provoking flavor to what is now a thin, meaningless gesture, remind yourself and tell the children of the curious origin of that custom, give a thought to our prehistoric Druid forefathers, still living on in our homes with every branch of holly and mistletoe we hang. It is good for the children, good for us, it gives a new and shapely perspective to life, to realize that the poorest and humblest of us have grandfathers, aeons of them, living, fearing, rejoicing, passing on to us their driving impulse to try to understand and to beautify life.

And don't forget, every time you focus the attention of your family on one of these age-old, profoundly human aspects of this grand old feast day, you lessen the strangle-hold on their minds of the acquisitive instinct so poisonously bloated by the commercial overemphasis on present-giving. For it is only overemphasis that is hurtful. Present-giving and present-receiving are not bad in themselves. To give well, generously, thoughtfully, to receive with pleasure, delicacy and gratitude—those are beautiful arts which every child should learn by practice. But it stands to reason that he has an infinitely better chance to learn them well, and not badly, if his attention is not solely concentrated on this part of his Christmas Day.

And of course, strangest and most incredible result of the modern distortion of Christmas, is our forgetfulness of what should be its dearest and most sacred meaning, its celebration of the birth of Christ, even to think of which, once, truly, brings tears of thankfulness to our eyes.

There is the day as we inherit it from our life-loving, deep-hearted ancestors, radiant with associations, evocative of emotions that run the gamut from simple light-hearted gaiety through the sweet poetry of symbolic old customs, to religious awe that shakes the heart and purifies the soul. If we do not open the door and let our boys and girls into all of these riches, rightfully theirs, we are cheating them. The child for whom we begin to prepare the Christmas festivals is, literally, the heir to all the ages. We steal the best of his birthright from him if, on Christmas Day, we give him nothing but presents.

➤ Please Pass the Smoked Salmon, ➤ the Sauerkraut, and the Christmas Cheer

All of us think that our way of celebrating Christmas is the right way. The best traditions, according to Norma Morin and Barbara Wagner, come when we take a little from everyone and mix them together. The memories of such traditions last forever.

An Ecumenical Gathering

Norma Morin

My father, who was Jewish, married my mother, a Methodist, when he was twenty years of age and she was nineteen. I was an only child, born on her twentieth birthday in Kentucky, April 23, 1926. They were originally Vermonters, and I eventually married a Vermonter. We all moved around quite a bit, but finally settled in Miami, Florida, where we lived for thirty-five years.

My husband and I had two children, a girl and a boy. As soon as we had located in Miami, we decided to establish a tradition of having my parents and any other relatives or friends available come to a breakfast on Christmas morning. (My husband, children, and I were Catholic, and and some of our friends are Baptist, so it was quite an ecumenical gathering!)

There was a wonderful kosher deli nearby where we got our supplies for our never-changing menu: Nova lox (smoked salmon), corned beef, cream cheese with chives, chopped liver, half-sour pickles, bialys (delectable crusty rolls), bagels, steaming hot coffee, plus a whitefish for my father, and pumpernickel. We'd say our prayers of thanks and then dig in.

After breakfast the children passed the gifts to each other from under the tree, and distributed them with great care. Each of us had one present at a time and everyone took his or her own turn amid many oohs and aahs. It was a very festive day, to say the least!

Our children are married and have their own family traditions now.

I built a home in North Carolina when we retired and provided a place with us for my parents. Plans don't always work out as envisioned, however. We moved to our new home in 1990. My father died in 1991, my mother died in 1992, and my dear husband died in 1993. But I still have very happy memories of our special tradition.

The Grit and the Yank

BARBARA WAGNER

My husband is a "Yankee" by birth, and I a "grit"—a term for Southerners which he acquired while a student at Duke. When we married, as is the case with everyone, we brought the customs and traditions from our two diverse backgrounds together. The result was a little from both plus a few new ones of our own. Many of these customs and traditions revolve around the celebration of Christmas and come from pleasant holiday memories.

His memories of the holidays included snow, that white stuff we seldom saw in eastern North Carolina and most certainly never on Christmas. Though sometimes there was a cold spell in early December, the twenty-fifth was usually warm, short-sleeve weather. White Christmases for me existed on Christmas-card pictures and in the carols we sang. Nevertheless, every year I dreamed of a white Christmas every year right along with Bing Crosby. That dream came true the first year we moved to his hometown of York, Pennsylvania. It started snowing on Christmas Eve and snowed all night. I'll never forget how beautiful it was on Christmas morning!

During my husband's childhood years Santa Claus put up and decorated the tree on Christmas Eve while he and his five siblings slept.

Farther South, my family put up the tree a week—or even two—before Christmas. The tree was part of the excitement and anticipation of the season. As an adult with my own children, I could not imagine putting up a tree on Christmas Eve. It always took us half the night to put together the toys that invariably had missing parts. Even Santa couldn't accomplish that feat! And so I won this tradition.

But then there was this thing about sauerkraut and turkey. Having been raised on traditional southern fare, I found it rather strange when my new in-laws served sauerkraut as a side dish with the Christmas turkey. Of course this reflected their German heritage. The closest thing to sauerkraut on my mother's Southern holiday table was a dish of collard greens. Eventually, however, I found this to be a good combination. The tart flavor of the kraut adds some zest to the turkey.

Today our children, now adults, think sauerkraut is essential to a Christmas meal. Maybe it brings back memories of their early years in Pennsylvania when Christmas always meant cold weather, maybe even snow, with a warm fire in the fireplace and a big family of a great-grandmother, grandparents, great-aunts and uncles, aunts, uncles, and cousins gathered to enjoy Christmas dinner complete with all the trimmings—including sauerkraut.

A Civil War Tradition

*JOHN PIERSON

My mother's mother was a Coxe from Utica, New York. On Christmas morning the Coxe family would line up outside the living room or wherever the presents had been left by Santa, youngest first and so on back to the oldest, hands on shoulders of the one before you. They would march into the room in step, chanting: "Hay foot, straw foot, belly full of bean soup, January, February, March. . . . Hay foot, straw foot . . ."

The chant was supposed to have come from the War between the States, when unlettered Union farm boys didn't know left from right. Their drill sergeants would stuff a piece of hay into the top of their right boot and a piece of straw into the left boot. These they could follow.

~ The Grand Illumination ~

*BETSY POWELL MULLEN AND TOM MULLEN

On eighteenth-century plantations "Christmas guns" were shot off on Christmas Eve and at the break of dawn on Christmas morning throughout the South. In fact, when I asked my New England–born father what was one of the first differences he noticed between the North and South when he came to North Carolina in the 1930s he instantly replied, "Fireworks. You southerners will use any excuse to set off fireworks." Colonial Williamsburg continues the tradition of the Christmas guns with their renowned Grand Illumination. The appeal is timeless.

Picture tens of thousands of people squeezed along a three-hundred-year-old street that's only a mile long. Imagine it being so cold that hot cider tastes more like iced tea. Feel the dull ache of standing on your feet for about three hours and being able to shuffle, if you're lucky, a few feet at a time.

There we are in the middle of it: two toddlers, a great-grandmother, two grandparents, one uncle, and thirty-something parents, all blissfully aware that our annual holiday kickoff is cold, crowded, and crazy.

And every year it's something we can't wait to do.

The Christmas season doesn't begin for us until we make the family pilgrimage to Colonial Williamsburg for the Grand Illumination, a decades-old Virginia tradition. Over the years, our family trek has expanded to include a spouse, one child, then another child and various friends. Still, on the surface, there's no real reason why we should go to Williamsburg on that day. We all live close enough to enjoy that city on any other day when it doesn't seem like half the world has come slogging down historic Duke of Gloucester Street and we are united in our disdain of cold and crowds. Still, the town casts a nostalgic spell over each of us for different reasons.

Like a mother calling children for supper, the Grand Illumination for us beckons every year to come share its graces, to take time to sit and be with family.

Most years, Grand Illumination falls on a frigid December day. The countdown to Christmas is reaching a fever pitch, and we're all precariously behind in our holiday shopping, rushed to the brink at the office, and pulled into so many different directions.

As we drive ourselves desperately and deeply into a pre-holiday frenzy, Grand Illumination forces us to stop for one day. It fills the afternoon with a leisurely peace and streaks the night sky with explosions that shout, "Stop. Look. Listen."

And we do.

The tradition of Grand Illumination has seeped into our souls.

No one is sure who started this tradition or why it began. As we grow older and our family expands, our traditions seem to have become more deliberate. With families today separated by distance and commitments, we can no longer count on the everyday rituals that held us together. There's no more lingering after dinner, generations gathered around the family table.

We try to keep those traditions alive, however, by passing them to our children. They recite the same blessings and bedtime prayers we did as children. We read the same books and sing the same songs. We make family dinner the cornerstone of the day. We share the same comforting foods on special occasions. We find new, creative ways to celebrate family and togetherness, traditions they can remember and pass to their children.

And whenever possible we come together to honor the time-tested traditions.

One year, when almost everyone was sick and the weather took a wintry turn, one member of our family took a friend to Grand Illumination, just to keep the tradition alive. Few things can keep us away. It forces us to stand still for a day and celebrate the season and each other.

We begin making plans for it early each fall: where we will meet, where we shall eat, where we will park our feet to watch the bonfires and fireworks and hear the softly sung songs that stir us so.

It brings us and binds us.

～ A Heartwarming Scrooge and ～ an Angel Named Jason

No time of year brings back more memories of our departed loved ones than does Christmas. But how warming and uplifting our memories are. As the young Ashlee Hoskins reminds us, remembering traditions can help us through hard times and help us relive the past rather than drowning in grief. And, Barry Troutman tells us, remembering angels can bring untold joy to others.

The year my father died I was worried that seeing *Scrooge* would break my mom's heart, and I hoped that her grief wouldn't spill over. She might forbid me to watch it. That would break my heart. To my amazement we watched it together, and she even enjoyed it. At that moment I respected her the most.

The rest of my Christmas vacation I never felt hollow or bleak because my mom had put aside her grief and relived precious moments of the past.

She had participated in a family tradition and made it increase in value in my heart.

It has been two years since that memorable night. Now that I am older, I understand that having family traditions unites a family's hearts.

Watching *Scrooge* is a family tradition that will be a part of me.

Ashlee M. Hoskins, middle school

➤ ➤

As I sit here I remember the autumn of 1988. I was expecting my second child. Unfortunately, complications developed and I lost Joshua during the eighth month. Holidays would be hard to bear. Joshua would not be here to help decorate the tree, carve our pumpkins, or to put his teeth under his pillow. There had to be something we could do to keep his memory alive.

One day in December, my daughter, Jennifer, and I were shopping. There were "angel trees" throughout the mall. An "angel tree" is a tree filled with paper angels, each one labeled with a child's name, age, and what they would like for Christmas. As we were browsing through the trees, we came upon an angel named Joshua. He wanted a teddy bear. We bought the most beautiful teddy bear we could find, wrapped it, and returned it with Joshua's name on it.

Now each and every year, we can't wait to browse through the angel trees. Of course, we always look for an angel named Joshua, but we also take several names and have lots of fun buying gifts for our angels.

Our Joshua tradition will always continue, not only at Christmas, but through the year. We know there's an angel in heaven with a smile on his face. And there's one down here with a grin, too.

Barry M. Troutman

➤ Tree's Arrival Brings Magic ➤ of the Holidays

BEA COLE

Put a group of fifty-plus Christmas lovers together and invariably you'll hear the same old sad song: "Remember how much fun we used to have when we'd go out in the woods and cut down our Christmas tree?"

My happy Christmas tree memories stem not from the countryside but from the yearly drive down the storybook-pretty Victorian Main Street of Danville, Virginia. There the nearby farmers sold the spare cedar and pine trees cut from their land to us "city folks." In the early dusk of the December days the trees were romantically beautiful. Invariably, when the tree we had chosen was standing straight in the wooden stand my father had nailed together, the tree either had a skinny or a flat side. No matter. Once it was dressed in red and green and frosted with silver icicles, it was the perfect tree.

That was all forty-odd years ago. Today I wander among blue spruces, Fraser firs, and Scotch pines strung along a brightly lighted Christmas-tree lot. These are perfectly shaped cultivated trees, painstakingly pruned by professional tree farmers. They are beautiful. They make me long for the simplicity and innocence of bygone days.

Lucky Bea Cole lives in New Hampshire where she has managed to reestablish that wished-for tradition of a homegrown Christmas tree. But that's just the beginning of the fun.

With a little more than a week before Christmas we finally added the Christmas tree to our home. We usually wait as long as we can because there isn't a lot of extra space in our house, but the impatient voices of our daughters won over.

During our nightly travels they had noticed that other people already had their trees up. The rich colors of the lights filled windows as we drove by.

This year we decided to make the harvesting of the tree a family outing. In the past, my husband, Pete, usually ventured out to buy a tree somewhere because we always had a baby or two running around. But now we have no more babies and are totally consumed in the world of the little girl. So it seemed like a good time to start our own family tree tradition.

Pete and I both remembered the excitement of Christmas tree hunting. It was always something that my family did as a group. Into the woods we'd go in search of the elusive "perfect" tree. I never really cared about the tree; one was as good as another. It was the sliding that I went for. After we had climbed up the side of Mount Welcome and found our tree, it was time to slide back down!

Our children seemed extremely excited about this Christmas tree hunt. We climbed but a short distance out back of our neighbors' property and stopped to inspect the crop. Immediately the older children began to explore the maze of trees. They were shouting about some critter tracks they had found while Dad cut down the tree.

The real fun began once we got the tree inside. Its scent filled the house as it stood in the bathroom drying out. The girls took regular turns going in to check on it. Then finally it was put in the stand to be decorated. Pete strung the lights as Alisha hopped around behind him, her excitement barely contained as she bounced off the tips of her toes with her arms waving at her sides. I began to wonder if I should grab her skirt lest she take off in flight.

Then Dad's job was done. The girls were handed their boxes as each child has her own ornaments. We watched as they studied and admired their favorite ones. Through the years family and friends have added to their collection.

Our little girls scurried back and forth, putting their decorations on the prickly branches. Melissa was lifted up and then she stretched out slender arms to add a painted mouse as Lindsey chuckled over an ornament inscribed "Baby's first Christmas." That was a long time ago for her. She was only three days old that first year. Finally their boxes were empty. Pete and I added our ornaments, and the job was done.

Then I sat back and admired our work. I realized that the Christmas tree is one of the best holiday traditions, not because of the gifts that come from beneath its spreading branches but because of the peace, joy, and happiness it brings for just being what it is—a tree adorned with love.

⁓ And for the Birds ⁓

My ninety-year-old parents have been bird lovers their whole lives long. In my childhood, as Christmas approached, Mother would always ask, "Who will feed the birds?" This signaled that it was time to make the birds' Christmas tree. We popped popcorn and strung it. Cranberry garlands were made. We set little clusters of grapes aside. Suet was wrapped into a ball by winding twine around it. But the most fun of all was spreading peanut butter on pinecones. When all was assembled, we tied bright red ribbons around the treats. We then decorated the birds' Christmas tree in our backyard. The reward then, and now, is watching cardinal red and blue jay blue Christmas colors mixed in among the sparrow brown and squirrel gray visitors to the tree.

To it you can also add apples and oranges through which you have strung a bit of fishing line to secure them to the limbs. These add even more color and carry out the traditional use of fruits in Christmas decoration.

I often hang pretty artificial fruits on my indoor tree as a reminder of what my grandfather said years ago.

He, like the Coles, cut down a pine tree from nearby woods. On it he hung real apples and oranges. "Everyone knows apples and oranges can't grow on an evergreen tree," he would say, quickly adding, "but once a year, for just a few days, we can pretend. And that is the magic of Christmas."

I was awakened by the sound of a robin's song this morning. My mom had poured birdseed in the bird feeder outside my window. I got up and went to the living room window and I saw the enormous tree that he had decorated yesterday.

We call this tree "the bird tree." It's like a Christmas tree, but instead of ornaments, there are birds. On the tree we put items that birds eat like birdseed, popcorn, cranberries, and apple slices.

When my great-grandfather lived in our house, he decorated the same tree. He mostly decorated it with the same things that we do. There seem to be more birds every year. They must know that the tree will always be there.

It's good to see that most of the birds survive the harsh winter. The birds in the tree give a certain light to our backyard. We can watch it from the dining room if we put the blinds up. This is my favorite tradition, and I hope we will continue to do it every year.

Daniel Wilt, middle school

~ *Christmas Tree* ~

AILEEN FISHER

I'll find me a spruce
in the cold white wood
with wide green boughs
and a snowy hood.

I'll pin on a star
with five gold spurs
to mark my spruce
from the pines and firs.

I'll make me a score
of suet balls
to tie to my spruce
when the cold dusk falls,

And I'll hear next day
from the sheltering trees,
the Christmas carols
of the chickadees.

～ The Irresistible Charm of Advent Cards ～

SHEILA STROUP

Many of our current Christmas traditions can be traced back to Europe and our immigrating ancestors. In my New England grandmother's trunk of letters (she never threw anything out!) I found this passage in a 1954 letter from her dear friend Ruth Boehner, an officer in the United States Air Force who had returned to Alabama after a tour of duty in Europe.

"I'm sending you an Advent card, and hope you have as much pleasure with it as I have had with mine these past years. I got acquainted with them overseas. Both the Swiss and Germans have lovely ones, and I thought you, too, might enjoy poking one of the "lids" daily. The first one I had after I came here caused much comment. Everyone is anxious to lift all the lids at once instead of day by day—but no fair peeking, you know!"

I recalled this note when reading Sheila Stroup's memories of her family's Advent card.

The first year we didn't get one I felt like something was missing from my December.

I think it was 1989, when Shannon and Keegan were at college and Claire had moved up to junior high and fancied herself too old for such things.

Having an Advent calendar taped to the refrigerator had been a family ritual since the early seventies when our older two began to understand what Christmas was about. It was a way for them to measure how long they had to wait until baby Jesus would appear in our Nativity set and Santa would arrive.

I can picture them at three, standing on a chair, opening the last window just before they went to bed on Christmas Eve. They were wearing red flannel pajamas from Sears, with tops striped like candy canes, and matching Christmas stockings.

Although they're twenty-six and no longer live at the Stroup house, Shannon and Keegan still put those stockings by the fireplace on Christmas Eve and hope for Santa.

Some traditions are hard to give up.

Going to buy the Advent calendar became a tradition, too. For us, it signified the beginning of the Christmas season.

We always got it at Carol's Corner Bookstore, a wonderful little shop in Covington, Louisiana, that held much more than books.

In December the store would get more crowded than usual. Holiday stories and little jars of homemade hot-pepper jelly would line the shelves, Santa would show up in the puppet theater, and a Christmas tree covered with tiny wooden ornaments would take up the center of the room.

Advent calendars were stuck everywhere. There were snowy woodland scenes, Nativity pictures, Victorian Christmas trees, and Scandinavian villages.

In fact, there were so many calendars to choose from that our yearly ritual always included a disagreement about which one we'd take home.

It wasn't too bad when Keegan and Shannon were small. Shannon would pick out an animal calendar, and Keegan would go along with her choice if I promised him he could open the first window and I let him get an ornament off Carol's tree.

But later, when the little sister came along, they always had a loud three-way argument.

"This one." "No, this one." "No, THIS one."

I'd give them the Sesame Street co-op-er-a-tion talk, and when that didn't work, I'd grit my teeth and say something like "Well, if you can't agree, we just won't get one this year."

At that point, Claire would throw herself on the floor and start to cry, and I'd back away from the annual holiday scene and pretend that my children belonged to somebody else.

When Shannon and Keegan finally gave in, we'd take Claire's choice home and tape it up on the refrigerator, and every night they'd fight over whose turn it was to open the window.

Now that Claire is eighteen and off at college, she's beginning to realize you never outgrow some things. She called me on November 30 and said, "I need an Advent calendar."

The thought of buying one herself never occurred to her evidently. "You're the mommy," she said, when I suggested it.

So of course I got her one.

I like the thought of her opening the little window every night, looking forward to Christmas and coming home.

Like Shannon, Keegan, and Claire, Celia Berger will also carry on the Advent tradition in her family, but her children won't be such an embarrassment to their mother in the card store, though there may be a little discord at home! Once the children are older, though, the true significance of the Advent wreath will take on a special meaning to those who celebrate it, as it has for Laurie Powell.

Every single year since I was in the second grade, right before the chilly month of December, my family gets down the things for the Advent wreath from the attic.

The Advent wreath is used to put five candles in. You are supposed to light one candle each week. The first four candles represent love, joy, hope, and peace. The very last candle that you light on Christmas Eve is white. It reminds us of Jesus Christ.

A lot of other people's wreaths are store-bought, but our Advent wreath is lovingly homemade. We get fresh greenery like pine which gives it a Christmasy smell. We wrap the greenery over the old piece of Styrofoam that we have used every year. The candles are a mixture of old and new.

Lighting the Advent wreath is a lot of fun! We sing and pray. My brother and I argue about who will light the candle or blow it out.

The Advent wreath is my favorite family tradition. The Advent wreath makes me feel happy to welcome Christmas.

Celia Matsen Berger, elementary school

The Christmas season is full of laughter, goodwill, and joy. In the Powell family, these characteristics come from not only the giving and receiving of gifts but also through the giving of one's heart. Is has become a tradition in our house to light an Advent wreath during the Christmas season and share with each other what we are truly thankful for. This time has become a memorable and touching part of our Christmas.

As the candles of the Advent wreath are lit, several Scriptures are read, and we pray together as a family. These actions establish a setting in which a person can expose one's heart.

Next comes my favorite part. We take turns expressing what we love the most about each other, our friends, or the Christmas holiday. My mom likes to speak last, which is probably a mistake, because by that time she is always crying.

During this time of fellowship, relationships are strengthened. A new light is shone on the people whom you know and trust best. It was during this time that I saw my older brother cry for the first time and watched my dying grandfather spend his last Christmas with us. Luckily I had this time to say thank you and I love you.

Family traditions create memories and bonds that last a lifetime. I have come to love and admire my family more through our Advent wreath.

Along with the lighted candles, a strong and burning love burns during this time that will stay in my heart forever.

Laurie Powell, high school

— Sleigh Bells in Cooleemee, 1945 —

*Elizabeth Burgess

The wonder of Christmas sleigh bells knows no geographical boundaries. When four mill buddies re-created that special magic for their children and neighbors in a small Southern town, they used sleigh bells brought many years earlier to this country from the faraway Alps. They never would have imagined that years later this North Carolina Christmas folly would be remembered halfway around the world—in the very Alps where the bells had first jingled so long ago.

On Christmas Eve 1945, in tiny Cooleemee in eastern North Carolina, the Erwin cotton mill friends—Scotty, Joe, Charlie, and my dad, Sam —turned into children. They laughed huge ho-ho-ho's and leaped across each other's backyards with a fine collection of sleigh bells draped across their winter coats and gloves.

Traditionally Charlie was allowed the first bell run, since it was his grandfather who had brought the bells to America from a village deep within the Bavarian Alps many years ago. Charlie made a test run to make sure his children were observing the cardinal rule: "If you hear anything, don't get up and don't look out the window, or Santa won't come." The rule worked for the younger kids since we didn't have TV or movies to give us clues to do otherwise, while the older ones feigned sleep until breakfast the next morning when they would laugh uncontrollably as their younger siblings talked of the bells.

Back in the garage, Charlie's waiting friends draped him in bells. Then in a slow prance he headed toward the sandbox, careful not to trip over the plank edges. With bells jingling he advanced past the tree swing and small woodshed. He pranced close under the children's window, then darted away to the garage. Polly, his wife, looked out the window, her mouth covered with her hand to hold in the laughter.

My dad, Sam, was outfitted next. He leaped out of the garage, turned left, then danced around the chicken coop. (Mom had cleaned out and sterilized the coop, then painted it pink. Now it served as the neighborhood playhouse.) Dad rounded the old tree stump, careful not to flip on the rock border gathered from the Yadkin River that held petunias in the summer, then ran the length of the hedge bordering Erwin Street doing some fancy leaps in the air. By now he was carried away by reindeer power, roaring out "Merry Christmas to all!"

He cut across the front yard where the thrift blazed purple in the summer then bounded back under our window where three-year-old

Bob had done some leaping of his own—into my bed, clinging to my shoulders, afraid Santa would leave because he wasn't asleep.

Daddy dashed toward the back fence where hollyhocks and sunflowers reached for the sun during the hot summers, and then rounded the chicken playhouse again.

He would have kept on, but Scotty chased him down. Only because it was my dad's first time as a bell ringer had be been granted the extra run. Our family had just moved east from Little Rock, Arkansas, where Dad was stationed on the Army Air Corps base. Charlie joked that they would allow extra time for him to shake the Casablanca sand out of his shoes, referring to his last tour of duty.

Joe's turn came next. As the crew moved down the driveway they realized that since Dr. Kavanaugh was still away with his war duties, they should run past his house, too. Agreeing on "right foot, left foot" to keep the rhythm smooth and believable, each runner grabbed a section of bell strap and ran. It worked.

At Scotty's house his wife, Frances, was slicing fruitcake and making coffee for the neighborhood's not quite grown-up children. Because his yard was covered in thickly rooted ivy, Scotty did his scene solo while the others waited in the kitchen, whispering and drinking coffee. Scotty made two rounds, passing Jane and Frankie's bedrooms on the front toward the street and little Ross's room in the rear of the house. For good measure he ran around the McNeillys' garden over to the edge of Reverend Royster's house. Undoubtedly that gave Becky Royster something to talk about at breakfast too.

Many years later, when I was teaching in Germany, my five-year-old son and I vacationed in the Austrian Alps during Christmas. We took a sleigh ride in the light snowfall on Christmas Eve. As the driver covered us with a heavy lap robe against the chill, the horses stood pawing the snow, their bells ringing soft and clear in the crisp air. White lights shimmered on the snow-laden trees. Wonderful smells escaped from the gasthauses. As we traveled through the village the jingle of the bells was a lilting chorus in the fading light of dusk.

I pulled my son's cap closer around his sweet face and wrapped my arms around his small body as the bells wrapped me in memories of my daddy, Charlie, Scotty, and Joe leaping across our backyard with sleigh bells announcing the arrival of Santa for all good children in Cooleemee.

⤳ Making the Most of What You Have ⤳

SARAH MORGAN

Like the timeless tradition of the Santa's sleigh bells, so the arrival of a dressed-up Santa Claus has been around since the nineteenth century. Here, from the Civil War diary of Sarah Morgan, is an account of a most unusual Christmas visit during a time when people used what they had.

While all goes on merrily, another rap comes, and enter Santa Claus, dressed in the old uniform of the Mexican war, with a tremendous cocked hat, and preposterous beard of false hair, which effectually conceal the face, and but for the mass of tangled short curls no one could guess that the individual was Bud. It was a device of the General's, which took us all by surprise. Santa Claus passes slowly around the circle, and pausing before each lady, draws from his basket a cake which he presents with a bow, while to each gentleman he presents a wineglass replenished from a most suspicious-looking black bottle which also reposes there.

Leaving us all wonder and laughter, Santa Claus retires with a basket much lighter than it had been at his entrance.

⤳ The Briny Taste of Christmas ⤳

*JOHN RICHARD WEBSTER

Hard times can spur traditions that are handed down even when better times roll around. Who would connect Spanish olives with Christmas morning?

Awakening on Christmas morning, my first thought is of Spanish olives. I can still taste their salty brine as memories of a special Christmas tradition flood across me.

My brothers and I passed over candy treats and sidestepped special toys, and, for a few minutes, ignored the other precious cargo of our Christmas stockings. Instead, first thing Christmas morning, we drank the brine from the small olive bottles so that we could eat some of the olives right away without spilling the liquid on the bedcovers. You see, once again Santa had brought olives.

Years earlier Santa Claus brought our mother olives in a bottle and placed them in her Christmas stocking. In those Depression years, Santa must have known that not only were olives affordable, they were mother's favorite food. Since Santa brought them to her, he most likely reasoned that her children would surely rejoice in finding olives in their stockings too.

There were other traditions. Mother's family was Swedish, so Christmas, especially Christmas Eve, was a special time of family and smorgasbord. And Mother's birthday—December 13, the fabled Saint Lucia day in Swedish folklore—was cause for special celebration. But what I cherished most of all were those little bottles of Spanish olives that made Christmas morning so special in our house.

⟶ And a Partridge in a Pear Tree ⟵

*DIANE W. TRAINOR

When was the last time you gathered around the piano and sang Christmas carols? Everyone used to, but these days it seems few continue to. After reading Diane Trainor's memory of the Christmas sing-along you might want to start the custom anew.

I was a young teenager in 1957, the Christmas Day afternoon that our family was invited to a party hosted by close friends. Children of all ages were included, making this an extra special occasion to be partying with adults! I was asked to play the piano for a carol sing for those gathered in the living room. One by one all of the guests gathered around the piano and were singing their hearts out, regardless of their musical ability.

Someone suggested that the men sing "We Three Kings." They tried to outsing one another. Some had surprisingly melodic voices. Unfortunately others had voices beyond description—those, of course, the loudest ones.

The children were asked to sing "Rudolph the Red-Nosed Reindeer," "Frosty the Snowman," and "Up on the Housetop." Most were eager to make their debut, singing at the top of their lungs and using tremendous animation. Others stood wide-eyed, swaying from side to side, one finger in their mouths.

Toward the end of the evening, someone decided to have a grand finale. After much discussion, "The Twelve Days of Christmas" was selected, not just to be sung, but to be acted out.

The impromptu sing-along was so talked about that the same family graciously invited everyone back the next year. This time guests arrived with kazoos, rhythm-band instruments, and one young man even brought his saxophone, which he was learning how to play. He sat beside me on the piano bench, all the while his mother smiled sweetly as he made a tremendous amount of noise.

Just as before, the evening was brought to a close with the singing and acting out of "The Twelve Days of Christmas." By now the experienced thespians realized that five gold rings and the partridge had to be acted by someone with a strong voice. As the years progressed, these became very special assignments and it was an honor to be chosen for the part.

Our friends hosted this party for nine years. Eventually I married and lived in a home with a large den. The first Christmas in that house, I was asked to host the Christmas Day extravaganza. I readily agreed. By now the group had outgrown the home where we first gathered. Anyway, that gracious host and hostess had done their duty. In my den we continued singing the same carols and songs the same way, with new children particularly enjoying their moment to shine.

The party became such a tradition that in 1967 my mother helped my daughter and niece make construction-paper covers for the songbooks. They carefully cut up old Christmas cards and glued them on the paper. They printed their name and the date. These works of art continue to be used and are actually being used by my daughter's children!

After my children were born, I added a tradition of having a birthday cake for the baby Jesus. All children in attendance gathered around the cake, sang "Happy birthday, dear Jesus, happy birthday to you," and blew out the candles. They were always reminded that we were gathered because it was Jesus' birthday. For many of the younger ones, this was the highlight of the party.

Thirty-eight years later "The Twelve Days of Christmas" continues to be the grand finale. Sadly, some of our beloved carolers are no longer with us and their parts are now played by adults who were young children or perhaps not even born when the first gathering occurred so long ago. I have continued to play the piano all of these years except one, when I visited my daughter and her family in Texas. Even that year I was there in a manner of speaking. My brother, the long-term music director for the extravaganza, taped my accompaniment to be available in my absence. That Christmas Day everyone sang along as usual, but to the video.

During these many years, I have extended an invitation not only to our family but also to friends who cannot be with their families on Christmas Day. Recently I saw someone in another town who had not attended our celebration for twelve years and with whom I had lost contact during that time. His first words to me were "Do you *still* have your party on Christmas Day?" After his comment, I decided that any event lasting thirty-eight years definitely qualifies as a tradition.

⇀ Hang High the Stockings ⇀

*SWANN BRANNON

One of my biggest complaints about Christmas today is the stockings. Oh, they're pretty enough, but the machine-loomed imitation needlepoint stockings are too perfect, and they're stiff—quite unlike the real homemade stockings I had as a little girl that were made from felt, scraps of fabric, or even a leftover sock. You could see the shape of the oranges, pecans, and little boxes in those stockings. Swann Brannon of Savannah, Georgia, paints this picture of a mantel hung with beautiful handmade Christmas stockings that capture the spirit not just of the season but of each family member.

Many years ago my mother began needlepointing elegant Christmas stockings as family Christmas gifts. In every design she captured the individual personality of each one of us.

To me, the holidays were truly upon us in early December when the stockings reappeared, carefully hung from my parents' mantel. I loved to admire the colorful designs and finger the rich texture of the velvet that backed each one.

Mine had swans swimming on a water-blue background.

My brother Charles's featured a "that's what little boys are made of" theme complete with snips and snails and puppy dog tails and a blond-haired little boy happily playing.

My sister Bess, whom my mother had always considered the free spirit of the family, had bright butterflies flying with streamers of red ribbon.

For Sara, the candy-loving sister, there was a stocking depicting an old-fashioned girl sitting in a chair with her favorite gray cat having "visions of sugarplums" while rich desserts and confections floated in her thoughts.

As mother's skill with her needle increased, so did the sophistication of the stockings.

My father's stocking featured Scrooge standing on a London street corner, but as an added twist, he also had Uga, our family's bulldog, and the University of Georgia's mascot (U. Ga.—get it?) in tow.

With her newfound ability, Mother fashioned a new, more grown-up stocking for Charlie. This one portrayed him on the sidelines of Sanford Stadium holding the leash of his now departed bulldog, Otto.

Reminiscent of Savannah's Waving Girl, my mother's own stocking is of an elegant lady in a full gown waving a flag from her home on Liberty Creek.

Over the years stockings have been added for new family members as well. Todd, a physical therapist, has a stocking depicting an elf repairing toys, and Shannon's love of the outdoors is decorated with a tent, campfire, and bike.

There is also a smaller stocking with the word "Baby" inscribed in pastels. It is reserved for each new addition to the family until an individualized stocking is bestowed. Nine-month-old Sara, Bees and Shannon's child, will use it this year.

It has been passed down from Margaret, age two and a half, daughter of Sara and Todd, who will receive a new stocking of her own featuring a jolly Santa with none other than Barney coming out of his sack.

I think with great appreciation of all the countless hours Mother has spent secretly stitching each one late into the night. Often the stocking design would be a surprise to its recipient, unveiled for the first time when it took its place with the others on Christmas morning.

During this time of giving, we spend numerous hours searching frantically for the perfect gifts for our friends and family. Perhaps the wisdom of the season really lies in simplicity. The gifts that are the most special are those that last for years and continue to grow in sentiment.

Our beautiful stockings are such gifts. They are heirlooms we will always cherish. For with each one, my mother has given to us the gift of her time, talent, and love.

⤳ A Dickens Christmas at the Old House ⤳

*NANCY A. RUHLING

Many people share the tradition of reading from a favorite book at Christmastime. "The Gift of the Magi," A Child's Christmas in Wales, and How Come Christmas? are favorites. Betty McCain, the honorable secretary of North Carolina's Department of Cultural Resources, once told me how every Christmas Eve the oldest member of the family, the granddaddy, always reads "The Night before Christmas" and "The Littlest Angel" to their four little granddaughters, the oldest of whom is five. For this yearly event they all cuddle up in the same big bed. This, she says, truly gives everyone the Christmas spirit.

But Dickens' beloved story, "A Christmas Carol," is the most treasured tale of all. To a little girl in Ferguson, Missouri, one never-to-be-forgotten Christmas her uncles brought enchantment to The Old House that most of us only dream about.

Every Christmas Eve, I read Dickens' "A Christmas Carol." It is a tradition I began long, long ago on one very special Christmas past when the slender antique volume was presented to me.

As soon as I open the pages, now yellowed and crumbling with age, I think not only of Tiny Tim and Scrooge, but of my two uncles, Glenn and Jim, and all the wonderfully imaginative Christmases they created for me.

My mother and I always celebrated Christmas at The Old House, the rambling Victorian farmstead in Ferguson, Missouri, that belonged to my uncles—Jim, the clever one, and Glenn, the romantic one. I thought The Old House was the most enchanting place I had ever seen because its attic was filled with all sorts of old-time treasures— coal-oil lamps, fancy lace collars and linens, high-button shoes and antique leather-bound books with gilt-edged pages.

I decided to call it The Old House because it was one of the first and grandest houses in the whole town.

And with its high-ceilinged rooms, dazzling crystal chandeliers, champagne-colored velvet draperies that puddled to the floor, stained glass windows and mansion-size fireplaces, The Old House was a sparkling Christmas sugarplum.

And one Christmas, the year of my eighth birthday, a fresh layer of snow, soft as a bunny's fur, made it magical. We had never spent the night at The Old House before, and I was feeling quite grown up because I was to sleep upstairs all by myself in The Rose Room, my favorite because of its old-fashioned flowered wallpaper and its big bird's-eye maple bedstead.

Going to The Old House for Christmas with Glenn and Jim was always an adventure that I eagerly anticipated. I had dreams of being a great writer, so on this particular year, Glenn and Jim decided to create a Dickens Christmas just for me.

Thus, upon our arrival on that snowy day, Christmas 1963 in The Old House became Christmas 1843 in Jolly Olde England. We knocked upon the front door, and Jim, dressed in a silk smoking jacket of an evergreen hue, and Glenn, clad in a Christmas-red vest I had made for him, greeted us with resounding shouts of, "Merry Christmas to all. God bless us, every one!" that echoed, in a game of hide-and-seek, playfully though the fourteen rooms of the house.

We dined by candlelight upon duck with orange sauce, and after- ward, Glenn, the gourmet cook in the family, brought out a flaming plum pudding, a brandied black bowling ball, which—just like Tiny Tim's—was crowned by a sprig of fresh holly. All declared it a masterpiece, right down to the last bite.

We decorated the ceiling-high tree with Jim's antique ornaments and golden lights, then all gathered around the old upright in The Music Room to sing carols while Glenn, accompanied by the cheery pop-pop-popping of the chestnuts roasting in the front parlor fireplace, played in a grandly elegant style.

As midnight and Christmas approached, from the downstairs library Glenn brought a small book, its brown suede cover emblazoned "A Christmas Carol" in bright gold letters, and by the light of our Christmas Eve fire, began reciting, "Marley was dead, to begin with." With these words, he brought Tiny Tim, Scrooge, and Christmas itself to life.

When he had uttered the last "God Bless Us, Every One" and had closed the book, he handed it to me. I ran my hand lovingly over its cover and read the frontispiece inscription, written in the faded blue script of a fountain pen: "To Nellis, Christmas 1872, 417 Adams, Ferguson, Missouri."

"This book belonged to the first little girl who ever lived in The Old House," Glenn told me. "It has been here so long that it is like a member of the family. Jim and I always thought it should stay here because it is part of the history of The Old House, but we want you to have it. It is the most important Christmas gift we give you this year aside from our love. When we're gone and this day is long forgotten, this little book and its story will always carry the spirit of Christmas to you."

As the years have gone by, my Christmases have changed. Glenn and Jim are gone and so is The Old House. But every Christmas Eve when I carefully open the fragile pages of that slender volume of "A Christmas Carol," it's Christmas once again at The Old House with Glenn and Jim.

And, like Tiny Tim, I feel greatly loved and blessed.

⇥ *That Hardy Perennial, Christmas* ⇤

Robert P. Tristram Coffin

If you do not have a favorite Christmas reading, try this next text. Its heartwarming message, written in the war year 1944, should serve as a reminder that the old traditions ring through, year after year.

Christmas is the oldest perennial, maybe, the human race has. It has outlasted all the hardiest perennials in the world, including phlox and sunflowers. Chances are, it will be here when even democracy and the common man are with the dodo and the Hittites, and uncommon seraphs of light run the dynamos of reformed man.

This holiday has outlasted them all except May Day because it is built squarely on four foundations of happiness: They are children, the color of the forest, songs, and fine food. In that order. You can't leave out a single one of these foundations for your Christmas in this year of our Lord 1944—War is no excuse. You must have them all. And luckily they are not so hard to find. Maybe food will be the hardest. But we still have a fair chance of getting some in our country.

There are plenty children left, and we ought to be thankful for them. For they come first on every Christmas list. Of course, it is nice if they are your own. But people who haven't any at all—or haven't any left in their own houses—can always borrow from their neighbors. They are one of the household necessities easier to borrow than salt or a pint measure. So you have no excuse for not having a set of small dresses and trousers sweeping the dust off your plush chairs at Yule-time. The supply of hungry and practically bottomless small boys and bright-eyed little girls is unlimited. You go over and borrow some next door.

For you need children to bring you the next necessary item—the forest. Not the whole woods, to be sure, but a good green part of it. Most fathers by the time they have children are too stiff in the joints to go and fetch in the Christmas tree and the fir boughs. And their eyes are not what they used to be at picking out the right shapes and sizes in trees. They can't climb as well as their sons. So they let their sons—or their ones borrowed for the day—take the sharp axe and go after greens.

Christmas has always been green. It took over that color early from the Druids. And the Druids knew what the color of the life everlasting was. It was the color of the holly, "that is greenest when the groves are bare." The pagan god of the woods was wise enough to hitch his go-cart to the Christmas feast the minute it came to northern Europe. And the Great God Green has lasted for that reason. The woods love to come indoors once a year, when the snow is deep outdoors, and enjoy the man-made sun on the hearth.

So send out the boys to get your tree. Even if you have to send them to the store for it. They will get something green and good for them by bringing it home on their shoulders. If you live in the smaller towns, the boys can go out and cut the tree for themselves and enter Christmas in the best fashion. A boy of nine grows three inches in the act. He holds his breath and walks around a hundred trees till he finds the right one. Then he fells it and comes home wading the snow, deep in the life everlasting to his blue or brown or black eyes. And the stars coming out early in the fields of the sky are no match for his eyes.

But once the tree and the green boughs are delivered at the house, the girls take over. The boys' work ends with their fixing a base for the tree. Maybe it is a backless chair turned legs up or a wastepaper basket weighted down. But the boys' job ends there. Let the girls fall to. Girls know better than boys where to place the tree and the boughs and make the room, for this one night in the year, the ancient forest we used to live in when we all wore skins or whiskers and heard the old wolves baying the moon outside our cave. Girls have the Christmas touch. They can run you up an oasis of palms out of balsam on the mantel and make a place for the Wisemen to kneel and give their gifts to the Holy Child. They can cut the child out of paper, if no small dolls are around. And the Wisemen, too.

To people who object to taking young children into Christmas partnership, when they are supposed to believe still that Santa Claus does it all, I can say they are talking a lot of nonsense. The veriest believer of a boy no taller than a man's lowest rib will believe all the harder in the Christmas Saint if he is allowed to trim up the house for his coming. What better way to belief is there than laying a green carpet for the mysterious feet that come in the night to bring gifts?

All hands, boys and girls, should have a part in trimming the tree. And they don't need tinsel or the spangles that were so plentiful before the war. Popcorn strings are better than glass or tinsel, and the popcorn has a good smell on balsam which boughten decorations never had. And they look more like snow. Popcorn balls there must be. The woman of the house can pour on the melted butter and molasses, and all the children can press the balls into shape and get stuck right onto Christmas hard and taste Christmas when they lick their paws. If mother, or the lady who is playing the part *pro tem,* can run up a batch of peanut and popcorn brittle, now that she has her hands in the molasses anyway, so much brighter for the eyes of the boys and girls.

The presents can be homemade, too. Little boys would rather have one cart with spool wheels than a dozen machines that wind up with a key and break down always before Christmas Day is half over. Rag dolls still feel best to young mothers. And if the older children can take part in making one another's gifts, so much the greener will the Christmas be.

The songs will come easy. Every child in the world knows two or three. And the more children you get together, the more songs will multiply. All grownups will remember the words to at least ten. There are more good green Yule songs than songs for any other feast on earth. And as they all are about the birth of a child and about cows and barnyards, those hardy perennials that never go out of date, they are all bound to be good. And the beauty of it all is that you don't have to be able to sing very well. Not at Christmas. It is the hour of amateurs, and green boughs and night and the stars cover over a man's incapacity to hit high C or even to carry a tune far. I say night and the stars, for every good Christmas song-time ought to overflow on the streets of the town and under neighbors' windows and make the welkin ring. If candles are blacked out at our windows, there is no law against our letting Christmas go in at the ears. And darkened streets invite the use of lanterns. So that puts the Christmas celebration right back where it began, among sweet-breathed kine getting their fodder by taperlight and lamplight.

The Christmas food comes last. But it is also mighty important. Especially if the children you have borrowed wear forked clothes and are growing at the rate of an inch per boy-hour! Such children take a lot of food at Christmas time.

Bulk and flavor are the essential things, though looks are pretty vital, too. I mean a goose is better than the more expensive and fashionable turkey. A goose sends a more heavenly fragrance through all the rooms of a house. And he takes a better brown in the oven and looks handsomer flanked by baked potatoes. He is also more traditional, having come down from our ancestral Europe and centuries when the turkey was a wild dream on the other side of the world, and no one dreamed of his being good to eat. A roast goose tastes about ten times better, too. He has more fat on him, and he has lived a jollier life than the snobbish turkey. These things count.

So let it be goose. And stuff him with mouldy breadcrumbs sprinkled with sage until he is of heroic size and a third larger than life. Keep the stuffing dry, as a foil to the rich giblet gravy. It is the marriage of dry and moist which makes a goose dinner the peak of all dinners. For another thing, you can show the children what kind of Winter it is going to be by the goose's breastbone. And I never knew a turkey to have such an interest in meteorology! Yes, a goose it *must* be. And turnip mashed and peppered brown, and cranberry jelly, made in star-shaped moulds in sympathy with the Star in the East, a whole star for every last boy and girl, and two or three for father—whose ceiling for cranberry jelly is practically infinity. The cranberries are another foil—a flavor sharp as the new moon to cut through the full moon of the fat of the roasted goose. And of course, being red, cranberry jelly goes perfectly with all the greens of the season in boughs and boys and piping shrill voices.

If you cannot afford a goose, then three fat ducks will have to do. They must be baked and stuffed the same way, only with a little more moisture in the stuffing. And all three ducks must come to table on the same platter. Three ducks add up to one goose, and are essential. For I am going on the principle that you have at least four of your own children plus five of your friends', or else have been loaned at least nine by the neighbors.

But it is really the pudding that makes Christmas. It has always been so, ever since our British forebears dyed their bodies blue and sang *Heigh-Ho, the Holly,* with the white bearded Druids beating out the tune with a goose's drumstick. The goose is just an excuse to work towards the vital part of the feast. He is just the appetizer and whetstone to put the children really on edge.

Now there are puddings and puddings, of course. But my Great-Aunt Sally's *Plain Apple-Pudding,* handed down to my mother, is the only one that will do. Plain!—that's a Yankee witticism for a thing as subtle and wise as the Indians. I think my Great-Aunt Sally's pudding came from the Abenaki Indians, too. Anyway, the apples for it came from the trees I am sure the Abenakis planted. They were very small and tough and sharp crabapples that grow wild in Maine pastures, turn deep red when the frost hits them, and have a taste like the smell of a wild Rose of Sharon and Western Hemisphere Cedars of Lebanon.

If you can't get that kind of apples, others will have to do. But you must cast your pudding big and boil it in a pail set in hot water inside a giant iron kettle. You start with a pint of flour, a teaspoon of cream of tartar and a half teaspoon of saleratus. You sift the flour and knead into it a teaspoonful of lard with your loving hands. Then comes the milk—old milk with the suggestion of souring. Stir this in. You slice the apples thin as rose petals and insinuate them into the mass gradually. Dash in half a teaspoon of salt, a thin powder of cinnamon, and three mystic drops of vanilla. Grease a large lard-pail, put your pudding in, cover it, and set it in the kettle. Blow up the fire. (It should be beechwood.) Boil your pudding right up and down hard for two or three solid hours.

When the pudding is done, turn it out of the pail, rush it to the table, and stand it before the children's starry eyes. And the man of the house will stand up—this is a man's work and requires strength and male finesse—and lasso the smoking mountain with a loop of string and slice off slice after slice to the pudding's base. Mother will pour on a thick lemon sauce, as each hot slab of steaming apples and heaven goes by. The little girls will nip at it delicately. But the little boys will bite it to its hot heart, burn their mouths till the tears flow down, but swallow it as the old Red Indians used to, and they will be on the outside of its glory and beaming and looking for more before the girls have barely begun. And Christmas will be in them deep!

Children, fir balsam, *God Rest You Merry Gentlemen,* and *Plain Apple-Pudding!* These four. These are the foundation of the hardy perennial men call Christmas.

⟶ The Christmas Pageant ⟵

MAUDE ZIMMER

"The Best Christmas Pageant Ever" was our family's favorite story. Its humor and playfulness struck a chord reminiscent of my former husband's mischievous boyhood. Our kids loved it and will undoubtedly read the story to their own children one day.

From real life, here is Maude Zimmer's recollection of the annual Christmas pageant in a small Louisiana town. The picture is one that will bring back memories of this typical all-American Christmas tradition that evolved down through the years stemming from the morality plays of medieval Europe.

Every year a Christmas pageant was produced by Miss Jessica, superintendent of our Sunday School. The themes might vary, but the principal actors remained the same: the Holy Family, the Wise Men, the Shepherds, and Angels, both large and small.

Miss Jessica struggled with a shortage of stage properties and a surplus of would-be thespians; but each year the ultimate production was invariably proclaimed a success by the capacity audience of parents and friends of the participants.

The stage was the elevated space between pulpit and front pews in the little church. A wheezy old organ provided music for anyone with strength enough to pedal and talent enough to operate the eccentric stops and keyboard. Standard scenery consisted of a large canvas backdrop in bright colors depicting the little town of Bethlehem nestling among the Judean hills.

At one climactic moment in every pageant the star of Bethlehem shone down. A thin spot in the backdrop was fashioned directly over the pictured town; and at the proper time Miss Jessica, standing on a high stool behind the canvas, placed a flashlight directly over the thin spot and flicked it on and off. The audience and actors alike thrilled to see the painted houses and hills illuminated thus by the brightly beaming "star."

In the space on each side of the pulpit screens were placed in lieu of dressing rooms and stage wings. Behind the screens the performers huddled, awaiting their cues; and sometimes, if the script called for it, an unseen choir crowded in with the children.

Wardrobes of the actors required more time than money. Wise men's apparel was fashioned from shawls which ordinarily served to cover pianos and elderly ladies; their rich jewels usually consisted of beads and bracelets borrowed from mothers and older sisters; and their gifts were presented in shoe boxes covered with gilt paint, or gaily decorated tea canisters.

Shepherds wore striped bathrobes and towel burnooses tied with scarves; and occasionally the more rugged ones appeared in burlap feed-bags or real sheepskins. Angels were attired in robes of white cheese-cloth with wide flowing sleeves. Their costumes, like the Palestinian backdrop, were carefully preserved and altered to fit the current incumbents.

The Virgin always wore a special blue dress made new every year; and the most beautiful baby doll in the community lay in a manger of fragrant hay covered by an immaculate white linen cloth.

Miss Jessica, with infinite wisdom, assembled the entire cast each time we practiced. Scriptural passages were read over and over, and songs were sung. By the time rehearsals were completed, each of us knew the whole pageant by heart.

Since there were no dressing rooms, we did not appear in costume until the night of the performance. Once this lack of a dress rehearsal nearly spelled disaster. That was the year Miss Jessica decided the angels could utilize the fancy paper-and-wire wings we had bought for the Mayday fairy drill at school. Little girls possessing wings automatically became angels; and when the choir sang "It Came Upon a Midnight Clear," we were to march from behind the screens, take our places on stage and execute a pantomime.

The choir began on schedule; but the angels remained fixed in their places, unable to budge.

The screens, overlapping like stage wings, had been placed too close together. The first angel was plainly visible to the audience, her straining torso thrust forward like the figurehead on the prow of a ship, vainly striving to free her wings which were tightly wedged between two screens.

It seemed fitting that one of the wise men should have the presence of mind to make a premature appearance, move the screen and release the angels in time for us to hurry onto the stage and act out the remainder of the song.

Miss Jessica's fame as a producer never went beyond the confines of The Village; but in faraway places her "children" still try to practice what we learned from her—to interpret the dear, familiar story in many ways and to recreate for ourselves every year the wonder and joy of the first Christmas.

⤳ The Best Christmases Are ⤶
the Old Christmases

One tongue-in-cheek futuristic Christmas essay I read suggested that the old customs will soon be abolished. For example, no longer will we kiss under mistletoe. After all mistletoe berries are poisonous, and "unhygienic, sloppy, and sentimental" kisses breed unscientific thinking. So just how do you keep the joy and mirth of the season? All of us, poets included, have long wrestled with this dilemma. Alice Williams Brotherton despaired the loss of the "good old-fashioned Chris'mas" at the turn of the century, as did Ogden Nash in his humorous 1935 poem.

⤳ I'm a-Pinin' for the Old Times ⤶

ALICE WILLIAMS BROTHERTON

A good old-fashioned Chris'mas, with the logs upon the hearth,
The table filled with feasters, an' the room a-roar 'ith mirth,
With the stockin's crammed to bu'stin, an' the medders piled 'ith snow,
A good old-fashioned Chris'mas like we had so long ago.

Now, that's the thing I'd like to see ag'in afore I die,
But Chris'mas in the city here—it's different, oh! my!
With the crowded hustle-bustle of the slushy, noisy street,
An' the scowl upon the faces of the strangers that you meet.

Oh! there's buyin', plenty of it, of a lot o' gorgeous toys:
An' it takes a mint o' money to please modern girls an' boys.
Why, I mind the time a jack-knife an' a toffy lump for me
Made my little heart an' stockin' jus' chock-full o' Chris'mas glee.

An' there's feastin'. Think of feedin' with these stuck-up city folk!
Why, ye have to speak in whispers, an' ye darsn't crack a joke.
Then remember how the tables looked, all crowded with your kin,
When you couldn't hear a whistle blow across the merry din!

You see, I'm so old-fashioned, like, I don't care much for style,
An' to eat your Chris'mas banquets here I wouldn't go a mile:
I'd rather have, like Solomon, a good yarb-dinner, set
With real old friends, than turtle soup with all the nobs you'd get.

There's my next-door neighbor Gurley—fancy how his brows 'u'd lift
If I'd holler "Merry Chris'mas! Caught, old fellow: Chris'mas gift!"
Goodness me, I'd like to try it! Guess he'd nearly have a fit.
Hang this city stiffness, anyway; I can't get used to it.

Then your heart it kept a-swellin' till it nearly bu'st your side,
An' by night your jaws were achin', with your smile four inches wide,
An' your enemy, the wo'st one, you would grab his hand an' say:
"Mebbe both of us was wrong, John; come, let's shake, it's Christmas Day!"

Mightly little Chris'mas spirit seems to dwell 'tween city walls,
Where each snow-flake brings a soot-flake for a brother as it falls;
Mighty little Chris'mas spirit! An' I'm a-pinin', don't you know,
For a good gold-fashioned Chris'mas, like we had so long ago.

⁓ Merry Christmas, Nearly Everybody ⁓

OGDEN NASH

Christmas time used to be the time when everybody loved everybody,
And even in the subway when everybody had their arms full of packages
   nobody shoved everybody.
People went around looking benevolent,
And goodwill was pleasingly prevalent,
And the cockles of people's hearts were all warm and cockley
And the weather acted more New Englandly and less Miamily,
And on Christmas Eve people would assemble their friends and merrily
   sing carols with them and merrily congeal with them,
And they sent Christmas cards and presents to people because they liked
   them and not because they hoped to put over a deal with them.
Yes, the good old Yuletide was indeed sublime,

But that was once upon a time,
  Because now everybody was somebody they are trying to blow to pieces or
  dismember,
And people can't concentrate properly on blowing other people to pieces
  properly if their minds are poisoned by thoughts suitable to the
  twenty-fifth of December.
Hence my thesis,
Which is that I think it is much nicer to have a nice Christmas than to blow
  somebody to pesis,
So please excuse me a moment while I momentarily take my mind off
  Tokio and Peiping and the Rebels and the Loyalists;
Forgive me if I temporarily ignore the disagreement between Mr. Lewis and
  the Economic Royalists;
This is not the season for tales of Der Fuehrer and his sportsmanship;
Call again on the twenty-sixth if you want to discuss the Chief Executive
  and his Supreme Courtmanship;
Christmas comes but once every Anno Domini,
And I want an old-fashioned one and I invite everybody who is on my
  side to enjoy it the way it ought to be enjoyed even though
  everybody on the other side will undoubtedly cover us with
  ignominy.

~ Nothing New About Christmas ~ Isn't It Great?

CLARK MORPHEW

If you yearn for these old ways and feel let down by too much change, don't despair. For as Clark Morphew, a clergyman in Saint Paul, Minnesota, points out, the old traditions still endure, though they may have a modern spin on them. That's the beauty of traditions. Each generation molds them to meet its needs.

Every Christmas I struggle to come up with a something that will uplift, inspire, and comfort, but this year I have nothing to write.

It's the same old Santa Claus, the same wrenching concern for the poor, the same baby Jesus gurgling in the manger. People scurry about trying to find the perfect gift. I get Christmas cards from old friends. We get a few cookies baked and then, bingo, it's all over and everyone sets out on the road to recovery.

I'm not depressed by this sameness. If Christmas changed every year, we would all be angry. Clip one whisker from Santa's beard and half the population would be outraged.

In fact it is that sameness that makes Christmas such a noble holiday. In a world where not much can be counted on to stay the same, Christmas does. And it's celebrated with pure American gusto precisely because we have seen it come and go for so many years. It's like an old friend coming for a visit.

But after twenty-five years of writing sermons and columns about Christmas, I have nothing new to write. I remember one year I wrote about people suffering at Christmas, and my parishioners complained so vociferously that no negative word ever again came from that pulpit on Christmas Eve. I thought they were going to storm the altar.

Another year a colleague told a little story about a pathetic rabbit in lieu of a traditional Christmas sermon. By New Year's they had the young pastor by the hide and were ready to toss him in a snowbank.

There isn't a preacher alive who has the stamina and emotional muscle to change Christmas. The faithful hordes will get you every time. They want their Christmas just like it was all the years before.

For instance, I pity those preachers who feel compelled every year to rant about how commercialized Christmas has become. I wonder if they realize their parishioners are going to bolt out of church at the first opportunity and head for the mall. And they'll spend infinitely more at the mall than they tossed in the offering bucket. A negative sermon at Christmas does nothing but erode the preacher's authority.

Sure we spend lots of money at Christmas, and most of us do it happily and lovingly. That will never change. So relax, preachers, and think of all the little children who will be thrilled on Christmas morning because mom and dad had the money to spend and were willing to fall into the commercial Christmas trap.

Think also about all the people who work in retail sales and depend on those weeks before Christmas to beef up their bank accounts. Think of it as commerce, and give thanks for the privilege of living in affluent America.

There's another thing that never changes at Christmas. The poor are always with us. Jesus said that a long time ago. But, I caution, he did not mean we could ignore the poor simply because there are always needy people in our world.

It's just the opposite, and that's why the red kettles come out at Christmas and why the nonprofits send out so many solicitations for funds. They know we're in a giving mood. And we know they are in need of some help. Do your charitable giving carefully, but please, do it faithfully as well.

I remember stepping outside a restaurant in California one evening shortly before Christmas and being surprised by a blind musician plucking on a guitar and singing Christmas carols. He had a bad location that didn't offer much foot traffic. There were hundreds of cars whizzing by on the street but few pilgrims walking past the restaurant.

I stood there for a few minutes listening to his songs and watching the tired expression on his face. It was a cold evening. His fingers were red and swollen and his face showed the pain. But he persevered.

I wondered why he was there. Was it to make enough extra money to buy a few presents? Or was he simply taking advantage of the giving season and getting to people when their defenses were down?

It also occurred to me that I was the luckiest man on the face of the earth. I had it all. And I knew in an instant, it was only a twist of fate that made him sight-impaired and me a seeing person.

I decided it didn't matter if I was a sucker for this scene. I had a few bucks left after shopping, so I dumped them into his old guitar case and walked away feeling like a king. Somehow that memory is Christmas for me.

⚊ *The Tradition Continues* ⚊

The Swedish Shoe Elf

One of the special aspects of the American Christmas is its blending of many traditions from varied sources. Besides the usual Santa and gifts, most of each family's unique traditions come in through the uniting of new family members, as Norma Morin recounted earlier in this book. But children all over the world are fascinated with how boys and girls live in other countries. Read how this kindergartner brought home a new, but old, tradition that became woven into his family's celebration and you will see that the possibilities for beginning new Christmas traditions are limitless.

You can take this idea a step further by having your children select a new or outgrown pair of their own shoes to give to a less fortunate child for Christmas. This makes your child a true Christmas elf.

Our Christmas is made up of many traditions from different countries. My favorite tradition is putting shoes under the Christmas tree. We started doing this in 1987.

In kindergarten, my sister had a friend from Sweden. She told us that if you put your shoes under the Christmas tree, you would get gifts: "We believe that elves bring the gifts. They always bring little gifts during the night. You can put only one pair of shoes under the Christmas tree. We start doing this ten days before Christmas. You have to be good to get a gift each night. It is so exciting when you get up and there is a gift in your shoe!"

I am glad that our Christmas is made up of many traditions from different countries.

Jason W. Carter, elementary school

The Kissing Ball: It's Not Just for Christmas

Each year when you hang the traditional kissing ball in the foyer or over the kitchen door, you are thinking romance. In reality, the tradition had nothing to do with lovers, but rather began as a way to soothe the feelings of warring factions.

Feuding neighbors and relatives are an inevitable part of life. The age-old question is how do you bring a peaceful conclusion to these unpleasant spats? These days arbitration boards and negotiating groups attempt to bring everyone around.

In the Amish community, where neighborly love is at the root of their traditions and beliefs, those who have wandered away from these teachings come together for a special day of fasting and meditation followed by a humbling service of foot-washing and a love feast.

A still older tradition is the kissing ball fashioned in the Middle Ages by our English ancestors. During the Christmas holidays, boughs of boxwood, evergreens, and of course, mistletoe were gathered. These were then stuck into a potato, which helped to keep the stems moist, and the ball was hung from a door ledge or ceiling beam. Everyone then gathered around the wassail bowl, that traditional drink of Christmas cheer. After the toasts were given, those who were known to have feuded and disagreed during the year were encouraged to meet beneath the kissing ball. Under this symbol of peace, they kissed and made up in the hope that the new year would bring renewed harmony and well-being to their communities and homes.

My Family's Christmas Play

If you enjoyed Maude Zimmer's account of the Christmas pageant, but think the old-fashioned Christmas play has no place in today's TV-oriented world, take heart! To Joy Davis, an elementary school student, this tradition is not only enjoyable, it is worth writing about and doing. You might even get the entire family involved, as Christopher Caldwell did. But if putting on the play is too much, you can adapt the idea into dressing up to make a Christmas-card picture the way Megan Casciere's family does.

My family tradition is special because not many people are in a play with their relatives at Christmas. Every Christmas the people in my mother's family go to my grandparents' house, and on Christmas Day the grandchildren present a Christmas play.

The tradition started when my older cousins were young. They decided to put on a Christmas play about the birth of Christ. The first play included music, singing, and characters from the nativity scene. The adults thought it was wonderful and encouraged the children to have a play every Christmas.

Even though we are organized, our play ends up being a disaster at times. Usually everyone wants to have the best part. One year all the Wise Men were girls and the children got grumpy during the rehearsal. After the play began, the shepherd would not go on stage, one Wise Man's crown fell off, and another one kept sticking her tongue out! But of course the adults thought it was one of the sweetest plays ever, since their children were in it.

I think it is fun being a part of such a special tradition, especially at Christmas.

Joy C. Davis, elementary school

One of my family traditions is getting together and putting on a Christmas play. Sometimes we plan the play on Thanksgiving and work on it all of December and put it on on Christmas Eve. The day before Christmas Eve, my family makes tickets, signs, props, and other things we need. We draw faces on the tickets and take them up at the time of the play and put them in a bowl. At the end of the show we draw one out of the bowl and whoever wins gets twenty-five cents' worth of foreign coins.

Christopher Caldwell, elementary school

Every year we make yearly Christmas cards from family snapshots. The first thing that you have to do is think of any idea. Then you have to make the outfits. My mom makes the scenery next. It does not take that long to find the props and to make the scenery.

The next thing you do is set up the scenes. I help my mom and dad set up the scenes so it will go faster. Then my dad's friend Mark takes the picture. That is my favorite part. Then you make a list of people to send the cards to.

The first yearly picture we did was my little brother Bryan dressed up as Rudolph, and Erin, Kaitlyn, and me dressed as the other reindeer. My mom dressed as Mrs. Claus. My dad dressed up as Santa Claus. We all got up on the roof. Then last of all, Mark took the picture.

The next year we dressed as presents. We had bows on our heads. We got into boxes. The boxes were wrapped in Christmas paper. We looked very funny.

Last year we dressed up as snowmen. We used blankets, sheets, and wire. I really like that Christmas picture.

Well, we better start thinking of a Christmas picture for this year.

Megan Casciere, elementary school

Secret Santa and a Midsummer Christmas

The childhood love of Christmas knows no season. For the Medlin family the often last-minute chore of gift-buying takes a more leisurely turn by beginning Christmas in July when the family is together for another occasion.

Our Medlin family tradition began as it always does every year at this time—in the middle of summer! Who could ever imagine thinking of Christmas in the middle of summer? Let me tell you, it is actually fun.

Imagine sitting around Grandma's dinner table eating her delicious food with thoughts of Christmas jumping through our heads. What a perfect situation! After we had eaten, we all went to the den for that long-awaited moment. Aunt Judy already had the folded names in the hat ready for each person to draw for Christmas. Each year this is done to cut down on the cost of gift-giving between the Medlin families. This is so exciting because we know we are going to get a gift from somebody, but we never know who. The rest of the year you spend your time trying to find that special gift for that special person.

When that special evening comes, I get so excited I almost pop! The conversations can't get over quick enough for the opening cere-mony. One by one, from person to person, we open the beautifully wrapped gifts. Finally the secret person is revealed. Expressions of surprise and gratefulness are exchanged, and there ends another Med-lin tradition.

Kiel Medlin, elementary school

Many families carry on the tradition of the secret Santa. The point is, though, to keep this special gift from becoming lost among all the other presents. Diane Mott Davidson, author of the Goldie Bear mystery series, manages to make these gifts stand alone by keeping the presents separate from the regular gift-giving time. She writes: "After the Christmas presents are opened, after Christ-mas dinner, we bring out the secret Santa presents. We open them in turn, and it is a great fun time. What has made it special for us as parents was helping the children shop for their secret Santa present when they were young. What they love about it is having a special, unique gift-giving experience as they play 'secret Santa' for one family member."

The Upside-Down Christmas Tree

In the best Christmas Day tradition, our family was taking a late afternoon drive to see the Christmas lights. We were rounding a curve when suddenly I spied an upside-down Christmas tree. "Stop!" I exclaimed, giving no thought to other cars. "Back up!" There, in the front foyer, fully lighted and decorated, was a Christmas tree, suspended from the ceiling, upside down. Needless to say, the next morning, I was on Susie Mitchell's doorstep.

Her unconventional, traditional tree came about a few years ago when Susie realized that their rambunctious kitten, Murphy—named for Murphy Brown, of course—would play havoc with a floor-to-ceiling tree. The solution was to raise the tree out of the kitten's climbing reach by hanging it from the ceiling. But once she decided to do that, Susie reasoned, why not go the mile and hang it upside down? It took her husband twenty seconds to hang it. It took her four and a half hours to decorate it.

What the Mitchells did not know was a tidbit of tradition I had picked up years ago. It seems that practical nineteenth-century Pennsylvanians often hung their smaller, tabletop Christmas trees from the ceiling, not to keep them from kittens' claws, but to protect them from nibbling mice. You see, the trees, decorated with morsels of cakes, cookies, and other sweets, were irresistible to the country mice.

Just in case you have any reason to hang a Christmas tree upside down, Susie Mitchell has learned over the years that an artificial tree works better than a live one. If the live tree has been netted for transportation, its branches tend to stay closed when the tree is hung upside down. An artificial tree's branches hold their shape better. To hide the trunk at the ceiling, Susie suggests a gathering of bows and birds. At the top—I mean the base, of the upside-down tree—attach a star. Voilà! A car-stopping tree.

The Christmas Doll

*NANCY MARLOWE

Little girls, dolls, and Christmastime meld to become one of the sweetest memories we hold of the season. Nancy Marlowe recalls how this moment became a special tradition for her. Should you adapt her tradition for your own child or grandchild, you will particularly enjoy reading the century-old poem that follows.

Born of thrift or necessity, it became a gift-giving tradition for my grandmother to choose one of the well-loved dolls given to my sister and me a Christmas or two earlier and to recycle it with a new wardrobe. Funny, we never missed the doll undergoing the makeover and never knew which one it would be until Christmas morning. We looked forward to these refurbished dolls more than to the new ones.

~ The Best-Loved of All ~

KATHARINE PYLE

Three new dolls sat on three little chairs,
  Waiting for Christmas day;
And they wondered, when she saw them,
  What the little girl would say.

They hoped that the nursery life was gay;
  And they hoped that they would find
The little girl often played with dolls;
  And they hoped that she was kind.

Near by sat an old doll neatly dressed
  In a new frock, black and red;
She smiled at the French dolls—"As to that,
  Don't feel afraid," she said.

The new dolls turned their waxen heads,
  And looked with a haughty stare,
As if they never had seen before
  That a doll was sitting there.

"Oh, we're not in the least afraid," said one
  "We are quite too fine and new;
But perhaps you yourself will find that now
  She will scarcely care for you."

The old doll shook her head and smiled:
  She smiled, although she knew
Her plaster nose was almost gone,
  And her cheeks were faded too.

And now it was day; in came the child,
  And there all gay and bright
Sat three new dolls in little chairs—
  It was a lovely sight.

> She praised their curls, and noticed too
> How finely they were dressed;
> But the old doll all the while was held
> Clasped close against her breast.

The Dolls' Christmas Party

What could be more delightful than a Christmas party to which all of the little girls bring their dolls? A dolls' Christmas party, where invitations are sent to the dolls and they are invited to bring their little girls! Instead of giving the little girls a Christmas gift, give each doll a gift of her very own tea set. Her little girl will enjoy playing with it all year long.

Have a Happy Yule, Y'all

One of my favorite Southern Christmas memories is the typical Texas scene I captured in a Beaumont, Texas, Mexican restaurant parking lot. There, on the grille of a pickup truck, was a holly wreath with a steer skull in the center. Perched above the Texas license plate, the wreath was humorous, festive, and very Texas.

Years later, when I was giving a talk in Dallas, as the slide of the scene flashed on the screen I remarked that if anyone knew where I could find such a skull, I'd love to know about it. A week later a handsome steer's skull arrived on my Raleigh doorstep. Within hours it was encircled with an evergreen wreath, its horns decorated with silver Christmas balls, and hung over my mantel for a touch of Texas in the Tar Heel State. It's now a tradition.

Old Christmas—A New Idea

I was standing somewhat impatiently in the cluster of shoppers waiting to have their last-minute Christmas gifts rung up and wrapped when the woman who, at last, had reached that enviable spot at the counter looked up and, in total bewilderment, asked, "Why am I dating all my checks July?"

We all understood. We all sympathized.

What we need to do, I chirped in my usual way, is celebrate Old Christmas.

To my surprise, no one there seemed to know my reference. It used to be a wonderful tradition when Christmas was a simpler time, and it is the origin of "The Twelve Days of Christmas," a song that all of us enjoy but few of us know the significance of.

In olden days the Christmas celebration ran from December 25 until Epiphany, January 6, the feast day of the Three Kings, commemorating the day the Wise Men arrived in Bethlehem and found the Christ Child. Because that was the day the first gifts were offered, in the early days of Christmas, many families exchanged gifts then. Over the years, though, as December 25 became Santa's visiting day, the significance of January 6 was forgotten except by a few who continued to observe "Old Christmas."

This is an almost-forgotten tradition we could recapture today, all the while making our frantic lives a little less stressful.

Image how wonderful it would be to avoid the Christmas crowds. Think how pleasant it would be to do your shopping on December 30 or 31, maybe even January 2, when the prices are right, and your packages can still arrive by January 6. I often celebrate Old Christmas and find the seemingly "late" gifts all the more special because they are unexpected. Unwrapping the extra gift can even take away some of the holiday blues that come with the big letdown after Christmas.

Just in case you don't want to wait till January 6, in New Orleans Christmas gifts traditionally were exchanged on New Year's Day.

Twelfth Night Cake

Not only was Twelfth Night a gift-giving time, it was also a time of tomfoolery and mischief, minstrels and masques, especially during the sixteenth and seventeenth centuries. Both Ben Jonson and Shakespeare wrote Twelfth Night plays. Should you wish to celebrate January 6 with a party, why not create an updated cake for the occasion in the tradition of the eighteenth century.

In those days the young unmarried men and women would feast on a beautifully decorated cake into which a pea was baked on one side and a bean on the other. The ladies were served slices from the side with the pea (remember the princess and the pea), and the men from the side with the bean. The man who found the bean became king for the night, and the lady who bit into the pea became his queen. Today you can use the Christmas cake pulls designed by Mary Landrum of Dallas, Texas, to capture the best of the old for today. Cake pulls are silver charms to which ribbons are attached and then placed under the cake or individual slices of cake or sweets. Each charm has a special meaning or promise associated with it. Who wouldn't like to find a silver Christmas tree in a delicious cake, pie, or brownie promising "boughs of joy," or a candy cane for "sweet memories." After the party they make lovely favors, or they can be worn on a charm bracelet.

Remember the Manger

The night before Christmas we have a meal, and some friends come over. We have straw under our plates to remind us that Jesus was born in a bed of hay.

Nicolas Paolina, elementary school

Giving, Without Getting Caught

*SUZY SCHNEIDER

Suzy Schneider of Jefferson City, Missouri, is right. Giving a charitable gift at Christmas is a widespread tradition. But she gives a little insight that might add special meaning to this cherished custom.

This Christmas tradition is simply a tradition of giving. I'm sure something similar is done by people all over. Several years ago we started getting a Christmas gift for someone who might not otherwise have much of a Christmas, and it's all done anonymously.

Our church has "The Giving Tree." Ornaments fashioned out of old Christmas cards are made by the children. On the back of each ornament is a brief description telling you about the recipient—male or female, adult or child, age, one or two suggested items, and clothing sizes if those are needed. Each person selects an ornament, and when we have found the perfect gift, we return it to the church already gift-wrapped, with the ornament tied to the outside of the package. The church distributes the gifts to the recipients.

For an adult gift, there is usually only one suggested item—maybe jeans, or a sweater. But in fulfilling that need, we also usually throw in a little something extra—a turtleneck to go with the sweater, or a pair of gloves to go with the jeans. If the child's gift requests clothing, he'll usually get it, but also something special—a book or a stuffed animal.

I used to think that finding gifts for children was more fun than for the adults. Then my dear husband pointed out that we are all God's children. (He's such a good man, really he is.) So now it's a real pleasure to find that ideal adult gift. It has to be something nice, something that will brighten someone's eyes on Christmas morning. After all, the three Wise Men came bearing the finest gifts they had to offer to the Christ Child.

There's something magical about not knowing the person to receive our gifts. That way we can't judge how "worthy" the recipient is. They just are. That's the way it should be.

As for the givers. We have the ability and the resources to help someone, man or woman, adult or child, to make someone's Christmas a little merrier than it might otherwise have been. I like to think of it as doing random acts of kindness, without getting caught!

An Indoor Manger Scene

I will always remember the time I was on a Miami radio show talking about Christmas traditions. Though it was a sultry 85 degrees outside, the air-conditioned studio was comfortable. Somehow, between the Christmas music and the typical decorations, I forgot I was in tropical Florida. When I mentioned something about a cozy hearth, I caught myself and added something to the effect of "But you don't have fireplaces." A listener promptly called in to say that many Florida homes have fireplaces just for looks and that at Christmas she used hers to create a manger scene. That's more than just a good idea. It is a tradition that Frances Parkinson Keyes speaks about in this poignant Christmas poem written in Alexandria, Virginia.

━ *My Library Fireplace* ━

FRANCES PARKINSON KEYES

. . . So come and share my hearth and home . . .

> *My library fireplace is wide,*
> *Its shining brasses glow;*
> *The easy chairs on either side*
> *Are comfortable and low.*
>
> *Secure and strong the hearthstone lies*
> *Beyond the deep-set grate,*
> *And marble columns smoothly rise*
> *To frame the hearth in state.*
>
> *The mantel shelf is marble too,*
> *A painting hangs above it—*
> *If you should see my library, you,*
> *Like me, would come to love it.*
>
> *On rainy days and chilly days*
> *The fire burns warm and bright,*
> *And when the darkness falls, it plays*
> *In lovely leaping light.*
>
> *But once a year on Christmas Eve,*
> *Stript clear of logs and brasses,*
> *It is made ready to receive*
> *The little lambs and asses,*

The quiet cows, the gentle sheep
That gather round a manger,
Where angels guard a Baby's sleep
And ward away all danger.

Bemused and meek St. Joseph stands
Near Wise Men from afar,
And Mary kneels, with folded hands,
Beneath a shining star.

And all the beauty, all the light
Embodied in the story
Of Christmas Eve is here, so bright,
The room reflects its glory.

So come and share my hearth and home
As often as you're able,
On gloomy days and cold—and come
To see my sacred stable,

Glad with the confidence that then
Together we'll receive
The blessing of Good Will to Men
That comes on Christmas Eve.

The Christmas Hearth and Staircase

The once essential fireplace was the scene of many Christmas traditions, now mainly forgotten. Yet their charm endures and these traditions could easily be reestablished in your home. They will, as Thomas Wolfe wrote in Look Homeward, Angel, *keep the doubter "devout." First there is the sending of Santa's list, for which an adult is needed to exclaim, "There it goes!" Wolfe described the event this way:*

Up the Chimney

THOMAS WOLFE

. . . Night after night in the late autumn and early winter, he would scrawl petitions to Santa Claus, listing interminably the gifts he wanted most, and transmitting each, with perfect trust, to the roaring chimney. As the flame took the paper from his hand and blew its charred ghost away with a howl, Gant would rush with him to the

"I 'M SURE I HEARD A FUNNY KNOCKING,
BUT NOTHING 'S IN THIS EMPTY STOCKING."

window, point to the stormy northern sky, and say: "There it goes! Do you see it?"

He saw it. He saw his prayer, winged with the stanch convoying winds, borne northward to the rimed quaint gables of Toyland, into frozen merry Elfland: heard the tiny silver anvil-tones, the deep-lunged laughter of the little men, the stabled cries of aerial reindeer. Gant saw and heard them, too.

If the magic of that moment captures you, you will surely want to add this easy and fanciful nineteenth-century tradition of Santa's sooty footprints to your Christmas Eve merriment. It seems that when the children began doubting whether or not Santa was coming down the chimney to bring their gifts, Papa, as nineteenth-century fathers were fondly called, would gather the family around the parlor fireplace. After stories and evening prayers, Papa would smother the fire so Santa wouldn't get burned. Once the children were asleep, the parents spread a white sheet on the hearth. Next morning the children found proof of Santa's visit in the sooty footprints he had left as he walked from the fireplace to the tree and back.

But how do you hold the anxious children back in the morning? John Pierson recounted the Civil War tradition of "Hay foot, straw foot" earlier in this book. This clever grandfather has another technique.

Every Christmas we go to our grandparents' house and on Christmas morning, my big brother and I wake up all the adults in the house. When we finish, my grandfather goes downstairs and gets scissors and orange juice. Why? Because there is a ribbon that holds us back from going downstairs. While he is putting the orange juice on the table, my brother and I get ready to go downstairs. Then my grandfather says, "On your mark. Get set. Go!"

He cuts the ribbon and we race downstairs and look at all the presents.
Annie Stefanovich, elementary school

Boxing Day Gifts

"Reward to the servauntes at Crystemas, with their aprons, xx s. Reward to the Clerk of the Kechyn, xiij s, iii d. Reward to the Baily of the husbandry, vi s, viij d. Reward to the Keeper of the Covent Garden, vi s. viij d." So Dame Agnes Merett, cellaress of Syon Convent at Isleworth, recorded her gifts of shillings and pence, in 1537.

Boxing Day, December 26, has long been celebrated in England and some other European countries as a day when monetary gifts are passed out to those who serve you during the year, be they household servants, employees, or public servants such as the mail carrier. One clever and very modern young woman who knew only that Boxing Day had an English origin, thought it was so named after the boxes everyone took home with them after shopping at Harrod's the day after Christmas!

These days, Boxing Day parties are becoming quite popular again. My friends Bill and Sally Creech in Raleigh throw a gala affair honoring their three sons who, now grown, are in town for the holidays. The Creech boys invite their youthful friends to the party and are instructed to bring their dates, friends, siblings, and parents. This way whole families are invited. For many of us it is a looked-forward-to once-a-year reunion with the younger generation, now wide-flung, that we might lose track of now that there are no longer car pools and soccer games.

The Family Tree, Christmas-Style

Almost every family has a stash of Christmas ornaments special to itself. My own Christmas tree most years is, as you would expect, a Southern Christmas tree hung with ornaments gathered from the places I have visited in connection with my book, Southern Christmas. *There's the Mississippi magnolia ornament and the Texas sheriff's star, the North Carolina sand dollar and the Georgia peach. But this idea shared by Minnesotan, Anita Warner, is the most special Christmas ornament idea of all.*

It began the year she and her husband, Steve, became engaged. Using a plain white Christmas ball and a fine-point indelible-ink felt pen, Steve wrote their names, the year, and the word "engaged." Every year since, the tradition has continued. Now that there are children, the entire family history is recalled each December as they unwrap the growing number of family ornaments, remember the past, and record that year's events.

Where's the Pickle?

"You are going to put the pickle tradition in, aren't you?" I heard repeatedly when I mentioned this book. If anyone else was within hearing range, before I

could answer, the question was followed by "What pickle tradition?" I wrote about it in Southern Christmas, *but here it is told by young John Fitzgerald, who plans to keep the tradition alive.*

On Christmas morning I have a special tradition. It all started when I was about three years old. My mom bought a pickle ornament. On Christmas morning she hid the pickle ornament, then told us to look for it. When my sister found it mom gave her a big candy bar imported from Germany. She also gave my brother and me each fun-size candy bars. The tradition is whoever finds the pickle gets the chocolate. I really like this tradition because if you are lucky you get chocolate. I am looking forward to finding the pickle this year.

This tradition comes from Germany. The pickle ornament looks exactly like a pickle. It is hard to find the pickle because it is green and blends in with the Christmas tree. The chocolate is from Germany also. It tastes very rich and good. When I grow up I will hide the pickle for my kids.

John Fitzgerald, elementary school

~ One Romance ~

THEODORE WATTS-DUNTON

Life still hath one romance that naught can bury—
Not Time himself, who coffins Life's romances—
For still will Christmas gild the year's mischances,
If Childhood comes, as here, to make him merry.

MAY YOU KEEP MERRIE THOUGHTS THROUGHOUT
THE YEAR!

Hanukkah

THE FEAST OF LIGHTS

⤙ *A Guiding Light* ⤙

HENNING COHEN AND TRISTRAM COFFIN

"Let the world see that we are Jews and that Judaism means light," writes Leo Trepp.

Each December homes across America become emblazoned with lights to commemorate Hanukkah (the Feast of Lights), Christmas, and Kwanzaa. Since pagan times religions and people around the world have long embraced the symbolism of light in their ceremonies and celebrations, but the traditional lighting of the Hanukkah candles one by one has a singular place in the world. The menorah itself, the nine-branch candlestick with four lights on either side of the center candle, or shammash, from which the others are ignited, symbolizes light, truth, and freedom. In times of peace the menorah shines brightly in a window so all may see it. In times of war and oppression it is lighted, but hidden from those who, upon seeing its flame, would bring harm to those to whom it means so much. The significance of the menorah and its place in Jewish life is not limited to Hanukkah, though, for often the emblem is engraved on tombstones, signifying that light, truth, and freedom guide us through life and death.

As with all of our traditions, knowing about the origins is the first step in understanding those emblems and symbols that we immediately identify with the celebrations and festivities. The Folklore of American Holidays *explains the eight-day festival this way:*

The story of Hanukkah is told in the first book of the Maccabees, in the *Apocrypha.* The Syrian king Antiochus Epiphanes in 162 B.C. ordered that an altar to the Greek god Zeus be placed in the Temple at Jerusalem. This provoked a successful rebellion led by Judah Maccabee, and the Temple was cleansed and rededicated. According to a Talmudic legend, only a limited amount of consecrated oil was available for relighting the perpetual lamp, but miraculously it lasted for eight days. Thus Hanukkah is known as the Feast of Lights and the Feast of Dedication. A *menorah* or lamp with eight candles is lighted, one on the first evening, and the number increases by one each night of the festival. It is a joyous holiday, celebrated with games, plays, gifts, and meals which feature *latkes,* or potato pancakes.

⁓ My Hanukkah Candles ⁓

PHILIP M. RASKIN

Eight little candles,
All in a line;
Eight little candles
Glitter and shine.

Eight little candles—
Each little flame,
Whispers a legend
Of honor and fame.

Eight little candles
Bashfully hide
The soul of a people,
Its hope and its pride. . . .

Eight little candles,
Sparklets of gold,
Stories of battles,
And heroes of old.

Heroes undaunted,
And noble, and true;
Heroes who knew
How to dare and to do;

Heroes who taught
The ages to be
That man can be brave,
And that man should be free. . . .

Eight little candles,
Look at them well,
Floods could not quench them,
Tempests not quell.

Modest and frail
Is their light—yet it cheers
A people in exile
Two thousand years. . . .

Eight little candles—
Their guttering gleams
Speak to my heart
In a language of dreams.

Light to my eye
Is their smile and their cheer,
Sweet to my ear
Is their whisper to hear.

"Courage, but courage,
Maccabee's brave son,
Fight for light—
And the battle is won."

⌁ Home Observances to ⌁ Celebrate the Season

Mae Shafter Rockland

Interestingly, when I began reading about Hanukkah I found the same contro-
versy surrounding this celebration that surrounds my traditional December
religious holy day, Christmas: too commercial, too many gifts, too little mean-
ing. In the first selection that follows, Mae Rockland explains the simple
origins of the Hanukkah customs and expresses her hope that this spirit can be
kept in the holiday observances.

I dread the Monday after Thanksgiving. It seems that no sooner has
the turkey carcass been put into the soup kettle than our entire nation
plunges into frenetic activity dictated by the shopping-days-until-
Christmas countdown. Jewish Americans become quietly schizo-
phrenic as we are pushed and pulled by the media, well-meaning
friends and colleagues, as well as our own children, themselves in the
throes of Santa-starvation. It would seem that, since Hanukkah usually
falls within a week or two of Christmas, the cure for "seasonitis"
(inflammation of the season) is readily at hand: play up Hanukkah.
Indeed, recent years have been witness to diverse forms of magnifica-
tion of what for centuries has been a minor holiday. During the late
1950's and early 1960's an aberration called the Hanukkah bush enjoyed a brief vogue. At that time a neighbor of mine built a six-foot-
tall plywood dreidel which was painted blue and white. This (to me
pitiful albeit honest) attempt to counter the pressures of the outside
world was annually set up in the entryway, decorated with flashing
electric lights, and surrounded by heaped gifts. And the same commercial interests that have sentimentalized and distorted Christmas so
that its profound spiritual and family qualities are all but lost in
glitter and greed are ready to go to work on Hanukkah as well.

If we are to keep Hanukkah from becoming swallowed up in the
general midwinter madness while it is coming out of the shadows and
growing in importance, we must take care to preserve its meaning and
integrity. With Hanukkah we need to exert added effort to make it a
holiday for adults as well as for children: when we as adults have
internalized the meaning of the Maccabees' fight for religious freedom
and feel its relevance for us today, we can go on to enjoy the light-
hearted aspects of the holiday with our children and friends, confident
in the knowledge that that which we offer unambivalently and with
enthusiasm will be received the same way. . . .

[Just as] the words of a Yiddish song—the "*kleyne likhtelakh*" [little lights]—remind us of tales of valor, bravery, and might in bygone days, the miracle of the oil has become a poetic substitution for the miracle of Jewish survival.

Any party or gathering will include the lamp-lighting ceremony; whichever way one chooses to interpret the flames, their light never fails to spread hope and joy. The candles are lit anytime after sunset, except on Friday night when they are lit immediately before the Sabbath candles. Whether you have one lamp for everyone to share or one for each participant, try to make certain that in the course of the holiday everyone—children, women, and men—will have an opportunity to kindle at least one light. The *shammash,* or servant light, is lit first. . . .

Women are to cease from their labors while the Hanukkah lights are burning. This custom, as well as that of eating cheese foods during Hanukkah, is in tribute to the brave Judith, who, it is said, lulled General Holofernes to sleep with a meal of wine and cheese and then cut off his head. When the head was exhibited on the town wall, Holofernes' troops took fright and deserted; thus the Jews of Bethulia were saved. Today, though cheese pancakes are still popular, the humbler potato *latke* has superseded them on most Hanukkah menus, and wine-and-cheese-tasting parties have become a contemporary way of commemorating Judith's valor.

While candle-lighting and food are central to a Hanukkah party . . . I'd like to make a few comments about decorations, invitations, games, and gift-giving. Try as I may to accommodate myself to the many requests I receive for ideas and workshops on Hanukkah decorations, I am very uneasy with the whole idea of "decorating for Hanukkah." I am aware that, with the world at large covered with visual manifestations of the Christmas season, there are many people who feel the need for a parallel Hanukkah display. . . .

My tendency is to avoid excess: to clean it up as the Maccabees did, and to use Hanukkah as a time for adding another Jewish artifact to my collection. For example, it's a good time to make a *mizrah* for an eastern wall that may not have one. I like to set out all the Hanukkah lamps I have and, after they are lit, to place them in the windows. Over the years my children and I have also accumulated quite a few dreidels. These are set out in a handsome bowl, along with another bowl of candy and nuts, to encourage anyone who wants to play. Other Hanukkah games, including a felt appliqué version of "pin the candle on the *hanukkiah*" and a new board game called "Aliyah," are also left around as invitations to play. For me the holiday atmosphere and warmth of the home are decoration enough.

Since the Middle Ages, playing games to while away the long

winter Hanukkah nights has been a popular domestic tradition. Old engravings, woodcuts, and paintings often show serene family scenes with the Hanukkah lights aglow in the window and the household engaged in playing games of cards, chess, and dreidel. It is said that the custom of playing dreidel originated during the Maccabean struggle—that when groups of pious Jews would gather to study the Torah, which had been outlawed by Antiochus, they would keep a dreidel on the table along with the holy books. If they were discovered by soldiers, they could protest that they had only gathered to gamble. There were spinning tops in the Greco-Roman period and the Jews may very well have been familiar with them, but we are more certain that the dreidel as we know it came to be strongly associated with Hanukkah among Ashkenazic Jews during the Middle Ages, when playing put-and-take with a spinning top marked with letters was a popular Christmas time diversion adopted by Jews.

Gift-giving at Hanukkah grew out of the older tradition of giving children Hanukkah gelt [money]. Just as I have always associated the Hanukkah lights with the spiritual victory in ancient Judea, I have linked the custom of giving children a few coins with the political aspect of the Maccabean triumph. When the Maccabees finally achieved independent status, one of the first things they did was to coin their own money—a governmental process we take for granted but which was a privilege won only after many battles. So even though I do give my children gifts at Hanukkah, I also give them coins. It is my custom to give them one penny on the first night, two the second, and so on, until by the end of the week they have accumulated the grand sum of thirty-six cents. This has a nice symbolic quality to it since the numerical values of the letters spelling "life" in Hebrew add up to eighteen, and thirty-six is twice eighteen.

Unless it gets out of hand, exchanging gifts at holiday time is a universally heartwarming custom. A grab bag is always fun and can be handled in a number of ways. Rather than the host's providing presents for everyone, the guests can be assigned other guests to bring gifts for, or everyone can simply bring some little thing to contribute to the grab bag and then randomly pull a package from the sack.

⇌ To Keep the Tradition ⇌

LEO TREPP

In this selection, we read how families continue these traditions today as part of their more relaxed 1990s celebration of Hanukkah.

The Lighting of the Menorah

The center of Hanukah celebration is the home; it is a family feast. The Talmud lays down the rules:

The Mitzvah [commandment] applies from sunset up to the time when traffic in the streets ceases. . . .

One [set of the] Hanukah lights [is sufficient] for the head of the house and his entire household; but those who wish to beautify [Mitzvah] have one for each person. . . .

It is our Mitzvah to place the Hanukah light at the door, outside; he who lives in an upper story shall place it at a window, facing the street. In times of danger it is sufficient to place it on a table. Raba said: He also must have a second lamp, as a source of the light he needs for use. If there is a flame in the room already, this is not necessary. . . .

We are to kindle the lights when it gets dark, that their light will illuminate the night around us. Ordinarily, we will light the candles as soon as night falls; if necessary, we may fulfill the Mitzvah any time before dawn.

On Friday evening, we cannot light the Hanukah candles at night, for the Sabbath forbids it. We, therefore, rely on the ruling that they can be kindled at dusk and do so *before* mother lights the Sabbath candles. But these Hanukah candles must be long enough to burn for at least one-half hour after nightfall.

At the end of the Sabbath, we cannot kindle the lights before Havdalah; but, knowing that the lights can be lit throughout the night, we kindle them immediately after Havdalah.

The Rabbis taught that there must be at least one light per household. If a Jew were very poor, one single candle would suffice. We no longer place the Menorah at the door it is too dangerous. But we do place it at the windows. Let the world see that we are Jews and that Judaism means light.

Card-Playing

Some hold that card playing has always been a passion with Jews. But the professional gambler was considered an undesirable person, not trustworthy as a witness in court. In some communities, card playing was, therefore, put under ban for the entire year except the period from Hanukah to the Fast of the Tenth of Tevet. By permitting it during this time, the Rabbis may have wished to give people an opportunity to get their hankering out of their system.

Special Celebrations and Special Dishes

The fifth day of Hanukah was set aside by eastern European Jewry as the night for a special feast for family and friends. This was the night when light had positively triumphed over darkness; five lights were burning; only three unlit candles were left.

It is customary to serve pancakes, Latkes, on Hanukah, and some families make it a point to serve milk dishes during the festival. Both these customs are connected with the special role of women at the Hanukah season.

⤚ *A Light Touch* ⤙

PHILLIP GOODMAN

When there is so much history and tradition associated with a religious holiday, sometimes the impression can be given that though this is a festive time, it must have an air of solemnity about it. Enjoy these humorous "interpretations" of the holiday as spoken by children and included in Phillip Goodman's book Rejoice in Thy Festival.

Never Postpone for Tomorrow

On the day before Hanukkah, a solicitous mother said to her son:

"You should do your homework now. Tomorrow is Hanukkah and you'll want to play with the *Dreidel*. Never postpone for tomorrow that which you can do today."

"If that's so," the child coyly responded, "give me the Hanukkah *Latkes* that you prepared for tomorrow."

Mother's Latkes

Leah: I'll bet you that my mother's *Latkes* are better than those your mother makes.

Rachel: My mother's *Latkes* are so delicious that even though I ate them several hours ago I still have the delicious taste in my mouth.

Leah: Not only do I have the taste of my mother's *Latkes* in my mouth even though I ate them yesterday but I can still feel them in my stomach.

Hanukkah Gifts

A teacher was telling his pupils that during Hanukkah they should receive a gift on each night of the holiday as part of the candle-lighting ceremony and celebration. Just as the brightness increases with each additional candle, so should the joy with each gift.

True to form, one pupil wanted to know: "Why isn't it exactly as with the candles? One gift the first night, two gifts the second night and so on."

~ *Creating a Menorah* ~

Because the ceremonial lighting of a candle occurs each day of Hanukkah, writers enjoy extolling the mystery and joy relating to the symbolic menorah. In the two selections that follow, we read about the careful crafting of a menorah and then enjoy a family's happy holiday time.

Yearning for the Beautiful

FROM *The Jewish Exponent,* April 17, 1914

What mystery had the generations which followed one another read into this form of art, at once so simple and natural? And our artist wondered to himself if it were not possible to animate again the withered form of the Menorah, to water its roots, as one would a tree. The mere sound of the name, which he now pronounced every evening to his children, gave him great pleasure. There was a lovable ring to the word when it came from the lips of little children.

On the first night the candle was lit and the origin of the holiday explained. The wonderful incident of the lights that strangely remained burning so long, the story of the return from the Babylonian exile, the second Temple, the Maccabees—our friend told his children all he knew. It was not very much, to be sure, but it served. When the second candle was lit, they repeated what he had told them, and though it had all been learned from him, it seemed to him quite new and beautiful. In the days that followed he waited keenly for the evenings, which became ever brighter. Candle after candle stood in the Menorah, and the father mused on the little candles with his children, till at length his reflections became too deep to be uttered before them.

When he had resolved to return to his people and to make open acknowledgment of his return, he had only thought he would be doing the honorable and rational thing. But he had never dreamed that he would find in it a gratification of his yearning for the beautiful. Yet nothing less was his good fortune. The Menorah with its many lights became a thing of beauty to inspire lofty thought. So, with his practiced hand, he drew a plan for a Menorah to present to his children the following year. He made free use of the motif of the right branching arms projecting right and left in one plane from the central stem. He did not hold himself bound by the rigid traditional form, but created directly from nature, unconcerned by other symbolisms also seeking expression. He was on the search for living beauty. Yet, though he gave the withered branch new life, he conformed to the law, to the gentle dignity of its being. It was a tree with slender branches; its ends were moulded into flower calyxes which would hold the lights.

The week passed with this absorbing labor. Then came the eighth day, when the whole row burns, even the faithful ninth, the servant, which on other nights is used only for the lighting of the others. A great splendor streamed from the Menorah. The children's eyes glistened. But for our friend all this was the symbol of the enkindling of a nation. When there is but one light, all is still dark, and the solitary light looks melancholy. Soon it finds one companion, then another, and another. The darkness must retreat. The light comes first to the young and the poor—then others join them who love justice, Truth, Liberty, Progress, Humanity, and Beauty. When all the candles burn, then we must all stand and rejoice over the achievements. And no office can be more blessed than that of a Servant of the Light.

~ *Hanukkah* ~

CECILIA G. GERSON

The hand of Time moves o'er the dial,
And guides the seasons through the year;
It drives the sorrow from our hearts—
Behold-the Feast of Lights is here!

The Feast of Lights old memories stir,
And pride within our breast soars high,
We live again in ancient days,
When Judah's glory was the cry.

We see the Maccabees of old
Bow low within the house of God;
Where Syrian hands defiled the halls,
Where Israel's patriarchs had trod.

Now light we tapers for their deeds;
Awak'ning in each heart a prayer,
That we may like the Maccabees
The glory and the valor share.

The Feast of Lights—a time when hope
Throws off the yoke of sorrow's rod,
To wing its way above the flames
That leap to glory and to God!

~ *The Yellow Candle* ~

SADIE ROSE WEILERSTEIN

Where would traditions be had we not had the craft of storytelling to bring them forward through the years? Stories, both written and oral, form the foundation of many of our traditions, especially those originating from biblical times. In her touching early twentieth-century story, Sadie Rose Weilerstein brings to life the significance of the welcoming, life-giving light of the menorah in a contemporary setting.

Suddenly he jumped to his feet. Hadn't father said, just before he left, that tonight was Hanukkah! Then he must light his candles right away, for hadn't father explained to him, while learning the blessing, that he must kindle the first yellow taper and say the strange Hebrew words just as soon as it got dark on the first night of Hanukkah? Bennie didn't understand just why he wasn't allowed to light the lamps, but would be permitted to light the Hanukkah candles; nor did he consider how worried his parents would be to have him striking matches unless they stood near to watch him. It was enough for him that it was Hanukkah at last and that he knew the difficult blessing, every word of it. Why, he wouldn't have to awaken poor mother to help him, which relieved him a good deal, as he felt somehow that she would get well quicker if she were allowed to sleep as long as she pleased. But how could he reach the menorah father had put away on the very top shelf, next to the candlesticks for *Shabbas*? Bennie was not easily daunted. Even if he couldn't use the menorah the first night, he was determined not to be cheated out of lighting the very first candle tonight. He couldn't reach the box of little yellow tapers that father had put away with the menorah, but on the lowest shelf he found just what he wanted—an old tin candlestick with a half-burned candle which mother sometimes used when she went down into the cellar, and didn't care to bother with a lamp.

Mrs. Roth always kept the box of matches well out of the reach of Bennie's active fingers, so he didn't trouble himself to look for them. Taking the candle he opened the stove door and thrust it into the flames. Walking very carefully, for he felt mother might consider what he was doing almost as naughty as playing with fire, he put the candle back into the holder and set it upon the window sill. Then, standing very straight, he slowly repeated the Hebrew benediction: *"Boruch atto Adonoi Elohenu Melech ho-olom asher kiddeshonu bemitzvosov vetsivonu lehadlik ner shel Hanukkoh."*

Sitting on the floor in the warm patch of light cast by the stove, Bennie ate his supper, looking proudly all the while at his candle, burning fine and straight in the window. When the dishes were all empty, he went to the window pane and amused himself by scraping off the frost with the kitchen knife. He wanted to see his candle throwing a pretty ribbon of light on the snow; he knew it would look nice, for he remembered how pretty the lamp in the kitchen window had appeared to him one night when they had come from town and had seen it shining as they drove up the hill. He wanted his candle to shine a long ways—just like a lamp—and, bringing out an old lantern which his father had once given him to play with, he set the light within it and again placed it before the carefully scraped pane. Then he sat down on the window sill, watching the snow flurries and wishing for father to come home.

Father came at last, bringing with him a tall, bearded man who carried a little black satchel and hurried into mother's room without saying a word. Father went after him and for a long time Bennie sat trembling beside his Hanukkah light, wondering what it was all about. After a very little while, although it seemed to Bennie that he had waited all night, father came back into the kitchen and took the little fellow in his arms. Bennie saw that he was crying and it frightened him, for he had never seen his father cry before. "Is mama very sick?" he asked.

"The doctor says she will get well," answered Mr. Roth, and his voice trembled. "You can't understand it all, Bennie boy, but there was something bad in her throat," and he added something about diphtheria, which meant nothing to Bennie, who just considered it one of the big words grown-up people were always using to confuse him. "But the doctor has just burned it all out and she will get well. Only if we hadn't come in time—" He stopped and shuddered. "Bennie, if you hadn't put your light in the window we might have been an hour later getting here and then the doctor says it would have been too late. Our lanterns went out at the top of the hill and the snow was so blinding that we might have floundered about half the night before we found the house. But your little candle helped us find the way."

"I said the blessing all right," Bennie told his father, "but was it all right not to use the regular menorah and a yellow candle?" he ended anxiously.

"You did just the right thing," his father assured him.

But Bennie was not satisfied. "Please, Papa," he pleaded, "please get down the yellow candle and let me light it and say the Hebrew for you. Please!"

Smiling a little uncertainly, Mr. Roth brought down the tin menorah and the box of yellow tapers. He gave Bennie one for the *Shammash,* explaining that it was to light the others, and watched him with the same twisted smile as the child adjusted and lit the first candle. *"Boruch atto Adonoi,"* began Bennie proudly, and he wondered why his father hid his face in his hands and started to cry all over again.

— *The Tradition Continues* —

Every Night Is Special

On Hanukkah, my family makes latkes, plays with dreidels, and has other neat traditions. There are eight nights of Hanukkah. Each night is very special.

Many years ago, Judah the Maccabee and his army fought for his Jewish rights. Even though they were a small army, they won the battle over the Syrians. When the Maccabees returned to their temple, they found it desecrated. When they tried to light the eternal light, they discovered that the Syrians had spilled all of the sacred oil except for one small container. It was unbelievable that this small amount of oil lasted eight days and nights until more oil could be bought.

I really enjoy latkes, lighting the menorah, and receiving presents on Hanukkah. Latkes are potato pancakes cooked in oil to remind us of the oil used to light the eternal light long ago. I think latkes are delicious. Every night on Hanukkah we light one more candle on our menorah and put it by the window to welcome strangers who may pass by and see the light. We also receive presents each night. A dreidel is a small top with Hebrew letters on it. We spin dreidels and play games with them. We can win money or candy.

To celebrate such a holiday different from most people makes me feel very dignified and proud. It makes me special . . . unlike anyone else.

Jacob Pinion, elementary school

Every year in December, my whole family comes to my house to sing, light candles, open presents, tell the story of the Festival of Lights, and eat. They come for Hanukkah!

In my house during Hanukkah, we hang colorful decorations; we play dreidel games; and we eat potato latkes, which are potato pancakes. My father tells the Hanukkah story while my mother cooks the food; however, only my grandmother can make the potato latkes. Hers are the best!

When we are finished eating, we all gather around the table with the menorah in the middle. We say the Hanukkah blessings and then we light the menorah. When we light the candles of the menorah, I remember the miracle of the eternal light. It feels neat that Jewish people all over the world are lighting the menorah at the same time we are.

It's important to me to have my family with me on the eighth day of Hanukkah. We have a chance to celebrate our Jewish heritage. I plan to continue this Hanukkah tradition with my children so it will stay a special tradition in my family from generation to generation.

Adam Roberts, elementary school

To Welcome Guests

From The Jewish Party Book *come these ideas, complete with historical references, to be adapted in modern-day celebrations of the wonderful Jewish holiday, Hanukkah, whose history inspires hope for all humankind.*

A WELCOME BANNER

Too often we think of a door as something to keep people out; how much nicer, especially at holiday time, to have the door itself extend a welcoming greeting. The last house I lived in had a glass panel in the front door. I made a batik cloth for it, incorporating a Hanukkah lamp and the phrase, ["Blessed shall you be when you enter"—Deuteronomy 28:6]. I chose this phrase because it was often used on Hanukkah lamps during the period when they were hung on the doorpost opposite the *mezuzah*. . . . Fabric banners for the door, incorporating holiday motifs, can be made either by printing on the fabric or with embroidery and appliqué.

HANUKKAH LAMPS

Jewish bookstores, synagogue gift shops, and in some locations department stores have an increasing variety of Hanukkah lamps for sale, or you may be fortunate enough to have an antique candelabrum. Or you may want to consider making your own *hanukkiah*. In recent years I have been making a new one every year. This gives me the sense of rededication which is what Hanukkah is all about. All the lamps I've made are not necessarily of equal quality; I don't think they will *all* be heirlooms, though I hope some will. I enjoy using the new lamp along with those made or bought in previous years. Having many lamps allows everyone present to light a lamp, thereby participating more fully in the celebration.

An easy way to approximate the feeling of the very early lamps is to simply accumulate nine small bottles or dishes and use them with candles or oil. The bottles India ink comes in, for example, are attractive and make nice little lamps. If you want to make an oil burning lamp, fill the bottle with salad oil and use a pipe cleaner or the string from a mop as a wick. Bukharan Jews often use inverted handleless teacups as candleholders for Hanukkah.

I brought back a three-inch-thick slab of tree trunk from last summer's vacation in Maine. Back in the city a friend with a power drill then made nine depressions one inch in diameter to hold utility-size candles.

FLAMING TEA

It is just as gratifying to prepare a special treat for adults as it is for children. An old Russian Hanukkah custom was to provide each guest with a glass of hot tea and several lumps of brandy-soaked sugar in a teaspoon. While songs were sung, a candle was passed around to ignite the spoons of sugar. When all the cubes were aglow, the burning brandy was poured into the tea. Since it is difficult to duplicate old customs in large groups without being stagey and artificial, this might be nice to try at dessert, with just family or a few friends.

MAY YOUR LOVE FOR THE PEOPLE NEVER CEASE!

Kwanzaa

THE CREATION OF A NEW TRADITION

~ Unity and Community ~

HAKI R. MADHUBUTI

"To best understand the inner beats of a people, you look at their special days and moments," writes Haki R. Madhubuti in his book, Kwanzaa. *"To really feel a people's thundering pulse, it is necessary to observe the celebrations of birth, naming, and baptism of their children; the rites of passage of their young men and women, plus their family reunions around special hours all confirm for that people (and denote for outsiders) an invaluable oneness that goes beyond the mere articulation of tradition."*

Time and time again I have been asked, "What do you know about Kwanzaa?" To simply say that this is a newly created and rapidly growing African-American holiday misses the mark. Most importantly Kwanzaa celebrates the principles of the black family and the unity of the African-American community.

To enjoy Kwanzaa to its fullest you need to understand the necessity for its creation. Behind its invention, as with all traditions, old or new, was the spirit of hope for the future that comes from understanding the past. For your enlightenment, here is Madhubuti's explanation.

The popularization and "advancement" of western culture has effectively eroded the traditions of many non-western people. Few people have endured this erosion and survived with their humanity intact as well as Black people in the United States. Ever and ever we survive and adopt and survive in a style that is uniquely Black but void of any liberating substance. Yet, somehow within such survival, many Blacks continue to struggle for recognition, selfhood, and cultural meaning and continuation. This struggle, in all of its complexity, may not be amply articulated by the Black elite, but it can be observed daily in the lives of Black people.

. . . In 1966, a young visionary living on the west coast who was also the founder and chairman of the Black Nationalist organization, US, conceived and created the only "indigenous non-heroic Black holiday in the United States," KWANZAA. Dr. Maulana Karenga . . . postulated that significant meaningful movement in the U.S. was improbable, if not impossible, without a cultural component (base). He felt that at the base of any movement must be the cultural imperatives that give the people a clear and precise sense of "identity, purpose and direction."

The word KWANZAA is "derived from the Swahili word, KWANZA, which means 'first' and is part of the phrase *Mantuda Ya Kwanza* (first fruits)." Dr. Karenga added the extra *"a"* to distinguish the Afro-American from the African. The ideas and conceptions of Kwanzaa developed out of the system of social and political thought of *Kawaida* (Tradition and Reason), also developed by Dr. Karenga.

KWANZAA is an affirmative expression of the best of Afro-American creativity dwelling on the positive rather than the negative. The roots of KWANZAA are continental African, but the branches and fruit are distinctly Afro-American. Dr. Karenga sought to make the natural and profound connection of Afro-American people to their ancestral beginnings, therefore, KWANZAA "as a holiday of the first fruits" comes directly out of the tradition of agricultural peoples of Africa, who celebrated and gave thanks for harvests at designated times during the year.

⸺ *The Seven Principles of Kwanzaa* ⸺

Dr. Maulana Karenga

What could be more noble than to create a new tradition for a people based on time-tested values held important and by all people, races, and ethnic groups throughout the world, a unified effort to advance the family and community?

Kwanzaa proponents adhere to seven principles or guides in their daily lives as set forth by Dr. Karenga in 1965. Known as Nguzo Saba, these are:

1. Umoja (Unity)—To strive for and maintain unity in the family, community, nation and race.
2. Kujichagulia (Self-determination)—To define ourselves, name ourselves, create for ourselves and speak for ourselves instead of being defined, named, created for and spoken for by others.
3. Ujima (Collective Work and Responsibility)—To build and maintain our community together and make our sisters' and brothers' problems our problems and to solve them together.
4. Ujamaa (Cooperative Economics)—To build and maintain our own stores, shops and other businesses and to profit from them together.
5. Nia (Purpose)—To make our collective vocation the building and developing our community in order to restore our people to their traditional greatness.
6. Kuumba (Creativity)—To do always as much as we can, in the way we can, in order to leave our community more beautiful and beneficial than we inherited it.
7. Imani (Faith)—To believe with all our heart in our people, our parents, our teachers, our leaders and the righteousness and victory of our struggle.

⭢ *The Tradition Continues* ⭠

The celebration of Kwanzaa begins the day after Christmas, runs through the following week, and is filled with feasting and gift-giving, ending with the Kwanzaa karamu. Here are suggestions and information to help you create a Kwanzaa celebration.

Celebrating Kwanzaa

Cedric McClester

As it is always better to get an early start, I suggest that you begin the first week in December by making a check list. On your list you should check for the following items: A *Kinara* (candle holder); *Mkeka* (place mat, preferably made of straw); *Mazao* (crops i.e. fruits and vegetables); *Vibunzi* (ears of corn to reflect the number of children in the household); *Kikombe cha umoja* (communal unity cup); *Mishumaa saba* (seven candles, one black, three red, and three green); and *Zwaidi* (gifts that are enriching).

It is important that the *Kinara* not be confused with the menorah. The *Kinara* holds seven candles to reflect the seven principles which are the foundation of Kwanzaa, while the menorah is a Jewish religious symbol that holds eight candles. If you don't have a *Kinara* and don't know where to get one, it is suggested that you use *"kuumba"* (creativity) and make one. A two by four or a piece of driftwood will do just fine, and screw-in candle holders can be purchased in most hardware stores. The *Mkeka* (place mat) shouldn't present a problem. While straw is suggested because it is traditional, cloth makes an adequate substitute. If cloth is used, one with an African print is preferred. The other symbols are easy to come by and warrant no further discussion other than to caution against placing the *Mazao* (crops) in a cornucopia which is Western. A plain straw basket or a bowl will do just fine.

One last note, even households with no children should place an ear of corn on the place mat to symbolize the African concept of social parenthood. All seven symbols are creatively placed on top of the place mat i.e. the symbols should be attractively arranged as they form the Kwanzaa centerpiece.

GIFT GIVING

Kuumba (creativity) is greatly encouraged. Not only is *Kuumba* one of the seven principles, it also brings a sense of personal satisfaction and puts one squarely into the spirit of Kwanzaa. Therefore, those symbols that can be made, should be made. To buy everything ready made is to burden Kwanzaa with the kind of commercialism that presently plagues Christmas. The giving of gifts during Kwanzaa does not contradict this, as gifts should be affordable and of an educational or artistic nature. Gifts are usually exchanged between parents and children and traditionally given on January 1st the last day of Kwanzaa. However gift giving during Kwanzaa may occur at any time.

DECORATING THE HOME

The *Kinara* along with the other symbols of Kwanzaa should dominate the room, which should be given an African motif. This is easily achieved and shouldn't result in too much expense. As the colors of Kwanzaa are black, red, and green, this should be kept in mind when decorating the home. Black, red, and green streamers, balloons, cloth, flowers, and African prints can be hung tastefully around the room. Original art and sculpture may be displayed as well.

THE LIBATION STATEMENT

It is tradition to pour libation in remembrance of the ancestors on all special occasions. Kwanzaa is such an occasion, as it provides us with an opportunity to reflect upon our African past and American present. Water is suggested as it holds the essence of life. Libation should be placed in a communal cup and poured in the direction of the four winds i.e. north, south, east, and west. It should then be passed among family members and guests who may either sip from the cup or make a sipping gesture.

For The Motherland cradle of civilization.
For the ancestors and their indomitable spirit.
For the elders from whom we can learn much.
For our youth who represent the promise for tomorrow.
For our people the original people.
For our struggle and in remembrance of those who have
  struggled on our behalf.
For Umoja the principle of unity which should guide us in
  all that we do.
For the creator who provides all things great and small.

THE KWANZAA KARAMU

The evening of December 31st has special significance because the Kwanzaa *karamu* [or feast] is held then. The *karamu* allows for cultural expression, as well as for feasting. There should be a wide variety of various foods as all attending should take responsibility for preparing a dish, or several dishes. Single persons may bring a dish or they may elect to bring fruit, bread or anything else that might enhance the meal.

It is important to decorate the place where the *karamu* will be held, (e.g. home, community center, church) in an African motif that utilizes a black, red, and green color scheme. A large Kwanzaa setting should dominate the room where the *karamu* will take place. A large *Mkeka* should be placed in the center of the floor where the food should be placed creatively and made accessible to all for self-service. Prior to and during the feast, an informative and entertaining program should be presented. Traditionally, the program involves welcoming, remembering, reassessment, recommitment and rejoicing, concluded by a farewell statement and call for greater unity.

Below is a suggested format for the *karamu* program, from a model by Dr. Karenga.

Kukaribisha (Welcoming)
Introductory Remarks and Recognition of Distinguished Guests and All Elders.
Cultural Expression (Songs, music, group dancing, poetry, performances, chants, unity circles, etc.)

Kukumbuka (Remembering)
Reflections of a Man, Woman and Child.
Cultural Expression.

Kuchunguza Tena Na Kutoa Ahadi Tena (Reassessment and Recommitment)
Introduction of Distinguished Guest Lecturer and Short Talk

Kushangilia (Rejoicing)
Tamshi la Tambiko (Libation Statement)
Kikombe cha Umoja (Unity Cup)
Kutoa Majina (Calling Names of Family Ancestors and Black Heroes)
Ngoma (Drums)
Karamu (Feast)
Cultural Expression

Tamshi la Tutaonana (The Farewell Statement)

FOODS FOR KWANZAA

From The Black Family Reunion Cookbook *by the National Council of Negro Women, Inc., here is a suggested menu for the Kwanzaa karamu, or feast.*

Kwanzaa Celebration Menu
Akara or Bean Balls
Deep Fried Maryland Crab Cakes
Okra Salad
Vegetarian Blackeyed Peas and Rice
Hoe Cakes
Pandowdy
Double Crust Blueberry Pie

Another suggestion comes from Eric Copage, author of Kwanzaa: An African-American Celebration of Culture and Cooking. *Prepare all the dishes from one specific African people or country, or try to select recipes from various lands. If holding a potluck supper, the guests might bring a dish from their ancestors' native land.*

Something That No One Can Take Away

I have no doubt that new traditions can have a meaningful and important place in our lives. This essay by middle school student Jamesina M. Douglas reinforces the necessity for traditions as we head into the twenty-first century.

Family traditions are a vital and important part of our heritage and well-being. Some cultures have different traditions that are celebrated at certain times of the year. One that is close to my heart is the celebration of Kwanzaa.

Kwanzaa, in my family, starts the day after Christmas and lasts six more days. At a young age, my parents taught me the meaning of Kwanzaa, which means "first fruit." My mom and dad usually take that week for a vacation. Each evening, family members light one of seven candles, which are three green, a black, and three red candles. The seven candles represent unity, self-determination, collective work and responsibility, cooperative economics, purpose, creativity, and faith. We usually discuss the principle of the day as we are lighting the candle. We may exchange homemade gifts, which sometimes include desserts, bookmarks, jewelry, et cetera. My favorite part is when we go to the Afro-American Culture Center in Charlotte, North Carolina. There we see dancers in traditional costumes doing native dancing. We also get to taste traditional African food.

I think this holiday will reflect on me as I grow older and teach it to coming family members. Kwanzaa not only teaches me about my ancestors, it also shows that if you have self-confidence you can be somebody. When someone lights a candle, you can feel all kinds of special things run through you. It is like you're free from all danger and harm that may frighten you. Kwanzaa lets me know that I am a descendant of royalty, and I know I have something that no one can take away.

Jamesina M. Douglas, middle school

CHAPTER 3

New Year's Day

THE BEST IS YET TO COME

~ Peas for Luck, Greens for Dollars ~

Being a born-and-bred Southerner, New Year's Day is my favorite traditional holiday—yes, even ahead of Christmas and Thanksgiving. Like Thanksgiving and May Day it is a totally noncommercial day—if you don't count the ball games, that is. And like Christmas it is a day filled with hope.

I never let the day go by without inviting friends for dinner. When I was living in Wisconsin years ago, our New Year's Day party was the talk of the neighborhood. My Scandinavian-descended northwestern friends had never heard of hog jowls, much less tasted black-eyed peas. I had so much trouble finding the peas—dried or canned—in the Madison grocery stores in 1966 that the next year I bought a supply in my hometown of Danville, Virginia, and took them back with me. The fresh collard greens and kale I found in an Asian specialty shop, but I gave up on locating any okra.

The word on a true Southern New Year's dinner seems to have spread around. A couple of years ago, with the publication of Southern Hospitality, *I had the fun of showing the meal off on* Good Morning, America. *To my way of thinking, it's the easiest, most delicious, and relaxed company meal you can prepare. Plus it gives you the perfect excuse to avoid the TV ball games, if that's your inclination. But best of all, the meal promises to bring you good luck through the rest of the year. The basic menu couldn't be simpler.*

Black-eyed Peas for Good Luck
Greens for a Prosperous Year
(You'll get a dollar for every green you eat. Then again,
some people say you'll get a dollar for every black-eyed pea.
So to be safe, eat lots of both.)
Cornbread Muffins with Silver Dollars Baked In
Pork in Some Form (Hog jowls are traditional,
but so are Virginia ham and country sausage.)

⁓ Hoppin' John ⁓

*SWANN BRANNON

Add to the basic menu side dishes of other "feel-good" food—I like grated sweet potato pudding, cheese grits, okra, and tomatoes—top it off with pecan pie and fruitcake, and you have the traditional Southern New Year's Day feast.

But farther south than my North Carolina and Virginia roots, in Savannah, Georgia, Swann Brannon would make a few adjustments to my menu. Oysters and hoppin' John make her day.

Hoppin' John. What a wonderful Southern tradition. New Year's Day would not be the same without it.

Back in the days when the University of Georgia was overlooked by the college bowl games, many of my childhood New Year's Days were spent at a Tybee oyster roast organized by the Clarke, Paulsen, Epting, and Wessel families.

Tybee was a wonderful place in the winter. It was always cold and often a little rainy, and somehow being on a summer island in January made the day special.

This gathering was held in a white house near the back river. Downstairs there were long, paper-covered tables near a roaring fire. Oysters were cooked the real way—on sheet metal under wet burlap sacks and then shoveled into a steaming mountain before you.

Upstairs there was another fire, crackling with fatwood, which was the primary source of warmth, since most beach houses did not have central heat. Archie, a longtime employee of the Wessel family, would cheerfully serve cinnamon cake and hot coffee to the ladies. I was allowed to have a cup mostly filled with cream and sugar, but it made me feel quite grown-up. (Rumor had it that there was homemade brandy available for the gentlemen in the attic, but I had no interest in spirits then.)

It was a fun day spent with family and friends and lots of children exploring closed-off rooms and musty-smelling shower stalls full of fishing rods, crab lines, and old life preservers.

In addition to oysters, the menu featured hot dogs and those little six-and-a-half-ounce bottles of Coca-Cola that are hard to find these days.

But it's the hoppin' John that stands out in my mind—the best I've ever tasted.

It was served from a stacked rice steamer. There was a heavenly aroma coming from the pans that mixed with the spicy scent of the special secret sauce (catsup, butter, and Tabasco), which was served to put on top.

People are very peculiar about their hoppin' John. Some consider cooked black-eyed peas close enough. Others qualify peas on rice as authentic.

In my opinion, the real hoppin' John is the kind that Franklin Dugger is famous for.

Brown cowpeas and rice are cooked together until the concoction is slightly dry yet still moist, with the rice taking on a faint beige color. The bits of bell pepper, celery, and onion are cooked until hardly identifiable.

This oyster roast always had the right kind of hoppin' John, and I loved it. Served on flimsy white paper plates with little plastics forks, it was heaven—and promised to bring good luck all year.

Somewhere in time, Georgia's luck and our coaches changed and suddenly our New Year's Days were spent at bowl games in other cities.

It seems like the farther away you get from home, the harder it is to find hoppin' John. We often had to rely on the kindness of a regionally sympathetic restaurant or postpone our New Year's celebration until we got home.

My mother's hoppin' John is some of the best. She also serves extra peas on the side and turnip greens (to bring you money) and roast pork. Although delicious, it's not quite the same hoppin' John from my youth.

The college bowls have again sadly passed the Bulldogs by. So this New Year's, my family will hold our own Tybee oyster roast. We'll have all the usual dishes and accompaniments, but the place of honor —the center of the table—belongs to the hoppin' John.

⤳ Pickles and Prayers ⤳

GLADYS TABER

Before New Year's Day, there is New Year's Eve. Everyone is familiar with the traditional celebrations in Times Square and in countless clubs, bars, and restaurants throughout the country. They are pretty much all the same. The homey gatherings are the ones we seem to remember the most.

The new year often comes accompanied by steeply falling temperatures and spitting snowstorms. In the city there is a lot of what Mama used to call "carrying-on." When the children were away at school or working in the city, Jill and I had a number of New Year's Eves by ourselves. We had a strong feeling of wanting to see the old year out beside our own fire, so we avoided the customary parties. We sometimes read aloud, we played our favorite records, and we talked about the year to come. I think of those New Year's Eves and am thankful we did not waste them while she was alive.

New Year's at Stillmeadow is a family occasion. Jill's daughter Dorothy and her husband Val and their two wonderful children come and fill the house with love and laughter. After dinner, the children toast marshmallows and popcorn too, and Holly hangs around the kitchen waiting for more turkey. After the children climb the ladder stairs and go to bed, the three of us settle down for a warm and comfortable talk. Jill used to say, "There is one thing about us, we are a verbal family." So we are!

Midnight comes all too soon, and we bring in a tray with freshly baked sourdough bread with cheese and salami and thin slices of ham and pickles. When the chimes ring out (over television to be sure), we hold hands and say our private prayers for the year to come. I couldn't wish for a better way to begin than this.

⤳ First the Revelry, Then the Food ⤳

MAYMIE RICHARDSON KRYTHE

When it comes right down to it, New Year's Day celebrations are as old as time immemorial, and our ancestors brought the traditions associated with the day with them from all corners of the world. Here, adapted from All About American Holidays, *are selected highlights that explain the most popular ways we continue to celebrate New Year's Day across the country.*

New Year's Day is the most important January holiday, and the only one the entire world observes, regardless of race or religious belief. No doubt the greeting, "Happy New Year!" in various languages has been most often heard around the globe. . . .

Mingled in with the old cry "Happy New Year!" is the raucous din of welcoming in a new year. Noisemaking on this date is one of the earliest and longest continued customs known to mankind. This idea is said to have come from Babylon and India, where hilarity and much noise accompanied their New Year observance. . . .

Here in the United States (especially in some southern sections) an old custom still exists—shooting off guns to greet a new year. It was brought in by early settlers over a hundred and fifty years ago.

Cherryville, North Carolina, still clings to this custom. Recently, forty or more citizens marched to the city hall. Each was armed with an ancient musket. At one minute after midnight, eighty-five-year-old Sidney Beam greeted the mayor with a shout, "Good morning to you, sir!" Then his companions sent "a shattering volley into the air." Next they marched around the streets and out into the country, shooting off their old weapons. These southern revelers saluted the new year on into the afternoon.

For centuries the pealing of bells has been an important part of the coming of New Year's Day, a pleasant and welcome sound. Charles Lamb once remarked that the most striking bell sound is "the peal that rings out the old year." . . .

Today around the globe church bells peal out as people gather on the streets at midnight to rejoice together. And modern man, in a lighter mood than his ancestors, greets New Year's Day, with the perennial noisemaking.

—◆◆—

Since New Year's Day is the time for reunions of families and friends, feasting naturally is a chief pastime. And throughout the world this holiday is associated with certain foods believed to bring good luck to the diners. Often, too, there is an exchange of dishes between friends. Some modern eating customs on this date can be traced to ancient eras. Serving sweets, for example, goes back to the time when sugar cane was discovered. A favorite Roman food was honey; apples dipped in honey were also a feature of Hebrew New Year's observances, which take place sometime between September 6 and October 5.

Since some American Indians associated New Year's Day with acorns and salmon, they made a ceremony of eating these foods at this time. In our southwestern states, Texas for instance, there was a belief that good fortune would come to those who ate black-eyed peas on January 1. This goes back to England from which settlers brought the idea to Virginia. Black-eyed peas were considered a delicacy from the time of our first President. And the turkey has long been the main dish on many tables in the United States when friends gather to honor a new year.

— • —

Calling on friends on New Year's Day is said to have been started centuries ago by the Chinese. And in the United States, especially in cities, such as New York, this custom began early. Dutch settlers are credited with beginning this pleasant practice. The men called on the women; so the ladies saw men friends at least once a year. It is said that George Washington was surprised by this custom when he went to New York, as the first elected Chief Executive. Gradually, the calling idea spread from the East coast to other states, and for many decades was a popular way of opening a new year.

Our first President started the precedent (which continued to this century) of holding open house for the general public on January 1. He and his wife, Martha Washington, continued such social affairs during the seven years the national capital was in Philadelphia. Although John and Abigail Adams moved into the White House in Washington, D.C., before it was completed, they managed to hold a reception there on New Year's Day in 1800.

Thomas Jefferson followed their example. In 1804, for example, he held open house, from twelve noon until 2 P.M. During this period, a large number of guests arrived, including government officials, diplomats, military officers, and even some Cherokee Indian chiefs, along with "most of the respectable people of Washington and Georgetown." On this notable occasion, the Marine band played, and "abundant refreshments" were served.

Other Chief Executives continued the custom for many years; also the wives of Cabinet members and various Washington social leaders received friends and constituents on New Year's Day.

In eastern cities like New York and Philadelphia, it was quite "the proper thing" to give and attend such annual functions. During the latter part of the last century, anyone who wanted to be considered in the upper social brackets took part in these social affairs.

It was customary for men to call on ladies on New Year's afternoon; for younger people to visit older friends, while women paid calls on each other the following day.

During the Gay Nineties, hostesses often announced in the newspapers the hours they would receive guests on this holiday. People arrived in their best finery—men in silk hats, with chamois skin gloves, and ladies in "stiff bombazine with sealskin tippets."

Callers placed their cards on trays in the reception hall, greeted the host and hostess, then went to the dining room, where tables held such substantial foods as roast beef, turkey, ham, relishes, along with all kinds of fancy pastries. Of course, punch and the traditional eggnog were dispensed in large quantities.

After their guests had departed, the host and hostess often made a round of calls on their friends. As a result, the affair became a real calling marathon. Persons rushed around in their "stylish turnouts," drawn by teams of matched horses, to see how many calls they could make. At times, undesirables managed to crash the parties; also guests who had imbibed too much at different homes sometimes caused hostesses embarrassment.

While Easterners were carrying on this New Year tradition, it is interesting to note what Westerners, in Southern California, for example, were doing to observe the amenities of this holiday.

Even in the 1850s, after the state had entered the Union and Los Angeles was just a small pueblo, her people always celebrated the coming of a new year. Some Angelenos attended midnight Mass at the old church, still standing at the plaza. Others showed their joy by shooting off guns and pistols.

On January 1 friends got together for roast turkey and "all the fixings." The *Los Angeles Star,* in January 1855, reported as follows: "Christmas and New Year's festivities are passing away with the usual accompaniments, namely bull fights, firing of crackers, fiestas, and fandangoes. In the city, cascarones commanded a premium, and many were complimented with them as a finishing touch to their head-dresses."

By 1877, many Angelenos were attending church services on the morning of New Year's Day; and later, prominent citizens entertained at their homes. "The ladies wore their prettiest smiles, and dispersed the customary refreshments in the most graceful and hospitable manner." It was said that a certain hostess entertained more than "thirty gentlemen in her parlor" at one time. That evening, the elite of the city gathered at Union Hall for a brilliant formal ball.

In those days people all over the United States were big eaters. If you had been invited to a New Year's Eve ball in the 1870's and 1880's after several hours of dancing, you and your partner would have joined the other guests in the dining room "to partake of" a meal that would fortify all sufficiently to continue the gay festivities until dawn. . . .

Gradually the custom of extensive calling on New Year's Day died out in most places. Nowadays, many socially minded persons prefer to celebrate the coming of the holiday by spending New Year's Eve in hotels and cafes. After a gala dinner, a floor show, and dancing, the noisemaking keeps up until midnight; then it reaches a crescendo, followed usually by a brief pause when the new year is welcomed in with "Should Auld Acquaintance Be Forgot," the song that has become associated with this annual event:

> *For auld lang syne, my dear,*
> *For auld lang syne,*
> *We'll take a cup of kindness, yet,*
> *For auld lang syne.*

Afterwards, the festivities are resumed and may last the rest of the night.

Because of the different time zones in the United States, the West can hear or see by means of radio or television, the earlier celebrations in the East, such as that in Times Square where pandemonium reigns when the old year is over.

While many Americans celebrate New Year's Eve in this hilarious fashion, others consider its arrival more seriously. Therefore, they "take stock" of themselves, review their mistakes and failures of the past months, and, following the advice of Sarah C. Woolsey, "Yesterday's errors let yesterday cover," resolve to do better.

Making New Year's resolutions has long been an American custom on this holiday. Even though some scoff at the idea, and few succeed in keeping all of their resolutions, we are encouraged in the attempt by the poet, Alfred Tennyson, who wrote:

> *I hold it truth with him who sings*
> *To one clear harp on divers tones*
> *That men may rise on stepping stones*
> *Of their dead selves to higher things.*

When numerous Americans are attending gay social events on New Year's Eve, others prefer to take part in Watch Night services at some church. These meetings are said to have originated with early Methodists. They held the first such gathering in this country at Philadelphia in 1770. Members left their homes, met for a season of prayer and praise, and after midnight bells had rung in a new year, these worshipers went thoughtfully to their homes.

Nowadays, in some churches, members and friends meet early for an informal program, and then enjoy an hour or so of good fellowship, with refreshments. Sometimes these exercises are followed by Holy Communion. The congregation is inspired by the religious aspect of the season, which "emphasizes the fundamental purpose of the new year—to bury the past and start anew."

Or the Watch Night service may begin at 11 P.M. in a candle-lighted sanctuary. There is special music; the minister gives a meditation on the significance of the hour; and all join in familiar hymns. There is a solemnity about the time and place; as midnight bells peal in the new year, they recall the words of Emily H. Miller: "The old goes out, but the glad young year comes newly in tomorrow."

At the Watch Night service in New York's noted Riverside Church, there is an "hour of great significance," then the carillon in the tower announces the arrival of a new year. It is a great contrast to the noisy observance in Times Square, but both are typical of the way the United States heralds the coming year. No matter how one celebrates, he no doubt will wish with William Cullen Bryant: "The good old year is with the past, oh be the new as kind!"

New Year's Day coincides with the Circumcision which is observed in the liturgical churches to commemorate the circumcision of Christ eight days after His birth, in accordance with Jewish practice. Members of these churches, the Anglican or Episcopal, the Roman Catholic, and the Greek Orthodox are expected to attend services either on New Year's Eve or New Year's Day.

On this holiday many Americans enjoy staying at home for family dinners or entertaining friends. Naturally the football enthusiasts who are unable to attend the Rose Bowl game watch it on the screen and later enjoy informal suppers.

Today our modern American celebration of New Year's Day is high-lighted by two famous events: in the East, at Philadelphia, the colorful Mummers' Parade is held, while the celebrated Pasadena Rose Tournament is staged in the West. Both have gained national acclaim; and annually millions of local people and tourists throng to see them.

The Mummers' Parade goes back to the time when the Swedish emigrants came over and settled along the Delaware River. At yuletide they kept up their celebration until New Year's Day. Dressed in grotesque outfits, they roamed around the towns and countryside in gay bands, creating fun for neighbors and townspeople. English settlers brought with them their traditional mummers' holiday plays. As the years went by, groups of Swedish masqueraders and English mummers paraded together on New Year's Day, shooting their firearms and making as much noise as possible.

Just before the famous Centennial of 1876 in Philadelphia, some of the citizens had organized the Silver Crown New Year's Association. This was the first large society to take part in the Mummers' Parade, which was still a rather unorganized affair. In 1901 the city government recognized the mummers and allowed them to stage a parade in which forty-two clubs joined. By 1930 this had become an important event, with prize money amounting to thirty thousand dollars.

In 1955 more than eight hundred thousand people witnessed the Mummers' Parade, a ten-hour long spectacle, presided over by King Momus. That year pink was the predominant color, but there were other costumes in varied pastel shades. These handsome outfits are fashioned from gleaming satin with fine embroidery work on them, and some are ornamented with spangles and sequins.

There was, as usual, much noise: shrieking sirens, firecrackers, and car horns, while clowns and other comics lampooned national and international celebrities. String bands, decorated with colorful plumes, marched to traditional banjo rhythms. The top prize of two thousand dollars was won by the Polish-American band, whose members did the can-can.

In 1957 the mummers staged their fifty-seventh annual parade. A crowd of several hundred thousand lined the four-mile route along Broad Street to the judges' stand at the City Hall. Philadelphia provided fifty-two thousand dollars in prize money that year for three classes of entrants: comic, fancy, and string. The comics were dressed to represent famous politicians, popular television personalities, and other notables. Preparations for this event had begun a year before; and in this parade twelve thousand mummers strutted along and gave New Year's Day a rousing official welcome.

One newspaper stated that the participants had spent about half a million dollars on their costumes. There were one hundred bands, and such old-time favorites as "Oh Dem Golden Slippers" and "Four-Leaf Clover" were often heard along the line of march. An unusual feature of this Mummers' Parade in the "City of Brotherly Love," is that no women are allowed in it. However, many men impersonate women in this colorful event.

Out on the Pacific coast, on this same holiday the Pasadena Tournament of Roses Parade is seen by millions of Californians, and by visitors from all over the world. It is always hailed as one of the best annual American festivals in the entire country.

Charles F. Holder, founder of the Valley Hunt Club, is really responsible for the first such parade, held in the city of Pasadena on January 1, 1886. On that day, members of the Hunt Club decorated their carriages and buggies with real flowers. After they had paraded around the town, they gathered that afternoon to watch varied athletic contests.

For several years the Valley Hunt Club financed the parade; then the city of Pasadena took over the responsibility. Finally the Tournament of Roses Association was formed as the permanent sponsor of this unique celebration.

This event has gone through several stages of development. At first it was just a parade of decorated vehicles, then floats were added and prizes given. In 1902 a football game was played in the afternoon. For several years chariot races were put on.

Each year since 1905 there has been a beautiful queen to rule over the event, and a celebrity has led the long procession as grand marshal. The Rose Parade has become a larger and more expensive affair with the passing years. Only *fresh* flowers can be used on a float; and one of these beautiful creations often costs several thousand dollars. A different theme is chosen yearly and all floats carry out the central idea. Numerous bands are interspersed between the exquisite floats, so the mood of gayety and celebration is sustained.

Another special feature of the parade is the sight of hundreds of spirited, prancing horses (including handsome golden palominos), their silver trappings glittering in the bright sunlight, as they are put through their paces by skilled riders.

Such headlines as the following described the 1959 parade:

1,500,000 HAIL DAZZLING ROSE PARADE
63 BRILLIANT FLOATS THRILL VAST THRONG

That year the top prize—the sweepstakes—was won by the city of Glendale, California:

The sweepstakes prize went to the city of Glendale, for its magnificent "Adventures in Fantasy."

It was a worthy champion—10,000 vanda orchids, 6,000 roses and innumerable narcissus and chrysanthemum blooms, fashioned into a sedan chair from which a queen of fantasy ruled a fairyland.

A canopy of strung orchids stretched above the chair and tiers of pink, lavender, and white chrysanthemums led upward to a platform where three princesses reposed on blossoms.

—*Long Beach Press-Telegram,*
January 2, 1959

It is estimated that over a million and a half people watch both the parade and the Rose Bowl football game between eastern and western teams, which was instituted in 1916 and has become a permanent afternoon feature on New Year's Day.

⇀ The Other American New Year ⇀ Chinese New Year in San Francisco

Somehow, say "New Year" and along with the images of Times Square or Guy Lombardo I see colorful Chinese dragons and hear the gonging bells associated with that other new year celebration, the Chinese New Year. Its popularity is sweeping across the country. I remember rushing out of the house one night in late January to see and hear the festivities at our neighborhood Chinese restaurant—yes, even in Raleigh, North Carolina.

Another time I was in San Francisco just before the occasion and saw the people gathering armfuls of flowers and vegetables along Grant Avenue to use in their celebration at home. Someday I hope to see the parade itself, but until then, I have an image in my mind's eye from these descriptions of that colorful and festive holiday.

A Time of Family Unity

Ben Fong-Torres

But while we had tricks and treats and Thanksgiving and Christmas, we also had Chinese New Year every February, or whenever the first day of each Lunar Year arrived. To us, the Chinese calendar was confusing, with New Year—and Mom's and Dad's birthdays—falling on different dates every year.

The Chinese also make New Year a two-week-long affair, and I never did figure out the difference between *Hon Neen* (which seemed to precede the actual New Year) and *Hoy Neen* (which meant "open year" and, presumably, the beginning of the new year). At some point, we knew that we'd receive *hoong bow*—little red envelopes containing a coin, given by adults to children to reward them for good manners and to wish them good luck.

I knew that, no matter how far from home, the children were expected to gather for dinner on those days in a show of family unity. Every year, our parents would put out their round, lacquered, wood platter—called by some a "tray of togetherness" and by others a "tray of prosperity"—with eight compartments for a variety of sweets— candied melon (for health), sugared coconut strips (togetherness), kumquat (prosperity), lichee nuts (strong family ties), melon seeds (dyed red to symbolize happiness), lotus seeds (many children), and longan (many good sons).

All over the house, there'd be bowls and platters piled high with oranges and tangerines, which meant good luck and wealth, and wherever Chinese visited during the two weeks of New Year celebration, they would bring gifts of fruit and go through an exercise of manners that befuddled us.

The hosts would chide the visitors for bringing oranges.

"Oh, not necessary," they would say, knowing full well that the gift was almost mandatory in Chinese tradition.

The guests would insist; the hosts would relent. Then, at the end of the visit, the hosts would pile the guests up with oranges and tangerines.

"Oh, no, no," the departing guests would protest, fully prepared to accept the exchange of fruit—which they would bring to their next hosts.

At dinner, every course, as with every aspect of the New Year celebration, was laden with symbolism and purpose. We had to have chicken, simply steamed and presented whole, indicating completeness. The same reasoning applied to fish, roast suckling pig with thick, crunchy skin and an even thicker layer of fat, and, as a yin-yang balance, a vegetarian dish called "Buddha's monk stew," composed of Chinese vermicelli (noodles, uncut, symbolize long life), fermented bean curd, cloud ears, tiger lily flowers, and gingko nuts.

Before dinner, we'd set off firecrackers outside the house—to ward off evil spirits—and create an echo of what for most Chinese was the highlight of New Year's: the parade through Chinatown, San Francisco, with its block-long golden dragon. We rarely made it over to *Dai Fow,* but contented ourselves with Oakland's street celebrations. On Webster and surrounding streets, teams of young lion dancers from judo and karate schools made the rounds of business establishments and family associations, which hired the lions to chase off bad influences with their supernatural powers. While neighbors and passersby gathered to watch, they performed amidst gongs, drums, and exploding firecrackers, and, at show's end, climbed high, ignoring lit fireworks at their feet, to snatch a string of *hoong bow*—red envelopes containing dollar bills—payment to the lions for warding off the demons.

I was fascinated by the lion's head, with the blinding primary colors, the bulging, bejeweled, fur-browed eyes and the pom poms springing out of its forehead. The lead dancer would hoist it over his head, thrust and jerk it up and about, and flap its extended tongue and white-whiskered lower jaw, dancing acrobatically with two other men who worked under a long, multicolored fabric train behind him, forming the body of the lion.

Back at the New Eastern, I'd take a cardboard box that had held eggs and, with paper, water colors, crayons, string, and fabrics Mother had left over from her garment work, fashion my own lion's head, complete with a flapping lower lip. Barry and Shirley were happy to pound on garbage can lids or a Quaker Oats box while I pranced around the backyard.

Our parents were delighted that we would embrace Chinese New Year with such enthusiasm.

～ Kissing Day ～

Bertha L. Heilbron

Radically different from the noisy street-festival activities of our twentieth-century Chinese-American New Year's Day celebration was the nineteenth-century Minnesota Indian tradition of "kissing day" as related in The Folklore of American Holidays *based on research by Bertha L. Heilbron.*

When missionaries began to work among the Minnesota Indians, particularly among the Chippewa of the North, they found that the natives made much of New Year's Day. They celebrated the holiday, which they called "Kissing day," after the manner of the French-Canadian traders and voyageurs. The puritanical religious leaders often were obliged, much against their wishes, to observe the day in the native manner. William T. Boutwell, who went to Leech Lake in 1833, found that the Indians there were in the habit of visiting the resident trader on January 1 to receive presents, "when all, male and female, old and young, must give and receive a kiss, a cake, or something else." They seemed to expect similar treatment from Boutwell, for on the first day of 1834 they caused the pious missionary considerable annoyance by appearing at his cabin at breakfast time. He relates the story as follows:

"Open came our door, and in came 5 or 6 women and as many children. An old squaw, with clean face, for once, came up and saluted me with, '*bonjour*,' giving her hand at the same time, which I received, returning her compliment, '*bonjour*.' But this was not all. She had been too long among Canadians not to learn some of their New Year Customs. She approached—approached so near, to give and receive a kiss, that I was obliged to give her a slip, and dodge! This vexed the old lady and provoked her to say, that I thought her too dirty. But pleased, or displeased, I was determined to give no countenance to a custom which I hated more than dirt."

At Red Lake twelve years later a band of missionaries planned a New Year's celebration which seemed to please the natives, who "honored" them "with a salute of two guns." The missionaries at this place recognized the Indian custom and took part in the celebration. According to Lucy M. Lewis, the wife of one of the missionaries, all the mission workers gathered at early dawn at the house of their leader, "the most convenient place to meet the Indians who assemble to give the greeting and receive a cake or two & a draught of sweetened water. It is the custom through the country to make calls and receive cakes." But instead of offering kisses, these Indians sang a "New Year's hymn learned in school for the occasion." The Red Lake missionaries marked New Year's Eve by assembling the pupils of the mission school and giving them presents. In 1845 the gifts consisted of flannel shirts for the boys and "short gowns" for the girls. The Indian children "came with cleaner faces & hands than usual," writes Mrs. Lewis, "as a little soap had previously been distributed."

— The Tradition Continues —

Hope. That's the basis of traditions. Throw in a measure of good luck and as these young people's pieces show, New Year's Eve and Day are brimming with anticipation of good times to come.

Each New Year's Eve, my family stays up to midnight watching New Year's Eve shows on television. One of my favorite televised scenes is from Times Square in New York City.

As a white dazzling ball descends and explodes into the number of the new year, my sister and I burst into the living room. We use her little toy musical instruments and play them as if we were part of a band in a parade. After that we each sip a small glass of wine or grape juice. While we hold our glasses, we pray to have a great new year. Finally we clink our glasses, say "Cheers," drink the contents, and go to bed.

While my family and I are celebrating, I feel tremendously ecstatic. The reason for this is because I know my family and I will have new snow, new trees, new flowers, new times to have fun and new times to do work, new times to jump in raked leaves, and new sunshine. I know my family and I will have all these things because it will be a brand new year.

As we celebrate on New Year's Eve, I think of the upcoming year. I think of how much fun my birthday, Christmas, Valentine's Day, the Fourth of July, and the other holidays will be during the new year.

Our New Year's Eve celebration is one of my favorite traditions. I look forward to it every year.

James E. Darst, middle school

⌁⌁

For decades my family has followed the age-old tradition of a male having to be the first to enter and walk through the house on New Year's Day. My ancestors believe this will bring them good luck.

So, at one minute past the stroke of midnight on New Year's Eve, my dad has to wake up, get dressed, and go walk through several houses. He first goes to my great-aunt's house where he finds them standing at the door waiting for him. They will not allow any female to enter their house until he has made his visit. Next, he walks through the house of the old lady who lives next door to them. Dad then does the same thing at my grandmother's house. From there he goes to my aunt's house and does the same thing there. He also might have to go to some friends' houses and walk through them.

Finally, when he finishes walking through all the houses, he comes back home and goes back to sleep to dream of another tradition that my family follows—that of having black-eyed peas and collard greens for our traditional New Year's dinner.

Daniel C. Bell, middle school

⌁⌁

We have a family tradition that has been the same as long as anyone can remember. It takes place on the first day of the year, New Year's Day. We always have the same meal, year after year. Moma might add a different dish, but there is always a pot of greens and a pot of black-eyed peas. Lucky for me, she does cook something else to go along with it. Moma says the greens stand for dollar bills and the black-eyed peas stand for pennies. Everybody tries to eat as much as they can.

The way Daddy and Moma eat, I wonder why we are not rich. But maybe things could be much worse. Moma and Daddy say we are very rich in some ways. We have a good home, good jobs, good health, and —most important—each other. I guess that is why we always thank God for what we do have. Could this be another family tradition? This would be a good one. I hope I learn to like these foods so I can help keep the New Year's tradition going on.

Lisa Nicole Jackson, elementary school

What you are about to read may sound a bit bizarre, but it's a fun celebration. My brother, Eric, and I work hard making homemade confetti a few days before New Year's Day. Then, on New Year's Eve, my mother makes banana pudding for us to eat while we try our best to make time fly by. Usually we watch the countdown on television.

After that, we put a divider in the center of the living room floor. When the clock finally strikes midnight, the competition begins. We put equal amounts of our homemade confetti on each side of the divider. Then, my dad and brother get on one side of the divider and my mom and I get on the other side. After I say "Go!" we see who can throw the most confetti on the other side. After we are all tired, we have to clean up for about an hour. Each following day, for some strange reason, we keep finding confetti in the most unusual places. I really like this family tradition. It's so much fun, and each year I count the days until we get to celebrate New Year's again.

Darlene Bryan, elementary school

I cannot wait until New Year's Eve because we always go to my grandparents who live here in Asheboro. On that night, at about 7:00 P.M., we always eat a big dinner that my grandmother prepares. Usually, we have duck or goose. Every New Year's, there is always that big bowl of yellow sauerkraut. Believe me, I don't touch it!

After we eat dinner and the kitchen is cleaned up, my grandma puts a big bowl of slightly cooked peas on the clean table. Along with the peas, a whole baked fish decorates the table. The family tradition has it that all of the peas must be eaten by midnight so the entire family will have good luck and no tears in the next year. The fish must remain on the table past midnight so everyone will have money in the new year. (I'm still waiting for mine!) We watch the New York Times Square countdown on television. Then at 12:00 A.M., we all drink a glass of champagne. New Year's Eve is certainly a treat for me!

Jeana Preimats, middle school

Every New Year's Eve, starting in 1990 when I was six years old, my family and I would eat collards with black-eyed peas for luck. The collards were dollar bills and the black-eyed peas were coins.

When we all were finished eating, we told about what we were going to improve on. Talking about the things we were going to do made me feel so good. The things we talked about were how to have a much better life, and how to improve on certain things. All through the year all my goals are coming true. Last year my goals were to improve on my cursive writing and to get along better with my sister. It's good luck to have traditions to help us think about ways that we can make our lives better.

Lindsay Inman, elementary school

I will always remember the way my family celebrates New Year's Day. We like to boil fifty-cent pieces in cabbage on New Year's Day. It may sound like a strange tradition to you. My parents have always said, "If you eat the cabbage and keep the money, it will bring you good luck. If you spend it, it would bring you bad luck. Even if you put cabbage on your plate and just take the money, it will bring you bad luck."

I put my money in a bag and stick it in my dresser drawer so no one will take it and bring me bad luck. No one in my family has ever spent their money because they don't want to have bad luck.

We will probably continue this tradition, so we will have good luck and lots of money.

Peticia Craigo, elementary school

New Year's Day is special for my family because we share the Holy Bread together. This happens every New Year at my family's house. The people in my house include my parents, sister Jaci, and me.

The Holy Bread we eat at New Year's was left over from Christmas. The Holy Bread was sent from my great-uncle Stryiki because he is a priest and lives in a monastery. When we're ready to eat, everybody sits at the table. When we're all seated, my dad gets some Holy Bread. He says something complimentary to each of us. After that, he breaks off a piece of bread for each of us. After we eat the Holy Bread, we feast on the food we have. My favorite foods are turkey, potatoes, corn, and black-eyed peas.

After we eat, I feel happy that we had the feast. I'm also joyful that the Lord forgave my sins.

Christopher James Wasek, elementary school

On New Year's Day, my family breaks bread. It is a Greek tradition that was brought from Cyprus by my great-grandmother.

My great-grandmother, Big Yia Yia (which is Greek for Grand-mother), bakes a special Greek bread and puts a dime in it. It is cut by the head of the family. We all pick one piece. Whoever has the dime in their bread is supposed to have good luck for the entire year. We take the bread home and eat it at breakfast that week. My mom likes to dunk her bread in coffee.

My great-grandmother is getting old, so my Little Yia Yia will hopefully keep the tradition going. I can't wait until I'm the grandmother so I can bake the bread and watch the joy on my family's faces while hoping for the treasured dime.

Lara Kristen Stroud, middle school

— A Toast for the Birds —

*SUSAN TORRANCE

When I told friends and strangers that I was working on The Book of American Traditions *the mail flowed in from across the country. One of the earliest letters I received came from Susan Torrance at the Armstrong County, Pennsylvania, Tourist Bureau in Kittanning, Pennsylvania. She wrote that upon first hearing about my request for traditions, she thought it would be easy to come up with one. "Then," she says, "I realized how automatic things are and it's hard to think of things as a tradition or as something that's not done everywhere or is anything special." But she enclosed the following tradition, which is one of my personal favorites of all I've received to date. It has nothing to do with teetotaling, because I traditionally toast New Year's with champagne. It has everything to do with friends and fun, optimistically looking ahead to the next year and remembering last year, and, of course, the birds.*

All who can make it home for the holiday try to arrive by dinnertime on New Year's Eve. At dinner, which is nothing fancy, the theme for the evening is announced. Each year a different person gets to come up with a theme for the New Year's Eve festivities. At some point during the evening, supplies (paper plates, construction paper, crayons, glue, markers, glitter, and so forth) are brought out so that everyone can make their hat portraying the theme for the party. Also, during the evening a jigsaw puzzle is started with the idea that it must be completed by midnight. Over the course of the evening people drift in and out of working on the puzzle and playing games like Uno. Some busy themselves with keeping the group in snacks and beverages.

It's usually around 11:00 P.M. when the person to drop the ball and the person to make the toast are chosen. An inflatable ball-shaped Christmas ornament or other round item is hung from the chandelier in the family room. When the countdown to midnight begins on television, the person selected lowers the ball in synchronization with the ball at Times Square. While this is happening the person chosen to make the toast is frantically making toast in the kitchen. (Yes, the bread-in-the-toaster kind of toast.)

The piece of toast made in the toaster is decorated with the number of the new year spelled in cinnamon hearts, frosting, or other cake decorations. The piece of toast is then cut in half. One half goes into the freezer for the next year. The half put in the freezer last year is found and cut into the correct number of pieces for the number of people present. When the new year arrives, the ball is dropped and everyone goes to the kitchen for a piece of the old year's toast.

It's taken to the back porch and thrown to the birds as all yell "Happy New Year!" Then all come back inside and get a little piece of half of the new year's toast (the half that wasn't put in the freezer for safekeeping). Thus the new year is properly "toasted." (By the way, no one gets drunk at the party. It's just good clean fun.)

My pipe is out, my glass is dry;
    My fire is almost ashes too;
But once again, before you go,
    And I prepare to meet the New:
Old Year! a parting word that's true,
    For we've been comrades, you and I—
I thank God for each day of you;
    There! bless you now! Old Year, good-bye!

Robert W. Service

CHAPTER 4

Valentine's Day

THIS ONE GOES OUT TO
THE ONE I LOVE

⟶ *When Love Rules the Day* ⟵

Roses, daisies, carnations, baby's breath, diamonds, perfume, heart-shaped boxes of candy, love letters. On no other day of the year is so much emphasis placed on doing something special for the one you love. Many couples become engaged or wed on February 14, hoping that this romantic day will bring them luck through the years.

Then there are those people who feel that Valentine's Day is just a greeting-card holiday and take the easy way out. This allows for much creativity on the part of those who really want to impress and surprise their sweethearts. Diamond rings are found at the bottom of champagne glasses. Messages of love are announced to the world on billboards, in the newspaper, and in the sky.

Bouquets of flowers shamelessly appear at even the most austere workplaces. True to the tradition, love rules the day.

⤚ Happy Valentine's Day ⤙

MAYMIE R. KRYTHE

Ever wonder how Valentine's Day began? It's easy to overlook a holiday's origins when you are focused on finding just the right gift for your valentine, but Maymie R. Krythe has done the research for you. She also tells the origins of many of America's Valentine's Day traditions.

Just before St. Valentine's Day, store windows feature valentines. Adults as well as children are attracted by the displays of artistic cards and gifts. Even though this holiday has lost some of its romance, many still like to observe it by sending affectionate messages or by giving gay parties.

There are conflicting ideas about the origin of St. Valentine's Day. Some sources say it goes back—perhaps to the third century—when there were hordes of hungry wolves outside Rome. The god, Lupercus, was said to watch over the shepherds and their flocks. Therefore, in February Romans celebrated a feast, called the Lupercalia, in his honor. Even after the danger from these fierce animals was over, people still observed this festival.

When Christianity became prevalent, the priests wanted their converts to give up former heathen practices. Therefore, the officials Christianized the ancient pagan celebration and called the Feast of Lupercalia St. Valentine's Day. Sometimes a priest placed names of different saints in a box or urn; the young people drew these names out; then during the following year each youth was supposed to emulate the life of the saint whose name he had drawn.

According to the Acta Sanctorum, there were actually eight men with the name, Valentine, seven of whose feast days were on February 14. Also on this date occurred "the veneration of the head of the eighth."

These men are said to have lived in different parts of the world, including Spain, Africa, Belgium, and France. However, the three most important ones were a priest, beheaded at Rome in 269, a bishop of Umbria (both of the third century), and the third, Valentine, who was put to death in Africa. Tradition has preserved several accounts of these saints—but some authorities believe many of the stories have no historical value.

One source states that a Valentine served as a priest at a beautiful temple during the reign of the cruel Emperor Claudius. Romans revered this priest, and young and old, rich and poor, thronged to his services. When the Emperor tried to recruit soldiers for his wars, he met much opposition. For the men did not want to leave their wives, families, or sweethearts. Then the angry monarch declared that no more marriages would be performed, and that all engagements were canceled.

This was not fair to young lovers—so Valentine thought—therefore, he secretly joined several couples. Claudius declared that no one, not even a priest, could defy him; so he threw Valentine into prison where he died. Then his friends got his body and buried it in a churchyard in Rome.

Another version is that St. Valentine was seized for helping some Christians; while in prison he cured a jailer's daughter of blindness. This made Claudius angrier than ever; he had Valentine beaten with clubs and then beheaded. His death is said to have occurred on February 14, 269 AD. In 496 Pope Gelasius set aside this date to honor him. Another legend says that Valentine fell in love with the jailer's daughter and wrote her letters, signed "From your Valentine."

So gradually as time passed this new Christian holiday became a time for exchanging love messages, and St. Valentine emerged as the patron saint of lovers.

Credit for creating the first worthwhile valentines in this country goes to Miss Esther Howland, a student at Mount Holyoke College a century or more ago. Her father, a stationer in Worcester, Massachusetts, used to import valentines from England, as did other American merchants.

However, Esther decided to create her own messages; as a result, she was one of our first career women. About 1830 she started to import lace, fine papers, and other supplies for her business. This grew so rapidly that she had to employ several assistants. Her brothers marketed her justly popular "Worcester" valentines, and sales amounted to about a hundred thousand dollars annually.

These messages remained at the height of their popularity in the United States until the Civil War era. Valentine's Day is said to have ranked next to Christmas in holiday importance. Many early valentines, hand-painted and expertly trimmed with lace work, are now collectors' items. Even though some have faded, we are still charmed by their delicate colors, unique designs, and tender sentiments.

In later decades valentines became less artistic and frequently they were overornamented—especially through the Gay Nineties—with garish decorations of spun glass, mother-of-pearl, imitation jewels, or silk fringe. So the finer handmade greetings gave way to unattractive, cheap-looking ones.

Another type that lessened the popularity of valentines was the "vinegar valentine," or so-called "comic." Printed on cheap paper, in crude colors, they were first concocted by a New York printer, John McLaughlin. Such messages ridiculed certain types of persons: old maids, teachers, and others. This unkind custom made many people unhappy; for the valentines were certainly not in tune with the real spirit of St. Valentine.

Fortunately, from the beginning of this century there has been quite a change in the missives sent on February 14. The heavy sentimentality of earlier days has given way to the "light touch." Naturally, too, living in the Space Age has affected our valentines.

At times a husband will "go all out" on this holiday to impress his wife. Some time ago the comedian, Garry Moore, hired four planes to do some sky writing. This included a heart three miles wide, pierced by an arrow, six miles long. Inside the heart were the names, "Garry and Nell."

Nowadays, adults usually purchase valentines to accompany a more elaborate gift, such as candy, flowers, or perfume. School children enjoy buying or making valentines for their friends and teachers; they like to baffle the receivers by printing the old "From guess who," on the messages. Even in quite modern schools youngsters want a gaily decorated box with a slot in the top where they can "mail" their valentines. Usually each classroom has one and the distribution at the end of the school day is eagerly awaited.

Naturally St. Valentine's Day, like some other holidays, has become commercialized. The designing and manufacturing of valentines is one of the most important parts of the greeting card business. (It is estimated that, in 1959 for example, at least 150 million such messages went through the United States mails.) Some artists give their entire time to planning these cards; and the charming verses are, of course, the work of real professionals.

And there's a certain city in Colorado, named Loveland, whose post office does a land office business around this special holiday. It all began in 1947 when some individuals sent their valentines to this town, where they were stamped with an appropriate crimson seal, and then remailed with the postmark, "Loveland," on them.

Even though today most of us don't care for the overly sentimental valentines of bygone days, we are glad that the spirit of good St. Valentine is still prevalent. For our simpler present-day greetings do convey the same good feelings that the older ones did. And no doubt the saint—whoever he was—is glad to know he started a custom that brings happiness to many persons.

~ Be Mine ~

Down through the years, valentine verses have seesawed from endearing to insulting and back again. These days the trend seems to be leaning toward beautifully illustrated cards accompanied by that unmistakable message "I love you." In The Romance of Greeting Cards, *Ernest Dudley Chase gathered this assortment of greetings that have been sent down through the years.*

Gee, but I like you, oh so much
I fain would hold your hand,
And win your promise to be mine,
But I haven't got the sand!

~ ~

I need not say I love you,
For well you know I do,
I cannot count the many times
I think and think of you
But every thought brings gladness
And Life holds brighter cheer,
And there's a song within my heart
Because I love you, Dear.

~ ~

Just for your own dear self alone
Is the message this brings to you
For the things I say this special day
Are just between us two.
I want you to know as the seasons go
That the ties of the past hold true,
And deep in my heart is a place apart
I have kept for you—just you!

~ ~

Here's a toast to your eyes
And a toast to your smile
I could say more—'cause I'm able
But if I toasted all your charming ways . . .
I'm afraid I'd be "under the table."

~ ~

Maybe you'll think I'm forward,
Maybe you'll think I'm bold,
But darn it all—I like you . . .
And it's high time you were told!

Some men have pep
And some men have looks
And some men wear clothes like fashion books,
And some have brains
And some have cheer
But you have everything, old dear!

But perhaps most outrageous of all was this humorous Valentine tradition contributed by Elizabeth H. Watkins.

It is my paternal grandfather, Harold A. Fletcher, a notorious tight-wad, who started a tradition in our family of not signing greeting cards. Every Valentine's Day I would receive a card without a signature. Of course, I knew who my secret admirer was, and that now I could use the card again! If Gramp really needed to sign a card for any reason, he would do it in pencil—stubbornly refusing to waste the card by using a pen.

~ First Valentine ~

GLADYS TABER

Remember the first valentine candy you received? I do. Carl Lowe walked miles out of his way to deliver that crimson-red heart-shaped cardboard box wrapped in red satin ribbon. No dozen or more long-stemmed American Beauty roses have ever been so welcomed or so appreciated.

Remember the valentines we made in school from doilies and red construction paper? They, too, meant everything to us at the time, but once we had delivered them, we quickly forgot about them. Imagine finding those outpourings of our childhood thoughts years later.

Gladys Taber did just that. She found a box containing all the valentine cards she had made and given to her mother. They brought back a flood of memories that we can all relate to.

Incidentally, in my heart of hearts . . . I'm still waiting for the violets.

Valentine the saint was a Christian martyr who died about 270 A.D. in Rome. I wonder whether he leans over "the gold bars of heaven" like Rossetti's "Blessed Damozel" and watches while on his day heavily ribboned boxes of candy and bouquets of roses in green waxen armor go merrily from one to another!

Perfume seems so appropriate to Valentine's Day as a token to "the object of one's affection" as the dictionary says with such reserve. Possibly perfume is more romantic than most things, for a whiff can transport us to the sandalwood groves or the land of far Araby.

Flowers certainly, for flowers breathe of young love. Roses especially. But when I was turning sixteen, my beau brought violets, a rare luxury. The cool dark purple was beautiful as a dream, the glossy pointed leaves framed the flowers, and the stems were wound with silver foil. The air on Olympus could not smell sweeter than those violets. I laid them on my pillow at night. It did not matter that in our little town by the time the violets had been carted in on the old sweating Northwestern train, they were half dead, nor that by the next day the leaves rusted, the flowers crimped with death. Those violets were immortal, for I can smell them yet.

I sprinkled them with cool water. I laid them in the icebox—too near the cake of river ice Mr. Lutz had just tonged in as it turned out —but never mind, I had my violets. The whole world was a blossoming garden to me!

Years later, after my little Mother died, I found a small box tied with pink ribbon in her big walnut dresser. In it were all the valentines I ever had made for her from the first wavering I love yu Mama to the erudite Sugar is sweet and so are You. From blue and pink crayon on oatmeal paper to a fancy deckle-edged pale blue paper with an original poem by the rising young writer aged fifteen.

So Mama was sentimental too! Who would have guessed it? As Papa and I emoted around like rockets, she was so quiet and serene and so sensible. And all the time she was saving those valentines!

This was a holiday for her to give parties, and oh the table frilly with rose-colored ribbons and shining with newly polished silver. Oh the little heart-shaped cakes, a bite apiece and cloud-pink with icing. The maple nut parfaits and the candied roseleaves. I remember these better than the main part of the dinner, naturally being young and dessert-minded. I can recall thin slices of rosy sugar-cured country ham, glazed with brown sugar and deep with clove. The vegetables I cannot remember at all. Sweet-potato soufflé was there. And thimble-sized light rolls.

This would be a faculty party when History and Latin and Geology and Mathematics would forget their differences and have a merry time. Followed by charades with a sedate Professor stamping around in an old bear rug being, naturally a BEAR.

The valentine tea would be more quiet, ladies only, and the clink of silver tongs on fair china cups as I passed and passed wee rolled and open sandwiches, eating several every time I turned around.

Followed a party for my gang. We just swarmed all over everything and ate like mastodons. Rolled up the Orientals and danced. Finished off with hot chocolate beaten with Mama's Mexican beater and with cinnamon spicing it, and dollops of heavy sweet whipped cream—plus the rest of the tiny heart cakes.

And finally, when Valentine's Day was really over, a whole half week of it, a moonlight walk with my beau along the snow-deep streets of the little town.

⇀ *The Tradition Continues* ↽

My favorite day is Valentine's Day. I don't know how it got started, but I like it. I like to make cards in art class and then give them to everyone in my class. We take construction paper and make hearts by folding the sheets in half and then cutting out a heart we stencil on. We also use paper lace and red ribbons to make our valentines prettier.

Last year I got a box of yummy chocolate from a secret admirer. I never found out who it was from, either. I like Valentine's Day!

Carmenita Scarfoni, elementary school

⇀ ↽

My favorite family tradition is our annual Valentine's Day party. We invite all the neighborhood children and their parents to come over to our house. When everyone arrives we exchange Valentine's cards. Later on we will eat a special red heart-shaped Valentine's cake. But the best of all is when the children go into the kitchen with my mom to make "Valentine's Day finger Jell-O." First we make red Jell-O with extra gelatin so it will be very firm. When it has congealed, we take heart-shaped Valentine's cookie cutters and cut out finger Jell-O. When we are through making the finger Jell-O, we place them on trays and serve the adults in the other rooms. They are very surprised at how good the Jell-O is, and we feel good that they like it.

Hilda Daniel, elementary school

THE FOURTEENTH OF FEBRUARY IS A DAY SACRED
TO SAINT VALENTINE! IT WAS A VERY ODD NOTION,
ALLUDED TO BY SHAKESPEARE, THAT ON THIS DAY
BIRDS BEGIN TO COUPLE; HENCE, PERHAPS, AROSE
THE CUSTOM OF SENDING ON THIS DAY LETTERS
CONTAINING PROFESSIONS OF LOVE AND AFFECTION.

Noah Webster

CHAPTER 5

Mardi Gras

WHEN EVERYONE RULES FOR A DAY

~ *Carnival Begins in January* ~

Don't let anyone in Mobile, Alabama, know that you think Mardi Gras began on these shores in New Orleans. The truth is, America's celebration of this most festive, colorful, and raucous of all the holidays began in Mobile on New Year's Eve in 1832 when a party of intoxicated young men created bedlam by parading along the streets, ringing in the new year with cowbells they had "borrowed" from the town's hardware store. They were dubbed the "Cowbellian de Rankin Society," and America's Mardi Gras was born.

Of course historians and folklorists tell us that Mardi Gras really had its origins in such pagan celebrations as Bacchanalia, Lupercalia, and Saturnalia—festivities that became Christianized and spread from Europe through the entire Western Hemisphere with the French and Spanish explorers. Along the way elements from Caribbean, African, African-American, Latin, Creole, and even English celebrations were added to the French and Spanish concept of Mardi Gras. Today, in Mobile, Alabama; New Orleans, Louisiana; Pensacola, Florida; and Galveston, Texas, Mardi Gras is a wonderful amalgamation of many cultures and ways.

But back to the Cowbellian de Rankin Society. Somewhere along the way —no one seems to know exactly when—instead of beginning the celebration of Mardi Gras on New Year's Eve—after all, there's already a reason to have a party on New Year's Eve—the party to send off Mardi Gras was pushed up to Twelfth Night, or January 6. In those early days, Christmas traditionally ran from Christmas Eve until January 6, also known as Old Christmas or Epiphany. What were the people going to do on the night of January 6 once the Christmas festivities were over? Surely there had to be some reason for a party. And so Mardi Gras began. In a nutshell, our ancestors in the Deep South finished one season of festivity and began another on January 6, Twelfth Night. That way they could keep frolicking from Christmas Eve all the way through Shrove Tuesday, also known as Fat Tuesday—the day before the fasting Lenten season preceding the Easter celebration began.

These days, that once Deep South celebration is spreading in popularity across the country. Of course churches of various denominations everywhere have long held traditional Shrove Tuesday pancake dinners in their church parlors. But the new Mardi Gras celebrations popping up in Boston and Reno and Des Moines are copied after the colorful and showy carnival events associated with the famed festivities in Mobile, New Orleans, and Rio de Janeiro.

These days few people can, or want to, party every night from January 6 until midnight Shrove Tuesday—though in New Orleans sometimes they try. So in the towns that attract tourists and visitors for their Mardi Gras celebrations the big thrust—the street parties, parades, and dances—falls during the four or five days just preceding Shrove Tuesday. By Thursday everything is in full swing and the weekend is completely given over to the festivities. Schools may even be closed on Monday and surely are on Tuesday. But with the stroke of midnight on Tuesday, and the breaking of dawn on Ash Wednesday, order is restored, life returns to normal, and the party's over for another year.

⚊ 150 Years of Masks, Throws, ⚊ and Parades

The adage "You had to have been there" is more applicable to Mardi Gras than to any other festive event that I can think of. The spirit and festivity and sheer number of events overwhelms you. Here, to give you a historical and *visual sense of what really transpires in New Orleans, the city synonymous with Mardi Gras, even if it wasn't the original home, are three descriptions that span the years.*

The first was written by Charles Lyell, an Englishman traveling in the States in the mid nineteenth century. He paints a vivid picture of the times, the celebration, and the city, all the while providing some insightful editorial comments.

A behind-the-scenes description written by Frances Parkinson Keyes in the late 1940s follows. A longtime resident of the city during her lifetime, Keyes takes us along on the daily activities of one of the Mardi Gras queens to explain what really happens and what it means to hold that honor.

Last is a 1990s look at a thoroughly modern celebration of this centuries-old tradition written by Bethany Bultman. The combination of these three great reads, plus Bultman's tour-guide description of where to go and what to do (a nun or nun-in-costume comes highly recommended) should send you packing to New Orleans—or, if you want the flavor but not the hassle of New Orleans, to Mobile—for next year's event.

The Old-Time Mardi Gras

CHARLES LYELL

February 23, 1846. The distance from Mobile to New Orleans is 175 miles by what is called the inland passage, or the channel between the islands and the mainland. . . . We sailed out of the beautiful bay of Mobile in the evening, in the coldest month of the year, yet the air was warm, and there was a haze like that of a summer's evening in England. Many gulls followed our ship, enticed by pieces of bread thrown out to them by the passengers, some of whom were displaying their skill in shooting the birds in mere wantonness. . . .

Next morning at daylight we found ourselves in Louisiana. We had already entered the large lagoon, called Lake Pontchartrain, by a narrow passage, and, having skirted its southern shore, had reached a point six miles north of New Orleans. Here we disembarked and entered the cars of a railway built on piles, which conveyed us in less than an hour to the great city, passing over swamps in which the tall cypress, hung with Spanish moss, was flourishing, and below it numerous shrubs just bursting into leaf. In many gardens of the suburbs, the almond and peach trees were in full blossom. In some places the blue-leaved palmetto and the leaves of a species of iris (*iris cuprea*) were very abundant. We saw a tavern called the Elysian Fields Coffee House, and some others with French inscriptions. There were also many houses with porte-cochères, high roofs, and volets, and many

lamps suspended from ropes attached to tall posts on each side of the road, as in the French capital. We might indeed have fancied that we were approaching Paris, but for the Negroes and mulattoes, and the large verandahs reminding us that the windows required protection from the sun's heat.

It was a pleasure to hear the French language spoken and to have our thoughts recalled to the most civilized parts of Europe by the aspect of a city, forming so great a contrast to the innumerable new towns we had lately beheld. The foreign appearance, moreover, of the inhabitants made me feel thankful that it was possible to roam freely and without hindrance over so large a continent—no bureaus for examining and signing of passports, no fortifications, no drawbridges, no closing of gates at a fixed hour in the evening, no waiting till they are opened in the morning, no custom houses separating one state from another, no overhauling of baggage by *gens d'armes* for the octroi; and yet as perfect a feeling of personal security as I ever felt in Germany or France.

The largest of the hotels, the St. Charles, being full, we obtained agreeable apartments at the St. Louis, in a part of the town where we heard French constantly spoken. Our rooms were fitted up in the French style, with muslin curtains and scarlet draperies. There was a finely proportioned drawing room, furnished *à la Louis Quatorze,* opening into a large dining room with sliding doors, where the boarders and the "transient visitors," as they are called in the United States, met at meals. The mistress of the hotel, a widow, presided at dinner, and we talked French with her and some of the attendants; but most of the servants of the house were Irish or German. There was a beautiful ballroom, in which preparations were making for a grand masked ball to be given the night after our arrival.

It was the last day of the Carnival. From the time we landed in New England to this hour, we seemed to have been in a country where all, whether rich or poor, were labouring from morning till night, without ever indulging in a holiday. I had sometimes thought that the national motto should be, "All work and no play." It was quite a novelty and a refreshing sight to see a whole population giving up their minds for a short season to amusement. There was a grand procession parading the streets, almost every one dressed in the most grotesque attire, troops of them on horseback, some in open carriages, with bands of music, and in a variety of costumes—some as Indians, with feathers in their heads, and one, a jolly fat man, as Mardi Gras himself.

All wore masks, and here and there in the crowd, or stationed in a balcony above, we saw persons armed with bags of flour, which they showered down copiously on any one who seemed particularly proud of his attire. The strangeness of the scene was not a little heightened by the blending of Negroes, quadroons, and mulattoes in the crowd; and we were amused by observing the ludicrous surprise, mixed with contempt, of several unmasked, stiff, grave Anglo-Americans from the north, who were witnessing for the first time what seemed to them so much mummery and tomfoolery. One wagoner, coming out of a cross-street, in his working-dress, drove his team of horses and vehicle heavily laden with cotton bales right through the procession, causing a long interruption.

The crowd seemed determined to allow nothing to disturb their good humour; but although many of the wealthy Protestant citizens take part in the ceremony, this rude intrusion struck me as a kind of foreshadowing of coming events, emblematic of the violent shock which the invasion of the Anglo-Americans is about to give to the old *regime* of Louisiana. A gentleman told me that, being last year in Rome, he had not seen so many masks at the Carnival there; and, in spite of the increase of Protestants, he thought there had been quite as much "flour and fun" this year as usual. The proportion, however, of strict Romanists is not so great as formerly, and tomorrow, they say, when Lent begins, there will be an end of the trade in masks; yet the butchers will sell nearly as much meat as ever. During the Carnival, the greater part of the French population keep open house, especially in the country. . . .

A few days after the carnival we had another opportunity of seeing a grand procession of the natives, without masks. The corps of all the different companies of firemen turned out in their uniform, drawing their engines dressed up with flowers, ribbons, and flags, and I never saw a finer set of young men. We could not help contrasting their healthy looks with the pale, sickly countenances of "the crackers," in the pine-woods of Georgia and Alabama, where we had been spending so many weeks. These men were almost all of them Creoles, and thoroughly acclimatized; and I soon found that if I wished to ingratiate myself with natives or permanent settlers in this city, the less surprise I expressed at the robust aspect of these young Creoles the better. The late Mr. Sydney Smith advised an English friend who was going to reside some years in Edinburgh to praise the climate: "When you arrive there it may rain, snow, or blow for many days, and they will assure you they never knew such a season before. If you would be popular, declare you think it the most delightful climate in the world."

Carnival Begins on Twelfth Night

FRANCES PARKINSON KEYES

Because World War II suspended the Mardi Gras—or Carnival, as it is called—celebrations, Queen Beverly, whom Frances Parkinson Keyes follows here, does not "feel the magic" of the late 1940s event she has been invited to reign over until she sees the royal regalia—the crowns, jewelry, and scepters —in the window of a department store. That's where we pick up the story.

Much as a prospective bride steals out of bed for another look at her wedding presents, Beverly gazed at the glittering ornaments destined for the Queen of Hermes. And at last came the great moment when they were hers to wear.

According to a time-honored custom, the Queen and her entire Court dressed at the home of the Krewe's President; lest this robing process should prove too much of a strain, they were offered refreshments in the form of sandwiches and champagne. Their pictures were taken together and they were escorted to the limousines which were waiting to convey them to City Hall. Then Beverly was suddenly confronted with another difficulty. The plumes which gave the finishing touch to her gorgeous headdress were thirteen inches high; she could not take her appointed place in the limousine without bending over almost double; and, if she did this, she could not lean out of the window, to bow and smile and wave to the populace which had long been foregathered to watch the triumphal progress. There was only one thing to do and it was promptly done: the rear seat of the limousine was detached from its normal place and put on the floor. Beverly sat down on it . . . as best she could. The motorcade started off with its special police escort. And the Queen, her white plumes waving from the most effective angle, graciously greeted the onlookers along the way.

At City Hall the Mayor and various other dignitaries, together with the previous year's Court of Hermes, were waiting to greet the new Court in the Mayor's parlor—an imposing apartment, elegantly furnished, lined with immense portraits and lighted with crystal chandeliers. A formal address of welcome from His Honor was accompanied by more champagne; then the sound of music heralded the approach of the parade and the arrival of the King, who would toast the Queen from his float. The dignitaries and the Courts hastened outside to take their appointed places on the reviewing stand, which, fortunately, presented no problems for a high headdress.

Down the street they came—the bands, the torch bearers, the floats, the maskers with their bags from which they tossed all sorts of glittering baubles to the waiting throngs. For the next hour, the procession wound down the street, filling it with tuneful hilarity and transforming it to a scene of splendor. Then, after the last salute had been given and the last float had passed from view, the Queen and her Maids were once more escorted to their limousines and, again with special police escort, went tearing off to the Court entrance of the Auditorium, where the striped awning overhead and the strip of spotless canvas across the sidewalk alike proclaimed that everything was in readiness for their reception.

According to usual procedure, the Grand March around the Auditorium marks the first triumphal appearance of the Queen there. At this particular ball, there was a slight variation from custom. The tableau represented a reception given by Louis XIV and his Queen to emissaries from all the countries represented in France during the glorious days of the *grand monarque.* Therefore, when the curtain went up, the King and Queen of Hermes were already on their thrones, the "emissaries" were approaching by the palace gates, and the Court of the previous year was ensconced on a balcony. The Grand March—and grand indeed it was—formed the climax and not the prelude to the ceremony.

This Carnival Season ended even more thrillingly than it had begun for Beverly: as current Queen of Hermes, she was entitled, like the Queens of the other major balls, to watch the great Mardi Gras parade. . . .

AND ENDS ON MARDI GRAS

. . . from the front of the Boston Club balcony, where it is reviewed by the Queen of Carnival; and, as a member of the Rex Court, she took an active part in the meeting of Rex and his Queen and Comus and his Queen, in their respective suites, in the presence of their joint Krewes and their chosen guests. This is the supreme moment toward which all celebrations have been converging, ever since the Twelfth Night cake was cut to disclose the golden bean for the Revelers' Queen and the silver beans for her Maids. The girls who, like Beverly (and some ancient Roman whose name I forget) can say, "All of this I saw, part of this I was," never need to say anything else, as far as New Orleans is concerned. However, it is exhilarating to hear a Carnival Queen's impressions from her own lips. And this is how Elizabeth Nicholson, who reigned at Mardi Gras in 1948, described them to Marjorie Roehl of the *New Orleans Item,* which brings out a series of special Carnival issues:

It's people cheering you and telling you they like you. It's like when you're small and wake up every few hours on Christmas Eve, wondering if it's morning yet. It's a tremendous thrill, gay and exciting and fun, but it's a little tense too. It's carrying fifty pounds of mantle and crown and sceptre and meeting the Comus Court with every one singing, "If Ever I Cease to Love." It's—well—it's really wonderful.

I got up at seven A.M. because I had to be breakfasted and ready by nine A.M. All of us had received innumerable cautions, both oral and in writing, BE PROMPT!

The Queen and her Maids appeared on the Boston Club balcony about eleven and stayed there, waving and smiling, until the parade was over. We wanted to stay and watch all the trucks, Miss Nicholson remembered. But as everything had to move on schedule, we went inside and had lunch about two P.M. Then at four I had to rush home and dress for the ball.

To carry your train more easily . . . you're harnessed into a canvas contraption under your dress. Your shoulders, ribs, waist and even your knees are strapped to your tram. That is supposed to make your balance easier. I was wearing high heels to make me a little taller and the more I thought of the possibility [of having my heels buckle under all this weight] the worse it seemed. So I had the shoes reinforced with metal. And that was heavy too. But at the time you don't notice the discomfort. Everything is too wonderful, too exciting. And then there's that tremendous climax of the meeting of Rex and Comus. And afterwards you go home, so sorry it's all over. It's only when you take the crown off you realize it was heavy.

Locally, the Comus Ball, which takes place on Mardi Gras at the same time as the Rex Ball, is generally considered the most select, though several others are quite as beautiful and many outsiders need to be reminded that all are private functions. The girl who reigns as Queen of Comus, like the girl who reigns as Queen of Rex, is always chosen from the most exclusive social circles and shares many of the latter's honors. In the Grand March, which brings the Balls to an end, Comus and Rex exchange partners; and, at the Queen's Supper which follows the Balls, the King of Carnival proudly takes his place between the two Queens. But when the feast is over and one last toast has been drunk in the inexhaustible champagne, the strains of the Carnival song, "If Ever I Cease to Love," die away in the distance and the gorgeous purple and green and gold flags come down from all the houses where former Queens live. And finally the lights go out.

Parades and Throws

BETHANY EWALD BULTMAN

There is no question that Mardi Gras is about parades. About 60 Carnival parades fill the schedule between January 6 and Ash Wednesday, particularly during the two and a half weeks before Mardi Gras. But the four-day Carnival weekend is when parading reaches its crescendo. The pages of the *Times-Picayune* should be able to supply you with the three parade routes and the list of who parades on each. Among those held during the four-day weekend are two super-parades. The first is the Endymion parade on Saturday, which bills itself as the largest non-military parade in the world. Endymion first paraded in 1967 and continues to make good its motto, "Throw 'til it hurts!" The second is the Bacchus parade on Sunday. Taken together, these krewes have a combined membership of 2,300 men, and each year toss to bystanders more than 1.5 million cups, 2.5 million doubloons, and 200,000 gross of beads.

The crowds who attend these celebrity-studded parades tend to be denser, louder, and more aggressive than at other parades. Because these events fall on the weekend, people drive in from a 300-mile (483-km) radius just for a chance to see the likes of Henry Winkler or Danny Kaye dressed up in crown and blond wig, and to have their tax attorney or former professor throw them handfuls of 12-inch (30-cm) pearl strands.

Carnival Day (Tuesday) is more for families. Eager parade-goers wake up before dawn and stake out a spot along a parade route. By 7:00 A.M., St. Charles Avenue is blanketed with parade-watching equipment and essentials: special ladders, folding deck chairs, ice chests, generators, crockpots filled with red beans, barbecue pits, and buckets of Popeye's fried chicken; and video cameras and hand-held TVs. Out in Metairie, across the river, and in St. Bernard Parish, the scene is repeated for the suburban parades. By nine o'clock the streets are filled with paraders, dressed in costume and strutting their stuff. The parades begin snaking through the streets in earnest by 11:00 A.M. A lot of the local high school bands also march in parades. The good ones will march in many parades, and the money they earn goes a long way to support their schools.

Anything goes on Mardi Gras Day. *Everyone* dons flamboyant costumes or bizarre make-up. Locals and out-of-towners stroll the streets dressed as packs of Energizer Rabbits, condoms, tap-dancing bottles of Chanel, the Rolling Stones, Nubian royalty, Oscar Wilde, the Romantic Poets, French Revolutionaries leading Marie Antoinette to the guillotine, and troupes of topless clowns. Some people dress as nuns; some nuns dress as bag ladies. Transvestitism reaches the pinnacle of the art form, as the French Quarter hosts one of the most elaborate gay beauty-and-costume contests in the world. Usually, the costumes worn in the Quarter are a great deal more lascivious than those worn by the families in Metairie and along St. Charles Avenue.

Each year New Orleans festers with rumors concerning the goings-on at Carnival season. As the old-line krewes pride themselves on secrecy, getting the scoop on who is doing what becomes part of the fun. Good sources for the skinny on what's happenin' are limousine drivers who have been booked to tote the royalty around; the lunch crowd at Galatoire's on Friday; the noon street-corner crowd around Common and Carondelet; alteration staff at Town & Country on St. Charles Avenue; awning installers; and the maids who work on Palmer Avenue and shop at Langenstein's on Arabella Street. Perennial rumors include: one (or all) of the krewes are bankrupt; Schwegmann's Giant Supermarket has sold out of ice picks; a rider in Iris threw her three-carat diamond to the crowd by mistake; or the real queen of Comus got pregnant and the new one is a last-minute replacement.

To get some meatier info, try visiting the Mardi Gras Museum—a 10,000 square-foot exhibition of Carnival films, memorabilia, traditions, costumes, sounds, and photographs that can be viewed year-round in the Rivertown section of South Kenner. Other collections of Carnival memorabilia include those of the Louisiana State Museum, and of the Germaine Wells Mardi Gras Museum, 813 Bienville Street on the second floor of Arnaud's Restaurant.

The biggest gossip in recent times has occurred in connection with the new nondiscrimination rules implemented by the city and aimed at the krewes. It all started in December of 1991, when Councilwoman Dorothy Mae Taylor co-authored an ordinance, MCS 14984, prohibiting race and sex discrimination by krewes. Those groups who had exclusive admissions policies were denied access to city services and parade permits. Of the 60 or so parading krewes, only three old-line krewes whose traditions stem from nineteenth-century elitist sensibilities viewed this as "cultural terrorism" and refused to comply: they were Mystick Krewe of *Comus,* the Knights of Momus, and the Krewe of Proteus. Also as a result of the ordinance, other krewes are changing their routes and schedules. It's best to consult the *Times-Picayune* for the most up-to-date parade information.

Krewe members aren't the only participants in the parades; marching or walking clubs feature prominently as well. The Jefferson City Buzzards is considered the oldest of marching clubs, as it was begun in 1890. They get going about 6:45 A.M. on Mardi Gras morning in the vicinity of Audubon Park and leisurely stroll toward the downtown madness. The Corner Club begins its day before 7:30 A.M. at the corner of Second and Annunciation streets. Pete Fountain's Half Fast Walking Club kicks off from Washington and Prytania streets about the same time.

Truck parades also feature prominently on Mardi Gras Day, when five of them follow the parade of Rex downtown (they follow Argus in another neighborhood). These are comprised of over 350 decorated flatbeds with nearly 15,000 costumed maskers. The trucks are decorated by families and friends who meet on the weekends and do all the decorating and costume-making themselves. In preparation for the parades the riders must get up before dawn, drive to the starting point of the parade, and wait for up to four hours to roll.

Throughout the parade, masked riders stand atop two- and three-tiered papier-mâché tractor-towed constructions from which they throw plastic cups, panties, and beads, as well as metal doubloons inscribed with the logo of the krewe, to the eager crowd. The riders often spend over $1,000 on their individual stock of "throws" to give out during the parade.

In the early days of the festivities, merry-makers used to carry bags of flour that they would throw at each other. When a mischievous few mixed pepper with their flour, the practice had to be discontinued and safer things thrown. These days, the typical throws are beads, "doubloons" (fake coins), and, in recent years, Zapp potato chips, which come packaged in Carnival colors. Probably the most valued throws are the hand-painted coconuts tossed by the krewe of Zulu. Onlookers vie energetically—sometimes boldly—to catch the most "stuff." In recent years, it's become more commonplace for women to expose their breasts than to shout the conventional phrase, "Throw me sumtin' Mista!" in return for a long strand of faux pearls. *Be warned—*

many an ordinarily gentle, little old sterling-headed grandmother will stomp your knuckles bloody for that aluminum doubloon, and that adorable tyke has no qualms about jerking your knees out from under you for a bamboo-and-rubber spear. Most importantly, never ever put your hand on the ground to pick up anything! If you want those beads or that doubloon, put your foot on it and don't lift your toe until you have it firmly in your hands.

Other tips for catching favors include taking a nun in habit with you, and standing under a street lamp: she'll be a favorite target for the good Catholics on the floats. Or make a posterboard sign that says "John" and hold it up at each float, figuring that there must be at least one guy named John on every float. Or cut a large bleach bottle in half and attach the spout to a broom handle so that you have a handy tool to hold up to the riders. Another version of this is to turn an umbrella inside out and hold it up to the floats. Some parade-goers with kids use a special 8- to 10-foot (2-m to 3-m) ladder fixed with a bench at the top for the little ones, while parents stand below balancing them. These pre-made parade ladders can be bought at many local hardware stores and cost about $60. Ladders should not be hooked together, placed at intersections or against barricades, or left unattended—or the police will confiscate them.

Those who live within walking distance from the parade routes sometimes joke that "Mardi Gras" must be an old Creole expression meaning, "May I use your bathroom?" Nowadays the city puts out a lot of Port-O-Lets, and restaurants and bars will let their patrons avail themselves of the facilities. Those groups who have large packs of newly toilet-trained kids or big drinkers in their party might consider renting a hotel room on the route.

The estimated size of the Mardi Gras crowd is based on the amount of trash generated. A good crowd is one that has produced 2,000 or more tons of refuse. Each parade is followed by the Sanitation Department with its street sweepers, water-and-brush trucks, and blowers. Watching them is almost as much fun as watching the parade.

⌐ The Tradition Continues ⌐

In these pages I admit that my favorite day-in, day-out tradition is starting out the week by calling my kids on Sunday. New Year's Day is my favorite holiday tradition. If I could pass on only one tradition to my children it would be a love for nature. But if I could wave a magic wand and spread one tradition across the entire country it would be hanging a Mardi Gras wreath on every door to bring color and smiles to those most dreary wintry months of January and February.

All that is needed is a wreath frame—be it a grapevine, wire, or Styrofoam type—green, gold, and purple ribbons, and whatever other Mardi Gras decorations you like—a sequined crown, fanciful plumes, the traditional masks, beads, or a costumed Mardi Gras doll. With the growing popularity of Mardi Gras, these accessories are sold in party and craft shops everywhere, and of course in New Orleans year-round. Let your imagination be your guide. After the first year you'll think your doorway looks bare without one. It's a wonderful way to slip out of the Christmas season into springtime.

> IF EVER I CEASE TO LOVE,
> IF EVER I CEASE TO LOVE,
> MAY THE FISH GET LEGS AND THE COWS LAY EGGS—
> IF EVER I CEASE TO LOVE!
>
> *Mardi Gras theme song*

CHAPTER 6

St. Patrick's Day

WE'RE ALL A WEE BIT IRISH

~ *"St. Patrick Was a Gentleman"* ~

HENRY BENNETT

Oh! St. Patrick was a gentleman,
Who came of decent people;
He built a church in Dublintown,
And on it put a steeple.
His father was a Gallagher;
His mother was a Brady;
His aunt was an O'Shaughnessy,
His uncle an O'Grady.
So, success attend St. Patrick's fist,
For he's a saint so clever;
O! he gave the snakes and toads a twist,
And bothered them forever!

The Wicklow hills are very high,
    And so's the Hill of Howth, sir;
But there's a hill much bigger still,
    Much higher nor them both, sir.
Twas on the top of this high hill
    St. Patrick preached his sarmint
That drove the frogs into the bogs,
    And banished all the varmint.
So, success attend St. Patrick's fist,
    For he's a saint so clever;
O! he gave the snakes and toads a twist,
    And bothered them forever!

➤ A Not-So-Irish Lass ➤

Picture this 1990s scene.

I agreed to help a friend, a good ole boy type, out by speaking to his professional group's March meeting to be held at one of the larger hotel chains —a Marriott, Hyatt, or Sheraton. My fiftyish friend—let's call him Jim— was dating an acquaintance of mine, a stunning, extraordinarily stylish, dark-haired forty-something woman. We'll call her Eileen.

"We'll have to have supper with the group," Jim told me. "But Eileen can join us around nine and we'll have a Saint Patrick's Day drink." I agreed.

The night of the talk, once the meeting adjourned Jim and I wandered out to the lounge where Eileen was waiting. "Excuse me for a moment," Jim said. Eileen and I jumped at the occasion for a little "girl talk."

Jim quickly reappeared with a previously ordered bouquet of green and white carnations. "Happy Saint Patrick's Day!" He beamed, thrusting the sterotypical arrangement toward Eileen.

I'll admit I was a little disappointed, I'm the redheaded Irish lass after all, but I tried not to show it. There was no mistaking Eileen's sentiments.

She looked at Jim in shocked amazement. "Don't you know I'm Jewish?" she grimaced.

"On March seventeenth we're all a little bit Irish," he grinned sheepishly.

Saint Patrick's Day Parades

CHARLES J. O'FAHEY

From The Folklore of American Holidays *comes this piece originally published in* Ethnicity II *(1975). Charles J. O'Fahey calls up his personal memories of Saint Patrick's Day to capture the traditions that surround this clearly ethnic day that almost everyone will claim kinship to, if not kinmanship with, just one day out of the year.*

Although the St. Patrick's Day parade may be the largest ethnic spectacle in the United States, many Irish-Americans feel ambivalent about it. On the one hand, the green lines painted on the parkways and the green paper hats appear vulgar and trite in contrast to the joyous array of symbols in the Italian *festa* or the Spanish-speaking community's fiesta. What Irish-American does not feel anger at the sight of a donkey cart bearing "The World's Worst Irish Tenor" or a pudgy young woman in a green T-shirt inscribed "Erin Go Bra-less"? How many of us are not weary of hearing the strident sounds of "Sweet Rosie O'Grady" and "When Irish Eyes Are Smiling" lunge out at us from the crowded bars along the parade route? Every year on March 17 I want to swear off clay pipes and blackthorns.

But then I see in my mind's eye my grandfather in top hat and morning suit, adorned with a sash across his chest proclaiming that the County Galway was his ancestral home. He always marched with a unit of the Ancient Order of Hibernians—like so many other AOH stalwarts who graced the parades in New York and Chicago and San Francisco 30 years ago. In Boston there are still memories of Mayor James Curley riding in the parade in a fur coat, piously shaking hands with priests and nuns along the way; of Grand Marshall Knocko McCormack (brother of former House Speaker John McCormack) heaving his 300 pounds onto a dray horse that hauled the ashcart for the City of Boston; of Up-Up Kelly, a Curley lieutenant, punctuating the mayor's St. Patrick's Day speech by jumping up every minute to applaud Curley's excoriation of the British and urging the audience to do likewise; of thirsty marchers thronging into P. J. Connelly's Bar for a "one and one"—a half-glass of blended whiskey and a dime glass of draft beer for a chaser. In those days the St. Patrick's Day parade had style and verve, and gave you a sense that the Irish had come from the docks and the railroad construction gangs to win a measure of acceptance in America.

In the nineteenth century, the Irish in America had no ambivalence about their enthusiasm for St. Patrick's Day parades. By the late 1840's the annual turnout in New York had dramatically increased with the coming of the Great Famine emigrants. In 1846 the *New York Herald* reported that during the St. Patrick's Day Mass at St. Columba's Church on 25th Street, the Reverend Joseph Burke preached on the life of the saint in the Irish language. The reporter commented: "The oration was all Greek to us; but to judge from the breathless silence which prevailed during its delivery, we saw that the audience was delighted with it." The New York press described the burgeoning parades of the 1850's and 1860's with increased detail. By 1870 the line of march looked like this: a platoon of policemen; the Sixty-Ninth Regiment; the Legion of St. Patrick; Men of Tipperary; 21 divisions of the Ancient Order of Hibernians; numerous parish benevolent societies and total abstinence units (e.g., "Father Mathew T.A.B. Society No. 2 of New York, 400 men" and "St. Bridget's R.C.T.A.B. Society, 1300 members"). Thirty-thousand men walked in the procession of 1870.

The parades of that day sometimes drew complaints from certain quarters. The *Irish Citizen* protested in 1868 that because so many German bands were hired, there weren't enough Irish airs in the parade: "We are aware that there are but a few Irish bands in the city, but if those who hire the German bands insisted on having Irish music . . . their demands would be attended to. We feel confident that nearly every man in the procession would prefer marching to one of the spirit-stirring airs with which they are familiar in the old land—if only played by a fife and drum—than to have their ears dinned with the *chef d'oeuvres* of some foreign composer, which could never awaken a responsive throb in their hearts, or impart a spring to their step."

But generally the Irish-American press praised the manly bearing of the marchers and the enthusiasm of the spectators or pointed out parade highlights. In 1863 the *Metropolitan Record* told of a group of boys, 10 to 16 years old, who in green jackets and black pantaloons carried two banners. One was inscribed "The Temperance Cadets of the Visitation of the Blessed Virgin" and the other read: "All's Right: Dad's Sober." In 1871 the *Irish Citizen* described "a triumphal car" drawn by 10 white horses "covered completely with green drapery, fringed with gold and ornamented with mottoes in gold." Surmounting this car was a huge bust of Daniel O'Connell and seated in front of the bust a certain Mr. McClean, "harp in hand, to represent the Irish minstrel."

McClean was described as a man "who stands six feet four in his stockings and is splendidly proportioned. Flowing white locks fell over his shoulders and on his head was a wreath of oak leaves, with acorns of gold. A long white plaited beard fell down on his breast. He wore a jacket and skirting, with a heavy cloak and drapery of saffron, trimmed with gold and green. About his waist was a red belt with a gold buckle. His tights were of saffron and his sandals scarlet. With golden bracelets, a large Tara brooch, set with jewels, and a small harp, which rested on his knee—his attire was complete."

To the rear of the bust rested in *papier-mache* an ancient Irish wolfhound "as large as a colt," bearing the legend "Gentle When Stroked; Fierce When Provoked." The car was preceded by a six foot seven inch "Irish Chieftain," with "his long-haired, herculean retainers and trumpeters." Obviously the Irish of that time in America revered symbols with origins in a distinctive, ancient culture.

⌁ A Wee Bit of Ireland in ⌁ Every American Town

MAYMIE R. KRYTHE

The larger Irish celebrations in Boston, New York, and even Savannah and Cleveland are well known and documented. Still, stop in any crossroads in America on March 17 and if you're not wearing green you'll get a disapproving look, or maybe even a pinch—the traditional "punishment" for not showing your loyalty to your Irish brothers on their day of days. As we learn next, so many Irishmen have moved to other lands through the years that it's only natural every town should be familiar with Irish ways. After all, Irish traditions are easy to adopt as your own. They are filled with goodwill, great cheer, and wishes of good luck for all.

Since Irishmen are adventurous souls, many of them emigrated and settled in various parts of the world; therefore, St. Patrick's Day has been observed round the globe.

It is said that the first celebration of this holiday in the United States took place in Boston. (General Washington had many Irishmen in his army.) The idea spread to other cities, including New York, and was sponsored by such groups as the Charitable Irish Society (founded in 1737), the Friendly Sons of St. Patrick (Philadelphia 1780), and the Ancient Order of Hibernians. The New York branch of the Friendly Sons of St. Patrick (founded 1784) was made up of both Roman Catholics and Presbyterians. The first president of this group was a Presbyterian.

There's a tradition that in 1762 a group of Irish celebrants met in a tavern near New York to celebrate St. Patrick's Day. They drank twenty toasts including this one: "May the enemies of Ireland never eat the bread or drink the whisky of it, but be tormented with itching, without benefit of scratching!"

By 1870 many Irish emigrants had settled in Los Angeles and had organized the St. Patrick's Benevolent Society. On his feast day, after attending Mass, the loyal sons of Ireland would seize their flags and join a parade in the saint's honor, with a band playing lively Irish tunes. In 1870, 150 members were served "a magnificent dinner" at the United States hotel. Father O'Leary was the orator of the day; humorous stories were told and many toasts were drunk.

As the band played "The Wearin' of the Green," this same organization paraded again the next year. Pupils of the school, directed by the Sisters of Charity, sang "The Hymn to St. Patrick." At the final celebration—a banquet—that evening, the speaker, John King, extolled Ireland; all joined in such songs as "Through Erin's Isle" and "The Twig of Shannon." When this organization celebrated in 1875, the chief speaker was Stephen M. White who later, as a United States Senator, fought for a free harbor for Los Angeles.

Irish celebrations are still popular on the Pacific coast. They are sponsored by such groups as the Ancient Order of Hibernians, Irish-American clubs, Friendly Sons of St. Patrick, and the Ulster Irish Associations of Southern California.

The festivities may consist of luncheons with top church officials as speakers or banquets where awards are sometimes given to outstanding artists of Irish extraction in the entertainment field. In the past these have included Dennis Day, Ann Blyth, George Murphy, and Maureen O'Hara.

All over the United States the day is one of rejoicing and merrymaking. Houses and halls are gaily decorated with flags, dolls, clay pipes, harps, and of course shamrocks. The sons of St. Patrick are a warmhearted lot, and all are welcome on the saint's day. Guests are expected to share the Irish stew and other refreshments, and to lend their voices to the singing of "The Wearin' of the Green," "Where the River Shannon Flows," "My Wild Irish Rose," and "When Irish Eyes Are Shinin'."

New York has long been known for its elaborate parade on St. Patrick's Day. It is said to have more Irishmen among its inhabitants than Ireland itself. In accord with the proverbial luck of the Irish, the weather usually is pleasant, bright, and clear. In 1959, a visitor, Henry O'Mara, head of Ireland's National Police, declared, "I never saw a parade like this in my life."

Today St. Patrick's Cathedral on Fifth Avenue, in New York, is the central point of the observance. For many blocks, this famous street is packed; usually more than a million persons turn out each year to see a Hundred Thousand Irish—or semi-Irish—parade along the avenue. There are many bands, with pipers, regiments of soldiers, mounted police, social, civic, and other Irish organizations. The paraders move jauntily along to the tune of such marching songs as "Garry Owen."

Some dance jigs, and all of course wear something green. Bands play old favorites including "Come Haste t' th' Wedding," "Sprig o'Shillelagh," "Top o'Cork Road," or "Munster Buttermilk."

Cleveland, Ohio, has many Irish citizens, and they too stage parades on this popular holiday. In 1952, the city had a big, special celebration when the Ancient Order of Hibernians put on its eighty-fifth annual banquet.

Even down South, March 17 is a "great day for the Irish." Many such emigrants settled in that part of the United States during the potato famines in Ireland. In Savannah, Georgia, not long ago there was a parade with music by eighteen bands and a dinner given by the Hibernians. In the city of Atlanta, shamrock dust was recently spread along the famous Peachtree Street, and the fire chief in top hat and full dress led the parade. Whenever the Irish get together on St. Patrick's Day, you hear such expressions as *Erin go bragh* ("Ireland Forever") and *Beannact Dia leat* ("God bless you").

The shamrock, Ireland's chief emblem, has a town named for it in Florida. Each year many persons send letters there to be stamped with the "Shamrock" postmark. And annually, tons of shamrock plants, with "a bit of the auld soil clinging to them," are flown across the Atlantic for March 17.

County Cork is the center of this shamrock trade, and it sends millions of these plants all over the world. The small town of Rosscarberry, with only three hundred inhabitants, is engaged in this industry, which is presided over by Mrs. Catherine O'Keefe ("Mrs. Shamrock," herself). All the villagers, young and old, spend weeks gathering the plants in meadows or on rock-strewn acres. Also, most of the people grow shamrocks in their own homes and gardens. So it's not surprising that this "little sprig has saved a dying village."

The "wearin' of the green" has long been featured in our country on St. Patrick's Day. Even business houses in various parts of the United States have taken up the idea. One dry cleaner in Massachusetts offered to clean free any green garment; and "Glory be 'tis a miracle" started an ad of the Muller Brothers, in Hollywood, California, that they would wash all green cars without charge on St. Patrick's Day.

In 1959 our national capital had a long-remembered celebration on this holiday, for smiling seventy-six-year-old President Sean O'Kelly of Eire was a guest there on March 17. He laid a wreath at the Tomb of the Unknown Soldier, addressed a joint session of Congress, had dinner with the Eisenhowers, and attended other functions.

During his visit Americans got a big surprise in regard to the association of the color green with the Irish. From the time the visitor arrived, he literally saw green everywhere. There was a long green carpet at the airport; President Eisenhower wore a green tie, and other officials, green socks. At the Congressional session, each member sported a green carnation.

Finally, at dinner that evening it was too much for the Irish President; he informed the guests that he and his countrymen do NOT like the color green. It is connected in their minds with too many unpleasant memories of the times when Ireland was not free. Now the old green flag is no longer the national ensign; also, the flag of the Irish President is blue with a white harp.

Since many Irishmen are outstanding citizens, not only here in the United States but all around the world, it is quite fitting for them to celebrate on March 17. And Robert Briscoe, the former Lord Mayor of Dublin, once said, "St. Patrick's Day for the Irish is one of the greatest milestones in its history. St. Patrick . . . brought to Ireland the great faith that Ireland still preserves and adheres to with such affection."

➳ The Tradition Continues ➳

On Saint Patrick's Day, which is a holiday celebrated on March 17 every year, my grandma Lane sets a big nice table all in green and white. She has Irish hats, napkins, Waterford glasses, and candles.

The whole family, which is about twenty aunts, uncles, and cousins, gets together to celebrate Saint Patrick's Day. For dinner we eat corned beef, cabbage, potatoes, carrots, and Irish bread.

Grandma plays Irish music and everyone sings. All the kids play games and have fun while the grandmas wash the dishes.

We can't wait for the cake made like a shamrock with green icing!

Saint Patrick was called the apostle of Ireland. It is said that Saint Patrick drove all the snakes out of Ireland.

Erin Mary Mettin, elementary school

Today is Saint Patrick's Day. My mother came up with a silly tradition that is unbelievable. Every Saint Patrick's Day, early in the morning, my sister and I have to take a "leprechaun bath." A leprechaun bath is when you take a bath in a tub filled with green water.

After our baths, we sit down to an Irish breakfast. My mom makes special four-leaf clover toast. We also have green punch and green grits. We have been doing this every year since my older sister was very small.

Raymond McCall, middle school

CHAPTER 7

The Spring Celebrations

Passover

OUT OF EGYPT

~ *A Watchful God* ~

The standard definition of Passover—the commemoration of the escape of the Jews from bondage in Egypt—misses the spirit and festivity of this happiest of Jewish holidays.

Historically, the name Passover (or Pesach) refers to God's sending an angel to slay the firstborn son in each Egyptian house while passing over the Jewish homes. The stunned Egyptians allowed the Jews, who had been held in bondage for 430 years, to escape. Thus the Israelite nation was born, making Passover both a religious and a secular celebration.

Theologically, the celebration of Passover reminds the Jews of God's powerful presence in history and that God, not any king or master, rules the earth and His people and that He watches over the oppressed. Each year Passover is celebrated with food and drink and joyfulness in the home and at the syna-gogue, coinciding with the Christian holiday of Easter.

To Prepare for Passover
ABRAHAM CAHAN

In 1899, Abraham Cahan, a reporter for the Commercial Advertiser, *vividly described the days before Passover on the Lower East Side of New York City.*

The Ghetto is in a flutter. This is *Erev Pesach* ("Eve of Passover"), the busiest season in the Jewish year. The great festival, which will begin on Saturday, March 25, is to last eight days. All cooking utensils must be changed; *matzo* (unleavened bread) must take the place of the ordinary loaves; the house and every member of the family must be adorned for the celebration of Israel's Independence Day.

Not a crumb of leavened bread is to be allowed in the house, and every vessel and every bit of food that comes in contact with them are *khometz* ("proscribed"). On the eve of the first day of Passover, there-fore, the head of the family, armed with a ladle, a feather brush, and a candle, inspects every crack and cranny in the house for lurking bits of leaven.

"Blessed art Thou, Our Lord, King of the World, Who hast sancti-fied us with Thy commandments and commanded us to clear the leaven!" The old man utters the benediction with special solemnity. The housewife follows him with smiling eyes, which seem to say: "Search away, Jacob! It will be a cold day in Tanus [July] when you catch a crumb after I have scrubbed and cleaned the house."

Springtime Joys in the Jewish Household
FROM THE *TAGEBLATT*

The joy of Passover is associated not only with the reason for the holiday. The preparations for the feast involve the whole family, and that delight is what we find in this turn-of-the-century piece that appeared in the Tageblatt. *Here we are given a more personal look at the symbolism and ceremony traditionally associated with this Festival of Freedom.*

What can compare with the joy of the Jewish housewife when she sees the ferment rising out of the hole in the *med* barrel? She knows then that her seder table will be *Yiddishlach*, and that the *arba kosos* will contain the nectar of the gods. Ah, the joy of *med* brewing, rivaled only by the delights, *eingemachts preglen.*

Did you ever help to brew med? I remember when I was a kid how jealously I prized that privilege.

We would be routed out of bed in time for an early breakfast. Clean, new wooden pails containing honey and bags of granulated sugar greeted our sleep-laden eyes. We would eat hastily and then roll up our sleeves and proceed to work. Water was poured into the honey, just enough to liquefy the sweet mass. Then a great stirring would ensue, until the honey was softened to the right degree of smoothness . . . a sheet of cheesecloth would be fastened over the top of a wash boiler, which we held on to for dear life. Water pails and pails of water, would then be strained through. Finally the bags containing the hops would be put into the wash boiler. Soon, as the concoction began to boil, the air in the house would become heavy with the pungent but not unpleasant odor of the hops.

Hour upon hour the boiling continued. Toward evening a solemn air of expectancy would overtake us: The *med* was about through boiling. First one would have a taste, and then another; we would smack our lips and pass judgment.

"It ought to boil a little longer," one would say.

"Ah, what do you know about making med?" would come the retort.

Finally the experts would compromise. . . . When the med was done brewing, the wash boiler was lifted off the stove and the sweet-bitter liquid, having cooled sufficiently, carefully ladled out and poured through a funnel into the med barrel, which meanwhile had been brought up from the cellar bin where it had been stored away since last *Pesach.*

In a day or two a little froth would appear around the bunghole of the *med* barrel. How complacently we would look about the house then. There was the *med* frothing and fermenting merrily; the bundles of *matzos* had the place of honor on the top of the bureau; the beets were souring, and all was ready for the gladsome *Pesach.* . . . Spring has many joys, but what joys of spring can compare with those that belong to the Jewish household?

⸺ *How the Sea Parted* ⸺

Passover is celebrated for seven days by Reform Jews and for eight days by Orthodox and Conservative Jews. An important commemoration of Passover comes on the seventh day when the story is told of the parting of the Red Sea to let the Israelites cross and the closing of the sea on the pursuing Egyptian army.

~ By the Red Sea ~
Hymn for the Seventh Day of Passover
Judah Halevi

When as a wall the sea
In heaps uplifted lay,
A new song unto Thee
Sang the redeemed that day.

Thou didst in his deceit
O'erwhelm the Egyptian's feet,
While Israel's footsteps fleet
How beautiful were they!

Jeshurun! all who see
Thy glory cry to Thee
"Who like thy God can be?"
Thus even our foes did say.

Oh! let thy banner soar
The scattered remnant o'er,
And gather them once more,
Like corn on harvest-day.

Who bear through all their line
Thy covenant's holy sign,
And to Thy name divine
Are sanctified alway.

Let all the world behold
Their token prized of old,
Who on their garments' fold
The thread of blue display.

Be then the truth made known
For whom, and whom alone,
The twisted fringe is shown,
The covenant kept this day.

Oh! let them, sanctified,
Once more with Thee abide,
Their sun shines far and wide,
And chase the clouds away.

The well-beloved declare
Thy praise in song and prayer:
"Who can with Thee compare,
O Lord of Hosts?" they say.

When as a wall the sea
In heaps uplifted lay,
A new song unto Thee
Sang the redeemed that day.

⟶ The Tradition Continues ⟵

My family traditions are Jewish traditions. My family and I always go
to the Passover. At this occasion, we have seder the first night. We go
to the temple for ten days. This is the first holiday of the year for me.

My next holiday is the Assembly. At the Assembly, I go down to
Virginia Beach. I go to the temple for seven days at this occasion. The
Assembly is where all business of the church is discussed.

Next, I celebrate Hanukkah, a Jewish holiday to replace Christmas.
I stay home for this holiday. I get gifts for eight days. Hanukkah starts
on December 9. This holiday ends eight days later. In this time I have
parties, eat turkey, and I stay up late and play cards. All together, I
get about twenty-four presents. I also give presents to all members of
my family. Last year I gave my mom a jewelry box. To me, Hanukkah
is the best holiday of the year.

Jewish holidays are not always the same time each year. They change
according to the Hebrew calendar.

I feel good about being Jewish. Not many people in the world are
Jewish. There are a lot of holidays that I enjoy. I enjoy being Jewish.

Moshe T. Thomas, middle school

Easter

ARISE, NEW HOPE AWAITS

~ Sleepers, Awake! ~

When I was growing up in Danville, Virginia, attending the Easter Sunday sunrise service in the quaint Moravian restoration of Old Salem in Winston-Salem, North Carolina, was a tradition. Cars and buses full of worshipers started out in the dark of night to arrive in the village just in time to see the lights in the old brick and timber houses come on as the sleeping town was awakened to a rousing chorus of "Sleepers, Awake!" played by a magnificent brass band.

While the moon was still high, thousands of visitors of every sect, creed, and race paraded from the steps of the Home Church, where they had gathered, to the nearby resting place of the Moravian dead, God's Acre, as Moravian cemeteries are called. When all were assembled, prayers were given and songs were sung, and antiphonal brass choruses were played while everyone awaited the dawning of Easter morn.

Silently and wondrously the bright moon that had lighted the worshipers' way slowly began to lose its glow as the sky turned from pitch black to an azure blue. Silently and wondrously a soft yellow-pink glow spread across the

181

earth. Then in a sudden burst from behind the majestic, newly budded and leafed trees in the east, the sun appeared.

In that emotionally charged moment the benediction was pronounced: "Go forth!" In the distance the last deep, compelling tones of the brass horns hung in the morning mist, bringing, for another year, the sacred service to an end. Yet few of the worshipers left. Peacefully, reverently, the guests lingered, wanting the moment, the morning, and the peace to last.

⚘ *Signs of Spring: Bright-Colored* ⚘ *Easter Eggs*

The egg as a symbol of the rebirth that comes with the Easter season and spring is deeply rooted in our European ancestry. Of course most famous are the exquisitely crafted Fabergé eggs, which are true works of art. First we read of the Russian Easter traditions, many of which are continued in the United States today, and then we learn about the craft of decorating eggs the Moravian way.

Russian Easters

PRISCILLA SAWYER LORD AND DANIEL J. FOLEY

On Easter morning a thousand bells rang the good news across the city. Anybody in Russia who desired could go to the church and ring the church bells on this day. In every dining room, tables were spread for the Easter feast. In the afternoon everyone went to visit friends; to forget even a single one was considered discourteous. Every table held the same fare, and the greeting was the same: "How kind of you! Come in! *Christohs voskress* (Christ is risen)!" All then kissed one another three times and proceeded to the feast. Every dish had to be sampled to please the hostess.

The whole city was in festival array as the crowds, all dressed in their Sunday best, paraded through the streets. Even the men displayed their vanity in brightly colored shirts of every hue. Their hair shone with pomade and their boots shone as well. For the women, flowered skirts and brilliantly colored scarves gave them the glamour they desired. As they met, they embraced, chatted, and exchanged Easter eggs, many of which vied with their owners in color and beauty of design. It was, in short, a day of great joy and merriment, one on which small presents were given to household servants and other employees. The parish priests—called "popes" because of their high caps and flowing beards, which gave them a venerable look—went around blessing food, exchanging pleasantries, eating, and enjoying a glass of cheer, usually vodka.

The dowager empress joined her son each year for Easter at Alexander Palace, where his entourage gathered to pay him tribute. These court receptions, resplendent with military uniforms, Arabs in turbans with shawls over their shoulders, ceremonial robes worn by the clergy, and the high fashion of royalty, included every level of Russian society. The gardeners with baskets of fruit and flowers, the blacksmiths, the cooks, the butlers, the scullions, the coachmen, the stablemen, and all the rest joined with the hundreds of visitors who gathered for the occasion. The fragrance of roses and lilacs filled the room. Protocol demanded that the emperor receive every employee, to whom he gave the traditional kisses and offered an Easter egg. Persons of lower rank were given large porcelain eggs made in the imperial factories while the dignitaries received smaller eggs made of stones from the Urals which were cut in the imperial factories.

On Easter weekend young ladies are given Easter charms shaped like eggs which may be any one of several semiprecious stones, such as lepidolite, quartz, jade, and the like. The more charms a girl receives, the more popular she is. These charms are worn on a necklace rather than a bracelet.

At Richmond, Maine, a colony of 300 or more Russian families celebrates Easter according to the calendar of the Eastern rite in a New World replica of an old Russian Orthodox church. Here in the United States, these Russian Americans and those in other communities practice their age-old religion in freedom. On Easter Eve, carrying icons, bright banners, censers, and the traditional Easter foods, the parishioners file in procession to the church. There, after a ceremony of old Slavonic church songs and readings, the Easter foods are blessed. These foods to be eaten on Easter Day itself are oddly shaped. There is the tall cylinder-shaped kulich (a rich coffee cake); the *paska*, a pyramid-shaped cheese enriched with eggs, raisins, and butter; there are also fruits, preserves, honey in the comb, meats and many, many colorful Easter eggs. Many of the foods are marked "XB" (*Christohs Voskress*).

Easter Day, wrote the Abbé d'Auteroche in his *Journey to Siberia* written in the late eighteenth century, was set apart for visiting in Russia. "A Russian came into my room, offered me his hand, and gave me, at the same time, an egg. Another followed, who also embraced [me], and gave me an egg. I gave him, in return, the egg which I had just before received. The men go to each other's houses in the morning, and introduce themselves by saying, 'Jesus Christ is risen.' The answer is, 'Yes, He is risen.' The people then embrace, give each other eggs, and drink brandy." Eggs were colored red with Brazilwood, and it was the custom for each parishioner to present one to the parish priest on Easter morning. They were also carried for several days following Easter. Persons of high station usually displayed gilded eggs, and greetings and eggs were exchanged in the home, in the marketplace or wherever friends met.

On Easter morning in Russia, in the Ukraine, and in Poland, the egg plays a significant part in the beginning of a joyful day. Before breakfast is served, the father of the household cuts an egg that has been previously blessed and distributes pieces to all the members of his family, wishing them a happy and holy Easter. Then the family sits down to a hearty breakfast with eggs aplenty.

Decorating Eggs: The Moravian Way

Edith E. Cutting

In the Triple Cities—Binghamton, Johnson City, and Endicott [New York] many people remember life in former European homes and treasure the traditional customs and designs, making them a part of the American tradition. Among these customs is that of the delicate and painstaking decoration of Easter eggs.

One of the outstanding types of design is that used most often by people of Slovak ancestry, particularly those who came from Moravia. These eggs are dark purple with white designs of birds or flowers. Both color and design have meaning. The traditional purple is almost black. Lighter shades may be used when the dark dye is not available. This purple represents the holiness of the Lenten season, for it is the color of the priests' vestments and the draperies used in the church at that time.

The white, of course, represents the joyous Easter Day. Because the lily of the valley is the national flower, it is one of the most frequently used motifs, though many conventionalized flowers and birds appear, symbolic of spring, of new life, and of love.

In the "old country," on Easter morning, each young man of the community, equipped with a lash braided of eight willow whips, visited the homes of the girls of the village. He tried to arrive before a girl was up in order to whip her from bed—the whipping being symbolic of the lashes received by our Lord before He was crucified— but she was usually ready with gifts to appease him before she received too many blows. These gifts were the Easter eggs, which each girl had carefully decorated, and one or more embroidered handkerchiefs, or for a fiancé, an embroidered shirt. On Easter Monday the girls whipped the boys out of bed and received in return gifts of candy, fruit, kerchiefs, or a gay skirt. They did not receive Easter eggs, for eggs were decorated by women and girls only. Although these customs are not followed closely in the Triple Cities, there are families in which the Easter lashes are still made, and there are women who still decorate Easter eggs with the traditional purple and white designs.

The eggs are boiled hard and, while still hot, are covered with a mixture of shellac, alcohol, and a purple dye that is now difficult to get. (Before World War II, many women had the dye sent to them by relatives in Czechoslovakia.) The dye must be one that will not penetrate the shell, or the clear white design where it is scraped off would be impossible. To give the egg a rich gloss, four or five layers are applied with a cloth dipped in this solution.

When the egg is dry, the designs are outlined on it with a small, three-cornered file. Then with the same file, the dye is carefully scraped off inside the outline to make leaves, shaded petals of flowers, or even words of Easter greeting. The individual floral or bird designs are often copied from eggs kept from past years; in fact, many are the traditional designs, like those embroidered on kerchiefs or skirts. But the completed designs vary, each person making whatever choice and arrangement of elements which may appeal to him. Naturally, the more delicate and complex the design, the lovelier the egg.

⟶ The White House Easter Egg Hunt ⟵

WILLIAM SEALE

The traditional Easter egg hunt at the White House is of such long standing that no one knows exactly when it began. Though an attempt was made to end the event, as surely as the Easter Bunny comes, each year the children of our nation's capital will gather for this frolic. William Seale tells us about the famed tradition of rolling Easter eggs on the White House lawn.

This Easter Monday custom had originated at the Capitol many years before, no one remembering exactly when; the children of Washington rolled their dyed eggs down the steep Western incline of Capitol Hill. By [President] Hayes' time several hundred children attended every year. Just after Easter in the year 1878 the Congress passed a law prohibiting the use of Capitol grounds and terraces as "playgrounds or otherwise."

Little attention was paid to this until Easter Monday 1879, when the Capitol police refused to admit the children to the grounds. A furor arose, and the children went to the grounds of the National Observatory and the White House, the latter apparently—even if not in fact at—the invitation of the President. "They laughed, yelled and played," reported the *Star.* "In rolling down with their eggs the girls —some of them pretty good size, too—were totally regardless of the extent of striped stockings displayed." The egg-rolling was enlivened by the appearance of a poor boy, "a ragged and dirty boy of 14," too old for egg-rolling, who snatched a basket of Easter eggs and fled through the gates and down the street, the children running in pursuit. Captured by the police, the boy returned the eggs, and the children cheered. Easter egg-rolling has been an annual event at the White House ever since.

⭢ Don't Forget the Easter Outfit ⭠

* LEE WILSON

Like that other traditional religious and secular holiday, Christmas, Easter has certain expectations associated with it. Attending church in proper attire was once much more a part of the day than it is now. You don't have to be from Ames, Tennessee, to identify with Lee Wilson's memories of the day.

All the Sundays of my childhood are compressed into one little wavy-edged black-and-white snapshot, which according to the date in the margin says was taken in March of 1956, when I was five years old. It is a photo of me and my three-year-old brother Mark, dressed in our Sunday best, standing on the lawn in front of the little white house where we lived with our mother and father; by the clothes we are wearing, I can tell that it is Easter Sunday.

My brother is dressed for church in a starched white shirt with long sleeves that hang slightly too far over his dimpled hands and a pair of short tan suspender-pants with sharp creases that emphasize his fat little knees. His blond hair is cut short over the ears but is long enough on top to allow for a carefully maneuvered rooster-crest wave. His white anklet socks and white lace-up shoes look like a baby girl's, but his figured clip-on bow tie, as silly as it looks, firmly declares his budding masculinity.

I am sure that my mother made my pastel cotton dress. With its puffed sleeves, lace-edged collar, and gathered skirt, it looks like twenty others I wore during the fifties. I am also wearing a frilly little

Easter bonnet that ties with a ribbon under my chin and have crooked my round arm, like any proper lady, elegantly through the handle of an Easter basket purse as silly as my brother's bow tie. My shoes and socks are black and white, respectively, those being the *only* colors for Sunday shoes and socks for well-brought-up little Southern girls in the fifties. I have a lot of hair for a five-year-old, with bangs cut short and straight and fat blonde curls, liberated at the last possible minute from pincurls that made me sleep badly and hurt my scalp.

But we are not smiling for the camera, my brother and I. He has poked out his lower lip and wrinkled his button nose and his nearly invisible blond eyebrows threaten to meet. You can even see furrows in his baby forehead. He is clearly unhappy about being dressed to his milk teeth in clothes he must keep clean. Even more eloquent than his scowl is the object in his right hand. Evidently my parents were not able to pry his fat fingers from around a white plastic horse from his favorite cowboys-and-Indians set. He is taking it with him to church, Easter or no, and doesn't give a rap for the ceremonial picture-taking that precedes our leaving in my father's old Studebaker for the ritual parade of finery that was Easter Sunday in the South.

At least he is looking at the camera. I have twisted my little rosebud face into the pained expression of a *grande dame* who has witnessed something unseemly and look at my delinquent brother with real chagrin, seeking, no doubt, to show him the error of his ways by literally frowning on his behavior. My peer pressure is, however, in vain. His lip continues to protrude and his scowl continues to disfigure his baby face.

My brother has been a banker for nearly fifteen years now. He wears tailored suits and has two children older than he and I were in my fifties photo and he long ago learned how to behave on ceremonial occasions. I, on the other hand, got a broken heart at twenty-five for my efforts at conformity and thereafter gave it up, except that I do occasionally put on a dress and heels and go home to Cornersville, Tennessee, to go to church with my parents. It makes my mother happy. I don't listen to sermons anymore, not even from preachers, so I spend the hour thinking about how my world has changed since I last wore black patent leather mary janes with white socks, but I sit up straight in the pew and put money in the collection plate and ask after the health of all the old ladies when the sermon is over. I don't have many illusions anymore, but my mother does, and, anyway, it's hard to be a real rebel after you've carried an Easter basket pocketbook to Sunday school and been prouder of it than anything in creation in 1956.

Minister Hopping Mad About Easter Bunny Hoopla

CLARK MORPHEW

Dressing up and Easter eggs are all part of the holiday, Clark Morphew concedes. But the Easter Bunny? The Reverend Larry Rice holds some dissenting thoughts on that subject, and he does something about it.

There's one Resurrection Day I'll never forget, because that was the day the Easter Bunny got killed, smashed on the road in roughly the size and shape of a dinner plate.

My children were little tykes, and they had found their Easter baskets early that morning. By the time I slid out of bed, great globs of sugar had already been consumed. As we set off for church, I noticed that the kids had the energy level of road runners on speed.

Naturally, they squirmed through worship and the church Easter breakfast, which, for each child, consisted of a glass of milk and a big, frosted doughnut. After that, they were really running around the dining hall, tipping over chairs and threatening the lives of kindly church people.

So, I made a marvelous suggestion that I was sure would drain their sugar-induced energy. "Children," I said, "let's see if we can find the Easter Bunny."

Deathly screams filled the room as they butted into the walls, climbed up the curtain on the stage and pelted the pastor with squished doughnut goo.

We piled into the car and headed for the road that goes through the forest. I had children stationed on all sides watching the woods for the Easter Bunny.

I had my eyes firmly fixed on the road when I saw the dreadful sight—a pair of bunny ears sticking up from the road, but there appeared to be no bunny body attached.

The body was there, all right. Apparently, a car tire had hit the luckless critter right behind the ears, which were preserved in perfect shape. But guessing from the shape of the bunny body, this rabbit would not be making any more egg deliveries.

As we passed over the flattened hare, I realized the children looking out the back window were going to be in a position to see the gory sight. Not wanting to traumatize my own flesh and blood, I hollered, "Kids, look ahead! I think the Easter Bunny just ran into the woods."

All eyes snapped toward the front. I looked in the rearview mirror and saw the rabbit ears swaying in the wake of our exhaust.

You may be wondering why I'm telling this gory story. You have a right to ask.

I will make a confession. I never have felt comfortable with the Easter Bunny. The character makes no sense to me. I can tolerate Santa Claus at Christmas, leprechauns on St. Patrick's Day and witches at Halloween.

But secretly, I have always thought the Easter Bunny was a ridiculous concept. Even children know rabbits don't lay eggs, and the creatures don't have the sense to deliver baskets of candy house to house.

I've always thought, if we're going to lie to our children on religious holidays, let's at least fib in a logical and intelligent way. Until now, I have kept this prejudice to myself.

But then, I discovered the Rev. Larry Rice, executive director of the New Life Evangelistic Center in St. Louis, who is so disgusted with the Easter Bunny concept that he has purchased hundreds of rabbits to feed to the poor in Missouri.

"People in this country are worshiping the rabbit instead of God," he said. "They're forgetting the true meaning of Easter, that it is a celebration of the resurrection of Jesus Christ."

To make a religious point, Rice bought about 1,400 rabbits, all butchered, frozen and ready to cook. And he's handing them out in St. Louis, Jefferson City, Columbia and Kansas City.

"There are 420,000 people in Missouri who run out of food by the end of the month," Rice said. "There are just a tremendous number of people who are hurting right now in this country. Instead of giving out little Easter bunnies that children can cuddle, we're giving out nutritious food."

Rice, by the way, has been on a hunger strike since Jan. 20, his 42nd birthday. He will eat his first full meal on Easter Sunday. Yes, Rice will break his fast by eating bunny with hundreds of people, most of them poor and homeless.

This isn't the first time Rice has used food to make a point. When state legislators were trying to decide if they should spend $9 million on football facilities, Rice bought them a free lunch.

He went to the state Capitol in Jefferson City and set up a buffalo-burger stand on the steps of the statehouse. He had a big sign that said, "Don't Be Buffaloed by Special Interest Groups." But the effort failed.

"They ate my buffalo burgers and still voted for the rich guys," Rice said. "Now things have deteriorated so badly that we're having to eat the Easter Bunny."

~ The Tradition Continues ~

An Easter egg hunt can be as much fun as a tree-decorating party—if you can get everyone to join in. For reluctant adults, try the trick Ann Grant of Brevard, North Carolina, told me about. Slip one-dollar or five-dollar bills into some of the openable plastic eggs intended to hold candy and let the word get around what you've done. Watch the grown-ups scramble!

Some New Twists to Easter Traditions

My sister-in-law from Connecticut has a wonderful children's Easter tradition. Now that her boys are grown and passing the tradition to their children, she has shared this approach with many of her friends.

Instead of simply awakening and finding an Easter basket or participating in the usual Easter egg hunt, Dee created a little more excitement for the boys. They were taught that when the Easter Bunny visits, he or she makes little nests throughout the house. Dee formed little nests of Easter grass and placed them everywhere. In each nest she placed two or three eggs or some Easter toys. The boys jumped out of bed on Easter morning to find an empty but beautifully ribboned and bowed basket waiting for them. They raced about the house finding nests and written clues as to where other nests might be found. It was a time of great merriment and of wonderful memories, a tradition that Dee's children can now experience with their children.

Betty Baker

The family tradition in my mom's family is cracking eggs. First you color your egg so it will look like the champion egg. Then each person holds his egg in his hand. Next a person hits the point of his egg on another person's egg. When the person's egg cracks, he or she is out of the event. The egg which did not crack stays in, and the person sees if he or she can be the champion. This takes place during Easter. Friends and relatives gather at each other's homes cracking eggs to see whose is the champion egg. This tradition started way back in biblical times. Simon, an egg merchant, carried Jesus' cross. When he came back to his eggs, he found out that they were all colored. Now coloring and cracking eggs still continues. I enjoy this tradition and I'm looking forward to next year.

Ross Davis, elementary school

At Easter, my family decorates Ukrainian Easter eggs using wax. This is a very slow process, but once the wax is removed, the egg is dipped in different colors, resulting in an outstanding decorative egg. After decorating the eggs, my family puts on their new Easter clothes and attends Midnight Mass. At Easter, all Russian Orthodox attend Midnight Mass the Saturday night before Easter Day. On Easter Day, my family takes food to church to be blessed by the priest.

Jill Sikes, elementary school

A family tradition of ours is to get together and have a party on Easter. We cook hot dogs and hamburgers on the grill. After that, we get our Easter baskets and get ready to hunt for plastic eggs. When my uncle Michael says go, we start looking for the eggs. Last year I won the prize for the most eggs found by the big kids. My uncle divides us into younger and older groups. When we get through picking up the eggs, my uncle counts to see who has the most eggs. Whoever has the most eggs in the younger and older groups wins a prize. But everyone gets something because for every egg you find you get a quarter for it. When you look for the eggs, you have to look under rocks, up in trees, in bushes, and in the dirt. After that, my uncle hides an alabaster egg. I have never found it yet, but I keep trying. It is usually hid the best. The young kids' eggs are easier to find, but the big kids are not allowed to look for the young kids' eggs. We have our parties at Guilford battleground park. When the hot dogs and hamburgers are done, we eat. We also have chips, potato salad, and chili beans. After we get done eating, some of the kids play ball. Then we see if any more eggs are left. Then we go home.

Andy Long, elementary school

IF EASTER EGGS WOULD ONLY HATCH,
MY, WOULDN'T THAT BE FUNNY!
Douglas Malloch

CHAPTER 8

Arbor Day

The Greening of America

⇀ *A New Tree, a New Beginning* ⇀

Our ancestors carefully carried fragile seeds and tree saplings from their home-lands to these shores. When, and if, those seeds sprouted and the trees thrived, ensuing generations would often gather the shoots and seeds from those second-generation trees for their new homesteads. Planting a tree to mark a new beginning or to claim new land is a time-honored tradition, as is the planting of a memorial tree. Thus it was particularly fitting that the two hundredth anniversary of George Washington's birth was so commemorated, explains Paul F. Hannah, for "When {one} places in the ground with his own hands a tree which is dedicated to Washington, the first president will become a real individual rather than a long-ago hero."

A Tree-Planting Memorial

Paul F. Hannah

An army many times larger than he ever commanded in life has been mobilized by the spirit of George Washington from the youth and adults of the land. Called into being by the Bicentennial Commission and the American Tree Association as an important part of the 1932 observance of the two-hundredth anniversary of the birth of George Washington, this army is planting trees. Each tree is a living monument to Washington, and will be dedicated to his memory on February 22 of next year [1932]. It is expected that before the great army disbands, ten million such memorials will have been planted.

The George Washington tree-planting idea has been acclaimed as one of the most significant phases of the coming bicentennial celebration. Fully supported by the press, the American Tree Association is reaching every corner of America, seeking unqualified cooperation in its plans. Individuals, clubs, patriotic organizations, and schools are joining in this unique tribute to Washington.

It is agreed that no more significant memorial than trees could be erected. Combining beauty with utility, symbolic of growth and power and gaining additional meaning from the planting by individual citizens, trees typify the national hero as no stone monolith could do. Their roots go deep into the soil, just as Washington's principles penetrate the national heart. Their firmness and solidity, combined with their steady growth, are indicative of the progressive yet sound Washingtonian principles of government.

It is as an educational idea, however, that the Washington memorial tree-planting program must gain the support of educators everywhere. Actual participation in national events forms the only method of giving them reality in a child's mind.

When he places in the ground with his own hands a tree which is dedicated to Washington, the first president will become a real individual rather than a long-ago hero, and his precepts will acquire a new meaning. Then, too, the thought of doing an act in common with thousands of children and adults all over the country will engender a national pride. Largely on the basis of this reasoning alone numerous educators have endorsed the Washington memorial tree-planting program as one of the most important national movements of the present day.

The primary idea of the project, however, is to drive home to citizens of all ages the necessity of forest conservation, particularly by reinvoking the conservation ideals of Washington and fixing in mind his principle of a self-reliant nation. A nation which uses timber more than four times faster than it grows it, which has one hundred million denuded, profitless acres and a constantly dwindling timber reserve, needs to hesitate in its plunge toward timber bankruptcy to consider the basic ideas that have fostered its growth.

John J. Tigert, former commissioner of education, once wrote: "There is no more important lesson for the American people to learn than the need of growing and conserving forests and trees. Our future development as a nation will largely hinge upon the success with which we can spread this gospel." Charles Lathrop Pack, president of the American Tree Association, has said, "if the nation will save the trees, the trees will save the nation."

No one can plant trees without learning something of forestry principles; no one can grow up in an atmosphere of tree planting without realizing its national importance. The bicentennial campaign gives every teacher or principal a lever whereby he may pry young America from an apathetic attitude toward forestry into wide-eyed understanding of the imperative need for forests.

There are scores of ways in which school children may participate practically in the bicentennial tree-planting program. The most useful plan is the creation of school and town forests. Such forests are sources of civic pride, they improve a community's appearance, and become powerful wage-earners.

Nearly every community has a worthless, desolate tract ideal for a forest, which might be donated by the owner, or sold for a nominal sum. The state in most cases will furnish trees at cost or free. The limitless planting power of hundreds of school children, ready at the call of educational leaders, is needed to create a lasting benefit at insignificant cost. What city would not be better for a George Washington Memorial Forest, a yearly income-producer and a permanent example of good husbandry?

Many a schoolhouse owes its being to the fact that a community forest paid for it. The town of Fryeburg, Maine, which in 1928 needed $7,500 for one of its school buildings, and found the funds on its own forest of white pine, represents but one of an increasing number of progressive municipalities. In Massachusetts eighty-six towns have established forests that return a revenue of from three to six dollars an acre for each of the 19,000 acres planted; and most of the money is spent in education.

The bicentennial program inspired the city of Grand Rapids to plant last December six thousand trees on a fifty-acre school forest, which shall serve as a demonstration area and school laboratory. More than sixty thousand trees will be planted, and each child will learn from this tract the value of forestry. The example of the Michigan city may be followed without difficulty everywhere.

No limit can be placed on the possibilities of tree-planting. Children who sing "America the Beautiful" each morning may help bring reality to the song by planting the roadsides of America with trees. Each corner of the school yard offers a suitable spot for a shade tree that future generations will love.

Approaches to buildings ought to be tree-flanked. In every case, the town or state roadway engineer, or shade-tree commission will lend valuable aid, advice, and suggestion.

The American Tree Association issues to each child or adult who plants a tree a special bicentennial certificate, a token of national gratitude for patriotic service. It hopes to list at least five million children on its honor roll, and be able to count on them to carry out Washington's principles of conservation.

⭢ *Family Trees* ⭠

DOUGLAS MALLOCH

You boast about your ancient line,
But listen, stranger, unto mine:

You trace your lineage afar,
Back to the heroes of a war
Fought that a country might be free;
Yea, farther—to a stormy sea
Where winter's angry billows tossed,
O'er which your Pilgrim Fathers crossed,
Nay, more—through yellow, dusty tomes
You trace your name to English homes
Before the distant, unknown West
Lay open to a world's behest;
Yea, back to days of those Crusades
When Turk and Christian crossed their blades,
You point with pride to ancient names,
To powered aires and painted dames;
You boast of this—your family tree;
Now listen, stranger, unto me:

When armored knights and gallant squires,
Your own beloved, honored sires,

Were in their infants' blankets rolled,
My fathers' youngest sons were old;
When they broke forth in infant tears
My fathers' heads were crowned with years;
Yea, ere the mighty Saxon host
Of which you sing had touched the coast,
My fathers, with time-furrowed brow,
Looked back as far as you look now,
Yea, when the Druids trod the wood,
My venerable fathers stood
And gazed through misty centuries
As far as even Memory sees.
When Britain's oldest first beheld
The light, my fathers then were eld.
You of the splendid ancestry,
Who boast about your family tree,

Consider, stranger, this of mine—
Bethink the lineage of a Pine.

⤳ *He Who Plants a Tree* ⤳

I firmly believe that legends and stories bring a rich and added dimension to our daily tasks. To instill a deeper appreciation of Mother Nature and the planet Earth in our younger children, take the time to read them the poems, legends, and stories that will widen their eyes and heighten their insight.

⮌ Trees Used in Games and Sports ⮌

MARY L. CURTIS

Think of all the games you play,
Baseball, tennis, and croquet,
Checkers, chess, and dominoes,
Games that everybody knows.

And the fun you have in school,
In the gym and in the pool,
Racing round the running track,
Jumping from the springboard's back.

Think of summer sports and fun,
Fishing, hunting with a gun,
Climbing trees, and paddling, too,
In a rowboat or canoe.

Games and good times by the score,
Those we've named and many more,
Each and every one of these
Depends on wood that comes from trees.

⮌ The Heart of the Tree ⮌

HENRY CUYLER BUNNER

What does he plant who plants a tree?
He plants the friend of sun and sky;
He plants the flag of breezes free;
The shaft of beauty, towering high;
He plants a home to heaven anigh
For song and mother-croon of bird
In hushed and happy twilight heard—
The treble of heaven's harmony—
These things he plants who plants a tree.

What does he plant who plants a tree?
He plants cool shade and tender rain,
And seed and bud of days to be,
And years that fade and flush again;
He plants the glory of the plain;

He plants the forest's heritage;
The harvest of a coming age;
The joy that unborn eyes shall see
These things he plants who plants a tree.

What does he plant who plants a tree?
He plants, in sap and leaf and wood,
In love of home and loyalty
And far-cast thought of civic good—
His blessings on the neighborhood
When in the hollow of His hand
Holds all the growth of all our land—
A nation's growth from sea to sea
Stirs in his heart who plants a tree.

— The Tradition Continues —

Greening Up Their Corner of Vermont

BEA COLE

As I walk along my country road, I breathe deeply. I can't help but be filled with wonder and pride.

The wonder comes from the beauty all around me. Cool air rises from our peaceful brook and touches my skin. I see the buds on the trees have gracefully unfolded like the limbs of a ballerina, producing leaves that look almost translucent. They hang suspended from the branches like green spiders.

When I reach home I notice that the grass has become a thick carpet on my back lawn, erasing the brown patches. The red nubs of our rhubarb have turned into a deep green ruffled mass and my tulips stand tightly wrapped, waiting to display their delicate splendor.

The pride I feel comes from the knowledge that we work together to keep our countryside clean. On April 30 we joined with our fellow neighbors for the 25th annual Green-Up Day.

The Balla Machree tractor and trailer were flanked by busy people removing paper, cans, and bottles from the roadside. The five children rode or walked along with us. Their presence was important as witnesses to the process because they are our future green-uppers. As we walked along on that beautiful day, I couldn't help but wonder when this whole thing got started. I remember cleaning up in the spring when I was younger, but I never knew the how and why.

Out of curiosity I called someone I thought might know the history of Green-Up Day. Frank Teagle was well informed on the subject since he's been a part of it since the beginning.

Green-Up Day began in 1970. It was started by Governor Deanne Davis who was a "real environmentalist," according to Teagle. In the beginning the process was set up and run by the state. They actually closed down the interstate to clean the roadside and set up alternative routes while it was being done. The volunteer turnout was outstanding and has since kept the custom alive.

Now of course each town is in charge of setting up and executing the Green-Up themselves. The job is not quite as overwhelming now as it was years ago, Teagle remembers. He believes that the Green-Up effort has bred more environmentally conscious people. This desire to keep our state clean was also responsible for the bottle bill in Vermont.

The annual Green-Up Day is done only in Vermont (although towns in other states do something similar). But to most of us that doesn't come as a big surprise. We Vermonters share common pride in the beauty of our state and a strong ambition to make sure it stays that way!

Making Trees Special

Every Earth Day, we plant a tree in our yard, and since it's my birthday, it has become a family tradition. In 1983, a year after I was born, we planted our first tree. It was a dogwood. We watched it grow until we moved. I would like to go back and see how tall it is today. Next came my poor oak tree on my second birthday. We had a drought and it didn't make it.

Over the next nine years, we planted a redbud, a maple, pear, cherry, spruce, Douglas fir, magnolia, birch, and a long-leaf pine. Like the ill-fated oak, the magnolia also perished. This time, while it was little, we had a flood and it drowned. The others, fortunately, are still growing today. We have planted so many trees in our yard that someday we may have to move our tradition to a park.

I like our tradition because all you have to do is either buy a little tree or plant a seed yourself and you have something that will hopefully make the earth a better place to live. I hope I hand this tradition to my children.

Corey P. Vernier, elementary school

In my family, we have a unique tradition. On everybody's birthday, we buy a tree for them. They choose a spot in the yard to plant it.

I have gotten a number of trees through the years. I have planted a crepe myrtle. Its flowers are pink. I have also gotten a Bradford pear.

In the future, its blossoms will be white. It is not mature enough to have blossoms yet. I also have a weeping cherry tree. Its blossoms will be purple. We just planted it for my eighth birthday on the twentieth of October.

I like getting the trees because I can tend to them. When they grow big, I can play in their shade. When I get big and look at my trees, I will remember my birthdays.

Alana McAllister Wilson, elementary school

In the backwoods of my grandfather's pasture, there is a humongous beech tree that is about 115 feet tall. It takes five people of average size to wrap around the trunk of it. It is a very special part of the heritage of my past relatives. This is because it has hundreds of names carved in it from my past ancestors.

My family has a tradition of having their name carved in it when one turns ten years of age. It is very magnificent to study and look at the tree. Present family members can see names dating all the way back to the mid 1800s. I remember the day when my name was carved in the tree. I went with my mom and dad to the spot by the creek, and my mom had to carve my name in because I was very short. It didn't take long for her to finish, but I was proud when she was done because my name would go down in history and never be erased.

I hope to someday help my grandchildren carve their names in the "Name Tree" and trace their heritage.

Jody Mills, middle school

IF YOU WANT YOUR NAME TO BE HELD IN GRATEFUL REMEMBRANCE, PLANT TREES; IF YOU WANT TO IMPROVE THE ROADSIDES IN YOUR TOWN, PLANT TREES; IF YOU WANT TO ADD BEAUTY TO THE SURROUNDINGS OF YOUR DWELLING, FOR YOUR OWN AND YOUR FRIENDS' EYES, PLANT TREES; IF YOU WOULD HAVE YOUR HOUSE AND GROUNDS MORE VALUABLE, TO KEEP OR TO SEE, PLANT TREES; IF ANY OF YOUR LAND IS NOT WELL ADAPTED FOR CULTIVATION OR PASTURAGE, CANNOT YOU PLANT TREES? IF YOU WANT PROPERTY THAT, LIKE MONEY AT INTEREST, WILL BE "GROWING WHILE YOU ARE SLEEPING," PLANT TREES.

Farmer's Almanac, 1860

CHAPTER 9

May Day

❧❧

It's May!

➤ *Gather Ye Rosebuds* ➤

Of all the traditional holidays, the one that once was enjoyed to the fullest, but today is mostly overlooked, is unquestionably May Day. The old books are so filled with May Day stories, poems, reminiscences, and crafts that you have to wonder what happened—especially these days, when we seem eager to add yet another work-free holiday to our calendars!

No celebration could be more lighthearted, spirited, or prettier. Everything about it lends itself to a party and gifts, even love and romance. But in the nineteenth century and, truthfully, even today, May Day was much more widely celebrated in the South than in the North. The festivities associated with the day were way too frivolous for the Puritans. In fact, on May 1, 1627, Plymouth Colony was horrified to find that Thomas Morton had erected a maypole at his home, Merry Mount Plantation. To make matters worse, it was rumored that Morton and others had been seen dancing with Indian squaws. To stop the activities, Governor Endicott had the pole chopped down and, worse yet, shipped the Anglican Morton back to England!

Despite May Day's "tainted reputation," to those of us with May Day memories there is no other day quite like it. May Day assemblies brought parents to school to see their scrubbed and dressed children frolic around the maypole—inside in colder climes and on the school lawns farther south. In college May Day was long anticipated. With trees and flowers budding, love was genuinely in the air. May Day courts were the order of the day followed by dances that night. Of course that has all gone by the by now that there are so few women's colleges left, and most of those would rather bring back home economics classes than stoop to having such a sexist celebration.

My own remembrances of the May Day I was five are as romantic as they come. My heart was filled with springtime dreams. That year, more than anything else I dreamed of having a May basket filled with yellow-eyed white daisies, graceful petticoatlike poppies, and silky pink roses just like the ones pictured in a storybook I had. At the handle of my basket there would be a profusion of long curlicue pink and blue ribbons.

I can still remember slipping out the back door and around the house to see if a May basket was waiting at my front door. My heart fell when I spied the lonesome gray front porch, as empty as it could be.

Well, I would certainly have to do something about that. Barefoot and still in my nightgown, I bounded through the dewy grass to the flower border, where I gathered a handful of spring flowers, blue and pink. Clutching the flowers I slipped back into the house, tiptoed through the kitchen, and burst into the dining room. I knew I'd find Mother there having her morning coffee. (Yes, people did such things back then.) "Happy May Day!" I squealed.

Years later I asked Mother if she ever had any idea how much I wanted a May basket when I was a little girl. She never had any inkling of my dream of dreams.

Thank goodness I had the chance to live out a little bit of that dream with my own daughter one May Day. She was in kindergarten at Story Book Farm. I dressed her in an aqua chiffon dress. I tied ribbons on the crown of a picture hat and bows around a leftover Easter basket. I filled it to overflowing with every spring flower I could find. Our photo album has more pictures of her taken that day than on any other single event.

May Day is too good to let it slip by. Like Thanksgiving, May first could be a sharing, festive, and very noncommercial day. It would take no more than a few flowers, a used basket, some recycled ribbon, and a light heart.

O SING TO THE LORD A FRESH NEW SONG!
Psalm 96

~ A Basket Full of Love ~

CHET HUNTLEY

Lest you think that May Day lives only in the hearts and memories of the "fairer sex" and Southerners, here, from Montana-born Chet Huntley's autobiography is a nostalgic recollection of that day before, as he said, it was turned into "a brash and chauvinistic holiday."

May Day, in those innocent years before the proletariat turned it into a brash and chauvinistic holiday, was touchingly observed by the youngsters . . . at least, in our town. It had more currency in Saco than in any other community I have ever known. Somewhat surreptitiously, we boys put aside the more predictable pursuits to labor absorbingly over our May Day baskets. With glue, scissors and watercolors we fashioned a basket for the "girl of our choosin'." It was filled with candies and small gifts and carried stealthily, with pounding heart and nagging trepidation, to the front door of the girl's house. Never, by our local rules, did the generous gift-giver reveal his identity. That was part of the game. Carefully, the handle of the May Day basket was fixed over the doorknob, then you knocked loudly and ran hell-bent for some predetermined hiding place.

I was singularly faithful to my fair Helen. Each May Day, I brought my heart and my basket to Helen Peterson's door and anticipated the next day at school, when I would watch her intently studying every boy in the class for some clue to the identity of her admirer. Desperately, I wanted her to guess that it was I, but simultaneously I was almost panic-stricken by the thought. Alas, I fear I was much too impassive. I am sure Helen never knew. One spring, she thanked Lee Taylor for her May Day basket!

⇀ *May Day Morning* ⇀

VIRGINIA SCOTT MINER

Oh, let's leave a basket of flowers today
For the little old lady who lives down our way!
We'll heap it with violets white and blue,
With a Jack-in-the-pulpit and windflowers too.

We'll make it of paper and line it with ferns,
Then hide—and we'll watch her surprise when she turns
And opens her door and looks out to see
Who in the world it could possibly be!

To Make a May Basket

SUSAN ALLEN TOTH

Early spring was probably the most exciting time in the North Woods, for then Mother took us to hunt for May-basket flowers. On a chilly Saturday morning when the sun finally broke from gray skies into the thin clear sunshine of early spring, Mother hung an old willow basket over her arm and led my sister and me to a hidden entrance into the woods a half-mile away from the house. Down a winding path, barely visible under the last patches of melting snow and moldly leaves, we followed Mother's sure steps, looking carefully as we walked for nearby flowers. Mother taught us how to find the delicate white Dutchman's-breeches and snowdrops and we gathered them into small bouquets with wild purple violets. At the end of the path, deeper into the woods than we ever dared go alone, was a small clearing with a large flat-topped stone in the center. . . . Mother said college students knew about this place and sometimes came here to have parties, so we must never go this far by ourselves. It was disappointing to know that someone had been here before us. But, protected by Mother, we weren't frightened about meeting any stranger, and we soon turned to scamper home, running ahead of her now, yelling and racing, while she followed slowly with the picnic basket full of flowers. When we got home, we had hot rolls and cocoa while we constructed little baskets out of colored paper to fill with flowers and leave at our neighbors' doors.

Happy Lei Day

It is most appropriate that the state that gives us of our most beautiful and exotic flowers, Hawaii, celebrates May Day, but of course there it is Lei Day, named for the lei, or wreath of flowers, worn around the neck.

⭢ The Tradition Continues ⭠

Thinking ahead to how to re-create May Day, you might take some ideas from Gladys Taber's memories of May Day at the turn of the century. (Incidentally, though she called Cape Cod home, Taber's American experiences ranged from New England to New Mexico and included the South.)

Reviving May Day Memories

GLADYS TABER

We used to wander dreamily down the wine-dark streets in the evening, when we were children, carrying our May baskets. They were little colored baskets woven of blue and lemon-yellow straw, and we lined them with soft moss, or fresh green leaves. All day long we had been down along the shining river, gathering sweet purple violets and buttercups, and little nameless pink and white blossoms. Then for special people we hid chocolates or jelly beans under the dewy flowers, and tied ribbon bows on the basket handles.

In twos and threes we went from house to house, slipping up on the porches and setting the baskets inside the screen doors, ringing the bell—oh, exciting and delicious moment—and then running like bunnies to the shrubbery where, giggling and whispering, we peeped out to watch the door open and the May basket go in!

The donor of a May basket was supposed to be secret, but there were always ways of knowing, and the one who made the prettiest May basket was stiff with pride for days.

We should preserve this custom, I think, and I hope the children of tomorrow may go out to the sunny meadows and spring woods and gather May flowers for the little reed baskets, and walk singing through the twilight to an early supper and the joy of giving May baskets.

Here are two more suggestions to add to the traditional walk in the woods or trip to the nursery to gather flowers and greenery—take an hour or so to make baskets for sick children, the elderly, or friends, and if you like to plan ahead, take a day in the fall to plant bulbs that will blossom in May to use for your May Day basket.

FOR FLOWERS THAT BLOOM ABOUT OUR FEET . . .
FATHER IN HEAVEN, WE THANK THEE!"
Ralph Waldo Emerson

CHAPTER 10

Mother's Day

❧❧

M *Is Still for Mother*

➤ Thoughts, Not Gifts ➤

It is amazing where casual conversations can lead. "What's your next book going to be about?" my future husband Bob Sexton asked me. "American traditions," I replied. "Like Mother's Day? I just saw a marker commemorating the home of Mother's Day in . . . ah, let's see, it must have been Grafton, West Virginia. Yes, about a block from the train station. You should see the beautiful tracks and junctions," he said, launching into the history of the old Baltimore and Ohio Railroad.

    I filed Grafton–Mother's Day away in my mind. Good thing I did. Some time later, when I was beginning to assemble information on that perennially favorite American celebration, I read, "The first Mother's Day was held in

Philadelphia on May 10, 1908." In another source I read, "The observance
of Mother's Day dates from May 1907. It began under the inspiration of
Miss Anna M. Jarvis of Philadelphia."

In no time I was on the phone to Grafton.

"Not so," said Bruce Miller at the Tygart Valley Development Authority.
"Philadelphia may be the home of brotherly love, but Grafton's the home of
motherly love."

In truth, I had thought Mother's Day was one of those fabricated, commercial holidays, probably created by a card or candy company. Nothing could be
more wrong. In fact, after establishing Mother's Day in commemoration of her
beloved mother, Ann Marie Reeves, Anna Jarvis fought vigorously to keep
Mother's Day free of commercialism.

Here, thanks to an offhand remark, I can relate the real story of how
Mother's Day originated. I never did hear the end of the railroad story. . . .

Ann Marie Reeves, in whose honor Mother's Day was first celebrated,
was the daughter of a Methodist minister who moved his family
including twelve-year-old Ann from Culpepper County, Virginia, to
Philippi, in what is now West Virginia, in 1845. Ann met and married
Granville E. Jarvis soon after her twentieth birthday. After their first
two children were born, she and her husband settled in Webster, West
Virginia, and would eventually have twelve children, eight of whom
died in infancy or childhood.

Despite these and other hardships, Ann Jarvis refused to become
bitter and was known for her unselfish and devoted service to her
community. Among her notable acts of community service was the
recruiting of women from Philippi, Pruntytown, Fetterman, and
Grafton to join Friendship Clubs (called Mother's Day Work Clubs in
another publication) in an effort to eliminate unsanitary conditions
and other perils of rural life.

During the Civil War when Union troops from Indiana, Ohio, and
Pennsylvania were stationed in Fetterman and an epidemic of typhoid
fever and measles broke out, General George R. Latham asked Mrs.
Jarvis and her Friendship Clubs for help. She and other local women
administered to the sick and were later commended for magnificent
services rendered to the sick soldiers. It seems that Mrs. Jarvis had a
way of bringing together people who could easily have been at odds.
This trait was further exemplified by the Mother's Friendship Day
festivities, which she organized in 1868 with the help of her fellow
club members to ease tensions between the Confederate and Union
soldiers from the area who had returned from the Civil War. Despite
the enormous potential for a confrontation of some sort to erupt, Mrs.
Jarvis and the other women pulled off a peaceful celebration, which

included renditions, sung by all, of "Way Down South in Dixie" and "The Star-Spangled Banner."

The Jarvises' daughter Anna was born in 1864 and attended school in Grafton, West Virginia, and Mary Baldwin College in Staunton, Virginia. Anna returned to Grafton to care for her blind sister Elsinore and taught school there for several years. At her father's death in 1902, all the Jarvis women moved to Philadelphia, Pennsylvania, to live with Anna's brother Claude. Three years later, on May 9, 1905, Ann Jarvis died and was buried in West Chester, Pennsylvania.

Anna, who often had heard her mother wishing for "someone, sometime, to establish a memorial mother's day for mothers living and dead," set to work bringing her mother's dream to life. The first Mother's Day was celebrated in Grafton, West Virginia, at Andrews Methodist Church on May 12, 1907, as a memorial service for Ann Jarvis. A telegram from her daughter, Anna, read during the service, defined the purpose of the day: to revive the dormant love and filial gratitude we owe to those who gave us birth; to renew a home tie for the absent; to obliterate family estrangement; to create a bond of brotherhood through wearing of a floral badge, the white carnation; to make us better children by getting us closer to the hearts of our good neighbors; to brighten the lives of good mothers; to have them know we appreciate them, though we do not often show it as we might. Anna Jarvis sent six hundred white carnations to this first service, with one being presented to each son, daughter, and father, and two to each mother.

Upon the advice of Philadelphia businessman John Wanamaker, Anna Jarvis began a campaign for the national observance of a day devoted to mothers. She wrote to everyone imaginable to garner support for her pet project, whether they were congressmen or evangelists. One year and about a thousand letters later, on May 10, 1908, at the request of Miss Jarvis, a fully prepared program was presented to the public at Andrews Methodist Church, while on the afternoon of the same day a similar service was conducted at Wanamaker's Auditorium in Philadelphia. The publicity surrounding this second celebration of Mother's Day was considerable, and in 1910, forty-five states, Puerto Rico, Hawaii, Canada, and Mexico joined in the celebration of Mother's Day.

In 1910, the governor of West Virginia issued the first Mother's Day proclamation; Oklahoma was next. In December 1912, the Mother's Day International Association was formed to promote the international observance of Mother's Day. Congress passed a joint resolution on May 17, 1914, to set aside the second Sunday in May as Mother's Day, and President Woodrow Wilson issued a proclamation two days later which requested that the Stars and Stripes be flown on this holiday:

> Now therefore, I, Woodrow Wilson, President of the United States, by virtue of the authority vested in me by the said joint resolution, do hereby direct all government officials to display the United States flag on all government buildings and to invite the people of the United States to display the flag at their homes or other suitable places on the second Sunday in May as a public expression of our love and reverence for the Mothers of our Country.
>
> In witness whereof, I have set my hand and caused the seal of the United States to be hereunto affixed.
>
> Done at the City of Washington this ninth day of May in the year of Our Lord One Thousand Nine Hundred and Fourteen, and of the Independence of the United States One Hundred and Thirty-eight.—Woodrow Wilson

Today, more than one hundred years after the formal establishment of Mother's Day, another group of selfless and industrious women in Grafton, West Virginia, led by Olive Crow, has restored the birthplace of the founder of Mother's Day, Anna M. Jarvis. Of the thousands of letters Anna wrote extolling her mother's virtues, this one sums up her life most poignantly:

> If this mother of eleven children [who lived], whose ambitions had been restrained by the ties of motherhood, homemaking, years of frail health, and finally the financial losses of my father, had led a selfish life and devoted herself as faithfully to her own pleasure and ambitions as she did to those of others, her achievements would undoubtedly have brought her unusual honors, and made her a woman of prominence in her undertakings.
>
> But after all, was she not a masterpiece as a Mother and gentlewoman—we who love her best as life's most precious gift to us, think so. When her sweet, peaceful face [is] called to mind, we feel that her triumph could not have been greater than in the noble Christian character that crowned her last days with glory.

~ All for a Good Cause ~

So just how did Mother's Day change from being a heartfelt, selfless day of simply saying thank you to your Mother into another commercialized holiday? This April 1934 editorial from Good Housekeeping *explains the emotional and commercial appeal the day has. The piece points up one of America's strongest and most admirable traditions—that of giving generously to help others.*

We yield—or does one say bow?—to the inevitable. But we do it whole heartedly and urge you to join us. Mothers' Day is going off the sentimental standard. Three years ago when several charitable organizations asked us to join in an appeal to make Mothers' Day a day of almsgiving, we told them we would have none of it, that there were plenty of other days for giving to the poor—even to poor mothers—and this one should remain as the day on which every one should give to his own mother some expression of his love and homage. We admitted that the whole thing was founded on sentiment, and that the day was being commercialized, but just the same we wanted Mothers' Day left alone. A lot of big, grown men—and women, too, though they do seem a bit nearer the mother heart—would feel a bit sheepish at ordinary times to say, even with a flower, "Mother, I love you," but not on this day. It is easy then—and those words need so much to be said that their saying should be made easy.

But now comes something else that is near to our heart and of a vital importance to mothers, too. In our February magazine, in her article "Every Baby Need a Mother," Genevieve Parkhurst told you about the mothers that died in childbirth—a number appallingly and unnecessarily large—and said that something should be done about it. Something is going to be done about it. The Maternity Center Association of New York—we have told you several times about its wonderful record—is leading in a nation-wide campaign to "Make Motherhood Safe for Mothers." So Mothers' Day—May 13th—is to be observed by women's clubs, men's clubs, medical societies, chambers of commerce, and other professional and civic groups who will join in community effort to this end. . . .

We see in this movement, which we heartily endorse, nothing that can do harm to the original purpose of Mothers' Day. Just the opposite. If it succeeds, there will be more mothers for sons and daughters to love and honor as the years go by.

⤳ Training Up the Children ⤳

MILTON S. MAYER

No question about it. Richard Scarry's What Do People Do All Day *was our family's favorite book. Langdon read the fireman episode over and over, while Joslin's favorite was the baker. Not surprisingly, mine was "A Mother's Work Is Never Done." Mothers have many important jobs, but topping the list is that of instilling strong values in their children, for as it is written in Proverbs 22:6, "Train up a child in the way he should go, and when he is old he will not depart from it." Mothers, and fathers too, shape their children's outlook on the world and pass on the strength of character that is essential to a meaningful and fulfilling life.*

Many famous children have credited their mothers for inspiring them to make their mark on the world. Milton S. Mayer's story of the Comptons tells about a remarkable early twentieth-century American family and one such mother.

Honorary Degrees are supposed to signify achievement—sometimes achievement in science or the arts, sometimes (though seldom openly) the achievement of the college in wheedling a new dormitory from a prosperous citizen. A few years ago Ohio's historic Western College for Women bestowed a doctorate of laws for neither of these reasons. To a woman, youthful at 74, it awarded the LL.D. "for outstanding achievement as wife and mother of Comptons."

The ceremony over, the new doctor hurried back to the welcome obscurity of an old frame house in Wooster, Ohio. Otelia Compton doesn't want to be famous, and she isn't. But her four children are.

Those who extol the virtues of heredity may examine with profit the Compton family tree. The ancestors of the first family of science were farmers and mechanics. The only one of them associated with scholarship was a carpenter who helped nail together the early buildings of Princeton. There was no reason to predict that the union of Elias Compton and Otelia Augspurger, two country schoolteachers, would produce columns in *Who's Who*.

Yet Karl, their oldest son, is a distinguished physicist, now president of the great scientific institution, Massachusetts Institute of Technology; Mary, the second child, is principal of a missionary school in India and wife of the president of Allahabad Christian College; Wilson, the third, is a noted economist and lawyer, and is general manager of the Lumber Manufacturers' Association; while Arthur, the "baby," is, at 45, one of the immortals of science—winner of the Nobel Prize in Physics.

How did it happen? The answer, according to the four famous Comptons, is contained in the old frame house in Wooster. Elias Compton was the beloved elder statesman of Ohio education; he taught philosophy at Wooster College for 45 years. But he always explained that he was just one of Otelia's boys. All credit was hers.

Otelia Compton, characteristically, denies that she has a recipe for rearing great men and women. She will admit that her children are "worthy," but what the world calls great has no significance for her. When Arthur won the world's highest award in science, her first words were, "I hope it doesn't turn his head." The only way I was able to pry her loose from her reticence was to get her into a good hot argument.

There is nothing unfair about picking an intellectual quarrel with this woman of 79; she is more than equal to it. She reads as ardently as any scholar. She thinks as nimbly as any logician. One day this summer her children kidded her about getting old. It seems she forgot to take her wristwatch off before her daily swim.

Cornered in her kitchen, Otelia Compton simply had to admit that she knows something about motherhood. There are her four children, with their total of 31 college and university degrees and their memberships in 39 learned societies. In addition, there are hundreds of boys and girls whose lives Otelia Compton shaped during the 35 years she spent directing the Presbyterian Church's two homes for the children of its missionaries.

Her formula is so old it is new, so orthodox it is radical, so commonplace that we have forgotten it and it startles us. "We used the Bible and common sense," she told me.

Did she think heredity important?

That was easy for the descendants of Alsatian farmers. "If you mean the theory that is handed down in a blue bloodstream, I don't think much of it. Lincoln's 'heredity' was nil. Dissolute Kings and worthless descendants of our 'best families' are pretty sad evidence. No, I've seen too many extraordinary men and women who were children of the common people to put much stock in that.

"But there *is* a kind of heredity that is all-important. That is the heredity of training. A child isn't likely to learn good habits from his parents unless they learned from *their* parents. Call that environment if you want to, or environmental heredity. But it is something that is handed down from generation to generation."

She feels strongly that too many Americans today are obsessed with the notion that their children "haven't got a chance." "This denial of the reality of opportunity," she says "suggests a return to the medieval psychology of a permanently degraded peasant class. Once parents decide their children haven't got a chance, they are not likely to give them one. And the children, in turn, become imbued with this paralyzing attitude of futility."

Certainly the four young Comptons would never have had a chance had their parents regarded limited means as insuperable. Elias Compton was earning $1400 a year while his wife was rearing four children and maintaining the kind of home a college community demands. The children all had their chores, but household duties—and here is an ingredient of the Compton recipe—were never allowed to interfere either with school work or the recreation that develops healthy bodies and sportsmanship.

If heredity is not the answer, I wanted to know, what is?

"The home."

"That's a pleasant platitude," I said.

"It's a forgotten platitude," she replied sharply. "The tragedy of American life is that the home is becoming incidental at a time when it is needed as never before. Parents forget that neither school nor the world can reform the finished product of a bad home. They forget that their children are their first responsibility.

"The first thing parents must remember is that their children are not likely to be any better than they are themselves. Mothers and fathers who wrangle and dissipate need not be surprised if their observant young ones take after them. The next thing is that parents must obtain the confidence of their children in all things if they do not want to make strangers of them and have them go to the boy on the street corner for advice. Number three is that parents must explain to the child every action that affects him, even at the early age when parents believe, usually mistakenly, that the child is incapable of understanding. Only thus will the child mature with the sense that justice has been done him and develop the impulse to be just himself.

"The mother or father who laughs at a youngster's 'foolish' ideas forgets that those ideas are not foolish to the child. When Arthur was 10 years old he wrote an essay taking issue with experts on why some elephants were three-toed and others five-toed. He brought it to me to read, and I had a hard time keeping from laughing. But I knew how seriously he took his ideas, so I sat down and worked on them with him."

Arthur—he of the Nobel Prize—was listening. "If you had laughed at me that day," he interrupted, "I think you would have killed my interest in research."

"The reason why many parents laugh at their children," Mrs. Compton went on, "is that they have no interest in the child's affairs. It isn't enough to encourage the child; the parents must *participate* in his interests. They must work *with* him, and if his interest turns out to be something about which they know nothing it is their business to educate themselves. If they don't the child will discover their ignorance and lose his respect for them."

When Karl Compton was 12, he wrote a "book" on Indian fighting. Mary was absorbed with linguistics. Wilson's devotion to the spitball made him the greatest college pitcher in the Middle West. Arthur, too, was a notable athlete, but his first love was astronomy. The combination of Indian fighting, linguistics, the spitball, and astronomy might have driven a lesser-woman to despair, but Otelia Compton mastered them all.

When the four children were still under 10 years of age their mother took them to the wilds of northern Michigan where they hewed a clearing and pitched a tent. There these urban-bred children learned simplicity and hard work. There they imbibed, as the mother of Comptons would have every town child imbibe, of the unity and mystery of Nature.

The boys all worked summers and in college, gaining priceless experience; and they all had their own bank accounts, "not," their mother explains, "because we wanted them to glorify money but because we wanted them to learn that money, however much or however little, should never be wasted."

Would she put hard work first in her lexicon? Mrs. Compton thought a moment. "Yes," she said, "I would. That is, hard work in the right direction. The child who has acquired such habits does not need anything else."

And what is the "right kind" of hard work?

"The kind of work that is good in itself."

"What's wrong with working for money?" I asked.

The mother of Comptons exploded. "Everything! To teach a child that moneymaking for the sake of money is worthy is to teach him that the only thing worth while is what the world calls success. That kind of success has nothing to do either with usefulness or happiness. Parents teach it and the schools teach it, and the result is an age that thinks that money means happiness. The man who lives for money never gets enough, and he thinks that that is why he isn't happy. The real reason is that he has had the wrong goal of life set before him."

What did she mean by parents and schools "teaching" that money is happiness?

"I mean all this talk about 'careers' and 'practical' training. Children should be taught how to think, and thinking isn't always practical. Children should be encouraged to develop their natural bents and not forced to choose a 'career.' When our children were still in high school, a friend asked Elias what they were going to be. His answer was, "I haven't asked them." Some of our neighbors thought we were silly when we bought Arthur a telescope and let him sit up all night studying the stars. It wasn't 'Practical'."

Yet it was his "impractical" love of the stars that brought him the Nobel Prize and something over $20,000; and in order that he might pursue his cosmic ray research, the University of Chicago equipped a $100,000 laboratory for him.

I thought of the four Comptons and I wondered if "impractical" parents weren't perhaps the most practical.

⟶ Lessons My Mother Taught Me ⟵

*EMYL JENKINS

It never fails. Put two generations of parents and grandparents together and soon someone begins complaining about the poor education today's youth is receiving. While the arguments and debates whirl around my head, I quietly remember those long-ago days before school buses and TV and recall my daily long walk home from school and the invaluable lessons that waited for me once I was there.

I can hear my mother now, saying to my father some thirty-five years ago as we drove down the old state highway, a paved but little traveled road, "We're coming up on that patch of phlox around this bend—now's the time to dig it up. Slow, now. Over there." She would always be right.

She had a sixth sense for where flowers grew along the side of the road, whether they had been scattered there by birds and the wind or were the sole remnants of a long-ago front yard. Together my parents would get out of the car, take the rain-rusted trowel out of the trunk, and head toward the patch of phlox, invisible to all but their eyes.

My job usually was to carry the day-old newspaper to wrap the plants in. And no matter how late it was when we got home that night, the phlox—or whatever flower my mother had begged, borrowed, or stolen that day—had to be put into the rock garden and watered. Then I'd promptly forget the day's events until months later, when Mother would remark, "Ah, that phlox is a little darker pink than I thought it would be. But it certainly is perfect next to the candytuft. Remind me to tell your father we must dig some more."

Though Mother loved her flowers and studied most diligently the various horticulture magazines she subscribed to, I always knew that to her, flowers were only metaphors for the larger lessons of life. I learned more philosophy in her garden than in any classroom.

Many an afternoon when I came home from grammar school I would find my mother, not playing bridge—the fashionable thing women did in the early 1950s—but kneeling on the linoleum pad Daddy had cut out for her to keep from soiling the already grass-stained knees of her gabardine slacks, digging bare-handed in her rock garden. While she planted and transplanted, weeded and pruned, I'd tell her about the day's events.

"Margaret Ann pushed her way in front of me at lunch today," I would remark, still angry.

"Remember, she's got an older brother," Mother would say gently. "I imagine there are times when she has to push to get her way at home. I'm sure she just forgot she was at school." Then Mother would add, "Oh, look at the littlest pansy plant over there. The tall ones with the big faces and the thick stalks are pushing it out. I think I'll move the sweet little one over here by the Johnny-jump-ups where it can be the biggest one." She didn't have to say another word.

One early spring morning—I must have been about eight or nine—when I came down to breakfast in a favorite Christmas-red and hunter-green gingham blouse tucked into my new pink-and-gray plaid skirt, Mother cheerfully remarked, "You've so many bright colors on, I think I should plant you in my garden rather than send you off to school!" I went upstairs and changed my blouse.

Our dinner-table conversation often included some casual reference to the garden, though it was seldom the topic of conversation.

"Have you seen dear Mrs. Brown lately?" Mother might begin. "I thought of her today when I was pulling the wild morning glories out from around the climbing roses. She's not had an easy life." Though Mother never compared Mrs. Brown to the long-suffering but proud roses, in my mind's eye I immediately knew those morning glories were Mrs. Brown's wild teenage daughters who ran away and didn't tell their mother where they were going until they were hours away from home.

Now that I have reached the age my mother was then, I understand that my mother's garden was her sanctuary. The place where, as Wordsworth said, "the heavy and the weary weight/of all this unintelligible world/is lightened." The place where she worked out her own problems and those of the world, as she saw them, while she tended her plants and flowers, day in and day out. In her garden, Mother put life into perspective.

For you see, people who garden do see things differently. They see life differently.

In solitude they take the time to pause, to reflect, to sort through problems big and small. In a garden people see the balance between the strong and the weak, the newborn and the time-weary. People who garden learn when to dig up and transplant, when it's just the right time to pinch a sprig off to spur new growth, and when it's better to let things well enough alone. They come to realize that overfeeding and overwatering are just as harmful as neglect. They know each day has its beginning and its ending, and that some days the dark will come before the daylight tasks can be completed. And most important, they find that time teaches them that all too often, no matter how they try, unannounced and unforeseen forces—the wind, a storm, even a neighbor's stray dog or cat—can undo all the toil and love one person has put into a garden.

But when such things happen, people who garden also see tomorrow's marigolds and zinnias and next year's larkspur and irises—and are ready to start anew.

⌐ *Valuable Gifts* ⌐

"Write it down! I won't remember it." How many times did you say that to your parents when they began telling you about Great-Aunt Mildred's first trip to the beach or your grandfather's first day at school, to say nothing of who is kin to whom on which side of the family?

Some of my fondest childhood memories are of sitting with my grandmother in the garden in spring listening to her tales of what my mother was like when she was just a girl. Funny how these memories seem to come back to you later in life. For one reason or another, some parents don't think it is important to share details of their lives with their children, but as we learn here, these glimpses of the past are sorely missed. Let Joseph Cooper's words convince you that it is worthwhile to cherish these memories, and then let Kent Collins's piece persuade you to take the time to write it down. After all, this is a legacy you can give to the family you will never see.

Mothers Can Give Another Valuable Gift to Their Young

JOSEPH F. COOPER

Mothers, please, give your children a gift this Mother's Day. Give the facts of your life—at least some of them—so that your children and theirs will not lose you.

I have lost my mother in the sense that she is unable to convey to me the facts of her life. She has suffered almost total memory loss; she will be 88 this summer. The only evidence of her vitality as a young woman is in photographs, undated, of her ice-skating and canoeing, of her on a ship and on a boardwalk. Judging by the clothes, the photos are from the 1920s and 1930s. But there aren't any notations about the places and the people in the photographs. The photos are scraps; there isn't any scrapbook. I wish I knew what she thought about and hoped for back then.

A Certificate of Honorable Service from the Army Air Forces 1 Fighter Command Aircraft Warning Service says she was "a loyal and faithful volunteer." It is dated May, 1944, Mitchell Field, New York. I try to picture her in an airfield bunker wearing earphones and moving miniature planes across a map as reports are relayed to her. I try to imagine what it was like. She never talked about this service.

The framed photos of my parents have no context. I don't know how they met or when they decided to marry. From their marriage certificate (Harrisburg, Pennsylvania, August 1945) and my father's discharge papers (Indiantown Gap Military Reservation, August 24, 1945), I can make a few assumptions. There is no other physical evidence at hand. Family and friends are gone.

My father died unexpectedly three years ago. The few times I broached the subject of his past, he asked why I wanted to know. I never had a good answer. He wasn't given to talking about such things, and my mother, I suspect, took her clues from him. And I was shy about probing into my parents' personal lives. I didn't imagine they had anything to hide, nothing scandalous or shocking or shameful. I was curious but reluctant to pursue matters they had no inclination to divulge. By the time I had the courage and clarity to ask my mother about her life, her responses were not reliable; they were interesting, and maybe revealing, but not reliable.

Did she actually work in her father's tobacco shop in 1915, at the age of 13? Did he leave her alone in the shop when he had to make a delivery? Was she scared? Did she have to work, and give up school, so her sisters could go on to higher education? Did she drive her brother's Pierce-Arrow to a lodge in the Poconos for a weekend? And did the young people gathered there come out to the front lawn to admire "her" car? What happened to my father's Army uniforms? Did she and my father go to Atlantic City for their honeymoon? During labor, in Pennsylvania Hospital in Philadelphia, was she really seen by a doctor who had attended FDR?

I think she went to great lengths for me. Did we walk all the way around the field behind our first apartment to get to the convent for music lessons? I remember (barely) holding a triangle. How many buses did she and I have to take to get me to Cub Scout meetings?

I remember neatly folded T-shirts and towels being packed for overnight camp. Or was it for ROTC boot camp? What did she think about when she sewed on my name tags? And when she saw me off? Did she wash and iron for every game? Our house was always neat and clean. I wonder what she thought about as she did the cooking and cleaning, day in and day out.

I have some sense of what she feared for me. I know she worried that my little forays into student politics might lead to the rough-and-tumble of real political endeavors. I don't know what she imagined for my future. I know she worried about my heart being broken. When things didn't go my way at school, in sports or at work, she'd console me by saying, "You'll be lucky in love." When I wasn't lucky in love, she said that I had a lot to be grateful for. I wonder if that was how she viewed her lot in life.

There are so many things about her I would like to know; so many things about our family I would like to know; so many things about me as a baby and a little boy I wish she could tell me. It was always too soon to ask. Now it is too late.

Wise Mothers Leave Warm Legacy

KENT S. COLLINS

In the mountains straddling North and South Carolina, a middle-aged man is quietly musing about his dearly departed mother:

"It's been a year now since Mother died. Her headstone is in place next to Dad's at the town cemetery. All the nice talk at church about how special she was, about her kindness and wit, have quieted finally. Only the neighbors talk about her regularly still—those people she talked with during her walks, those people she watched after when sick, those people she counted on and who counted on her."

This man and his sisters returned to their mother's home a few months back to pick and choose among the treasures, the junk and the memories. The house is up for sale and when it's gone, only the headstones will be left.

"Now we wonder," he writes "what Mother really left us. Several miles and several months removed, we are left to wonder what made this lady special. The list looks so simple. But the magic of each remembrance will forever make us, her children, wonder. And worry some. Are we doing it Mother's way? What lessons should we call up? What example might we follow? What principles do we pass on to her grandchildren?"

This is not the melancholy sentiment of a sad man in mid-life crisis. It is the quest for a road map for the rest of life. If elderly parents knew their grown children would need such a map, they might do things differently. Conversely, if the children knew they would some day want a map, they too might do things a little differently.

"Mother left a legacy of kindness," this man explains. "We all think we are kind people. But if we are, why don't the rest of us get reactions like Mother got? Was her kindness simply doing things for other people? No, it was more than visiting a sick friend, carrying in dinner for a woman whose husband was away, delivering a casserole for the friend with surprise house guests. Her kindness was in her attitude about doing those things. It radiated to others, and it seemed to echo back to her.

"Mother was also special because she guarded her relationships with her children. She did not treat us equally, but she came across as being fair. Our individual needs got her attention, even when she gave unequally of her time and money. She coaxed us towards good mates, guided us in raising good children, and never showed disgust when we weren't so good."

The legacy any of us leaves our offspring is casually developed— maybe recklessly—over time. But someday it will be preciously or painfully remembered. No house-building, career-building or wealth-building compares in ultimate importance to this legacy building.

Retirement is a good time to build—or remodel—a legacy. Retirees have the time to do it, the experiences from which to forge it. Most of all, retirees have the need to do it. A legacy like the one left to this Carolina man will be treasured by many people for many years.

⤙ How We Kept Mother's Day ⤚

STEPHEN LEACOCK

So how will you celebrate Mother's Day? Much like Thanksgiving and Christmas, the routine seems to repeat itself year after year—breakfast in bed, a card, telephone calls, lunch or dinner out, flowers. How about putting a little twist on the day?

One year our family decided to have a special celebration of Mother's Day, as a token of appreciation for all the sacrifices that Mother had made for us. After breakfast we had arranged, as a surprise, to hire a car and take her for a beautiful drive in the country. Mother was rarely able to have a treat like that, because she was busy in the house nearly all the time.

But on the very morning of the day, we changed the plan a little, because it occurred to Father that it would be even better to take Mother fishing. As the car was hired and paid for, we might as well use it to drive up into the hills where the streams are. As Father said, if you just go driving you have a sense of aimlessness, but if you are going to fish there is a definite purpose that heightens the enjoyment.

So we all felt it would be nicer for Mother to have a definite purpose; and anyway, Father had just got a new rod the day before, which he said Mother could use if she wanted to; only Mother said she would much rather watch him fish than try to fish herself.

So we got her to make up a sandwich lunch in case we got hungry, though of course we were to come home again to a big festive dinner.

Well, when the car came to the door, it turned out that there wasn't as much room in it as we had supposed, because we hadn't reckoned on Father's fishing gear and the lunch, and it was plain that we couldn't all get in.

Father said not to mind him, that he could just as well stay home and put in the time working in the garden. He said that we were not to let the fact that he had not had a real holiday for three years stand in our way; he wanted us to go right ahead and not to mind him.

But of course we all felt that it would never do to let Father stay home, especially as we knew he would make trouble if he did. The two girls, Anna and Mary, would have stayed and gotten dinner, only it seemed such a pity to, on a lovely day like this, having their new hats. But they said that Mother had only to say the word and they'd gladly stay home and work. Will and I would have dropped out, but we wouldn't have been any use in getting the dinner.

So in the end it was decided that Mother would stay home and just have a lovely restful day around the house, and get the dinner. Also it turned out to be just a bit raw out-of-doors, and Father said he would never forgive himself if he dragged Mother round the country and let her take a severe cold. He said it was our duty to let Mother get all the rest and quiet she could, after all she had done for all of us, and that young people seldom realize how much quiet means to people who are getting old. He could still stand the racket, but he was glad to shelter Mother from it.

Well, we had the loveliest day up among the hills, and Father caught such big specimens that he felt sure that Mother couldn't have landed them anyway, if she had been fishing for them. Will and I fished too, and the two girls met some young men friends along the stream, and so we all had a splendid time.

We sat down to a roast turkey when we got back. Mother had to get up a good bit during the meal fetching things, but at the end Father said she simply mustn't do it, that he wanted her to spare herself, and he got up and fetched the walnuts from the sideboard himself.

The dinner was great fun, and when it was over all of us wanted to help clear the things up and wash the dishes, only Mother said that she would really much rather do it, and so we let her, because we wanted to humor her.

It was late when it was all over, and when we kissed Mother before going to bed, she said it had been the most wonderful day in her life, and I think there were tears in her eyes.

⁓ On Mother's Day ⁓

AILEEN FISHER

On Mother's Day we got up first
so full of plans we almost burst.

We started breakfast right away
as our surprise for Mother's Day.

We picked some flowers, then hurried back
to make the coffee—rather black.

We wrapped our gifts and wrote a card
and boiled the eggs—a little hard.

And then we sang a serenade,
which burned the toast, I am afraid.

But Mother said, Amidst our cheers,
"Oh, what a big surprise, my dears,

I've not had such a treat in years."
And she was smiling to her ears!

← The Tradition Continues ←

After spending months, even years, asking of others, "What is your favorite tradition?" finally it happened. I was at the New Orleans home of my friend Katherine de Montluzin when another guest turned to me and asked, "What's your favorite tradition?"

Combine my love for customs and memories with my habit of making everything into a tradition (according to my children), there becomes so much to choose from that selecting just one was a tall order. Finally, though, I did. It brought out the mother in me. It's calling my children on Sunday nights—whether they're at home or not.

We have a tradition in our house that happens every year. On Mother's Day, my father and I treat my mom very, very nice. My mother gets to sleep in late on this day and watch anything she wants on TV. Her favorite show is *Star Trek.*

We clean the house for her. My dad washes the floor and I pick things up.

We also take her to a movie. My dad takes her to a scary movie while I stay at my grandma's. My parents pick me up after the movie.

My dad and I give my mom a card. I get to pick out the card that goes to my mom. My dad picks out the card that is for my grandma.

I feel good about this tradition because all of the other days my mother is good to me and takes care of me, and I want to be nice to her and take care of her on this day.

Rebecca Cannon, elementary school

← ←

Today was Mother's Day! When we all finished our breakfast, we gave Mama her Mother's Day cards. It was a time of happiness for us all.

Later on, we all went to the Davises' pond like we always do on this special day. It was a silent, beautiful place with nature's surprises waiting to be explored all around us.

My father, sister, and brother went fishing on the pond in an old aluminum canoe, while my mother and I stayed on shore struggling to put a cute, innocent cricket on the hook. Our fishing pole broke, so we blew grass to keep ourselves entertained until it was time to go.

By the end of the day, it was time to end our family tradition by releasing all the fish we caught. Then we all left for home.

After dinner, we kissed Mama good night and wished her a happy Mother's Day.

Melissa Ann Graham, middle school

On Mother's Day I always buy my mom something. I buy her glass figurines or something she needs for our house. She always likes the things I buy for her. My mom always tells me that I do not need to buy her anything just as long as she has me.

Then my mom and I go out to eat breakfast at a place she like to go. I want to pay for her breakfast, but she will not let me.

When we go home, we sit down and do what she wants to do. I also tell her how very much I love and appreciate her.

When it is Mother's Day, I do not give my mom a hard time because it is her day and I want her to enjoy it.

Mother's Day is special, just like my mom. She is very important and loving to me. I love her with all my heart.

Stephanie Fields, elementary school

I HAVE PRAISED MANY LOVED ONES IN MY SONG,
    AND YET I STAND
BEFORE HER SHRINE, TO WHOM ALL THINGS BELONG,
    WITH EMPTY HAND.

Theresa Helburn

CHAPTER 11

The Fourth of July

WE HOLD THESE TRUTHS

~ A Day to Be Kept in Remembrance ~

*EMYL JENKINS

I asked my New England born-and-bred father, "Daddy, what was the biggest difference you found between the North and the South when you crossed the Mason-Dixon line back in 1936?"

"Firecrackers," he said. "You Southerners will use any excuse to set off firecrackers. We only had them for the Fourth of July."

Daddy quickly adapted to our ways, and every year I was the enviable neighborhood kid when the Fourth rolled around because Daddy made sure that he had an ample supply of sparklers, Roman candles, firecrackers, bottle rockets—any of the legally obtainable fireworks of the late 1940s.

Mother didn't approve.

A few years ago when Daddy took his grandchildren—*my* precious little ones—out in the driveway to set off his booty of saved and hidden fireworks bought to thrill them, I understood. In my girlhood, though, I complained bitterly, calling Mother a killjoy and other appropriately insulting names.

Of course Daddy loved fireworks. They are as much a part of a little boy's character as snips and snails and puppy dogs' tails. And my father grew up in Massachusetts where holidays were few and far between back then, so the Fourth of July was magical indeed. Many's the time Daddy would tell me how, when his father went to school, Thanksgiving was the last real holiday until the Fourth of July. But then what a celebration!

To prove his point, he read to me from a well-worn 1898 history textbook, *Building the Nation.* (I'm awfully glad my New England family never threw anything away. Those old musty books have certainly come in handy over the years!)

" 'In the New England States the Fourth of July was celebrated as in no other section of the country,' " he read, his voice filled with patriotic pride. " 'At sunrise there was firing of cannon and ringing of bells. Later in the day there was mustering of soldiers, picnics, orations, rehearsing the patriotism and heroism of the men who achieved the independence of the nation, drinking of beer' " (he laughed a little as if transformed to the young boy stealing a sip) " 'lemonade, and rum-punch. It was the nation's birth,' " he continued, " 'and the beginning of a new order of things in human government. It was felt that such a day ought to be forever kept in remembrance.' " (He cleared his throat, no doubt recalling his World War II days in the navy and the unsung patriotic deeds he had witnessed at sea and the European front.) " 'President John Adams said that it ought ever to be celebrated, and the people agreed with him. Old and young—men, women, and children—all participating in the enjoyments, to keep alive their love of country.' "

Old and young—men, women, and children. . . .

I've thought about that statement a lot over the last few years when our society has seemed to become more fragmented than drawn together. Where is that unswerving national spirit of togetherness we once had? It seems it wasn't that long ago, when I think how recently my own childhood was.

Oh, I know the answer. And I must shoulder some of the blame even as I pose the question.

More than once I spoke up and protested our role in Vietnam. I still do. I blame a fair share of our country's and the world's present ills on that regrettable war. But we cannot rewrite history. Everyone knows that, though some people would like to erase the words and change the events that do not fit their political or social agendas.

What can we do to reawaken a sense of pride in our country? Like so many ideals, this sounds so simple, but it is so hard to achieve. How would I start? Ironically by acknowledging that which seems to be gnawing away at us—our diversity.

You see, I spend many hours every month riding in taxicabs in cities like New York, Miami, Los Angeles, Atlanta, Houston, New Orleans, and even Raleigh. (How else do you get to and from the airport?) Almost always the driver is an immigrant. I have a curious mind and so I begin the conversation.

"What country are you from?" I usually ask as an opening question.

You'd be amazed how many times I have been told in a thick foreign accent, "I'm from America."

How do we recapture some of our lost patriotism?

Talk to those who are Americans by choice, not by birth. And begin your family tradition of *celebrating* the Fourth of July, fireworks and all, old and young—men, women, and children—all participating in the enjoyment to keep alive their love of country.

— Have a Musical Fourth —

ANNIQUE DUNNING

"The Stars and Stripes Forever," "You're a Grand Old Flag," "Yankee Doodle Dandy." Even if we don't know all the words, we can hum along when the Boston Pops strikes up its patriotic medley. Thanks to information supplied by Caleb Cochran in the Boston Pops press office, here's how the traditional Fourth of July concert began long before television brought this memorable event into our homes across the country.

In 1881, Henry Lee Higginson, the founder of the Boston Symphony Orchestra, wrote of his wish to present in Boston "concerts of a lighter kind of music." The first Boston Pops concert, on July 11, 1885, represented the fulfillment of his dream. Called the Promenade Concerts until 1900, they combined light classical music, tunes from current hits of the musical theater, and an occasional novelty number.

On July 4, 1929, Arthur Fiedler, a young violinist with the Boston Symphony Orchestra, initiated through his own efforts the free outdoor concerts by an orchestra of Boston Symphony musicians which have come to be known as the Esplanade Concerts. Soon the Esplanade series became a favorite annual attraction, attracting audiences drawn from all ages and all walks of life from in and out of Boston.

In towns across the country, free open-air concerts performed by brass ensembles in gazebos and shells were all the rage at the turn of the century. This was different. This was a symphonic ensemble, the sort you expected to see perform in a grand symphony hall.

There was another difference as well. The Esplanade Concerts were played without enclosure, gates, or ticket windows. Today, just as in the 1930s, when you step from the sidewalk onto a vast lawn facing the stage, you are in a grand out-of-doors auditorium. You settle on the grass, stand on the outskirts, or hire a chair for a dime, which means you grab one up from a stockpile and put it in any unoccupied territory you like. No matter how affluent you may be, you cannot reserve a seat.

In 1973 David Mugar and Arthur Fiedler organized the first of the Fourth of July Boston Pops concerts. From then it has grown steadily larger and more elaborate until today, the computer-programmed fireworks display, which lasts for nearly half an hour, takes almost a week to set up and dismantle on barges in the Charles River. When the entrance to the grounds opens at six on the morning of the Fourth, the line of people who began gathering the night before streams in. And on the Charles River captains and skippers are jockeying for prime position

Michael Manning, a special reporter to the *Boston Globe,* in 1995, described the atmosphere at America's favorite birthday party this way:

> If you've never been to the Hatch Shell for the Fourth, you've missed an extraordinary community exercise. The crowd is on the scale of a Vatican Easter address, but the atmosphere is that of the traditional Sunday afternoon brass band concert on the town green. Of course, the band is an 80-piece professional orchestra, the gazebo is a parabolic reflector buttressed by an Olympian amplification system, and the green is that stretch of land extending from the Longfellow Bridge to Boston University.
>
> As the concert hour draws near, the audience grows increasingly restive. There are more and louder outbreaks of spontaneous applause, more children being lofted playfully into the air, more group-oriented games being invented and exhausted. There are red, white, and blue—festooned papier-mâché hats, people done up as Uncle Sam, the Statue of Liberty, the Liberty Bell, and things you don't know who they are. It is more fun on a larger scale than is permitted in one place on any other day of the year.

⁓ When We Were Americans, First ⁓

RUSSELL McLAUCHLIN

Less than a mile from what used to be the middle of Detroit, Alfred Street runs at right angles to Woodward Avenue. The neighborhood, like the city, has undergone many changes since Russell McLauchlin, a newspaperman in Detroit in the 1940s, grew up there. In his remembrance of an old-fashioned Fourth of July, he describes an event in a time when we were all Americans.

An intense and flaming patriotism was a prevailing characteristic of every 10-year-old on Alfred Street. Sir Walter would have found no need for head-shaking over any of us. There breathed no lad with soul so dead who never to himself had said, in effect, "The United States of America is the greatest place which could possibly be imagined."

There survived, to be sure, small prejudices in favor of England, not altogether quenched by the tales we heard, at home and in school, concerning disagreeable British practices in the years preceding 1776. England was doubtless an enemy; but, as between England and any other Old World realm whatsoever, there could be no question of choice. For the story of England included shining biographies of men whom we passionately admired. No really "bad" country could have accommodated the career of Nelson.

But it annoyed us a little, nevertheless, to realize that our most useful possession—our speech—was called "English." That seemed too great a concession to the political origins of our own land. With the ultimate in heroism, we were told, our dauntless forefathers had broken forevermore the tie. Then why, we wondered, advertise that tie in every word we uttered?

For we all believed—German, Irish, French, Jewish, or whatever we were—that our private American backgrounds went directly to the Plymouth Colony and that our own family blood had been the price of liberty in the Revolutionary war; and this was, generally speaking, far indeed from the fact, in a mid-western city, long ago.

My own family-line, for instance, went into Canada and was composed of what are called United Empire Loyalists, whose forebears took a poor view of the American Rebellion. My only direct ancestors, in any way connected with that conflict, shed their blood for King George III. But I didn't really grasp that embarrassing fact until Alfred Street had long been a memory.

So, being passionate patriots and feeling a shade of irritation at the official title of our native speech, we did the best we could by way of editing.

"Listen to that man," we used to say, laughing heartily at his language. "He can't talk United States."

This love of country touched its annual peak, naturally, on the Fourth of July when it was the custom to arise with the sun and, collecting on somebody's lawn, produce the ultimate in noise. Carefully hoarded nickels had supplied most of us with many packages of firecrackers and there were even, in the possession of the more favored, a few -reat, cylindrical explosives called "cannon crackers," which were properly detonated beneath an overturned tin pan.

All these noise-makers were touched off by sticks of a slow-burning material called "punk," which later appeared in more stylish form as the "joss-stick," useful for the discouragement of mosquitoes on summer evenings.

And always, in these early morning noise sessions, there arose some sufficiently spendthrift nature to lavish an entire package of firecrackers in one great series of explosions. When, some two-score years later, we learned of the atomic bomb and the possibility of its starting a chain of disintegrating actions, I'm sure it reminded us all of the rich boy in the neighborhood who, with a grand gesture, used to sacrifice a whole package of firecrackers at once.

Also, we had cap-pistols, which made a mild and unsatisfactory sound but were of comfortably convincing outline. We had torpedoes which could be dropped on the sidewalk with a heartening racket. We had tiny projectiles which, when ignited, pursued a swift and eccentric course on any flat surface and were universally called by a name nowadays forbidden in the interests of interracial amity. And we had odd little chemical pyramids which, when touched by burning punk, poured forth horrible-looking, solid streams of substance and were called "snakes."

These snakes were not peculiar to the Fourth of July. They could also produce a strong effect in conjunction with a small Rabelaisian device called a "Sooner Dog." I'm sure that every boy on Alfred Street, at some time or other in his boyhood, acquired a Sooner Dog and employed it with satisfaction until discovery and confiscation took place. Sooner Dogs, I have reason to believe, are still obtainable in this republic; but nowadays, of course, they are popular only in the most remote and degraded communities.

The early morning excess of patriotism, which was an unvarying Fourth of July visitation, declined for want of ammunition, long before breakfast time. Only the thrifty conserved their firecrackers for use later on. Most of us were disconsolately bereft of the means of celebration by half-past-six, and it seemed an incalculable time from then till sundown, when the family supply of fireworks was to be expended in a silent but spectacular display. So the Fourth of July, after its brave beginning, usually turned into one of the least exhilarating holidays of the year. It necessarily involved a 12 or 13 hour stretch with nothing to do at all. Compared with Christmas, the incomparable, or Thanksgiving, the day of surfeit, it was a remarkably dull time; although it had been anticipated for months and had absorbed all our savings through a period of denial beginning long before the last day of school. But our patriotism was proof against that annual, summertime frustration and may, indeed, have grown to greater strength in recompense.

I recall for instance, a neighborhood gathering on Washington's Birthday when, with utmost gravity, we sat and attended, while various youthful scholars gave talks on the Landing of the Pilgrims, the Battle of Gettysburg, Valley Forge and the Sinking of the *Maine.* The historical lore exhibited in those addresses may have been questionable; one lad, as example, telling the tale of a "handful" of Yankees, destroying a huge, rebellious host on Gettysburg's bloody acres. But of earnestness there was a plenty.

And none of the young patriots at that gathering was more devoted than the single present descendant of the Red Coat power, who stood up to read what he was pleased to call "an Ode," by himself composed to compliment impartially General Washington and the National Emblem. This work of art, written when its author was just 10 years old, was received with such wondering enthusiasm by all the neighbors of whatever age, that its final stanza is reproduced for the benefit of patriots of a later period.

The "Ode," then, concluded as follows:

> *We love thee, for thy every stripe*
> *Is hued with brightest red;*
> *And thy stars shine above the men*
> *And heroes who are dead,*
> *We love our country, every tree*
> *And every hill and crag;*
> *But most of all do we love thee,*
> *Our own, our native Flag!*

Observe, please, the precocious talent which made a verb of "hue"; the sensible concession that some of the men sleeping beneath Old Glory's folds might not have been heroic; the strongly inspirational reference to American topography; and the paraphrase of a classic in the last line.

Be sure that patriotism was no dead letter, on old Alfred Street!

~ A Grand Old Fourth of July ~

CHET HUNTLEY

In the frontier land of Montana, Chet Huntley began looking forward to the Fourth of July as soon as the memories of Christmas began to fade. Montana and the Fourth seem a natural match to anyone who has beheld the beauty of the land and the ruggedness of the people.

On the Fourth of July there was certain to be a celebration somewhere. One year it was held at the little forlorn village of Whitewater, near the border. Another time it was in Saco, but frequently it was held in the grove of trees along the Milk River.

We children began to anticipate the Fourth about the time the memories of Christmas had faded. There was the inevitable rodeo, usually a baseball game, perhaps a fabulous band which played real music in an improvised bandstand gaily decorated with bunting, and from which the congressman or the country agricultural agent delivered his Fourth of July address. There were foot races for men, women and boys; potato races, sack races and backing-up races for Model T's. Carnival entrepreneurs appeared with little booths in which the customer threw baseballs at various targets and won kewpie dolls. There were booths where rings were thrown over the heads of canes and the canes had various denominations of currency attached to them. Operators of the old shell game were there, and there were shooting galleries and early varieties of bingo. One year there was a concession in which the men threw baseballs at a target, and if they hit the bull's eye it tripped a mechanism, causing a heavily painted young woman to be thrown backward off her perch far enough to reveal her bottom for an instant. Grandma caught me observing that one and hustled me away. She almost demanded to see the man in charge of the picnic for an explanation of what that hussy was doing on the grounds. The ranch families brought huge picnic lunches and ate them in the shade of the big trees. There were refreshment stands with hot dogs, lemonade, ice cream and cotton candy for sale. I dipped into my savings to buy a few firecrackers and made a pest out of myself until they had been exploded. At night there was a fireworks display, then the grove was turned into magic as the Japanese lanterns were lit, an orchestra struck up, and the couples were whirled on the improvised floor. Grandpa was the best "caller" of the square dance in the entire area, and he would send the couples through the promenade, then "gents to the inside and ladies to the out," and call for "the grand right and left." It was all so great, so grand, so noisy, that a small country boy could barely endure it.

The Story of "The Star-Spangled Banner"

JAMES PARTON

Everyone enjoys Fourth of July fireworks and festivity. But how much brighter the display would be if we were to envision the bombs bursting in air that inspired the song that binds all Americans together, "The Star-Spangled Banner." Today few people know the inspiration behind our national anthem. Yet a few verses vividly capture the American spirit of our country's early years. This recounting, written in 1885, explains the events leading up to the fateful night when our fledgling country's independence hung in the balance and tells why a brilliant burst of fireworks in the sky should touch each one of our hearts.

A piece of news was borne across the Atlantic Ocean in May, 1814, which chilled with apprehension every American heart: Napoleon Bonaparte had been overcome by the allied armies of Europe, and was safely imprisoned on the island of Elba!

This intelligence notified the American people that the fleets and armies of Great Britain, which for twelve years had been waging war with France, were now disengaged, and would have little to do, and would be free to overwhelm and crush the Republic of the United States.

We were then in the second year of that contest with Great Britain which we still call the War of 1812. It was a summer of alarm, and the whole coast was alive with the bustle of defensive preparation.

The invasion came. The enemy's ships entered Chesapeake Bay about the first of June, a fleet of frigates and lighter vessels.

In August Admiral Cockburn entered the bay in a great ship of eight guns, bringing with him a fleet and three or four thousand soldiers, which increased the British force in those waters to twenty-three men-of-war and an army of ten thousand troops and marines.

Every one knows what followed. The country was invaded, Washington was sacked and pillaged and its public building burned. The enemy retired with considerable loss, it is true, but triumphant and exulting.

It was a dearly-bought victory, for it silenced opposition to the war, kindled the national feeling, and enlisted every heart in the country's defense.

A few days after, the British forces made their second attempt upon that coast. Baltimore, then a city of forty thousand inhabitants, enriched by the prosperous commerce of the last quarter of a century, would have been a valuable prize, and would have given the foe a hold of the shores of the Chesapeake, from which they would have been dislodged with difficulty. Washington was but a straggling village, without military value. Baltimore was a commanding position, capable of being defended.

Two miles below the city, on a point of land jutting into the water, stood then, and now stands, Fort McHenry, so named for one of the early statesmen of Maryland. Sturdy arms and willing hearts had been laboring there for many weeks, to strengthen its fortifications and get additional guns into position, under the direction of Lieutenant-Colonel George Armistead.

The time had been well employed, and the gallant commander had a modest confidence in his ability to repel the imposing fleet of Cockburn, which now consisted of more than forty vessels, and carried seven thousand troops. The fate of Baltimore depended absolutely upon his holding this position.

The star-spangled banner which floated over the fort had been made by a lady of Baltimore, Mrs. Mary Pickergill, aided by her daughter. These ladies, full of the patriotic feeling of the hour, made a flag worthy of the importance of the occasion. It contained four hundred yards of bunting. It was so large that the ladies were obliged to spread it out in the malt-house of a neighboring brewery.

When Mrs. Pickergill's daughter was an old lady of seventy-six years, she used to describe the scene.

"I remember," she wrote, "seeing my mother down on the floor placing the stars. After the completion of the flag she superintended the topping of it, having it fastened in the most secure manner to prevent its being torn away by balls. The wisdom of her precaution was shown during the engagement, many shots piercing it, but it still remained firm to the staff. . . . My mother worked many nights until twelve o'clock to complete it in a given time."

The reader will see in a moment the significance of this statement. But for the firm and faithful stitching of these two patriotic ladies, we should probably have had no song of the Star-Spangled Banner.

September the sixth, the great British fleet left its anchorage in Chesapeake Bay and sailed for Baltimore; and entered the Patapsco River, upon which the city stands, five days after. Twelve miles below Baltimore, they landed seven thousand men. Happily, the brave Marylanders and Pennsylvanians were ready for them.

Three thousand militiamen, volunteers from Maryland and Pennsylvania, commanded by General John Stricker, well-posted and well-entrenched, withstood this great force, killed their commander, General Ross, and forced them finally to abandon the attack.

While these events were occurring, the great vessels in the British fleet moved up the river, anchored before Fort McHenry, and began to pour upon it that tempest of shot, shell and rockets, which the author of our song has commemorated. Every gun was heard in Baltimore. We can well imagine the feelings of its inhabitants during the twenty-four hours of its continuance.

The author of the song, Francis Scott Key, was not a combatant in the battle, although he witnessed it from beginning to end. During the first operations on that coast Admiral Cockburn and several officers of the British army occupied as their head-quarters a house at Marlborough, belonging to an aged physician of the place, Dr. Beanes, whom they detained as a prisoner lest he should send news of their landing to Baltimore.

He was a particular friend of Mr. Key and of his family. Hearing that the doctor was about to be carried off by the enemy, Key obtained permission from the commanding general of the American forces to go to the British fleet under a flag of truce, and make an attempt to procure the old gentleman's release. In a letter to his mother, written just as he was about to start upon this errand of friendship, he wrote, "I hope to return in about eight or ten days, though it is uncertain, as I do not know where to find the fleet."

He set sail from Baltimore about the third of September, and found the British fleet at the mouth of the Patuxent, bound for the attack on Fort McHenry. He went on board the vessel of Admiral Cockburn, to whom he stated his errand, and asked for the release of Dr. Beanes.

The admiral received him with utmost civility, but informed him that he could not comply at present with his request, and was obliged even to detain Key himself and his vessel until the operation upon Fort McHenry was concluded.

The admiral's vessel being over-crowded, he sent the American gentlemen on board of the frigate *Surprise,* commanded by his son, Sir Thomas Cochrane; where they spent the night, and thus moved on to the attack.

During the bombardment of the fort, Mr. Key and his friends, including Dr. Beanes, were sent on board their own little vessel under a guard of marines, and thus they were afforded an opportunity to witness the action.

Of all the thousands of human beings within hearing of that bombardment, there was probably not one so fitted by nature and education to be moved by it. Francis S. Key, then thirty-five years of age, a lawyer in good standing at the distinguished bar of his native State, was son of John Ross Key, an officer in the army of the Revolution.

He had been noted from his youth up for the ardor of his patriotism, and he had attempted more than once to celebrate in verse the gallant deeds of his countrymen. He had a habit of dashing down lines and stanzas that occurred to him on any odd scrap of paper that came first to his hand, and several of his poems were gathered up by his friends from the litter of his office.

All day the bombardment continued without cessation. During the whole night they remained on deck, following with their eyes the continuous arcs of fire from the enemy's ships to the fort.

The anxiety of the poet, and the little company of Americans about him, grew only more intense when darkness covered the scene, and they could form no conception of the progress or the probable issue of the strife.

Suddenly, about three in the morning, the firing ceased. As they were anchored at some distance from the British vessels, they were utterly at a loss to interpret this mysterious silence.

Had the fort surrendered?

As they walked up and down the deck of their vessel in the darkness and silence of the night, they kept going to the binnacle to look at their watches to see how many minutes more must elapse before they could discern whether the flag over Fort McHenry was the star-spangled banner, or the union jack of England.

The daylight dawned at length. With a thrill of triumph and gratitude, they saw that "our flag was still there." They soon perceived from many other signs that the attack, both by land and sea, had failed and that Baltimore was safe. They could see with their glasses the wounded troops carried on board the ships, and at last the whole British army re-embarking.

A few minutes after the dawn of that glorious day, when the poet first felt sure of the issue of the battle, the impulse to express his feelings in verse rushed upon him. He found in his pocket a letter, and he wrote upon the back of it the first lines of the song. In the excitement of the hour he could not go on with his task, but he wrote some further brief notes and lines upon the letter.

Some lines he retained in his memory without making any record of them. When his guard of marines left him free to hoist anchor, and sail for the city, he wrote out the song on the way, very nearly as it now reads, and on reaching his hotel in Baltimore, he made a clean copy of it.

The next morning he showed it to his brother-in-law, Judge Nicholson, Chief Justice of Maryland, who, judge as he was, had commanded a company of volunteers in Fort McHenry during the bombardment.

We may be sure that *such* a judge read the song with no critical eye. So delighted was he with it, that he sent it round to a printer, Benjamin Edes, who had also commanded a company of troops in the late operations. An apprentice, Samuel Sands, instantly set it in type, and in less than an hour it was distributed all over the city of Baltimore, received by every one with enthusiasm.

But what is a song without music? An old Baltimore soldier told in after years how the words came to be so happily wedded to the music to which it has ever since been sung.

A group of volunteers lay scattered over one of the green hills near Baltimore a day or two after the bombardment.

"Have you heard Francis Key's poem?" said a member of the company, who had just come in from the town.

He took a copy of it from his pocket, and read it aloud to them as they lay upon the grass. It was called for again. He read it a second time, and a third, more soldiers gathering about to hear it, until the whole regiment seemed to be present.

An actor, named Ferdinand Durang, who was also a soldier, sprang up, rushed into a tent, seized his brother's music-book, used by both of them for their flutes, examined piece after piece and at length cried out—"Boys, I have hit it!"

He had selected the air of a favorite old English song, called "To Anacreon in Heaven," written by John Stafford Smith, about the year 1772. It was composed for a musical club which met at the Crown and Anchor tavern in London, frequented by Dr. Johnson and Sir Johua Reynolds.

As soon as Ferdinand Durang had selected the music, he mounted a stool, and sung it to his assembled comrades with all the fire and spirit of which he was capable. An eye-witness says, "How the men shouted and clapped! for never was there a wedding of poetry to music made under such inspiring influences. Getting a brief furlough, the Brothers Durang sang it in public soon after. It was caught up in the camps, and sung around the bivouac fires, and whistled in the streets; and when peace was declared, and we scattered to our homes, it was carried to thousands of firesides as the most precious relic of the War of 1812."

The flag of Fort McHenry, which inspired the song of Francis Key, still exists in a tolerable state of preservation. Colonel Armistead caused it to be taken down from the staff after the battle, and its honorable wounds bound about by the very ladies who had made it. It was ever after carefully preserved.

He left it to his widow, who in turn bequeathed it to their youngest daughter, born under it in Fort McHenry after the bombardment; and she in turn left it to her son, Mr. Eban Appleton, of Yonkers, New York, who now possesses it.

It was raised over Fort McHenry for the last time September 14, 1824, at the reception of Gen. Lafayette.

The author of the song died at Baltimore, in 1843, aged sixty-four years, and in 1857 a small volume of his poems was published in the city of New York. He has living descendants.

❧ The Star-Spangled Banner ❧

Francis Scott Key

Oh, say, can you see by the dawn's early light,
What so proudly we hailed at the twilight's last gleaming?
Whose broad stripes and bright stars, through the perilous fight,
O'er the ramparts we watched were so gallantly streaming?
And the rockets' red glare, the bombs bursting in air,
Gave proof through the night that our flag was still there.
Oh, say, does that star-spangled banner yet wave
O'er the land of the free and the home of the brave?

On the shore, dimly seen through the mists of the deep,
Where the foe's haughty host in dread silence reposes,
What is that which the breeze, o'er the towering steep,
As it fitfully blows, half conceals, half discloses?
Now it catches the gleam of the morning's first beam,
In full glory reflected now shines on the stream.
'Tis the star-spangled banner! Oh, long may it wave
O'er the land of the free and the home of the brave!

And where is that band who so vauntingly swore
That the havoc of war and the battle's confusion
A home and a country should leave us no more?
Their blood has washed out their foul footsteps' pollution.
No refuge could save the hireling and slave
From the terror of flight, or the gloom of the grave:
And the star-spangled banner in triumph doth wave
O'er the land of the free and the home of the brave!

Oh, thus be it ever, when freemen shall stand
Between their loved homes and the war's desolation!
Blessed with victory and peace, may the heaven-rescued land
Praise the Power that hath made and preserved us a nation.
Then conquer we must, when our cause it is just,
And this be our motto, "In God is our trust,"
And the star-spangled banner in triumph shall wave
O'er the land of the free and the home of the brave!

~ The Land of the Free ~

What does the Fourth of July mean to you? Does it mean a picnic, fireworks, celebrations, parades? We all know that what we are celebrating is the anniversary of the signing of the Declaration of Independence in Philadelphia in 1776. Even though we did not officially become a nation at that time, this date signifies our intent to break away from Great Britain and start our own country, free from monarchy. So as you read the following poems, keep in mind that we live in the greatest country on earth, an ever-changing nation that can continue to be the land of the free for as long as its citizens continue to be brave.

~ The Boy and the Flag ~

EDGAR A. GUEST

I want my boy to love his home,
His Mother, yes, and me:
I want him, wheresoe'er he'll roam,
With us in thought to be.
I want him to love what is fine,
Nor let his standards drag,
But, Oh! I want that boy of mine
To love his country's flag!

I want him when he older grows
To love all things of earth;
And Oh! I want him when he knows,
To choose the things of worth.
I want him to the heights to climb
Nor let ambition lag;
But, Oh! I want him all the time
To love his country's flag.

I want my boy to know the best,
I want him to be great;
I want him in Life's distant West,
Prepared for any fate.
I want him to be simple, too,
Though clever, ne'er to brag,
But, Oh! I want him, through and through,
To love his country's flag.

I want my boy to be a man,
    And yet, in distant years,
I pray that he'll have eyes that can
    Not quite keep back the tears
When, coming from some foreign shore
    And alien scenes that fag,
Borne on its native breeze, once more
    He sees his country's flag.

~ Rites of Young Patriots ~

*SUSAN ROSE

All of you came to spend the night
so you could gather Queen Anne's Lace
from the roadside at dusk,
bring it to the well-house bench
where half-gallon jars stood filled,
colored red and blue
by pills left from dyeing Easter eggs.

All of you ran next morning to look,
to see insipid pink
where you had hoped for red,
a disappointing greenish-blue
and some stems that had simply
drooped and died.
Lawrence, botanist-philosopher at five, told me
the only color you could count on was the purple speck.

All of you stood on the porch steps, hands over hearts,
and while Pa-pa raised the flag, you pledged allegiance,
led by whichever grandchild was youngest
and could repeat it without prompting.
Do you remember the year it was Sarah's turn—
she was convulsed with giggles—
and how Pa-pa from the top step conducted
"O beautiful for Spacious Skies!"

I thought you had forgotten those days
until you called from Boston

to wish me a Happy Fourth of July,
say you were looking forward to the fireworks
and ask if the Queen Anne's Lace
was blooming by the roadside near the mailbox.

— Fourth of July in the Olden Time —

J. L. HERRING

There wasn't much made over the Stars and Stripes in the years following the Civil War when the rough and ready men of the Georgia wire-grass country and their families got together for their midsummer celebration. It was the Confederate flag that lingered in their memory. But the tradition of the Fourth of July gathering continued nonetheless, complete with the obligatory patriotic speech, barbecue, and an old-fashioned dance for the young at heart.

"Oh, Lordy, Ma; Jack Kilcrease has drunk seventeen cups o' coffee, and now it's all gone."

The plaintive wail of the bereaved caused some of the eaters nearby to turn their heads and look, but their attention was brief. Four or five deep, they stood by long lines of tables, the men outside, the women inside, with hands full of barbecued meat and cornbread, jaws working, and pocketknives cutting from time to time liberal portions to supply the vacancy the expanded swallows created.

The one feature of the festival of forty years ago in which time has wrought little change is the barbecue. There is a difference in detail now, but the essentials are about the same as half a century gone.

Then there was not much of a display of Old Glory, for too many men were alive to whom the flag brought unpleasant memories; but the speech was pretty much the same; the barbecue almost the same —only the people were different.

The beeves, the hogs, the goats and the sheep had been killed the day before, and brought in by the contributors during the afternoon. In the long pits fires of oak wood, hauled from a distant grove, had been burning all day; now a bed of embers glowed their length. Near by there was a burning heap of oak logs, to replace the coals from time to time.

On spits of oak laid across the pits, the meat rested—usually a quarter of beef cut in half; a hog, sheep or goat split lengthwise. Under this, all night the fires were kept going, the meat being turned occasionally as it slowly cooked. It was this deliberate, gradually broiling process, that gave the barbecue its flavor. From time to time the chief cook's first assistant passed up one side and down the other of the pits, and with a mop on a short handle basted the roasting meat from a bucket containing salt, pepper, and various seasoning condiments. For barbecue in those days was seasoned in the cooking.

All night long the cooks kept their vigil, for constant supervision was the price of well-cooked meats, and on the cook the success of the day depended.

Many were the yarns told—principally personal recollections of the war just passed, for usually it was veterans who were supervising the cooking—during the night around the fire. When morning came, the cooks were gaunt-faced and egg-eyed, but their task was not done, for the meat must be cooked up to the hour the tables were placed, and then the fire withdrawn just in time to allow the meat to cool enough to cut.

About nine o'clock the crowd began to arrive. They came in buggies, a few in two-horse wagons, but a great many in horse-carts, the man on the horse, the family balanced in the cart over the axle; still others on horseback, but a great many, hundreds in fact, on foot, for little was thought of a ten-mile walk in those days.

After each newcomer had made a round of inspection of the barbecue pits, each expressing his opinion of how it ought to be done, they gathered under the shade of the pines, to swap gossip and neighborhood news, trade horses, or crack jokes.

There was a lemonade stand with its hardworked force, for ice had been hauled many miles, at great expense, and the weak compound was swallowed more for the cooling "kick" than for any ingredients it was supposed to contain. Of watermelons there were none, for they did not ripen so early then.

Near the stand were many boys, with long breeches and watering mouths, gazing on what they had not the money to buy. They had been the rounds of the pits, inhaling the savory odor of the cooking meats until hunger drove away even the smart from bare feet that had incautiously stepped on live coals.

Only too close by was the grocery, where stronger liquors were sold, and where later in the day a row started which afterwards bereaved two families.

A small platform had been built, covered with brush and floored with borrowed plank. Here the orator of the day held forth. The Fourth of July speech then was much the speech of today. The tail feathers of the eagle were yanked until the bird of freedom screamed, and the adherents of the more or less famous politician applauded according to their devotion or enthusiasm, liquid or mental, while the urchins looking on and understanding not, wished he would quit, so dinner could come. The babies cried, the young folks courted, a group near by laughed at a joke, sundry matrons swapped confidences and dipped snuff—all within plain hearing of the speaker who heroically stuck to the job.

Everything must end, and at last the speaking was over. Up from the pits, tubs and cedar piggins of the meat were carried and distributed along the tables, these innocent of even paper covering. There was no Brunswick stew in those days; no pickles, nor trimmings, but the [pie] was there in abundance for every man to eat his fill, and for many of the provident to carry off a supply against the day to come.

The housewives had brought great stacks of pone cornbread—there was no baker's bread to be had—and this was cut and distributed with the meats. Then the wives brought forward trunks and baskets and from these what looked like an inexhaustible supply of good things to eat, and added them to the cue on the tables. Many could not miss, even for a meal, the cup of coffee, and to supply them, pots had been set on the coals near the pits until their contents boiled. It was when he diminished the supply in sight that a thirsty citizen provoked the boy to protest.

Those people did not know much of the delicacies, but they brought to the meal appetites of plowhands and the digestions of rail-splitters. It was no small task to feed them but the men in charge knew what to provide for, and at last they were fed. Then hot-foot for the well, and crowd and push for the water that after all is the only perfect quencher of thirst.

After dinner, the speaker gone, the platform gave place to the fiddlers, the straw-beaters, the caller and the dancing couples. Despite the July heat, despite the perspiration that made rags of the home-laundered shirts and collars and caused the color to "run" in many a beloved calico dress, until the shades of evening drove them home, the dancing went on, ever-changing individuals, but the same thing in form. There we leave them, the old folks hitching up for the homeward journey, the young folks still stepping lively to the jingling tune of the "Arkansaw Traveler," or one of his many kindred, or:

> *Johnny, get your hair cut, hair cut, hair cut,*
> *Johnny, get your hair cut, shave and shine,*
> *Johnny, get your hair cut, hair cut, hair cut;*
> *Johnny, get your hair cut, just like mine.*

~ Our Uncle Sam ~

"Just where did Uncle Sam come from?" the eager-faced kid asked. It took a little searching to find the answer, but here it is. The tall, lanky, red-, white-, and blue-outfitted Uncle Sam we know today was drawn from the character, "Brother Jonathan," in The Contrast, *America's first comedy, written by Royall Tyler. It debuted in New York in 1787.*

~ The Tradition Continues ~

TIPPY CANOES (AND SPLINTERS, TOO)

HAMPTON SIDES

While others are puttering around on their sailboats and yachts, a group of hardy preservationists are keeping alive that relic of colonial days, the Chesapeake log canoe. Hampton Sides gives us the background of this endangered species and then takes us along on the annual Fourth of July race on the Miles River in St. Michaels, Maryland.

Log canoes trace their lineage back to the Indians of the Chesapeake, who were known to hack their Stout vessels from whole tree trunks. (It's not clear, however, where they stood on the question of the six-second handicap.) When Captain John Smith explored the Chesapeake in 1608, he was surprised to find 50-foot canoes that would bear as many as 40 men. "These they make of one tree," he noted, "by burning and scratching away the coles with stones and shells, till they have made it in the forme of a Trough."

If somewhat crude in construction, those dugouts could not be faulted for their seaworthiness or speed; Capt. Smith marveled that they "will row faster than our barges." Soon the colonists had adapted the Indian technique, fashioning craft from several logs instead of one and adding sails. With proud faded names like *Persistence, Tenacious* and *Flying Cloud,* the log canoes have acutely rigged masts, stiletto sterns and prows, and entirely too much canvas for their own good. And because they have no weighted keel, they're extremely tippy and prone to capsize. This is where the boards figure in. To counterbalance their exaggerated heel, lag canoes make use of long "hiking" planks that are cantilevered over the windward side of the boat. In response to shifting winds, the crew members (specifically, "boardmen") shinny up and down these varnished sticks of lumber, practicing the fine art of human ballast.

During the ante-bellum period, most Eastern Shore plantations had slaves skilled in canoe construction and maintenance. Over time, the log canoe became a kind of riverine pickup truck, used by oyster tongers and commercial fishermen to navigate the shoals and narrows of the bay. When the British blockaded the Chesapeake during the War of 1812, the swift, shallow-draft canoe proved crucial in eluding the enemy.

Log-canoe racing is said to have started informally among commercial fishermen: At the close of the day, the first waterman to reach the docks with his catch got the premium price. The earliest recorded race was sailed off St. Michaels in 1859. The owner of the pokiest boat was awarded a ham skin, "so he could grease her and do better next time."

In 1880, the U.S. Census reported 6,300 log canoes on the Chesapeake. But with the arrival of steam (and then gasoline) engines, the sailing vessels were left to rot in weedy coves and marshes. By the 1930s, log canoes were used only for recreational sailing, and their future was uncertain. "The sport of racing seems doomed," lamented M. V. Brewington in his definitive 1937 book, *Chesapeake Log Canoes.* "Probably less than ten men are now living who are capable of turning out a successful canoe. They whose knowing eyes and skilled hands brought the canoe to the height of its perfection are fast going."

Today, at the first puff of wind, we immediately sense the boat heeling, like some prehistoric beast turning in its sleep. It's unsettling to be in a vessel this large that's also this precarious, and I instantly understand why log canoes are made exclusively for river sailing: They'd soon flip in the open waters and heavier winds of the Chesapeake Bay.

Now Captain Penwell is yelling, "Out, Out, out!" We boardmen slam the 16-foot-long hiking boards into place under the inside lip of the leeward gunwale, and scramble halfway up the boards on the windward side. "I mean *all the way out!*" Penwell cries, grimacing at the water pouring in. Now we lean farther out over the water, feeling the cool spray on our dangling legs. For a moment the boat has righted herself, and Penwell is tolerably happy. But suddenly the wind shifts again, forcing *Jay Dee* to tack. We scramble madly back down the planks, but not quickly enough to avoid getting soaked by the waterline that has suddenly risen to meet us. We must reverse ourselves— removing the heavy boards, lodging them in the other side and scooting back out. And so it goes, all afternoon, this frantic seesaw game with wind and water.

To be in a log canoe is to be ill at ease. Something is always in need of desperate correction. Every moment is lived with the awareness that catastrophe is imminent. It's not a sport for holiday cruisers, gin-and-tonics in hand. Stay on a log canoe long enough and you'll get ulcers.

Right now, though, mostly what we're getting is blisters, bad ones, and they're smarting all the worse from the constant gush of salt water. Still, we boardmen have begun to develop a kind of galley-slave camaraderie, and the suffering somehow feels good, or at least less bad, for the sharing.

What in the beginning had felt awkward and unsteady has become intuitive. I've begun to develop a sixth sense for the caprice of the wind and the answered heavings of the canoe, and I imagine myself as a bubble floating in a mason's level.

At times, when *Jay Dee* is planing smoothly and the sails are full, there is a faint hum that seems to emanate from somewhere deep in the hull, as if the ghosts of the old boatwrights were sighing with content. That's what I'm hearing at least, as my mind begins to drift on this crystalline day on the Miles. But a boardman can't afford to daydream. The wind comes around, and Penwell is all over us again —"Out! Out! Out! *All the way out!*" Later, at the bar, a few of us boardmen from the *Jay Dee* close out the afternoon comparing blisters, strawberries and other honorable flesh wounds.

"Ooooooh."

"Nice!"

"Very tasty."

Now the two last log canoes straggle in from the Miles and glide to their respective slips. An elderly St. Michaels woman, wife of one of the more avid sailors, has been sitting at the bar watching the boats return, and she interrupts our little dermatology seminar. "Look at them," she says to me, her eyes nearly brimming with tears. "They're like swans. For us, summer doesn't start out here until the first race of the season. And today we know it's finally summer—because the swans are back."

Appalachia's Annual Anvil Shoot

Until recently revived at the Museum of Appalachia, in Norris, Tennessee, few people had ever heard of an anvil shoot, let alone seen the dramatic event. This method of celebration is deeply rooted in our country's history. Tradition says that it was used to celebrate the nation's independence, Christmas, and even Davy Crockett's election to the U.S. Congress. Also early settlers reportedly fired anvils in hopes of making Indians believe it was cannon fire.

Anvil shooting involves placing one anvil upside down on the ground and filling its cavity with a fine grade of black powder. A second anvil is placed upright on top of the first anvil. The powder is ignited by a fuse. The top anvil is thrust some forty to sixty feet into the air. The earth literally shakes; and the deafening boom, it is said, can be heard as far away as fifteen miles.

~ An Out-of-Doors Holiday ~

Reading the many traditions sent in about Fourth of July celebrations, you see one thread runs through them all. Just as we dream of a white Christmas, we hope for a sunny Fourth.

Our family doesn't play softball very often, but every Fourth of July on our Vermont farm we have a big game in the middle of the afternoon.

Grandchildren, grandparents, friends, neighbors, the summer minister and family and whoever else come to the newly mown hayfield for "the game." The all-age crowd arrives with dogs, mitts, lounge chairs, jugs of water and lemonade, and every kind of hat. Players range from two to ninety, and teams are evened out. After the game, we usually have a swim in the pond, followed by a potluck picnic.

The softball game has been a family tradition for twenty-one years now, ever since Granny picked a Fourth of July afternoon to die of cancer. She held out till all the family had arrived for the weekend and had gone out to play the first family game of softball. When the game was over, word quietly spread up and down the valley that she had died. Ever since then the "big game" brings us all together to celebrate summer.

Cheers!

Susan Urstadt

The Fourth of July is a very special day because it is my birthday and America's birthday. Every morning on the Fourth of July, my mom cooks pancakes. One of these pancakes has the age I am. After I eat my pancakes, I have a party and invite all my friends. At the end, I open my presents that my friends give me, and at nighttime we go see fireworks and they go *boooom!*

Jennifer Leech, elementary school

Today is July Fourth, our country's birthday and my sister's birthday. In my family, we have a tradition of celebrating birthdays. Our tradition is when a child in the family has a birthday, the uncles, aunts, grandparents, and cousins come to my grandparents' house. We have a big dinner and cake, too! I like it because this tradition is ours only.

Jessica Honea, elementary school

On Independence Day my family and I travel to Youngsville, North Carolina. That's where my dad's family has a family reunion. Actually we go a few days before. My aunt and uncle own a farm. It's huge, with cows, horses, chickens, dogs, and even a bull.

The first thing we do when we arrive is find our aunt and uncle. They give us a program. The program tells us about the activities and the times and places they occur. It also contains a map of the rooms and campsites where different families stay. My family always stays in the blue guesthouse. Usually my sister arrives first, so my sister, brother, and I get straight to work helping everyone prepare for a week of fun and excitement.

On Independence Day we all go down to the big lake. Everyone takes a seat and watches the show. Bursting fireworks fill the sky with a colorful sensation that makes you feel happy that you're there.

Throughout the week everyone is always doing something. On this farm there is no such thing as boredom. We ride horses, play tennis, basketball, golf, go on nature walks, and tons more. One particular activity that takes place is the talent show. This year my cousin and I did a tap duet to "Jump, Shout, Boogie." Everyone enjoys this part of the reunion.

By the time the week is over, everyone is exhausted. We always dread the long drive back to our hometown.

This is my favorite family tradition because everyone enjoys and has the most fun when you're around the people we know, love, and trust most.

Shelly Shoe, elementary school

Every year, my daddy's family gets together on the Fourth of July to celebrate Independence Day. We go to my uncle Mike's house in Raeford. Family members also come from Florida. We participate in all kinds of pool games, like pool volleyball, and diving and splashing contests. There is much enjoyment as we splash the cool blue water on each other. We cook thick, juicy hamburgers and hot dogs, and lots of other good foods. It is always a part of our tradition to eat a juicy red watermelon, which is grown by my uncle in his garden. Finally we all go see the fireworks at Aberdeen Lake. The red, beautiful fireworks explode in the air. A joyful feeling goes through my body.

Justin Walters, elementary school

On the Fourth of July every summer, I go to the beach with my family. I go swimming with my mama or my uncle Louie. We all sit out on our deck at night to watch firecrackers. Every time one comes up, I jump. I like it!

Jordan Phillips, elementary school

Around July Fourth, the Funderburk family flies into Myrtle Beach from as far away as New Orleans and Seattle to participate in the family reunion. The highlight of our weekend is entering the Fourth of July boat parade. The children think of slogans to express that year's theme, while my aunts gather costumes and decorations. Grandma buys everything from pajamas to pinwheels decorated with an American motif. The boat is transformed into a patriotic vessel with sparkly streamers, balloons, and wind socks. Once my sister and I even tap-danced in American flag bathing suits on a platform my uncle made, while the rest of the family sang.

About 11:00 A.M. on July Fourth we line up our tour de force among the other gaily decorated boats. As we move by the crowds, everyone smiles and sings loudly. Afterward we eat a red, white, and blue dessert while waiting for a telephone call. Last year the call came and we were thrilled to receive second place in the Most Patriotic division. This year we didn't win an award, but our picture appeared in the *Sun News*.

My family's Fourth of July tradition is special because we unite as a family that is usually separated by thousands of miles. Winning the boat parade is not important; it is the time we get to spend together that is valuable.

Our Fourth of July celebration is more than an expression of the American spirit. It is an expression of the American family and the love that holds it together across the miles.

Jill M. Pelhan, high school

To Capture a Moment
in America's History

*LIZ SEYMOUR

Looking for a way to capture the historical importance and reverence our forefathers felt for this most patriotic of all American holidays? Read how Liz Seymour's family has put meaning into the day without sacrificing any of the fun.

In 1959 when my parents and my aunt and uncle began getting their families together on Cape Cod we could all squeeze into one wide-bodied Rambler station wagon, but our extended family has long since outgrown both the Rambler and the weathered old house that we used to rent on the dunes. We still get together every summer, but now we stay prosaically and comfortably in a motel on Route 6 and go to the beach every day in a caravan of rental cars and family vans.

The reunion always takes place over the long Fourth of July weekend. It has become so much a part of our lives that time and place have merged: we talk of "going to the Fourth of July," of events happening "during Cape Cod." Widely scattered now up and down the East Coast and on both sides of the Atlantic, we can seldom all make it to the Fourth of July at once, but we stay in touch and compare notes year after year. The numbers may change, we have discovered, the weekend may be a little hotter or a little cooler than it was the year before, a new baby or a new spouse may have joined the group (or, sadly, left it), but the essential rhythm never varies.

On the evening of the Fourth itself we carry our chairs and coolers down the long wooden steps to Nauset Beach. We set up in a semicircle facing the ocean with an American flag planted in our midst and make toasts to each other with rum and fried clams. As we talk, the sky over the ocean turns pink and the foamy waves take on an incandescence in the afterglow of the sunset. Our shadows grow longer and longer on the sand in front of us until the sun disappears over the dunes and all the shadows are swallowed up in the dusk. Up the beach the gigantic lantern of Nauset Light begins its stately revolutions.

Before the light is completely gone, my uncle pulls out a bound copy of the Declaration of Independence and passes it down the line. The person sitting at the end of the row begins: "When in the Course of human events, it becomes necessary . . ." The children run up from the water's edge and take their places, getting help with the hard words: "We hold these truths to be self-evident, that all men are created equal, that they are endowed by their Creator with certain unalienable Rights . . ." In the twilight we hold a flashlight over the page to see the words: "that among these are Life, Liberty and the pursuit of Happiness."

The Declaration goes up the circle, each person reading a couple of sentences: hesitant childish voices, ringing oratorical voices, ironic teenage voices, shy voices, puzzled voices, flamboyant voices. Thanks to our visitors over the years we have heard Thomas Jefferson's beautiful words in a French accent, a German accent, a Mexican accent, and even in the clipped accent of Great Britain itself. When we come to the end of the circle we just send it around again until we come to the ringing conclusion: "And for the support of this Declaration, with a firm reliance on the protection of Divine Providence, we mutually pledge to each other our Lives, our Fortunes and our sacred Honor."

Then we read the names, listed alphabetically in our edition, cheering for the signers from our own states; the last name, always read with great flourish and applause, is George Wythe of Virginia, the man who taught law to Thomas Jefferson. Before he puts the book away, my uncle records the date on the end paper; visitors, new spouses, and children who have just learned to read are noted in the back.

It's usually dark by the time we climb the stairs, sleeping babies over our shoulders and a chill evening wind blowing up the beach. The next day or the day after, we say good-bye and go back to the various places that the pursuit of happiness has taken us. The Declaration, shaken clean of sand, returns to a shelf in Connecticut. It's not a bad thing to be reminded occasionally that it is the mutual pledge of independence and interdependence declared two hundred and twenty years ago in Philadelphia that makes a nation, or a family, or a world go.

THERE MAY NOT BE MUCH LIBERTY
AROUND THE WORLD TODAY
BUT ALWAYS BY THE GRACE OF GOD
WE HAVE THE U.S.A.
AND WHILE THE STARS AND STRIPES STILL FLY
ALL PEOPLES MAY BE SURE
THAT JUSTICE, TRUTH, EQUALITY
AND FREEDOM WILL ENDURE.
AS LONG AS WE HAVE WISDOM AND
WE KNOW THAT WE ARE RIGHT

AND WE CONTINUE TO MAINTAIN
OUR MILITARY MIGHT
WE DO NOT WANT TO RULE THE WORLD
WITH ALL ITS FERTILE SOD
WE ONLY STRIVE TO CONQUER SOULS
AND BRING THEM BACK TO GOD
WE HOPE WITH ALL OUR HEARTS THAT WE
SHALL LIVE TO SEE THE DAY
WHEN PEACE WILL FLOURISH EVERYWHERE
AS IN OUR U.S.A.

James J. Metcalfe

CHAPTER 12

Halloween

THE GOBLINS WILL GET YOU IF YOU DON'T WATCH OUT!

~ *A Night Meant for Mischief* ~

"It's nice to be a little teeny, tiny bit scared," are the first words of Olive Beaupré Miller's Halloween poem. That's the tingly feeling I love to remember when Halloween rolls around. My idea of a good-time horror show is The Little Shop of Horrors. *Leave those gruesome* Halloween I *and* II *and on ad nauseam films for someone else. Watching Margaret O'Brien's Halloween scene in* Meet Me in St. Louis *makes me as frightened as I want to be, though I have to admit I could be called a lightweight* Rocky Horror Picture Show *groupie.*

Once upon a time Halloween was a lot more fun, or so it seems to me. The frights were tingly, not shattering. That's the spirit that Ray Rheinhart fondly remembers, when the spookiest of nights was filled with mischief in his hometown of Hoboken, New Jersey. That was expected. Halloween was to those adolescent boys more than a holiday. It was one of life's rites of passage.

Hallowe'en Mischief

*RAY RHEINHART

When I was growing up across the Hudson River from midtown Manhattan in Hoboken, New Jersey, just a few years before television taught us differently, Hallowe'en was not a time of trick-or-treating —at least not treating. I can't even remember carved pumpkins, although late October inevitably brought pomegranates (which we called Chinese apples) to the Italian greengrocer on the corner.

No, on the night of October 31 there was only mischief. The adult world could not buy us off with candy or shiny pennies. They didn't even try.

Instead, they braced themselves for the inevitable Walpurgis Night of hyper male adolescents who could barely wait for the sun to go down. Once it was dark, any metal garbage pail left unsecured was unceremoniously tossed down the stone steps that led to the basements of the city's brick and brownstone row houses. The clatter of metal against concrete usually continued right up to midnight. If there was a cast-iron fence around a property, the gates were likely to be stolen. Of course, clean car windows were targets for the milky scrawls of soap bars.

Boys filled socks with flour, knotted the socks, and then chased screaming girls. A blow to the head or shoulders would leave a ghostly print. The prettier the girl, the more likely she was to be dusted with flour. There was no doubt in anyone's mind that this fact was part of the natural order of things.

Some of the older boys from the rougher end of the city would add a handful of rocks to the flour. These instruments of terror tended to be reserved for small boys who quickly developed a scared animal's wariness whenever a male with acne crossed the street in their direction. This, too, was part of the natural order. It wasn't just the adults who prayed for a day of cold rain.

Not until television became a fixture in most of our homes did we learn that kids from Portland, Maine, to Portland, Oregon, were practicing a seasonal extortion. Dressed in all manner of costumes, the children of sitcom parents were going from door to door, offering a choice to the adult world, which they, in turn, seemed (amazingly!) to welcome: Hand over the loot and we won't scatter your garbage.

This instantly struck us as a far more gratifying way of seizing control of the night. With that bite from the televised Tree of Knowledge, Hallowe'en was never the same.

~ A Halloween Party ~

ANNIE FELLOWS JOHNSTON

Other than in a child's book designed for Halloween, I have never seen so many wonderful ideas collected in one place as there are in this one chapter in The Little Colonel's Holidays. *You can glean the ideas while losing yourself in the sort of carefree, wholesome story that you, your mother, or your grandmother used to read on rainy afternoons. I'll wager that by the time you finish this truly haunting and hilarious Halloween tale you'll be ready to re-create many of these wonderful, but sadly now forgotten, Halloween traditions from the turn of the century.*

Nothing worse than rats and spiders haunted the old house of Hartwell Hollow, but set far back from the road in a tangle of vines and cedars, it looked lonely and neglected enough to give rise to almost any report. The long unused road, winding among the rockeries from gate to house, was hidden by a rank growth of grass and mullein. From one of the trees beside it an aged grape-vine swung down its long snaky limbs, as if a bunch of giant serpents had been caught up in a writhing mass and left to dangle from tree-top to earth. Cobwebs veiled the windows, and dead leaves had drifted across the porches until they lay knee-deep in some of the corners.

As Miss Allison paused in front of the doorstep with the keys, a snake glided across her path and disappeared in one of the tangled rockeries. Both the coloured women who were with her jumped back, and one screamed.

"It won't hurt you, Sylvia," said Miss Allison, laughingly. "An old poet who owned this place when I was a child made pets of all the snakes, and even brought some up from the woods as he did the wild flowers. That is a perfectly harmless kind."

"Maybe so, honey," said old Sylvia, with a wag of her turbaned head, "but I 'spise 'em all, I sho'ly do. It's a bad sign to meet up wid one right on de do'step. If it wasn't fo' you, Miss Allison, I wouldn't put foot in such a house. An' I tell you pointedly, what I says is gospel truth, if I ketch sound of a han't, so much as even a rustlin' on de flo', ole Sylvia gwine out'n a windah fo' you kin say scat! Don't ketch dis ole niggah foolin' roun' long whar ghos'es is. Pete's got to go in first an' open de house."

But not even the rats interrupted Sylvia in her sweeping and garnishing, and by four o'clock all the rooms which were to be used were as clean as three of Mrs. MacIntyre's best trained servants could make them.

"Even ole Miss would call that clean," said Sylvia, looking around on the white floors and shining window-panes with a satisfied air.

Mrs. Sherman had driven down some time before, with a carriage-load of jack-o'-lanterns, and was now arranging them in rows on all the old-fashioned black mantels. She looked around as Sylvia spoke.

"It would have been spookier to have left the dust and cobwebs," she said, "but this is certainly nicer and more cheerful."

Fires were blazing on every hearth, in parlour, dining-room, and hall, to dissipate the dampness of the long unused rooms. A kettle was singing on the kitchen stove, and tables and chairs had been brought over and arranged in the empty rooms. All that the woods could contribute in the way of crimson berries, trailing vines, and late autumn leaves had been brought in to brighten the bare walls and festoon the uncurtained windows. The chestnuts, the apples, the tubs of water, the lead, and everything else necessary for the working of the charms was in readiness; the refreshments were in the pantry, and on the kitchen table Lloyd [nicknamed the Little Colonel] was arranging the ingredients for the fate cake.

"There couldn't be a bettah place for a Halloween pahty," she said, looking around the rooms when all was done. "No mattah how much we romp and play, there's nothing that can be hurt. Won't it look shivery when all the jack-o'-lanterns are lighted? Just as if some old ogah of a Bluebeard lived heah, who kept the heads of all his wives and neighbours sittin' around on all the mantels an' shelves."

It was in the ruddy glow of the last bright October sunset that they drove away from the house to go home to dinner. Even then the grounds looked desolate and forlorn; but it was doubly gruesome when they came back at night. The Little Colonel and her mother were first to arrive. They had offered to come early and light the lanterns, as Miss Allison was expecting all her nieces and nephews on the seven o'clock train, and wanted to go down to meet them.

The wind was blowing in fitful gusts, rustling the dead leaves and swaying the snaky branches of the grape-vine until they seemed startlingly alive. Now and then the moon looked out like a pale bleared eye.

"It is a real Tam O'Shanter night," said Miss Allison, as she led the way up the winding walk to the front door. "I can easily imagine witches flying over my head. Can't you?" she asked, turning to the little group surrounding her. There were eight children. For not only Ranald and his sisters had come with Malcolm and Keith, but Rob Moore and his cousin Anna had been invited to come out from town to try their fortunes at Hartwell Hollow, and spend the night in the Valley where they always passed their happy summers.

"Oh, auntie! What's that?" cried little Elise, holding tightly to Miss Allison's hand, as she caught sight of Lloyd's old Popocatepetl, grinning a welcome by the front door. He looked like a mammoth dragon, spouting fire from nose, eyes, and mouth.

Elise clung a little closer to Miss Allison's side as they drew nearer. "What awful teeth it's got, hasn't it?"

"Nothing but grains of corn, dear. Lloyd stuck them in. You haven't forgotten the Little Colonel, have you? She is inside the house now, waiting to see you." Then Miss Allison turned to the others. "Step high, children, every one of you, when you come to this broomstick lying across the door-sill. Be sure to step over it, or some witch might slip in with you. It is the only way to keep them out on Halloween. Step high, Elise! Here we go!"

"That's one of the nice things about auntie," Kitty confided to Anna Moore as they followed. "She acts as if she really believes those old charms, and that makes them seem so real that we enjoy them so much more."

The Little Colonel, waiting in the hall for the guests to arrive, had been feeling a little shy about renewing her acquaintance with Ranald and his sisters. It seemed to her that they must have seen so much and learned so much in their trip around the world, that they would not care to talk about ordinary matters. But when they all came tumbling in over the broomstick, they seemed to tumble at the same time from the pedestals where her imagination had placed them, back into the old familiar footing just where they had been before they went away.

Lloyd had thought about Ranald many times since Miss Allison's account of him had made him a hero in her eyes. She could not think of him in any way but as dressed in a uniform, riding along under fluttering flags to the sound of martial music. So when Miss Allison called, "Here is the captain, Little Colonel," her face flushed as if she were about to meet some distinguished stranger. But it was the same quiet Ranald who greeted her, much taller than when he went away, but dressed just like the other boys, and not even bronzed by his long marches under the tropical sun. The year that had passed since his return had blotted out all trace of his soldier life in his appearance, except, perhaps, the military erectness with which he held himself.

Kitty, after catching Lloyd by the shoulders for an impulsive hug and kiss, started at once to examine the haunted house. "There'll be mischief brewing in a little bit, I'll promise you," said Miss Allison, as Kitty's head with its short black hair dodged past her, and there was a flash of a red dress up the stairway. "She is looking for the 'ghos'es' that Sylvia told her were up there."

Elise clung to Allison's hand, for the little sister wanted the protection of the big one, in those ghostly-looking rooms, lighted only by the fires and the yellow gleam of those rows of weird, uncanny jack-o'-lantern faces. Like Kitty, both Allison and Elise had big dark eyes that might have been the pride of a Spanish senorita, they were so large and lustrous. Kitty's curls had been cut, but theirs hung thick and long on their shoulders. The sight of them moved Rob to a compliment.

"You and Anna Moore make me think of night and morning," he said, looking from Anna's golden hair to Allison's dusky curls. "One is so light and one is so black. You ought to go around together all the time. You look fine together."

"Rob is growing up," laughed Anne. "Two years ago he wouldn't have thought about making pretty speeches about our hair; he'd just have pulled it."

"Here comes a whole crowd of people," exclaimed Allison, as the door opened again. "I wonder how many of the girls I'll know. Oh, there's Corinne and Katie and Margery and Julia Forrest. Why, nobody seems to have changed a bit. Come on, Lloyd, let's go and speak to them."

"I'm glad that everybody is coming early," said Lloyd, "so that we can begin the fate cake."

That was the first performance. When the guests had all arrived, they were taken into the kitchen. Under the ban of silence (for the speaking of a word would have broken the charm) they stood around the table, giggling as the cake was concocted, out of a cup of salt, a cup of flour, and enough water to make a thick batter. A ring, a thimble, a dime, and a button were dropped into it, and each guest gave the mixture a solemn stir before the pan was put into the oven, and left in charge of old Mom Beck.

By that time the two tubs of water had been carried into the hall. Several dozen apples were set afloat in them, with a folded strip of paper pinned to each bearing a hidden name. By the time these had been lifted out by their stems in the teeth of the laughing contestants, the lead was melted ready to use.

They tried their fate with that next, pouring a little out into a plate of water, to see into what shapes the drops would instantly harden. Strangely enough, Ranald's took the shape of a sword. Malcolm's was a lion and Keith's a ship, the Little Colonel's a star and Rob's a spur. Some could have been called almost anything, like the one little Elise found in her plate. She could not decide whether to call it a sugar-bowl or a chicken. But Miss Allison explained them all, giving some funny meaning to each, and setting them all to laughing with the queer fortunes she declared these lead drops predicted.

They tried all the old customs they had ever heard of. They popped chestnuts on a shovel, they counted apple-seeds, they threw the parings over their heads to see what initials they would form in falling. They blindfolded each other and groped across the room to the table, on which stood three saucers, one filled with ashes, one with water, and one standing empty, to see whether life, death, or single blessedness awaited them in the coming year.

In the midst of these games Kitty beckoned the boys aside and led them out on the porch. "What do you think?" she whispered. "After all the trouble auntie has taken to plan different entertainments, Cora Ferris isn't satisfied. I heard her talking to some of the older girls. She told Eliza Hughes that she expected some excitement when she came, and that she was dying to go down cellar backward with a looking-glass in one hand and a candle in the other. You know if you do that, the person whom you're to marry will come and look over your shoulder, and you can see him in the glass.

"The girls begged her not to, and told her that she'd be frightened to death if she saw anybody, but she whispered to Eliza that she knew she wouldn't be scared, for she was sure Walter Cummins was her fate, and would have to be down in the cellar if she tried the charm, and that she wouldn't be afraid of going into a lion's den if she thought Walter would be there. And Eliza giggled and threatened to tell, and Cora got red and put her hand over Eliza's mouth, and carried on awfully silly. It made me tired. But she's bound to go down cellar after awhile, and somebody has told Walter what she said, and he's going, just for fun. Now I think it would be lots of fun to watch Walter, and keep him from going, on some excuse or another, and then one of you boys look over her shoulder."

"Rob, you're the biggest, and almost as tall as Walter. You ought to be the one to go," suggested Keith.

"Down in that spook cellar?" demanded Rob. "Not much, Keithie, my son. I might see something myself, without the help of a looking-glass or candle. I am not afraid of flesh and blood, but I vow I'm not ready to have my hair turn white in a single night. I have been brought up on stories of the haunts that live in that cellar. My old black mammy used to live here, and she has made me feel as if my blood had turned to ice-water, lots of times, with her tales."

"You go, captain," said Malcolm, turning to Ranald. "You've been under fire, and oughtn't to be afraid of anything. You've got a reputation to keep up, and here is a chance for you to show the stuff you are made of."

"I am not afraid of the cellar," said the little captain, stoutly, "but I'm not going to be the one to look over her shoulder into the looking-glass. I don't want to run any risk of marrying that fat Cora Ferris."

A shout of laughter went up at his answer.

"You won't have to, goosey," said Rob. "There's nothing in those old signs."

"Well, I am not going to take any chances with her," he persisted, backing up against the wall. That settled it. They could have moved the rock foundation of the house itself easier than the captain, when he took that kind of a stand. Looking at it from Ranald's point of view, none of the boys were willing to go down cellar, for they could easily imagine how the others would tease them afterward. Kitty's prank would have fallen through, if she had not been quicker than a weasel at planning mischief.

"What's to hinder fixing up a dummy man, and putting him down there?" she suggested. "You boys can run home and get Uncle Harry's rubber boots, and his old slouch hat, and some pillows, and that military cape that Ginger's father left there, and she'll think it is an army officer that's she's going to marry. Won't she be fooled?"

The boys were as quick to act as Kitty was to plan. A noisy game of blind man's buff was going on inside the house, so no one missed the conspirators, although they were gone for some time.

"We just ran home a minute for something," was Keith's excuse, when he and Malcolm and Ranald came in, red-faced and breathless. Rob and Kitty were still in the cellar, putting the finishing touches to the army officer. Kitty was recklessly fastening the dummy together with big safety-pins, regardless of the holes she was making in her Uncle Harry's high rubber hunting-boots.

"Isn't he a dandy!" exclaimed Rob, putting the slouched hat on the pillow head at a fierce angle, and fastening the military cape up around the chin as far as possible. "Come on now, Kitty, let us make our escape before anybody comes."

Meanwhile, the boys had corralled Walter Cummins, and Cora, seeing him leave the room, thought that the proper time had come. Slipping the hand-mirror from the dressing-table in the room where they had left their wraps, she took a candle from one of the jack-o'-

lanterns on the side porch, and signaled the girls who had agreed to follow her. She was nearly sixteen, but the three girls who groped their way across the courtyard in the flickering light of her candle were much younger.

The cellar was entered from the courtyard, by an old-fashioned door, the kind best adapted to sliding, and it took the united strength of all the girls to lift it. A rush of cold, damp air greeted them, and an earthy smell that would have checked the enthusiasm of any girl less sentimental than Cora.

"I am frightened to death, girls," she confessed at the last moment, her teeth chattering. Yet she was not so frightened as she would have been had she not been sure that Walter had gone down the steps ahead of her.

"Hold the door open," she said, preparing to back slowly down. Her fluffy light hair stood out like an aureole in the yellow candle-light, and the face reflected in the hand-mirror was pretty enough to answer every requirement of the old spell, despite the silly simper on her lips. When she was nearly at the bottom of the cellar steps she began the old rhyme: "If in this glass his face I see, then my true love will marry me."

But the couplet ended in a scream, so terrifying, so ear-splitting, so blood-curdling, that Katie dropped in a cold, trembling little heap on the ground, and Eliza Hughes sank down on top of Katie, weak and shivering. Cora had seen the pillow-man in the cellar. Dropping the looking-glass with a crash, but clinging desperately to the candle, she dashed up the steps shrieking at every breath. Just at the top she stepped on the front of her skirt, and fell sprawling forward. She dropped the candle then, but not before it had touched her hair and set it afire.

The soft fluffy bangs blazed up like tow, and too terrified to move, Eliza Hughes still sat on top of Katie, screaming louder than Cora had done. The sight brought Katie to her senses, however, and scrambling up from under Eliza, she flew at Cora and began beating out the fire with her bare hands. Cora, who had not discovered that her hair was ablaze, did not know what to make of such strange treatment. Her first thought was that Katie had gone crazy with fright, and that was why she had flown at her and begun to beat her on the head. It was all over in an instant, and the fire put out so quickly that only Cora's bangs were scorched, and Katie's fingers but slightly burned.

But the screams had reached through the uproar of blind man's buff, and the whole party poured out into the courtyard to see what had happened. There was great excitement for a little while, and Kitty, enjoying the confusion she had stirred up, giggled as she listened to Cora's startling description of the man that had peeped over her shoulder. "He didn't look like any one I'd ever seen before," she declared. "He was tall and handsome and dressed like a soldier."

"Oh, surely not, Cora," answered Miss Allison, who saw that some of the little girls gathered around her were badly frightened. "That couldn't be, you know. The cellar is quite empty. Give me the candle, and I'll go down and show you."

"Oh, no, please, auntie, don't go down," cried Kitty, seeing that the time had come to confess. "It is just a Halloween joke. We didn't suppose that Cora would be scared. We just wanted to tease her because she seemed so sure that she would find Walter down there. Go and bring him up, boys."

Ranald and Rob started down the stairs, with Keith carrying a candle, and Malcolm calling for Walter to come on and help carry out his rival. The four boys, picking up the dummy as if it had been a real man, carried it up the steps and laid it carefully on the ground. So comical did it look with its pudgy pillow face, that everybody laughed except Cora. She was furiously angry, and not all Kitty's penitent speeches or the boys' polite apologies could appease her. If it had not been for Miss Allison she would have flounced home in high displeasure. But she as usual poured oil on the troubled waters, and talked in such a tactful way of her harum-scarum niece's many pranks, that there was no resisting such an appeal. She allowed herself to be led back to the house, but she would not join in any of the games.

"Mom Beck says I'll have bad luck for seven years because I broke that looking-glass," she said, mournfully.

"Oh, nonsense!" exclaimed Miss Allison. "Don't give it another thought, dear, it is only an old negro superstition."

She might have added that it was to herself and her brother the ill luck had come, since it was her silver mirror that was broken, and Harry's rubber boots that would be henceforth useless for wading because of the holes thoughtless Kitty had made in them with safety-pins, when she fastened them to the pillows.

Refreshments were served soon after they went back to the house. Not the cakes and ices that usually attended parties in the Valley, but things suggestive of Halloween. Pop-corn, nuts, and apples, doughnuts and molasses candy. Then the fate cake was cut, and everybody took a slice to carry home to dream on.

"Eat it the last thing before you retire," said Miss Allison. "Then walk to bed backwards without taking a drink of water or speaking another word tonight. It is so salty that it is likely you will dream of being thirsty, and of somebody bringing you water. They say if you dream of its being brought in a golden goblet you will marry into wealth. If in a tin cup poverty will be your lot. The kind of vessel you see in your dream will decide your fate. Ah, Walter got the button in his slice. That means he will be an old bachelor and sew his own buttons on all his life."

Anna Moore got the dime, and Eliza Hughes the ring, which foretold that she would be the first one in the company to have a wedding. The thimble fell to no one, as it slipped out between two slices in the cutting. "That means none of us will be old maids," said little Elise. Miss Allison slipped it on Kitty's finger. "To mend your mischievous ways with," she said, and everybody who had enjoyed the pillow-man laughed.

The moon was hiding behind a cloud when at last the merry party said good-night, so Miss Allison provided each little group with a jack-o'-lantern to light them on their homeward way. As the grotesque yellow heads with their grinning fire-faces went bobbing down the lonely road, it was well for Tam O'Shanter that he need not pass that way. All the witches of Alloway Kirk could not have made such a weird procession. Well, too, for old Ichabod Crane that he need not ride that night through the shadowy Valley. One pumpkin, in the hands of the headless rider, had been enough to banish him from Sleepy Hollow for ever. What would have happened no one can tell, could he have met the long procession of bodiless heads that straggled through the gate that Halloween, from the haunted house of Hartwell Hollow.

⇀ The Tradition Continues ↽

Think about this. Why not turn the treat aspect of Halloween into a giving time? This holiday comes just as cold weather is approaching and the wants of the needy are increasing. These days we hear constant warnings about allowing your children to eat the candy and treats they gather. So why not have the goblins at your house trick-or-treat for canned goods to give to the local food bank and have treats waiting for them at home as a reward for their good deeds?

Today my extended family is meeting at Aunt Linda's farm for our annual pumpkin-carving reunion. We usually meet every year around Halloween to carve pumpkins, visit with relatives, and decorate the yard. This year my uncle bought forty pumpkins for us to carve. My uncle Bruce, who is a very talented pumpkin artist, always has an awesome new idea for his pumpkins. Last year he made a pumpkin snowman out of three pumpkins and two long gourds. The year before last, he used two pumpkins to make a witch that had brown corn-silk hair, a gourd with warts for the nose, and black corn kernels for her teeth. But for those of us who are less skilled, Uncle Bruce buys a book that we can use to trace faces on the pumpkins. While we carve pumpkins, my grandmother collects all the seeds and roasts them for a snack for us. Usually the night before Halloween, we set out the lit pumpkins so people can come and see our legendary pumpkins. The small town my aunt lives in knows our family goes all out for Halloween. Hopefully, this year we'll have some great new ideas and another terrific crowd.

Desta G. Lingg, high school

Well, it's that time of year again. It's the time when the air begins to get a little chilly, and the leaves on the trees change color and fall to the ground. The pumpkins have just been harvested and are ready for carving. Yes, it is now time for Halloween.

That brings me to one of the many traditions that takes place around my household. Ever since I can remember, every Halloween Eve, the children in my family would gather up the carving knives and head on out to the picnic table. There we work for hours, struggling to see who could make the best jack-o'-lantern. On Halloween night we would set them out on the porch, put lit candles in them, and watch the frightening faces glow.

Though most of my brothers and sisters are grown up and have their own families to carve pumpkins with, my brother and I keep the tradition alive. Every year on October 30, we select the best carving knives and head out to the picnic table.

Mary Tate, middle school

Every year on Halloween, a tradition in my family is to decorate our house like an abandoned house. We hide candy. Mom buys a Frankenstein. We put grapes all over the floor, so people can step on them. We pretend they are eyeballs. We put water in the attic and pour it down on people. We all help make fake skulls and put red lights in them. They look ugly.

It's real scary, but I like it. Everyone helps. We eat pumpkin pie. We eat pumpkin seeds. We eat a big bag of Hershey's. We get a big scoop of ice cream. Then we go trick-or-treating. When we get home, we put our candy away. Then we go to bed. Celebrating Halloween makes me feel happy. It's real important to me to have fun with my family.

Leonard Dewayne Utley, elementary school

I like to decorate for Halloween. Mom or Dad goes up to the attic to get the decorations. Justin and I help them. We will put out a big cobweb across the porch. It scares everybody. Lots of the big kids like it, but the little kids are scared. We have lights we put up. Two of the lights are a ghost and a pumpkin. We also like to put on scary music. It scares people. I like the music. Dad likes to dress up like Dracula. We dress up, too. People like our costumes. We like to go trick-or-treating. It is fun. We get lots of candy. We also go to two carnivals. We get lots of candy at the carnivals. That's all we do for Halloween.

Ryan Kennedy, elementary school

Every year, hundreds of people come to get spooked by the ghosts and goblins at the "Mace Place," which happens to be my home. This year we had a tour of my frightening house, free of charge. I think it is pretty scary, though my friends won't admit it.

We have some scary scenes such as a graveyard scene, a "mad scientist" scene, and a dining room scene! Tonight one of our friends got so scared he almost jumped through our TV screen. We use a lot of scary effects such as a fog machine, creepy sound effects, and these disgusting-looking masks, but what I think really scares them is the eerie tricks done with lighting and mirrors.

Good night and have a happy Halloween!

Christopher Mace, middle school

Every year, my family has Halloween breakfast. Everybody gets up at 5:30 A.M. and goes downstairs to eat breakfast. It is very dark outside in the morning at that time of the year, and my parents like to put the lights on dim to make it even spookier!

My parents are dressed up in masks and spooky clothes. We have a pumpkin in the middle of the table that has been carved and has a candle glowing inside. The kitchen is decorated with skeletons, a pumpkin, goblins, witches, and all sorts of Halloween decoration. There is Halloween candy, books, gifts, and toys at everyone's place mat and also a candle that shines wildly. My parents say that the pumpkin in the middle of the table brings all of the goodies to our Halloween breakfast every year. I know that is not true, but everyone likes to kid about it!

We eat doughnuts and drink coffee, for breakfast—that is, everyone except my dad and my sister, who don't like coffee! The scary Halloween breakfast ends about 7:00 A.M. with a lot of laughter and jokes. Everyone goes to their room and gets in their normal clothes and starts their normal day.

Ryan R. Greenwood, elementary school

One of our family traditions is baling hay and putting it on a trailer pulled by a tractor so we can have a hay ride on Halloween. It's a lot of hard work. When I'm done, I feel really tired and stressed out. Sweat is just pouring from my head. It's a lot of work getting hay, but it's lots of fun going on the ride. Our family invites friends and other people to come along. That's why we have a big trailer. We start at my grandpa and grandma's house. We go around lots of back roads and end up at my mom's house. Then we go back. As we are on our way to my mom's house, we ask people that live on that road if they want to come along. It's really fun and makes you feel good. When the whole thing is done, it is normally around 12:00 and 1:00 at night. It's really dark and spooky. It gives you the creeps. When the whole thing is done, everyone is either asleep or very tired. When we go back to my grandma and grandpa's house, everyone goes home. The next day we all help and put the hay in my grandpa's truck. Then we take it to a farm. That's really tiring. Your whole body feels sore when you're done. The whole thing is lots of fun. That's why I'm glad it's one of our family traditions.

Shawn Miller, middle school

Each Halloween season, the Raleigh, North Carolina, Parks and Recreation Department sponsors a scarecrow decoration party. It started out as a contest, but it was decided each scarecrow deserved a prize, and so now it is just a fun way for everyone to try their hand at this craft. The event started when Anne Burney told her daughter Susan, who works at the Pullen Park site, decorating scarecrows would be a good idea. On the Saturday before Thanksgiving toddlers and adults and all in-between ages gather to find the scarecrow forms in place and lots of recyclable material there to get them started. Most people bring their own scraps and cloth, pumpkins and gourds, and have an idea in mind, but if you just happen by, as I did one year, you can hop out of the car and start right in. Last year there were fifty or so scarecrows created by some two-hundred-plus people who picnicked, created, and enjoyed the live music provided by a local band. I call that a great Halloween tradition.

BLACK AND GOLD, BLACK AND GOLD,
    NOTHING IN BETWEEN—
WHEN THE WORLD TURNS BLACK AND GOLD,
    THEN IT'S HALLOWE'EN!
                                    Nancy Byrd Turner

CHAPTER 13

Those Other Days

THE BEST OF THE REST

~ Any Excuse for a Celebration ~

The following is a list of those other days that you may or may not have heard about, but that do, in fact, exist. These are the days that might give you an excuse for throwing a party, taking a day off from work—"Hey, I'm not working on Alamo Day; my friend Bob is from Texas!"—or starting your own traditions. Incidentally, each state has its own day, the day it joined the Union. Visit your library and find out your state's day and have a State's Day party.

In truth, you can use any of these days to real advantage. Even the most frivolous of events can be turned into a celebration and a good cause. When my New Orleans friends Bill and Peggy Gershuny were looking for a way to raise money for AIDS research and care, they invited their friends over to celebrate the one hundredth anniversary of the martini. (A most appropriate theme for that city of spirit and spirits.) To add to the fun, they asked their guests to

269

come armed with their favorite martini glasses, shakers, and stirrers. The night yielded money, fun, and great stories.

Or you could just start your own "other day" tradition. That's what Thomas E. Saxe, Jr., president of the White Tower restaurant chain, did back in 1949. He was on vacation in Sarasota, Florida, when that American favorite, the rocking chair, worked its charm and wove its spell on the overworked and weary executive. He founded the Sittin' Starin' 'N' Rockin' Club (SS&RC). What could be more American?

Here to get you started are just a few of those other days.

April Fool's Day: A Day of Mirth

The first of April, some do say
Is set apart for All Fools' Day
But why the people call it so
Nor I, nor they themselves, do know.

POOR ROBIN'S ALMANAC, 1760

Earlier in the century April Fool's Day was more widely celebrated than it is today. Could be that this traditional day of simple frivolity is fading away. What a shame, because it gives everyone the opportunity to be a little mischievous in this sometimes too-serious world.

April Fool's Day is traced back to the days of court jesters in England where the victim of the harmless jokes played on April 1 was called the "April fool." When I was a child, I spent March 31 scheming with friends and thinking up our own silly tricks. April 1 started and ended with some sort of joke on our parents or siblings. As you can see from the following poem, story, and essay, the day can still hold fun and merriment.

⭢ A New Kind of Trick ⭠

VIOLA RUTH LOWE

April Fool's Day doesn't have to have bad pranks associated with it. If you have children you may want to share Viola Ruth Lowe's concept of a goodnatured and well-intentioned trick. You may even want to use the day as an excuse to perform a thoughtful deed yourself.

"Tomorrow will be the First of April," said Dick to his twin sister Daisy. "Do let's think out a really good joke to play on someone."

Daisy put down the doll's dress she was making.

"I have been thinking lots about it, Dick," she said, "and I've got a perfectly lovely idea for a new sort of April-fool trick."

"Well, tell me what it is," said her brother, and he listened to her plan.

"I say, Daisy, it *is* a good idea," he murmured. "Let's go and see about it now."

Now Betty, an old crippled flower-seller, lived in a tiny tumble-down cottage not far from the twins' house, and the very next morning Daisy and Dick hurried to her door. They knew that at that time Betty would be out selling her primroses and violets, and would not return until midday.

On his arm Dick carried a big, covered-in basket, while Daisy was loaded with several exciting looking parcels. They knew that the old woman's cottage door would be open, for, as she had once told them, "there isn't anything worth stealing in my place." So the twins had no difficulty in letting themselves in, and for the next hour they were very busy indeed.

Daisy, who had often helped her mother, scurried round with dust-pan and brush, washed the dishes, and put sweet country flowers in a bowl on the little round table.

But first of all she had spread a clean white cloth, and on it were to be found a crusty loaf, fresh creamy butter, home-made jam, some crisp short-bread, a plum cake—which Daisy had made herself, with mother's help—and a tin of sardines which Dick had bought out of his own pocket money.

"It's far and away the best April-fool surprise we shall have ever worked," the little girl said happily.

"Yes," agreed Dick slowly. "It is rather jolly doing things for people who can't afford to do them for themselves, isn't it, Daisy?"

And just then they heard old Betty's footsteps outside, and quick as lightning the two children hid themselves under the table, breathless with excitement.

In came the old lady, and at sight of the changed room she stood still with a little cry of surprise. Dick and Daisy could wait no longer.

"It's April the first!" they cried, scrambling out from under the table, and they felt it was quite the nicest trick they had ever played on anyone.

➤ April Fool ➤

ELEANOR HAMMOND

Small April sobbed
"I'm going to cry!
Please give me a cloud
To wipe my eye!"

Then, "April Fool!"
She laughed instead
And smiled a rainbow
Overhead!

➤ The Tradition Continues ➤

When no one seems to have any contributions or suggestions for me, that's pretty good proof that it is time to go to an earlier generation of books for ideas on how to bring back a fading tradition. Here are some ideas gleaned from a fifty-plus-year-old book, Days We Celebrate. *They can be adapted to today, or done in the same old way.*

Open some English walnuts carefully, take out the meats, and put inside the shell some wee favor or a little folded paper, saying "April Fool." Tiny dolls, little bits of paste jewelry, and miniature animals are all appropriate surprises. Each shell may contain a penny or a dime if you like. Glue the shells together, and no one will suspect that the nuts are not what they seem.

Having friends over for dinner on or near April 1? Everyone loves dessert. Why not serve an April Fool's Day dinner where the meal is served backwards: beginning with ice cream and ending with soup? From *Ideas for Entertaining,* a book published in 1905, here are other ideas of how to serve your amusing meal in an unconventional and good-humored manner:

Soup in teacups with teaspoons
Crackers in a covered vegetable dish
Sliced meat arranged on a cake stand
Mashed potatoes in berry bowls

Gravy in individual sauce dishes
Peas poured from a water pitcher into glass tumblers
Vegetable on the bread plate
Bread in the salad bowl
Tea in soup bowls with teaspoons
Dessert on dinner plates

Columbus Day

Or what about Columbus Day? If it weren't for a quick CNN clip of the annual New York City Columbus Day parade, chances are October 12 would slip by without most people giving it a second thought. Because banks, federal offices, and post offices are closed—if not on October 12, then on the Monday closest to the day—we are slightly inconvenienced, but our attention to the day ends there.

Because my Southern grandfather's birthday happened to fall on Columbus Day, it has always been a red-letter day for me. As recently as the 1950s, Columbus Day was treated with reverence and respect. These days if it is mentioned at all—other than for the parade—usually it is surrounded by the controversial question, Who really discovered America? So we're back to the same sort of thankless debate as Where was the first Thanksgiving? What is important is that someone came and others followed. Most significantly this is the one patriotic holiday that is celebrated throughout the Americas, North and South. Here to set the stage for Columbus Day are a few lines from a poem by Edgar Guest. Then from the 1892 Youth's Companion we have a reading and a poem that were recited in schools throughout the nation on the four hundredth anniversary of Columbus's voyage to the Americas. These should get you started.

❧ The Things That Haven't Been Done Before ❧

EDGAR A. GUEST

The things that haven't been done before,
Those are the things to try;
Columbus dreamed of an unknown shore
At the rim of the far-flung sky.

The Meaning of the Four Centuries

FROM *THE YOUTH'S COMPANION*, 1892

The spectacle America presents this day is without precedent in history. From ocean to ocean, in city, village, and country-side, the children of the States are marshaled and marching under the banner of the nation; and with them the people are gathering around the school-house.

Men are recognizing to-day the most impressive anniversary since Rome celebrated her thousandth year. . . .

As no prophet among our fathers on the 300th anniversary of America could have pictured what the new century would do, so no man can this day reach out and grasp the hundred years upon which the nation is now entering. On the victorious results of the completed centuries, the principles of Americanism will build our fifth century. Its material progress is beyond our conception, but we may be sure that in the social relations of men with men, the most triumphant gains are to be expected. America's fourth century has been glorious; America's fifth century must be made happy.

One institution more than any other has wrought out the achievements of the past, and is to-day the most trusted for the future. Our fathers in their wisdom knew that the foundations of liberty, fraternity, and equality, must be universal education. The free school, therefore, was conceived as the corner-stone of the Republic. Washington and Jefferson recognized that the education of citizens is not the prerogative of church or of other private interest; that while religious training belongs to the church, and while technical and higher culture may be given by private institution—the training of citizens in the common knowledge and the common duties of citizenship belongs irrevocably to the State. . . .

To-day America's fifth century begins. The world's twentieth century will soon be here. To the 13,000,000 now in the American schools the command of the coming years belongs. We, the youth of America, who to-day unite to march as one army under the sacred flag, understand our duty. We pledge ourselves that the flag shall not be stained; and that America shall mean equal opportunity and justice for every citizen, and brotherhood for the world.

Other Celebrations

With those examples of what can be done on these seldom celebrated but full-of-potential days, here are some of the days that lend themselves to entertaining, to history, and to starting new traditions.

January 31: Karamu is a feast celebrated by African-Americans, with ceremonies, cultural expressions, and a magnificent buffet. The celebration traditionally occurs on the night of Kuumba (January 31).

February 1: National Freedom Day commemorates the signing of the Thirteenth Amendment to the Constitution by President Abraham Lincoln in 1865. This amendment abolished slavery and has been formally observed since a presidential proclamation of 1949.

February 2: Groundhog Day is traditionally the midpoint of winter. On this day a groundhog, or woodchuck, is observed to see if, upon leaving his burrow, he sees his shadow and returns for six more weeks of winter, or if winter is almost over.

February 12: Race Relations Day is dedicated to understanding among all races and is observed on the Sunday nearest Abraham Lincoln's birthday.

February 19: Presidents' Day commemorates the birthdays of George Washington and Abraham Lincoln.

February 29: Bachelors' Day (Leap Year Day).

March 6: Alamo Day commemorates the end of the Mexican siege of the Alamo in 1836.

March 12: Girl Scouts Day.

March 15: The Ides of March.

April 13: Thomas Jefferson's birthday, 1743.

April 14: Pan-American Day, begun in 1931, honors the first international conference of American states held in 1890.

April 19: Patriots' Day commemorates the first battle of the Revolutionary War, which occurred in 1775 at Lexington and Concord.

April 22: Earth Day, first observed internationally in 1970 to raise awareness of the need for worldwide conservation of natural resources.

May 5: Cinco de Mayo is widely celebrated in cities and towns with large Mexican-American populations. It commemorates the defeat of the French at the Battle of Puebla in 1867, and is becoming a popular celebration in the bars and "watering holes" in America.

May 13: Indian Day, sponsored by the Society of American Indians, was first celebrated in 1916 to honor the American Indian. Date varies from state to state.

May 18: Armed Forces Day (third Saturday in May).

May 22: Jumping Frog Jubilee Day, observed in Angels Camp, California, features an event inspired by a short story by Mark Twain.

May 30: Memorial Day or Decoration Day was first celebrated on May 30, but is now observed on the last Monday in May. Several locations claim the "original" Memorial Day commemoration to the Confederate dead, but the day is a national legal holiday.

June 14: Flag Day has been celebrated since the eighteenth century and commemorates the adoption of the Stars and Stripes by the Continental Congress in 1777.

June 19: Father's Day.

June 19: Juneteenth is an unofficial holiday observed by thousands of African-Americans primarily in some Southern states. The holiday originated in Texas during the Civil War period, when news of the Emancipation Proclamation signed by President Abraham Lincoln in September 1862, to become effective on January 1, 1863, did not reach Texas slaves until June 1865. The slaves immediately left the plantations, congregated in the cities, and began celebrating their freedom by praying, feasting, dancing, and singing.

July 4: Hannibal, Missouri, observes Tom Sawyer Fence-Painting Day with a contest based on the famous episode in Mark Twain's *Tom Sawyer.*

July 14: Bastille Day, the French national holiday, commemorates the storming of the Bastille, a Paris prison, in 1789.

August 1: Sports Day.

August 19: National Aviation Day, honoring the Wright Brothers and other pioneering aviators.

September 3: Labor Day (the first Monday in September) became a federal holiday in 1894. It was founded by Peter J. Maguire in tribute to American industrial workers. Traditionally the last weekend of summer.

September 7: Grandfather's Day.

September 17: Citizenship Day honors new Americans and is the beginning of Constitution Week.

September 20: Harvest Moon Days occurs during the period of the full moon nearest the autumn equinox and is a time for traditional harvest festivals across the United States.

September 21: World Peace Day.

September 23: Frontier Day was begun in Cheyenne, Wyoming, in 1897, and pays tribute to the pioneers of the West. The date varies from state to state.

September 28: Good Neighbor Day (the fourth Sunday in September) is observed in the United States to promote good relationships among neighbors and acquaintances.

October 1: Agricultural Fair Day, anniversary of the first agricultural fair held on October 1, 1810, in Pittsfield, Massachusetts. The fair became the forerunner of today's popular state fairs.

October 7: Child Health Day (the first Monday in October) was proclaimed on May 1, 1928.

October 9: Leif Eriksson Day is celebrated in Wisconsin, Minnesota, and other states in the United States, as it is in Iceland and Norway, to honor the landing of Norsemen in Vinland, Newfoundland, in A.D. 1000.

October 15: World Poetry Day.

October 18: Sweetest Day (the third Saturday in October) originated as a day for spreading cheer among the unfortunate. It affords an excellent opportunity to do something nice for someone else.

October 24: United Nations Day commemorates the founding of the United Nations, 1945.

October 28: Statue of Liberty Dedication Day, 1886.

October 31: National Magic Day is celebrated on the anniversary of the death of Harry Houdini, 1926, and honors the skills of magicians.

November 8: Dunce Day is the anniversary of the death of Duns Scotus in 1308, the medieval scholar from whose name the word "dunce" is derived. Dunce Day provides modern-day pranksters with an excuse to act up.

November 9: Sadie Hawkins Day was created in 1938 by cartoonist Al Capp for his comic strip *Li'l Abner* as an occasion upon which the unmarried women of Dogpatch could pursue eligible bachelors. Currently celebrated with school dances where girls invite boys.

November 11: Veterans Day.

November 19: Discovery Day is celebrated in Puerto Rico in honor of the day in 1493 when, on his second voyage, Columbus discovered Puerto Rico.

December 15: Bill of Rights Day honors the ratification of the first ten amendments to the Constitution.

December 16: Boston Tea Party Day celebrates the anniversary of the Boston Tea Party of 1773 when, in order to protest the tax established by the crown on tea, angry colonists dumped a British vessel's shipload of tea into Boston Harbor. This was one of the major events leading up to the American Revolution.

December 21: Forefathers' Day commemorates the landing of the Pilgrims in 1620 in Plymouth, Massachusetts.

December 26: Boxing Day, a legal holiday observed throughout the British Commonwealth on the day following Christmas, began as a day when gifts were given to those in service by their employers.

PART TWO
RITES OF PASSAGE

CHAPTER 14

Births, Christenings, and Birthdays

THE SONS AND DAUGHTERS OF LIFE

~ Speak to Us of Children ~

KAHLIL GIBRAN

The minister of the First Congregational Church in Webster, Massachusetts, began one of our family's traditions. When my father left New England to go to Charlotte, North Carolina, in the 1930s, the Reverend Hubert Allenby gave him a copy of Kahlil Gibran's The Prophet. *My father, a serious and educated man, read and reread the book and soon began giving it as a gift for any occasion—weddings, Christmas, birthdays, and of course to others who were about to chart new waters. There was always a copy of the book on*

Daddy's desk or the bookshelf in the den, and I began reading Gibran's powerful words at a young age. I still do so today and often give the book as a present, especially to those who are embarking on a new journey in life.

I can think of no more fitting words to use at the beginning of this section on that opening rite of passage, birth, than these written by the Lebanese mystical poet, philosopher, and artist who moved to the United States in the 1910s and was immediately claimed as one of our own.

And a woman who held a babe against her bosom said, "Speak to us of Children."
They are the sons and daughters of Life's longing for itself.
They come through you but not from you,
And though they are with you yet they belong not to you.

You may give them your love but not your thoughts,
For they have their own thoughts.
You may house their bodies but not their souls,
For their souls dwell in the house of tomorrow, which you cannot visit, not even in your dreams.
You may strive to be like them, but seek not to make them like you.
For life goes not backward nor tarries with yesterday.
You are the bows from which your children as living arrows are sent forth.
The archer sees the mark upon the path of the infinite, and He bends you with His might that His arrows may go swift and far.
Let your bending in the Archer's hand be for gladness;
For even as he loves the arrow that flies, so He loves also the bow that is stable.

⁓ *The Birthday* ⁓

Lee Smith

All cultures and people have untold numbers of traditions surrounding the birth of a child. In the northeastern United States, the entire community of Woodlands Indians would gather just before the expected baby was born and begin an enactment of a birth, pretending that another woman was in labor, thus protecting the real mother and child from the spirit of death. Miles away and years later, well-intended godparents can sometimes be caught pinching a baby at the baptismal font, for it is said that a baby who cries while being christened will have a lifetime of good luck. In Lee Smith's popular story, Oral

History, *we read of the many old Southern mountain traditions that transpire at the time of birth, from dusting the baby with ashes taken from between the chimney rocks for good luck to burying the borning quilt.*

Pricey Jane give out a little scream and I push down, and out pops that baby as easy as pie. I'll swear it didn't take a half hour, it was the easiest baby I ever birthed. It was so easy it like to got me spooked, and I'll admit it. As I said I expected the worst. They is something special about this baby, I says to myself, and sure enough she was the prettiest baby girl I have ever seed before or since, come out with a full head of pale yaller hair like Almarine, not a mark on her noplace. She screws up her little mouth till it looks like a bow and then she cries out real healthy-like. Pricey Jane smiled the sweetest smile.

"Let me have my baby, Granny," she said, and I did.

And it were a funny thing. Even how 'twas the easiest baby I ever birthed, I was plumb wore out. I cut the cord and tied the strippy cloths and let Rhoda and Mrs. Crouse get on with it. I sets myself down by the fire to rest, and I set there the whole time while the rest of them was a-carrying on and finishing.

Here's what they do—you ring your bell, and Almarine done it, and all the womenfolks and gals come from all over, carrying food. There's no little girls can come, nor yet no singular women. They'll eat and they'll drink, and Almarine has got some corn liquor there ready, along with gingerbread Pricey Jane made herself when she figured her time was nigh, and directly they'll dust the baby with dust from between the chimney-rocks, for luck, and then they'll take the ax outen under the bed where you put it to cut the pain.

And then they'll take it and chop up the man's hat iffen they can find it—and Almarine had left his a-laying right out in plain view he was that worrit. And then they'll take and bury the borning quilt and then they'll go on home, and they done all of it, me watching it all like a dream. I couldn't make no difference twixt dream and day.

"Poor old Granny," Pricey Jane said when they left. The firelight was a-jumping everywhere and it seemed like her voice was a song. I could see them gold earrings a-shining. Almarine was right up there on the bed-tick by her, and Eli had him a bunch of dried cobs on the floor, a-building a house of his own.

"Come and sleep here," Pricey Jane says, but she should have knowed I won't. I don't sleep noplace but my own bed in my house on Hurricane Mountain. I knowed it was time to go.

Once I stood up I felt good on my feet, and my feet was ready to travel. I looked back at them all from the door. The firelight flowed all over everybody, casting such a glow. The new baby was sound asleep in that cradle what Almarine made, and her hair shined out in that light.

"Wait, Granny," says Almarine. "What ought we to call the baby?"

I says, "Name her Dory. Hit means gold."

⟁ Monday's Child Is Fair of Face ⟁

ANONYMOUS

Monday's child is fair of face,
Tuesday's child is full of grace,
Wednesday's child is full of woe,
Thursday's child has far to go,
Friday's child is loving and giving,
Saturday's child works hard for a living,
And the child that is born on the Sabbath day
Is bonny and blithe, and good and gay.

⟁ The Master of Your Heart ⟁

LOUISE ERDRICH

The typical experience of today's mothers, whether they give birth in super-sterilized maternity wards or in comfortable rooms intended to look almost like their own bedrooms, is much different from those of the past. Then or now, when the cigars have been passed out, the phone calls have been put in to distant friends and relatives, and the anxious well-wishers who were on hand to see the newborn have left, it is those first few hours spent with a newborn child that are some of any parent's most precious memories.

The first night of our baby's life is spent on her father's chest, held just there, in the bed or the rocking chair. I think of the German expression for the way a pregnant woman carries her child under her heart. Now it is Michael's turn to carry our baby over his. And he does. She curls there, hunched in a doll-size flannel gown, a cotton cap. Beside them, my breasts filling painfully, astoundingly, I'm too tender and bumpy to sleep on. So I rest lightly but profoundly, and in exhausted relief. My heart is an ordinary ex-smoker's, so-so runner's, diligent untroubled ticker, anyway. His is more complex. It beats faster, booms louder, swishes his blood through an extra flourish of artery. Michael's is a diagnosed Wolff-Parkinson-White heart with a more complicated beat. Each daughter finds her first wonder in its samba knock.

— Just for the Record —

By now the moving children's contributions included in "The Tradition Continues" sections have undoubtedly convinced you of how important it is to them that you continue to pass on the traditions that they cherish. One of the best ways to ensure the perpetuity of a family's most loved activities is to keep a family log. John Lagemann has found that it can even help you avoid the unpleasant experience of a trip to the doctor's office!

We Keep a Family Log

John Kord Lagemann

Recently the whole family tried to figure out where Kord, our ten-year old son, had lost his wrist watch. Then we remembered a possible clue —and we located the watch hanging on a fence in a friend's back yard. What gave us the clue? Kord had duly noted a neighborhood baseball game in the family log.

Our log is just an ordinary loose-leaf notebook, crammed with a varied assortment of letters, mementos, pictures and jotted entries. But actually it's much more than that. It tells us what our family life is all about. It reminds us of that epoch when the youngsters were too little to eat without spilling, when they found it hard to comb their hair. The small exciting gossip of the first day of school comes back, the problems of early married life, a forgotten face, the joyous details of family Christmases. Little events become bigger when they're written down.

The log started on that day in the hospital when I saw our firstborn son through the door of the delivery room. On the back of an envelope I jotted down a note to him: "We're calling you Kord. You're well formed, bigger than most babies, healthy spring water and unmistakably male. And your mother is more beautiful than ever."

This penciled scrawl turned up later in a folder of letters my wife and I wrote each other during the war. We kept the folder on a handy bookshelf, and from then on our log just grew. By means of it we slow the onrush of time: last year or ten years ago seems as real to us as yesterday—and it's all a part of today. And, going back to written entries, we're often surprised how rich in detail they seem when compared with our unaided memories.

Our log has helped every member of the family take his own measure in relation to the events around him. Kord, criticizing his younger brother, Jay, for "making faces with his voice," discovers in the log that he himself did the same thing a few years back. Now, when Jay does something to annoy him Kord may tell him: "It's just a phase you're going through."

Also, my wife, Betzy, and I can laugh at earlier mistakes and apply to present problems the lessons that somehow escaped us while we were experiencing them. How often the log has pulled us out of a fit of depression by reminding us of other occasions when our fears proved groundless, when seemingly irreconcilable differences turned out to be trifles!

For most persons the first decade of life is a fog of forgetfulness lit up by occasional flashes of memory. The parents of our childhood do not emerge as distinct, three-dimensional human beings until after our adolescence—when we are busy declaring our independence of them. So, to our log we have added such things as photographs of Betzy and myself in our youngster days, and some reminiscent letters our mothers wrote. "I'm not sure I would have you two as children," Kord told me after reading some of these letters the other day. Well, neither my wife nor I was a model child, but we feel that we have lost none of our boys' respect in letting them know this. We think they'll understand *themselves* better because the log gives them a chance to share *our* childhood years.

The log is a wonderful reminder of something grownups often forget—that every age, day and hour of life has its own immediate value. "Wait till you're older," we keep telling children, as if life didn't really begin till 18 or 21 or 40. Actually children are not, as Jay once put it, "living on approval." For their part, swapping experiences and keeping the log with grownups makes them feel understood and appreciated. When two generations meet on common ground in this way, both reap a profit.

It is easy to start a family log and fun to keep it. The simplest way is to gather together in a sturdy binder or loose-leaf notebook the records which have already accumulated and then add to them whenever the spirit moves you. Don't make a chore of it. It's the spontaneous contributions which make it a living family story. The children will want to get in all kinds of trivialities and irrelevancies—let them do it. Many of these entries bring back the flavor of past times as more sensible things never could.

My wife has found that the log is a space-saver. Instead of having letters, photographs and notes scattered about in drawers and closet shelves, they're clamped neatly into binders—in chronological order.

This filing of family data serves another practical purpose in any household. Out in the country last summer, for instance, Jay stepped on a rusty nail. When did the children have their last anti-tetanus shot? The log's answer saved the unpleasantness of another injection.

"Here's one for the book" has become a family expression. Each of us, we find, is on the lookout for fresh observations on the world about us. And they're all recorded exactly as they come out—family words and phrases which would doubtless have been lost if we hadn't written them down.

A good deal of the history of our times creeps into the lot—history as experienced in the everyday lives of a family. Inflation, taxes, the atom bomb, Communism, the threat of World War III—all those turn up in stories about school drills, clothes drives, civil-defense classes, the business of making ends meet.

One of the best things our log has done for our children is to give them a feeling of confidence. By putting them in touch with the past, it gives them faith in the future. Their sense of security in belonging, to a going concern has been strengthened by the stories we have written down about their grandparents and great-grandparents—personalities who are very real to them despite the fact that some of them died long before Kord and Jay were born.

Life today is very different from the past when children grew up in a kind of kinship community, a world of grandparents and uncles and aunts, a world reduced to an intimate scale in which children could orient themselves to all the great experiences of life—birth, death, work, marriage. Now American families are often isolated by half a continent from their nearest kinsfolk.

What will our children have to look back on as symbols of home? Certainly not the rented apartment or the rapidly changing suburban neighborhood where they are growing up. If they are to "go home again" it will not be to the old homestead but to the family log and the memories it keeps alive. Yes, if our home ever caught fire, you can guess what we would all think of saving first: our family log.

Christenings

➤ To Save the Dear Child's Soul ➤

"My dear Grace," the model christening invitation begins in my mother's 1924 edition of The Book of Etiquette. *"The baby is to be christened next Sunday at four o'clock at the Brick Church and both Harry and I are anxious to have you present. I think Harry Jr. would be also if he were old enough to know what it is all about. Cordially yours, Alice F. Duncan."*

In olden days, children were christened, or baptized, within just a few days of birth. Many mothers were unable to attend these ceremonies because they had not yet fully recovered from childbirth. Imagine the bewilderment of a child born in the winter months who had barely had time to adjust to his new surroundings in a measure of comfort before a warm fire before being taken from his mother's arms, bundled up, taken to the meeting-house, and christened over a baptismal bowl in which the ice had just been broken!

Mothers had to content themselves either with having a dinner for the midwife and neighbors who were present and assisted during the birth—in which, needless to say, she didn't take much part—or with a little celebratory caudle enjoyed with these women at her bedside. (This tradition continued into the twentieth century.) Alternatively, a dinner was held for these women sometime within a week or so after the birth. In the latter case, unless a woman was lucky enough to have considerable resources, she probably did most of the preparation herself. Judge Samuel Sewall of Boston recorded in his diary that a dinner for seventeen women took place two weeks after the birth of one of his children. Boiled pork, beef, and fowls; roast beef and "minc'd pyes"; cheese and pies and tarts were served. Knowing this, we modern mothers can be thankful for the medical technology that contributes to low infant mortality rates—and for catered christening parties!

As we see in the following passage by the popular columnist and writer Dee Hardie, christenings can be postponed almost indefinitely. At least in that situation the child has been named. You see, it is said that one reason why traditionally the mother was not allowed to attend the child's christening was so the father would have the privilege of naming the little one!

The Christening

Dee Hardie

The half-mile road up our hill was passable if you had a strong constitution and quick reflexes. It had caused comment, well-deserved. And
so we bowed to progress, and to the bank. Our country pebbled lane,
our uneven mosaic, became a direct route, a gray macadam road.

It was such an occasion that we had our third Thornhill party—we
christened the road. We invited all those who had braved it before—
the milkman, the postman, our laundry man, and other friends. One
even brought a present, his broken axle.

We strung ribbons across, put up pseudo Burma Shave signs that
were so clever I can't remember a one. Our most prominent lawyer,
Frank, who first introduced us to Thornhill, wore a top hat. Sitting
high on the back of an open convertible, he cut away at the ribbons,
making a speech at every clip. And the barn, for the very first time,
served as a banquet hall.

Since we had christened a road, Agnes didn't see why we couldn't
get around to christening her third grandchild, Tommy. "Surely" said
Agnes, who never missed a Sunday of church, "you *should* have Tommy
baptized before the next baby is born." Everyone, it seems, was getting
nervous.

Todd and Louise had been christened as babes in arms, but Tommy
was seventeen months old, walking around with abandon where angels
feared to tread. And still not blessed. But then he was always different.
While the other two children were towheaded blondes, his hair was
shiny dark brown. His dimple, the only one in the family, was deep
and irresistible.

We talked a young minister into performing the rites on the front
lawn of Thornhill. I wanted, even then, continuity. Agnes, with some
grace, accepted the site, but gave the service some substance, she
thought, by producing a small bottle of water from the River Jordan.
She and Harry had visited the Holy Land during the winter. This
water was a special prize she had carried home for her grandson's
christening. Moments before the service she and Mabel thought we
should boil the water to insure against impurities. After all it had
been a long trip, and how many wash their laundry in the River
Jordan? So boil it we did—completely away. And so little Tommy, in
a white suit and bare feet, was christened, quite in order, with water
from the stream at Thornhill, where the watercress grows.

Birthdays

➤ Growing Up and Older ➤

In this youth-oriented time in which we are living, accepting birthdays seems to be one of life's unwanted tribulations. Ridiculous, I say, because I belong to the Dorothy Canfield school of thought that says our lives are made richer by memories and more meaningful by our experiences. Here, first, are some memories many of us share of former birthdays, and then Canfield's declaration of why fifty (or sixty or seventy) doesn't (or shouldn't) hurt.

Birthday Parties

SUSAN ALLEN TOTH

I must have enjoyed those first birthday parties, which I remember for frilly dresses, pin-the-tail-on-the-donkey, crepe-paper streamers, and of course the presents. Mostly we gave each other paper dolls, stationery with little dots printed on it, and colored beads of bath oil in see-through plastic boxes. Even knowing what to expect, I was always frantic with excitement when I sat in front of my heap of wrapped presents with their gaudy tissue papers and corkscrew-curled ribbons. Birthdays were better than Christmas because I got all the attention as well as all the presents. I picked the flavor of ice cream, stuck the candy letters on the cake, and got to cut them out of the frosting. I chose the games and the paper napkins. I was the Birthday Girl: queen for a day. All the rest of my life I've expected my birthdays to have that same excitement, and when they don't, I'm childishly disappointed. If my birthday wears uneventfully on, and nothing happens, I become cross and then self-pitying. Finally I go to bed in a profound funk, haunted by a phantom party.

All the girls wanted to go on having birthday parties. After kindergarten, boys stopped attending, but we girls conspicuously observed each passing year. We felt we had special limits to our lives, particularly a certain number of years, perhaps twenty-five to thirty, to get married. Birthdays all led up to marriage, when life stopped. By late junior high school, when our mothers no longer gave parties for us, we girls arranged them for each other. To keep things fair, and cheap, we decided every year exactly what identical gift to give each other and then pooled resources to buy it. Our senior year in high school, for our last round of birthday parties, we chose a blue satin garter with white lace in a padded white satin box. It was extravagant, from Carole's, an elegant store, and intended, as a fancily lettered card instructed us, to be "something new and something blue" to wear at one's wedding. Though none of us had weddings in the offing, we knew that at eighteen they were edging closer. After the birthday girl opened her garter, we shared some ice cream at the Rainbow Café and went off together to an afternoon movie. But this round, we felt self-conscious. Now that we were well into our teens, girls didn't usually have real parties unless there were boys.

I Am Fifty—And It Doesn't Hurt!

Dorothy Canfield

Do you remember the little girl who asked if it didn't feel queer for a few days after you grew up? I think of her when people ask me how I feel about being middle-aged. The answer is, "You don't feel anything sensational. You just go on living."

Of course I realize that I am no exception to the laws which make all women around 50 very different from what they were at 20. To take, first, the most obvious change, and one that has always provided a theme for melancholy poems—the inexorable passing of the smooth-skinned, bright-haired radiance of youth. Why have I been so little troubled by this change?

The 1914–18 war taught me a lesson on that point. I spent much time in France, in contact with the direst needs. We, who were doing what we could to help, desperately needed reinforcements. To be of any use, our reinforcements must be capable of endurance, perseverance, self-forgetfulness. We came to distrust bright eyes and gleaming young hair. In our minds these pretty signs of physical youth became associated with childishness, fickleness, lack of conscience. We could not always provide the "something exciting" without which they would not stick at a long, tiresome job till it was done. Would not? Apparently they could not. For dependability is a quality almost impossible to youth, but natural to the middle-aged tastes.

Remembering the heartfelt liking we had in our war work for the plain, middle-aged faces of the women who could be counted on to stick it out, no matter what came, I do not now feel desolately that the world has no more welcome for me.

A young poet would, of course, be horrified at my resigned satisfaction. But bring to mind the fact that 99.5 percent of good lyric poetry always has been written by young people who are brilliantly improvising on a subject they know nothing about.

Being middle-aged is a nice change from being young. Honestly, I mean it. One of the traits of human nature about which there is unanimity of opinion is its love for change. When I was a young lady —that is what we were 30 years ago—I was anything but superior to the pleasures of young ladyhood. I "adored" opening the long pasteboard box which meant a bouquet from an admirer. I loved maple-nut sundaes to distraction and there never was a girl, I am sure, who more heartily delighted in West Point hops. But suppose that by some miracle I should now look young again and should be invited to dance once a week for the rest of this session at West Point, as I used to do. I'd rush into it as enthusiastically as I should carry out a sentence to play tag for an hour a day.

I still quite naturally enjoy playing tennis, riding horseback, skating, and mountain climbing. It is true I don't engage in these sports as ferociously as I did at 20, and for a good reason. I don't need to, or care to. At 20 I was like nearly everybody else of that age, frightfully uncertain—half of the time at least—of deserving to be in the world at all, and as a result was frightfully anxious to prove my worth to myself in the only way youth knows—by beating somebody else at something.

Here is one of the pleasures of middle age of which nobody breathes a word to you beforehand: the deliciousness of outgrowing that neuralgia of youthful pain at being surpassed in anything. This change is not due to greater magnanimity—rather to the fact that moderately successful, healthy-minded older people have found an excuse for existence in some job that the world seems to want done, which, after a fashion, they seem competent to do.

My gentle old uncle, when the cat had settled down to sleep in his favorite soft chair, used always to leave her there and sit upon a hard chair till she woke up and went away. When we remonstrated with him, he answered, "A cat has so few pleasures compared with those open to me." I have something of the same feeling about the boy who beats me in a race on the ice. He does *so* enjoy beating somebody. And there is so much else that I can enjoy of which he doesn't dream. For one thing, I can consciously, disinterestedly, relish the physical delights of the exercise, the miraculous knife-edge poise, the gliding speed, the tingling air, the beauties of the frosty trees. I enjoy these things far more than he does, or than I did at his age, freed as I am now from his single reason for being on the ice: either beating, or learning to beat, somebody else.

Understand me, I do not make the claim that I enjoy my corner of the pond more than that magnificent, long-legged kid out there, racing from one end of the hockey field to the other in eagle-like swoops. He is enjoying a wild, physical intoxication which gets considerably dimmed by the years. But as far as that goes, his physical intoxication is not so wild as that of a group of little children who, with faces of pure joy, are merely scuffling along on a slide at one end of the pond. The point is that we are all, in different ways suitable to our ages, having a glorious time. The young couple who swing dreamily around and around, hands clasped, are not the only ones to enjoy the ice.

I use skating, of course, as a convenient symbol for the way life is taken at different ages. Now, you will note that of all those age-groups on the ice, I, being the oldest, am the only one who has any notion that *everybody* is having a good time. Although the 14-year-old kid may be amused by "the kids without even any skates," he is not sorry for them, because he remembers that ages ago he used to enjoy sliding. But it is real pity he feels for the poor fish who's got tied up with a girl and has to steer her around. And probably his pity is even greater for the grayhaired woman who seems to think that cutting circles is skating. The young couple know, of course, that the hockey-playing boys who have not yet found their mates are having some sort of childish good time, but they are convinced that it must be awful to be so old as to have gray hair, with your first love far behind you.

The trouble, you see, is that they don't trust the future. Young people seldom do. They are afraid to. They are so impressed with the present that what they can't get now, this instant, seems lost forever.

Is it true, as people say, that youth is naturally happier than age because the one lives on hopes, the other on memories, and that while you can change hopes to suit yourself, memories persist in staying more or less the way they actually happened? Stuff and nonsense! Hope's always left, no matter what afflictions have come out of Pandora's box. It's not a question of an age limit. From cradle to grave the favorite slogan of every mother's son and daughter is: "I've learned my mistakes. Hereafter everything I tackle is going to go over big."

The fear of approaching old age? Having arrived at an age which seemed to me at 20 as forlorn as 80 does to me now, and perceiving that a change of tastes and desire has gone along with a change in age, I cannot help guessing that if I continue to yield myself naturally to the rhythm of the years, I shall find the inner time-table making as close and accurate connection for me then as now.

~ Births: The Tradition Continues ~
What's in a Name

Every year when the list of most popular names appears I cannot help but wonder what's wrong with the good old names. Of course even the old-fashioned names began sometime and each generation must create its own names to reflect the mood of the times. Take Mary, for example. It is my first name, and was my aunt's. I'm sure she was given the name because, as the popular song at the time of her birth says, "It's a grand old name." The young girls who wrote the following essays are proud of their family names and, as you see, the name carried through the generations does not have to be a first name.

The name Sophia has for many years been passed to the second girl in each generation. My relatives on my dad's side of the family are Cuban. It's been a custom for many years for my family to pass on the name Sophia. I'm glad I have the name Sophia because I can pass it on to my children's children.

Sophia Pensado, elementary school

The tradition in my family is the middle name Ann. It started with my great-great-grandmother. She was born on August 21, 1889. Her name was Mary Ann. Mary was named after her mother.

My great-great-grandmother had a set of twins who were born on August 20, 1923. The girl was named Mary Ann. She had a daughter who was named Neddy Ann. On February 9, 1942, my great-grandmother had another daughter who was named Barbara Ann. She had a daughter named Sherrie Ann. My grandmother named my mom Kevin Ann. When I was born, Mom named me Beth Ann.

This has been a tradition in my family for 104 years. I will follow the family tradition if I have a daughter. This family tradition may have run for a longer period of time than 104 years, but no family member can remember any further back. I feel that this tradition is very good because it makes me feel good to know that I have the same name as all the girls before me. Even though I don't know my ancestors, I feel close to them.

Beth Ann Endsley, elementary school

From Tiny Acorns

The thirteen-year-old who penned this next passage when asked to write about traditions probably didn't realize that he had struck on an age-old custom practiced in Europe and the Middle East, but what a good idea!

A tradition that I think would be most interesting is to plant a tree when a child is born and let it grow with the child. By the time the tree is nice and big, the child can climb in its branches and sit in its cool shade. The child and the tree would be lifelong companions. If a tree was planted every time a baby was born, we could grow acres of cool green forest every day. This would, in my opinion, be a wonderful tradition. When each person has a birthday, a tree will be included as well. I wish my parents had done this for me.

J. C., middle school

I remembered this tradition when I was buying pansies and anemone bulbs last fall at Buchanan's Nursery. While paying the bill, I noticed a sign: Discover the Pleasure of Giving Plants for the New Baby. Something about the way it was phrased made me pause. "Whose idea was that?" I asked. This letter from Don Risser explains it all.

My wife and I have been waiting for quite some time to have children. Just recently we agreed to adopt three-week-old twins (a boy and a girl) from the Republic of Georgia, formerly part of Russia. We are ecstatic to say the least!

The idea of giving plants for the birth of a child is not only mine. Many people have planted trees and shrubs for a new baby so the child can watch it grow as he grows—hopefully cultivating new gardeners.

Don Risser

⤳ Christenings: The Tradition Continues ⤳

From Bryce Reveley, a master restorer of antique textiles, who also has wonderful suggestions for continuing traditions that are included in the wedding section, here are ways to make a christening ceremony all the more meaningful by using family heirlooms.

The antique skirt of a circa 1900 lingerie (batiste and lace) wedding dress becomes the christening dress for the first child, and then it is used for each subsequent child, sometimes with the names and birth dates of the children who have been baptized or christened in it embroidered on the dress itself or on the slip. The most names I have ever seen embroidered on a christening dress is thirteen, with the names David and Roger repeated for the boys and Mary and Claire for the girls. The quality of the embroidery varied from the exquisite work of nuns to the lowly quality of some harassed mother who obviously hated to sew but did not want to stop the family tradition of personalizing the dress. I have also seen wedding veils used as the overskirts for christening gowns, and sometimes the net and appliqués of lace are even embellished with pearls. The wedding handkerchief, which is traditionally carried, can also become a christening cap with three stitches and a little bit of ribbon, and if need be, the cap can become a handkerchief just by snipping away the three stitches!

Bryce Reveley

My great-grandmother made a baptismal gown and First Communion dress. The gown was for all her twelve children, and the dress was for Meme's five daughters. My grandma got to keep the gown and dress. My mom and my three aunts have all worn the pretty white dress to First Communion. My mom and all her brothers and sisters wore the baptismal gown. Now the gown has been worn by all my cousins, boys and girls. The Communion dress had been worn by all my girl cousins.

I will wear the dress next. I will keep it nice for my daughters. It will make me feel happy if my daughters keep the gown and dress for their daughters and sons. This is a tradition to pass on for many years. I am glad I was part of this tradition. It is very special to me.

Gena F. Paulk, elementary school

My family has lots of traditions, but my favorite one is about a christening gown. About one hundred years ago, my great-great-
grandmother made a lovely ivory gown. She wove the material and
laced and sewed them together. She did not have a sewing machine,
so she sewed the gown by hand. Every child in my family has been
christened in this gown. Everyone has complimented the gown. My
mom has the gown now. Someday she will pass it to my sisters,
brother, and me. This is one of our family traditions.

Ashley Christopher, elementary school

*If the child is truly an infant, the way my daughter, Joslin, was when she
was christened at three-weeks-old so that some family members could attend
who otherwise could not have, a soft baby pillow is a lovely addition to
the christening service. I used a pillowcase that her great-grandmother had
monogrammed for her grandfather, my father, some sixty years earlier.*

*Incidentally, I have also seen pillowcases for the yet unborn baby embroidered
with the names of the brothers and sisters surrounding a big question mark in
the center.*

➤ Birthdays: The Tradition Continues ➤

*How do you keep siblings happy when the other children's birthdays roll
around? Andrea Miele wrote, telling about a tradition her mother started
when she and her sisters were young.*

I have a most wonderful mother, who spent the better part of her life
making my life and my sisters' lives as delightful as possible. She is a
dear, considerate woman who helped to shape me into a confident
compassionate lady.

She adores her three daughters, and our happiness and development
was of utmost concern to her. For that reason she came up with the
notion of the Birthday Fairies.

When it was one of our birthdays and the natural emphasis would
be on us, she was always cautious not to alienate the other two sisters
or have them get hurt feelings. She created something called Birthday
Fairies that would leave small trinket gifts for the other children also.
Nothing extravagant that would take away from the actual birthday
child's celebration, but just a reminder that the sisters were loved too!
What an easy way of having children learn to celebrate along with the
birthday child, and not be jealous or envious.

A grand conclusion to this story is that we are grown women, and have carried on the tradition of Birthday Fairies! The trinkets are no longer necessary, but the Birthday Fairies are still a living, breathing entity in our birthday festivities symbolic of a light, joyous memory and a fanciful recollection!

Andrea Miele

My family has a tradition that we carry out every year. It is about my brother, Brandon, who has Down's syndrome. The tradition began when Brandon had heart surgery in 1989. We celebrate it every February 7. We call it a new heart party because he has a new heart and he enjoys it. My whole family comes and we have fun with Brandon at his party, and he has fun also. He has a heart cake with candles for each year he has had a new heart party. The cake always has stitches made from frosting, and the cake always says, "Bless My Mended Heart!"

Faith Wilson, elementary school

Each year on my son's birthday, I save the newspapers so that he can see what was happening throughout his lifetime. He's twenty-five now. Some of the papers are yellowed. I should have preserved them better, but I hope he will look back on them someday and enjoy the headlines.

Bee Weddington

— A Patriotic Birthday —

Have you ever thought of using an unusual birthday as a springboard for a gentle, amusing, and never-to-be-forgotten history lesson? It could be great fun if you accompany it with a cake and possibly music, the way David Tomsky does. The possibilities are limitless. A trip to the library, or even the chapter in this book, "Those Other Days," will get you started. Do a little more digging into the background of the birthday and you'll have a grand surprise for your family or co-workers.

The first time, it gave me quite a start. I was out of town and called back in to pick up my messages via that new invention, voice mail. Suddenly the entire Marine Corps Band was blaring "The Marines' Hymn" into my ear! "Oh, Dave!" I laughed. "Only you!"

My friend David F. Tomsky, Lieutenant Colonel USMC (Retired), is a die-hard marine who isn't going to let November 10 go by without reminding everyone he can that this is the proud day of the birth of the United States Marine Corps. He'll even tell you that the Corps predates our nation's birthday. And when he plays "The Marines' Hymn" for you, he's just carrying on a tradition. In David's own words:

Wherever marines gather on November 10 (and they do gather, around the globe), they salute the birth of the Corps in traditional ceremonial fashion. Part of that tradition is a decorated Marine Corps birthday cake, the reading of a traditional marine commandant's birthday message, and most important, the playing of "The Marines' Hymn." It's not really the birthday until "From the halls of Montezuma . . ." rings out. Now I'm retired, I have been left to my own devices to honor the Corps each November 10. My personal tribute has come to involve bringing a portable cassette recorder to work on that date and subsequently playing the Marine Band's rendition of "The Marines' Hymn," loudly and repeatedly, throughout the day. By doing so, I honor the Corps, continue to participate in a time-honored tradition, and annually remind both myself and my bemused co-workers from whence I came. Semper Fidelis.

To Dave's story, I would add this additional bit of fascinating history told in Thomas Jefferson and Music *by Helen Cripe:*

Jefferson enters the story of the Marine Band through that old enemy of the historian, tradition. Tradition says that he and Colonel Burrows went out horseback riding one day and discussed, among other things, the Marine Band. Jefferson thought that they were pretty bad and supposedly suggested enlisting some musicians in Italy as Marine and bringing them back either as a new band or to augment the existing one. Wherever the idea came from, Burrows, in 1803, told Captain John Hall, who was with Commander Edward Preble's squadron in the Mediterranean, to enlist the Italians. Hall enlisted eighteen Italians and bought instruments, much to the consternation of Colonel Burrows's successor, who knew nothing of any such orders. The Italians and their families arrived in Washington on September 19, 1805. They were not impressed —their "captain," Gaetano Caruso, said that they "arrived in a desert; in fact a place containing some two or three taverns, with a few scattering cottages or log huts, called the City of Washington, the Metropolis of the United States of America."

It is not clear whether they were a separate band or were added to the original one. Eventually all but six of them resigned from the corps, but several future leaders of the band came from the remaining six and their families.

And so the Marine Band was organized in 1800 in Washington at the suggestion of Colonel William Ward Burrows, first commandant of the United States Marine Corps. He also recommended that the corps enlist young boys specifically as musicians to be trained to be fifers and drummers.

These days, every year I mark November 10 on my calendar.

— The Joy of Sharing —

During my years as an antiques appraiser I was often struck by how many things a family accumulates and then hides away, only to be "found" years later—usually when cleaning out an estate.

This made me begin to think about how much better it is to give the things you love to those you love while they can appreciate the gifts as a sharing gesture. Think about this. Just as the young girls of long ago had hope chests, so you can begin a lifelong chest of treasures for your son or daughter, if not at birth then on one of their early birthdays.

Each year select a family heirloom and put the child's name on it. Either you can continue to use the object or you can pack it away in the drawer or chest designated for that child's gifts. If you continue to use it, take a photograph of the item and write a note to the child saying that this is his or her gift for such-and-such a birthday, along with any family history you wish to include. Seal the note and put it in the appropriate place. Later, when your child moves away or marries, or when it is just the right time, present these wonderful gifts. What a bounty!

— Selu —

MariJo Moore

Aware of what is happening to the children
Corn Woman walks the fields, carrying knowledge
from where the good medicine grows.

Pulling truths from stalks of corn
leaning into the winds, the teachings of long ago
become renewed with every grain the children swallow.

Keep in mind that you
are part of the whole, she reminds them.
The future is planted within you.

Give to yourselves lives to be proud of.
Treat yourselves and others
always with respect.

The rocks are listening. The trees are listening.
The eagles are listening. The rivers are listening.
And the children?

They are destined to hear
the sounds of the sacred grains of wisdom
growing inside their hearts.

CHAPTER 15

Courtships, Weddings, and Anniversaries

LOVE MAKES THE WORLD GO 'ROUND

— Something Old, Something New —

*EMYL JENKINS

Like most of my girlfriends, I was a dreamy sort back in my youth. It was inevitable in those days when the lyrics of songs included phrases like "Fairy tales can come true" and our movie fare was *Cinderella* and the original *Father of the Bride*. But most important, as you'll discover when you read the excerpt I have chosen from *Maid of Honor* on page 333, because I read the Little Colonel books, my fate as an incurable romantic was sealed.

Though I never cared much for baby dolls, I was awfully fond of my bride doll. She had a long, tapering dirty-blond pageboy and wore a simple white satin dress. She must have had a veil, but it has long since disappeared. My doll—if she had a name, I don't remember it —was a Christmas present the year I was seven, the same year I was the flower girl in my uncle's wedding. I loved every minute of that long walk down the aisle in my powder-puff pink dress with long sleeves, and I lived on the dream of it for years.

Mario Lanza's "Be My Love" topped the pop charts when I was in junior high, and Grace Kelly married Prince Rainier during my sophomore year in high school. As if that wasn't enough, I went to an all-girl college (we never heard of the term "single-sex" back then), Mary Washington in Fredericksburg, Virginia. The fact that there were no boys closer than the marine lieutenants at Quantico or the college boys at U. Va. or Washington and Lee added a distinct aura of romance and mystery to the dating scene.

Other than getting an unexpected but hoped-for weeknight telephone call from your current beau, the most exciting event that transpired in our safe and sanctimonious dorms was when one of the girls on your hall got pinned to the man of her dreams. Sue and Jim. Garnette and Bill. Peggy and Walter. The names were coupled on our lips for eternity.

Marriage was a holy state, and one we all looked forward to—usually as soon after graduation as possible. To add to the glamour of it all, because of the school's geographical location, several girls married West Point, Annapolis, VMI, or Quantico men in elaborate military weddings complete with an arch of crossed swords—or sabers if the groom was a navy man—and dress uniforms. I distinctly remember that by second semester of the senior year there were more copies of bride magazines than textbooks in some of my friends' rooms.

How times have changed. As I write this my own daughter, Joslin, is planning her wedding. It is going to be a wonderful occasion, a true May Day wedding with joyful music and flowers galore. Best of all, she is wearing my wedding dress. What a wonderful tradition and one that is cherished in many families!

Before taking the dress to be altered, though, I dug out my old wedding album to see how the skirt fell and exactly where the sleeves ended. A bittersweet feeling came over me as I turned the pages of those black-and-white wedding photographs of a thirty-year marriage that ended in divorce. But then most of life's happiest moments wear a sad halo. Can't let those pesky shadows become dark clouds, I was thinking when my eyes fell on a worn paperback in the same drawer where I kept the album. The cover, that of a pouting bride, left no doubt this was a 1960s wedding guide, one that I must have used and surely could still relate to. I turned to the chapter "Divorced Parents' Invitations."

"Never under any circumstances," I read, "may the names of both divorced parents appear on the same ceremony invitation or on the combination ceremony and reception invitation." Oh, dear! Joslin's already printed invitations begin:

Emyl Joslin Jenkins
Dr. Clauston Levi Jenkins, junior
request the honour of your presence
at the marriage of their daughter
Mary Joslin Asbill
to

Mr. Michael William Hultzapple

The more I read, the more I learned that almost everything we were doing for this dream wedding was, according to the 1960s etiquette book, dead wrong. The final straw came when I read that if the bride's father is giving (read "paying for") the reception and has remarried, "the real mother can take no active part in receiving the guests." Me? Fade into the background? Dream on.

While I may bemoan that today's generation is more likely to hear Ugly Kid Joe sing "I hate everything about you," than listen to Frank Sinatra croon, "Fairy tales can come true," and their idea of a wedding movie is *Sixteen Candles*, not *Father of the Bride*, still I'm awfully glad that my daughter can have both of her parents' names on her wedding invitation and that my delightful former husband, Clauston, his charming wife, Beth, and I can all greet the wedding guests at the reception.

Joslin and Mike will have a beautiful, joyful wedding filled with scores of old traditions. Kira Theuer, Mike's seven-year-old cousin, is the flower girl. My daughter is wearing my now vintage wedding dress. The minister who christened Joslin, and who has since retired and moved away, is making a special trip to Raleigh to marry her. He will read the wedding service from Joslin's great-grandmother's Book of Common Prayer. Just before she walks down the aisle, Joslin will slip the sixpence my friend Louise Talley brought to her from London into her shoe.

As for the *new* way we're doing some things at the wedding—that's just the beginning of some new family traditions.

～ Apache Song ～

ANONYMOUS

Now you will feel no rain,
for each of you will be a shelter to the other.

Now you will feel no cold,
for each of you will be warmth to the other.

Now there is no loneliness for you;
now there is no more loneliness.

Now you are two bodies,
but there is only one life before you.

Go now to your dwelling place,
to enter into your days together.

And may your days be good
and long on the earth.

～ The Properly Attired Bride ～

*Just when did it become the tradition for the bride to wear white? It must
have been sometime between the Civil War years and the 1880s. Many lavishly
beautiful and colorful velvet and silk nineteenth-century wedding dresses have
been preserved, but this 1859 description from Monroe City, Missouri, docu-
ments the style of a true American-style wedding dress:*

Her wedding dress was fashioned with a tight bodice, a
necklace neckline and dropped shoulders with flowing sleeves.
The material used was linsey-woolsey, a mixture of woolen
threads woven through linen threads, a cloth never made commercially but produced only on American farms and plantations.

Julia's dress had shadowy blocks of light and dark gray 5″
high and 3″ wide, which formed stripes going around her
5-yard skirt. The gray was broken by a 2″ band of wine-colored
wool and natural linen stripes alternating. The gown was lined
throughout with a fine tan mercerized corded material. The
lining had pockets for whale bone stays; a small pocket was

placed at the waist and a larger one in the fold of the skirt. Every tiny stitch had been put in by hand with loving care.

This is quite in contrast with the next description, taken from an 1880s etiquette book. The advice to the bride is also quite entertaining:

The bride should retire to rest early on the evening preceding the wedding, although the ceremony may not take place until the next evening. She should avoid all fatigue and excitement, and endeavor to look as fresh and blooming as possible on the all-important occasion.

The bride generally takes breakfast in her own room, and remains there until the hour arrives for her to resign herself to the hands of her maidens to be dressed for the altar. It is the bridesmaidens' privilege to perform this service.

After she is dressed she remains in her room till her carriage is announced, or, when the wedding is at the house, until it is time for her to descend to the drawing-room. The bride's carriage is invariably the last to leave the house, and it contains but one occupant besides herself—namely, her father or the person who is to give her away.

With regard to the dress of the bride, it is simply impossible to lay down a rule. It is governed by the fashion of the day, but is always white for a maiden, and of light colors for a widow contracting a second marriage. According to the present fashion, the attire of the former is that of a white moiré antique dress, with a very long train, or a plain white silk, with a lace skirt over it; wreath of orange blossoms, a Honiton lace veil, descending almost to the ground. Of course, the gloves should be white, and the shoes or boots of white kid, or white satin, as the case may be.

The brides of these days certainly followed those instructions to the letter if they could, for in The Shattered Dream, *the daybook of Margaret Sloan, a Southern bride at the turn of the century, the entry for Wednesday, April 18, 1900, reads, "We all attended the Tonsand-Mall wedding at the Stone Church at 7:30, and she was as pretty a bride as I have seen in a long while, attired in white organdie trimmed in white satin ribbon, with veil and orange blossoms."*

Today the traditional vision of "the bride wore white" still is permanently ingrained in every woman's mind. I'll always remember the scene in Bull Durham *when worldly-wise Millie, preparing for her wedding, asked her friend, "Annie, do you think I deserve to wear white?" to which Annie replied, "Honey, we all* deserve *to wear white."*

⟶ The First Step: Courting ⟵

"It's really wonderful to be courted," I remarked the other day when an unexpected bouquet of flowers arrived from Bob. Only when my friend looked at me in amazement and replied, "Courted! I haven't thought of that word in years," did I realize how totally nostalgic, romantic, and old-fashioned I am when it comes to matters of the heart.

In the old days courting played a most important part in one's social life, especially in those areas of the country where homesteads and plantations were far apart. The courting visits were carefully planned and greatly looked forward to in those days before automobiles and airplanes. This passage from Old Louisiana *describes the well-chaperoned mid-nineteenth-century courting scene, complete with happy ending.*

Propriety First

LYLE SAXON

After time had passed and the young family of my grandfather Watson had grown apace, he moved to Panola Plantation, on the Mississippi River in Louisiana, but not far from Natchez, Mississippi. Five of his daughters had married and it would soon be my mother's turn. She had just returned from Nazareth, Kentucky, where she had been for three or four years, finishing her education. She was graduated under able instruction of Sister Columbia Carroll, a niece of John Carroll of Carollton. Many of the Louisiana planters sent their daughters to school at Nazareth. The first time my mother saw my father, he had come to Nazareth to see a cousin of his who was to graduate with my mother. A crowd of girls (unknown to the good nuns) were peeping through the blinds of one of the rooms that overlooked the lawn in front of the school. The big chestnut horse that the young planter from Louisiana was riding, broke away from his master and went racing over the garden with Mr. Dix in full pursuit. Little did the young daughter of Mr. Watson think that before a year rolled away she would meet the rich young planter in Natchez and that he would fall in love with her.

Their meeting took place at his great-aunt's country house, "The Vale." He was playing on his violin, accompanied by his cousin, Miss Gailhard. When she (Miss Watson) entered the parlor, he lifted his eyes from the music and saw the girl who was afterward to become his wife, he did not play any more, but spent the rest of the evening talking to her. When my mother returned to Panola Plantation, the young planter paid frequent visits, while his overseer attended to his interest at home.

~ The Marriage Tree ~

PAUL WILSTACH

And for those who couldn't wait, there were the marriage trees. . . .

Whoever heard elsewhere of Marriage Trees? They show them on
Eastern Shore. They stand on the line between Maryland and Virginia.
This division between the two colonies was made in 1663, and in
running the line, Scarburgh and Calvert selected a number of sturdy
old oak trees as boundary monuments. On the northern side of this
line the Maryland justices and parsons made marriage easier for run-
aways from "farther down," and many young couples never journeyed
into Maryland beyond the shade of the north side of the "marriage
oak," where they found the joiner waiting for his fee.

~ To Indulge in Bundling ~

EDWIN MITCHELL

*"I trust you're going to include bundling in the traditions," one of my New
Orleans friends smiled mischievously, undoubtedly thinking to himself "that's
one way to get back at those oh-so-pure Yankees!"*

*"Bundling?" my own kids responded when I asked them if they had ever
heard of the tradition. "Sounds like something you do with a baseball bat, or
something you add to a fire," one of them remarked.*

*Surprised that they had not heard of the practice, I went on to explain it.
They thought I was kidding, so I rounded up this piece by Edwin Mitchell
from* It's an Old New England Custom. *My children have never looked at
their New England forefathers in the same way since.*

What is the truth about the old New England custom of bundling,
which had its rise in the severe weather conditions which prevail
throughout the region during part of the year? Was this antique
winter sport as innocent as some have said it was, or was it, as others
have alleged, a low and immoral practice? New England has long been
taunted with this unpuritan custom which permitted a young courting couple to spend the night together in the same bed either fully or
only partly clad. It flourished, paradoxically enough, while the shadow
of Calvin was still over the land and the private life of everyone was
the intimate concern of the whole community, especially of those
ardent investigators into local sin—the clergy.

Yet there were clergymen who condoned bundling, and some who even approved the custom. Others actually engaged in the practice themselves. One candidate for ordination, who later became a distinguished minister, wooed a number of girls, with at least one of whom, according to an entry in his diary, he bundled *magna cum voluptate*.

The Rev. Samuel Peters, author of the *General History of Connecticut* (1781), gave bundling a clean bill of health. He said it was not only a Christian custom, but a very polite and prudent one. The modesty of Connecticut females was such, he declared, that it would have been accounted the greatest rudeness to mention to a lady a garter or leg, yet it was thought but a piece of civility to ask her to bundle. But Mr. Peters as a social historian is unreliable. He had a rich talent for invention, one of his most notorious hoaxes being the spurious code of blue laws, which he promulgated out of whole cloth in the same work in which he discussed bundling. Yet there were people who shared his opinion that bundling was an innocent pastime, a view reflected in the following contemporary lines:

> Let coat and shift be turned adrift,
> And breeches take their flight,
> An honest man and virgin can
> Lie quiet all the night.

But when western Massachusetts became a hotbed of bundling Jonathan Edwards at Northampton raised his voice in stern warning against the custom, the consequences of which were only too evident in the number of babies born in less than the orthodox period after marriage. All over New England during the period of the Great Revival couple after couple stood up in open meeting and confessed to sexual intimacy before marriage.

In 1781, the Rev. Mr. Haven of Dedham, Massachusetts, shocked at the increase of sexual incontinence in his vicinage, attacked the growing sin in a memorable discourse in which he attributed the fault "to the custom then prevalent of females admitting young men to their beds who sought their company with intentions of marriage." The trouble was, of course, that marriage did not necessarily follow a course of bundling, and unless nature called a halt and precipitated a choice by the girl, there was danger that indulgence in the custom would lead to promiscuity.

It must be said, however, that despite the fact that bundling was done under cover in the dark, there was nothing furtive about it. Parents took the custom as a matter of course, the mother and sisters of the fortunate girl often helping to tuck the courting couple in bed together. Everything was done without self-consciousness. At the same time the extreme temptation involved in the situation was recognized, as the girl was frequently swathed like a mummy, or her legs were tied together, or a dividing board or other object placed between the bundlers and sleigh bells attached to the bed. But love laughs at token safeguards of this kind, and whether a case turned out to be one of guilt or innocence, conquest or control, rested ultimately, as it always has, with the young people themselves.

It has been claimed that one of the economic elements centering in the custom was the practical importance to a couple of knowing in advance of marriage whether or not they could have children to aid them in the struggle of life. It is true that bundling was a country custom; children were valuable assets in the agricultural life of the time, and apparently no special stigma attached to anyone if a baby was born seven months after marriage; but to say that young people married to solve the labor problem is to rule out romantic love and place matrimony on a rather sordid plane. The upper strata of New England town society, which did not practice bundling, admittedly took a decidedly mercenary view of marriage, as is shown by all the bickering and litigation there was over marriage settlements, but even among these people marriages were not contracted exclusively on a basis of mutual gain in worldly goods.

The conditions which favored bundling among rustic New Englanders were poorness of communications and the necessity of conserving heat and light. A country youth who had worked hard from sunrise to sunset all the week would set out on Saturday night to see his best girl. Habitations were widely spaced in those days, and the young man might have to walk from six to a dozen miles to reach the girl's house. The week end from sundown Saturday to sundown Sunday was practically the only time he had for courting. Families were large and houses small, with all beds occupied, and while the young couple could have sat up all night, this would have necessitated the expenditure of light and fuel which were too precious to be wasted in this way. So instead of turning the young man out in the cold, he and the girl enjoyed each others company in comfort by lying snugly together under the quilts in her feather bed.

Although this week-end country custom was extremely popular throughout New England, it neither originated here nor was it confined exclusively to New England. New Englanders blamed it on the Dutch, and the Dutch on the New Englanders. An amusing passage in Washington Irving's *Knickerbocker's History of New York,* ascribes bundling to the inventive genius of the Connecticut Yankees, who, it is said, practiced it to keep up a harmony of interests and to promote the population:

"They multiplied to a degree," Irving wrote, "which would be incredible to any man unacquainted with the marvelous fecundity of this young country. This amazing increase may, indeed, be partly ascribed to a singular custom prevalent among them, commonly known by the name of *bundling*—a superstitious rite observed by the young people of both sexes, with which they usually terminate their festivities, and which was kept up with religious strictness by the more bigoted and vulgar of the community.

"This ceremony was likewise, in those primitive times, considered as an indispensable preliminary to matrimony; their courtships commencing where ours usually finish, by which means they acquired that intimate acquaintance with each other before marriage, which has been pronounced by philosophers the sure basis of a happy union. Thus early did this cunning and ingenious people display a shrewdness at making a bargain, which has ever since distinguished them, and a strict adherence to the good old vulgar maxim about 'buying a pig in a poke.'

"To this sagacious custom, therefore, do I chiefly attribute the unparalleled increase of the Yanokie or Yankee tribe; for it is a certain fact, well authenticated by court records and parish registers, that wherever the practice of bundling prevailed, there was an amazing number of sturdy brats annually born unto the state, without the licence of the law or the benefit of clergy. Neither did the irregularity of their birth operate in the least to their disparagement. On the contrary, they grew up a long-sided, raw-boned race of whoreson whalers, wood cutters, fishermen and peddlers; and strapping corn-fed wenches, who by their united efforts tended marvelously toward populating those notable tracts of country called Nantucket, Piscataway and Cape Cod."

The Conjugal Bed

Herman Melville

How it is I know not; but there is no place like a bed for confidential disclosures between friends. Man and wife, they say, there open the very bottom of their souls to each other; and some old couples often lie and chat over old times till nearly morning.

Actually, when the record-breaking winter of 1996 blanketed the sunny South with arctic air, many of us who were without electricity, water, or phones for several days would have cheerfully agreed that bundling can have its place, especially when firewood is hard to come by. Here are two stanzas from a 1786 ballad in favor of bundling:

> *Nature's request is give me rest,*
> *Our bodies seek repose.*
> *Night is the time and 'tis no crime*
> *To bundle in our cloaths.*

> *Since in a bed, a man and maid*
> *May bundle and be chaste:*
> *It doth no good to burn up wood,*
> *It is a needless waste.*

~ *"Dear Father-of@Bride.to.Be* ~ *May I Please Marry Your Daughter?"*

Bob Levy

So today's children don't know about bundling. "Thank goodness!" the prude in me sighs. "Are you kidding?" replies my 1990s self. "Bundling? Who needs it in today's anything-goes world?"

If there is one thing I have learned from compiling the hundreds of traditions that make up this book, it is that the members of every generation are going to create new traditions to fit their lifestyle. Today in place of bundling there's cybercourting.

Job searches via the Internet? Commonplace. Bridge games on the Internet? Constantly. But asking for a young lady's hand in marriage via the Internet?

It happened last month. Instead of journeying all the way from

South Carolina to Fredericksburg, Va., to ask whether he could ask The Question, Kinny Vinson simply sent an e-mail query to Patrick McCarthy, father of Tracy.

"Pat," began Kinny, with admirable directness, "over my spring break, Tracy and I will be going to Pigeon Forge, Tenn., for a short vacation. I am planning on proposing to her during that trip, and would like to ask you for your permission.

"I know that this is a very informal way of doing so, but it is different. Anyway, all that Tracy knows is that we are going out of town for a few days and that we are going somewhere in Tennessee, so be sure not to let the cat out of the bag before then.

"Hope to hear back from you very soon."

Kinny did.

"He mailed me back right after, saying he approved and he hoped I would make her happy," said Kinny, who's a mechanical engineering student at the University of South Carolina. "It was kind of a nice way of doing it, because we have a written record of what I said and what he said."

Kinny added that he didn't figure Patrick would be offended by his cyberrequest, since the two men are dedicated hackers who discuss computers all the time.

The bride-to-be was a bit abashed by her intended's methodology. "When he said he had done it over the Internet, I said, 'Anybody could have read this!'" Tracy recalled.

But she was delighted to accept Kinny's proposal just the same. The couple plans to set a date soon, probably for May 1996.

How did it feel for Kinny's message to come chugging into an unsuspecting Dad's work station? "I was flattered that in this day and age, he had honored an old tradition," said Patrick, who works as a computer program manager.

"I wrote back to him telling him I appreciated him letting us know. I really didn't expect him to do it this way, but he's an engineer, so I guess it makes sense."

The mother of the bride-to-be, Karen McCarthy, knew that March 3 was supposed to be Bended Knee Day down in Pigeon Forge. But by the eighth, Tracy hadn't called. So Karen called Kinny's mother and learned that the couple hadn't left their home town of Columbia, South Carolina, until March 8. Tracy's "jumping up and down call" came soon after.

Will wedding invitations go out via the Internet? No one's saying, but understandably, suspicions abound.

~ So Many Details! ~

JOHN SIMCOX HOLMES

At the turn of the century, John Simcox Holmes, a graduate of the Yale School of Forestry, became bethrothed to Miss Emilie Rose Smedes of Washington, D.C. Holmes wrote this endearing love letter, now in the Southern Historical Collection at the University of North Carolina, while he was working as a state forester in Asheville, North Carolina. In between passages telling Emilie about his work and friends there, John writes about their upcoming November 1, 1909, wedding and honeymoon plans. Those excerpts follow.

> Tuesday, Oct. 5
> 6:15 P.M.

Yes, my darling, I got your kiss, but it wasn't a very good one. You will have to supplement it later on. You will do that for me won't you? Your dear little note written just 30 hours ago is most welcome, as it is 36 hours since I heard from you. . . .

Now dear, you must tell me what flowers you would like on the 1st. Do you carry them in church? & does Miss Henrietta? Red roses? or white? or something else. Be sure to let me know, so that I can write & engage them. I wrote to engage the berth, I mean stateroom "for myself & wife." That certainly sounds nice, doesn't it? I said No. 16 (or 18). This is the most forward stateroom on deck on the port side. They all seem much about the same on that boat, but the most forward is further from the smell & the noise of the machinery.

I have about 115 names on my list & there will be probably 15 or 20 more making about 130-140. Will complete it soon. I am so afraid of leaving out people who might feel hurt. About 55 or 60 of these go to the Forest Service. Tell me if that is larger or less than your list.

My dearest one, I love you & want you. Bless you. Are you keeping well in the midst of all this rush & hurry? Don't do too much. You had much better leave something undone than get run down.

> God keep you, my own,
> *Your Jack*

⤙ A Moveable Wedding ⤚

LYLE SAXON

While making the necessary plans for my daughter Joslin's wedding, over and over we were given the same advice: "Just don't get upset if everything isn't absolutely perfect. Something is bound to go amiss." Inevitably, some little glitch seems to be part of the wedding tradition, but hopefully none calling for the extreme measure the bride's father had to go to for the nineteenth-century wedding described here.

Sallie was a ward of my father's, and everyone called her a beautiful girl. Her father and mother were dead and she lived with us after she left school. In those days, young girls did literally nothing. She sat in the sun and entertained her many beaux, and finally selected the handsomest, or the richest among the crowd that came a-courting. It was necessary—or so they thought—that she must attend all the balls and parties, and must spend part of the season at least in New Orleans, at Mardi Gras balls and at the French Opera. She gave house parties on the plantation and entertained her friends from New Orleans in return.

Cousin Sallie had, among her suitors, a young man that she had met at Green Brier, White Sulphur Springs [then Virginia, now West Virginia]. He was a rich man's son from the upper part of Mississippi and did very little but enjoy himself. Both my cousin Sallie and he were well mated in this respect. He came down to visit her at Bralston; and as the time approached for the wedding, every steamboat that stopped at Fairview Landing brought boxes of drygoods and beautiful costumes for her trousseau. The wedding dress was of brocaded white satin, with a veil of fine white lace, and the contrast to her brunette type was calculated to produce a beautiful effect. The old Bralston home was a long rambling house, one story high. The front door opened directly into the double parlors. The parlors, on her wedding day, had been made into a bower of roses and formed a lovely setting for the bridal party. The back gallery was laid with the wedding supper. A caterer came up from New Orleans to supervise everything. All was in readiness for the wedding; the guests had arrived and bridegroom, with the minister and best man. They stood in their appointed places and the bride entered from the library on my father's arm. Truly she appeared a dream of beauty. The bridegroom handed his license to the old minister to glance over before beginning the ceremony and a look of amazement came over the old gentleman's face. He spoke out so everyone in the room could hear:

"Well, Mr. Owen, the license is made out for the wedding to take place in Mississippi, and here we are in Louisiana!"

"Consternation!"

"Of course the wedding will have to be postponed until the mistake is rectified," the minister said.

"But," said the young man, "cannot some way be found out of the difficulty? The wedding must take place this evening. All of our plans will be upset."

The old minister said that he could see no way out of the difficulty. Then my father said something to the bride, who smiled and nodded her head. Then my father spoke up and said: "What is to prevent my calling up several of my men and letting them bring the required number of skiffs to the landing; then let the bridal party with the minister and guests get in the boats, row across the river to the Mississippi side. The young people can be married on the sandbar, then return home for the supper and dancing."

All acceded to this proposal, and the skiffs were brought. The negroes came trouping from the quarters. Dozens of skiffs appeared. The bride and bridegroom and the guests—about twenty-five young girls and forty young men, not to mention the older people, the minister and the children, rowed across the river, and standing on the sandbar beside the Mississippi the ceremony was completed. "How romantic! How beautiful!" everyone said.

When the minister held up his hand in blessing, the plantation bell rang out from across the water, and we could hear the negroes cheering on the opposite bank of the stream.

⟶ The Presence of Your ⟵ Company Is Requested

Weddings invariably bring out the best in all of us. To the religious among us, weddings are a metaphor for rebirth. To the romantic, weddings give dreams a chance to come true. To most of us, weddings embody hope in its deepest sense.

In today's world, chances are great that someone close to you, a friend or family member, will marry someone quite unlike himself or herself. County marries city. Californian marries New Yorker. Youth marries age. Jew marries Gentile. Black marries white. Regardless of the differences, as Homer wrote in The Odyssey, *"There is nothing nobler or more admirable than when two people who see eye to eye keep house as man and wife, confounding their enemies and delighting their friends."*

Weddings, unlike any other of our rites of passage in life, bring us together in a festive setting. Surrounded by laughter and food, new understandings and friendships are formed. Even in the old days, cultural and religious differences were dissolved at the altar. I know my mother always told me that I became an Episcopalian when a brawny Irish Catholic lad gave his heart to a Presbyterian Scottish lass.

To celebrate that admirable union, here from assorted sources are descriptions of wedding traditions gathered far and wide that continue today—many now being blended together as new families are formed. As always, the Bard said it best:

> *A contract of eternal bond of love,*
> *Confirm'd by mutual joining of your hands,*
> *Attested by the holy close of lips,*
> *Strengthen'd by interchangement of your rings;*
> *And all the ceremony of this compact*
> *Sealed in my function, by my testimony.*
>
> William Shakespeare, Twelfth Night

⟶ *The Shivaree* ⟵

JESSAMYN WEST

Ever heard of a shivaree? I don't believe I had until I reread Jessamyn West's book, The Friendly Persuasion, *a short time back. I was giving a talk at Conner Prairie, a wonderful restoration outside of Indianapolis, and wanted to refresh my memory about the early settlers of that area. Certainly I did not remember this wedding-night practice from my first 1950s reading of the touching story of Quakers during the Civil War era.*

A shivaree is a French peasant wedding tradition brought to this country by the Acadians and still occasionally practiced today. Originally a crowd would gather where the newly married couple were spending their first conjugal night and boisterously "serenade" them with disruptive, playful songs and noises accompanied by pots and pans. Today a shivaree combines good fun with a dose of devilment, much like decorating the getaway car. Usually the couple expects to be "shivareed" and is prepared for the event by having coins to toss out to the crowd, which of course breaks up the merriment.

She [Elspeth] was almost asleep when she heard from down the road the first shots of the shivaree, the banging of milk pans and the clanging of bells. Mel Venters looked away from the fire. "What's going on?" he asked. "Where's all that noise coming from?"

"From the shivaree," Elspeth told him. "They're shivareeing Uncle

Stephen and Aunt Lidy. . . . They'll stand out on the balcony . . . and bow to the people. Then," she said, clutching her jack-in-the-box, which she had forgotten to put down, "they'll bow to each other and kiss." . . .

There was a blaze of light from the torches and lanterns of the people who had come for the shivaree, but the house itself was still dark, the balcony empty. Mel's sleigh cut hissing up the driveway and the crowd, seeing who had arrived, shouted and pounded louder than before.

"Hi Mel, come to have your last look at the bride?"

Mel said nothing, either to Elspeth or the shivaree-ers, but brought up his sleigh, sharply and deftly, in their midst.

"She ain't here," someone yelled to him. "Neither one's here. They've flown the coop."

"Go on, Mel, you ask the bride to come out," they shouted. "You got a way with women. She'll do it for you, Mel."

They seemed to know what they were talking about; lights showed through the upstairs windows while they were still calling on Mel to ask the bride to come out. They redoubled their shouting then and in a minute or two Elspeth saw Uncle Stephen open the door onto the balcony then turn back, give his hand to Aunt Lidy, who stepped out and took her place beside him. Uncle Stephen had on his black suit, but Aunt Lidy was in a long red dress, a dressing gown, perhaps; something that in the flicker of light from torches and lanterns looked to Elspeth like a dress which might have had a crown about it, or a garland of flowers. Aunt Lidy's dark hair was uncoiled and hung about her face and down her shoulders in rippling tongues of black.

Uncle Stephen called out, "Hello, folks," and waved and said, "I sure did," to someone who yelled, "You sure picked a looker, Steve," but Aunt Lidy said nothing. She simply stood there very quietly with the red-gold of the torches and lanterns on her face, looking down at the crowd sometimes, but more often smiling and watching Uncle Stephen as he and the shivaree-ers shouted back and forth to each other. . . .

Then Aunt Lidy did what Elspeth had said she would: she made toward the crowd beneath her a slight bowing movement, then laid her arms, very solemnly and slowly, as if thinking what she's doing, about Uncle Stephen's neck and kissed him, just as seriously and just as slowly. No one of all the shivaree-ers yelled or hooted—because the kiss did not seem playful, but almost a part of the wedding ceremony, dignified and holy. . . .

When [Elspeth] looked back at the balcony Aunt Lidy was standing as before and Uncle Stephen had his arm about her shoulders. He leaned over the balcony and spoke in a matter-of-fact way. "There's food in the house, folks, and warm drinks. Come in and welcome."

Elspeth came in with the shivaree-ers, but grandma hustled her upstairs before the eating and drinking started. In bed she lay listening to the night's many sounds. The sounds, at first from belowstairs: the shouting and talking and singing, then the pawing and neighing of horses and sound of sleigh bells growing fine and thin as the bells of China in the frosty air, and finally the sounds of grandpa's and grandma's talking.

— "Running Up" the Bridegroom —

J. L. HERRING

Good-natured horseplay and revelry are an expected part of country weddings. This account of "running up" the bridegroom describes a custom in the wiregrass country of Georgia. Note also the time of the year—Christmas. Long ago when ours was an agrarian country, December, not June, was the favored month for weddings. The farmers and planters had to be in their fields during the summer. Winter was a more leisurely time.

Bang! Whoop! Whoo-e-e! "Here they come!"

To the crack of revolvers, the pop of seventeen-foot cow-whips, cheers and rebel yells the cavalcade, over fifty strong, came in sight over the hill. Down the slope, through the vale and up the rise to the homestead they rode, yelling like Indians and with a thunder like a cavalry charge.

In front rode the bridegroom, on either side his groomsmen. The galloping, yelling, shooting crowd behind were his chosen friends, companions of boyhood and early manhood, today gathered from a radius of forty miles to pay him this tribute of friendship and esteem, according to a time-honored Wiregrass Georgia custom, known as "running up" the bridegroom.

We had passed the crowd half an hour before as we drove to the home of the bride, sitting on their horses in a thicket of pines, awaiting the coming of the groom and his best men. Now they nearly overtook us as they came, like a whirlwind, bringing her lover to his bride.

Without slackening speed, up to the gate they came, the groom and his men springing from their still-prancing horses, reined suddenly back upon their haunches. The reins were caught by ready hands, and the honor guests of the day went in.

The marriage was the union of two of the oldest families of Wire-grass Georgia. Sturdy pioneers, stockmen, their fathers numbered their acres as their cattle and sheep, in terms of thousands. For many weeks the news had gone out that the marriage day approached and on this balmy morning the day before Christmas, from all points of the compass they gathered. Coming in wagon, in buggy, on horseback, in ox cart and afoot, a day's journey was accounted as only one to a next-door neighbor, for distances were magnificent then and settlements few.

The homestead consisted of the "big house" built of logs, in double-pen, with broad piazzas on either side. The chimneys were of stick and clay, well-built and substantial; the roof of boards rived from straight-grained pine, the floor hewn from the same useful tree.

Across the white, sanded, tree-shaded yard one hundred feet away, stood the kitchen, with its gaping fireplace; back a little the smoke-house, and farther to the rear the corn crib, all constructed of logs, the universal building material.

In the house, in the yard, even outside the gate for some distance the guests were gathered in groups and couples. Inside the house was a bustle of preparation. Everywhere in the decorations was the festive green and white, cedar boughs and arbor-vitae dipped in flour, symbols of the wedding time. In vases, on mantels, everywhere the clusters could be hung, they were in evidence, with occasional strings of red "bachelor buttons," and a few brilliant prince-feathers and coxcombs.

Out on the front piazza walked the bride, blushing like a June morning, with her maids on either side. Dressed in virginal white, with delicate touches of color in ribbons at neck and waist, and wreaths of evergreen on their hair.

As the groom and his party met them, they turned and faced the preacher, a patriarch and the head of one of the families. In a simple ceremony, he spoke the words that united the young pair for life—for there were no divorces among those people.

Then came the next great event of the day—dinner. For a week, the mother with a corps of assistants had been preparing for this. Great stacks of potato custards, mountains of ginger cakes and cookies, piles of crullers, immense chicken pot-pies, baked chicken, turkey, boiled ham, beef roast and venison sliced, sausage, souse, pork—all of the plenty of this home of plenty, among a people whose watchword was hospitality, and who would have esteemed it a lasting reproach for a guest to leave hungry.

No house could hold that crowd, and the tables were set, end-to-end, across the glistening yard. Not much silver, but snowy linen and glistening glass; vases filled with cedar, white and green, and flowers. Great Pound-cakes alternated with layer, cinnamon and angel, the more solid cakes all frosted and garnished with green. In the center was the bride's cake, pyramided, one upon the other, a red apple on the apex, frosted and garnished in colors. Its cutting marked the advent of the wedding-party.

Talk about eating! To eat was considered an accomplishment then. The tables would seat hundreds, and as fast as one appetite was satisfied, its owner rose and another took his place. A dozen negroes, in long white aprons, their wool festooned with feathers of the turkey and chicken of many colors, were kept on the jump supplying viands that ever disappeared.

The feast began soon after noon, and as the shades of evening came, they were still eating.

Those were good people, good times, and good customs; all are gone now. This is a new age, but no better one, and precious memories are those of the days and the people who are no more.

The bride, fulfilling her destiny of wifehood and motherhood, was long since claimed by the pale groom, Death; the groom is now on the threshold of old age, but perhaps in retrospect there comes again to him as to the writer, clearer even than yesterday, the sunny morning of Christmas eve, when friends "run him up" to the home of the love of his youth.

⁓ How to Recognize a Jewish Wedding ⁓

VERA LEE

Are you tired of the same lovely but often solemn and sometimes even teary-eyed wedding ceremonies? If you are unfamiliar with the Jewish ceremony, Vera Lee explains the differences between Christian and Jewish weddings. If you have never attended one, you may be surprised at how exciting a Jewish wedding really is. From beginning to end, a Jewish wedding offers an exciting start to a marriage.

The modern Jewish wedding doesn't differ radically from a Christian one, but it has a number of important symbols and traditions that clearly set it apart.

There is first of all the *ketubah,* the Hebrew marriage contract dating from the end of the first century and still in use today. Much like the ancient Egyptian contract, the *ketubah* was designed mainly to assure the bride's legal status and protect her rights. But that contract, often just a formality these days, is not a conspicuous feature of most marriage ceremonies.

If we actually attend a Jewish wedding—whether at the home of a blue-collar worker or at a posh Park Avenue temple—we are immediately aware of some very visible symbols that mark the wedding as a Jewish one.

Of course there are the *yamulkes,* those little beanie caps (usually white for weddings) worn by the rabbi, the groom, the wedding party and male guests.

Then, instead of an altar you will see a *huppah,* an improvised canopy attached to four poles, under which the couple will be wed. (The origin of that custom is now lost, but other Middle Eastern civilizations have used bamboo posts topped with boughs and leaves at their weddings.)

The procession down the aisle is different, too. In most Christian marriages, the father of the bride walks to the altar to give his daughter away, while the other parents sit teary-eyed in their pews. At a Jewish wedding, usually both parents of the bride and groom will escort their children to the *huppah,* demonstrating involvement of the whole family.

And there is that exotic tradition: the breaking of the glass. After the ceremony has been recited in Hebrew and English, the groom stomps on a glass (wrapped in cloth in order not to bloody anyone) as people applaud or shout *"mazeltov"* (congratulations).

The broken glass symbol has many interpretations. For some, it signifies the frailty of human happiness; for others, it refers to the destruction of the Israelite Temple in the year 70 A.D. In the past, some Jewish husbands have insisted that it means they will have all the authority in the household. (Who would dare say that these days?) But one of the oldest and most common interpretations of broken glass at weddings is the easing of sexual penetration on the first night of marriage.

(Sicily, Greece and England, among other countries, have also had the custom of breaking glass at weddings. In the Greek village of Epirus today, when the bride leaves her house, she kicks a glass of wine placed at her doorstep. If it breaks, the marriage will be successful.)

The festivities at a Jewish wedding reception will nearly always include, besides ballroom dancing, a round of that lively Israeli circle dance, the *hora.* At times, it may be accompanied by a real old-world *klezmer* band, combining Eastern European Jewish themes and traces of modern jazz.

Next comes the grand finale. As in other cultures, the Jewish bride and groom are considered royalty, at least for a day. So they are each enthroned and their chairs are lifted high in the air over the dancing, cheering guests.

When couples are aloft, you will usually see them each clutching one end of a handkerchief or cloth napkin. This symbolizes their union, but it also reminds us that in former times Jewish couples, even married ones, were not allowed to touch each other in public.

Sometimes, in their enthusiasm, the bridal party will also hoist up the chairs containing the couple's parents. That can get a bit hairy, however, especially if mom and dad are unaccustomed to levitation outside a 747.

Now, traditionally, one of a Jewish mother's main goals in life was to marry off all her children. That—besides being a perfect house-keeper—was a sure sign of her success. So if by chance the bride or groom is the last child to be married off, you may see and participate in the joyful *krentsl* dance.

The mother of the last marriageable child is crowned with a wreath of leaves, a *krentsl* (a Yiddish diminutive of *kranz,* the German word for "wreath").

Then family and friends surround the lucky lady and joyfully dance around her.

Meanwhile, a sumptuous meal, sometimes lasting hours, will bring the event to its conclusion.

So, if you knew nothing about Jewish weddings before reading this, now you can say when you go to one, "By jove, this is a Jewish wedding!"

— *Jumping the Broom* —

HARRIETTE COLE

When a family wedding is eminent, the mother-of-the-bride becomes an avid reader of newspaper wedding and engagement announcements. That's how I learned that Pamela Dorese Hudson and William Henry Daniel had included the old African wedding tradition of "jumping the broom" at their Richmond, Virginia, reception. "The attending guests joined the couple in the symbolic jump," I read. I had to know more. Harriette Cole's history of this touching tradition adapted below reinforces how important traditions are, even in the worst of times, and how, during times of oppression, they help a people. How wonderful that this inspired tradition has bridged the continents and the centuries.

Not long after the beginning of Slavery, Africans were . . . denied the right to marry in the eyes of the law. Yet the enslaved were spiritual people who had been taught rituals that began as early as childhood to prepare them for that big step into family life. How could they succumb to this denial?

They could not. So they became inventive. Out of their creativity came the tradition of jumping the broom. The broom itself held spiritual significance for many African peoples, representing the beginning of homemaking for a couple. For the Kgatla people of southern Africa, it was customary, for example, on the day after the wedding for the bride to help the other women in the family to sweep the courtyard clean, thereby symbolizing her willingness and obligation to assist in housework at her in-laws' residence until the Couple moved to their own home. During slavery, to the ever-present beat of the talking drum, a couple would literally jump over a broom into the seat of matrimony. Today, this tradition and many others are finding their way back into the wedding ceremony.

Slave narratives and other early nineteenth-century documentation reveal the ways in which slave couples did their jumping. With the master's permission a couple was allowed to stand before witnesses, pledge their devotion to each other, and finally jump over a broom, which would indicate their step into married life. Below is a slave marriage ceremony supplement, found in the sheet music—dated Sunday, September 9, 1900—to the song "At an Ole Virginia Wedding":

> Dark an' stormy may come de wedder;
> I jines dis he-male an' dis she'male togedder.
> Let none, but Him dat makes de, thunder,
> Put dis he-male, and dis she-male asunder.
> I darefor 'nounce you bofe de same.
> Be good, go 'long, an' keep up yo' name.
> De broomstick's jumped, de world not wide.
> She's now yo' own. Salute yo' bride!

Following are two versions of jumping the broom from *Bullwhip Days: The Slaves Remember* by James Mellon. What's especially revealing is that in both instances the master of the plantation encouraged and blessed the union of "his" slaves. In the first passage the slave Joe Rawls reminisces about his wedding at the turn of the century.

Well, dey jis lay de broom down, 'n' dem what's gwine ter git marry walks out 'n' steps ober dat broom bofe togedder, 'n' de ole massa, he say, "I now pronounce you man 'n' wife" 'n' den dey was marry. Dat was all dey was t'it—no ce'mony, no license, no nothin', jis' marryin'.

The second passage is a description of the wedding ceremony of a woman named Tempie Durham. After an elaborate wedding, complete with food, drink, and formal ceremony, the groom had to leave to go back to his owner's plantation nearby. The couple was never allowed to live together. They did have eleven children, which prompted Tempie to write, "I was worth a heap to Marse George, 'kaze I had so many chillun." Here's her version of jumping the broom:

> After Uncle Edmond said de las' words over me an' Exter, Marse George got to have his little fun. He say, "Come on, Exter, you an' Tempie got to jump over de broomstick backwards. You go to do dat to see which one gwine be boss of your househol'." Everbody come stan' roun' to watch. Marse George hold de broom 'bout a foot high off de floor. De one dat jump over it backwards an' never touch de handle gwine boss de house, an' if bofe of dem jump over widout touchin' it, dey ain't gwine be no bossin'; de jus' gwine be 'genial.
>
> I jumped fus', an' you ought to seed me. I sailed right over dat broomstick, same as a cricket. But when Exter jump, he done had a big dram an' his feets was so big an' clumsy dat dey got all tangled up in dat broom, an' he fell headlong. Marse George, he laugh an' laugh, an' tole, Exter he gwine be bossed till he skeered to speak less'n I tole, him to speak.

The practice of jumping the broom is the most widely known wedding ritual born in the African-American community, thanks to Alex Haley's epic family saga *Roots,* in the dramatic scene in which Kunta Kinte and Bell took their step into married life. Since the 1970s countless African-American couples have incorporated this tradition into their weddings with the intention of creating a bridge between them and their cultural heritage. No matter how Western or cultural African-American ceremonies may be, that one act binds thousands of couples together in solidarity.

The use of traditions that have been either borrowed from African shores or from the Caribbean, or that were born anew here, spans much farther than this one practice. In many cases, Black couples don't even realize they are part of our own tradition. Take, for instance, the lesser-known tradition of crossing sticks. Artist Lloyd Toone unearthed an early-1900s family wedding portrait from Chase City, Virginia, featuring a couple crossing two strong sticks, one more sign of holy matrimony. . . . Symbolizing the strength and vitality of trees, the staff-like sticks were crossed to honor and bless the new life that was about to begin. . . . Among the Samburu of Kenya, sticks were also used during wedding celebrations by the groom to brand the beloved cattle that he would give his wife to finalize their vows.

Cultural links can be found throughout the process of getting married, from the food we eat, to the way we dress, to the rituals we perform at the ceremony. For example, just the thought of preparing West Indian Black Cake, not to mention eating it, whets an African-American palate. Along with plain old delicious pound cake, it is a remnant of our Caribbean and African legacies that frequently finds its way onto wedding dessert tables today. Our current desire to decorate our hair with vibrant dyes of burnished red and braids adorned with cowrie shells dates back centuries to the custom of covering hair with a mixture of red ochre and animal fat on special occasions, and of wearing the plentiful cowrie shells to encourage fertility. The revived practice of pouring libation to the ancestors and offering a prayer of supplication to them dates back possibly to the beginning of time and has been incorporated into many contemporary ceremonies.

The common denominator for our people the world over is *family*. In some African societies a marriage is not official until a libation has been poured and a prayer offered requesting grace from those family members who have passed. In countless African tribes from the east, the west, and the southernmost points, inclusion of nuclear and extended family members throughout the process of marriage has been a given. Even today parents in some African societies still arrange marriages for their children. It is customary in Ghana for aunts and other elders to play private detective, running what amounts to a background check on a future spouse to determine that person's reputation, health and wealth status, family heritage, and other vital information. Aunts, cousins, and older female relatives throughout West Africa often take the role of "wedding consultant," helping to secure all the details of the courtship and ceremony.

Family elders impart detailed counseling once a couple has received the requisite permission from both sets of parents. For young women the messages come both in whispered tones and in group meetings when female elders share insights on the duties of a wife—everything from how to cook food and clean house to how to make love. In Liberia there is even a special school, called Sande Society, to which young girls between ages six and ten go for several years to learn the art of homemaking. Many African societies tend to be male-centered, and young men surely don't get off the hook when it comes to marital duty. Their fathers, mothers, and community elders teach them the ways of providing for their families. Lessons vary depending upon the nature of the group's income, and whether it is based on agriculture, mining, hunting, or other means. African communities commonly practice rituals through which boys must pass to reach manhood and during which they receive all of the lessons that they need to function as adults. If a generalization can be made about a continent of people, it is that African families tend to be close-knit even today, though they may be sewn together a bit differently than their African-American counterparts.

An African Wedding Benediction

Divine helpers, come! Keep watch all night! Rather than see the bridegroom so much as damage his toenail, may the good spirits go ahead of him. May the bride not so much as damage her fingernail! The good spirits will be their cushion so that not a hair of their heads shall be harmed.

And you, all you good wedding guests waiting in the shadows, come out into the light! May the light follow you!

— The Chinese-American Ringbearer —

BEN FONG-TORRES

I never see a child dressed in his or her finest clothes going into a church for a wedding, usually holding on to an adult's hand, that I do not remember Bill and Margaret Kable's wedding. Seated in the pew immediately in front of me, Margaret's little niece was picture-book perfect in her finest summer outfit. She sat so still, as instructed by her eager parents, that soon she fell dead asleep. She awakened just as the bride and groom were walking out of the church, accompanied by the blaring organ. Needless to say, the tears flowed.

Ben Fong-Torres knew he had to be on his best behavior when he was the ring bearer in an elaborate San Francisco wedding. And yes, he, too, fell asleep, but not until he treated us to this view of a traditional, exuberant Chinese-American wedding celebration as seen through a child's eyes.

I did not know what a wedding was. At age six in the fall of 1951, all I knew was that I was going to be involved in a big one.

One of Grace Fung's sons was getting married, and somehow, among Grace and her husband Jack and my parents, it was decided that I'd make a perfect ringbearer.

I could tell it was a big deal by the way my parents spoke to me. My father always spoke firmly, but with an agreeable laugh, while my mother offered the gentle touch, a softness leavened by the under-standing that in our house, she handled most of the discipline. Now, as they told me of my responsibilities, I sensed that I was about to do something grown-up. This wasn't just going to school, or joining my siblings in a simple chore, or singing a song at the neighborhood grocery. This was stand-alone time.

"Fung Moo and Fung Bok are our good, good friends," my mother said. "It's a big wedding, several hundred people. You'll have to practice and make sure you do it right. You don't want to *seet-meen*—lose face."

No, I wouldn't want to . . . *what?*

"How can I lose my face?" I asked.

She laughed.

"Losing face means disgrace, loss of respect for your family. So you must be good."

We went shopping at Roos Brothers, a downtown store that, to my amazement, stocked only men's clothing. We'd always gone to big department stores or to Pay Less for clothes—to wherever the sales were.

At Roos Brothers, my parents picked out a rental tuxedo for me. Now I knew for certain that this was a big deal. It was a vanilla white, double-breasted tux with pleated black pants and patent leather shoes.

I remember the sensations of trying on the formal wear, of standing in front of the tall mirrors, of the clerks checking the fit. I looked so different. This was more adult than almost anything I'd seen my own father wear. With this on, I knew that I could never lose my face.

My job, as I learned at the rehearsals, was simple: to hold an embroidered pink satin pillow bearing the wedding rings and to march quietly down the aisle to a point between the bride and groom —Nancy and Wayman—and the minister. There, I'd keep the rings within reach of the minister, and when the pillow was empty, I'd take a step back.

I was thrilled. It was my first chance to perform in front of a big crowd of strangers, and I couldn't wait for September 16 to come.

To accommodate a party of more than three hundred, the Fungs decided to have the ceremonies and banquet in *Dai Fow*—"Big Town," as the Chinese referred to San Francisco—and on the appointed Sunday afternoon, 360 people filled the pews of the San Francisco Presbyterian Church on Stockton Street.

To me, the wedding was one big show, with grown-up men in tuxedoes just like mine, eight bridesmaids in chiffon dresses of various pastel colors, and the organist now playing the music I'd heard so many times at rehearsals. I felt row after row of eyes on me as I walked slowly down the aisle with the rings. It was, I would later learn, a typical Chinese-American wedding, the exchange of vows taking place in a Western church, in English, followed by a big Chinese banquet laden with food and rituals from the Far East.

The *yum-choy*—the banquet—was at Sun Hung Heung, a stately old restaurant in Chinatown. I wasn't allowed to stay up for all of it, but it was my first glimpse of the festivity with which the Chinese celebrated special occasions. The dining room was twice the size of our own at the New Eastern. Like ours, the walls were paneled in dark wood, but here they were decorated with panels of red and gold banners wishing the bride and groom good luck and fortune. Family members, friends, and representatives of family associations made short speeches, most of them in Cantonese. And a roomful of big round tables held a feast of dishes I would come to know well at banquets in the years ahead. There was the fanciest soup in existence, made of shark fin, representing power and prosperity; a parade of poultry dishes—chicken, squab, and a crispy roast duck—with steamed buns you could peel into flat pieces to sandwich around slices of duck. There were oblong dishes of huge black mushrooms with oyster sauce, of diced chicken with cashew nuts, of steamed whole fish, all to be washed down with tea, orange soda, or every Chinese kid's favorite: Belfast sparkling cider. Some of the adults, mostly the men, would drink a pungent rice whiskey called *Mm-ga-pei,* a taste most Chinese children never grew to acquire.

While my parents joined in the toasting, staying well into the evening, I slept in a room in the back.

Then it was back to normal life at our two homes, the flat on Eighth Street and the New Eastern Cafe.

President Grant, Father of the Bride

WILLIAM SEALE

In the absence of a presidential wedding, we've had to rely on the president's children for those White House galas in recent years. I remember the Johnson and Nixon daughters' marriages most vividly. Who today would know that during the dark post–Civil War years of our country President Ulysses S. Grant's daughter, Nellie, was treated to a White House ceremony that was famous well into the twentieth century and would make those more recent weddings pale in comparison? Nellie's was truly a lavish wedding. No president could ever get away with such extravagance in today's world.

The most publicized social event of the administration of Ulysses S. Grant was the marriage of the President's only daughter, Nellie. At the outset the Grants intended to exclude the press, but at the last minute they decided to drop this plan, and reporters attended in sufficient numbers to take down every detail. The Grants apparently played no favorites, for the major papers of the United States and many in Europe were represented and ran firsthand accounts. Few social occasions at the White House have so wholly captured the American people as Nellie Grant's wedding.

The year 1874 dawned joyously with the announcement to the press. Preparations commenced at the White House. The East Room, torn up by remodeling when Nellie returned from Europe the previous fall, by mid-March stood gleaming in white and gold and "Pure Greek" glory, awaiting the wedding of the decade.

Valentino Melah was to arrange things. He knew that the Grants wanted Nellie to marry like a princess. The knowledge that both the United States and Great Britain would be watching made this the paramount challenge of the "professor's" White House career. As White House events went, it was small, with only 250 cards sent out, yet every effort was expended to make it flawless. As late as 1907 it was recalled as "one of the most brilliant weddings ever given in the United States." The papers were filled with wedding news throughout the winter and spring of 1874. Not until the engraved cards were distributed was the date, May 21, announced.

Mrs. Grant and Nellie traveled by private railroad car to New York to purchase materials and meet with fashionable dressmakers. Whom they patronized is not known. New York had a plentiful supply of elegant modistes, fresh from the fallen Paris of Napoleon III. The press was assured that Miss Nellie's trousseau would have been manufactured in Paris had there been the time for proper fittings, but all that actually came from Europe was point lace for the wedding dress itself. Purchased in Brussels, the point lace was formed into a great "wavy" overskirt of "horizontal lines" that covered the white satin wedding gown and fell out behind it over the six-foot train.

Quite a large sum was spent on Nellie's trousseau, which included morning dresses, afternoon dresses, "gaslight" dresses, and opera costumes—each with shawls and fans. Reporters were shown "silks of every hue and color . . . shawls from India . . . parasols with superb ivory handles, muslin dresses with French-worked flounces, others with puffs and lace inserting. There are gauzes, grenadines, and hats for every costume, slippers for every evening dress, and the lingerie is so fine and dainty that the sight of it brings delight to every feminine heart that rejoices in delicate embroidery, soft lace, and fine needlework."

Because of the limited quarters in the house, most of the family's out-of-town guests stayed in hotels on Pennsylvania Avenue. On the morning of the 21st, those honored with invitations began to emerge at approximately quarter past ten and slowly proceed to the north side of the White House. It was for most of them only a short distance, but walking for all but the native Washingtonians—who were great walkers—would have been unthinkable. Pedestrians were admitted through the pedestrian gate, while those in carriages had the double iron gates of the White House pulled aside.

At the north door the guests were ushered across the stair hall to the left and into the dimly lighted East Room, where all the curtains and shades were closed and where tubbed palms and fruit trees from the conservatory were lined up orchard-like to suggest a tropical garden. Before the crimson curtains of the great Venetian window a dais had been erected and covered with Turkish carpets. From a tall floral arch on the dais hung a large bell made of white roses, over the spot where the marriage ceremony would take place.

Shortly before 11, the three East Room chandeliers were lighted with long-handled "lighters," then those in the transverse hall, sending off the usual whiff of gas to mingle with the heavy odor of flowers. The Marine Band, in the hall outside, stood poised but silent as the wedding procession marched down the grand staircase. Young Sartoris and his best man, Nellie's oldest brother, Fred, led the way. Next came Mrs. Grant and the two younger boys. Then came the eight bridesmaids dressed exactly alike in white satin, with overskirts of white illusion and wide sashes that extended into trains. As they reached the level floor of the hall, an attendant scattered flowers over the trailing drapery.

After passing through the Blue and Green Rooms to the center of the East Room, the bridesmaids halted in a semicircle before the dais. Sartoris and Fred Grant took their places on the left of the Methodist preacher, the Reverend Otis H. Tiffany. Nellie entered the room last, on the arm of her father.

She was met by Sartoris beneath the central chandelier, and with him she ascended the dais, where she could be seen by all the guests.

Flowers were everywhere. Nellie's veil was held in her high-piled hair by a wreath of white orchids and green leaves, interspersed with sweet-smelling orange blossoms. The bridal bouquet presented by her parents was of white flowers arranged on a mother-of-pearl fan. Her gift from the groom was not the customary bouquet, but a loose mass of white flowers "of the rarest kind," ordered from the best florist in New York and rushed to Washington on the night train. Placed on the dais on a large silver tray, they were interpreted by newspaper reporters and correspondents as Love's Offering to Nellie Grant.

When the ceremony was over, a receiving line formed before the dais. The Marine Band now began to play music from Rossini, Bellini, Verdi, and Brahms. Those who had passed along the line could view the gorgeous floral tributes in the parlors. Every surface held artistic pieces, Victorian dreams of beauty. A mahogany table in the center of the Green Room held a tall bouquet of lilies, with a card at the base: "Compliments of Mrs. Hicks, No. 10 West Fourteenth Street, New York." On the white marble table in the Red Room was a gilded calling-card basket covered over with artificial insects.

Upstairs, the Oval Room was draped in white muslin, rather like a tent, to make it look less like a library; the wedding gifts were exhibited there in rather curious categories according to the stores where they were purchased. The cards of the givers drew as much curiosity as the gifts, which included earrings, cameos, flounces of rare lace, fans of silk and satin, "antique" candlesticks, gold knives, forks, spoons, candles painted with flowers, tea and coffee services, punch bowls, salt cellars, fruit knives, glove-boxes, and numerous other items.

At 11:30 the doors of the State Dining Room were folded back to reveal Melah's fairyland, curtains pulled closed, gas blazing overhead, and candles twinkling on the table and sideboards. The wedding cake was a mighty white pyramid in the center of the table, exploding from the top, so it seemed, with white blossoms that cascaded down one side. From the cake, ropes of flowers, roses, and white orchids extended almost to the ends of the long white table. This arrangement imitated to some extent the shape of the old plateau, which was no longer in favor with Mrs. Grant. At the ends of the table, large silver trays were piled high with flowers and diminutive red, white, and blue flags bearing the sentiments "Success to the President," "Hail, Columbia," "Success to the Army," and "Success to the Navy."

Oddly, only the bridal party, the immediate family, and intimate guests were seated. Everyone else waited outside in the parlors where food and wine were passed. Breakfast was served on the "Flower Set," and the menu on each plate, hand-lettered in the office of Octavius Pruden, was rolled up like a diploma. The feast began with soft-shell crab on toast, followed by lamb, beef, wild duck, and chicken. Nellie's wedding cake was served with chocolate pudding and baskets of chilled fruits, as well as water ices and ice cream. The principal drink was not wine but Roman punch, the strong, icy whiskey beverage drunk between courses to clear the palate for the next serving.

Nellie retired to the second floor at about noon to prepare for her departure. The crowd in the dining room broke up, with guests there rejoining the others in the parlors and halls, while waiters moved about distributing little ribboned boxes containing pieces of wedding cake as favors for the ladies. At last Mr. and Mrs. Sartoris descended the grand staircase and passed through the glass screen to the carriage that stood waiting for them in the north portico.

The streets were thick with spectators applauding and cheering. Guards had been stationed at all the gates to prohibit the uninvited from entering, but people had pressed to the fence and climbed the trees along the streets. At the windows of the Treasury, clerks and other office workers looked down at the prince and princess in their carriage, rolling toward the station. The press reported that little of the people's work was done that day. Babcock, in command of the carriage leading the bridal procession, hurried the line of vehicles to the luxurious palace car that would take the newlyweds to New York, where they would set sail for their home in England.

⏤ *The Picture-Perfect Wedding* ⏤

Annie Fellows Johnston

Mendelssohn's "Wedding March," a rose arbor, harps, violins, hundreds of scented candles, the charms in the bride's cake. Leave it to the Little Colonel, also known as Lloyd Sherman, to participate in the most wonderful fictional wedding ever to be held when her chum Eugenia is married. And, oh, yes, the charms in the bride's cake are a tradition even the most modern bride can have. It's included in "The Tradition Continues." To understand some of the traditional customs that take place at the wedding, here first is the background scene, and then we jump ahead to the wedding day.

The old Colonel, hearing the call, "The mail's here," opened the door of his den, and joined the group in the hall where Betty proceeded to sort out the letters. A registered package from Stuart was the first thing that Eugenia tore open, and the others looked up from their letters at her pleased exclamation:

"Oh, it's the charms for the bride's cake!"

"Ornaments for the top?" asked Rob, as she lifted the layer of jeweller's cotton and disclosed a small gold thimble, and a narrow wedding ring.

"No! Who ever heard of such a thing!" she laughed. "Haven't you heard of the traditional charms that must be baked in a bride's cake? It is a token of the fate one may expect who finds it in his slice of cake. Eliot taught me the old rhyme:

> *'Four tokens must the bride'scake hold:*
> *A silver shilling and a ring of gold,*
> *A crystal charm good luck to symbol,*
> *And for the spinster's hand a thimble.'*

"Eliot firmly believes that the tokens are a prophecy, for years ago, at her cousin's wedding in England, she got the spinster's thimble. The girl who found the ring was married within the year, and the one who found the shilling shortly came into an inheritance. True, it didn't amount to much—about five pounds—but the coincidence firmly convinced Eliot of the truth of the superstition. In this country people usually take a dime instead of a shilling, but I told Stuart that I wanted to follow the custom strictly to the letter. And look what a dear he is! Here is a bona fide English shilling, that he took the trouble to get for me."

Phil took up the bit of silver she had placed beside the thimble and the ring, and looked it over critically. "Well, I'll declare!" he exclaimed. "That was Aunt Patricia's old shilling! I'd swear to it. See the way the hole is punched, just between those two ugly old heads? And I remember the dent just below the date. Looks as if some one had tried to bite it. Aunt Patricia used to keep it in her treasure-box with her gold beads and other keepsakes."

The old Colonel, who had once had a fad for collecting coins, and owned a large assortment, held out his hand for it. Adjusting his glasses, he examined it carefully. "Ah! Most interesting," he observed. "Coined in the reign of 'Bloody Mary,' and bearing the heads of Queen Mary and King Philip. You remember this shilling is mentioned in Butler's *'Hudibras'*:

> *'Still amorous and fond of billing,*
> *Like Philip and Mary on a shilling.'*

"You couldn't have a more appropriate token for your cake, my dear," he said to Eugenia with a smile. Then he laid it on the table, and taking up his papers, passed back into his den.

"That's the first time I ever heard my name in a poem," said Phil. "By rights I ought to draw that shilling in my share of cake. If I do I shall take it as a sign that history is going to repeat itself, and shall look around for a ladye-love named Mary. Now I know a dozen songs with that name, and such things always come in handy when 'a frog he would a-wooing go.' There's 'My Highland Mary' and 'Mary of

Argyle,' and 'Mistress Mary, quite contrary,' and 'Mary, call the cattle home, across the sands of Dee'!"

As he rattled thoughtlessly on, nothing was farther from his thoughts than the self-conscious little Mary just behind him. Nobody saw her face grow red, however, for Lloyd's exclamation over the last token made every one crowd around her to see.

It was a small heart-shaped charm of crystal, probably intended for a watch-fob. There was a four-leaf clover, somehow mysteriously imbedded in the centre.

"That ought to be doubly lucky," said Eugenia. "Oh, *what* a dear Stuart was to take so much trouble to get the very nicest things. They couldn't be more suitable." . . .

The wedding was all that Mrs. Sherman had planned, everything falling into place as beautifully and naturally as the unfolding of a flower. The assembled guests seated in the great bower of roses heard a low, soft trembling of harp-strings deepen into chords. Then to this accompaniment two violins began the wedding-march, and the great gate of roses swung wide. As Stuart and his best man entered from a side door and took their places at the altar in front of the old minister, the rest of the bridal party came down the stairs: Betty and Miles Bradford first, Joyce and Rob, then the maid of honor walking alone with her armful of roses. After her came the bride with her hand on her father's arm.

Just at that instant some one outside drew back the shutters in the bay-window, and a flood of late afternoon sunshine streamed across the room, the last golden rays of the perfect June day making a path of light from the gate of roses to the white altar. It shone full across Eugenia's face, down on the long-trained shimmering satin, the little gleaming slippers, the filmy veil that enveloped her, the pearls that glimmered white on her white throat.

Eliot, standing in a corner, nervously watching every movement with twitching lips, relaxed into a smile. "It's a good omen!" she said, half under her breath, then gave a startled glance around to see if any one had heard her speak at such an improper time.

The music grew softer now, so faint and low it seemed the mere shadow of sound. Above the rare sweetness of that undertone of harp and violins rose the words of the ceremony: "*I, Stuart, take thee, Eugenia, to be my wedded wife.*"

Mary, standing at her post by the rose gate, felt a queer little chill creep over her. It was so solemn, so very much more solemn than she had imagined it would be. She wondered how she would feel if the time ever came for her to stand in Eugenia's place, and plight her faith to some man in that way—*"for better, for worse, for richer, for poorer, in sickness and in health, until death us do part."*

Eliot was crying softly in her corner now. Yes, getting married was a terribly solemn thing. It didn't end with the ceremony and the pretty clothes and the shower of congratulations. That was only the beginning. *"For better, for worse,"*—that might mean all sorts of trouble and heartache. *"Sickness and death,"*—it meant to be bound all one's life to one person, morning, noon, and night. How very, very careful one would have to be in choosing,—and then suppose one made a mistake and thought the man she was marrying was good and honest and true, and he wasn't! It would be all the same, for *"for better, for worse,"* ran the vow, *"until death us do part."*

Then and there, holding fast to the gate of roses, Mary made up her mind that she could never, never screw her courage up to the point of taking the vows Eugenia was taking, as she stood with her hand clasped in Stuart's, and the late sunshine of the sweet June day streaming down on her like a benediction.

"It's lots safer to be an old maid," thought Mary. "I'll take my chances getting the diamond leaf some other way than marrying. Anyhow, if I ever should make a choice, I'll ask somebody else's opinion, like I do when I go shopping, so I'll be sure I'm getting a real prince, and not an imitation one."

It was all over in another moment. Harp and violins burst into the joyful notes of Mendelssohn's march, and Stuart and Eugenia turned from the altar to pass through the rose gate together. Lloyd and Phil followed, then the other attendants in the order of their entrance. On the wide porch, screened and canopied with smilax and roses, a cool green out-of-doors reception-room had been made. Here they stood to receive their guests.

Mary, in all the glory of her pink chiffon dress and satin slippers, stood at the end of the receiving line, feeling that this one experience was well worth the long journey from Arizona. So thoroughly did she delight in her part of the affair, and so heartily did she enter into her duties, that more than one guest passed on, smiling at her evident enjoyment.

"I wish this wedding could last a week," she confided to Lieutenant Logan, when he paused beside her. "Don't you know, they did in the fairytales, some of them. There was 'feasting and merrymaking for seventy days and seventy nights.' This one is going by so fast that it will soon be train-time. I don't suppose they care," she added, with a nod toward the bride, "for they're going to spend their honeymoon in a Gold of Ophir rose garden, where there are goldfish in the fountains, and real orange-blossoms. It's out in California, at Mister Stuart's grandfather's. Elsie, his sister, couldn't come, so they're going out to see her, and take her a piece of every kind of cake we have to-night, and a sample of every kind of bonbon. Don't you wonder who'll get the charms in the bride's cake? That's the only reason I am glad the clock is going so fast. It will soon be time to cut the cake, and I'm wild to see who gets the things in it."

The last glow of the sunset was still tinting the sky with a tender pink when they were summoned to the dining-room, but indoors it had grown so dim that a hundred rose-colored candles had been lighted. Again the music of harp and violins floated through the rose-scented rooms. As Mary glanced around at the festive scene, the tables gleaming with silver and cut glass, the beautiful costumes, the smiling faces, a line from her old school reader kept running through her mind: *"And all went merry as a marriage-bell! And all went merry as a marriage-bell!"*

It repeated itself over and over, through all the gay murmur of voices as the supper went on, through the flowery speech of the old Colonel when he stood to propose a toast, through the happy tinkle of laughter when Stuart responded, through the thrilling moment when at last the bride rose to cut the mammoth cake. In her nervous excitement, Mary actually began to chant the line aloud, as the first slice was lifted from the great silver salver: "All went merry—" Then she clapped her hand over her mouth, but nobody had noticed, for Allison had drawn the wedding-ring, and a chorus of laughing congratulations was drowning out every other sound.

As the cake passed on from guest to guest, Betty cried out that she had found the thimble. Then Lloyd held up the crystal charm, the one the bride had said was doubly lucky, because it held imbedded in its centre a four-leaved clover. Nearly every slice had been crumbled as soon as it was taken, in search of a hidden token, but Mary, who had not dared to hope that she might draw one, began leisurely eating her share. Suddenly her teeth met on something hard and flat, and glancing down, she saw the edge of a coin protruding from the scrap of cake she held.

"Oh, it's the shilling!" she exclaimed, in such open-mouthed astonishment that every one laughed, and for the next few moments she was the centre of the congratulations. Eugenia took a narrow white ribbon from one of the dream-cake boxes, and passed it through the hole in the shilling, so that she could hang it around her neck.

"Destined to great wealth!" said Rob, with mock solemnity. "I always did think I'd like to marry an heiress. I'll wait for you, Mary."

"No," interrupted Phil, laughing, "fate has decreed that I should be the lucky man. Don't you see that it is Philip's head with Mary's on that shilling?"

"Whew!" teased Kitty. "Two proposals in one evening, Mary. See what the charm has done for you already!"

Mary knew that they were joking, but she turned the color of her dress, and sat twiddling the coin between her thumb and finger, too embarrassed to look up. They sat so long at the table that it was almost train-time when Eugenia went upstairs to put on her travelling-dress. She made a pretty picture, pausing midway up the stairs in her bridal array, the veil thrown back, and her happy face looking down on the girls gathered below. Leaning far over the banister with the bridal bouquet in her hands, she called:

> "Now look, ye pretty maidens, standing all a-row,
> The one who catches this, the next bouquet shall throw."

There was a laughing scramble and a dozen hands were outstretched to receive it. "Oh, Joyce caught it! Joyce caught it!" cried Mary, dancing up and down on the tips of her toes, and clapping her hands over her mouth to stifle the squeal of delight that had almost escaped. "Now, some day I can be maid of honor."

"So that's why you are so happy over your sister's good fortune, is it?" asked Phil, bent on teasing her every time opportunity offered.

"No," was the indignant answer. "That is some of the reason, but I'm gladdest because she didn't get left out of everything. She didn't get one of the cake charms, so I hoped she would catch the bouquet."

When the carriage drove away at last, a row of shiny black faces was lined up each side of the avenue. All the Gibbs children were there, and Aunt Cindy's other grandchildren, with their hands full of rice.

"Speed 'em well, chillun!" called old Cindy, waving her apron. The rice fell in showers on the top of the departing carriage, and two little white slippers were sent flying along after it, with such force that they nearly struck Eliot, sitting beside the coachman. Tired as she was, she turned to smile approval, for the slippers were a good omen, too, in her opinion, and she was happy to think that everything about her Miss Eugenia's wedding had been carried out properly, down to this last propitious detail.

As the slippers struck the ground, quick as a cat, M'haley darted forward to grab them. "Them slippahs is mates!" she announced, gleefully, "and I'm goin' to tote 'em home for we-all's wedding. I kain't squeeze into 'em myself, but Ca'line Allison suah kin."

Once more, and for the last time, Eugenia leaned out of the carriage to look back at the dear faces she was leaving. But there was no sadness in the farewell. Her prince was beside her, and the Gold of Ophir rose-garden lay ahead.

⟷ Wanting the Best for Our Daughters ⟷

BESS STREETER ALDRICH

"In a community where there have been few lines drawn, one does not begin to draw them at wedding times," wrote Bess Streeter Aldrich, a writer now little known but once considered one of America's most truthful depicters of midwestern life. I remembered that line when I was told of a lovely old-timey tradition that still exists in some of America's small towns. No formal wedding invitations are sent out. Instead, a notice runs in the town's newspaper inviting everyone who knows the bride and groom to gather at the church for the wedding ceremony.

In this lovely and touching wedding scene from A Lantern in Her Hand, *we glimpse the wedding presents our grandmothers and great-grandmothers cherished and share the wishes that every mother has ever felt for her daughter's wedding—to have for her the very best.*

And then Margaret's dress was to be made and all the wedding to be planned. Margaret said she had her heart set on a navy blue silk with white ruching and—

Her mother stopped her. "Don't you . . ." Abbie was wistful. "Don't you wish we could afford a white satin dress and white slippers and a veil?"

"No, Mother . . . the navy blue silk is just what I want. As long as Fred and I are going right to the rooms over the drug store, I want my clothes to be suitable and I might never have use for a white satin again. Besides, now that I'm going to live in Lincoln, I want to save every penny toward painting supplies. I'm never happier than when I'm opening up the paint-box and getting at the oil and brushes. You know, Mother, my housework won't be much . . . just think . . . those few tiny rooms to keep and not any of the work there is here on the farm . . . and I'm going into my painting for all it's worth. I can't explain it to you, Mother, but there's something in me . . . that if I could just get down on canvas the way the cottonwoods look against the sky, or the way the prairie looks at sunset with the pink light . . ." she broke off. "Oh, I suppose you think I'm daffy . . . you wouldn't understand."

Abbie, at the east kitchen window, looked over the low rolling hills where the last of the May sunshine lay in yellow-pink pools on the prairie. Her lips trembled a little. "Yes, I would," she said simply. "I'd understand."

And then, quite suddenly, it was the night of the wedding. The moon slipped up from a fleecy cloud-bed and with silvery congratulations swung low over the farmhouse behind the cedars. The whole countryside was there. In a community where there have been few lines drawn, one does not begin to draw them at wedding times. The lane road held all manner of vehicles,—lumber-wagons, buggies, phaetons, carts, surreys, hayracks. The Lutzes were all there and all of the Reinmuellers but Emil, who sat on a milk stool in the barn at home all evening and sulked. Sarah Lutz looked stylish in her tight-fitting black dress of stiff silk, with jet earrings against her rosy cheeks. Christine had a new blue calico gathered on full at the waistline.

Mack surprised them all by driving up the lane road in a shining, black buggy with canary yellow wheels, yellow lines over the horse's black back, and a yellow whip. He drove over to the Lutz's and came back with Emma Lutz, who was trying her best not to look important.

The presents were all in the sitting-room, the small things on tables. There were two red plush chairs, a stylish castor, a green glass pitcher with frosted glasses, three lamps with snow scenes on the globes, several hand-made splashers and tidies, and enough cold meat and pickle forks to supply a garrison of soldiers with fighting equipment. Gus and Christine, out of deference to the literary tastes of the family, had bought: a huge volume, their decision over the purchase having been based upon weight rather than content, and which now, upon inspection, proved to be *Twenty Lessons in Etiquette.*

Some time before the ceremony Abbie climbed the uncarpeted pine stairs with the little calf-skin-covered chest under her arm. Just as her mother had climbed the sapling ladder in the old log cabin, she was thinking. Wasn't life queer? Such a little while ago, it seemed. Where had the time gone? Blown away by the winds you could not stop,— ticked off by the clock hands you could not stay.

Margaret was nearly dressed. Her blue silk, with its fifteen yards of goods, was looped back modishly over a bustle, the train dragging behind her with stylish abandon. Abbie sat down on the edge of her daughter's bed, the chest in her lap. "You know, Margaret, it was always a kind-of dream of mine that by the time you were married, we'd be well enough off to do a lot of things for you. I always saw you in my mind dressed in white with a veil and slippers,—not just that I wanted you dressed that one way,—but I mean as a sort of symbol,—that we'd be able to do all the things for you that should rightfully go with the pearls. But," Abbie's voice broke a little and she stopped to steady it,—"things don't always turn out just as we dream,—and we're not able to do much for you. But anyway, you shall wear the pearls to-night if you want to."

Margaret, holding up her long dress, crossed the rag-carpeted floor in little swift happy steps, and threw young arms around her mother.

"I know all you've done for me, Mother." She took Abbie's rough hands in her own firm ones and held them to her lips. "And it's *everything*,—just *everything* that you could do. Never as long as I live can I ever repay it." There were tears in the young girl's eyes and to keep them back, she said lightly, "No, thanks, Mother, dear. I'm all right with my lovely blue silk and the white silk ruching at my neck. Keep them for Isabelle or baby Grace. You and father will be well-fixed in a few years. The land will be higher. You're having good crops now and by the time Isabelle is married, your dream can come true. And besides, Mother, dear," she put her young cheek against Abbie's, "you know that when you marry the man you love, you don't need jewels to make you happy."

Yes, yes,—how the words came back, borne on the breeze of memories! How swiftly the clock hands had gone around! Abbie could not speak. She must shed no tears on her little girl's wedding day. So, she only patted her and kissed her, smiling at her through a thousand unshed tears. And you, who have seen your mother smile when you left her,—or have smiled at your daughter's leaving,—know it is the most courageous smile of all.

⚊ *A Mother to Her Daughter* ⚊

EMMA GRAY TRIGG

One of the loveliest poems I have ever read was written by an almost unknown Virginia poet of the 1930s, Emma Gray Trigg. Though honored by prizes and praised by other poets, Trigg's poems do not find their way into modern anthologies. I have given this poem to my daughter as a gift to carry her through life. I remembered it when rereading Bess Streeter Aldrich's moving description of "the most courageous smile of all."

> *What will you take from me*
> *For your wayfaring?*
> *What shall I have to give*
> *You would be sharing?*

When you are lonely,
  Travelling long,
When your feet falter
  You will need song.

Music to march by,
  Silver and gold,
Fire for warming you
  If it be cold;

These things will comfort you,
  Carry you far
On the road you are going.
  But if a star

Tempt you to follow,
  Wings will be needed,
Wings for your flying,
  Strong, unimpeded.

These I have fashioned
  From pinions of light,
Caught as they fell
  From a swift bird in flight.

I give you for courage
  A light heart that sings,
And I who have never flown,
  Give you my wings.

~ To My Dear and Loving Husband ~

ANNE BRADSTREET

In 1678, almost two centuries before Elizabeth Barrett wrote the immortal
lines to her beloved Robert Browning, "How do I love thee? Let me count the
ways," Anne Bradstreet, America's first noteworthy poet, wrote "To My Dear
and Loving Husband." She had married Simon Bradstreet in England when
she was only sixteen. Together, in 1630, they journeyed to the Massachusetts
Bay Colony on the Arabella where they had eight children and made countless
contributions, he to government, she to literature.

If ever two were one, then surely we.
If ever man were loved by wife, then thee;
If ever wife was happy in a man,
Compare with me ye women if you can.
I prize thy love more than whole mines of gold,
Or all the riches that the East doth hold.
My love is such that rivers cannot quench,
Nor ought but love from thee give recompense.
Thy love is such I can no way repay;
The heavens reward thee manifold, I pray.
Then while we live, in love let's so persever,
That when we live no more we may live ever.

— The Tradition Continues —

A Heavenly Ham

Cynthia Blyth Halsey

Little could my then future son-in-law, Pennsylvania-born-and-bred Mike Hultzapple, know that he had won forever a place in my heart when he announced that the one thing he wanted for his Southern wedding reception was ham biscuits. These are essential at every Southern wedding reception, even before the Civil War, as this amusing account testifies. I found it in Worth Remembering, *a little book put together in commemoration of the one hundredth anniversary of the United Daughters of the Confederacy by the New York Chapter in 1963. This story was contributed by Cynthia Blyth Halsey and was told to her by her father, Harvey Randolph Halsey.*

There should be a special dish for a wedding dinner . . . but heaven only knew where it was to come from when Major Charles Seldon married Miss James. Rations were thin in Northern Virginia after April of 1865. The bride and her mother combed the smoke house, ransacked the cellar . . . and finally rested from their search in front of the great hall fire. "Only heaven knows where we'll get anything. It looks like a choice of johny cake with bacon . . . or without." But heaven did know . . . because as they stood there a 15 pound ham fell down the chimney and landed with a crash at their feet.

No it wasn't a miracle. It seems that they'd hung the ham to cure in the old chimney because the smoke house was unsafe. This one had been forgotten . . . and the suspending rope had frayed through just at the right time. A merry wedding followed.

Something Borrowed, Something Blue

BRYCE REVELEY

My New Orleans friend Bryce Reveley has a national reputation for magically restoring antique lace and textiles. I knew she would have wonderful wedding traditions to share with today's brides. Here are her words, which remind us that these treasures that have a permanent place in our lives are also very delicate. How glad I am that my own daughter, Joslin, was not at all deterred from wearing my wedding dress by her parents' divorce. Also, don't overlook the suggestion of adding your own touch to a family heirloom dress, especially if the groom's mother, grandmother, or sister has a suitable piece of fabric or lace—maybe even a bedspread!

Continuity takes many forms in the spectra of our lives. The heirlooms I deal with every day as a textile conservator remind me of the need for continuity and for traditions. Wedding traditions are deep-seated, stretching back for centuries, although the old saw, "Something old, something new, something borrowed, something blue," dates from the nineteenth century. The desire to share not only customs but also physical mementos such as wedding gowns, veils, and handkerchiefs reminds us all of our most basic human need—sharing common experiences.

In the past twenty years I have worked with seven brides in one family on their 150-year-old family heirloom. The way that it came to me is sad, but it has a happy outcome.

In 1970, a modern bride decided to clean this ancient dress by putting it in the washing machine. And she did get it really clean. However, the lace and the dress needed a great deal of tender loving care in order to make it usable for the next cousin's wedding which was coming up in a few months. In order to keep another catastrophe from happening, I told the family that if I worked on the dress and properly restored it, they had to promise me that I would be the only one to clean and restore it, should the need ever arise again. I have now cleaned it seven times, and each time a cousin or a sister uses it, something new is added—a bit of lace from the other side of the family, some blue ribbons, or whatever—but that which is added can be removed for the next wearing.

Another family heirloom that I have seen on three occasions involves a bit of subterfuge on my part. When I first saw the family wedding "veil," I was somewhat confounded by its position of importance as a veil. It had deep flounces on three sides trimmed with lovely hand-made lace, and in the center of the veil, complete with exquisite lace appliqués, was a life-size basket of recognizable flowers: roses, margarites, forget-me-nots, ivy—the flora that one associates with weddings. When the bride tried it on (it needed a good cleaning and blocking, and had a few small rents in it), I saw the basket of flowers very clearly through the net right at derriere level. It was at this point I recognized the "veil" as a bedspread, but in this family it had been used for several generations as a veil. Since 1979 I have cleaned and restored the "veil" three times. Each time I have caught myself writing on the invoice "bedspread," only to have to start over again. For you see, in this family the tradition is to wear the family basket-lace veil just as all other women in the family have done for over seventy years!

The rites of passage in all of our lives also carry a talismanlike quality I feel, helps to soothe and to perpetuate our human needs and our desire for continuity. Frequently I hear that a girl may not want to wear her mother's wedding dress because her mother and father are divorced and the dress may therefore be "unlucky." Other girls less threatened by such ideas, nevertheless will blithely buy a "new" gown at thrift shop or a vintage clothing store because it is both beautiful and inexpensive—but without giving a thought about why or how it got there in the first place. A friend of mine has in his shop the entire wedding party ensemble: wedding gown and veil and five American Beauty satin bridesmaids' dresses. They have been there for years. Why? Because the original wedding was canceled just a few days before it was to take place.

Speaking of laundry, one of the cutest ideas for a humorous surprise for a just-engaged young lady comes from my dear friend Charlotte Goodwin. Seems that one summer during her teenage years she had so many beaux that one day when she was out on a date, her mother made paper dolls which looked like the different boys and strung them up on a clothesline across Charlotte's room. If the intended bride has had her pick of young men, the chosen fellow could be made the champion, with his competition strung along behind. Another variation on the idea would be to cut out figures of a bridal party—bride, groom, attendants—and string these up.

⤙ To Liven Up a Party ⤚

When writing Pleasures of the Garden, *I came upon a delightful Victorian floral parlor game that is wonderfully suited to a bridesmaids' party or shower, especially when the bride's friends may not know one another well. That happens often these days when a bride invites a childhood friend from one town, college friends from other cities, and work friends who just happen to have been brought together through their employment to her wedding or as attendants. The game's old-fashioned quality, plus its humor and natural prettiness, makes it a guaranteed icebreaker. The purpose is to foretell each girl's suitor's or intended husband's personality in "the language of flowers."*

To prepare, make a bouquet of many different flowers gathered from the florist or from your garden, or use silk flowers bought at a craft shop. Use an appropriate Victorian vase to add to the charm and authenticity of the game. (Incidentally, the bouquet makes a wonderful decoration piece until the end of the party, when the game is played.)

Have as many small gift cards and envelopes as there are flowers. If possible, use pretty floral-motif gift cards. On each card write a flower's secret meaning, put it in an envelope, and punch a hole through a corner. Run a thin satin ribbon through the hole and tie it to the corresponding flower.

At the party each guest then draws a flower from the bouquet and learns her paramour's secret character, reading it aloud, of course. Here are some suggestion for your bouquet and its message, but a list of the language of flowers is readily available in many books: violet, modest; white or pink hyacinth, playful; dark blue or purple hyacinth, mournful; primrose, candid; daisy, an early riser; pansy, kind and thoughtful; daffodil, daring; geranium, stupid; sprig of myrtle, devoted; marigold, rich; lily, pure; stock, hasty; pink rose, haughty; red rose, loving; tulip, proud; jasmine, amiable; foxglove, deceitful; aster, changeable; oak leaves, hospitable.

The Language of Flowers

If the language of flowers catches your imagination, here are some suggestions for special love-message bouquets.

"LET THE BONDS OF MARRIAGE UNITE US."

Blue convolvulus	Bonds
Ivy	Marriage
A few blades of straw	Unite us

"I LOVE YOU AND I HOPE YOU WILL MARRY ME."

Rose	Love
Daisy	Hope
Ivy	Marriage

"I LOVE YOUR PASSION AND LIGHTNESS."

Rose	Love
Purple velvet	Passion
Larkspur	Lightness

"MY MESSAGE IS I LOVE YOU."

Iris	Message
Rose	Love

~ *A Charming Tradition* ~

On page 333 the charming tradition of cake pulls is explained. Symbolic sterling silver charms are now commercially available from Mary Landrum in Dallas, Texas, and specialty shops everywhere. They are lovely and can be kept forever. In fact, charm bracelets decorated with the different "pulls" gathered from weddings were once quite fashionable. Should you wish to create your own charms or buy inexpensive wooden or plastic items from craft shops, below are some objects you can use and what they symbolize. Or now that you have read about the flower game, you could use pressed flowers that symbolize good wishes and love, or even make up your own symbols. I enjoy rummaging through the jewelry boxes at antique shops and flea markets to gather up items that can be used as pulls. Whatever you use, place the objects, either unwrapped as you would the silver charms, or in a small envelope like those designed to hold coins available at a hobby shop, or use gift-card envelopes on the plate on which the wedding cake will be placed. Attach a pretty ribbon to the charm or to the envelope, after punching a hole in it. You may include the meaning of the object on a tag if you think it is needed.

Wedding bell or wedding ring: the next to marry
Shamrock or horseshoe: blessed with good luck
Coin: great fortune and wealth
Heart: guaranteed to find true love
Engagement ring: the next to be engaged
Baby or carriage: to be blessed with children
Pineapple: a hospitable home
Wishing well: wishes will come true
House: a loving home
Letter, phone, or typewriter: good news

~ *Everything Old Is New Again* ~

There is no end to the list of old and new wedding traditions. Several people have told me that they heard such detailed descriptions and stories about their parents' wedding so often that they thought they had actually been there! To my way of thinking, it is charming to combine some of the old ways with new ways. Here are just a few ideas:

If a wedding ring is sitting idle in a jewelry box, it should be passed to the newlyweds. It doesn't have to be "the" wedding ring. It can be worn on a chain or a bracelet and given the light of day again. Or the gold can be melted down and combined with other metal to create a special token for the wedding day. The possibilities are endless.

A prayer or reading used at another generation's wedding can be incorporated into a service where the bride and groom write their own vows.

Look at your mother's or grandmother's wedding or family album. Can the cake be copied? Can you use the same knife they used to cut the cake? Could you duplicate your mother's bridal bouquet? Do your parents have the glasses they used to toast each other? Can some of the music at the wedding or reception be the same? Ask your parents what moment they remember most fondly from their own wedding and see if it can be re-created. Could you return to their honeymoon site?

From my friend, Liz Seymour, here are two ideas you may want to incorporate as new traditions in your wedding:

If large or extended families are meeting for the first time, try using "family tree" name tags explaining each person's relationship to the marrying couple. For example, "Ellen Smith, Charlotte's oldest sister"; "Harry Parks, Jim's cousin from Oregon." It's a great conversation opener and memory jogger.

To add festivity to the reception, attach custom-made wine or sparkling juice labels to the bottles using the bride's and groom's names:

Margaret et Marc
Vin de table
9 juin 1996

Chateau Margaret et Marc
New Rochelle, New York
9 juin 1996

~ Even Children Are Romantic ~

I'll admit that even I was a little amazed when some of the children's essays involved wedding traditions. Considering my own romantic view of life as a child, I shouldn't have been.

I was outraged! Why do we have to go to their house every year at the end of November? And don't give me all that tradition junk. Well, I went this year, but never again!

You see, we go to the Lockmans' house annually for Thanksgiving dinner. Every year the group gets larger because the Lockmans have three grown daughters. One is married, one is engaged, and one has a boyfriend. After the blessing had been given and everyone made that quick first step to dive into the turkey, the boyfriend's voice interrupted abruptly. "In the spirit of Thanksgiving," Scott said melancholically, "I have one request." He said this with one arm around Mr. Lockman and the other pulling out a diamond ring from his pocket. Oh, no, I thought. I knew what was coming. The next words out of his mouth, while propping himself up on one knee, were "Jonjie, will you marry me?" The answer was "Yes!" Every woman in the room was crying. Then we sat down to eat, talking about one subject, marriage.

When we finally left, I asked happily, "So can we do this again next year?"

Andy Glenn Allen, middle school

~ ~

Today I was talking to my mom. She told me about a family tradition. In my family, when the youngest woman gets married she gets an antique trunk.

On the day of the wedding, the mother of the bride puts her daughter's clothes in the trunk and gives it to her as a surprise after her wedding. The bride takes it with her and keeps it until her daughter gets married.

This trunk has been passed from my great-great-grandmother to my great-grandmother, then to my grandmother, and now my mother has it. On the day of my mom's wedding, my grandmother packed my mom's clothes in the trunk. My grandmother had planned to give it to my mother at the end of the reception. Before the wedding, my mom went up to her room to get dressed. She opened the closet only to find that the only thing that was in her closet was her wedding dress. She went to find her mother and tell her that someone had stolen her clothes. When my grandmother found out how upset my mom was, she had to tell her what was going on, and it ruined the whole thing.

My mom told me about the trunk because she didn't want me to do the same thing she did. Someday I will get the trunk. The trunk is beautiful and I am glad that I will be able to have a family heirloom.

Sharee Hartsell, middle school

To Be Used Often

The card with the wedding present said that it should be used often. So for twenty-five years the picnic basket has needed only the food and a destination for a picnic. Sometimes the basket has held specialties like pâté, crusty bread, and nectarines. Other times more plebeian fare has been packed—bologna sandwiches and iced tea.

The picnic basket has been opened on a mountaintop swathed in a cold, wet fog. It has gone to the beach and come home with grains of damp golden sand. Picnics have been packed in the basket and taken to city parks and mountain meadows, on hot summer days and snowy winter ones.

Once the basket was taken on what was to be a romantic meal near a log cabin, shaded by black walnut trees. However, several hundred other people were already there to take part in a living history reenactment. That time the basket provided us the key to a new hobby, a spreading circle of close friends, and a new career.

Ducky and Dr. Griff, we did what you said—we've used your gift often. The picnic basket has become the symbol of our favorite family tradition.

Margaret Marquis

Tree-Trimming Shower

The Christmas pickle is a well-known tradition. Young Kristen Frye wrote that in her family a pickle is given as a special wedding gift to each newlywed couple as a way of ensuring that they will be able to enjoy this family tradition at Christmas. "This gives the pickle great importance," she writes. "I will always consider this my favorite family tradition."

A tree-trimming party is a wonderful theme for a bridal shower. With so many year-round Christmas shops these days, you can have such a party any time of year and ensure that the young couple's first Christmas tree need not be threadbare. Be sure they receive a pickle!

The Kneeling Cushion

In the nondemoninational circa 1840 chapel at Mordecai Historic Park in Raleigh, North Carolina, the wedding couple kneels on one cushion symbolic of their unity. Its lovely handworked needlepoint design incorporates traditional themes representing life's riches: the dove for peace and tranquillity, a hummingbird for industry, wine for sacramental blessing, honeysuckle for sweetness, and lilies of the valley for happiness.

And Don't Forget the Anniversaries

The comic scene of the forgetful husband arriving home empty-handed from work on his anniversary night to be met by a tearful wife isn't the figment of a writer's imagination. It happens. In fact, Bob and I were married on my birthday, June 26. "That way," Bob said, "I can forget two important days and only spend one night in the doghouse." I'm sure anniversary celebrations began as so many traditions did, as an excuse to celebrate, especially in long-ago times when life was much harder and less leisurely than today and, I'm sure many readers are thinking to themselves, when divorce was not as prevalent. Actually, the high incidence of divorce should make every anniversary even more of a celebration today.

Using the customary chart of anniversaries as a guide for gift-giving isn't a bad idea when flowers and candy seem too prosaic. As many imaginative gifts come in paper, wood, and tin as in silver and jade and the anniversary themes are great to build a party around as well.

One of the most enjoyable anniversary parties I know about happens each year when Dee and John Mason of Asheville, North Carolina, throw their "Let Them Eat Cake" party.

It seems that their wedding cake was mistakenly delivered to the wrong club. Dee was such a happy bride that she didn't even miss the cake until the time came for the traditional cutting; then it was too late to do anything about it. Now John and Dee celebrate their anniversary by ordering a beautiful wedding cake and inviting their friends to their belated, but now traditional, wedding cake party.

ANNIVERSARIES

First—Paper	Thirtieth—Ivory
Fifth—Wood	Thirty-fifth—Jade or coral
Tenth—Tin	Fortieth—Ruby
Twelfth—Silk	Forty-fifth—Sapphire
Fifteenth—Crystal	Fiftieth—Gold
Twentieth—China	Fifty-fifth—Emerald
Twenty-fifth—Silver	Sixtieth—Diamond

Imaginative Anniversary Invitations

A wonderful nineteenth-century etiquette book suggests the printing of invitations to a fifth (wooden) anniversary party on a thin sheet of wood, the tenth (tin) anniversary party on a sheet of tinfoil, and of course the twentieth (china) anniversary party on a surface resembling chinaware. With the wide array of beautiful paper products and printing available today, use your imagination to come up with unique ways to celebrate and continue this time-tested tradition.

A Year to Remember

Yves Durant, with whom I co-hosted Georgia Public Television's nationally shown holiday show, Wining and Dining with Yves Durant, *has this wonderful suggestion for an anniversary present. Select a wine from the year of the marriage. But if, in the case of a major anniversary, the wines are too expensive, then buy a good wine for the current year and write on it, "On the occasion of your twentieth (or whatever) anniversary. To be enjoyed on your twenty-fifth (or other) anniversary."*

HEAR THE MELLOW WEDDING BELLS—
GOLDEN BELLS!
WHAT A WORLD OF HAPPINESS THEIR HARMONY FORETELLS!
Edgar Allan Poe

CHAPTER 16

Funerals and Burials

REMEMBERING OUR DEPARTED ONES

~ A Beautiful, Peaceful Place ~

Remember when every country church had its own graveyard? Remember when every town had a master stonecutter who chiseled out roses and ivy and a line or two of poetry on tombstones? That was my great-uncle Will's profession. He was a craftsman and a sculptor.

I think of him sometimes as I whiz down highways and pass the totally insipid, treeless, and monument-free modern cemeteries located alongside these easy-access roads.

Where are the tombstones to mark a lifetime, now past, whose secret stories would make us weep and laugh? Where are the crepe myrtles and maple trees to bloom and give shelter to singing birds?

The only flowers I see are plastic. The only signs of life I ever detect are long lawn-mower lines left on perfectly manicured grass.

I love cemeteries. Always have. Some people call me morbid. I reply that never am I more aware of life's bounties than when, in the cemeteries of the old, I am surrounded by century-old trees, singing birds, and beautiful monuments that denote memories of rich stories of our bittersweet past.

When writing this book I learned that I am not alone in my longings. Others love them too. May the tradition continue.

Decoration Day
*Leon Hamrick

A writer once wrote "you can't go home again." But thanks to a Southern tradition many of us do each year on a Sunday called Decoration Day or, more simply, "The Decoration."

"The Decoration" is really no more than a memorial weekend when families from near and far gather. Together, they spruce up the grounds of cemeteries where family and friends are buried, place flowers on graves of loved ones, and enjoy a common fellowship which has no parallel.

People come for different reasons. Memories of loved ones; family ties; the need for, and to be, family; celebrations; remembrances of friends; and friendships—all are magnetic attractions for these special days and pilgrimages of faith.

As a boy, I looked forward to the Decoration as the time when we were able to see cousins, aunts, uncles, and friends for perhaps the only time during a year. In addition, as the day approached, visions which later turned into reality lurked in the recesses of my mind. Family and community tables laden with all sorts of mouthwatering food were everywhere. Piles of golden brown fried chicken, bowls of favorite vegetables such as creamed corn, green beans, and sliced tomatoes, deviled eggs and potato salad—all were very prominent offerings. As if this weren't enough, a storehouse of lemon and chocolate pies with meringue piled high, brown-crusted berry and cobbler pies, and multilayered chocolate, coconut, and fruit-filled cakes added significantly to the bountiful spreads prepared by loving mothers, grandmothers, aunts, sisters, and cousins. There also was a wonderful blend of iced tea prepared and flavored with fruit juices and served from a large thermos by Uncle Dow, a favorite relative.

After the morning service, as we gathered for the meal, I'm sure other young folks joined in silently wishing for the excessively long blessing to end so the real reason for the gathering—the meal—could begin.

After dinner there was always congregational singing with quartets, duets, trios, and other combinations of musicians taking part. Everyone particularly enjoyed the talented Darnell family. Traditional hymns such as "The Old Rugged Cross," "Amazing Grace," and "Beulah Land" shared time with more modern gospel songs, "Telephone to

Glory," "Railway to Heaven," "Turn Your Radio On." Put all together, they told the same story.

Younger children used this afternoon time for play along the wooded trails behind the brush arbor, which has long since been replaced by a more permanent open tin-roofed structure (but it still has a sawdust-covered dirt floor).

During the warm afternoon, play was interrupted for a short walk to a temporary roadside stand at the filling station just a stone's throw away from where the road forked. Here a nickel saved for the occasion would buy a much dreamed of Popsicle.

Those were wonderful and special times which nurtured faith and love, family, and friends. Those were the times which propelled us into faith relationships and helped to begin the molding process of what we were and were to become. Blessed days!

A few weeks ago on that traditional second weekend in June, my wife, Bunny, my sister, Bonnie, and my cousins Bob and Spence slowly and deliberately walked through the cemetery, which had been cleaned off and decorated by local residents and visiting families; we were pleased and grateful.

As we looked at grave markers and dates of life spans, refreshing our memories while learning and relearning family history, we talked and tried to recall events and words attributed to our forebears whose memories we were honoring by our presence.

One of the events is worth repeating, not only because it is humorous but also because it tells us something about the people and times three-quarters of a century ago.

At that time, history would suggest that singing was even a greater part of our celebrations and worship than it is today.

My grandfather, Robert Taylor Hamrick, known also to his many friends and acquaintances as Uncle Bob, was rather robust and had a sizable "bay window." In spite of this he was an ardent and expressive song leader. On this particular Sunday while he was very actively lifting his arms toward the rafters and the heavens, Grandpa's suspenders broke loose from his trousers and down went his pants, exposing knee-length underwear known in those days as BVDs.

Well, Grandpa, without the slightest hesitation, reached down and yanked his pants back into place as he loudly commanded the congregation to, "Sing on, brothers, sing on!"

Bunny and I have been married since early June 1949. Each year when the second Sunday of June rolls around, we always remember fondly—and with a chuckle—our first Decoration together. As Bunny tells it, I told her to be ready to go "up home" on the next weekend for the Decoration. Being a city girl and not wanting to appear dumb to her new husband, she went to her mother and asked what was "The Decoration." Her mother told her it was a day set aside where people came back to their home cemeteries and decorated the graves of loved ones with flowers. Not fully understanding, Bunny thought this was rather ghoulish and was soon to be pleasantly surprised by the experience of that first Decoration. She also was appreciative of my mother's explanation the night before concerning proper Decoration protocol. Bunny learned about the spreading out and partaking of the food at our common tables. She even learned to be particular about whose food one ate. Of course Mother didn't tell her that directly. She said something like, "You know what I mean."

Those who haven't attended a Decoration have missed wonderful opportunities for fellowship with near and far relatives and new and old friends. You certainly need to plan for, or even create, the next one!

No matter what your own memory of that gathering place may be, or however you may regard what you experience there—be it in personal relationships, recollections of loved ones who have crossed that great divide, images of the past, or communion with the Holy Spirit —your inner self is bound to be touched and your journey of faith forever affected.

～ To Bury Our Dead ～

Tourists flock to the cemeteries of New Orleans to see the magnificent aboveground vaults in that legendary city built below sea level. But in the 1950s in the little bayou town of Plattenville, Frances Parkinson Keyes came upon another cemetery on the special springtime occasion honoring Saint Faustine, a martyred maiden. It was a stirring sight to see the freshly whitewashed tombs in candlelight and quite a contrast to the New Orleans tradition. Sadly, the procession is no longer held, but the cemeteries of New Orleans remain— complete with hair-raising stories.

To Build and Bury Aboveground

LURA ROBINSON

Visitors to New Orleans usually include the cemeteries in their tours of inspection. While the choice of tombs on view ranges from those of dashing pirates and voodoo queens to statesmen and Confederate heroes, there must be some significance in the fact that Easterners almost unanimously ask to see the tomb built by Josie Arlington, the highly successful madam of Storyville, where a bronze virgin raps unavailingly at a red granite door. Near by is the distinctive Moriarity monument, a tall shaft surrounded by the four life-size female figures of Faith, Hope, and Charity—and Mrs. Moriarity.

While a marked degree of individuality is exhibited in the construction and decoration of its tombs, New Orleans apparently never cared much for the expressive epitaph. Aside from the inscriptions on tombs of the young men who died on the field of honor, perhaps the most provocative epitaph is the one that consists of two simple words, "My Husband." Did the deceased live through his mortal span with no other qualifications. Was he Pierre Dubois, José Gonzales, or Joe Doakes? His name, if he had one, is not given. What manner of woman consigned this poor male soul to immortal anonymity?

It is on All Saints' Day, of course, that the New Orleans cemeteries present their "Sunday-best" appearance. A week before the event, great bustling and scrubbing and trimming and weeding go on behind the thick walls. When November 1 dawns, almost the entire population joins in a crisscrossing procession to the thirty-odd cemeteries of the city. Solemn, yet enjoyable in its way, the occasion brings a turnout rivaling that for the Mardi Gras. In at least one of the old cemeteries, a fence carefully separates the Catholic from the Protestant section. Yet the wholesale observance of All Saints' Day, originally a Catholic custom, has been embraced unstintingly by other faiths.

With armloads of flowers entire families march to the houses of their dead, some bringing lunch and spending the day among the tombs. A family of means which dares decorate its vault with a dozen carnations in lieu of the more expensive cabbage-size chrysanthemums can look for year-round censure. Yet, a handful of wild flowers or a wreath of beads and human hair that has been in use for generations is acceptable from the poor. The measure of grief for the deceased is in the size and quality of the November 1 floral tribute, which in turn is measured against the financial status of the remaining members of the family. So almost any New Orleanian can count with extraordinary certainty on a suitable All Saints' Day remembrance annually after departing this world—whether the remembrance be for his own sake or for the customary yardstick of alert alive neighbors.

All Saints' Day at Plattenville, Louisiana

Frances Parkinson Keyes

The sturdy little brick church at Plattenville, which I first saw from the bridge, is the scene every spring of a festival honoring St. Faustine, whose regally robed statue is among the many artistic treasures of this richly ornamented sanctuary. On this occasion, St. Faustine is removed from her shrine and paraded along the bayou, under ecclesiastical auspices, accompanied by a group of little girls, wearing costumes patterned after hers and reviving the legends about her. In quaintness and charm, this festival rivals the celebration of the feast of St. Amico. But for eerie beauty, no ceremony in which a bayou forms an integral part of the setting can equal the observance of All Saints' on the Bayou des Oies and Bayou Barataria.

In the "Lafitte Country" through which these bayous flow, the people bury their dead in great white tombs by the waterside; and when twilight comes on "Toussaint" they illumine the graves with tall flickering candles and keep prayerful watch in their proud small cemeteries throughout the night. The first candles are lighted without any signal except the instinct of the worshippers that now is the time. No formalities begin the rite. One by one the lights flicker into being. A breeze over the bayou fans the minute flames, giving them visible life. Night, falling suddenly, finds the beautiful scene complete.

The cemeteries are transformed. Freshly whitewashed tombs, which look bare and old by day, take on new colors. Their façades are adorned by shadows, their outlines softened. A translucence like that of marble disguises the roughness of cement. On this night, the tombs of Barataria are as splendid as those of the mighty anywhere in the world.

Silhouetted against the white tombs, worshippers move from grave to grave, carrying more and more flowers, more and more candles. Not one comes empty-handed. At least one candle must be lighted in memory of every kinsman and every friend who has gone on ahead, by those left behind. Death and the ceremonies of those remembering the dead are not austere mysteries to these celebrants, but intimate and friendly rites of communion with well-remembered friends whose lives continue in another world.

Dead? They are not dead. They live in the community they helped to hew out of the wilderness, in generations of children reared to useful citizenship, in the blessed freedom they defended through the centuries with their blood. And they will always live in the pilgrimage of undying remembrance, made on this day of every year, to the silent cities, briefly aglow with light.

~ *Telling the Bees* ~

JOHN GREENLEAF WHITTIER

Far north of Louisiana, in Appalachia and in New England, you may have heard the expression "Telling the Bees," but not fully understood its meaning. The great American poet John Greenleaf Whittier wrote a simple poem, "Telling the Bees," in 1858, after the death of his mother, Mary. In the words of Whittier himself, telling the bees was "a remarkable custom, brought from the Old Country, {which} formerly prevailed in the rural districts of New England. On the death of a member of the family, the bees were at once informed of the event, and their hives dressed in mourning. This ceremonial was supposed to be necessary to prevent the swarms from leaving their hives and seeking a new home." We pick up Whittier's ballad and then move to North Carolina and a recounting by the popular Southern writer Sharyn McCrumb of her family's "Telling the Bees" tradition.

I can see it all now—the slantwise rain
    Of light through the leaves,
The sundown's blaze on her window-pane,
    The bloom of her roses under the eaves.

Just the same as the month before,—
    The house and the trees,
The barn's brown gable, the vine by the door,—
    Nothing changed but the hive of bees.

Before them, under the garden wall,
    Forward and back,
Went drearily singing the chore-girl small,
    Draping each hive with a shred of black.

Trembling, I listened: the summer sun
    Had the chill of snow;
For I knew she was telling the bees of one
    Gone on the journey we all must go!

Then I said to myself, "My Mary weeps
    For the dead to-day;
Happy her blind old grandsire sleeps
    The fret and the pain of his age away."

But her dog whined low; on the doorway sill,
    With his cane to his chin,

The old man sat; and the chore-girl still
Sung to the bees stealing out and in.

And the song she was singing ever since
In my ear sounds on:—
"Stay at home, pretty bees, fly not hence!
"Mistress Mary is dead and gone!"

⮜ Telling the Bees: A Family Tradition ⮞

*SHARYN MCCRUMB

My great-uncle France really did "tell the bees."

I am descended from Scots-Irish pioneers who settled in the spine of the Smoky Mountains in western North Carolina in 1790, when the Appalachians were the frontier, dividing the gentrified east coast from the wilderness beyond. These first settlers built cabins out of rot-resistant chestnut logs, and shingled the roof with oak, because oak splits thin and straight. They hunted in the deep forests as the Cherokees had done, and they farmed their narrow valley along the Toe River.

They were a self-sufficient bunch in those days. They had to be. Town was a two-day ride from the farmstead, and money was limited to what you could earn selling fur pelts to the traders: fox, bear, deer, mink. They carved utensils from wood or horn, made soap in the fireplace kettle, using hog fat and hickory ashes. About the only items that had to be purchased were iron and gunpowder.

They used honey instead of sugar, and for that they kept bees. But where did you get the bees? Great-uncle France was a bee tracker. He probably learned the skill from his grandfather, Mose Honeycutt, mountain man and bear hunter. Some of the Arrowoods—the ones I take after—went in for book learning, and there is a passel of preachers in the family tree, and a couple of college professors, but France was a throwback to the woodsmen who forged that Wilderness Road, heading away from civilization.

When France wanted to get a beehive started, he began by sitting for hours by a creek in the woods on an April morning, watching for wild bees, who came to the stream to drink at intervals between pollen-gathering. Finally he would follow one that seemed headed for home—making a bee line for home, in fact. That's where the expression came from.

Uncle France would get only a few yards before he lost the scout bee—maybe he'd stop at a big chesnut a few paces deeper into the woods. He'd wait there by the tree for the next bee to skim by, and he'd follow that one a few yards farther along. When he lost sight of that bee, he'd wait until the next one flew by. Finally, this tenuous process would lead him to the bee tree, where the hive was located. He hoped to find the hive in a sourwood or basswood tree, the two best trees for honey. Bees loved the sweet flowers on those trees, and they would produce rich, distinctly flavored honey.

If the hive was on an assessible branch, France would cut off the tree limb and take the whole hive home with him. Stung now—he was used to stings. If he couldn't get the hive intact, he would mark the tree and come back in a day or so with his bee gum—a three-foot section of a hollowed-out black gum tree, which he was planning to use as the hive's home in domesticity. Then he would cut down the tree and split open the trunk, relocating some of the honeycomb into his bee gum. When the queen bee was found and put into the new bee gum, the hive would follow. Then he would leave the bees to settle overnight in their new abode. The next morning he would put a sack over the bee gum and haul it home, bees and all.

Once the hive was installed in a "bee gum" in the backyard, France would have a ready supply of honey and wax for the family's needs. But in some strange way, the bees seemed to become part of the family. Mountain beekeepers swore that the bees knew things. Within the family.

If there was a death in the family, Uncle France used to take some of the black crepe people used for mourning and cut it into thin streamers. He'd go out to his bee gums first thing in the morning, and while he was tying the streamer on the bee gum, he would solemnly inform the hive of the death. "Reckon you know that poor Davy passed away," he might say. "You stay here, though. No need to be leaving. It was the Lord's will." And then on to the next hive, and the next.

And the bees stayed.

➤ Remembering the Living and the Dead ➤

LLOYD C. DOUGLAS

Say "funeral" and most people are overcome by sadness. But even funerals have their humorous side when the performance becomes a part of your daily life. Lloyd C. Douglas was the son of a minister who grew up to become a minister himself. But he is best known for his powerful novel, later made into the movie,

Magnificent Obsession. *This recollection recalls many traditions well known to everyone whose ancestors can be traced to a rural turn-of-the-century American home.*

My papa was in great demand for funeral services; and, if the weather wasn't too bad, he would take me along. Nearly all funerals, at that time, were held in a church, and the graveyard was always an important part of the church property; an appropriate place for it, I think. The "funeral parlor" and the secular, commercialized, noisily advertised cemetery were yet to appear.

Well within the scope of my lifetime there have been fundamental changes in our general attitude toward the dead. I hope it will not depress you if I speak of them.

Today, if there is a death in the family, by natural causes, the physician or the nurse or a neighbor phones a mortician who arrives in an ambulance with a promptness exceeded only by the Fire Department. The family, still upset emotionally by their bereavement (for, no matter how long the loved one had been ill, the immediate relatives are never quite prepared for the shock), have been herded into a room where they will be unaware of proceedings. The mortician's men quickly and quietly tiptoe out of the house with the so recently vacated tenement of clay; by the time the family strolls back to the bedchamber, everything has been put to rights. It is as if father or mother or sister Mamie or little Jimmy had never lived there.

And that night, and the next one, sister Mamie (we will say) who had been sick so long that she dreaded to meet strangers, shares communal lodging with a dozen or more in a sort of public dormitory for the dead.

Now I fully agree with you that the real Mamie, who was Mamie, is gone; and that her frail little body is not our precious Mamie at all. But this modern practice of permitting our dead to be grabbed up, while still warm, by total strangers, and hustled at top speed to a place of business, to be impersonally operated on by embalmers and beauticians, is the most cold-blooded performance that our era of efficiency and assembly line production has achieved.

Of course the old way of handling these sad affairs was immeasurably worse. There were a couple of days when mortality had much the best of it over any calm consideration of the spiritual Life Eternal. The home was full of the confusion of distant relatives, friends of the family, neighbors, and comparative strangers who had come out of curiosity, expecting to be shown the corpse, preferably by the next of kin, who was thoroughly worn out before the torture was ended.

I think it would be a good thing if every church had a little chapel where the remains of our departed could be taken, after having been embalmed in the privacy of the home. That might help to solve the dilemma. As the matter stands today, the Church, which should be prepared to offer the physical equipment and spiritual counsel so urgently needed on such occasions, is missing a great opportunity to be of service.

The typical country funeral of sixty years ago was an event of general public interest.

Papa and I would drive first to the bereaved home and head the long procession of buggies and carriages to the church. Usually the remains of the deceased would be conveyed in a hearse provided by an undertaker from a neighboring town who was primarily a furniture dealer. In that case he would have brought a coffin with him.

At the church door, everybody but the drivers would disembark. Papa would get out and I (feeling very important) would drive to the first vacant hitching rack; and, having made sure our horse wouldn't get into trouble, I would slip into one of the rear pews. The church would be full; and in one of the "Amen corners" (a group of about four pews on either side of the pulpit platform) a choir of twenty or more adults, mostly young farmers' wives, would be ready to go into action at the appearance of the funeral cortege.

It would be entering now, Papa leading; and the choir would shrilly blast the peace of the countryside:

Uh-sleep in JEEZ-ZUZ-Bless-ud sleep,
From which none EV-VER wakes to weep.

By now the coffin, in the hands of a half-dozen husky farmers, is squeezing through the narrow aisle, followed by the close relatives, in the order of their relationship, the men leaving their hats on. I do not know why the men kept their hats on. Papa thought the custom might have originated with the idea that the male relatives were so stricken with grief that they forgot to take their hats off.

I know that my papa never willfully tried to make these sorrowing people cry. What he had to say was spoken in calmness and reassurance. But it was obvious that the choir would be contented with nothing less than an emotional storm. In their opinion, that's what funerals were for; to give the bereaved a chance to cry it all out.

Indeed it was common practice, in the country, for an officiating minister to stress the family's loneliness and "the vacant chair" until the whole congregation would have lost all control of its emotions, and would be howling like dogs.

Papa used to tell us of an old "Pennsylvania Dutch" preacher who specialized in such performances. Once, according to Papa's recollection, the good old man, while "preaching the funeral" of an octogenarian, said, "Now ven you get home, vadder vill not be dere. You vill set down to dinner, and vadder vill not be dere. You vill go to vadder's bedroom to see dat he is comfortable, and vadder vill not be dere. Everywhere dere vill be a lackancy!"

But I must get on—and out of this gruesome subject. I'm half-sorry now that I ever got you into it, though I do think it is of quite important psychological interest.

Now the funeral sermon is ended and it is time to "view the remains." Beginning with the rear pews, presumably occupied by those farthest removed from the close neighbors, long-time friends and the relatives, the audience marches slowly forward to pass the coffin; mothers lifting up bewildered three-year-old tots for their last (and probably their first) look at the deceased.

This seems an endless business. The tension mounts as the procession begins to draw upon the forward pews containing cousins once or twice removed. Now, at last, the immediate family huddles about the coffin, in a complete breakdown. More likely than not, the cold face is kissed. I have seen a mother tuck a warm shawl around the throat and shoulders of the departed.

There is more singing: "Shall We Gather at the RIV-VER?"

We are out in the cemetery now, at the graveside, where a great heap of black soil and yellow clay is held back by a pile of fence rails. Leather lines, borrowed from some farmer's team, are looped under the coffin, and strong arms lower it into the flimsy pine rough-box, the lid to which quickly follows. Papa reads the conventional "Forasmuch as it hath pleased Almighty God . . . we commit this body to the ground: Earth to earth."

A neighbor, with a shovel heaped high with dirt, would dump it onto the lid of the rough-box, and an anguished cry would burst forth from the family.

"Ashes to ashes."

Another shovelful bounced and rattled on the rough-box, and another wail came from the bereaved.

"Dust to dust."

More dirt and more crying. Then the shovels really went to it with a vim. At least a dozen men joined in the prompt filling of the grave. The fence rails were tossed aside; and, in less time than it takes to tell it, the grave would be shaped to the age-old pattern.

Then everybody grew quiet and Papa would be ready to pronounce the benediction. But before he did that, he would say, "Friends are invited to return to the family residence for refreshments."

Now that it was all over, the community felt an immediate sensation of relief, and made no bones about it. The men, amazingly cheered, strolled out to the hitching racks, discussing their crops on the way. The women, who had barely spoken to one another, ambled out in groups, lightheartedly exchanging news of their families.

At the residence of the bereaved, a dozen or more of the women living in the neighborhood had set long tables in the dooryard, under the trees, loaded with heaping platters of fried chicken, cold baked ham, potato salad, pickled beets, deviled eggs, homemade bread, fruit preserves, every known variety of pie, and beautiful cakes with white icing and glamorized by little red cinnamon drops.

Naturally the women of the family received tender attention. They could smile now. It was a wan, weary little smile, but it was a smile; for they had cried until they could cry no more. And the men of the family, who had been out in the barn, were patted on the shoulder by the neighbors who had put the teams away in their stalls and filled their feed boxes with the right amount of oats. Then the men would gather around the table. They were hungry. Within an hour, you wouldn't have guessed that any of these people had attended a funeral. They had cried it all out. I used to cry, too, even when I had never seen a member of this family before. Some kindhearted woman, seeing the Reverend's little boy with swollen eyes, would bring him another drumstick.

During the thirty years of my own ministry, great changes came to pass in the conduct of funerals. Now, at the appointed hour, a limousine calls for the family. At the mortuary, the casket, surrounded by floral gifts from friends, is already waiting for the service.

The officiating clergyman is ready, too. Perhaps he pauses, before entering the small chancel, to shake hands with the mourners who are tucked away, out of the view of the friends who have come to pay their respects. The funeral service is brief and usually impersonal. When it is ended, all the friends of the family go their way, and the relatives are quietly sneaked out a rear door and into the limousine for the ride to the cemetery. There the earth has been carted away. Rugs, in imitation of green grass, cover all the raw spots on the ground. The grave is lined with some green fabric. The casket is waiting on a mechanical chassis, well covered with flowers. If it is an inclement day, a commodious tent has been erected to keep the weather out.

The minister reads from a little black book, and the casket, almost imperceptibly, apparently of its own volition, begins to descend. (When these gadgets first came in vogue, they frequently got stuck, refusing either to complete the job or back up. On these embarrassing occasions, a male relative would remain to see the matter through, while the rest of the family was packed off home at 30 mph.)

But, assuming that everything is working properly, the casket begins its descent while the minister reads from his liturgy. When he arrives at "Earth to earth," the mortician lets a handful of rose petals flutter down.

Everybody is spared the shock of seeing shovels in action. The bereaved may have wept quietly, but there has been no emotional release; much less emotional collapse.

That is still to come! They take all their unrelieved grief home with them. They take it to bed with them. It may darken their days. It may make them a perplexing problem to their best friends. It sometimes takes them to the psychiatrist.

No, I'm not recommending a return to the old way of dealing with this most painful of all the dilemmas faced by lonely people who have survived their best-beloved. I am sure the old way was much too heartrending. But the modern way, which refuses to permit any measure of relief and hides away the sorrowing ones from so much as a handclasp and a sympathetic pat on the shoulder, is wrong; all wrong, and nothing less or else than wrong.

The first funeral I ever conducted was held in our church, but the interment was to be in a country graveyard many miles from town. As I had very few country parishioners, I did not own a horse and buggy. The bereaved family was poor. We wanted to spare these good people any unnecessary expense; so the undertaker drove the hearse and I sat perched high beside him.

It was a very hot day. The graveyard, evidently not used much, was overgrown with tall timothy bay. The old caretaker, who apparently hadn't cared very far beyond the call of duty, met our little cortege at the open gate.

"I don't know jest how yer a-goin' t' make out," he 'lowed. "The boys ran into a yallerjackets' nest; and they's a-buzzin' around right thick like at the grave."

But this was no time to abandon the business that had brought us here. We drove on to the graveside. I firmly intend to spare you the details of this event. The committal service was brief and to the point. If I left anything out, there were no complaints. The relatives were too busy fighting yellowjackets to pay much attention to what we had come to do. Nobody lingered.

As boy and man, I think I have seen about everything happen to disturb the orderly procedure of a funeral.

Once, during the early days of my ministry, on the half-mile trip from large the church to the cemetery, the team attached to the pall-bearers' conveyance, frightened by the band, ran away.

The deceased, prominent in county politics, had been an incorrigible "jiner." In the procession, far ahead of clergy, hearse, pallbearers, family, etc., marched, in full uniform, the Knights Templar, I.O.O.F., Modern Woodmen, Junior Order of American Mechanics, Elks, Moose, and more.

The frightened horses took off for the country by the shortest route which lay straight ahead. At full gallop they plunged through the long files of marching men who scurried to the fences making no effort to defend themselves with the axes and swords with which they were armed.

At a funeral I conducted, some twenty-five years ago, a belated family of relatives arrived at the cemetery after the casket had been lowered to what had been referred to as its last resting place, and firmly insisted on seeing Auntie. Everybody but the protagonists of this idea thought that it was an immensely foolish thing to do; but the late-comers held their ground. It took a long time, but we did it. A lot of relatives weren't on speaking terms when they left for home.

In that same cemetery I once quite unintentionally lost a whole procession of out-of-town people. In Akron, Ohio, there is an old cemetery, far out in the country when it was established, but more recently encircled by the rapidly growing city. Akron is a hilly place, and this cemetery is an ideal spot to get lost in unless you are familiar with its winding roads. Customarily the undertaker sent a car for me, so I had never paid very close attention to the geography of that burial ground. On this particular occasion, an interment was to be made here by people living some fifty miles away. I was to have the committal service at the grave, and I had phoned my friend the undertaker that I would drive my own car as I had another errand to do immediately afterward.

Someone from the undertaker's establishment met me at the gate and piloted me to the grave. The out-of-town people had already arrived. After the committal service was over, and I had said good-bye to my new friends from a distance, I climbed into my car and drove away. As I proceeded, it began to occur to me that I couldn't recognize anything but the half-dozen cars I saw in my mirror.

Around and around we went, over little hills and through unfamiliar valleys, my pursuers relentlessly keeping up. I indecorously gave my engine more gas and so did the hapless strangers who had a right to believe that I could be trusted to lead them out of their predicament.

Now, to my horror, we began racing through tortuous roads, which I recognized! Surely we had been this way before; maybe a couple of times before! Then, to my immeasurable relief, my pursuers left me. I had taken a right turn and they had gone straight ahead. So I turned around quickly and followed them. Eventually they found an exit. If the strangers hadn't become suspicious of my leadership, we might all be driving around in that cemetery yet. I never met any of these people afterward: I never wanted to, though they had impressed me as being well worth a further acquaintance.

Late in my papa's life, one of his old cronies told him a story that amused him very much, apropos of the odd situations which occasionally turn up in the course of a clergyman's life.

There was to be a home funeral service for an elderly person whose church, at the time, was without a minister. A retired clergyman, living in a city some distance away, had promised to come and officiate; but, at the last minute, when the house was full and running over with relatives and friends, a telegram was received, stating that the minister had missed the only available train that would get him there in time.

One of the neighbors remembered that a young clergyman, of another denomination, had just moved into the community; so somebody was dispatched to request his immediate attention to the predicament. The young man cheerfully consented and presently arrived, out of breath but full of importance, to find the house packed and waiting to get on with it.

Without pausing to make inquiries about the deceased, not even knowing whether the departed was a man or a woman, the young man launched upon a beautiful discourse about Death and the Life to Come; but after he had referred to "our transformed loved one," and "the departed spirit," so redundantly that he had begun to feel the urgent need of some more personal pronouns, he edged toward a woman seated within reach of a whisper, and asked, behind his hand, "Brother or sister?" And she replied, "Cousin."

The Grieving Throngs

Michael Gold

Lest you think that that American scene could only happen in the Midwest or South, here is the same tradition described from the vantage point of a young Jewish boy growing up in New York City. He paints a vivid scene of the working-class immigrant Jewish funeral of the time.

I liked to go to funerals with the Jewish coach drivers. What glorious summer fun! Nathan was a tall Jewish ox, with a red, hard face like a chunk of rust iron. His blustering manner had earned him many a black eye and bloody face. It was a warm bright morning. Three

coaches rolled down the ramp of the livery stable on their way to a
funeral. Then out bounced Nathan, cursing his horses. I begged him
to let me go along. He was grouchy, but slowed down. I scrambled up
beside him on the tall seat.

Three coaches and a hearse: a poor man's funeral. We rolled through
the hurly-burly East Side. The sporty young drivers joked from coach
to coach. The horses jerked and skipped. Nathan cursed them.

"You she-devil!" he roared in Yiddish at his white horse. "Steady
down, or I'll kick in your belly!"

He tugged at the checkrein and cut the mare's mouth until it bled.
But she was nervous; horses have their moods.

We came to the tenement of the corpse. Many pushcarts had to be
cursed out of the way. We lined the curb. There was a crowd gathered.
Weddings, sewer repairs, accidents, fire, and murders, all are food for
the crowd. Even funerals.

The coffin was brought down by four pale men with black beards.
Then came the wife and children in black, meekly weeping. The
family was so poor that they had not the courage to weep flamboyantly.

But some of the neighbors did. It was their pleasure. They made an
awful hullabaloo. It pierced one's marrow. The East Side women have
a strange keening wail, almost Gaelic. They chant the virtues of the
dead sweatshop slave, and the sorrow of his family.

They fling themselves about in an orgy of grief. It unpacks their
hearts, but is hell on the bystanders.

These mourners egg on the widow; they don't want her to hide her
grief; she must break down and scream and faint or the funeral is not
perfect.

I sat on the high driver's seat and watched; I felt official and
important somehow.

Then came the ride across the Brooklyn Bridge, with the incredible
sweep of New York below us. The river was packed tight, a street
with tugboat traffic. Mammoth skyscrapers cut into the sky like the
teeth of a saw. The smoke of factories smeared the bright blue air.
Horns boomed and wailed. Brooklyn lay low and passive on the
horizon.

"A man is crazy to live in Brooklyn," said Nathan, the driver,
pointing with his whip toward that side. "My God, it is as dead as a
cemetery; no excitement, no nothing! Look, Mikey, down there. That's
the navy yard. That's where they keep the American warships. Sailors
are a lot of Irish bums. Once I had a fight with a sailor and knocked
his tooth out. He called me a Jew."

"Ain't you a Jew?" I asked timidly, as my greedy eyes drank in the
panorama.

"Of course I'm a Jew," said Nathan in his rough, iron voice. "I'm proud I'm a Jew, but no Irish bum can call me one."

"Why?" I asked.

I was very logical when I was seven years old.

"Why?" Nathan mimicked me with a sneer. "Why? You tell a kid something, and he asks why? Kids give me a headache!" He spat his disgust into the river. The blob fell a third of a mile.

They put the coffin in the ground. The old rabbi in a shiny high hat chanted a long sonorous poem in Hebrew, a prayer for dead Jews. A woman screamed; it was the dead man's wife. She tried to throw herself into the grave. Her weeping friends restrained her. The graveyard trees waved strangely. The graveyard sun was strange. The gravediggers shoveled earth into the grave. I felt lonesome and bewildered. I wanted to cry like the rest, but was ashamed because of Nathan.

Then it was all over. All of us went to a restaurant at the entrance to the cemetery and ate platters of sour cream, pot cheese, and black bread, the Jewish funeral food. Even the widow ate. Nathan gave me half of his portion. Then we rode home over the bridge.

I was glad to feel the East Side again engulf our coach. I lost my vague funeral loneliness in the hurly-burly of my street.

— Notes of a Native Son —

JAMES BALDWIN

It is said that birth and death are life's two experiences which all humankind shares. Yet in every culture the ceremonies and services associated with these two events are rich in their uniqueness and vary widely from country to country, from religion to religion.

James Baldwin is considered one of this century's greatest American essayists. His moving and insightful account of his father's funeral reminds us that, though the years between one's birth and death are shaped by outside forces— places of birth, race, religion, geography, occupation, opportunities, traditions, and just plain chance—in that final tribute to us, our funerals, the summing-up of our lives will be reduced to the singular memory of us held in the mind's eye of each person who knew us.

The chapel was full, but not packed, and very quiet. There were, mainly, my father's relatives, and his children, and here and there I saw faces I had not seen since childhood, the faces of my father's one-time friends. They were very dark and solemn now, seeming somehow to suggest that they had known all along that something like this would happen. Chief among the mourners was my aunt, who had quarreled with my father all his life; by which I do not mean to suggest that her mourning was insincere or that she had not loved him. I suppose that she was one of the few people in the world who had, and their incessant quarreling proved precisely the strength of the tie that bound them. The only other person in the world, as far as I knew, whose relationship to my father rivaled my aunt's in depth was my mother, who was not there.

It seemed to me, of course, that it was a very long funeral. But it was, if anything, a rather shorter funeral than most, nor, since there were no overwhelming, uncontrollable expressions of grief, could it be called—if I dare to use the word—successful. The minister who preached my father's funeral sermon was one of the few my father had still been seeing as he neared his end. He presented to us in his sermon a man whom none of us had ever seen—a man thoughtful, patient, and forbearing, a Christian inspiration to all who knew him, and a model for his children. And no doubt the children, in their disturbed and guilty state, were almost ready to believe this; he had been remote enough to be anything and, anyway, the shock of the incontrovertible, that it was really our father lying up there in that casket, prepared the mind for anything. His sister moaned and this grief-stricken moaning was taken as corroboration. The other faces held a dark, noncommittal thoughtfulness. This was not the man they had known, but they had scarcely expected to be confronted with *him;* this was, in a sense deeper than questions of fact, the man they had not known, and the man they had not known may have been the real one. The real man, whoever he had been, had suffered and now he was dead: this was all that was sure and all that mattered now. Every man in the chapel hoped that when his hour came he, too, would be eulogized, which is to say forgiven, and that all of his lapses, greeds, errors, and strayings from the truth would be invested with coherence and looked upon with charity. This was perhaps the last thing human beings could give each other and it was what they demanded, after all, of the Lord. Only the Lord saw the midnight tears, only He was present when one of His children, moaning and wringing hands, paced up and down the room. When one slapped one's child in anger the recoil in the heart reverberated through heaven and became part of the pain of the universe. And when the children were hungry and sullen and distrustful and one watched them, daily, growing wilder, and further away, and running headlong into danger, it was the Lord who knew what the charged heart endured as the strap was laid to the backside; the Lord alone who knew what one would have said if one had had, like the Lord, the gift of the living word. It was the Lord who knew of the impossibility every parent in that room faced: how to prepare the child for the day when the child would be despised and how to *create* in the child—by what means?—a stronger antidote to this poison than one had found for oneself. The avenues, side streets, bars, billiard halls, hospitals, police stations, and even the playgrounds of Harlem—not to mention the houses of correction, the jails, and the morgue—testified to the potency of the poison while remaining silent as to the efficacy of whatever antidote, irresistibly raising the question of whether or not such an antidote existed; raising, which was worse, the question of whether or not an antidote was desirable; perhaps poison should be fought with poison. With these several schisms in the mind and with more terrors in the heart than could be named, it was better not to judge the man who had gone down under an impossible burden. It was better to remember: *Thou knowest this man's fall, but thou knowest not his wrassling.*

While the preacher talked and I watched the children—years of changing their diapers, scrubbing them, slapping them, taking them to school, and scolding them had had the perhaps inevitable result of making me love them, though I am not sure I knew this then—my mind was busily breaking out with a rash of disconnected impressions. Snatches of popular songs, indecent jokes, bits of books I had read, movie sequences, faces, voices, political issues—I thought I was going mad; all these impressions suspended, as it were, in the solution of the faint nausea produced in me by the heat and liquor. For a moment I had the impression that my alcoholic breath, inefficiently disguised with chewing gum, filled the entire chapel. Then someone began singing one of my father's favorite songs and, abruptly, I was with him, sitting on his knee, in the hot, enormous, crowded church which was the first church we attended. It was the Abyssinian Baptist Church on 138th Street. We had not gone there long. With this image, a host of others came. I had forgotten, in the rage of my growing up, how proud my father had been of me when I was little. Apparently, I had had a voice and my father had liked to show me off before the members of the church. I had forgotten what he had looked like when he was pleased but now I remembered that he had always been grinning with pleasure when my solos ended. I even remembered certain expressions on his face when he teased my mother—had he loved her? I would never know. And when had it all begun to change? For now it seemed that he had not always been cruel. I remembered being taken for a haircut and scraping my knee on the footrest of the barber's chair and I remembered my father's face as he soothed my crying and applied the stinging iodine. Then I remembered our fights, fights which had been of the worst possible kind because my technique had been silence.

I remembered the one time in all our life together when we had really spoken to each other.

It was on a Sunday and it must have been shortly before I left home. We were walking, just the two of us, in our usual silence, to or from church. I was in high school and had been doing a lot of writing and I was, at about this time, the editor of the high school magazine. But I had also been a Young Minister and had been preaching from the pulpit. Lately, I had been taking fewer engagements and preached as rarely as possible. It was said in the church, quite truthfully, that I was "cooling off."

My father asked me abruptly, "You'd rather write than preach, wouldn't you?"

I was astonished at his question—because it was a real question. I answered, "Yes."

That was all we said. It was awful to remember that that was all we had ever said.

The casket now was opened and the mourners were being led up the aisle to look for the last time on the deceased. The assumption was that the family was too overcome with grief to be allowed to make this journey alone and I watched while my aunt was led to the casket and, muffled in black, and shaking, led back to her seat. I disapproved of forcing the children to look on their dead father, considering that the shock of his death, or, more truthfully, the shock of death as a reality, was already a little more than a child could bear, but my judgment in this matter had been overruled and there they were, bewildered and frightened and very small, being led, one by one, to the casket. But there is also something very gallant about children at such moments. It has something to do with their silence and gravity and with the fact that one cannot help them. Their legs, somehow, seem *exposed,* so that it is at once incredible and terribly clear that their legs are all they have to hold them up. I had not wanted to go to the casket myself and I certainly had not wished to be led there, but there was no way of avoiding either of these forms. One of the deacons led me up and I looked on my father's face.

I cannot say that it looked like him at all. His blackness had been equivocated by powder and there was no suggestion in that casket of what his power had or could have been. He was simply an old man dead, and it was hard to believe that he had ever given anyone either joy or pain. Yet, his life filled that room. Further up the avenue his wife was holding his newborn child. Life and death so close together, and love and hatred, and right and wrong, said something to me which I did not want to hear concerning man, concerning the life of man.

~ For Each of Us, a Resting Place ~

In Moravian communities across the country, Easter is celebrated with a sunrise service held in "God's Acre," the cemetery where the brothers and sisters are sleeping. The tradition began in 1732 in Hernhut, Germany, where a group of young Moravian men held an Easter service in a graveyard so they could celebrate Christ's symbolic rising and greet the morning with hymns of praise. It quickly spread to this country, and to me this tradition speaks of the mystery and beauty of the cemetery which far surpasses its ghoulish connotations of murder mysteries and gory tales.

Should you visit the Old Salem, North Carolina, Moravian Easter ceremonies you will see no fancy bonnets, frills, or bows, or any of the latest fashions in the predawn gathering. But you will hear a brass band whose sweet hymns echo through the primeval trees to welcome the rising sun and happy morning.

There will be no pink and yellow Easter baskets filled to the brim with colorfully dyed eggs and long-eared chocolate candy bunnies. But there will be warm, plump hot cross buns like those which peasants sold, but kings ate, in medieval days.

And there is a magical spell.

It begins when the dark, heavy cloud of night is lifted by dawn's soft colors and the morning sun spreads light upon the earth and the throngs of devout worshipers. It is a wondrous scene—a time of untold beauty and joy, hopefulness and thanksgiving, which comes when a deep personal experience is shared with other people.

That scene is captured throughout the country, at many graveyards and in churches of many denominations, because the tradition has spread beyond the Moravian faith.

The quiet meditation experienced and inspiration gathered among the tombstones of the dead tells us about our American heritage—our people, their hopes, dreams, lives, and deaths. As the highly acclaimed mystery writer Elizabeth Daniels Squire explains, "The people who came before me lived in a dangerous world and most of their tombstones seemed to say they'd been brave about it."

My favorite cemetery is in Virginia City, Nevada. Walking among the graves of those who traveled so far—from Ireland and Italy, China and Germany—to the barren and bare bowels of the unknown West when they heard about the Comstock Lode, today's troubles and pettiness come into perspective.

Nowhere is there more tradition to be found than in America's cemeteries. We should enjoy them more.

Told in a Cemetery

*Betsy Humphreys

As I followed a string of car lights up Carolina Street in Valdese, I felt the excitement of the day, even though it was still dark. I passed a family walking along the side of the road headed in my direction. They were making the Easter morning pilgrimage in the traditional style of the first Waldensians in Burke County—that is, they were traveling on foot to the cemetery that crests the hill and spills down toward the town side.

I pulled into the cemetery and saw that many had already gathered and were standing in small groups. Tombstones loomed in this shadowy world. I tried not to walk on graves but found myself dead center between a row of headstones and footstones and sidestepped quickly, shamed by my carelessness.

I leaned over slightly to read the names of families who had come from the Italian Alps to a 10,000-acre plot of North Carolina wilderness over one hundred years ago. They had pledged to "strive to be witnesses to the Truth through our conduct, our words, our activity, and our entire lives." Despite hardships that at times led to near-starvation and economic despair, these Waldensians prevailed over their circumstances. The tombstones that took me almost no effort to read stand as memorials to these pioneers who put immeasurable effort into their tasks. There are Rivoire, Bounous, Tron, and more.

Many of the graves were decorated with flowers, brought by loved ones the previous day. In this way the present-day Waldensians are like their religious neighbors, the Moravians, who clean and decorate their families' gravesites each Easter Saturday.

As I stood with the gathering crowd, I saw people talking quietly. Most would glance occasionally to the east, where the sun would soon rise from behind a wooded hill. The air was cool but not biting.

Soon a small group of teenage trumpeters began the familiar hymn, *"Jesus Christ Is Risen Today,"* announcing that Easter had arrived. The Reverend Kirk Allen, then interim pastor at Waldensian Presbyterian Church, read the unsettling story from Luke that defies all common sense. Then he preached, appropriately, on the theme of "Too Good to Be True." As he talked, a fireball sunrise assured us that this was no ordinary day.

It represents the unbelievable, unprovable by scientific methods. Yet this is truth for millions who are lifted into hope through the claim of One risen after death by murder.

It is absurd to some, yet on that hill, in that slowly warming, slowly lightening cemetery, the ultimate promise was repeated: Here is all the life and sustenance you will ever need.

~ *The Best She Could* ~

Back in 1963, when visiting my former husband's ancestral home in tiny Ridge Spring, South Carolina, we drove over to the cemetery in nearby Ward. The obligatory visit was part of the regional and family indoctrination. I will never forget the sight of the lifesize statue that Colonel Clinton Ward erected to himself. Next to it, dwarfed by comparison, a simple pillow tombstone marked his wife's grave. It read, "She hath done what she could" (Mark 14:8). Many's the time I have thought that is the summation of my own life.

Actually, the art, if one dares to call it so, of writing epitaphs surely reached its height in the late eighteenth and early nineteenth century. Today we seldom seem to inscribe much more than names and years into tombstones, but mystery writer Elizabeth Daniels Squire takes us on a trip back to a time when the tradition was otherwise.

The Summation of a Life

* Elizabeth Daniels Squire

A graveyard is full of mysteries waiting to intrigue. I learned that when I was a child. Wherever we traveled, my father would stop the car and go look at old cemeteries—the ones with tombstones tilted by time and grayed with moss. He looked for the history made real: tombstones for soldiers in the Civil War, or the stone for one entire family that died together in a yellow fever epidemic. And I understood from the large number of small carved lambs, and the tiny stones for babies and small children, that once it had been an accomplishment just to grow up. The people who came before me lived in a dangerous world and most of their tombstones seemed to say they'd been brave about it.

A father (1808–1882) in a graveyard near Asheville, North Carolina, rates these words: *"I have fought the good fight, I have finished my course. I have kept the faith."* Not too far away, a tombstone bears a carved hand that points straight up to heaven.

Markers are so varied, from plain flat stones with inscriptions to large stone tree-stump-shaped markers for deceased members of the Woodmen of the World, from the stone angel carved by Thomas

Wolfe's father, for example, to some homemade markers we found in a small family plot. Someone had cut squared-off holes in the ground above the graves, then poured in cement. Then the names and dates of the departed were written in the wet cement. Whatever their resources, these people cared.

I like to examine tombstones, which can hold the summation of a life or at least explain how it ended. I admire the explicitness of the story in the small space on some stones:

"Thad Sherrill, Son of Jason (and) Clarissa 1846–1898. Bushwhacked on Mt. Creek by George Maney. Maney lynched by Mob In Murphy 1899, Hanging Him To Upper Valley River Bridge." So says an inscription in the Old Mother Church cemetery in Robbinsville, North Carolina. The kernel of a larger story of hate and revenge.

And more personal tragedies are spelled out too. In a small family resting place outside of Asheville, a large stone bears the almost life-size picture of the motorcycle on which the young man buried there was killed.

But visiting graveyards has never depressed me. It's made me aware that I'd better make the most of my life. Because, as an old hymn says: *We are only here for a little while.*

My father, who had a great zest for being alive, looked for something to laugh about on tombstones. He had a great affection for my aunt Emily, my mother's sister. But, almost as an antidote for the sadness at her graveside service, he found a joke on my great-grandparents' tombstone. They share a monument in beautiful Spanish moss–draped Oakdale Cemetery in Wilmington, North Carolina. He died first, and so the stone said, "Here Lies Robert Rufus Bridgers." And his family put a Bible verse: *"He rests from his labors."* When his wife died, her name was added to the gravestone. So the stone now reads: *"Here lies Robert Rufus Bridgers—He rests from his labors—and his wife Margaret Elizabeth Bridgers."*

Fortunately, that whole branch of my family seems to be endowed with a good sense of humor so I didn't expect them to mind when I used that inscription, in the first chapter of one of my mystery novels, *Remember the Alibi.* The mystery begins—where else?—in an old cemetery.

In real life, tombstones can solve mysteries. My husband, like my late father, is a tombstone aficionado. This helped him figure out his great-great-grandmother's Hungarian connection. You see, his staunch Yankee family had staunch Yankee names, except for several men in the family with the exotic name Bela, which is the Hungarian version of "Benjamin." How on earth, my husband wondered, had that name come down to him from a great-great-uncle? Perhaps, he suspected, his great-great-grandmother had had a secret affair with a wild Hungarian.

But when we went to the green and peaceful family resting place in Riverton, Connecticut, he found the gravestone of his Great-Great-Uncle Bela Squire. Nearby he also found the stone of Dr. John Bela, whose inscription made clear he had been community doctor for many years. So my husband figures the name Bela honors the doctor who brought an ancestor into the world. In gratitude after a difficult birth, perhaps. Stones often hint at more than will fit into the chiseled inscription.

Graveyards anchor family history for many people, I find. They make it seem more real than just the names in a county courthouse record book or a family Bible.

Sometimes, a burial place is a reminder of a painful mystery that changes the lives of those who are still alive. Not far from my ancestors in the Wilmington cemetery is the Kenan family plot. My husband found it, and called me over to look. Because there lies Mary Lily Kenan Flagler Bingham (1867–1917).

We'd heard her story. Rumors about her death were still around in 1986 and helped cause the rather public Bingham family dissension that led up to the sale of the family-owned paper, The *Louisville Courier-Journal*. Mary Lily was the widow of Florida real estate and railroad magnate Henry M. Flagler when she married Judge Robert Worth Bingham, publisher of the *Courier-Journal*. A scant few months later, she died under strange circumstances. Rumors said her husband might be to blame. Her fortune helped develop the paper. And that fact is said to have helped fuel family dissension. Meanwhile Mary Lily lies in peace under the swaying Spanish moss. A mystery forever.

I, being Southern and aware of both near and far relationships, know that I am related to Colonel Bingham, who may or may not have caused his wife's death and who helped create a great newspaper. We are both descended from a far away ancestor who was a governor. And I come down from other creators of newspapers, and also from a pirate and other rather imperfect types. I can visit the graves of ancestors who flourished and those who definitely did not. I am a multitude.

I am the past as well as the present. There are graves to prove it. That's tradition, right?

And perhaps that is what makes a graveside service so moving at a time of loss. We need the comfort of the ritual—the hopeful words about the hereafter, the heads bowed, remembering. And there's also comfort in the fact that *this particular* loved one has now become part of the history and tradition commemorated in *this* place. So, comforted, we feel free to be glad to be alive, and even to laugh.

I ask friends what they remember about old graveyards and often it's the funny stones, not the sadness. Like the one I'm told about in Beaufort, South Carolina, that says, "You see, I told you I was sick," and the one in Murphy, North Carolina, which says, "Thanks for the dance."

➤ Sounds in the Stillness ➤

Growing up the child of a Yankee father and a Southern mother, I never cared much for the Civil War. Years later I jokingly remarked that the unwritten battle of the war was the one that was waged at our dinner table night after night after night.

Still, I knew the vastly different Blue-and-Gray points of view being voiced had nothing to do with my parents' present-day lives or my own. The war was over, whether you liked the ending or not. Those past events had played a part in shaping the present, and they certainly merited being remembered, but "The War" was not worth being blown out of proportion.

Luckily, today's generation has Ken Burns's poignant television saga of the Civil War to help heal many leftover wounds. But that takes hours to view. A generation earlier, Nell Ahern captured the heart of the war when she visited the grave sites created for the soldiers who fought in that war.

To capture the poignancy of her piece, we must remember that those graveyards were not formal cemeteries designed and specified as burial places. Those graveyards were backyards and farmlands, north and south. They are hallowed ground.

Whether the site be a cemetery or a graveyard, these can be healing places.

On the 100th Anniversary of the Outbreak of the Civil War—March 1961

NELL GILES AHERN

THE GHOSTS OF FALLEN HEROES SPEAK TO THE
VISITOR WHO CAN HEAR THEM.

It's a fine thing, my husband says, for a tourist to have a hobby: read about it in the winter, walk over it and look at it in the summer. And so we have old battlefields. They're one way to rout a New Englander out of his six provinces and send him wheeling to visit his wife's southern relations. From second-cousin Laura, who lives near Gettysburg, to my brother William, near Vicksburg, we have visited every battlefield of the Civil War.

But home again in Boston, I am seized with nostalgia as I begin a thank-you letter to Aunt Dollie for her pickled peaches recipe (first time she's let it out of the South). I hear the needling sound of summer rain on an umbrella. Chickamauga, that was, where we stooped to read each historic marker.

The sound of rain . . . the time of day . . . the pain of growing up and leaving home . . . this speaks to me from every battlefield of the War. What happened at Shiloh, at Petersburg, at Bull Run is not a dead event, but a personal experience.

And what is this nation made of but people like me? We've grown up on a shady street in a medium-size town somewhere, close to cousins and uncles and brothers. And now we are scattered all over the country. I had forgotten the taste of pickled peaches. I hadn't remembered the cadence of Uncle David's voice. But when I went south again, when I tasted and listened, my homeland came rushing back to me.

How personal was this nation's struggle for maturity, we discovered one sultry day in Virginia, shortly after noon. We were looking for the battlefield at Five Forks, on a country road that led only to a sleepy old house sitting in a dirt yard swept clean with a broom. I stepped up on the plank porch to knock. The house, beyond the open door, held its breath. At last I heard a bed creak, and bare footsteps over a broad floor. A sleepy-eyed woman appeared.

"I've spoiled your nap," I said. "I'm sorry." She said that was all right. I asked her if she knew anything about the battlefield at Five Forks.

"It's right here," she said. Her gesture swept the yard and the woods beyond, where Pickett's men and horses nearly 100 years ago had waited through a black night for a bloody day. Her grandparents had told about bodies limp as grain sacks, a screaming hell of men and horses. "You couldn't put a foot down between corpses."

If Five Forks is the smallest battlefield we have visited, the largest is the territory around Petersburg . . . about 170 square miles. Nearby are Williamsburg and the plantations along the James River. The country is beautiful.

At the National Military Park, we drove first to the museum, asked for a guide map, looked at the collection in the museum cases. We read a letter from a Yankee soldier whose conscience troubled him. He was one of the Pennsylvania regiment who had dug the mine, filled it with black powder, to explode in the face of the Confederacy in the Battle of the Crater.

We took a six-mile drive through the battlefield, stopping often to walk along the trenches. The stillness is immense. And yet, the ghosts speak as plainly as the mockingbird splitting his throat up there in a cedar tree.

On another battlefield, we sensed the nightmare quality of the War. One sweltering Sunday afternoon, we followed a country-thin road through the maze of swamp and underbrush where the Battle of the Wilderness was fought. There was nobody. Then all of a sudden an old Ford and a black man shining with sweat standing beside it, drinking a can of beer. As we squeezed past, he threw back his head and burst into spine-chilling laughter.

At broad noon in southern Tennessee, we walked onto the Battle-field at Shiloh. A light breeze carried soft, slurred, young voices. A bus stopped, the doors folded back, and young black children scrambled out, each holding high his fat paper sack of lunch. Their murmuring recalled the subdued hum of bees in a field of daisies.

I remember Shiloh for the graves. In the blank light of noon, the headstones were dazzling white. Row after row, we stopped to read the names: "Unidentified" . . . "Unidentified" . . . "Known only to God." In the long painful reach toward maturity, so much nameless valor thrown away.

South from Shiloh lives my brother William, and a morning's ride beyond him lies Vicksburg, shrine of the siege that broke the Confederacy on the Fourth of July, 1863. At the Hospitality Information Booth, a hostess suggested that if we were interested in the battle, we'd better see the whole city.

Nobody can say (for sure) that God was on the side of the Confederacy, but the Mississippi River certainly was. Look down from the bluffs of Vicksburg today, and you don't see Old Man River. In Grant's day, you did. To isolate the city from the river (which made it a Gibraltar), Grant's engineers dug a canal across the hairpin neck of land. Strangely, the water wouldn't flow. The plan failed. So Grant, instead, imposed an iron ring of starvation, and that succeeded. Ironically, the Mississippi River waited thirteen years—too late to help Grant—and broke through the canal.

While Grant was taking Vicksburg, Lee lost Gettysburg. This northernmost battlefield of the Civil War is by all odds the most famous, the most tactically interesting, and one of the bloodiest in history. In three days here, 51,000 men were lost, and here, four months later, Lincoln made them immortal. At Gettysburg a superb job has been done by the National Park Service. A guided tour doubles the experience.

Finally, it all must end in the stillness at Appomattox. Whatever time of day we've gone there, the sun is shining, a blade of grass throws a shadow. In a cinnamon rosebush sits a bird's nest . . . empty. In the deserted village there is the McLean House, where Lee surrendered to Grant on Palm Sunday, 1865. It isn't empty by any means. There's a lot of furniture in it and it is open to tourists. There's the old jail, a tavern, a country store. But there is not one sound.

Even when people lived here, Appomattox Court House was an out-of-the-way place. Wilmer McLean moved here from Manassas to escape the war. It followed him to his parlor, as though Destiny had singled him out, collared him against his own wall, and said, "Face it. Every man must."

Under the open pink sky at Manassas one evening we walked across the fields to the Henry House. At the grave of old Mrs. Henry, who demanded to be carried back from safety to die in her own bed, I felt again the nostalgia which the battlefields of the Civil War evoke. Why is this so true? Why are these historic sites so endlessly fascinating?

The growing pains of this nation belong to me and to all the millions of people like me. The experience is personal. This the ghosts seem to say, at a cross roads named Five Forks . . . through a Yankee soldier's conscience at Petersburg . . . in the shock of terrible laughter in the Wilderness . . . in the nameless valor thrown away at Shiloh . . . through the courage of embattled Vicksburg . . . the slaughter at Gettysburg . . . and at last the stillness at Appomattox.

These are the things we shall go back to hear again.

~ Slave Cemetery Restoration ~

SUSAN ROSE

Hillsborough, North Carolina, is a charming and most historical town that traces its roots back to pre-Revolutionary days. The restoration of the old slave cemetery in that Southern town in the 1980s inspired poet Susan Rose to pen these words.

In this silent grove they lie beneath the earth
In quietude they never found in their time

Of masters, overseers, "pattyrollers," Ku Klux Klan.
We have descended from these dead, descended from their owners.

On grassy slopes cracked tombstones, righted markers,
Faint lettering on flagstone slabs tell
When they lived and died—
Scratched roughly on a molded concrete lamb—June 1863–April 1864.

Poison ivy vines twist round the trunks of ancient oaks
Like furry ropes. Their tendrils, cut off higher than
A man can reach, hang loose, stems severed from their roots.
Their dying leaves wave in the breeze like flags of freedom.

These buried never knew of Little Rock or Martin Luther King.
We hear speeches to dedicate the marker
Where their names are listed;
We sing together, "We Shall Overcome."

⟶ The Tradition Continues ⟵

Remembering Keeps the Past Alive

I have never understood why parents try to shelter their children from death. If we do not learn as children that life will end, then how can we learn the value of storing away joyful moments and treasuring each day? As Kahlil Gibran said, "Remembrance is a form of meeting." Farewells and sadness, grieving and mourning, should be part of the healthy life. Otherwise we lose the meaning of the word "remember" when we speak of those who are gone. As these children's sketches show, learning early on the rich traditions that accompany death and are celebrated in the cemetery can help take away fears. They create continuity, one generation with the next.

When my grandfather died, we sprinkled soil brought from Scotland around his grave just as he had done to my great-grandfather's grave when he passed away in 1980. This is special to my family because we are Scottish descendants. Neither my grandfather nor my great-grandfather ever stepped foot on Scottish soil, but they spoke often of our Scottish heritage and encouraged our family to remember that we are members of the Clan McDonald.

Our tartan is prominent throughout our house. My mom has a kilt and Dad always wears his tartan tie to special family gatherings. In 1991, my family spent two weeks in Great Britain and had the opportunity to visit Edinburgh, where we collected some Scottish soil to bring home.

I am expected to carry on this tradition of placing soil from Scotland on the grave of the passing generation. This is a tradition that I am proud of, and hopefully my children will have the opportunity and desire to continue it for many years to come. Everyone should be proud of their heritage. My family's tradition makes me proud to be Scottish.

Neil McDonald, middle school

⇥ ⇤

Today, I was playing with my doll that reminds me of my great-aunt Eula Mae. I remembered the family tradition that she helped start. It was a very unusual tradition called the Dawsey Family Cemetery Day.

It happens at the town cemetery in Aynor, South Carolina, the town where my mom's family was born and raised. The ones who do not still live there try to come back for "Cemetery Day." It is always held the day before Mother's Day.

We wear old clothes and bring rakes, shovels, flowers, fertilizer, and supplies to clean the tombstones. We work all morning. Then we turn on the sprinkler system and water everything. The kids always get wet, too. That is my favorite part.

Afterwards, we go to my great-aunt's house, which is close-by, for lunch. My uncle talks about family history. Sometimes we sing songs. The kids have a talent show. Sometimes grown-ups participate. The kids are usually better.

"Cemetery Day" is special, but it will be sad this year because my great-aunt Eula Mae has died. She loved her family, especially the kids. "Cemetery Day" will be even more special from now on. It will help me remember her.

Stephanie Simpkins, elementary school

⇥ Memorial Day ⇤

Memorial Day was once as important a day as the Fourth of July. Today it has gotten lost among other, more recently added holidays and celebrations. It really doesn't matter what calendar day you use, but the tradition of combining a family reunion with a return visit to a family cemetery plot is worth the time and trouble. For Pat Rhyne the event brings together the generations bearing flowers and food, for worship and remembering. These are elements that bring out the best in each of us and create memories for the future.

What better tradition can there be than to remember our family members on a special day? On the third Sunday in May, our extended family members (brothers, sisters, aunts, uncles, and cousins by the dozens) attend Oak Grove Methodist Church in Ellenboro, North Carolina, for Memorial, or Homecoming. The family turns out in large numbers for this special day.

On Saturday we decorate fourteen graves with flowers. It's truly a tradition, as family members cut and arrange flowers and then transport them to the cemetery. Following this, there is a lot of cooking to be done as Sunday approaches.

On Sunday we gather for church, followed by dinner on the grounds. There is quite an array of food to enjoy as we sample each other's cooking.

Our family is especially proud of this tradition, because Oak Grove Methodist Church was founded by my husband's great-great-great-great-grandfather, Jeremiah Blanton, in 1893.

Pat Rhyne

⤚ *Flowers for Remembrance* ⤙

When I was younger, red tissue-paper poppies were worn for Veterans Day. In elementary school I even had to memorize the lines, "In Flanders fields the poppies blow/Between the crosses, row on row." Only recently I learned why red poppies were associated with death. In the Victorian era, certain flowers represented human emotions and sentiments. Traditionally, flowers are sent to the bereaved. This gentle expression can be made all the more meaningful by sending this bouquet of remembrance: red poppies for consolation, a red geranium for melancholy, snowdrops for hope in sorrow, and ivy for friendship.

K. D. Oana, a popular writer of children's books, reminded me of an Old World custom—spreading rose petals on grave sites for All Souls' Day or All Saints' Day. This symbolic gesture is founded on the belief of the soul's immortality. This year, on Columbus Day, my grandfather's birthday, I took the petals from some of the last roses of the season to his grave and placed them on the family's marker, which bears the verse he chose:

> *Let not Death appall thee,*
> *For beyond the tomb*
> *God Himself shall call thee,*
> *When the roses bloom.*

HOW ENDURING ARE OUR BODIES, AFTER ALL! THE
FORMS OF OUR BROTHERS AND SISTERS, OUR
PARENTS AND CHILDREN AND WIVES, LIE STILL IN
THE HILLS AND FIELDS AROUND US.

Henry David Thoreau

PART THREE

SHARING AND
TOGETHERNESS

CHAPTER 17

Home and Family Time

FAMILY TRADITIONS

⟶ *Traditions Begin with You* ⟵

American families are rooted in traditions. In fact, a recent poll (I guess poll-taking could be called a new tradition of sorts) showed that 41 percent of baby boomer families put more emphasis on traditions than their parents did! About 87 percent thought traditions should be passed on.

The beauty of traditions in America is that usually they are a combination of old ways gathered from north and south, east and west, and all cultures of the world, and then melded together through marriage and remarriage. The beauty is that as each family branch or generation takes them up, every tradition becomes richer and takes on its own character.

Family traditions inhabit every corner of our lives. For many, dinnertime is a family tradition—whether to learn good manners or come together for fellowship, or both. For others who do not have that time together, a family tradition can be a father-and-son walk in the woods or a mother-and-daughter shopping trip. A family tradition can be passing on an heirloom or a name. Owning your own piece of land is certainly a tradition born of the American dream. So is the right to an education. And the good life.

Where do these traditions begin? With you.

What are they? As Claire Whitcomb, an editor of Victoria magazine who co-authored Great American Anecdotes with her father, John, writes, anything can be a tradition. Family traditions are as varied and special as each family.

Tradition!

*CLAIRE WHITCOMB

In my family it was understood. Do something twice and you have a tradition on your hands.

"It's a tradition!" my father would say, gesturing like a band conductor (you could almost hear the swell of the trumpet section). Then he'd get out cookie sheets for pizzas, a household specialty made with refrigerator roll dough which, after various experiments, evolved into a Sunday afternoon fixture.

"It's a tradition," my mother would say tenderly, when we returned from piano lessons bearing nosegays of wildflowers picked in the woods.

Anything could become a tradition. Writing a poem for a birthday present. Poring through cookbooks to find an ethnic specialty for Sunday dinner. Driving home from church and "directing" my father, who would turn anywhere we wanted and pretend to be hopelessly lost, even though he managed to arrive at our corner on schedule.

Back when my brother had a buzz cut that colored eggs could be balanced upon, the Easter rabbit took it upon himself to hide our presents throughout the house. In due course birthday presents, Mother's Day gifts, and graduation cards had to be hunted for high in curtain valances, low in the baseboard heating. Sometimes they dangled by a ribbon from the fireplace flue or from the brace that held up the dining table leaves. Today presents for the grandchildren (as well as the grandparents) are hidden in spots that newcomers can scarcely find, but my brother and I know by heart.

Almost every birthday picture of me as a girl shows an angel food cake with orange icing ablaze with candles. Almost every memory I have of schoolday mornings includes my father, filling his coffee thermos and making a liverwurst sandwich to take to work.

The difference between tradition and being set in one's ways is slim. Tradition, after all, is nothing more than habit fired by enthusiasm. And my family was an ardent keeper of habits.

We liked nothing better than days that unfolded as predictably as the placement of toothbrushes in a bathroom holder. We mourned sofa fabric that frayed and couldn't be replaced because styles had changed. We hated to outgrow things, so my mother bought fuzzy brown-bear bathrobes in a multiple of sizes, guaranteeing furry comfort from kindergarten to sixth grade.

During the do-your-own-thing late sixties and early seventies we may as well have been living in Tibet. The only radical idea I can remember permeating the family sanctuary was my mother's decision to redecorate the rec room. I remember viewing this unaccustomed burst of spontaneity with skepticism, but with a willingness to adjust. The dog, however, proved recalcitrant. Blinded by cataracts when she was a puppy, she navigated the house by memory, whimpering at the spot where the sofa used to be, hoping to be asked up. In heartbroken haste, my mother returned the uprooted sofa legs and rocking chair runners to their ancient grooves in the linoleum.

Now that I have a child of my own, a toddler who can't pass a light switch without begging to flick it on, I understand how early the joy of repetition is learned. I also understand that my parents were toddlers in their own way, teetering on unstable legs, trying to create a happy household out of memories of impermanence—coal that was never sure to be in the bin, rent that was never sure to be paid, and other by-products of the Depression. I don't know how they acquired the skill, but somewhere along the path to parenthood, they learned to polish the simplest moments of joy until they shone like a string of Christmas lights, illuminating their children's way to adulthood.

My brother and I grew up knowing that the future was a well-charted terrain, that flags would be dutifully stuck in the brick planter on the Fourth of July, that Dad would always wear a red tie on Christmas, and that strawberry ice cream sodas (never any other flavor) would be the reward of a lengthy shopping expedition.

Today some of my family's traditions lie in storage, waiting for grandchildren old enough to appreciate them. But when my brother and I go home to visit, the rituals that still work are set out before us like the rose china we always used on Christmas morning.

And when we are ready to leave, my mother with her bad ankle and my father with his bad knees walk us to the car and then jump up and down and wave madly. My husband, son, and I drive slowly up the hill, waiting while they hurry to the front door and wave again. Why? It's a tradition, of course.

⟶ I Never Knew My Grandfather ⟵

*EMYL JENKINS

To my way of thinking, family traditions are carried on not just in our activities but in our thoughts—and my thoughts are often triggered by the sight of objects that I choose to have around me. We pass these material objects on within our families and among our friends as a way of keeping the past alive. My grandfather's overstuffed chair, my aunt's favorite picture, the cut-glass carafe which Mrs. Patrick gave me from her own collection when I was married . . . these are vestiges of the past that are part of my family tradition. To Catherine Hamrick, it is a maple table. Those who say objects are only "things" and mean nothing to them have missed one of the great pleasures of life—the tradition of remembering the people who once cherished them.

I never knew my grandfather, but I think of him often. I thought about him this morning in fact, when I filled the white-and-gold flower-encrusted Victorian vases he loved with Gerbera daisies, blue irises, yellow roses, spidery Queen Anne's lace, pink larkspur, and trailing English ivy.

From family pictures pasted in black leather photograph albums I know what he looked like. He parted his hair in the middle, wore fashionable high collars, and rarely smiled—at least for the camera. As he aged, gentle wrinkles and permanently embedded laugh lines belied the seriousness of his poses.

His high-set forehead always reminds me of my father; his dark, piercing eyes are those of my daughter, Joslin. No matter how hard I try, I cannot find one thing about him that resembles me! Yet I did inherit something as distinctive as a fingerprint, something more endearing than the shape of his face or the color of his hair. I inherited his love for beautiful and interesting treasures from the past.

A New England banker, my grandfather loved and collected eighteenth- and nineteenth-century antiques. During the 1920s he became interested in the pressed glass that had been made in Sandwich, Massachusetts, some fifty or seventy years earlier. As a young girl growing up in the South in the 1950s, I loved the patterns on the glass—blackberry boughs, cornucopias, lacy hearts, and sunbursts. Today I appreciate his eye for beauty even more. In many ways, his antiques reveal far more about him than the photographs that captured his image for posterity.

My grandfather is part of my everyday life—from the opaque blue-white tiebacks that hold back the curtains to let the morning sun in to the whale-oil lamp in my guest room.

In my desk are little treasures. I must have been about sixteen when I found the buttonhook in a box along with a single cuff link and a gold-plated watch chain my grandfather had put away for safekeeping. And sometime in my youth I ferreted out a wide gold band inset with three deep blue stones across the front. Though I haven't any idea whether the stones are real or not, I wear the ring almost every day.

With many of my grandfather's possessions came wonderful stories. Whenever Mother used a certain china bowl, I would hear little tales about my grandfather's collecting adventures, his treks along back roads, his finds at country auctions. From these stories I learned that "things" are more than material objects. They are tokens, footprints of people's lives. And to make their importance clear, my grandfather, in his own meticulous way (perhaps not trusting the family's storytelling abilities) often documented his fine purchases.

Like many of his generation and his profession, he was a precise record keeper. Among his papers is the inventory he made of his many possessions, which were entered in two separate columns.

The first listed those pieces—primarily furniture—he had inherited from various family members. After each entry, my grandfather recorded to whom each piece had belonged, the person's relation to him, and in many instances the relative's dates. From this column I know that the 1800 Chippendale secretary-bookcase, the 1760 Queen Anne highboy base that now has a new top, and the 1810 cherry candlestand are all family pieces that have been passed on from one generation to the next, just as they will eventually be passed on to my children.

More interesting in its own way is the second column. Here my grandfather listed those pieces he purchased or received from non–family members—mostly small decorative objects, china and glass. My grandfather took great care to document these pieces as carefully as the family pieces. Many of these notations are followed by the names of the previous owners. Some even show how much he paid for them. From this list I learned about the eighteenth-century handleless china cup and saucer I have on my desk, bought from Mrs. Shaw who lived a few houses down the block. The brass school bell my father always lovingly polished came from the two-room schoolhouse my grandfather attended in western Massachusetts. And the fragile coin silver spoon I keep wrapped in tissue paper in a drawer in the dining room was a prize given for good conduct to one of his teachers when she was a child, which she then gave to him.

No, I never knew my grandfather, but the objects he gathered around him speak of a rich imagination no photograph can ever capture. Whenever my friends ask me where I get my love for antiques, I secretly smile and think about my grandfather with his hair parted in the middle and my daughter's eyes.

Keep This Table

*CATHERINE HAMRICK

There's an anthropological theory in my family: Thousands of years ago, women and children skulked in the cave while hunters and gatherers fled to the forest. This behavior continued even after the cave gave way to the kitchen and the forest to the den and television.

In the slow hours after Sunday dinner, the menfolk in my family fall heavily on the couches. My father rhythmically punches the remote control until his thumb fails and the television drones to an audience unaware.

But the women—four generations of us—linger at the kitchen table for the last sip of coffee, pink lipstick rimming our cups. We nibble pound cake and spoon vanilla ice cream, then curse all men with skinny thighs. We curl napkin corners and tease each other about the men we might have married and plan the lives of yet unborn children.

We lean our elbows on the maple table that has stood for twenty-five years through mischief, arguments, tears, and joy. I have sought its sturdiness on winter nights and laid my head on it, immersing myself in the physical comfort of childhood. It's an instinctive gesture, like the movement of a small animal that dumbly nudges for its mother's warmth.

At that table I first learned the rituals my mother held dear: "Keep your napkin in your lap . . . For heaven's sake, don't shovel your food . . . Don't gulp . . . Sip slowly . . . No milk cartons on the table, PLEASE . . . Pick up the bowl when you pass the squash, don't shove it at your sister . . . Never crumple your napkin and throw it on your plate. I don't care if it IS paper . . . Tell me you enjoyed it; this is the one time you can fib . . . No, you may not turn on the television; it disrupts my digestion."

Usually our dinner table decorum disintegrated into a debacle. Feuds are commonplace in large families, and we carried our battles to the meal. Since yelling warranted more terrifying punishment, the major weapon at dinner was the silent treatment. You ignored your foe by holding a napkin to your face and blocking that person from view. In this spiteful game, any eye contact admitted defeat. Several times I simultaneously held napkins to either side of my head to avoid any peripheral sight of my sisters. With my hands thus occupied, I starved—the price for my silent crusade.

But the kitchen was more than a place for eating. For years it doubled as a studio for school projects and as a study for those baffled by "new" math and literature. With the table serving as a workbench, we stirred up salt maps for all seven continents and at least twenty-five states. Using plaster of Paris, I once sculpted the ridges and valleys found on the Atlantic Ocean's floor on a plywood board. Unfortunately, my mother nearly ruptured a disk when she helped me lug it to the station wagon. "It's a fine project," she puffed, "but how about a salt map of Antarctica next time?"

Short on patience, my father hunched over more than one algebra book and my mother looked for meaning in *Animal Farm* and *1984* at least five times. Whenever she contemplated George Orwell, she sighed and wondered what happened to *Romeo and Juliet.* She still grimaces when she remembers T. S. Eliot and "Ash Wednesday," preferring the simpler thoughts of William Wordsworth and his sea of daffodils.

However, not all was sweetness and light. Rebellion slammed its brutish fist on the maple table, threatening to split it in half. We raged over egocentric concerns—rock 'n' roll, cars, curfews, and hemlines—and parleyed over serious issues like peace, nuclear power, the women's movement, and presidential elections.

And my parents stood in the eye of the storm, always calm. Once, declaring myself an existentialist and denouncing religion as "bad faith," I glared at my mother and waited for her to cry. "Well," she shrugged, "if you're not attending church this morning, please bake the bourgeois potatoes. Even those of lofty philosophical thought have to come down from the mountain and eat with us mundane folks."

We children spent most of our adolescence lurking in hermetically sealed bedrooms. Contact with our parents meant blasting them with the Rolling Stones, David Bowie, or Jethro Tull. Later some of us fled to Europe or Colorado, others to New Orleans. But we all returned home, and the kitchen table remained intact despite its cracks.

And now we gather around it, held by memory. There my mother cut out and sewed at least ten formals, hemming them desperately while our dates watched my father snore through several innings of Braves baseball. There I offered my first boyfriend a chocolate chip cookie, and he kissed me instead. (How sweet it was!) There my grandmother recited the family tree, along with the life history of every cousin thrice removed. There in her steady captain's chair, my mother held each daughter who wept over a lost love. And there my father has served his Christmas breakfast every year, complete with country-fried ham, redeye gravy, and buttermilk biscuits dripping with honey or muscadine preserves.

These days I often eat at a coffee table, my 275-calorie fat-free, taste-free frozen dinner before me. Still, habit persists. I turn off the television and put my napkin in my lap and think of the hands that held one another as dinner was blessed at the kitchen table. The thought in itself is a benediction.

Blessed be the tie that binds.

⇀ From Generation to Generation ⇌

Grandfathers, grandmothers, mothers, fathers. Over and over, when I asked "What is your favorite tradition?" the first words of the answer were "My grandfather (or grandmother) always . . ." This was followed, as Paul Harvey would say, by the rest of the story. As we adapt the traditions of those closest to us, be they our blood or adopted family or even a community or neighborhood, to our lives, we carry the past into the future with us. Lincoln Steffens treats the mirror image he sees within his own family with nostalgia and humor. And he changes the course, when needed.

The Influence of My Father on My Son
LINCOLN STEFFENS

If my father could watch my son for a while, he might realize his own immortality. A glance would not suffice. My brown-eyed, brown-haired son does not look like my red-headed, blue-eyed father. Not a bit. And the immortality I speak of has not taken on the angelic form my good father expected. The child is more like his grandfather than that. My father would invite me sweetly to come and sit on a stool at his feet, and, as I let myself trustingly down, he would gently kick the seat from under me—and laugh. I should like to have had him see his little grandson plant his sled on the basement doormat and call me out to stumble over the trap—and laugh. In both cases the victim, the devilish spirit, and the laugh were the same. So I say that if my father had the time to give to the observation of my son he might realize, if not his immortality, then the partial continuity of his character, disposition, and certainly his influence upon his line, and be—not satisfied, perhaps, but convinced, surprised, and—let me guess—amused or embarrassed.

He would be amused to see Pete, a child of six, who did not know his grandfather, wave his hand in the identical gesture my father used to make to indicate that a questionable assertion of his was obvious or final and decisive. I was highly pleased myself when I first noticed it and recognized my father. I called it an inheritance direct from him till my matter-of-fact wife showed me that I had the same wave and used it in saying I didn't.

My son's mother, by the way, spoils many of our most wonderful fancies, Pete's and mine, and that's why he and I have agreed upon a sentiment which we say in unison behind her back, and sometimes in her presence. We sing: "Pete and Papa are wonderful. Mama and Anna [the maid] are ab-surd."

My father would be amused at that, anyhow. He would say, "Sssh! Don't say such things," but he would recognize in it himself and his son and his wife and my mother. He and I were often in cahoots against my mother, affectionately, on the side. Mothers do not always understand a fellow.

He would have been surprised and he might have been embarrassed when I did not rebuke my son, as he would have rebuked his son, for tripping his father over that sled. This I'll call indirect inheritance. My father, the practical joker, did not care for practical jokes on himself; he did not encourage the practice in me. I saw and I have reacted against this inconsistency with my son. I tease, too; I don't approve of it, but my father and my grandfather in me make me play tricks on my boy, so I have to let him have some fun with me. But my son inherits the benefit of at least one half of my father's fault.

My father required me to honor my father and my mother too much to put up games on them. I did on occasion. (That's how I know that my son can't help it.) I let my father mount my pony one afternoon in time to ride past the neighboring brewery just as the engineer let off steam, and my father was pitched off; and I laughed behind a tree, where, however, my father found me and— Well, I don't do to my little boy what he did to his little boy. I feel my father in me want to, but I remember him and my feelings, and I laugh. The family laugh at the family trait.

My son "honors" his mother, as I did mine. He would not plant a sled for his mother, as I would not for mine. On the other hand, if my son breaks something, he will run to tell me about it first, and then, when his mother discovers the wreck, he backs into my arms and bids her not to speak of it.

"Daddy minded that," he says.

I asked him once why it was that he respected his mother and had no fear of me.

"Oh," he said, "you are a funny man. You can get mad, like Mama, but you laugh. And—and anybody that laughs can't—can't do—what Mama does."

My father would have been surprised to hear this, as I was. My father was slower but he was severer than my mother, who was quick but light and irregular in discipline. It is just so in my son's family. My mother would thump me sharply on the head with a thimble or a spoon if I became too noisy with the whistle when I was playing I was a steamboat captain. She had no sense of the dignity of command. My father seemed always to know not only what I was doing, but what I was being. He had too much respect for a steamboat captain to humiliate me before my crew. If I committed a crime, he would not break into the scene and spoil it; he would say quietly, between him and me, "I'll see you to-morrow morning right after breakfast about this." Now I find that I preferred my father's way and I take it with his grandson, who likewise prefers it. His mother will call suddenly: "Pete! It's bedtime," when she thinks of it, and off he must go, regardless of his occupation. I look first, to see that he is busy with, say, an important building operation, and I would no more interrupt him than I would a crooked contractor. If it's late, I join my builder, we finish the job, and then he goes satisfied to bed, the day's work done.

One improvement I have learned from my childhood experience with my father; I do not threaten punishment in the morning. That was awful. Late into the night I would lie awake tossing and wondering what he was going to do to me. Usually he did nothing. A quiet, impressive "talking to" was all I got. And no doubt his idea was that the postponement of penalty—to save himself from acting in anger—would set me to thinking and be punishment enough, but my father did not visualize the anxiety, the agony of my sleepless hours of anticipation. Hence it is that I do visualize a bad night, and so we go to bed in Pete's house with a clean slate and a happy morrow to wake up to. No hangovers for us, and I am pretty sure Pete feels this benefit he has from my correction of my father's error. At the end of a "serious talk" the boy and I had one day, he rested a moment, then got up and said: "Well, that's all over, isn't it?" and I assured him it was. "We'll forget it now, Pete, and never mention it again."

~ *Mother to Son* ~

Langston Hughes

Well, son, I'll tell you:
Life for me ain't been no crystal stair.
It's had tacks in it,
And splinters,
And boards torn up,
And places with no carpet on the floor—
Bare.
But all the time
I'se been a-climbin' on,
And reachin' landin's
And turnin' corners,
And sometimes goin' in the dark
Where there ain't been no light.
So, boy, don't you turn back.
Don't you set down on the steps
'Cause you finds it kinder hard.
Don't you fall now—
For I'se still goin', honey,
I'se still climbin',
And life for me ain't been no crystal stair.

~ *The Road We Choose to Take* ~

When my children were young and playing their stereos at a deafening volume, a friend had a child who was constantly playing the drums. This did not bother us one bit. We lived too far away to even hear them. But other neighbors were constantly complaining about the noise and the parents' refusal to curb the ruckus. "Our kid is going to be a drummer," they told their angry neighbors, "so let him play!" Guess what? The child grew up and became a professional drummer. His dreams came true.

Why am I mentioning this? Read Louisa May Alcott's wonderful story of her youth and you will see how a young child's dreams, combined with inspiring examples of adults and the encouragement and understanding of parents, can shape his or her future.

Remember also that in today's world, where there are so many choices, your children may choose a path uncharted by either parents or peers. That has been the course taken by many great people. I recall Pete Hamill's vivid words from his powerful book, A Drinking Life, about his departure from the ways of his

rough Brooklyn neighborhood: "Of one thing I was certain: In that neighbor-
hood the bad guys never went to the library.

"I carried those books home, consumed them like food, then brought their
stories and characters and lessons down to the streets with me. I couldn't really
tell my friends about them. But they were real in my head. They often peopled
my dreams and they helped give me a sense that the streets were not everything."

My Childhood

Louisa May Alcott

One of my earliest memories is of playing with books in my father's study, building towers and bridges of the big dictionaries, looking at pictures, pretending to read, and scribbling on blank pages whenever pen or pencil could be found. Many of these first attempts at authorship still exist, and I often wonder if these childish plays did not influence my after life, since books have been my greatest comfort, castle-building a never-failing delight, and scribbling a very profitable amusement.

Another very vivid recollection is of the day when running after my hoop I fell into the Frog Pond and was rescued by a black boy, becoming a friend to the colored race then and there, though my mother always declared that I was an abolitionist at the age of three.

During the Garrison riot in Boston the portrait of George Thompson was hidden under a bed in our house for safe-keeping, and I am told that I used to go and comfort "the good man who helped poor slaves" in his captivity. However that may be, the conversion was genuine, and my greatest pride is in the fact that I have lived to know the brave men and women who did so much for the cause, and that I had a very small share in the war which put an end to a great wrong.

Being born on the birthday of Columbus I seem to have something of my patron saint's spirit of adventure, and running away was one of the delights of my childhood. Many a social lunch have I shared with hospitable Irish beggar children, as we ate our crusts, cold potatoes and salt fish on voyages of discovery among the ash heaps of the waste land that then lay where the Albany station now stands.

Many an impromptu picnic have I had on the dear old Common, with strange boys, pretty babies and friendly dogs, who always seemed to feel that this reckless young person needed looking after.

On one occasion the town-crier found me fast asleep at nine o'clock at night, on a door-step in Bedford Street, with my head pillowed on the curly breast of a big Newfoundland, who was with difficulty

persuaded to release the scary little wanderer who had sobbed herself to sleep there.

I often smile as I pass that door, and never forget to give a grateful pat to every big dog I meet, for never have I slept more soundly than on that dusty step, nor found a better friend than the noble animal who watched over the lost baby so faithfully.

My father's school was the only one I ever went to, and when this was broken up because he introduced methods now all the fashion, our lessons went on at home, for he was always sure of four little pupils who firmly believed in their teacher, though they have not done him all the credit he deserved.

I never liked arithmetic or grammar, and dodged these branches on all occasions; but reading, composition, history and geography I enjoyed, as well as the stories read to us with a skill which made the dullest charming and useful.

"Pilgrim's Progress," Krummacher's "Parables," Miss Edgeworth, and the best of the dear old fairy tales made that hour the pleasantest of our day. On Sundays we had a simple service of Bible stories, hymns, and conversation about the state of our little consciences and the conduct of our childish lives which never will be forgotten.

Walks each morning round the Common while in the city, and long tramps over hill and dale when our home was in the country, were a part of our education, as well as every sort of housework, for which I have always been very grateful, since such knowledge makes one independent in these days of domestic tribulation with the help who are too often only hindrances.

Needle-work began early, and at ten my skilful sister made a linen shirt beautifully, while at twelve I set up as a doll's dress-maker, with my sign out, and wonderful models in my window. All the children employed me, and my turbans were the rage at one time to the great dismay of the neighbors' hens, who were hotly hunted down, that I might tweak out their downiest feathers to adorn the dolls' head-gear.

Active exercise was my delight from the time when as a child of six I drove my hoop round that Common without stopping, to the days when I did my twenty miles in five hours and went to a party in the evening.

I always thought I must have been a deer or a horse in some former state, because it was such a joy to run. No boy could be my friend till I had beaten him in a race, and no girl if she refused to climb trees, leap fences and be a tomboy.

My wise mother, anxious to give me a strong body to support a lively brain, turned me loose in the country and let me run wild, learning of nature what no books can teach, and being led, as those who truly love her seldom fail to be,

"Through nature up to nature's God."

I remember running over the hills just at dawn one summer morning and pausing to rest in the silent woods saw, through an arch of trees, the sun rise over river, hill and wide green meadows as I never saw it before.

Something born of the lovely hour, a happy mood, and the unfolding aspirations of a child's soul seemed to bring me very near to God, and in the hush of that morning hour I always felt that I "got religion" as the phrase goes. A new and vital sense of His presence, tender and sustaining as a father's arms, came to me then, never to change through forty years of life's vicissitudes, but to grow stronger for the sharp discipline of poverty and pain, sorrow and success.

Those Concord days were the happiest of my life, for we had charming playmates in the little Emersons, Channings, Hawthornes and Goodwins, with the illustrious parents and their friends to enjoy our pranks and share our excursions.

Plays in the barn were a favorite amusement, and we dramatized the fairy tales in great style. Our giant came tumbling off a loft when Jack cut down the squash vine running up a ladder to represent the immortal bean. Cinderella rolled away in a vast pumpkin, and a long, black pudding was lowered by invisible hands to fasten itself on the nose of the woman who wasted her three wishes.

Little pilgrims journeyed over the hills with scrip and staff and cockle-shells in their hats; elves held their pretty revels among the pines, and "Peter Wilkins' " flying ladies came swinging down on the birch tree-tops. Lords and ladies haunted the garden, and mermaids splashed in the bath-house of woven willows over the brook.

People wondered at our frolics, but enjoyed them, and droll stories are still told of the adventures of those days. Mr. Emerson and Margaret Fuller were visiting my parents one afternoon, and the conversation having turned to the ever interesting subject of education, Miss Fuller said:

"Well, Mr. Alcott, you have been able to carry out your methods in your own family, and I should like to see your model children."

She did in a few moments, for as the guests stood on the door steps a wild uproar approached, and round the corner of the house came a wheelbarrow holding baby May arrayed as a queen; I was the horse, bitted and bridled and driven by my elder sister Anna, while Lizzie played dog and barked as loud as her gentle voice permitted.

All were shouting and wild with fun which, however, came to a sudden end as we espied the stately group before us, for my foot tripped, and down we all went in a laughing heap, while my mother put a climax to the joke by saying with a dramatic wave of the hand:

"Here are the model children, Miss Fuller."

My sentimental period began at fifteen when I fell to writing romances, poems, a "heart journal," and dreaming dreams of a splendid future.

Browsing over Mr. Emerson's library I found "Goethe's Correspondence with a Child," and was at once fired with the desire to be a second Bettina, making my father's friend my Goethe. So I wrote letters to him, but was wise enough never to send them, left wild flowers on the door-steps of my "Master," sung Mignon's song in very bad German under his window, and was fond of wandering by moonlight, or sitting in a cherry-tree at midnight till the owls scared me to bed.

The girlish folly did not last long, and the letters were burnt years ago, but Goethe is still my favorite author, and Emerson remained my beloved "Master" while he lived, doing more for me, as for many another young soul, than he ever knew, by the simple beauty of his life, the truth and wisdom of his books, the example of a good, great man untempted and unspoiled by the world which he made nobler while in it, and left the richer when he went.

The trials of life began about this time, and my happy childhood ended. Money is never plentiful in a philosopher's house, and even the maternal pelican could not supply all our wants on the small income which was freely shared with every needy soul who asked for help.

Fugitive slaves were sheltered under our roof, and my first pupil was a very black George Washington whom I taught to write on the hearth with charcoal, his big fingers finding pen and pencil unmanageable.

Motherless girls seeking protection were guarded among us; hungry travellers sent on to our door to be fed and warmed, and if the philosopher happened to own two coats the best went to a needy brother, for these were practical Christians who had the most perfect faith in Providence, and never found it betrayed.

In those days the prophets were not honored in their own land, and Concord had not yet discovered her great men. It was a sort of refuge for reformers of all sorts whom the good natives regarded as lunatics, harmless but amusing.

My father went away to hold his classes and conversations, and we women folk began to feel that we also might do something. So one gloomy November day we decided to move to Boston and try our fate again after some years in the wilderness.

My father's prospect was as promising as a philosopher's ever is in a money-making world, my mother's friends offered her a good salary as their missionary to the poor, and my sister and I hoped to teach. It was an anxious council, and always preferring action to discussion, I took a brisk run over the hill and then settled down for "a good think" in my favorite retreat.

It was an old cart-wheel, half hidden in grass under the locusts where I used to sit to wrestle with my sums, and usually forget them scribbling verses or fairy tales on my slate instead. Perched on the hub I surveyed the prospect and found it rather gloomy, with leafless trees, sere grass, leaden sky and frosty air, but the hopeful heart of fifteen beat warmly under the old red shawl, visions of success gave the gray clouds a silver lining, and I said defiantly, as I shook my fist at fate embodied in a crow cawing dismally on the fence near by, "I will do something by-and-by. Don't care what, teach, sew, act, write, anything to help the family; and I'll be rich and famous and happy before I die, see if I won't!"

Startled by this audacious outburst the crow flew away, but the old wheel creaked as if it began to turn at that moment, stirred by the intense desire of an ambitious girl to work for those she loved and find some reward when the duty was done.

I did not mind the omen then, and returned to the house cold but resolute. I think I began to shoulder my burden then and there, for when the free country life ended the wild colt soon learned to tug in harness, only breaking loose now and then for a taste of beloved liberty.

My sisters and I had cherished fine dreams of a home in the city, but when we found ourselves in a small house at the South End with not a tree in sight, only a back yard to play in, and no money to buy any of the splendors before us, we all rebelled and longed for the country again.

Anna soon found little pupils, and trudged away each morning to her daily task, pausing at the corner to wave her hand to me in answer to my salute with the duster. My father went to his classes at his room down town, mother to her all-absorbing poor, the little girls to school, and I was left to keep house, feeling like a caged sea-gull as I washed dishes and cooked in the basement kitchen where my prospect was limited to a procession of muddy boots.

Good drill, but very hard, and my only consolation was the evening reunion when all met with such varied reports of the day's adventures, we could not fail to find both amusement and instruction.

Father brought news from the upper world, and the wise, good people who adorned it; mother, usually much dilapidated because she *would* give away her clothes, with sad tales of suffering and sin from the darker side of life; gentle Anna a modest account of her success as teacher, for even at seventeen her sweet nature won all who knew her, and her patience quelled the most rebellious pupil.

My reports were usually a mixture of the tragic and the comic, and the children poured their small joys and woes into the family bosom where comfort and sympathy were always to be found.

Then we youngsters adjourned to the kitchen for our fun, which usually consisted of writing, dressing and acting a series of remarkable plays. In one I remember I took five parts and Anna four, with lightning changes of costume, and characters varying from a Greek prince in silver armor to a murderer in chains.

It was good training for memory and fingers, for we recited pages without a fault, and made every sort of property from a harp to a fairy's spangled wings. Later we acted Shakespeare, and Hamlet was my favorite hero, played with a gloomy glare and a tragic stalk which I have never seen surpassed.

But we were now beginning to play our parts on a real stage, and to know something of the pathetic side of life with its hard facts, irksome duties, many temptations and the daily sacrifice of self. Fortunately we had the truest, tenderest of guides and guards, and so learned the sweet uses of adversity, the value of honest work, the beautiful law of compensation which gives more than it takes, and the real significance of life.

At sixteen I began to teach twenty pupils, and for ten years learned to know and love children. The story writing went on all the while with the usual trials of beginners. Fairy tales told the Emersons made the first printed book, and "Hospital Sketches" the first successful one.

Every experience went into the chauldron to come out as froth, or evaporate in smoke, till time and suffering strengthened and clarified the mixture of truth and fancy, and a wholesome draught for children began to flow pleasantly and profitably.

So the omen proved a true one, and the wheel of fortune turned slowly, till the girl of fifteen found herself a woman of fifty with her prophetic dream beautifully realized, her duty done, her reward far greater than she deserved.

⟿ A Song of Greatness ⟿

CHIPPEWA INDIAN SONG

When I hear the old men
Telling of heroes,
Telling of great deeds
Of ancient days,
When I hear them telling,
Then I think within me
I too am one of these.

When I hear the people
Praising great ones,
Then I know that I too
Shall be esteemed,
I too when my time comes
Shall do mightily.

⟿ Boy and Father ⟿

CARL SANDBURG

We, neither adults nor children, cannot all be great. But, Carl Sandburg reminds us, childhood dreams do shape young adolescents for the future. Heed his words. Adults' actions also form the foundations and traditions on which children build their lives.

The boy Alexander understands his father to be a famous lawyer.
The leather law books of Alexander's father fill a room like hay in a barn.
Alexander has asked his father to let him build a house like bricklayers build,
  a house with walls and roofs made of big leather law books.

The rain beats on the windows
And raindrops run down the window glass
And the raindrops slide off the green blinds down the siding.
The boy Alexander dreams of Napoleon in John C. Abbott's history,
Napoleon the grand and lonely man wronged, Napoleon in his life
wronged and in his memory wronged.
The boy Alexander dreams of the cat Alice saw, the cat fading off into the
dark and leaving the teeth of its Cheshire smile lighting the gloom.

Buffaloes, blizzards, way down in Texas, in the panhandle of Texas
snuggling close to New Mexico,
These creep into Alexander's dreaming by the window when his father
talks with strange men about land down in Deaf Smith County.
Alexander's father tells the strange men: Five years ago we ran a Ford out
on the prairie and chased antelopes.

Only once or twice in a long while has Alexander heard his father say "my
first wife" so-and-so and such-and-such.
A few times softly the father has told Alexander, "Your mother . . . was a
beautiful woman . . . but we won't talk about her."
Always Alexander listens with a keen listen when he hears his father
mention "my first wife" or "Alexander's mother."

Alexander's father smokes a cigar and the Episcopal rector smokes a cigar
and the words come often; mystery of life, mystery of life.
These two come into Alexander's head blurry and gray while the rain
beats on the windows and the raindrops run down the window glass
and the raindrops slide off the green blinds and down the siding.
These and: There is a God, there must be a God, how can there be rain or
sun unless there is a God?

So from the wrongs of Napoleon and the Cheshire cat smile on to the
buffaloes and blizzards of Texas and on to his mother and to
God, so the blurry gray rain dreams of Alexander have gone on
five minutes, maybe ten, keeping slow easy time to the rain-
drops on the window glass and raindrops sliding off the green
blinds and down the siding.

~ Old-Fashioned Playtime ~

So many wonderful traditions that young parents and older grandparents love
to pass down to the next generation come from their own fondest childhood

memories. Across the country, attics and basements, trunks and closets, are filled with the toys from childhood—which brings up a tradition too often lost in today's hurried world: the tradition of play. Wonderful childhood games and books are essential to developing our talents and our character. The child, boy or girl, who, often to his parents' dismay, takes the wheels off every toy truck, train, and car within sight may be tomorrow's engineer. The children whose parents read to them learn joys that will last them all their lives.

Take Booth Tarkington's words to heart. They were written over eighty years ago, but they are forever young. They come from The Little Gentleman. *Mr. Kinosling, a "self-engrossed young man" and guest at the Schofield house for dinner, is speaking.*

In Praise of Boyhood

BOOTH TARKINGTON

"Boyhood is the age of relaxation; one is playful, light, free, unfettered. One runs and leaps and enjoys oneself with one's little companions. It is good for the little lads to play with their friends; they jostle, push, and wrestle, and simulate little, happy struggles with one another in harmless conflict. The young muscles are toughening. It is good. Boyish chivalry develops, enlarges, expands. The young learn quickly, intuitively, spontaneously. They perceive the obligations of noblesse oblige. They begin to comprehend the necessity of caste and its requirements. They learn what birth means—ah, that is, they learn what it means to be well born. They learn courtesy in their games; they learn politeness, consideration for one another in their pastimes, amusements, lighter occupations. I make it my pleasure to join them often, for I sympathize with them in all their little wholesome joys as well as in their little bothers and perplexities. I understand them, you see; and let me tell you it is no easy matter to understand the little lads and lassies."

➤ *Leisure* ➤

WILLIAM HENRY DAVIES

What is this life if, full of care,
We have no time to stand and stare.

No time to stand beneath the boughs
And stare as long as sheep or cows.

No time to see, when woods we pass,
Where squirrels hide their nuts in grass.

No time to see, in broad daylight,
Streams full of stars like skies at night.

No time to turn at Beauty's glance,
And watch her feet, how they can dance.

No time to wait till her mouth can
Enrich the smile her eyes began.

A poor life this, is full of care,
We have no time to stand and stare.

⁓ *Mother Shows Us Off* ⁓

CLARENCE DAY

Since time immemorial, children have loved to listen to stories about their
parents, grandparents, and great-grandparents, their lives, and the times in
which they lived. What did they do? What games did they play? What were
their parents and grandparents like?

Over and over, when reading the traditions submitted by the next generation,
I learned that the best part of family reunions was hearing the stories that
were told. This wonderful firsthand remembrance by Clarence Day, the author
of such American classics as Life with Father *and* Life with Mother, *the author*
recounts a time when children dreamed of pirate ships instead of stealth jets,
and formal visits and reciting poetry in the parlor were part of everyday life.
Those traditions may have been lost, but reading about them is just as much
fun as ever. There is also much to be learned about the role of "champion" that
the mother played in turn-of-the-century families.

Mother was sure that her four boys were the best little boys in New
York. Other people didn't always agree with her, but usually she didn't
know it. Little May Lewis, who lived around the corner in Forty-
eighth Street, for instance, had a nurse who used to warn her to keep
away from those redheaded Day boys. If Mother had ever heard of this
she wouldn't have waited a second; she'd have pinned a big hat on her
own wavy red hair right away, and grabbed up her muff and her
gloves, and gone racing around to the Lewises to tell them that their

nurse was quite wrong, and that her boys never did anything they shouldn't, or gave her a moment's uneasiness. And she'd have burst in upon them so impetuously, in her haste to defend us, and spoken so fast and so vehemently, that it would have been impossible for any of them to calm her down. In fact, when polite persons attempted to do this, as to smooth over an awkward situation, it added to Mother's annoyance. She felt that they were trying to get away from the point she was making. She said they were "just talking nonsense." But nobody ever had time enough anyhow to calm Mother down. She would rush to our defense, stun the enemy, and hurry straight out.

Not that May Lewis' nurse was our enemy; she was merely more realistic than Mother, and she probably had seen enough of the way we played on the streets to know that a little girl had better go and play somewhere else. Mother's firm belief, however, was that we never really meant to be rough, and that anyway we were privileged characters because we were boys. All males, Mother instinctively felt, were a special kind of creation. They owed certain duties to women and girls, but they also had certain rights.

I used to feel that it was kind of inconvenient to have her be so very proud of us. Somehow it seemed to make it obligatory on us not to disappoint Mother—or at least not to fail her any oftener than we could help. But it also implanted in us such a high opinion of ourselves, as good boys, that when we did get into trouble it appeared to us to be accidental. Accidental and therefore excusable. We were ready to be sincerely repentant, but we didn't expect to be punished.

Father's attitude was different from Mother's. He often remarked, "I know boys." His standards of behavior for children were as high as hers were, or higher, and he was only too ready to believe that we hadn't lived up to them. At such times it did us very little good to explain that we had got into this or that scrape "by accident." "Of course it was 'by accident,' " he would impatiently roar, as though it was unthinkable that any boy could mean to defy him; "but it's your business to see to it that accidents of this sort don't happen. And a spanking will probably assist you to bear that in mind."

"Oh, not this time, Clare," Mother begged him one Saturday, when he was saying this to me. "Clarence didn't really mean to knock off the cabman's hat with his little snowball." I fully agreed with her. I had hoped to do it, but when I succeeded I had been immensely surprised—so surprised that I hadn't been quick enough to make good my retreat. Also, I hadn't known that Father was inside the cab. I didn't feel more than half guilty.

But Father said again, "I know boys," and proceeded to give me a spanking.

When he had finished he went down to the club for an afternoon game of billiards, and as the snow had now turned to rain I went up to the nursery. It was Delia's afternoon out—she was Harold's nurse —so Mother told us three older boys to let Harold play with us, and see that he didn't get hurt.

There was always some unfinished game going on in the nursery. We kept our wooden blocks and marbles and our lead soldiers there, and the wars they were in never stopped. In a few minutes we were so busy that I had forgotten my spanking. Harold, being too small to fight, had been put up on the bed. He held a piece of an old curtain rod up to his eye, as a spyglass, and with this he swept the horizon and chanted to himself, "Ship ahoy!" We others were laying in a supply of ammunition for a battle at sea.

We had invented a man called Captain Sinkem, a lean privateer, and he had been ravaging the wooden-block coasts of the nursery for days. He had originally belonged to a lead-soldier regiment of Turkish Zouaves. His face had been battered in long ago, giving him a sinister look, and his baggy red trousers added to his piratical air. His ships had been made by ourselves out of old *Youth's Companions*, on the model of the famous Civil War ironclad *Merrimac*. There was a picture of her in our storybooks, looking evil and strong, with sloping bulwarks, a thick, covered top, and a ram at her bow. Her simple triangular shape made her easy to copy, at least in our hasty style. We could build an ironclad in ten minutes. Some numbers of the *Youth's Companion* were thicker than others, but even the thin ones, when folded up, made pretty good warships, and ships that had hulls of many layers were almost impregnable. It was no wonder that Captain Sinkem had done a lot of ravaging in them. He had ravaged one coast so hard that he had bumped it all out of shape.

We always played fair in our games between good men and bad, though it really was much more exciting when the wicked man won. Of course he had to be conquered in the end and die a horrible death, but somehow a game began to get dull as soon as the good man had triumphed.

In this particular game, after vigorously acting for Sinkem, we had manned the forts and fired all our marbles at his ships. But in vain. They had merely bounced off the thick paper bulwarks. At each bounce Captain Sinkem and his pirates had cheered wildly.

Now, however, a new character, Admiral Harry Broadside, had built some ironclads, too, and with these he had fended off Sinkem's ships. This was all very well as far as it went, but it didn't content Admiral Harry. He was an officer of our little lead Life Guards, and he was dressed in jack boots and white pants and a tall bearskin hat, and his martial ambitions were correspondingly haughty and fierce. His one idea was to destroy Sinkem's fleet altogether.

What he needed for this was new ammunition of a more deadly type. We suddenly remembered a box of old rocks, which we had been told not to play with. Mother loved to have us have a good time, and she never interfered with our fun, but she had warned us that if we threw those awful rocks at our soldiers we'd hurt ourselves with them. And Father had said indignantly that they were his old geology specimens, and that they weren't meant to be thrown around at all. He said that we ought to study them. He had collected them one at a time, in his boyhood, he told us, some of them from way up in Harlem, and some in the hills where the city afterward built Central Park, and he described how he had scrambled down gullies and dug in the slopes, and where he had found the purplish chunk of pudding stone and the silvery mica, and the commonplace-looking lumps of feldspar and hornstone and quartz.

If we had listened to him we might have learned something about the earth, after all, to add to our school education, which was concerned almost solely with the history and the tongues of mankind. But as the history of mankind, in our schoolbooks, consisted chiefly of wars, all we wanted to use Father's specimens for was ammunition.

We got the box down from the closet and divided the rocks into piles. Now we could have a fine battle. The only crews we had to man our vessels were our lead soldiers, of course, and they certainly made peculiar-looking sailors, but they were better than nothing. We marched them aboard in their helmets and plumes and red jackets. Harold tried to get off the bed to help us, but we forcibly put him back on, and gave him a trumpet to console him and made him ship's bugler. He tooted a shrill croaky blast and the fleets put to sea—that is to say, Admiral Broadside's vessels sailed away from the fireplace and Captain Sinkem's came out from under the bed and dashed around the floor rapidly, each fleet blowing sirens and loud warning blasts at the enemy, and the two opposing commanders shouting sneers and taunts and threats at each other. Then amid cheers and roars from the crews, and yells of "Boom!" with each shot, we stood off and threw Father's rocks as hard as we could at the ironclads.

They did far more damage than our marbles. Two ships were knocked over. The thin ones soon began to look battered. Harry Broadside's big flagship, the *Disdain,* had only a few rips and dents, but Sinkem's was covered with scars. It looked as though he was now faced with death and destruction at last. I called upon him to surrender —I was acting for Admiral Harry—and George, who was acting for the captain, began to look worried. He picked up the pudding-stone rock, which was especially jagged, and hurled it despairingly at my flagship. It struck square on a gap in a crease which had been loosened already, and the next moment the *Disdain* opened up and spilled her crew into the sea.

In the midst of the terrific excitement that this bull's-eye created, while George was dancing around and shouting "Surrender! Surrender yourself!" and while poor Admiral Harry was trying to swim to some other vessel, we became aware that Bridget, the waitress, was there in the room.

"Your mother want you," she said.

"Oh, Bridget! Not *now*? She doesn't want us this very minute!"

"Yes, this very minute, and ten minutes before this by rights," Bridget said. "Haven't I been standing here telling you so at the top of me voice, and you boys rackety-banging around on the floor with them rocks, and screeching as if you'd have yourselves killed without the police in to quiet you!"

We knew we had done wrong to take Father's rocks out of the closet. Now we'd got into trouble. We pulled Harold off the bed and started downstairs.

"Alanna machree! Would ye look at ye's!" Bridget expostulated. "Wash them dirty hands first. You can't go in the parlor like that. Come ye here, Har'l, till I run the comb through your hair before you go down to the quality."

"The parlor?" we shouted. "Then it's callers!"

"Sairtainly it's callers," said Bridget. "A lady with a grand, shiny bird in her hat—you'd think it was a duck by the size of it—and her old uncle with her."

We were immensely relieved. If it had been an order to stop throwing the rocks, that would have been a calamity; but callers, though of course they were a nuisance, would only take a few minutes.

It must be a terrible thing for modern children when a caller arrives, and when they have to sit down in the sitting room and be introduced, and the visitor tries to make conversation and they are supposed to be social. There was never anything so artificial as that in the eighties. Not in our home, at least. Children were children, and grown-ups were grown-ups, and the two weren't expected to mix. We boys liked our uncles and aunts and a few old family friends, but we looked upon other grown-ups as foreigners. And they felt that same way toward us.

There was nothing to regret about this that I can see. Quite the contrary. The Victorians had too much common sense to converse with children as though they were human beings. If Mother had had a daughter she might have wished her to be social, but she didn't really expect that of us. She understood little boys.

On the other hand, she did want her friends to have a look at us sometimes. She wanted to show us off to them and let them see what we were like. So when we were sent for, we generally had to speak pieces.

Mother had had to speak pieces herself in her childhood. It was the conventional thing to do in a parlor. It was like shaking hands. What the feelings of the visitors were about it I do not know, but it somehow solved the problem of how to get children in and then out again. Mother had recited so well at her school that she had been given a book as a prize: *Legends of the Madonna,* by Mrs. Jameson. (It had been presented to her "for perfect recitations in poetry, with the affectionate wishes of H. B. Haines, 10 Gramercy Park, 1870.") It was a nice-looking little volume, published by Ticknor and Fields, but when I looked it over it seemed rather soulful and dull; and judging by its very new appearance, Mother never had read it.

George didn't like speaking pieces. He looked worried as we started downstairs. I didn't mind, because it never took long and we were always allowed to go afterward. We slid down the banisters and landed in a bunch in the hall.

The parlor was a long, narrow room. It was full of plush chairs and ottomans and vases and roomy glass cabinets—a good room for boys to keep out of. We opened the sliding doors and shoved and pushed one another against the dark curtains, struggling to see which of us could achieve safety by going in last. Any boy who wasn't last usually got tweaked from behind as he entered. This made him fairly spring into the room, which was apt to flatter the callers.

This afternoon one of us must have pinched Harold a trifle too hard. He not only leaped convulsively through the curtains but went in with a shriek. "Hush, darling," said Mother. "This is Miss Wilkinson. Say how do you do to her." We lined up in a row and were all introduced one by one, and—prompted by Mother—we told Miss Wilkinson our names and our ages.

Remembering what Bridget had said, I stared at the bird on Miss Wilkinson's hat. There were no birds around in the streets except sparrows in winter, but ladies' hats more than made up for it. I had never seen a blue jay in the open, or a bobwhite or a swallow, but I saw plenty of them—on ladies. Miss Wilkinson's specimen was even more interesting. He was a large bird with prominent eyes and a ruby red breast like a robin's. His long wings stood stiffly out, and his attitude was that of flight—he looked as though he was about to swoop at the carpet and snatch up a fish—yet in spite of all this he was reposing in a pink curlicue nest, made of some light filmy stuff, such as chiffon. I wondered if there were eggs in it. It would have been hard to find out, for the nest constituted the crown of Miss Wilkinson's hat, and the heads of several gold hatpins projected from each side and in front. Sticking out in the air, opposite to the heads, were the pins' sharp, gleaming points, one of them so long that I thought it might skewer George in the eye. He was nearest.

"Clarence will speak his piece first," Mother said. She looked at me encouragingly and I saw her lips form the first words. I took a long breath and plunged in:

> "On Linden, when the sun was low,
> All bloodless lay the untrodden snow;
> And dark as winter was the flow
> Of Iser, rolling rapidly."

In retrospect this selection of mine seems gruesome, but I never thought of it that way. I had chosen it because there was a picture in the book of bearded soldiers in helmets, with black, flowing plumes, marching at night through the snow, waving their sabers, blowing trumpets and lighting their way with flaming torches, very splendid and ominous.

> "Then shook the hills with thunder riven;
> Then rushed the steed, to battle driven;
> And louder than the bolts of heaven
> Far flashed the red artillery."

All up and down Madison Avenue and in the side streets other little boys of the eighties were either reciting poems about battles or playing with their toy soldiers—even Willie Smith, who lived on the corner and who was much the fattest and most phlegmatic boy whom we knew.

Wars seemed to be done with in those days, except small ones in faraway places which didn't half count, and we thought of them only as romantic affairs, like Ivanhoe's tournaments.

The nearer I came to the doleful end of Hohenlinden, the more cheerful I got. Mother was forming each word for me too. I recited the final stanza contentedly:

> "Few, few shall part, where many meet!
> The snow shall be their winding-sheet,
> And every turf beneath their feet
> Shall be a soldier's sepulchre."

Miss Wilkinson's uncle stroked his mustache and said "Excellent, excellent," but Mother shook her head at him, saying "Sh-h," and motioning for George to speak next. George looked down at the light-blue and gray carpet and, fixing his eyes on a particular spot, he stumbled through "The Charge of the Light Brigade" in a small, depressed voice. I forget what came next. It was Blenheim, I think. At any rate, it was about death and battles. Miss Wilkinson smiled in a vacant way and preened herself busily. Her hands fluttered about, as she smoothed her flowing velvet skirt of rich purple, and adjusted her veil, and poked at the bird in her hat, and felt of a leaf on our rubber tree.

Everybody brightened up a little when Harold's turn came. He was last, he was chubby, and—as Mother explained—he was too small yet to say a whole poem. Mother smiled lovingly at him as he knitted his brows and began:

> "Forever float zat standard sheet
> Where bweezy fo-bit

" 'Where breathes the foe but falls,' darling," Mother said softly.

Harold reddened with embarrassment at being called "darling" in public, and set his fat little jaws with an obstinate look. "Where bweezy," he repeated:

> "Where bweezy fo-bit falls afore us,
> Wif fweedom's soil beneath our feet,
> An' fweedom's banner stweaming o'er us."

He bowed with a jerk. The performance was over. "Such good boys," Mother said to Miss Wilkinson proudly, as we started out. We tried not to run as we left, but we went through the door in a jiffy, and in the hall there was such a rush for the stairs that Harold fell down with a bang, and was kicked in the head.

Whenever Harold got hurt, which was perhaps rather often, the important thing to do was to choke him. If we had tried to comfort him first, his wails would have brought Mother up on the run. We also had found by experience that it was a great mistake to choke him in silence, because that silence itself would make Mother suspect that something dreadful had happened. Consequently, while choking our indignant brother, we had to make joyful sounds. This must often have given us the appearance of peculiarly hardhearted fiends.

On this occasion, Harold was instantly jerked to his feet with our hands over his mouth. The other two boys began whispering and cheering, in a loud nervous manner, and while Harold was struggling for breath I shook my fist at him.

"But you knocked me down," he said.

"All right," I said, "I'll let you hit me back. I'll let you knock me down, honest, no fooling. You can do it the minute we get to the top of the stairs."

"But I'm hurt in two places."

"Well, if you'll shut up about it," I said, "you can knock George down too."

"What *are* you doing, boys?" Mother called from the parlor in horror. "You aren't knocking each other down, are you!" We heard her start for the door.

"We were just fooling, Mamma," George explained reassuringly as she came through the curtains. Harold was on his way upstairs by that time. He was in a hurry to get to the landing, where he was to have his revenge.

Mother stood there a moment, but there didn't seem to be anything wrong. She said that we mustn't disappoint her like this and make a bad impression on everybody by being so noisy and rough when we were leaving the parlor.

"No," we said. "We didn't mean to."

"And if any boy hits one of his brothers I'll have to have Papa spank him."

Dead silence.

She went back in to those tiresome callers. It was all their fault, really, we felt. The second she disappeared through the curtains, we dashed up the stairs.

At the landing we stopped. Harold was waiting for us, eagerly shouting, "You promised, you promised!" I let him knock me down as agreed. His eyes shone as he punched away at me with his soft little fists.

"Now it's your turn, George," I ordered.

George wasn't at all in the mood to be knocked down, however. He said that the last time he had allowed Harold to do it, Harold had given him a kick on the shins. We were wrangling about this, when Mother again came to the door.

"Why, boys," she said to us reproachfully. We rushed off to the nursery.

As we slammed the door shut, we forgot all about the callers and Mother and everything else; Harold even forgot about hitting George, in our haste to get back to our battle. There was Admiral Harry, patiently waiting, bobbing around in the waves, and Captain Sinker's ships were more than ready to go on with their fire. Harold sprang up on the bed and sounded a bugle call, George shouted "Surrender!" and the cannonade began again exactly where it had left off.

⌐ Gone Fishing ⌐

Boys will be boys! Thank goodness. Playing marbles, minor fisticuffs, pirates sailing on bobbing waves—and no image of childhood would be complete without the tradition of fishing. It is a tradition that knows no age boundaries.

⌐ An Angler to His Son ⌐

JAMES COLEMAN HARWOOD

You spoiled a fishing trip, young man—
  A heinous, grievous sin—
You did not even wire to say
  'Twas likely you'd drop in.

You've made a world of worry, too,
  For such a tiny cub;
And, on the scales, you'd scarcely weigh
  As much as one big chub!

Yet, now you're here, you're welcome; but
  You've got a debt to pay—
When you're grown and go a-fishing, why,
  You owe your Dad one day.

⌐ Let's Go for a Ride ⌐

Remember your first car ride? I bet not. Nowadays we take for granted the luxury and excitement of the automobile. We carefully put our little ones in car seats and buckle them into their safety belts. That's most important. But imagine what it must have been like to have your family own the first car in town—not to mention no traffic rules to follow, and maybe no brakes on the newly invented and not yet perfected auto. Our automobiles and we have, as they say, come a long way, baby.

Family Excursion

EMILY KIMBROUGH

Grandmother Kimbrough called our house one evening about six o'clock. I was washing my hands for supper and I heard Mother answer, because the telephone was in the back hall just across from the bathroom door. It hung so high on the wall that, stretching up to reach the mouthpiece, she always sounded a little breathless. Whenever I talked into it, I had to stand on a chair. All children did. There was a calendar hanging in our kitchen that showed a little girl with yellow curls, and wearing only a pair of panties. She was standing on a chair, and saying into the telephone, so the printing underneath read,

"Is 'oo there, Santa Claus?"

I listened to Mother's conversation, of course, and in a minute or two it was well evident to me that something was going on. I heard her say, "We'll come right up; Hal's home. Don't worry, Mother."

And she hung up. . . .

Mother and Daddy came out the front door, and hurried up the street. I let them get a little ahead of me, and then scuttled after them. It was early Spring, but chilly. Mother had snatched her golf cape off the hatrack in the vestibule, and was hooking it at the throat as they passed me. I had not stopped to put on any kind of a coat lest I be caught, but I was too excited to feel cold. I knew something was up, and I knew that if I were caught I would be given a sharp spank in the rear and sent home. This made the suspense almost unbearable. I passed the Ross's house safely—they were our next-door neighbors— and then the Vatets'. After that there was a bad stretch, because there was a vacant field with no protecting shrubbery—nothing to hide behind until clear across Vine Street where Lydia Rich's house stood on the corner.

When Mother and Daddy reached the corner, they saw my two uncles and aunts hurrying along Vine Street, and waited for them. By the time they had all met and started off together, they were so busy talking that it was safe for me to pass the field and cross the street behind them. I was not allowed to cross the street alone, so that if I had been discovered then, I could expect the application of Daddy's bedroom slipper, but not one of them looked back. And by the time we had passed the Richs' and reached the big house itself, I was at their heels like a puppy. They stopped so abruptly in fact, that I very nearly walked up the back of Mother's legs before I could stop myself. She turned around, saw me, and all she said was,

"Out of the way, dear," and pushed me a little, nowhere in particular.

I knew then that whatever had stopped them must be awful, and I raced around in front of them with my heart pounding. I thought it must be something dead on the sidewalk, so I put my hands over my eyes and then looked down between them, but I couldn't see anything. I took my hands away and still I couldn't see anything. I looked back at the family, all of them, and they were staring into the street. There, against the curb, right at the carriage block, was a great, black *thing*. It had a top, with straps at the corners to tie it down. There was a front seat and a back seat. Far in front of the front seat were shining brass lamps. I could not imagine what the contraption was for, unless it was some kind of a couch to go in the Turkish corner of the library, except that it had big wheels.

Grandmother Kimbrough stood on the carriage block, with her back to the *thing*.

Barely five feet two, never weighing more than ninety-six pounds, she was as quick and sharp as a dragon-fly. Her dark eyes were flashing from one member of the family to another. She pushed up her hair off her forehead in a nervous gesture, that soft brown hair which was a constant exasperation to her.

"Why can't it turn gray, the pesky thing?" I heard her demand frequently. "Every respectable woman my age has gray hair. People will think I touch it up."

She folded her arms tight across her chest, a Napoleon on the carriage block I would remember her.

"Your father," she said grimly, "has bought an auto*mo*bile."

Grandfather was standing at the head of the *thing*. He looked very handsome, I thought, and not excited. I had never seen him look excited, nor even worried. Once I had heard him say to Uncle Frank, "If you're worrying about that, Frank, then I'll stop worrying. One is enough."

Everybody started talking at once. Aunt Huda said you could get coats with bonnets and veils to match. They kept the dust off, and were the latest style. She was going to write to her sister Bertha in New York and ask her to send her an outfit. Aunt Helen was talking to Grandmother, telling her not to be upset, that it would be lovely. She had heard they were very safe, and she knew that Father Kimbrough would be careful. The boys—that is, my father and my two uncles, but I called them that because everyone else did—started over to the automobile itself. They were talking about machinery. Grandfather called out,

"Mr. Lockhart, I would like you to meet my sons, Hal and Frank Lloyd."

I had not seen that there was somebody on the couch; but a man climbed down from it, and was introduced to us. He had driven the automobile from the factory and was going to stay for two weeks to teach Grandfather, and see that it was all right. . . .

Early in the morning my grandfather rode out to his factory in the machine, the trained expert, Mr. Lockhart, at the wheel. Some time later, about ten o'clock, he telephoned my grandmother and asked if she had been to market. She said that Noah, who was the hired man, was just bringing around Prince. Well, Grandfather told her, if she would care to drive down town in the new auto instead, he and Mr. Lockhart would come for her in about twenty minutes. A mental conflict must have rocked her. There was the danger of the infernal machine, the fact that the night before she had declared she would never set foot in it and Grandfather could go back with it to Kokomo, the knowledge that it was the first one in the town, and the recollection of Aunt Huda saying that it was the most stylish thing you could have, everyone in the East was getting one, her sister Bertha had told her so.

When Grandfather arrived about half an hour later, Prince was back in the barn, and Grandmother was standing on the carriage block. At the sight of him, however, she jumped off and backed away, because he was at the wheel and the mechanic from Kokomo was sitting beside him.

"Charles," Grandmother said, "I will not put my foot in this carriage, with you driving. Why, you don't know anything about the crazy thing."

Grandfather told her that he had been driving that morning for two hours, and that Mr. Lockhart considered him extremely apt. Furthermore, he did, after all, build bridges and might therefore be supposed to know something about machinery. The steering contrivance was not unlike driving a horse, once you accustomed yourself to minor differences. But if Grandmother were nervous she had better have Prince brought around again.

Grandmother climbed into the back seat and sat down.

"I will die with you," she said with obscure menace, "and you will always be sorry."

She bounced herself down on the black leather cushion with all the vehemence of her ninety-six pounds and slammed the door, thwarting Mr. Lockhart, who had come round to perform that little courtesy.

Mr. Lockhart reported to Grandfather that she was safely aboard, and Grandfather recited aloud the steps toward putting the machine in motion. The left foot down, the right hand over and back, the right hand then on the steering wheel throttle. And with that a roar convulsed the machine so that it sprang into the air, and stopped dead. Mr. Lockhart got out, went around in front, released an iron bar from a leather loop, ground it a few times and the engine roared again. Grandmother was already out and on her way back to the house. But Mr. Lockhart coaxed her in again. Grandfather called out that he knew exactly the cause of the mishap. It was not the fault of the engine but of his own misjudgment of the allotment of gasoline. The machine moved ahead once more, in jumps, but it kept going. Grandmother grabbed the carriage strap nearest her. They turned the corner on Monroe Street, and she held on with both hands.

A great many people saw them go up Main Street, and witnessed the unusual behavior of Mr. Meeks, the butter and egg man. He was a sturdy man with a round face that was almost as red in the Winter as in the Summer. His hands were red, too, with cracks running up and down across them on both sides. He was a farmer and worked hard but he loved to tell jokes and to laugh, slapping his big red hand down as if he were spanking himself when he was especially tickled. Once a week he brought in butter and eggs to regular customers. When the automobile with Grandfather driving it passed him, he was just getting out of his buggy at the house next to Mr. Bernard's little store. The horse went up over the sidewalk into the yard and one of the shafts of the buggy got stuck between the fence palings. Grandfather called out that he was distressed but couldn't stop. People who didn't see it could scarcely believe what Mr. Meeks did. He turned around in the yard and shook his fist after Grandfather. Grandmother had her eyes closed in such angry determination that she didn't see it.

Of course Grandmother knew every inch of the way by heart. A railroad track ran along the first cross street beyond Mr. Bernard's little store. This was a branch line of the Pennsylvania Railroad and carried only freight but it did cut right across the town and people always drew in their horses to look up and down before they crossed the track. Grandfather didn't draw in the machine. He was concerned about Mr. Meeks' horse being stuck in the fence and not quite sure, furthermore, of the process of stopping, so he just bumped over the tracks without even slowing down. It jarred Grandmother but she kept her eyes closed. Fortunately there wasn't a freight train coming. . . .

Grandfather came all the way up Main Street with no trouble; none of the horses along the curb shied; he didn't get caught in the trolley track nor have any difficulty about the trolley. The trolley wasn't even in sight. He was very pleased when he got to the corner of Main and Walnut. He even took one hand off the steering wheel to wave at the policeman, whose mouth dropped wide open at the sight of this vehicle. That pleased Grandfather, too. So he turned around and said loudly and cheerfully, "Where do you wish to go, Margaret?"

His voice was so loud and so close that it made her open her eyes, and when she saw that his face was turned toward her, and not out toward the road, she screamed at him,

"Mr. Topps's, Mr. Topps's!"

The shrillness of her tone and her agitation must, in turn, have startled him, for he jumped perceptibly as he turned his head back to the front again. And in the passage he caught sight of Mr. Topps's butcher shop. With a sweep that would have brought around the mighty Oceanic, "Greyhound of the Seas," he swung the wheel, and the machine responded. Up over the curb they went, across the sidewalk, and, cleaving a sharp, broad wake, straight through Mr. Topps's plate glass window to the very dot of their destination, the meat counter itself. There, shuddering, the carriage stopped.

Mr. Topps stood on the other side of the counter about two feet away from the front lamps, his cleaver upheld in his right hand, his eyes staring, his teeth bared in an unnatural grin. There *had* been two or three other people in the shop when the conveyance approached the window, but the sight of Mr. Topps's face had caused them to turn and see what was coming upon them. So they too were now on the far side of the counter with him.

When the clatter of falling glass stopped, Grandfather spoke out of the awesome silence.

"This, Margaret," he announced, "is where you said you wanted to come."

⌐ *Sentimental Journey* ⌐

*SAM STEPHENSON

Just as the automobile changed, so did the road and scenery that sprinkled those byways that took us on family adventures. The thing about us today is that we want to get everyplace in a hurry, but we miss the sights of the countryside. Admit it: no canned soft drink bought at a convenience store has ever tasted like the nectar drunk from a long-necked bottle in a country store. Sam Stephenson, whose road-trip adventures follow, is still a young man in his twenties. But he is living proof that you don't have to be over fifty to be filled with nostaglia. With memories like these of the recent 1980s, it is little wonder that the next generation will hold its traditions dear.

North Carolina Highway 54 was the only way to get to Chapel Hill from Raleigh before superhighway U.S. I-40 opened between the two towns in the late 1980s. Highway 54 is still there, but nobody takes it for more than a few miles at a time, because I-40 is wider and smoother and it quickens the trip by several minutes. The convenience and speed offered by the advancements of I-40 have turned 54 into a seldom-used artifact, much like the passenger train and the written letter.

For decades, Highway 54 was unavoidable by anyone traveling to Chapel Hill from eastern North Carolina, or from the entire eastern seaboard, for that matter, since interstate highways 1 and 95 run well east through the state. It was a brutal twenty-three miles of supposed highway. The road was barely wide enough for one of those vintage Buicks, much less two, and the shoulder along the road seemed to be a sea of mud, even during a summer drought. Highway 54 had inclines, declines, virtual 90-degree turns, and ridiculous combinations of all three that certainly could not pass inspections based on the current Department of Transportation codes. If mythology tells us that any worthwhile journey contains countless perils, then the journey to Chapel Hill from Raleigh on Highway 54 portended an Eden-like conclusion to the trip. And it usually was; even conservatives who said that walls should be built around Chapel Hill to protect innocent citizens from Communists and weirdos must admit that the curious quaintness and placidity of Chapel Hill made it unique and desirable. Chapel Hill was a village that was also the home of the University of North Carolina, and the two collaborated to create a locality where time and space knew different boundaries than the rest of the world, or at least the rest of North Carolina. Highway 54 must have had something to do with that. If it was easy to get there, then Chapel Hill surely would not have been so different or so appealing.

As a kid, some of my grandest times were my family's trips to Chapel Hill. My hometown of Washington, North Carolina (also known as Little Washington or the Original Washington, to distinguish it from the larger, but younger, Washington, D.C.), is about 130 miles east of Chapel Hill, and it used to take us a solid three hours to get there in our car. Chapel Hill was a land of fantasy for me. I was born there and spent the first few weeks of my life there, though this is not a fond memory for my family, since I was born dangerously premature and barely made it through those first weeks. Still, I thought it was neat to have been born in Chapel Hill.

My father and brothers attended college and graduate school there, and since most little boys want to emulate their father and older brothers to some degree, I dearly wanted to go to college there, too.

The UNC Tarheels played in Chapel Hill and most of my boyhood heroes were their stars of the gridiron or hardwood. Everything about Chapel Hill thrilled me: the pizza was the best; the toy stores had everything in the Sears catalog; the restaurants had free refills on Coca-Cola; Tarheel memorabilia abounded. And if you kept your eyes open, you might glimpse one of the famous athletes on Franklin Street. To me, Chapel Hill was the exotic place that you went, if you were lucky, after you were finished being a kid.

My family's trips to Chapel Hill occurred several times each year, and I marked them with an extraordinary amount of anticipation. When we were fortunate enough to have tickets we would go to see the Tarheels play, or to see my brothers when they were in school, or both. We would leave Washington early in the morning with a cooler full of ham biscuits and soft drinks, and I always took my pillow for sleeping on the trip back home. I waited all year for those trips, and my expectations were almost always met.

There were a number of ways to get to Chapel Hill from Washington, but none of them involved four-lane highways except the beltline bypass around Raleigh, which could have had twenty lanes and it would not have mattered. It was a treacherous drive along backroads filled with tractors and laced with small intersections, but it did not really get tough until we got off Raleigh's beltline and got on Highway 54.

Everybody detested Route 54, except me. To me, 54 was the gateway to Chapel Hill. When we reached the skinny road with mysterious dips and hidden turns, I knew that we were almost there. I used to plant my face to the windows in the backseat and peer hopefully at each interesting object that passed by. I knew how much time was left on our trip when we passed the huge painted rock on the right, the junkyard full of dilapidated cars on the left, or the 7-Eleven convenience store. When the derogatory, sometimes profane, comments about the road came from the front seat, I chuckled and knew that we were almost there. My excitement and anticipation levels grew with each slithering mile. Usually, on days when the Tarheels were playing at home, the traffic on 54 would come to a dead standstill about five miles outside of town and creep its way in. I did not mind this. I came to expect it. It was just a traditional part of the trip—and a wonderful trip it always was.

Last year, with my childhood trips a distant memory, I found myself in the position of living in Chapel Hill and working full-time in Raleigh. I was working hard and studying hard, trying to succeed in our world, and making plans for the future. Each day I would hop on U.S. Highway I-40 and cruise back and forth between home and work.

The commute on I-40, with the usual heavy traffic, was not effortless, but it was significantly faster than driving on Highway 54, even with no traffic.

One typical day last spring, I left work in Raleigh and headed home, driving into a rush-hour sunset. I turned my radio on just in time to hear the current traffic report: "Commuters traveling west on Highway 40 will find a major delay waiting for them. There are two different car accidents that have stopped traffic in two places between Raleigh and Chapel Hill and officials are estimating the delay to be at least one hour. Westbound commuters are urged to take an alternate route." This was terrible news. The "alternate route" was, of course, Highway 54, but I was only concerned with the extra time that my trip was going to take, not the route itself.

I had not traveled on Highway 54 in over ten years, but that did not occur to me right away. Once I got on 54, the only thing I could think about was how enraged I was that I was going to be late getting home. I was grasping the steering wheel as if it were playing tug-of-war with my car's chassis. In this age of convenience and technological advancement, I was being forced to travel home on a second-rate, pothole-filled track of asphalt that was filled with local drivers who never came within 10 miles per hour of the speed limit. I did not need this.

Then a funny thing happened. Just as impatience was beginning to threaten my judgment, I passed a small Little League–size baseball field off to the right of the road. Suddenly and unexpectedly I was awash in floods of warm memories of my childhood in general and my family trips to Chapel Hill in particular. Having been a Little Leaguer myself in Washington, that baseball field had been my favorite landmark during my childhood trips to Chapel Hill.

I had always wondered how good the kids were who played on that field, and if my best pitch could strike them out. The outfield fence looked a short distance from home plate to me, and I often had commented to my dad that I could hit home runs if I ever played there, and he always nodded assuredly. From that point on, my trip home on 54 was a revelatory experience. I recognized every twist, turn, and dip in the road, and most of the structures alongside it. I felt like I had gone back in time. No, I *had* gone back in time.

There were a few new, obligatory shopping centers and apartment complexes along the old road, but otherwise it was the same Highway 54. The painted rock, the junkyard, and other monuments of my youthful exuberance were still there, albeit in an older, weathered condition, but so am I. I even stopped at the 7-Eleven for a soda (it was no longer named 7-Eleven, but that did not matter). In spirit, I had returned to the optimistic, hopeful days of my youth and to the customary pleasure that my family's trips had provided me.

I have not had many chances to turn back the clock in recent years, but that unintended drive on Highway 54 last year offered me one. I could never have had such an experience on the superhighway U.S. 40. I do not think that I will choose to travel the archaic route again, but I will, at the least, take the modern "advanced" road with a different perspective, aware of its benefits, but also more aware of its limitations.

⟶ A Walk in the Woods ⟵
and the Joy of the Great Outdoors

Who knows? The tradition of the family trip can begin with that first walk in the woods, especially when those first ventures create an abiding love of nature that leads you to decide to explore more of God's great out-of-doors. Strangely enough, though I spent three years of my youth living in what I would call the country—in a tiny rural town—I never remember walking in the woods. Maybe it's because they were all around. On the other hand, I'd use any excuse to grab my kids up—one a toddler, the other still in a stroller— and head out to the closest clump of trees in our city environment. Could be that's why my now young adult children choose to spend their leisure hours hiking and camping out. It's always been a wonderful tradition for families, especially in America's unequaled national parks.

A Spruce, a Fir, an Unknown Tree
BARRY LOPEZ

When I was a boy my father took me into the woods and tried to teach me the difference between a spruce and a fir. To this day I confuse the two, but I have learned to tell the difference between a birch and an aspen and that, they say, is something.

What my father had in mind, of course, was not a lesson in the naming of trees. If he had not felt the urge to introduce trees to someone else, he probably never would have bothered to learn their names anyway. For all I know, he could not tell the difference between a spruce and a fir either. Trees fascinated him and that, really, was all there was to it for my father.

In the years since, I, too grew close to the trees and spent many an hour wandering contented in the woods.

What it is about trees that attracts and holds us I do not know. It's more than their size, more than the color of their leaves in the fall, more than the chattering squirrels and flapping birds that nest in the crooks of their limbs. It has something to do, I think, with the less obvious things: The way a spray of leaves filters light, the way trees sleep so darkly in the winter, the way a grove of redwoods will snag a cloud of mist on the tips of the topmost branches, and, holding it there, will milk the moisture from it. It is the way the trees sound in a storm, talking to one another, passing the wind around. It's walking silently over forest floors padded with decades of fallen pine needles and coming to the realization that everything in the forest depends entirely on one thing; the tree.

If you have ever stood alone in the pine barrens in New Jersey, or out on the desert in southern California among the Joshua trees, or along the rocky coast of Maine, you know something else of trees: They can sink their roots in the most miserable of soils and find life. And if you have ever stood among the hemlock and red cedar in the rain forest on Washington's Olympic Peninsula, or in a mangrove swamp in Louisiana, you know they can sink their roots into the very richest of soils and not grow fat.

Lay your hand on the slippery flank of a madrone, or feel the knotty flesh of an oak, or heft a piece of cherrywood in one hand and alder in the other and you will know what the scientist, the dendrologist, knows of trees. It is not until you try to open an acorn with your fingers, or listen to the crunch of oak leaves crackling underfoot, or watch the half dollar leaves of a quaking aspen shudder light in a summer breeze, or smell a eucalyptus that you really begin to understand something of trees.

When I was a boy, I remember sitting in New York's Central Park and watching the wind push a dry maple leaf across the smooth, blacktop path. It was arched up like a legless crab, and it scraped over the blacktop like a rake over concrete. I watched it for a long time, and then I went and picked it up. It crumpled in my hand like thin brown glass.

Another day when I was walking in the woods with my father, we crossed through a thicket of low branches and I caught my foot, falling headlong over a rotting redwood. I picked myself up and was aware of the hundreds of trees and plants that had sprouted from that immense, rotting carcass. The damp, dark brown fibers clung to my wool shirt for days after, as though they were trying to hitch a ride somewhere, as though they were still alive.

There is a strangeness about the way trees live. They huddle together like the redwoods to catch a cloud. They persevere like the bristlecone pine for four thousand years on a rocky cliff. Killed by disease or fire they still go on standing for years. A row of poplars, strung along a creek bank or around a house, breaks a prairie wind in half.

Perhaps though, in the end, it is the eternal presence of trees that catches hold of our imaginations for good. Each year they provide us with two million gallons of maple syrup, give us seven million telephone poles, 160 million board feet of burial caskets, 640,000 barrels of turpentine and a million and a half board feet of toothpicks. And yet the huge forests go on standing year after year. Seasons cycle, more lumber mills and pulp mills are built, and the forests are still there. You are almost afraid to wonder how it is possible.

Anyone who has wandered off into the woods for an afternoon has known something of their eerie presence, and has known that their silence can be frightening. There is a wisdom about them, especially when they are old. It is as if they were all privy to some great, dark secret, something held deep within them, buried beneath that silent silence.

Who has not stood on a hillside of Eastern hardwoods late in the afternoon and not looked once or twice over his shoulder at fleeting shadows. In the rain forest of the Pacific Coast, thick with moss and fern, littered with massive fallen trunks, it is as though you stood in the dark heart of another world. The silence is deafening; growth is too slow to perceive; the ground beneath you is like sponge. The air is damp, and thick enough to feel. It is to bridge that silence, perhaps, that we come, eventually, to learn their names. It eases the uneasiness to know a spruce from a fir, but it dulls the mystery, too.

It occurred to me, long after that walk in the woods with my father, that after he had told me the names of the trees he never again asked me what they were. I never learned them, and as I said, I do not think he ever did either. He was too smart for that. He knew there was more to trees than names, and let me find out the rest for myself.

~ The People and the Canyon ~

Laurence Critchell

One of America's greatest traditions is caring for, loving, and preserving our natural resources and our national parks. It is there, Laurence Critchell reminds us, that we also find another one of our country's greatest resources— people from near and far.

There is something different about the camping ground at the Grand Canyon, and I think it is this curious mixture of eternity and the brief, sweet, poignant span of our human lives. I remember the night when Mary and I first came there. We had been driving along the canyon ridge at twilight, in the immense loneliness that descends over all the vastness after sundown. We might have been a thousand miles from man. Yet there he was, in all those flickering fires and sweet warm songs, and in some way hard to understand you felt at once that you had come to something as eternal as the canyon.

We stumbled on a little boy of seven or eight who all but challenged us. "My name's David," he said. "What's yours?"

We told him.

"You'd better camp over there," he said, hitching his belt like an old frontiersman. "This here belongs to Dad."

"This here" was just a few square feet of grassy earth and David's right of eminent domain. We staked our own claim in the darkness and added one more fire—and the fragrance of frankfurters and beans —to all the other comfortable, homely evidences of man.

The public camping grounds on the south rim of the Grand Canyon are neither for those who like their wilderness pure nor for those who hold to any kind of distinction between one man and another. There is a kind of huge natural democracy about the place. Here are the friendly ones, who are grateful for what has been provided and a little in awe of the immense canopy of stars and that brooding nearness of the canyon. If you have trouble with your fire, as we did, someone is going to help you out. If you lack a necessity, like a hatchet or a flashlight, just walk twenty or thirty feet and borrow one from a total stranger. In the darkness, in the drifting wood smoke, in the common reason for being there, you find a quality that is infinitely remote from the atomic age. The devil is not there at all.

Mr. and Mrs. Burt Karcy of Washington, Iowa, had a trailer about thirty feet from where we slept. They were sitting out in camp chairs listening to the singing before they went to bed. He was a retired salesman of farm machines, and every summer they spent a few weeks on the south rim of the canyon.

"Sometimes we go to the north rim," he said. "There's a forest there —what's the name of it?"

"The Kaibab," said Mrs. Karcy.

"That's it. Beautiful place. But—well, there's more people here. And then we have the hotel—once in a while we go up there for a real meal."

"Burt," said Mrs. Karcy.

He grinned and patted her hand. "Just like to give her a break once in a while . . ."

The Kendziorskis were on the other side of us, along with David and his eminent domain. Al Kendziorski was a machinist with Douglas Aircraft at Santa Monica. He was a young, lean, dark-faced man with a beautiful Polish wife—and David—and an eighteen-month-old baby, who slept in a hammock in the car.

"Kinda crazy to come out here with a baby," said Al. "But I dunno —we get a kick out of it."

"Al built a carrying sling," said Mrs. Kendziorski. "You should see it."

"That's so we can hike," said the man with a grin. "We're going to try it down the canyon."

"Who carries it?" asked Mary.

"Oh, Al does," said Mrs. Kendziorski, with that peculiar satisfaction of a young woman who has married a strong man.

Across the clearing from where we slept that night, a group of youngsters from Pasadena Junior High School, who had come with their chaperones in an old-fashioned bus, sat around the campfire and sang songs. They were young—their voices were high and sweet and true, and it was beautiful to hear them as we lay there on the pine-fragrant earth watching the smoke of their campfire drift up to the stars. The songs they sang were the old familiar ones, reaching far back, back into the times they had never known—

> *I want a girl*
> *Just like the girl*
> *Who married dear old Dad . . .*

This was not just that huge democracy of the camping grounds, but something that moved the heart. As the fires began to die out all over the forest, we had the feeling that everybody was listening to them—the Karcys in their trailer, the Kendziorskis in their sleeping bags, and all the other people who were lying on the earth around us.

And then at last even the youngsters' fire died, the last sparks trailed up to the stars, and they sang that most beautiful of evening hymns—

> *Holy, Holy, Holy,*
> *Lord God of Hosts—*
> *Heaven and earth are full of Thee*
> *Heaven and earth are praising Thee . . .*

Mind you, there is no charge for all of this.

There is just a moment before dawn when you can almost sense the ages of time that are running quietly along in that great river at the bottom of the canyon. It is not something you can bear for more than an instant. Mary and I had walked down in the blackness to the canyon's rim and stood there waiting for the sunrise. Everything had become almost unearthly still—not the chirrup of a bird, not the crackle of a twig, nothing. Just that solitude, that vast gulf of space, and time running on from the beginning of the world to the infinitely distant end.

As I say, you can only bear it for a fraction of a second. Then, if you are wise, you had better clasp hands and wait impatiently and watch with enormous gratitude as the shadows lighten and the black turns blue and the birds awaken and all at once, for perhaps the trillionth time, there is that wonderful crescendo of gold as the whole world of the canyon is suddenly blazing with sun.

We went back hungrily for breakfast. The camp was already up; everywhere we could smell bacon frying. Blue smoke drifted through the trees. Strangers smiled and said good morning. Around the old bus from Pasadena Junior High there was a bustle of activity. Al Kendziorski was building a fire. Mrs. Karcy was carrying a towel and a brush through the trees. And David, his feet planted on our few square feet of camping ground, faced a family who had just arrived.

"Sorry," he said, hitching up his belt with immense confidence, "this belongs to a friend."

～ *Family Dining* ～

With memories of irresistible food aromas and nature's stunning beauty all intertwining in our minds, step into the family home to relive another type of traditional feast—the midcentury family meal. Writer Susan Williams acknowledges that the all-together family-sitdown meal has changed since Victorian times, just as the configuration of the house has changed. Gone is the parlor. The living room has replaced it. Yet to come is the family room. Still, family dining has a purpose and closeness about it that many of us feel we are losing today. But never fear. As Pat Ethridge, the host of CNN's Parenting Today *show reminds us, as long as there is popcorn for rainy days, the tradition of family laughter and comfort around the table will remain with us.*

From Dining to Grabbing a Bite

*SUSAN WILLIAMS

I am a middle-class baby boomer. My mother, like many middle-class women during the 1950s and 1960s, embraced our home as her primary occupation. We lived in a Cape Cod house in the suburbs, a house with a living room, dining room, and breakfast room. Although each of these three rooms functioned in different ways, all served ultimately to house and reinforce the daily rituals of dining for our family.

Each morning we would assemble in the breakfast room, where my mother would make sure that we drank our orange juice and took a daily vitamin. She would then offer us cereal, toast, bacon (always bacon), and eggs. Our breakfast room, like many postwar houses, had a large picture window, through which we often watched a family of pheasants feed in the backyard. That pheasant family seemed a reassuring reflection of our own family: mother tending her flock, the chicks clambering along behind, never straying too far, and the elegantly plumed father at a reserved distance.

Sometimes we ate lunch in the breakfast room as well—if we were home, that is. On Saturdays, we might have Campbell's onion soup cleverly dressed up as French onion soup through the addition of melba toast and Kraft Parmesan cheese. Another Saturday lunch favorite was sardines, usually served on party rye, accompanied by Cheddar cheese and a side of tomato soup. Later, we came to love Snow's clam chowder, dressed up with a pat of butter, freshly ground pepper, and a splash of sherry. Sometimes these Saturday lunches migrated out into the living room. My mother would bring a tray with mugs of soup and sandwich makings and place it in front of the sofa on the butler's

table that she and my father had received as a wedding gift. My sister and I were fascinated by the way the sides of that table were hinged, so that the entire table could be picked up and carried—although it never was in our house. These casual meals taught us much about improvisation and imbued us with a lifelong confidence in our ability to dress up ordinary occasions, to add a measure of excitement and theatricality to our lives.

As far as meals went, however, dinner was the main event of the day. As soon as we were old enough to sit at the table, we dined together as a family every evening that my parents were home, in the dining room. Our dining room had a corner cupboard with glass doors, where my mother stored her wedding china and glasses. There was also a chest of drawers that served as a sideboard, where silver flatware and table linens resided. The first job I ever learned was setting the table. I would take the placemats and napkins from one of the drawers, forks, knives, and spoons from another, put glasses at each place, fill the glasses, and finally light the candles. Throughout our childhood, my sister and I alternated between setting and clearing the table on a weekly basis. We both hated clearing, but loved blowing out the candles.

During dinner we conversed. We discussed the events of our various days, planned future activities, and frequently aired family grievances. We were expected to behave ourselves at dinner, to be civilized and courteous. We did not begin to eat until my mother had lifted her fork, and we did not leave the table without asking to be excused. The array of manners increased as we approached our teenage years. My father began to insist that we remain standing until my mother had seated herself. By then my sister and I were aware that dinner was an important family event, and that it was about more than just eating. In many ways, it was a final gift for us from our parents before we fledged, a gift that included daily doses of family togetherness as well as final instructions in civility and self-discipline.

Our dinner menus were structured by my mother's brief stint as a student of cooking at Mechanic's Institute, where she had learned about nutrition as well as about culinary finesse. We always had a well-rounded menu that included meat, vegetables, a starch—usually some form of potatoes because my father disliked rice—salad, and dessert. My mother was an excellent cook. She loved to experiment with new recipes and exotic ingredients, which usually meant anything imported, frozen, or sauced—Stouffer's spinach soufflé, for example. For more mundane meals, when she and my father were going out for dinner, we had chicken chow mein (canned, with a side of Chinese noodles), or a can of chicken stew topped with refrigerator biscuits and baked in the oven. Although we consumed these meals in the basement family room, in front of the television, we were aware that there was a "homemade" aspect to them that conveyed my mother's domestic concern for the well-being of her family even in her absence. Although on those evenings we ate off of TV trays, they were still set with placemats and napkins, fork on the left, knife, spoon, and milk glass on the right. The formality that governed dining room meals, a formality calculated through successive generations of women in my family to ensure civility, carried over even to our most prosaic kids' dinners.

I still value these food-centered family memories. They have provided me with a lifelong sense of well-being, of being safe and cared for, like the baby pheasants in the backyard. The lessons in middle-class gentility that I learned at my parents' dinner table continue to shape my expectations about social interactions—that there will be a measure of dignity, mutual respect, and formality. These dining traditions, a lingering product of a Victorian mentality and devised to reinforce and stabilize class relations, may seem anachronistic in today's multicultural world. And yet, civility—the art of making oneself liked and courted—must survive if we all are to live together in harmony. If we fail to pass on these lessons of the family dinner table to subsequent generations, people with diverse cultural expectations risk losing one of their basic means of social mediation.

Popcorn When It Rains

* PAT ETHRIDGE

It was there when it mattered most. On those cold, dreary days of my childhood, Mama made sure it was there. When it rained, she made popcorn. Every time. I could count on it, on grey, autumn afternoons when I walked home from school feeling as bleak as the November sky. Then the door would open, and I could hear the playful squeals of my younger brother and sisters, and Mama would greet me with a smile and remind me it was a popcorn day.

We all delighted in gathering around as Mama shook the shiny, copper-bottomed pot over the blue flames on the old gas stove. We would wait and watch in wide-eyed wonderment as the golden kernels began to sizzle in the hot oil. And when we heard the first pop, we would giggle the hearty giggles of children, laughing until our stomachs ached and our eyes teared and the fluffy, white clouds of corn finally pushed the lid off the pot. Mama would pour it into a big wooden bowl and sprinkle it with salt and place it atop the red Formica-and-chrome kitchen table. We would scramble to our seats and grab handfuls to spread on paper napkins and gobble the popcorn with glee.

It was there when it mattered most: comfort food I could count on. A simple family tradition with an element of surprise.

Making a Meal of Popcorn

One of the very rewards of asking, "What is your favorite tradition?" was learning how many ways the same tradition could be played out within a family. It might be compared to musical variations on a theme. Betty Baker is another proponent of popcorn. Her family could literally make a meal of it. Betty's account also gives us insight into how traditions sometimes just happen.

We often had such large meals in the day on Sundays that we were not really hungry at dinnertime. Sometimes we would just pop a big bowl of popcorn and gather around to chat or to watch a TV program that appealed to the entire family. It seems that through the years there was always some kind of family programming on that evening more than others. A popcorn dinner certainly is not the kind of thing you plan to do on a regular basis, but, as in many instances, doing it once or twice creates a spontaneous tradition. Suddenly the children were coming in from play or their dad in from yard work and all at once everyone was ready for popcorn night. So it began and continued. Take it from the chief cook and dishwasher—this was a tradition I wanted to encourage!

Betty Baker

⚊ Mother-and-Daughter Time ⚊

From small-town Ames, Iowa, to the big city of Des Moines was a long trip just to go shopping, but the wonderful times young girls had with their mothers made for a lifetime of memories. Then, as now, shopping is more than just a buying time. It is a looked-forward-to time of togetherness, especially when there's time for lunch.

Pleated Skirts and Lemon Sauce

SUSAN ALLEN TOTH

Mrs. Harbinger's daughter Kristy and I were good friends, as were Vanessa and my mother, and if we all went together, my mother wouldn't have to drive alone. My mother hated driving; she clutched the steering wheel so tightly her knuckles were white. I don't know how she managed our yearly [vacation] trips to Minnesota. She always spoke of going to Des Moines as if it were a dangerous safari from which we might not be likely to return. Mrs. Harbinger was more sanguine.

A day shopping in Des Moines was a great occasion. Early after breakfast we'd set out, dressed in our best as though we were off to church, a snack packed in a paper bag, car carefully stoked with gas and oil. Past the outskirts of Ames, into the open countryside, we picked up speed exhilaratingly until we eventually found ourselves stuck behind a slow-moving semi-trailer truck. Then, if Mrs. Harbinger drove, we braced ourselves, peered out the window, watched for coming traffic, and shouted encouragement. "It's okay!" "There's a yellow line ahead!" "I can't see over the next hill!" Finally Mrs. Harbinger pulled out, stepped on the gas, and we held our breath for the endless wait alongside the truck until we were safely back into our own lane. If my mother drove, we had a different tactic. We followed the truck until one or more of us became visibly restless. "Hazel," Mrs. Harbinger would turn and say gently to my mother. Then my mother was forced to act. But she didn't pass. Instead she looked for some place to pull off the road, preferably a truck stop or gas station. "Let's just take a break," she said, turning off the ignition. Then we climbed out, used the bathroom, bought a Coke or a candy bar. It gave the semi enough time to pull far ahead of us so we wouldn't run the chance of getting stuck behind it again.

Once inside the city limits of Des Moines, we followed a maze of streets none of us except Mrs. Harbinger really knew, block after block of bedraggled-looking houses, small warehouses, strange churches. Central Des Moines was not especially attractive. When we reached a main street near downtown, we looked anxiously for the one parking lot we always used, hoping it wouldn't be filled. Then Kristy Harbinger and I walked as fast as we could, urging our mothers along, until we got to Younkers.

Younkers Department Store was a confusing marvel to a young girl from Ames. Occupying a small city block, it had not just one but several entrances. We always used the one with a visitors' book, where you could leave messages for friends: "Hazel—come to the French Room at 4 P.M."; "Vanessa and Kristy: wait for us in the Tearoom at 11." Shopping in Younkers was a social affair, punctuated by coffee in the morning, lunch in the Tearoom later. Inside the store I wandered in a happy daze among the infinite departments. Unlike any store in Ames, Younkers had more than one counter that sold sweaters, more than one dark corner for shoes. I never completely mastered its layout. Just when I thought I had compared every price and variation of shortsleeved, round-collared white cotton blouses, an item which in Ames would have one coarse broadcloth style cheap at Penney's and a fancier pocketed style less cheaply at Marty's, I would find a new strain blooming in an overlooked corner of Younkers.

Bargains seemed to leap out at me from unexpected places: heaps of reduced Irish-linen handkerchiefs on top of the shiny glass notions counter, "End-of-the-Month Clearance" signs over dirndl skirts in Misses' Separates, and of course always the possibility of a hidden wonder in the French Room. There my mother and I would meet before lunch, knowing whoever had been there first would have already culled its possibilities for the other to consider. The French Room was Younkers' version of elegance. It was a large room, thickly carpeted, lined with mirrors, entered through heavy gold-framed glass doors that swung shut to close off the ordinary bustling world of everyday Younkers. Usually you had to ask to have clothes brought out, a tactic that effectively discouraged casual bargain-hunters like Mother and myself. But sometimes the French Room had a Special Clearance, advertised by a discreetly lettered sign on the heavy glass door. Then we would go in, heading straight for the rack with telltale price tags against the wall. We looked at the tags first, then at the clothes. Sometimes my mother would try on a dress, while I looked, almost always in vain, for something that wouldn't look too old or funny but would still say, quietly, "The French Room" on its gold-and-white label. Once, in high school, I bought a long-sleeved rayon shirt with gay multicolored flowers on a white background. It came from a different world from the one of white round collars. But the first time I wore it, and perspired—in a French Room blouse, a lady didn't sweat—all the colors ran together, so I had to keep my arms pinned close to my sides whenever I wore it. Still, I knew it was elegant, and once, before it had been reduced, it had cost $14.95. Just for a blouse. That was what one expected from the French Room.

After our foray to the French Room, Mother and I would lunch in Younkers' Tearoom, among a roomful of ladies, all talking loudly. We ordered things we couldn't get at the Rainbow Cafe at home: onion soup, chicken a la king, English muffins. For dessert, gingerbread with lemon sauce. Joined by the Harbingers, we would compare purchases, pulling each one triumphantly from its dark green Younkers sack for inspection. Then we would map out our afternoon, dividing it among the handful of smaller but intriguing shops that lined the block across the street. Regretfully, since I'd always see some unvisited counter, some last unexamined "Bargain" sign, we'd ride the escalators down two floors to the main exit. Escalators were unique to Younkers in all Iowa then; there was a single escalator in Younkers' Cedar Rapids store, I'd heard, but I'd never been there. As a child I was thrilled by the folding stairs that disappeared into flatness. But even when older, I loved to ride majestically up and down, surveying Younkers below as if its spread-out departments were my private fiefdoms. In the car on the way home, we'd open all the packages again, exclaiming over each other's surprises, marveling at reductions, and comparing successes. To have found a size 12 navy-blue pleated skirt when the only one seen in Ames had been size 8 was a vindication of our whole trip. If only, we thought, we could shop in the Des Moines Younkers every day.

⇀ A Place of My Own ⇀

One dream seems to run through every American family—the hope of owning a piece of land and your own home. This tradition has been echoed down through the years since the first settlers claimed land and hewed logs—from Roanoke Island in the sixteenth century to California in the eighteenth. There, we declare, "I can lead the good life." Comfort, peace, continuity, family— these are the joys that await us. And sometimes, as David Grayson discovered, much, much more.

All This Is Mine

DAVID GRAYSON

HOW SWEET THE WEST WIND SOUNDS IN MY OWN TREES:
HOW GRACEFUL CLIMB THESE SHADOWS ON MY HILL.

Always as I travel, I think, "Here I am, let anything happen!"

I do not want to know the future; knowledge is too certain, too cold, too real.

It is true that I have not always met the fine adventure nor won the friend, but if I had, what should I have more to look for at other turnings and other hilltops?

The afternoon of my purchase was one of the great afternoons of my life. When Horace put me down at my gate, I did not go at once to the house; I did not wish, then, to talk with Harriet. The things I had with myself were too important. I skulked toward my barn, compelling myself to walk slowly until I reached the corner, where I broke into an eager run as though the old Nick himself were after me. Behind the barn I dropped down on the grass, panting with laughter, and not without some of the shame a man feels at being a boy. Close along the side of the barn, as I sat there in the cool of the shade, I could see a tangled mat of smartweed and catnip, and the boards of the barn, brown and weather-beaten, and the gables above with mud swallows' nests, now deserted; and it struck me suddenly, as I observed these homely pleasant things:

"All this is mine."

I sprang up and drew a long breath.

"Mine," I said.

It came to me then like an inspiration that I might now go out and take formal possession of my farm. I might experience the emotion of a landowner. I might swell with dignity and importance for once, at least.

So I started at the fence corner back of the barn and walked straight up through the pasture, keeping close to my boundaries, that I might not miss a single rod of my acres. And, oh, it was a prime afternoon! The Lord made it! Sunshine—and autumn haze—and red trees—and yellow fields—and blue distances above the faraway town. And the air had a tang which got into a man's blood and set him chanting all the poetry he ever knew.

"I climb that was a clod,
I run whose steps were slow,
I reap the very wheat of God
That once had none to sow!"

So I walked up the margin of my field looking broadly about me:
and presently, I began to examine my fences—*my* fences—with a
critical eye. I considered the quality of the soil, though in truth I was
not much of a judge of such matters. I gloated over my plowed land,
lying there open and passive in the sunshine. I said of this tree: "It is
mine," and of its companion beyond the fence: "It is my neighbour's."
Deeply and sharply within myself I drew the line between *meum and
tuum*: for only thus, by comparing ourselves with our neighbours, can
we come to the true realisation of property. Occasionally I stopped to
pick up a stone and cast it over the fence, thinking with some truculence
that my neighbour would probably throw it back again. Never
mind, I had it out of *my* field. Once, with eager surplusage of energy,
I pulled down a dead and partly rotten oak stub, long an eye-sore,
with an important feeling of proprietorship. I could do anything I
liked. The farm was *mine.*

How sweet an emotion is possession! What charm is inherent in
ownership! What a foundation for vanity, even for the greater quality
of self-respect, lies in a little property! I fell to thinking of the excellent
wording of the old books in which land is called "real property,"
or "real estate." Money we may possess, or goods or chattels, but they
give no such impression of mineness as the feeling that one's feet rest
upon soil that is his: that part of the deep earth is his with all the
water upon it, all small animals that creep or crawl in the holes of it,
all birds or insects that fly in the air above it, all trees, shrubs, flowers,
and grass that grow upon it, all houses, barns and fences—all his. As
I strode along that afternoon I fed upon possession. I rolled the sweet
morsel of ownership under my tongue. I seemed to set my feet down
more firmly on the good earth. I straightened my shoulders: *this land
was mine.* I picked up a clod of earth and let it crumble and drop
through my fingers: it gave me a peculiar and poignant feeling of
possession. I can understand why the miser enjoys the very physical
contact of his gold. Every sense I possessed, sight, hearing, smell,
touch, fed upon the new joy.

At one corner of my upper field the fence crosses an abrupt ravine
upon leggy stilts. My line skirts the slope halfway up. My neighbour
owns the crown of the hill which he has shorn until it resembles the
tonsured pate of a monk. Every rain brings the light soil down the

ravine and lays it like a hand of infertility upon my farm. It had always bothered me, this wastage; and as I looked across my fence I thought to myself:

"I must have that hill. I will buy it. I will set the fence farther up, I will plant the slope. It is no age of tonsures either in religion or agriculture."

The very vision of widened acres set my thoughts on fire. In imagination I extended my farm upon all sides, thinking how much better I could handle my land than my neighbours. I dwelt avariciously upon more possessions: I thought with discontent of my poverty. More land I wanted. I was enveloped in clouds of envy. I coveted my neighbour's land: I felt myself superior and Horace inferior: I was consumed with black vanity.

So I dealt hotly with these thoughts until I reached the top of the ridge at the farther corner of my land. It is the highest point on the farm.

For a moment I stood looking about me on a wonderful prospect of serene beauty. As it came to me—hills, fields, woods—the fever which had been consuming me died down. I thought how the world stretched away from my fences—just such fields—for a thousand miles, and in each small enclosure a man as hot as I with the passion of possession. How they all envied, and hated, in their longing for more land! How property kept them apart, prevented the close, confident touch of friendship, how it separated lovers and ruined families! Of all obstacles to that free democracy of which we dream, is there a greater than property?

I was ashamed. Deep shame covered me. How little of the earth, after all, I said, lies within the limits of my fences. And I looked out upon the perfect beauty of the world around me, and I saw how little excited it was, how placid, how undemanding.

I had come here to be free and already this farm, which I thought of so fondly as my possession, was coming to possess me. Ownership is an appetite like hunger or thirst, and as we may eat to gluttony and drink to drunkenness so we may possess to avarice. How many men have I seen who, though they regard themselves as models of temperance, wear the marks of unbridled indulgence of the passion of possession, and how like gluttony or licentiousness it sets its sure sign upon their faces.

I said to myself, Why should any man fence himself in? And why hope to enlarge one's world by the creeping acquisition of a few acres to his farm? I thought of the old scientist, who, laying his hand upon the grass, remarked: "Everything under my hand is a miracle"—forgetting that everything outside was also a miracle.

As I stood there I glanced across the broad valley wherein lies the most of my farm, to the field of buckwheat which belongs to Horace. For an instant it gave me the illusion of a hill on fire: for the late sun shone full on the thick ripe stalks of the buckwheat, giving forth an abundant red glory that blessed the eye. Horace had been proud of his crop, smacking his lips at the prospect of winter pancakes, and here I was entering his field and taking without hindrance another crop, a crop gathered not with hands nor stored in granaries: a wonderful crop, which, once gathered, may long be fed upon and yet remain unconsumed.

So I looked across the countryside; a group of elms here, a tufted hilltop there, the smooth verdure of pastures, the rich brown of new-plowed fields—and the odours, and the sounds of the country—all cropped by me. How little the fences keep me out: I do not regard titles, nor consider boundaries. I enter either by day or by night, but not secretly. Taking my fill, I leave as much as I find.

And thus standing upon the highest hill in my upper pasture, I thought of the quoted saying of a certain old abbot of the middle ages —"He that is a true monk considers nothing as belonging to him except a lyre."

What finer spirit? Who shall step forth freer than he who goes with nothing save his lyre? He shall sing as he goes: he shall not be held down nor fenced in.

With a lifting of the soul I thought of that old abbot, how smooth his brow, how catholic his interest, how serene his outlook, how free his friendships, how unlimited his whole life. Nothing but a lyre!

So I made a covenant there with myself. I said: "I shall use, not be used. I do not limit myself here. I shall not allow possessions to come between me and my life or my friends."

For a time—how long I do not know—I stood thinking. Presently I discovered, moving slowly along the margin of the field below me, the old professor with his tin botany box. And somehow I had no feeling that he was intruding upon my new land. His walk was slow and methodical, his head and even his shoulders were bent—almost habitually—from looking close upon the earth, and from time to time he stooped, and once he knelt to examine some object that attracted his eye. It seemed appropriate that he should thus kneel to the earth. So he gathered *his* crop and fences did not keep him out nor titles disturb him. He also was free! It gave me at that moment a peculiar pleasure to have him on my land, to know that I was, if unconsciously, raising other crops than I knew. I felt friendship for this old professor: I could understand him, I thought. And I said aloud but in a low tone, as though I were addressing him:

—Do not apologise, friend, when you come into my field. You do not interrupt me. What you have come for is of more importance at this moment than corn. Who is it that says I must plow so many furrows this day? Come in, friend, and sit here on these clods: we will sweeten the evening with fine words. We will invest our time not in corn, or in cash, but in life.—

I walked with confidence down the hill toward the professor. So engrossed was he with his employment that he did not see me until I was within a few paces of him. When he looked up at me it was as though his eyes returned from some far journey. I felt at first out of focus, unplaced, and only gradually coming into view. In his hand he held a lump of earth containing a thrifty young plant of the purple cone-flower, having several blossoms. He worked at the lump deftly, delicately, so that the earth, pinched, powdered and shaken out, fell between his fingers, leaving the knotty yellow roots in his hand. I marked how firm, slow, brown, the old man was, how little obtrusive in my field. One foot rested in a furrow, the other was set among the grass of the margin, near the fence—his place, I thought.

His first words, though of little moment in themselves, gave me a curious satisfaction, as when a coin, tested, rings true gold, or a hero, tried, is heroic.

"I have rarely," he said, "seen a finer display of rudbeckia than this, along these old fences."

If he had referred to me, or questioned, or apologised, I should have been disappointed. He did not say, "your fences," he said "these fences," as though they were as much his as mine. And he spoke in his own world, knowing that if I could enter I would, but that if I could not, no stooping to me would avail either of us.

"It has been a good autumn for flowers," I said inanely, for so many things were flying through my mind that I could not at once think of the great particular words, which should bring us together. At first I thought my chance had passed, but he seemed to see something in me after all, for he said:

"Here is a peculiarly large specimen of the rudbeckia. Observe the deep purple of the cone, and the bright yellow of the petals. Here is another that grew hardly two feet away, in the grass near the fence where the rails and the blackberry bushes have shaded it. How small and undeveloped it is."

"They crowd up to the plowed land," I observed.

"Yes, they reach out for a better chance in life—like men. With more room, better food, freer air, you see how much finer they grow."

It was curious to me, having hitherto barely observed the cone-flowers along my fences, save as a colour of beauty, how simply we fell to talking of them as though in truth they were people like ourselves, having our desires and possessed of our capabilities. It gave me then, for the first time, the feeling which has since meant such varied enjoyment, of the peopling of the woods.

"See here," he said, "how different the character of these individuals. They are all of the same species. They all grow along this fence within two or three rods; but observe the difference not only in size but in colouring, in the shape of the petals, in the proportions of the cone. What does it all mean? Why, nature trying one of her endless experiments. She sows here broadly, trying to produce better cone-flowers. A few she plants on the edge of the field in the hope that they may escape the plow. If they grow, better food and more sunshine produce more and larger flowers."

So we talked, or rather he talked, finding in me an eager listener. And what he called botany seemed to me to be life. Of birth, of growth, of reproduction, of death, he spoke, and his flowers became sentient creatures under my eyes.

And thus the sun went down and the purple mists crept silently along the distant low spots, and all the great, great mysteries came and stood before me beckoning and questioning. They came and they stood, and out of the cone-flower, as the old professor spoke, I seemed to catch a glimmer of the true light. I reflected how truly everything is in anything. If one could really understand a cone-flower he could understand this Earth. Botany was only one road toward the Explanation.

Always I hope that some traveler may have more news of the way than I, and sooner or later, I find I must make inquiry of the direction of every thoughtful man I meet. And I have always had especial hope of those who study the sciences: they ask such intimate questions of nature. Theology possesses a vain-gloriousness which places its faith in human theories; but science, at its best, is humble before nature herself. It has no thesis to defend: it is content to kneel upon the earth, in the way of my friend, the old professor, and ask the simplest questions, hoping for some true reply.

I wondered, then, what the professor thought, after his years of work, of the Mystery; and finally, not without confusion, I asked him. He listened, for the first time ceasing to dig, shake out and arrange his specimens. When I had stopped speaking he remained for a moment silent, then he looked at me with a new regard. Finally he quoted quietly, but with a deep note in his voice:

"Canst thou by searching find God? Canst thou find out the Almighty unto perfection? It is as high as heaven: what canst thou do? deeper than hell, what canst thou know?"

When the professor had spoken we stood for a moment silent, then he smiled and said briskly:

"I have been a botanist for fifty-four years. When I was a boy I believed implicitly in God. I prayed to him, having a vision of him— a person—before my eyes. As I grew older I concluded that there was no God. I dismissed him from the universe. I believed only in what I could see, or hear, or feel. I talked about Nature and Reality."

He paused, the smile still lighting his face, evidently recalling to himself the old days. I did not interrupt him. Finally he turned to me and said abruptly:

"And now—it seems to me—there is nothing but God."

As he said this he lifted his arm with a peculiar gesture that seemed to take in the whole world.

For a time we were both silent. When I left him I offered my hand and told him I hoped I might become his friend. So I turned my face toward home. Evening was falling, and as I walked I heard the crows calling, and the air was keen and cool, and I thought deep thoughts.

And so I stepped into the darkened stable. I could not see the outlines of the horse or the cow, but knowing the place so well I could easily get about. I heard the horse step aside with a soft expectant whinny. I smelled the smell of milk, the musty, sharp odour of dry hay, the pungent smell of manure, not unpleasant. And the stable was warm after the cool of the fields with a sort of animal warmth that struck into me soothingly. I spoke in a low voice and laid my hand on the horse's flank. The flesh quivered and shrunk away from my touch —coming back confidently, warmly. I ran my hand along his back and up his hairy neck. I felt his sensitive nose in my hand. "You shall have your oats," I said, and I gave him to eat. Then I spoke as gently to the cow, and she stood aside to be milked.

And afterward I came out into the clear bright night, and the air was sweet and cool, and my dog came bounding to meet me. So I carried the milk into the house, and Harriet said in her heartiest tone:

"You are late, David. But sit up, I have kept the biscuits warm."

And that night my sleep was sound.

～ Old Log House ～

James S. Tippett

On a little green knoll
At the edge of the wood
My great great grandmother's
First house stood.

The house was of logs
My grandmother said
With one big room
And a lean-to shed.

The logs were cut
And the house was raised
By pioneer men
In the olden days.

I like to hear
My grandmother tell
How they built the fireplace
And dug the well.

They split the shingles
They filled each chink;
It's a house of which
I like to think.

Forever and ever
I wish I could
Live in a house
At the edge of a wood.

～ The Tradition Continues ～

In addition to the good times and closeness that come from family traditions, these times also provide the chance for adults to slip in painless history lessons and begin building good habits that will be invaluable in adulthood. Author Susan Newman's wonderfully practical suggestions can turn simple but needed tasks into happy events that can be building blocks for the next generation's good habits as well as help you gather together a treasure trove of tangible *memories which your children will later be able to share with their own families.*

Starting Traditions with Your Children . . . And Keeping Them Alive

SUSAN NEWMAN

Whatever and however you celebrate with children, start or continue traditions. It's never too early to begin building ritual into family life. When children are young, many things you do for them and with them may seem insignificant, but all will be appreciated in years to come.

Every holiday—be it George Washington's Birthday or Christmas —offers fertile ground for creating positive and strong family unity. You create the memories they will eventually cherish.

- Cooking Specialist: Ask for cooking help. Turn one child into a stuffing mixer, another into a potato masher, pie dough roller, or ingredient chef. Assign the same tasks each Thanksgiving; children quickly become both proud and protective of their "product."
- A Caring Christmas: With the children, search closets and chests for coats, clothing, toys, and canned foods to give to the homeless and needy each year.
- Strawberry Pancakes: Establish a traditional Christmas morning breakfast in your house—a special kind of pancakes, sticky buns, fancy omelets, or jelly-filled crepes.
- Toast Master: Allow each child to make a toast or offer thanks for a holiday meal. As children get older, their toasts longer, alternate speakers from year to year.
- Little Holidays, Big Deal: Make a big deal out of the small holidays. Drop green food coloring into the mashed potatoes or a batch of cookie dough on Saint Patrick's Day; bring home a cherry pie for George Washington's Birthday; buy candied apples for Halloween, small flags for July Fourth.
- All Heart: Buy heart-shaped baking pans—you'll use them every year to bake a Valentine's Day cake. Use red food coloring to turn the icing pink.
- Say "Cheese": Every Mother's Day and Father's Day have someone take a few family photos. Save the best shot from each year. As they accumulate, put four or five of them together in an album or frame. It's a colorful record of the passing years.

Childhood is an adventure, a journey to be joined by parents whenever possible. By grabbing pockets of time together—a few minutes here and there—you create pleasant traditions and memories for both you and your children.

Children's reactions are unpredictable. You never know which tradition or off-beat, spur-of-the-moment idea will become an oft-repeated "little thing long remembered"—embedded happily and fondly in their minds forever.

- Fantasy: For car trips, waiting rooms or when there is nothing to do or say, make up and develop stories about people you don't really know. The policeman you just passed lives in a huge castle; the nurse in the doctor's office is a ballet dancer at night. There's no age limit on story-telling.
- Awards Ceremony: At the last dinner or lunch of every vacation present awards to each of the children, other family members or guests. Awards need not be fancy: an empty box of cereal to the best eater, a tennis ball to the most enthusiastic sportsman, a used paperback to the person who read the most, fake candy lips to the most congenial, a comic book to the funniest. Make up awards to fit the activities you've engaged in.
- Red Envelopes: Instead of just handing over gift money or allowance, put it in colored envelopes. The envelope quickly becomes a welcomed sight and a unique family custom.
- Happy Un-Birthday to You: Choose a day roughly six months from a child's real birthday and deem it her un-birthday. Give it a quirky name and let her choose what she would like to wear, to do, and to eat.
- Remembrances of Things Past: Take pictures of your child's room every few years so she will be able to recall it as it was. Also photograph the exterior of your home(s) and your child's school(s).
- From the Library of . . . : Put aside favorite books for you and your child to reminisce about or for him to give to his own children years from now.
- My Teddy: Carefully wrap and tuck away your youngster's favorite teddy bear, stuffed animal, or doll when she has outgrown it.

❦ A Measure of Time ❦

*Margaret Maron

Despite our changing lifestyles so clearly mirrored in today's landscape, even we city dwellers are unwilling to let go of the tradition of the ancestral home. Popular novelist Margaret Maron is fortunate enough to have lived in her home long enough to measure a family's growth.

In our home is a wall that partitions the kitchen from the dining room. The wall is eight inches wide and for more than twenty-five years, our closest friends and their children (and now their grandchildren, too) have stood there at the butt end of it, to be measured in their stocking feet. Small lines indicate their varying heights and each line is named and dated in permanent ink. In the early years when we repainted the interior, I used to transfer the marks to paper and back. Now there's such a flurry of names and dates that we no longer paint that end of the wall.

We usually have a pig picking in the summer and a Christmas "sing" in December—big sprawling extended-family parties; and always, before the evening is over, some child will tug at my hand and ask, "Is it time to put us on the wall yet?" They love to see how much they've grown in the six months or year since they were last measured. So do their parents and grandparents. The littlest ones are often apprehensive when their shoes come off and they're told to stand up straight with heels touching the baseboard. The older ones step up eagerly.

Here's my nephew Scott at five years old, at eight, twelve, and finally topping the wall at six feet four inches when he was twenty. Here's his son William at six months. And here's my eighty-nine-year-old mother, a full inch shorter now than she was twenty years ago. A handful of October dates mark the week-long celebration when our son was married here at the farm. It was the first time that his New York cousins had met his Florida cousins and everyone who'd grown had to go on the wall, including our brand new daughter-in-law.

I look at this wonderfully messy reflection of advancing growth marks and am always reminded of Ogden Nash's bittersweet verse, "The Middle"—

> *When I remember bygone days*
> *I think how evening follows morn;*
> *So many I loved were not yet dead,*
> *So many I love were not yet born.*

⤙ A Welcoming Message ⤚

ARTIE E. APPLETON

How to turn the dream house of your childless years into the playhouse of your child-full years has long been a problem. I know I had to face up to the reality when little hands began reaching for the beautiful porcelain figurines and plates I had inherited from my New England grandfather. I continued a tradition my mother had started with me. I let each child hold whatever object he or she wished, under supervision, and talked about what made it pretty or interesting, or just irresistible to those little fingers. These, I said, were adult toys that had to be treated very carefully and were not half as much fun as the children's own toys. It seems to have worked. Although I raised a husky football- and baseball-playing son and a rambunctious—almost tomboyish at times—daughter, the only object that was ever broken was a vase knocked over by Little Kitty. I hope they'll carry this family tradition on.

Another, and bolder, way to approach the problem was described in the November 1944 issue of American Home. *It only requires a paintbrush and imagination, though I'll be the first to admit that undoubtedly you will want to choose your own 1990s colors!*

At first, the stairway seemed impossible. Goodbye to any dream of a gracious curved stairway! This one was uncompromisingly dark and steep—until we painted the treads a tile red, matching the hall floor, and the hand-rail and risers the same light blue we used with such cheerful results in the living room cupboards and bookcases. And on the risers, interspersed with peasant decals, we lettered in a white script the old sampler verse:

> *Come in the evening,*
> *Come in the morning;*
> *Come when you're looked for,*
> *Come without warning.*

The stairway I cried over has been transformed into a conversation feature, and it carries a warm note of welcome for our guests. As for the children, of course they adore it!

⁓ A Family Record ⁓
The Hand That Rocks the Cradle

During my years as an antiques appraiser, how often I heard, "This cradle has been slept in by five generations of my family." But had I asked the proud owner to name those babes, chances are the list would stop at the third or possibly fourth generation's name—and that's just the direct line. What about the cousins? To ensure that this family information will be continued, take the time to write down the names and, if possible, the birth date of each child who has slept in the cradle or bed, sat in the high chair, or whatever. It doesn't cost that much to have these names engraved on a small brass plaque that can be tacked on the bottom of the piece. Just be sure to leave room for more names to be added in the future.

This tradition can also be adapted to a child's first "big bed," or even to a marriage bed. When I remarried, Bob and I ordered a queen-size bed (a new tradition in itself) from the Lexington Furniture Company. When setting it up, we were astounded to see the date 6.26.96, the day the bed was made, and our wedding day, stamped on the inside rail. Needless to say, next to the date we carved our initials.

⁓ Building Traditions ⁓

Our young contributors echo the many pleasures and values their elders extolled throughout this family tradition section of the book. Every one of the traditions submitted below reinforces the importance of continuity in our lives, particularly at this time when so much is changing so rapidly. We begin by learning the delight that comes when tasks and chores become relabeled "family traditions" and end with that special event—the family reunion. In between are pieces filled with ideas from every walk of life, covering a multitude of topics and activities, and from all seasons of the year. Surely you will want to adapt some to your own lives.

Each fall when the trees are pretty with colors, my family and I go to the mountains to gather pine needles. Even before I was born, I got to go, but didn't know it. Dad, Mom, my little sister, Brentlee, Grandmom, and other family and friends and I go up the steep hill under the tall evergreens to rake pine needles. Dad said that in the fall they are real golden in color, like the golden-egg color. We use them at home in our yard. I like to rake and I'll help hold the bag for my dad to fill with pine needles, but my favorite thing to do is rolling those big bags down the steep hill toward the truck. They sure can roll a long way by themselves. One time, somehow I got up on top of a bag when it was rolling and it rolled over me. It just kept right on going. We all laughed. Mom thought that I was hurt. We all have fun. Maybe you can go with us sometime too.

Emileigh West, elementary school

Cutting firewood is one of my favorite things to do each year. My dad cuts the wood and Mom and I load the wood that Dad cuts. My brother helps with odds and ends like picking up light wood that Dad cut and going to get cakes, drinks, and other stuff out of the house. My family cuts and loads wood two times each year. The exciting thing about loading wood is I feel like I'm helping my family and not being lazy and careless. My dad takes the tractor and hooks the trailer of wood to the tractor. After he does that, he cranks the tractor up and pulls the trailer so he can pull the trailer to the shed so all of us can unload the wood and stack it up against the shed. When it comes fall and winter, Dad busts the wood and then he burns it. After all the wood is burned and winter is over, we go cut wood again. So far we have had a busy fall and we have cut lots of wood for winter.

Jessica Diane Roten, elementary school

Lest you think all the fun chores are country- or farm-oriented . . .

My family has always had family traditions. Ever since I was old enough to remember, my dad and I washed the cars every Saturday morning. My dad would make me get up early. Then we would wash the cars. Sometimes we would check all the parts of the car to make sure they were okay and even wax the car. When I was little, I remember it as a fun time. I got to play with the hose. As I got older, I was always busy. I never had any time to talk to my dad. I used Saturday mornings to find out what was happening in his life and to let him know about mine.

This tradition has always been important to me. It has taught me a lot. I have learned to respect my property and other people's property. When I get a car, I am going to take good care of it and wash it every Saturday morning. When I do, I will think of my dad and the great Saturday mornings we had together.

Christine Vandry, high school

My family tradition happens every Christmas morning when we deliver Meals on Wheels to shut-in people who usually don't have the muscles or bones to even walk out the door, or they don't have a lot of money to go buy themselves a Christmas Breakfast.

So what we do first is wake up, open all our presents, look them over, have a cup of hot chocolate, get dressed, and leave. We drive to the hospital loading dock to get the food and a list of the people who will get the food. Every year we assign a navigator in our family. This year is my year to navigate. When the navigator directs us to the home, we go in and deliver the food. Sometimes we like to go in and talk for a while. We do this until the list is finished.

Then we go to my grandma's house for a big Christmas brunch. This tradition helps us to remember the true meaning of Christmas.

Sassy Bencini, elementary school

Family Gatherings

If you don't think a family reunion is important, take a moment to read about this family's Camp Beach. You'll quickly see that when this tradition brings everyone together it is a time when the children begin sorting out life's characters and roles as played out in the family setting.

Every two years the most amazing collection of people come together on North Carolina's Outer Banks. It is not a convention, it is not a club. It is my family reunion. Some live in the country and some in the city, but every other year they arrive at the beach for two weeks of family summer camp.

My favorite is Aunt Boo who comes all the way from Texas. She works hard there, buying clothes for a department store chain, so when she comes to the beach, she wants to play. She is still young, so she plays with all her nieces and nephews. She is the only one of Mom's seven brothers and sisters who doesn't have kids. She likes to Rollerblade, ride the wave, and play on Mom's all-sister volleyball team. They don't beat the boys, but they argue longer and usually get the point.

When I go to the beach with my cousins, it seems like I have the biggest family in America. Everyone is different, but everyone likes to laugh and cook and eat Uncle Terry's grilled chicken. Uncle Chuck and Uncle Terry read the fat newspapers and go for doughnut runs. They get the wrong ones and no one will eat them. They are hurt and say they won't go on a doughnut run again. But they do.

Uncle Chuck brings his office to the beach. He is a lawyer, but tells everyone else not to ever be one. In his free time he likes to ride his bike, win at volleyball, and count beach towels.

My aunt Nanny is the funniest of all. She loses her glasses on the first day and spends the rest of the vacation going from house to house looking for them. She wears her sunglasses at night until she finds them. She looks funny. She likes beach hats.

Getting to see my family is fun. I like this tradition of Camp Beach!

Hillary Klug, elementary school

Family Heirlooms, Family Memories

Rings, watches, even school bells become part of a family's tradition when they are passed down through the generations. These tangible links with the past help build respect for treasured objects while keeping family history alive.

In my family, we have an antique ring that is passed down to the firstborn girl in each generation.

The ring was bought around 1888 by Lily, a nice of my great-great-grandfather, Hiram. Lily was the firstborn girl in her family. She bought the ring for her daughter, Gladys, who was Lily's firstborn girl. Gladys was a very spoiled girl. She was given everything she wanted, but she wouldn't take care of the things she had. The ring Lily bought her was very expensive. She was afraid that Gladys would get careless and lose the ring, so she asked my great-grandmother Jane if she would take care of it and continue the tradition of handing it down to the firstborn girl. Jane agreed.

Jane wore the ring for a little while until my grandmother, Janet, was old enough to wear it. My mother, Kim, was the next to wear the ring. I am a firstborn girl, and when I am old enough, I will be able to wear it.

I hope that I too will have a girl one day so she can be a part of this family tradition.

Melissa Kennerly, middle school

Today started off as just one of those days until about eight o'clock this evening when my nephew, Brandon, was born. This was a very special day for my entire family because my great-grandfather, who passed away in 1980, bought gold pocket watches for each of his living grandchildren to have when they were older. In addition, my grandfather left one last wish that his personal pocket watch, which was given to him by his great-grandfather, would go to his first great-grandchild. He also left a small note inside, which said, "I hope that you will cherish this watch as much as I did when it was given to me by my great-grandfather. Now it is a part of a new generation and I hope that it will be passed down to your first great-grandchild and continue to be passed down for many generations to come." One day when Brandon is old enough to realize the value of this special gift, we will present the watch to him and tell the special story behind it.

Joni Rouse, middle school

— —

There have been a lot of teachers in my family for generations. Two of my great-aunts and my great-grandmother were teachers. They taught back in the days when there was a one-room schoolhouse and the teachers had to ring a handbell to start classes.

My great-grandmother saved her handbell so that she could pass it down to her oldest daughter. Her oldest daughter is now my grandmother. Not long ago, my grandmother passed the bell down to her oldest daughter, my aunt Donna.

Donna has been a teacher for twenty years. She is very proud to have the bell. To Donna, the bell represents generations of hard work and dedication in her family. She is proud to know that one day she will be able to pass the bell to her only daughter, Lindsay.

Teaching and the passing down of the school bell is a tradition in my family. The school bell is part of my family's past. It is nice to have the tradition of passing on the bell in my family.

Blair Keith, elementary school

Family Fun Nights

The importance of having a traditional family time together, whether it be once a week or once a year, with both parents or just one present, cannot be overstressed. Not only is it a tradition, it can spawn many other traditions.

But how can you make this an uninterrupted time when it is hard enough to get the family together? Because I was a working mother and welcomed the excuse to eat out, often our family-talk-things-over night was combined with supper out. But for those who stay at home, Jessica Peak's mother makes a tape for the answering machine that says, "Sorry, it is Family Night at the Peaks. If you will leave your name and number, we will be happy to return your call as soon as possible." Follow that suggestion and you may even inspire your friends to consider keeping a family night.

I have a family with many traditions, that's because I have a large family! The one I want to tell you about is Friday Family Fun Night. My whole family likes this tradition.

Last Friday night we played blindman's bluff. Even my baby sister laughed when we played that game. We also play charades or maybe the telephone game. My favorite is treasure hunt. My parents set up clues all over the house, inside and out. Then my sister, brother, and I go and find the clues. A funny place for a clue is Dad's chest because he takes off running. Yes, Family Fun Night is *fabulous!*

Joshua Scott Strnad, elementary school

Girls' Night Out is the time I spend with my mom once a year. It is very important to me because I don't get to spend a lot of time with Mom. She works two jobs, and I sometimes don't get to see Mom at all during the day. Every year we go out together. We go to the movies and then to Pizza Hut. While we eat, we talk about my problems. This makes me feel real special. I know she cares. Family traditions have a great influence on me and my life.

Gilda Brockington, elementary school

Every Saturday morning at about 8:00 A.M., my dad and I go out to eat breakfast at Sunrise Biscuit. Sunrise Biscuit makes the best biscuits in Henderson. At least, I think so. My dad says that Saturday mornings are "just for the guys," and I think he enjoys taking me out for breakfast. We have tons of great memories.

James T. Jenkins, middle school

We have lots of traditions in our family. The one I like best is the mother-daughter cookie party. My mommy and I have this party for our friends every year around Christmastime. We have done this for three years now. This is how it works. Each of my friends and their mommies make three dozen of their favorite Christmas cookies. They bring all of these cookies to my house. We put one dozen on the table to share with everybody. We divide the other two dozen cookies into groups and put them into beautiful Christmas bags. Each girl takes home a sample of all the different cookies. Last year we made snowball cookies that were *great!* Yum! Yum! My friends really dress up for this party. They look so cute. My mommy's friends dress up, too. I am really looking forward to this year's cookie party!

Alexandra Smith, elementary school

If you don't have a family tradition, "Get one!"

Our family tradition is called Solo Time. We have Solo Time at Christmas, Thanksgiving, Easter, and other holiday dinners.

Our whole family participates in it. Even from far away. Everyone loves Solo Time, especially my mother, because she likes to laugh at me and my brother when it comes our turn. We usually sing my favorite songs, "Silent Night" or a gospel song.

One of my daddy's brothers plays the flute, and my grandmother's sister plays the guitar and piano. I'm also learning to play the clarinet and organ.

My grandmother likes singing "How Great Thou Art." My other grandmother doesn't sing because she is too shy.

After we finish and everyone has sung a song except my grandmother, we talk about how each other is doing. My family especially wants to catch up with my uncles who live far away.

I hope you have enjoyed my family tradition. Traditions sure are fun.

Selena Fay McLellan, middle school

— —

Do you ever need to talk to someone in your family? Well, if someone in my family wants to talk, we wait until Monday night when we have a family meeting. We can always talk about anything that bothers us or we feel needs to change. This might be about earning allowances, spending more time together, doing something on the weekend, or just getting out more. You can always ask what you need to know and get straight answers from my parents. Once I know my family has listened to me, I'm always in a great mood. Family meetings are a great tradition that work for me!

Sarah Hinson, elementary school

— —

Our family tradition that I like the most is when we light the fireplace for the first time in the fall. We all gather around the fireplace and read Bible stories and later we listen to Christmas music. That let's me know that Christmas is near.

Dad puts logs in the fireplace and newspaper to build a fire. We enjoy the crackling sound the logs make.

Mom prepares hot cocoa with marshmallows for everyone. We turn off all the lights and lie by the fireplace in our sleeping bags while Mom or Dad reads to us. Sometimes we take turns reading.

Puffy, the cat, sits nearby while we listen to the stories. We hug and pet Puffy and cuddle her.

I have a wonderful family—my mom and dad, two sisters, and me. Sometimes my grandmother joins us around the fireplace. I also have a dog named Chauncey. We are one big happy family when we sit by our fireplace.

After the fire dies out, we hug, say our prayers, and go to bed.

Jeffrey Lamar Rodgers, elementary school

Begin Early

How do you create a love for books and a respect for Mother Earth? You begin the family tradition written about by middle school student June Javens. Reading June's piece brought to mind this charming poem which should melt every father's heart.

I can't wait till bedtime, my favorite moment of the day. Every night my sister and I make our bedding in the living room. We make herbal tea and get any cookies my dad has bought. Then my sister and I pour the tea in nice ceramic mugs with sayings on them like "Live each day to the fullest."

We bring the cookies on paper plates and put them next to the tea in the living room. Then we yell, "Dad, we're ready!"

Dad settles in his armchair, takes a sip of tea, and begins to read Tolkien's books. This has become a tradition. He started with *The Hobbit,* but now we are in *The Fellowship of the Ring.* I like Tolkien's books because the setting is a distant time and place.

It's a cozy feeling to be snug under blankets during winter with a fire going, sipping fragrant herbal tea, listening to the continuing tale of Middle Earth. At times the book is so suspenseful that I jump up and disturb the reading. My dad always seems not to read enough. We usually beg for more. I wish my dad could read on and on.

June Javens, middle school

➤ *Father's Story* ➤

ELIZABETH MADOX ROBERTS

We put more coal on the big red fire,
  And while we are waiting for dinner to cook,
Our father comes and tells us about
  A story that he has read in a book.

And Charles and Will and Dick and I
  And all of us but Clarence are there.
And some of us sit on Father's legs,
  But one has to sit on the little red chair.

And when we are sitting very still,
  He sings us a song or tells a piece;
He sings "Dan Tucker Went to Town,"
  Or he tells us about the golden fleece.

He tells us about the golden wool,
  And some of it is about a boy
Named Jason, and about a ship,
  And some is about a town called Troy.

And while he is telling or singing it through,
  I stand by his arm, for that is my place.
And I push my fingers into his skin
  To make little dents in his big round face.

Many different types of family traditions have been passed down
through the centuries. My immediate family, which consists of six
children and two adults, has many traditions that are enjoyed and
appreciated by all. Some are Christmas, Easter, Thanksgiving, and
other major holidays. We also like to go to church together on Sundays
and buy each other Christmas and birthday gifts. All of these are
important, but above all I believe that reading every night is one of
the most important traditions in my family.

My father and mother read to me every night from the time I was
born until I could read on my own, which was long before kindergarten. Now I read on my own every night before I go to bed and in my
spare time. I enjoy reading, and do not consider it a chore, but rather
a privilege. On the long road to a good education that lies ahead, I
will continue to read to gain new knowledge and understand about
life. This is my heritage, and I will do my part to pass it on to the
next generation.

Rebekah Griggs, middle school

The Comfort of Family Traditions

*Family traditions do not have to be "monumental," Donna Culton, a high
school student, reminds us. They can be comforting and reassuring. They can
even help to build our confidence in uncertain times. Could there be better
evidence that we should begin our traditions early and keep them through life?*

My mom calls my brother in from his outside play with a bellowing
holler. Dad reluctantly turns off the TV and ventures into my room to
get me off the phone. One by one we trickle to the dinner table and

fall haphazardly into our chairs. Mom gently reminds us that she is not our slave, and we grudgingly form a four-man line to pile food on our plates buffet style.

Once we've digested a few morsels, life starts to return to our sullen faces. Slowly we loosen up and someone breaks a smile. As the meal proceeds we each begin to share the events of our day and humorous stories sure to make everyone else roll with laughter. The climax is reached when we are laughing, talking, and eating all at once.

There you have it. That is our family tradition and we do it every night. It may not seem monumental, but after a day of trials and pressures it is nice to feel loved.

Life may seem to roll onward and never let up, making us feel lost or scared, but I have an escape. Once a day, I'm reminded that I'll never be alone, and that no matter what happens, I'll always be a part of a unit, a structure, a love—a family.

Donna Culton, high school

➤ ➤

February, in my opinion, is the dreariest month of the year. It seems to be neither winter nor spring. Rain mists continuously down upon the world. It is no longer frigid outside, with melting snow leaving the ground bleak and damp. No birds sing, as all nature seems to stand still, waiting for February to pass. This month, the shortest of the year, takes the longest to disappear. When March finally arrives, everything awakens and rejoices. Birds return home, flowers bud, and faint green leaves appear on the trees once again.

My family plans a picnic at the end of each February to celebrate its passing. As we set out through the woods behind our house, we spy animals awakening from their long winter sleep. We walk until we get to our special place by the creek, and sit down under an ancient tree.

Years ago, someone in love carved their initials in its bark. Rays of sunshine filter softly through the branches over us. We spread out blankets beside the creek, admiring its foamy white and crystal clear surface. We are content that spring is finally here.

Kimberly Sanders, middle school

➤ ➤

July 19 is my favorite day of the year, except for Christmas. That is the day we have the Miller family reunion. Relatives from all over the country come to Millers Hollow in Kentucky where most of them grew up.

We have the reunion in a beautiful meadow where the old log cabin where my grandpa was raised sits. While the grown-ups are preparing the feast, the children go swimming in Millers Pond.

It's really exciting seeing everyone and how much they change year after year. Some can't make it every year, but when they do, they usually have changed a lot.

I usually eat so much, you would think it was Thanksgiving dinner.

After the feast, we all sit around and the elders tell us stories about the old days. To me, this is the best part of the day.

I sit and try to picture what it would be like "living in the old days," as my grandpa says. I think this is the part of the day everyone looks forward to. The silence is great as the one telling the story speaks.

Days like this make life special.

Leia Gallagher, elementary school

The Human Pyramid is a recording of our family's ups and downs, literally! The setting is my grandparents' backyard, where at every family gathering for the last twenty-five years, we take time out to form a human pyramid.

We group according to weight class, which varies from year to year. The featherweights at the top eventually drop down to the heavy-weight bases. The lightest of us all crowns the top.

The mood is jovial. It is a time of hugs and occasional bickering, when a former lightweight has eaten his way down to basehood.

Our pyramid serves as a photographic time line of our family, past and present. Each year another edition is placed in our photo album to re-create the day for posterity.

The tension rises as I prepare for my ascent to the peak. I remind myself not to look down or risk plunging to my death. Will I ever make it to the top of Mount Cellulite?

To me, this tradition has helped us, as a family, bond and laugh together. It gives us a common link when sometimes we may be drift-ing apart because of distance, personality conflicts, and fast-paced lives!

William Isenhour, high school

"You are special today" is a quote written on a red plate that each member of my family has eaten dinner off of at one time or another. The special occasions range from winning a game to having a birthday to being inducted into an honor society to being accepted into college. There is a wam feeling you get when you realize how much family support means to you. The red plate has come out when something hasn't gone your way too, to make sure you know the rest of the family still believes in you. I always enjoy seeing "the plate of plates" appear at the table, whether the occasion is for me or another family member. I am looking forward to continuing this special tradition in my future family.

Bridget Busby, middle school

Tomorrow we will follow our family tradition of going to the state fair in Raleigh, North Carolina. Thirty years of my daddy's life, and all of my life, we've gone to the state fair. He always uses his birthday money.

I can already smell the hot dogs, onions, and livestock. I can feel my little sister's sticky hands and the cotton candy in her hair. I can already hear my daddy fussing about finding a parking space and throwing money away on rides. I can taste the delicious funnel cakes with white powder piled up like snow. I can see the double Ferris wheel touch the sky while people scream and laugh.

After we walk about ten miles and the night chill makes us put on our coats, which Mom has held all day, we head toward the car. My parents will argue about which gate we came in. Daddy will carry my little sister and moan about his feet, head, and back hurting.

Daddy will say that we'll skip the fair next year, but that doesn't worry me because he is always the first one to say something about going.

It's a family tradition!

April Holly Cannady, elementary school

Times Change, Traditions Change

We look to the older generation to carry on our family traditions. Sometimes, without our knowing it, our elders may have changed their own ways, as David Godley recounts in this humorous story about his parents and his family's new family tradition.

A few years after my parents were happily married, my father had some socks with holes in the toes. He asked my mother to darn them, but she didn't know how.

"I will ask your mother to teach me how to darn socks," she told him.

The next time they went to my grandmother's house, they carried the socks.

"Granny," Mother said, "can you teach me how to darn socks?"

"I'll be happy to teach you how I darn socks," said Granny. She took the socks, walked to the trash can, threw the socks in, and said, "Darn socks!"

Because of my grandmother, we still darn socks the same way today.

David Loyd Godley, elementary school

So what do you do these days when the family grows up and moves away? Not everyone goes to the old homestead for a family reunion. You might want to try what my longtime friends, the Weinsteins, did and find a "park."

It's nearly time to pack for "Charlotte Park," a child's name for our family togetherness.

Our trips began when our young daughters became scattered and we looked for ways to get together for ordinary weekends as well as holidays. We located a spot nearly halfway for each of us—the growing city of Charlotte, North Carolina, which in no way resembles a park. A rented motel room and picnic-style Chinese food made a weekend trip easy enough for all of us.

The girls married. We wondered how each new son-in-law would take to these "Charlotte Park" weekends. We added some popcorn, TV ball games, golf matches, and a few more motel rooms.

When the first two grandchildren came along, we snapped photos, passed around the babies, and baby-sat while frazzled new parents snuck out for a few hours. We invented motel games like, Hey, You Guys! requiring only two lively two-year-olds and an empty closet.

The trips to Charlotte now come every few months. Our daughters, once little girls themselves, have grown even closer in adulthood. Their husbands are learning to appreciate each other's strengths and differences. And we grandparents get to bask in the glory of family.

But the biggest mark of success came when three-year-old Matt began to cry, "Mommy, I don't want to go home. I want to stay here. I love Charlotte Park!"

Harriette S. Weinstein

THE YOUTH OF AMERICA IS THEIR OLDEST
TRADITION. IT HAS BEEN GOING ON NOW FOR
THREE HUNDRED YEARS.

Oscar Wilde

CHAPTER 18

Food and Drink

LIPS SMACK, EYES FLASH

~ The Tail End Tale ~

*EMYL JENKINS

There's little question about it. Having spent years gathering, reading, and sorting through traditions, I'm quite sure that Thanksgiving is the most American of all of our traditions and Christmas has the largest number of traditions associated with it. But the one tradition story I was told the most times is that of the roasting pan. I heard it first from my cousin's young daughter, Melissa Mathews. Since then, I've been asked, "You do know about cutting off the end of the roast, don't you?" more times than I can count. Just in case you haven't heard it . . .

Seems a little girl was watching her mother prepare a roast. As her mother proceeded to cut off the end of the roast, the child asked, "Mother, why do you cut off the end of the roast before you cook it?"

465

to which the mother matter-of-factly replied, "Oh, you always do that."

Realizing that there really was no good reason for why she did it, other than the fact that *her* mother had always cut off the end of the roast, the mother asked her mother, "Mother, why do you cut off the end of the roast?" The grandmother replied, "Oh, you always do that." But no more had she answered than she realized she didn't know why she cut off the end of the roast other than the fact that *her* mother had always done it.

And so the grandmother asked her mother, "Mother, why did you always cut off the end of the roast?"

"Because," the great-grandmother replied, "the roast was too big for the pan."

If that isn't enough evidence of how important culinary and dining traditions are, think about the notes scribbled in the well-worn cookbooks that are passed down through a family: "Aunt Margaret's best pound cake" or "Papa's favorite chicken fricassee." Recipes are legacies in their own right.

Add to that the place food has in every type of traditional celebration and there is little question that some of our favorite memories and traditions can be traced to the dining room or the picnic table, from the christening party to the funeral wake. In fact, preparing the funeral food to take to a friend's home when there has been a death in the family remains one of the very oldest and most important traditions in my part of the world, the South. It is comparable to the covered dish church dinner of old. And the more rural the setting, the bigger a deal is it.

I will always remember the events surrounding the food when my mother-in-law died in 1972. A paralyzing February ice storm compounded our sorrow and complicated our necessary travel from Raleigh, North Carolina, to her home in southern South Carolina. We were grasping for any cheer we could find.

"At least we'll eat well," my former husband, Clauston, said, choking back his grief.

That's what he thought!

It's true that when we arrived at his mother's old home place in that tiny hamlet, now lived in by his uncle and aunt, we found that the neighbors had outdone themselves.

The hunt board truly was a groaning board. It sagged in the middle under the weight of ham biscuits, bowls filled with rice, greens, and pinto beans, a rump roast and an eye of the round, every variety of casserole—each with the cream of mushroom soup delicately crisped and browned around the edges, rows of coconut, caramel, and chocolate cakes and pecan, fruit, and chess pies.

Rounding out the scrumptious smorgasbord was the usual complement of watermelon, mustard, and orka pickles and a rainbow of congealed salads—lime, lemon, and mandarin orange, plus cheerful red tomato aspic garnished with paper-thin olive slices.

The appropriately named "comfort food" feast would be waiting for us after the dreaded church and graveyard services. But when we returned to the house, the spread had disappeared. In its place, on the kitchen table no less, were a couple of platters of sandwich-meat sandwiches on white bread, a plate of brownies, and a carefully counted-out selection of salad squares.

"What happened to the *food?*" the family moaned in unison.

"Oh, I put it up in the freezer," Aunt Mattie Mae replied matter-offactly. That smart woman, the aunt-by-marriage, wasn't about to let a swarm of her in-laws devour the food she could ration out for suppers for months to come!

Years later, the family still walked past that freezer, paused, and sighed.

Remembering this, I began thinking. In these days of memorial services held weeks, sometimes months, after the dear departed has been buried, what is going to happen to the tradition of funeral food? After all, as Maryln Schwartz told the world in *A Southern Belle Primer,* the proper Southern belle not only has at least one good black dress, she also keeps a store of three casseroles in the freezer "so if someone passes on unexpectedly, she's got enough turkey tetrazzini to cover any event."

In truth, Southerners have no lock on funeral food. Its origins go back through the centuries to all countries and all religions.

In America's Colonial days the custom was to serve wine and "funeral biscuits" after the burial service, a tradition brought from England. But those were no ordinary biscuits. They were more like ginger-flavored cookies than biscuits, and they were symbolically decorated for the occasion with roses (life snipped in the bud), plumes (black plumes on coaches and horses signified a funeral procession), roosters (representing resurrection), hearts, cherubs, and even hourglasses. These shortbread-like delicacies were so much a part of the funeral tradition that eighteenth-century bakers working in large metropolitan areas advertised these specialties.

By the later nineteenth century, a more generous funeral table had become the vogue, especially when families living far apart returned home when there was a death. They had to be fed, so the neighbors pitched in by bringing favorite dishes.

In the Pennsylvania Dutch country that meant Funeral Pie, or "Rosina Boi." According to John Hadamuscin, the author of *Sweet*

Indulgences and *Home for Christmas,* the Amish were particularly fond of pies and this one could be made year-round because boxed raisins were always available.

Funeral pie remains such a staple in the Northeast that John reports often there are five or six funeral pies on the table. This made me wonder what would happen if a family got five pies and no meat or, in the South, all biscuits and no casseroles?

I called John Edgerton, author of *Southern Cooking* and a staunch Tennessean, to get his opinion of today's funeral food offerings. John said he has given the subject of funeral food so much thought that he's come up with a homemade tongue-in-cheek hypothesis that goes something like this: You can measure the esteem of the deceased by the food selection that is brought to the home.

To support his theory John admits that when someone he really cares about dies, he would not dare take a Styrofoam container of store-bought barbecue around to the house. That is when he whips up his favorite pound cake and makes a topping of peaches and cream or raspberries or strawberries, or another one of his favorites, Pecan Bourbon Cake.

But not everyone has John Edgerton's time, talent, or philosophy. No need to despair, John says comfortingly. A gift of funeral food given in the spirit of "helping out" rather than tickling the palate is another option.

He remembers that when his father-in-law died, one of the most thoughtful gifts was a pound of bacon, a dozen eggs, a dozen biscuits, and a pound of coffee, "so nobody would have to worry about breakfast." That, Edgerton says, really goes to the heart of the matter of funeral food—caring and sharing.

Will D. Campbell sums up that generous spirit in *Brother to a Dragonfly:* "Somehow in rural Southern culture, food is always the first thought of neighbors when there is trouble. Taking a gift of food is something they can do and not feel uncomfortable. It is something they do not have to explain or discuss or feel self-conscious about. It means, 'I love you. And I am sorry for what you are going through, and I will share as much of your burden as I can.' "

Still, there are certain social parameters every Southerner observes, even while sharing another's burden, and no Southern belle or gent would be caught dead taking a barrel of Kentucky Fried Chicken to a grieving family. You see, in the South it has long been a custom for the funeral home to present the family with two memorial books: a Register, which the guests sign, and a Food Book. For those unfamiliar with it, the Food Book is the equivalent of a bride's gift book. It has numbered lines for the name of the dish and the person who brought each dish, along with a removable numbered sticker intended to be put on the bottom of the corresponding container.

This procedure was intended to facilitate returning the right container to the right person. But as anyone who has ever helped out in the kitchen when there's been a death in the family knows, this sticker method is a great help in the secret taste test that goes on behind closed doors. Furthermore, no matter how great original-recipe KFC tastes, somehow having future generations know that you were the one who brought it just doesn't seem de rigueur—at least in the South.

And the rest of the country?

"Well, when I told a lady from California about our funeral food," Edgerton said, "she insisted that if anybody brought food to the family out there it would be considered gauche."

That sentiment was echoed by my Colorado friend and author, Diane Mott Davidson. It seems that funeral food in the Rocky Mountains is ordered from a caterer and delivered, Domino pizza–style, to the house. Diane, an intellectual and frustrated analyst at heart, but a great mystery writer, explained the benefits of this procedure. "The caterer, knowing that people are low at this time, prepares food which provides the grieving friends and family the chance to work out their emotions. Funeral goers need action food, not passive food," she said. "At a christening, everyone is happy and opening presents, so you serve prepared sandwiches or brownies. But at a funeral you want foods that require piling on—like fajitas or strawberry shortcake."

Diane ought to know. The protagonist of her popular books is Goldy Bear, a caterer who invariably gets caught up in murder capers.

Funeral Pie, Lethal Layers, Bourbon Cake, Chile Relleno Torta? Just what is the perfect funeral food these days? Today, newspapers and TV commercials are full of plan-ahead, do-it-yourself funeral-arrangement ads. Shouldn't your funeral food be included in your plans as well, especially considering the old saying, "Your funeral's your last great party; you just miss it by a few days"?

Think about it. This is one time you wouldn't have to "eat healthy."

With that in mind, but without asking too much from my busy friends—except maybe John Edgerton, whom I will expect to bring both the pound cake and the bourbon cake—here are a few of my choices, along with the obligatory melt-in-the-mouth buttered biscuits and Virginia ham and a heaping bowl of potato salad.

First, there would be Chicken Divan, then Vidalia Onion Cheese Dip. (The dip would meet Diane Mott Davidson's "action food" requirement.) For vegetables, I'd like two casseroles. First there's the standard one-dish, can't-be-beat string bean casserole that even a child, or the world's busiest person, can mix together. Then, because I can't be positive if I'll be going to the Southern side of heaven or not, I'd like for someone to take the time to make a turnip-green soufflé.

And what would a visit to the house be if you didn't find the expected deviled eggs (could this be a pagan throwback to when earthlings offered gifts of food to the gods) and fried chicken? This is where the Food Book becomes really important. Deviled eggs just taste better when they are served in one of those specially designed round dishes with hollowed-out elliptical cups with a crowing rooster in the center. You have to get the dish back. As an extra precaution, many seasoned funeral food bearers dab an identifying dot of fingernail polish (it won't come off in the wash) on the underside of their plates.

Now, about the obligatory fried chicken. I suggest you forget about propriety, swing by Kentucky Fried Chicken, and make your purchase. Then, in the privacy of your own home, pile high the breasts, wings, and thighs on your grandmother's Haviland platter. Now you're ready to pay your respects. Incidentally, since deviled eggs and fried chicken are finger food, they also meet Diane Mott Davidson's requirement for keeping the grieving eaters busy.

Finally, for family and guests who want to nibble but not eat a full-fledged meal (they're still concerned about eating healthy), I'd suggest the cheese straws found at every Southern party, wedding, and funeral. In truth these goodies might be called a twentieth-century version of the funeral biscuits. Cheese straws are particularly great with bourbon, which reminds me of another one of my favorite funeral-food stories.

The year was 1947. Times were still hard following World War II when the revered Jacques Busbee, of North Carolina's Jugtown pottery fame, died in May. His wife, Julianna, asked my mother, a family friend, to sit with her during Mr. Busbee's cremation.

Later, when Mother told some friends of this dubious honor, they, in their Southern way, asked, "What did you take to Mrs. Busbee?" Without flinching Mother replied, "A pair of nylon stockings—they were impossible to get back then—and a bottle of whiskey. You always need a bottle of whiskey."

And, I would add, you don't have to return the container.

~ Sunday Meal with Papa ~

CORNELIA OTIS SKINNER

We complain that we can't get the family together for meals these days. It's really not a new predicament. In the nineteenth century farming fathers often toiled in the fields until the sun set, and since the invention of the automobile, traveling fathers have taken to the road, making it impossible to be with their families for the evening meal. But Sunday was different. Everyone, everywhere held the Sunday midday meal as a sacred family time with Father seated at the place of honor at the table. During the early years of the century, Otis Skinner was a well-known stage actor who was seldom home at dinnertime. While he performed in New York, his family lived near Bryn Mawr, Pennsylania. In the following passage, his daughter, Cornelia Otis Skinner, herself a popular actress and author of Our Hearts Were Young and Gay, *recalled her father's robust and comforting presence on that special family day.*

Sunday meant a large midday meal. And to make it more festive, Father usually brought with him a bottle of claret, of which I would be given a little thimbleful carefully watered. The salad course was in the nature of a ceremony, as Father always mixed the dressing. I can't recall a single meal when he was home, even on occasions of formal dinner parties, when Father failed to mix the salad dressing in a great wooden bowl, patinated with countless rubbings of garlic, slatherings of the best Italian olive oil, and guiltless of the sacrilege of soap and water. In this he tossed and tossed the lettuce until it was soaked and dripping and, as the French have it, beautifully "fatigued." How often in later years have I thought with longing of Father's salads when there has been placed before me some gag-worthy woman's-club concoction of fruit, mint jelly, and grated nuts, topped off with a maraschino cherry and chilled in the icebox to tastelessness, which is, I suppose, one thing in its favor.

Evening supper was generally oyster stew, or Father's favorite after-the-show meal, a bowl of crackers and milk. Then, for a brief time, he'd read aloud from Grimm or Hans Andersen, and as I grew sleepy he'd lift me up and carry me piggy-back up the steep cupboard staircase, tuck me into bed himself, and hear my prayers. Then he'd blow out the candle and say, "Goodnight, Person," and go back to Mother and the sweet-smelling fire, and I'd lie listening to the comforting drone of their voices. . . .

⤙ Let Us Break Bread Together ⤚

JANICE HOLT GILES

Henry and Janice Giles built a home and life together in Knifley, Kentucky. From there Janice wrote columns and books that captured their rural life. This "around-the-table" excerpt gives us an insight into people, traditions, and ways that we could not have gained had Thanksgiving dinner not brought these diverse, but well-intended, neighbors together.

This was Thanksgiving week.

As we all gathered around the traditional turkey, I imagine that most of us remembered to be grateful for the big and important things, such as freedom and health, the love of family and friends, and enough of this world's goods that we are not in want. I gave thanks for those things, too, but there are also some very special things which give my life added richness.

For the twinkle in my husband's eye. I take for granted his love, for in a good marriage love is something so basic and unseparable that it is hardly necessary to speak of it. It speaks for itself and like food and sleep and breath, it is always there. But it is a happy boon that my husband should have so grand a sense of humor. That his everyday speech should be so pungent with it and his wit that it is a constant delight to me, that we should often laugh together. It makes him a very special companion. It also smooths over some rough places and takes even unkindnesses to him or to me in good stride.

We suffered an unkindness on Thanksgiving Day, which our humor turned aside and made nothing of.

We had such a big feast that it was really a banquet. The turkey was enormous. We had dressing and giblet gravy and sweet potato pudding and cranberry sauce and mashed potatoes (smashed potatoes, as Scotty calls them), a green salad and celery and olives and pumpkin pie.

It was too much for us, but one cannot really cook a small Thanksgiving dinner. About the middle of the morning we said, "Why don't we invite every lonely person in the neighborhood to have Thanksgiving dinner with us?"

As you know, there are always people who live alone, especially on our ridge—they are old and their families have died, or they are widows and widowers. So Henry got the big old black Buick out of the garage and went up and down the ridge and collected up the people. There were Henry's old Uncle Milt Giles, the patriarch of our branch of Gileses, and Betsy Ann, his wife, both quite old now, whose children are all living "off," and could not come home for Thanksgiving.

There was old Jake Bottoms, whose wife is dead and whose children are also grown and could not be with him. There was old Jim Corbin, who is almost blind, who never married and who, since his mother died, lives entirely alone in a tiny little house on the other side of Jake's place.

There were Mrs. Jenkins and Lizzie. Mrs. Jenkins is a widow whose husband has long since been dead. Lizzie has never married. They are very poor and because Mrs. Jenkins is mortally afraid of fire they are almost always cold during the winter because she will not have a big enough fire to keep her house warm.

We told them all to "come as they were." So the men wore their nice, faded overalls and clean shirts. Like James Agee, I think faded blue overalls are the most beautiful clothing any countryman can wear. The blue is soft and the overalls are so free and comfortable.

But Mrs. Jenkins, Lizzie and Betsy Ann put on fresh aprons. We are ridgerunners, you know—foothill Appalachians. The apron is the badge of the Appalachian woman. If you visit me in my home, catch me unexpectedly, you will find me wearing an apron. I am definitely an "apron woman." But one must always put on a fresh one to receive guests, or to visit. I was honored that Mrs. Jenkins and Lizzie and Betsy Ann wore their best and newest aprons. And so did I.

They all enjoyed the dinner, ate hugely, and we enjoyed having them. The unkindness came at the beginning of the meal when Henry asked Uncle Milt to say grace—or ask the blessing, as it is said here. He prayed very sweetly until the very end. Then he asked God to forgive Henry and me for "not being Christians." "They know not what they do, Lord," he said, "forgive them."

Henry and I are not orthodox ridge Christians, that is, we are not "Bible Christians." I have been a long time learning that Bible Christians do not believe in denominations. They can find nothing in the Bible which says there shall be Baptists, Methodists, Presbyterians and, especially, Catholics. Bible Christians, therefore, believe it is a sin to belong to a denomination or church. To use any kind of church literature except the Bible is a sin, because that is "adding to the Bible" and at some place in the Bible, in Revelation I believe, there is a group of verses that says definitely that adding to or taking from the Bible is a sin which condemns one to hell.

Few people, even the missionaries who have come into this country, understand this ingrained belief of the Kentucky mountaineers, for they are inarticulate about it. "The Bible says"—and this is their creed, their theology, their faith.

In a way they do have a point. They say Jesus did not say, "Repent, be baptized and follow me through the doors of a church." The *people,* they say, are the church. One must repent, confess one's sins, be baptized. Then one has been saved and is a Christian. But his name is on no church roll and on no account will he have it there.

They say, too, that where "one or two are gathered together in my name, there am I." And they are right, there, too. They do have a building down the ridge, which they call the "meeting house." It is entirely nondenominational, and anybody at all who feels called on to preach may do so. Mostly the "meetings" are just a gathering of the people, the singing of a few songs together, some praying and testifying. When one of the older people decides they should have a communion service, they have one, but it is not held regularly. And they are always baptized in a running stream.

I was baptized in the Christian Church but later became a Presbyterian. But *I was* immersed, not sprinkled. Henry was baptized in Green River and grew up in the Bible Christian way. But he is considered to have backslid because he drinks a highball every evening.

Uncle Milt is a very good old man, according to his lights. He truly did not think we were Christians. But I felt my hackles rise as he sat at my table. Fortunately I looked at Henry, whose eyes were twinkling. Solemnly Henry said, "Amen," as the prayer ended. And the food began to be passed around without further comment.

Uncle Milt took seconds and thirds of everything and he did pay me a high compliment when he said to Henry, "Your woman is a good cook, Henry. She may be flighty and traipsey, but she's got a good hand with biscuits, makes good coffee and that pie was as good as any I ever et."

Henry thanked him, then added, "My woman is a good woman in every way, sir."

The old man sniffed, belched, got up from the table and said to *his* woman, "Well, Betsy Ann. Time to be goin' home."

Betsy Ann dutifully tied on her head scarf and followed him out the door and six steps behind him down the road to their own home, which is just around the bend from us.

Everybody left shortly. It is the ridge way, I suppose. No visiting after eating. But it was a good dinner, and very little of it was left.

～ The Embroidery Club ～

MARJORIE KINNAN RAWLINGS

At first glance you may wonder what place an Embroidery Club could have in the culinary section. As we know, a meal or food is often only an excuse to get people together. Likewise a club meeting may only be an excuse to eat. In this piece from Cross Creek Cookery, *we are also reminded that deep down we always hope that no one else can prepare our favorite recipes quite as well as we can.*

Mother was some time in being invited to join the Embroidery Club, and I think that Aunt Jenny, a charter member, dangled it before her nose so that she should be properly grateful when the great moment came. After having been several times a guest, Mother's appreciation of good food, her embroidery and her general acceptability were finally approved, and the day came when it was her week to entertain. The ladies used "Embroidery" as an excuse for their weekly meeting, but although a certain amount of cut-work doilies was eventually completed, a certain amount of hand-embroidered pillow-slips, tea-aprons and utterly useless and indefinable knick-knacks meant for Christmas presents, the real purpose of the Embroidery Club was to eat. This they did with a twittering and a gusto that would have left the plates and platters clean if the mode had not been to provide more than could possibly be eaten. Our own suppers or dinners on Mother's day were a continuation of the noon's luncheon, and I looked forward to these with unholy zeal. Mother herself was usually unable farther to partake, ill in bed with a sick headache, brought on by the nervous tension caused by trying to outdo the previous eleven Embroidery Club luncheons.

Let not the suspicious dismiss Mother's egg croquettes and jellied chicken without trying them. . . . I [had the recipe] slipped from under my nose by my dearest friend, whom I had evaded on the subject for the reason that she herself would not go near the kitchen, but left all to any passing cook. It seemed to me that the dish should be made with loving hands or not at all. My friend was caught in the great Kentucky flood and I invited her and her children to stay with me at the Creek until she could return to her home. She brought, on vacation, her cook of the moment, who slyly watched me prepare the croquettes. It seemed that the Louisville Country Club also serves a delicious egg croquette, whose ingredients it guards with its life. My friend expected to return to Louisville and flaunt the dish. I was again delighted when she later reported the theft of my recipe, and that the results were not quite right.

~ Serving Up Your Best ~

Those of us who grew up in the post–World War II era remember how special it was when our families piled into the car and drove to a Chinese restaurant for chow mein. It didn't happen often. First of all, no one ate out more than once every week or two—especially on any day other than Sunday. And then, you had to live in a fairly sizable town for there to be an Asian community to support such a place.

Other than the food of your region—the New England boiled dinner, Southern ham biscuits, Midwestern beef, Northwestern salmon—most Americans only flirted with exotic food when it came in a can or as a frozen TV dinner or, best of all, when it was cooked by a friend who had learned ethnic or regional dishes from a family member. I remember how my parents' friends loved to come to our Virginia home when my Southern mother cooked Boston baked beans and brown bread the way my Yankee grandmother, her mother-in-law, had taught her. To this day I remember everyone watching while Daddy sliced the piping hot brown bread, just removed from the can, with a length of string.

Slowly world-class chefs began waking up our appetites and our appreciation for all sorts of dishes. Soon we knew what boeuf bourguignon, sukiyaki, escargots, and spanikopita were, and experimenting with beef Stroganoff and babas au rhum recipes in our own kitchens. How far we've come.

Now even modest-sized towns can boast of good authentic Chinese and Italian restaurants. We confidently cruise along superhighways, knowing we can easily "run to the border" or drop in at a Jade Garden. But to my way of thinking we've lost something in all this. A part of the fun of travel used to be eating the food of those far-from-home American places we were visiting. It was a real treat to eat at Durgin Park in Boston, Chez Panisse in Berkeley, and Antoine's in the French Quarter of New Orleans, to say nothing of the hot dog stands on Coney Island, the walk-away crab bars along San Franciso's Fisherman's Wharf, and the barbecue shacks sprinkled along every Southern road.

The tradition of regional food is so important that Marjorie Kinnan Rawlings, author of the Pulitzer Prize–winning novel The Yearling, *described the commotion she started when she included a friend's fish chowder in her entertaining book* Cross Creek Cookery:

"I described his fish chowder, 'uncorrupted by alien elements such as peas and tomatoes, that make a poor thing of any New England chowder.' I thought that I had started another War between the States, for half of New England, it seemed to me, descended on me with disturbed and sometimes virulent letters, crying that no true New England chowder used peas and tomatoes. Somewhere in my past I had eaten Manhattan chowder, and had been misinformed as to its background. Let me here make amends, and proclaim that Ed's fish chowder

is almost identical with the best New England chowder—EXCEPT that New Englanders who tried his recipe, from Cross Creek, wrote me humbly that his was as good or better. One generous soul wrote me that her elderly mother, a New Englander from the days of the Mayflower, sighed on partaking of Ed's recipe and said, 'Daughter, this is it. Don't ever bother again with Grandfather's receipt.' Another New Englander, marooned in California, tried it and wrote that passing cars slowed down by their gate as the aroma was wafted on the air, and a multi-motored bomber overhead 'dipped its wings in salute.' "

From Charleston to California, regional fare is one of our most cherished traditions. It defines us as a people and makes the good life even better.

Rice, Grits, and She-Crabs

ROBERT MALLOY

Charlestonians love to eat, and their meals, being based on old-fashioned ways, are plentiful and varied. And Charleston cookery has been applauded by gourmets time out of mind. The city is no place for one on a diet, unless, like Mark Tapley, he wants a chance to come out strong in the face of temptation.

An ancient wheeze holds that the Charlestonians are the Chinese of America because they eat rice and worship their ancestors. Of course it goes only part way, for those who have no particularly brilliant ancestors to worship eat rice too. Everybody eats rice, at least once a day.

This probably gives radical dietitians the horrors, for the Charleston rice, eaten in such quantities, is the polished grain, robbed of all its nutritive mineral-rich coatings, and containing very little else but starch. But the variety of diet crank who insists on eating the shuck along with the corn can shudder if he likes. Charleston will probably go on eating its polished rice until some atomic infernal machine destroys the crop all over the world. And then what would Charleston be like, one wonders.

The growing of rice in the New World originated right in the neighborhood, the grain was long a chief crop, and Charleston knows how to cook it. You pick any discolored grains out of the amount you have chosen to cook—in older days this was a ritual which allowed Negro cooks to rest their bones while sitting out on the back piazza —wash the talc or other coating off in several waters, pour the moistened grain into salted boiling water and boil for about half an hour. Then the rice is put into a colander or strainer, rinsed with hot water, and put over a kettle (or on the back of the stove) to dry.

The result, ideally, is a snowy mass of distinct grains, each separate from the other but each tender and plump. The half-dried kernels, more like popping corn or dried beans, that are sometimes served in Chinese restaurants, are not rice as Charleston knows it, and neither is the gluey, lumpy mass that often results from unskillful cooking or ignorance of what rice should be.

This snowy dish of simon-pure Charleston rice is the Boston bean of the city. It is served for dinner, barring acts of God, seven times a week. Generally speaking, it is covered with gravy. Informally it may be put into soup or moistened with the soup. Charlestonians find it good in various ways; they require only that it be present at the table. If it tastes to you like so much laundry starch, that is your loss. Connoisseurs are reputed to be able, like wine tasters, to distinguish between the various kinds, which ought to prove that rice has a flavor after all.

There are, in addition, all kinds of rice dishes, chiefly in the form of a pilau (which Charleston calls a "pilloo"). As elsewhere the term denotes a flavored or garnished rice, the most ordinary variety being a dish hopped up with tomato sauce and cloves and salt pork. Another pilau is made with chicken giblets and cloves—but there are chicken pilau, okra pilau, shrimp, and squab, and all sorts of fancy varieties. You can even have rice croquettes and some people in Charleston even eat rice pudding. It is traditional that the serving of rice with fish is taboo, probably because of the absence of gravy. But if the rice is really hot there is no better sauce than butter.

Another rice treat, and perhaps the best of them all, is the dish known as Hopping John (and don't ask me why). This is a combination of rice, cow peas, and salt pork or ham, seasoned with a good deal of pepper. The outcome is a walnut brown in color, delicately flavored with the somewhat earthen taste of the cow peas. Possibly the taste has to be acquired but it's worth it.

Second only to rice as a staple is hominy, or what is called in some parts of the South "grits" and in the North "hominy grits." It is usually served for breakfast, although when I was in Charleston in 1946 there was a shortage of it. The essential thing is to have it well done until it is creamy in texture, with the grains well swollen, for this really brings out the flavor. A large lump of butter is placed on the hot hominy and either (a) allowed to melt or (b) stirred in, giving the hominy a rich cream color. The best accompanying food is shrimp, served ice cold. The cold shrimp is taken on the fork, enveloped in the hot, smooth, buttery hominy, preferably from the outside edge (there is a Negro saying "his mouth ain't 'fraid o' nuttin' but hot hominy" which explains this) and then conveyed to the proper spot. Hogshead cheese, eggs, fish, salt roe, steak, chops—anything goes well with hominy; beef à l'Alsacienne (marinated beef served cold) was a favorite with us under the name bouillie-salade.

Breakfast, when I was a boy, used to consist of one such combination, preceded by fruit, and/or radishes, a small dish of oatmeal or other cereal with the usual milk, butter, and sugar, and followed by muffins, hot bread, biscuits, pancakes, or waffles. It usually got us through the day at school until "recess," when we had a sandwich or two and an apple or some cake. On days when we were at home, the eleven o'clock sustainer was often left-over breakfast bread or biscuits or muffins with a liberal addition of molasses.

Dinner in Charleston used to mean the early afternoon meal, anywhere from half-past one to three o'clock, the lateness depending on the social station, customs, or pretentiousness of the family. The official closing of the cotton exchange used to be at two-thirty, which has been assumed to be the reason for the three o'clock dinner custom. It seemed to me that more people were having dinner at night than ever before; Charleston has spread out and not everyone can get home to dinner at midday. Children, naturally, are hungry early and often but it seems to me now that the later you have that dinner the better, for you are not much good for anything the rest of the afternoon with one of those dinners inside and weighing you down. Perhaps Charleston needs, for the sake of energy, to give up that midday meal and substitute crackers and milk. This could be put into effect about as easily as having *Uncle Tom's Cabin* made required reading in the schools.

Every family, of course, has its favorite dinner dishes. One that is especially good with the rice and meat is a baked custard made of boiled sweet potatoes, mashed with milk, cream, eggs, and butter, and flavored with sugar and cinnamon. In my family this was called *gâteau-patate*. There are various chicken and turkey dishes; and the ways of preparing fish are endless.

Charleston, like all seaports, is a great spot for sea food. The local fishermen bring in whiting, porgies, shrimp, and hencrabs. You can buy them at the markets, naturally, but the calls of the vendors used to be a Charleston institution. They varied from simple announcements, such as "Raw swimp!" prolonged and almost like a chant (cf. "strawberries" in other cities), to ditties, such as

> *De porgy walk an' the porgy talk*
> *An' de porgy eat wid a knife and fork—*
> *Por—gee!*

and to elaborate litanies celebrating the virtues of "she crabs," various vegetables, fruit, and delicacies. Most of the vendors used to come from James Island. Their equipment ranged from baskets carried on the head up through wheelbarrows, and pushcarts, to wagons with a huge vari-colored umbrella, decorated with advertising, over the driver's seat. Some of their cries were incomprehensible; one old woman used to call out something that sounded like "Annie buyee." When imitated by the unfeeling young, she proved a dead shot with an Irish potato.

Long ago there used to be a "honey man"—not in the sense of the words as now applied to privy cleaners—and there was a knotted and gnarled mauma named Chloe who exercised the profession of midwife and peddled "groundnut cakes" with a hoarse croak. These chewy disks of molasses and peanuts were once a cent apiece, germs and all.

Labor Day was the occasion on which these vendors had their festival. They paraded down King Street. Of late years the custom has become tourist-infected, with prizes given for the most original entries. In my childhood it was simple and almost primitive. The vendors then were picturesque, some ragged, and plentiful, and they were around from early morning to the middle of the day.

Supper, oddly enough, for a city that eats so fully, was often a slim meal in my childhood. There were a lot of superstitions among the old people concerning what it was proper to eat at night and what would invariably be fatal. Among the reputedly lethal articles of nocturnal diet were such harmless things as cheese and bananas; there was probably just as little reason for the others being included, whatever they were.

And of course there were the fruit cakes and puddings and other desserts, each one a prized recipe, or "receipt," and loyally supported against all others. One particularly horrible dessert was made of ginger and sweet potatoes, cooked to a sticky semi-transparent jelly that looked like solidified sea water. But there were many good sweet things to eat. For instance, the incomparable sugar figs, the red variety that are eaten skin and all, grew virtually wild in Charleston. There were lemon figs, which had to be skinned, and pound figs, great black ones; and there were persimmons, which some people consider insipid. Children used to like Chinese jujubes, which grew here and there. These were tiny russet fruits, the size of a small olive with a similar pit; the pith was crisp and not unlike apple flesh. They were the color of fine polished calfskin. If you really were hard up, there were sugarberries, or hackberries (I am speaking of juvenile appetites now) lying around. Each one was the size of a small currant, and beneath the skin there was a sweet layer about one-thousandth of an inch thick. The rest was a large seed.

A Hearty and Abundant Life

LEE SHIPPEY

It is an interesting fact not generally known in California that much of what is called Spanish cookery there is of Indian origin. The wife of the owner of a "Spanish restaurant" in San Gabriel visited Spain a few years ago and found that the Spaniards knew nothing of tortillas, tamales, frijoles (beans), as the Mexicans cook them, and other foods common to the "Spanish" restaurants of California. In fact, she says that when she went to Stockholm, later in the same tour, she found the Swedes better acquainted with some of those dishes than the Spaniards were, for the seafaring Swedes had picked up many recipes which fitted in well with ship cookery. Corn, beans, rice, and garbanza, peas are all native to Mexico and had to be introduced into Spain. "Jerky," or dried meat, was also of Indian origin. The Indians ground corn with their *metates,* added jerky and chile peppers, garlic, onions, and other native herbs. The seed of the purple sage, wild grapes, blackberries, gooseberries, water cress and several other greens were also native, and the plains Indians dried many of them.

The rancheros had only a light breakfast on arising but returned at nine o'clock for the *almuerzo,* consisting of chile-flavored sausages, fried beans, tortillas, sweet curd cheese, red wine, and, when it was obtainable, coffee. When the mid-day angelus sounded they stopped work, wherever they were, to bow their heads in thanks for having been sustained so long on such scanty rations and then rode home for a lunch of broth, meat and vegetables something like the New England boiled dinner, pigweed salad, tortillas, red wine, or coffee. And fried beans, of course, "beans, more beans and warmed-over beans being the order of every day," according to Mrs. de Packman. From dawn to night, there was never a meal without them. After that they took a siesta and didn't eat anything till the *marienda,* which was afternoon tea in the home, though it was the word for a picnic when outdoors. That collation was often only herb tea (yerba buena or some other wild herb) and little cakes, or a cooling drink made of orange-blossom wine, *chia,* and sweetened water, served with *tostados* (crisp corn wafers) and *conserva* (preserved fruit).

Having held back thus all day, the ranchero had to have a really substantial dinner, especially if he had honored guests, which usually he did. Mrs. de Packman gives us this account of a real *boda,* or formal dinner.

"The guests approaching announce themselves, calling out: 'Hail, gracious queen!' *El patron* and his household in chorus respond: 'Through the glory of God granted.' 'Come in, come in, my good friends!' urges the patron. 'Fortunate are the eyes that look upon you!'

"With open arms the patrón greets his guests and leads them in and the men drink toasts to the ladies with much ceremony while saying: 'I extend my arm. I crook my elbow. By all the living saints, to our hostess!' and then, 'I drink to all.' "

Then came the servants with filled dishes, and here is a sample menu:

Chicken meat-ball soup
Tongue salad and toasted red chile sauce
Roast fowl drenched with red chile sauce
Young chicken stewed with rice and served
with tomato and green chile relish
Leafy green salad
Tamales and enchiladas
Beans
Tortillas
Red wine and white wine
Turnovers, buns, shortbreads, and fruit dainties
Candied pumpkin   Boiled custard
Angelica wine

Maybe it isn't such a wonder that, thus fueled up, they could dance for two or three days and nights. Nor is it surprising that General Vallejo, for whom the city of Vallejo is named, needed fifty house servants.

That gives an idea of the simple, gay, hearty, and abundant life the Americans found when they flooded into California following the war with Mexico. It was a life born of the wealth and prodigality of nature, the abundance of products of the soil. The Americans tried to outdo it with the splendors money can buy, as, suddenly and unexpectedly, the wealth of gold and silver turned bartenders into magnates, pick-and-shovel men into lords of palaces, and at least one humble river-boat clerk into the most fabulous banker in American history, but theirs was a frenzied splendor and a spurious glory as compared to the pastoral days.

Abenaki Clambake

ROBERT P. TRISTRAM COFFIN

One of America's most loved and oldest culinary traditions is the New England clambake. Robert P. Tristram Coffin paints this scene of a truly early clambake, held long before grates and sides of old cookstoves, to say nothing of electric stoves and steamers, took the romance out of the occasion.

The Indians invented the clambake, and they are the authorities on it.

Of course you won't be able to get the Indians for your clambake. For they were the tall, straight-nosed, Greek profiled Abenakis, not the squat-faced, Mongolian-like Indians on the buffalo nickel, still extant in Oklahoma and points west. They were the good-looking Indians on the penny of my boyhood. They were the Greek gods James Fenimore Cooper put into his novels. They existed in eastern North America, in spite of what critics debunking *The Leatherstocking Tales,* and everything else, declare, with a superior snicker. But the last of these Classical Indians disappeared about two hundred years ago.

It's too bad, but you will have to manage without these bronzed assistants, who smelled of bayberry and spruce spills, at your feast. But I will do. For, you see, I have the Abenakis' greatest art in my fingertips. It was passed right on down to me through seven generations of New England clambakers who sat at the feet of the Abenaki masters. I am not so sure but what I am an improvement on the Indians. For I have worked out some extra little flourishes those Indians never knew about. I think I will make a capital substitute.

And the Abenakis' clams are still here in Maine, singing. Singing like larks, at high water. And they are even more important than I or the Indians as the basis for the best seabanquet eaten on any of the coasts of this old world.

When I say clams, I mean clams. I don't mean what New Yorkers miscall clams. I don't mean little-necks or cherrystones. Those round bivalves are nothing but quahaugs. That is the correct Abenaki word for them. They grow on my Maine coast in abundance. We raise most of the ones New Yorkers eat. This is where the best New Yorker round-clams come from.

Quahaugs are all right, in their way. It should be the *au naturel* way, though. They are never to know heat in any form. They are never to be cooked. They are to be eaten raw, palpitating still on their azured shells. Rhode Island cooks them, with the added indignity of vegetables thrown in, and calls the double ruin clam chowder. It isn't clam, and it isn't chowder. Not the kind I or other experts make. It is a kind of vegetable soup, spoiled by a sea-creature whose cooking is a tragic mistake. When quahaugs are cooked, they lose whatever little flavor they ever had, and they become a little bit harder than gutta-percha. Fried or baked, it is the same sad story. A cooked quahaug is the most inedible thing in the world and has about as much flavor as fried teakwood chips. There's a price on Rhode Islanders' heads in Maine. The bounty is about $2.25. All seasons are open.

I myself, if I do say so, am an expert quahaug sheller. Shelling quahaugs is also a secret handed down from the Abenaki. My inexpert friends commit mayhem when they try to open quahaugs. They go at them with a cleaver or a hammer. They startle these naturally shy and retiring creatures, and the pseudo-clams shut themselves up for the duration tighter than the exit-hinges on the Hot Place. It takes me hours to cajole and calm the little things down so I can defrock them gently of their shells. A short knife, resting lightly along the ball of the thumb of the open hand, while I talk with my friends and look else whither, the quahaug placed almost casually but expertly against the blade, a slight, seductive pressure—and the succulent, raw pseudo-clam is lying before your eyes, trembling with surprise in his mauve juice, ready to be swallowed. No shock, no violence.

The quahaug is good raw. As an hors d'oeuvre. That is what the Abenakis used him for. He is a good whetstone to sharpen the appetite for the real splendor to come. So I often open a few dozen of the medium-sized quahaugs—those just old enough to vote—as a prelude to my baked clams.

The clams to be baked may be eaten raw, too. But only the fool-hardy do that. And they strangle and choke, cough and shed tears for hours for their pains. They miss the essential flavor also, for true clams must go through the fires of tribulation to come out their ecstatic best. Real clams are thin and oval, like fragile vases, and you have to mine them deep in the mud. The poor imitations of clams—quahaugs —lie stupidly just under the surface. Anybody can find them. It takes an artist to get the authentic clams.

Getting the clams is an art, let me assure you. You hunt them at low tide. You trace them by the shower of diamonds they send up into the sun at the sound of your footsteps. The clams think you are the flood tide, returning, and the naive creatures expel the seawater they have been perusing for microscopic living food all during the ebb tide and prepare to inhale another houseful of ocean to comb for their next feast. Their greed betrays them to their mortal enemy. Then it is you surprise them. Inserting your pronged hoe well ahead of their fountaining holes, you suddenly turn them up to the light, their umber muscles bulging between their blue-green shells. When you have your clam-rocker full, you set the slatted basket in the tide's way and rock the sand gently from your bushel of coming joy.

I say bushel, but here I am thinking of just myself and a friend or two. For a fair-sized family or covey or drove of friends, you will need to have two or three bushels. There is no moderation when clams are baked my way. Some of my friends have been known to eat a half bushel of my baked clams apiece at one sitting. And they had to continue in a sitting posture a long time. They couldn't get up. But did they mind? Not they!

Next comes the fire. For clams are not to be cooked on any civilized stove. They are edible cooked that way. But it is not the way of genius. Not the Abenaki way. The Abenakis and I cook clams in the open, under the whole high blue and blazing Summer sky, under the blazing sun, and with the wind snowed with a thousand seagulls. It is on a bay where the whitecaps come rolling in from Spain, where bayberry leaves and fir needles scorch in the sun and mackerel-hawks are going over like white arrows, that clams are to be cooked and eaten at their best.

Collect the spars and ribs, rimy with salt, from ancient ships, drift-wood turned to slabs of sheer silver by the tide and the wind, wood that has come in from far places over the sea. With some dead spruce brush, set your heap of driftwood ablaze. Build the kind of fire the Greeks in Homer would build to burn the body of Achilles or Aga-memnon on. Let the wind carry it high to the sky. When the blaze falls, and you have rubies and topazes of living coals left a foot deep, throw yourself into the flooding tide and dredge up armfuls of rock-weed. The rockweed must be growing, you must tear it out by the roots, and bring it in with the sea dripping from it. Heave these green sprays with blossoms of orange balloons growing on them upon your bed of coals. Pile the rockweed on six inches deep. Leave a breathing hole for the fire at one end, so your embers will live under your wet seaweed. Then pour on your bushel of clams, squealing and spurting diamonds of surprise. And after that, throw on new armfuls of rock-weed and cover the clams over deep from sight. Set yourself down by your barrow and let her steam. Shell and eat your quahaugs now if you will. Talk and smoke and sing. You have nothing more to do. Use your nose for your timer. Possess yourself in patience, and wait for the feast to cook itself.

There are foolish-minded people who erect stonewalls and build middens to cook their clams on. There are silly ones who use grates and sides of old cookstoves. They are wasting their time. And no iron should touch the clams. There are people who use a sailcloth over the rockweed, but they deserve hanging. All that is needed is a bed of coals, a pile of rockweed, and clams just out of the Atlantic in between the hot and cool halves of this natural sandwich.

There are misguided souls who chuck into the seaweed ears of corn, lobsters, potatoes, even chickens. They are the effete and degenerate who commit the Unpardonable Sin in the eyes of the old Indians—mix foods. The Abenakis kept their flesh and their fish, their fowl and their vegetables separate. The clams alone are enough. No steamed lobster can hold a candle to a clam steamed in seaweed. Chickens and corn subtract from the feast. Put all your eggs into one steaming basket, and have all your eggs clams. You can have buttered bread if you want to. You can serve it to your more capacious friends, as a safety measure. But I prefer to have my clams unupholstered, untainted by corn, uncontaminated by wheat, pure, essential, alone.

If your whole family is at the shore—and is as large and hungry as mine—or if you have as many friends as I suddenly discover I have when my clams begin to carol in their own juice and fill the whole August day with their fragrance; you will need to multiply your bonfires. Make your beds of coals in a series, timed each a quarter of an hour after each. In this way your clams will mature in a sequence. As soon as your assembled clan have eaten one barrow empty and reduced it to a heap of shells, you can all rise and move on to the next barrow and start right in new at renewing your youth like the eagle's on clams martyred in seaweed.

The steam thickens upon your barrow. An odor of clam juice mingled with the subtle aroma of iodine in the weed, salt, and the magic of old ocean begins to spread out over the world and to enter your brain and your soul.

It is the time. You roll back the roof of your barrow. And a half bushel of bliss lies before you. The shells of your clams are sprung wide. You roll up your sleeves and sail in. Plates are no use, forks are no use. All you need is your fingers. You snatch a red-hot clam, the juice scalds your fingers, but you toss it from one hand to the other, to keep it from burning you mortally, upend the shell and sip the juice from the gaping crack, then rip off the upper shell, seize the lower with your left thumb clamped over the snout, holding it down, and you tear out the golden-brown meat with one snatch of your right thumb and forefinger. The snout comes off on the discarded shell clean as a whistle. You open your watering mouth, tip back your head, and drop down your clam.

There are no words for what follows. It is a song without words. I do not know what happens to that common little Maine clam in there during that half hour in that hot rockweed. Something apocalyptic takes place all right. That clam comes out stellified. It melts on your tongue. Even the black head—which serves merely as a handle to sop your clam by in the melted butter and which has to be bitten off and thrown away when you eat clams steamed in the conventional kettle —even that dissolves at the tongue's touch. I don't know what has happened. But I can say this much. You swallow something that is part deep smoke, part bright blue sky, part the deep blue sea, part the sharpness and zest which is Maine, part that unforgettable and match-less taste of burnt meat. That tender small clam tastes like the elixir of life. Maybe it is the iodine in the rockweed. Maybe it is the very soul of rockweed brought out by fire. Maybe it is the soul of fire. Maybe it is the life in your old ships' timbers that made the coals. Maybe it is the soul of the sea. Whatever it is, it is a taste you will remember all the days of your life, a taste that will haunt you down the years. Now it rocks you to your marrow. And you rock back and forth on your hams in rapture.

You snatch another clam out and another. You have to fight your way in through the reaching arms of your friends. They may bite your fingers in their excitement, mistaking them for clams in the steam that hangs over the flavorsome mound. You may bite them. In this feast no holds are barred. No one stands on politeness. There are no manners, let alone morals. No one consults courtesy. Each man for himself. And heaven help the woman that gets in the man's way!

It is the way the old Abenakis used to eat these same clams baked in rockweed. You squat on your hams as they squat on theirs. You yell as they yelled when a clam spills hot blood down your naked arm. You eat like the wolf, and your pile of shells grows high around you. All along the Maine coast are the mounds of the shells of the ancestors of these clams. The Indians left whole mountains of clamshells behind them as monuments to their happiness. You are adding new foothills to very ancient Sierras of bygone succulence. The Egyptians left their pyramids, the Romans their triumphal arches. But you are adding your stones to a finer monument, a monument to men's worship of the great deity Hunger, a monument to glad Gastronomy.

And, if you have eyes to see such thin, azure substances, you will need only to look around over your shoulder, and there you will behold a whole blue sky full of ghosts of the ancient Abenakis leaning over you, and their thin, thin mouths are watering, and a fire brighter than those of the Happy Hunting Grounds is blazing in their eyes.

I don't know how many hundreds of clambakes I have made in my time. I have made plenty. But each time I sit on my heels at one, the flavor of the clams is new to me, and I eat just as wildly and youthfully as ever. If I had the choice of deaths, I know what mine would be. It would be to eat so many baked clams that I would perish anyway, and then have some merciful friend shoot me over the pile of empty, smoking shells just as I bit into the last clam. But no friend would do that office of mercy for me. He would be too all-fired busy trying to seize that last, last clam out of my fingers to eat it himself!

~ Sugar Time ~

RUSSELL MCLAUCHLIN

Think of a New England winter and images of silvery-gray buckets gathering sweet maple syrup come to mind. This culinary tradition has been part of the life-blood of the Yankee family life since the eighteenth century, especially in Vermont, where a family's hard work was turned into a sweet treat for others' pleasure.

And, when I speak of maple syrup, there comes to my mind any cold, snowy Saturday morning of my boyhood. My grandmother would summon all the young inhabitants of Alfred Street and, giving each a plate, bid him cover the same with snow. Meanwhile, she would have prepared a great kettle of boiled-down syrup, piping hot. And into her big, old-fashioned kitchen we would storm, each with his snow-covered plate, and onto the snow she would ladle great slathers of the steaming syrup. This would congeal into the most delicious candy that anybody ever tasted in all his life.

Cane Grinding Time

J. L. HERRING

Far from New England and the maple trees lie the sugarcane fields of the sunny South. From the wiregrass country of Georgia to the flatlands of Louisiana, sugarcane-grinding time is a two-hundred-year plus tradition that continues today.

It is cane-grinding time in South Georgia, by some miscalled sugar-boiling time—although little sugar is made, and by others called syrup-boiling time, but it is not the syrup that draws the crowds. The cotton has been picked, the corn is in the crib, the potatoes have been banked and with the heavy work of the harvest over, the manufacture of the sugar cane into the year's supply of syrup is made the occasion of a merry making among the young folks.

This is down where the wiregrass covers the sloping hillsides and the pines still murmur and sigh in the passing breeze. The first frost has touched the waving blades of the tall sugar cane and given warning to the watchful husbandman.

First the cane mill, which has lain idle for a year is overhauled. It is a crude affair, two big iron rollers set vertically on a pine log frame. The forest has been searched for a stooping sapling with just the right crook and this is cut and fitted in place for a lever, the lower end almost touching the ground, the upper swinging in the air as a balance. The iron kettle—like the mill rollers a product of a Georgia foundry—is set in a furnace of clay.

Another day is spent in preparation. With wooden paddles, sharpened on one edge, the leaves are stripped from the standing cane. A stroke with a butcher or drawing-knife takes off the top and with an adz or hoe the stalks are cut. Then they are loaded on the handy ox-cart and dumped at the mill.

The first shafts of coming dawn are aslant the horizon and the air is keen and cold when the faithful mule is led out and by means of the plow gear hitched to the lever's end. Then for the animal begins the weary tread-mill round, which lasts far into the night. A lad of the family, too young for heavy work, is selected to feed, and with home-made mits to temper the cold stalks, grasps a cane as the mule is started. Between the slowly turning rollers he thrusts the smaller end; there are creaks and groans from the long unused mill, a snap of splitting stalk and the juice gushes forth. Along a small trough in the mill frame it runs into a barrel, covered with layers of coarse sacking to catch the impurities.

On the other side of the mill the cane pulp (pummy) falls and this is carried off by the feeder's assistant, who also keeps the pile of cane replenished. When there is a kettle full of juice a fire of lightwood is started in the furnace and soon the flames, like a beckoning banner, surmount the short chimney's mouth. As the juice boils the foreign matter arises in scum, and this is carefully skimmed off. Untiring vigilance in the boiling is the price of good syrup. Gradually the color changes from a dirty green to a rich amber and then to a golden red. The aroma arising suggests the confectioner's workshop and soon tiny, bursting bubbles attest that the work is done.

Then help is called and the fire drawn; hastily two men dip the boiling liquid into pails which are emptied into a trough (hewn from a cypress log). As soon as the syrup is out, fresh juice which is ready at hand is poured into the kettle and the work goes on.

As the shades of night fall, the neighbors, young and old, gather, for no man grinds cane alone. True, about as much is sometimes chewed, drunk in juice or eaten as syrup "foam" as the owner retains for his own use, but who would live for himself alone and what matter, so long as there is plenty for all?

The first visit of the young people is to the juice-barrel. There, with a clean fresh gourd, deep draughts are taken of the liquid, ambrosial in its peculiar delicious sweetness. Then to the syrup trough, with tiny paddles made from cane peels is scooped up the foam which has gathered in nooks in candied form.

Then, until the late hours of the night, the older folks sit around the front of the blazing furnace and swap yarns or crack jokes. By the light of a lightwood-knot fire near by the young ones play "Twistifica-tion," "London Bridge," and many kindred games, while on the pile of soft "pummies" there is many a wrestle and feat of strength among the young athletes. The bearded men grouped around the furnace, the steaming kettle and its attendant, from whose beard and eyebrows the condensed moisture hangs; the shouts of laughter from the young merry-makers; the plodding mule making his weary rounds, the groaning mill and gushing juice form a scene not soon forgotten.

In a few days when the "skimmings" ferment—there is cane beer, delicious with its sweet-sour taste, and still later "buck" from the same stuff, now at a stage when only the initiated can appreciate it, ready for the hard drinker or the wildcat still.

⇀ *The Kitchen I Love* ↽

GLADYS TABER

There is little question that the benefits gathered from our culinary traditions extend far beyond the stove or table. We instantly think of the conversation, conviviality, and knowledge that is exchanged during the food preparation and consumption. Many a woman has told me that she learned more about life and her own mother and grandmother, and even her siblings, while helping in the kitchen than she did from any other source or experience.

Gladys Taber, who chronicled her life on Cape Cod in scores of books and articles, shows us how the objects we use to prepare and enhance our food and dining add another dimension to our lives, our tasks, and our outlook on life.

As I was stirring the lentil soup today, I reflected that every woman must have a favorite utensil. I am deeply devoted to a certain wooden spoon. It has worn down at the edges and has a faintly pinky glow from having stirred so many ruby jellies and jams. But I always reach for it, it fits so comfortably in my hand and stirs so well, and it feels like a companion. We have been through a lot together, crises of sticking chili sauce or carrots in a precarious state. I am very fond of the old black iron spider too.

I love the new gadgets, the shining utensils, the smooth modern efficiency, but I still like to have the old friends right there within reach.

Small things can be important anyway. A spoon, a pan, a special dish, they make one's kitchen peculiarly one's own.

Small jobs can be important too. Washing the milk glass would never go down in history as an achievement, but how good I feel after I have done it! I sit down and look at the old corner cupboard and think about the days when the milk glass was made—and all the people who cherished it, and they did cherish it or it would have been broken long ago. The swan compote has the swans forever swimming on their white stream, the lacy edge plates are lacier than ever. And the little log cabin looks as if tiny folks must be inside, snug and happy. The hens look out at the world with a fierce eye as they sit on the woven basket dishes. The little sleighs look as if they were ready to take on passengers and skim over imaginary snows. I can imagine the tiny figures, waving muffs as they glide away.

We used to set the table with milk glass on a dark-green linen cloth to bring out the translucence, but now we are growing lazy. For the milk glass has to be washed by hand, the torrid heat of the dishwasher cracks the lacy edges. After all this is old, and needs gentle warm suds.

So we use the Leeds which is tough in fibre. Steve and Olive have a complete ironstone collection, and this is lovely as well as practical, for the dishwasher cannot crack it. Their dinner table, set by the big window overlooking the trout stream, is beautiful to see for one seldom does see every single thing in a collection. They even use the tall handleless cups for the coffee, and when I hold one in my hand and feel the good warmth coming through, I wonder why anybody ever put handles on cups at all. Olive uses the big tureens with the acorn tops on the covers for her hot dishes, and she even has an ironstone ladle in perfect condition.

Good wine may need no bush, I always think, but good food is enhanced by being served on such lovely dishes.

Connie collects mugs, and this has been a fine idea. She serves hot soups in them, as well as hot chocolate and tea, uses them for chips or bread sticks. Small ones make cigarette holders, a big pinky one holds an African violet. I like best the small ones that say "Remember Me."

Or "I love you." We have a footed milk glass mug which should, by rights, go with hers. It has four little paws for feet, and I cannot imagine how anyone dreamed them up.

We use milk-glass cups to hold pencils, milk glass on the bureaus and the bathroom dressing table, and milk-glass lamps on the mantel. And so even though we don't eat from our collection, we do use it. I feel strongly that a collection should be used. We keep the milk-glass candlestick in constant use and the H-and-L bowls for fruit, and in season, I do bouquets in everything from saltcellars to spoonholders.

Of course, as I say rather often, a collection is only really the memories that go in it. You cannot go in and write a check and own a collection. A collection means to collect. It means piece by piece. It means remember the day we found this in the junk pile at the auction? Remember the dear old ladies that found the matching tiny tureens with one wee ladle? Remember that darling woman who said this piece was her grandmother's but she had only one and it should go with ours?

At its best, it also means you figure the pennies. You give up something to get that swan compote. You save and pinch and squeeze and then proudly buy the eight Gothic plates all at once, all eight.

And oh, the excitement of having one square, blue, wheat-design vase and years later finding a mate in Maine or Vermont.

One piece we have not, and may never have. A friend of ours has it, a long, narrow, covered dish, with a lady's hand elegantly laid on top. On one finger is a ring *with* a green stone in it, and the stone is still there, after all the years of living that hand must have done. I do not covet things, but I wish I could once find one like this.

This friend is a very wise woman. She is the one who started us on the milk glass in the beginning. We had a great deal of illness and sorrow in our families and life had a grey visage for us.

"Collect something," said she, "there is nothing like collecting to revive your interest in life. Try milk glass."

And she helped us find our first small piece. From then on we were so busy scouring around that we got a lot of exercise and had less time to brood over our troubles.

Grandma's Cookie Cutters

The brilliant hues of crimson, orange, and yellow leaves combined with the thin glistening coat of frost I awoke to this morning are sending me a clear message.

It will be sugar cookie time very soon, time for my kitchen to become covered in a thin layer of flour as I measure, roll out dough, and bake. The aromas always take me back to Grandma's kitchen, where I first learned how special cutout cookies were. I reminisce on the seasons past when Grandma came to Mother's and we would bake enough Christmas cookies for our family and friends. The years passed, and one Christmas Grandma gave me her cookie cutters: a star, a bell, a Santa with a pack, a wreath. . . . I then introduced the cookie tradition to two eager small boys. Those first few years we carried on the tradition there were several misshapen cookies hidden under a thick layer of frosting.

This year, as the tradition continues, those small boys are in high school and college, but we will still make Grandma's cookies. They will be sent to North Carolina, Philadelphia, and Buffalo, and kept here for family and friends.

Grandma, the Christmas season just wouldn't be the same without your very special sugar cookies. Thank you.

Jacqueline Grose

It's All in the Preparation

FRANCES PARKINSON KEYES

Despite my incurable love for all things old, I must admit that the gadgets and kitchenware in today's enticingly outfitted gourmet shops are most attractive. Combine the specialty items fashioned from gleaming copper and stainless steel with the memory of succulent dishes we can order at fine restaurants and sometimes I can be sorely tempted. Then I remind myself that my 1941 vintage kitchen is already overflowing. Further, I have no eager culinary assistants to skim and stir. At that point I go home, take down a book like Frances Parkinson Keyes's Dinner at Antoine's, *filled with scrumptious food scenes, and I feel quite satisfied. Come with me to New Orleans where food reigns supreme to enjoy a succulent dish at Antoine's.*

"Well, at last! Here comes the ducks! Keep quiet, all of you, while I watch Roy. I don't want to be disturbed. Remember it's four years since I've seen this."

Roy Alciatore had entered the room and was greeting the guests while his assistants kindled the flames beneath two chafing dishes. Over one of these, the breast filets of the ducks, which had been roasted and carved in the kitchen, were now set simmering. Over the other, a shallow copper skillet, silver-lined, was carefully heated while a lump of butter softened and melted. The gleaming silver device, part of which resembled a letter press, was now moved forward on the sideboard, and as the screw was turned to put more and more pressure on the chopped duck carcasses in its silver cylinder, the expressed juices were caught in a porcelain bowl. Roy skilfully blended these with various wines and spices over the flickering alcohol flame of his burner. Then he added cream and brandy, almost drop by drop; from a tiny pepper mill he dusted a few grains of freshly ground white pepper into the chocolate-colored sauce, just before this was decanted over the filets.

During the ritual, the guests had left the table and crowded about the masterpiece-in-preparation. Now they returned to their places, murmuring their appreciation as the dish was served and the Château Nénin was poured.

"Uncle, it's scrumptious!" Ruth exclaimed. "I'm never going to eat duck any other way again, as long as I live."

"That's a large order. You haven't a duck press, for one thing."

" 'Yes, Virginia, there is a Santa Claus,' " quoted Aldridge sardonically.

"And I'll write Santa Claus to bring me one."

"Can't we concentrate on anything except food?" Amélie inquired. "First we had a long dissertation on *hauîtres Foch,* and now we've had a professional demonstration of duck pressing. I wish—"

~ *Party On* ~

Sandra Johnson LaRouche

Ever noticed how every winter your newspaper carries an article about how to beat the winter blahs? When the Raleigh News and Observer called me last year near Mardi Gras time I replied in a heartbeat, "Put on some Zydeco music, cook red beans and rice, and invite the neighbors over." Had the call come a little earlier, or later, I might have suggested, "Put on some Texas blues, cook a pot of chili, and invite your neighbors over." In my maturity I've learned to keep parties simple. That's a lesson Sandra LaRouche learned the hard way and relates with great humor.

"Many Are Cold But Few Are Frozen" was the opening line in the invitation to one of my first big parties. It was in the decade that brought you fondue pots and flocked wallpaper. Both are making a comeback, isn't that a scary thought?

I had envisioned the evening over and over in my mind. It would be one of those magic moments, everything would be white, silver or crystal—a Buffet Blanc, our annual Twelfth Night Party turned in what would become the legendary January Thaw.

In my daydream the fragrance of one dozen cinnamon-dusted baked apples each studded with exactly twelve cloves would overwhelm guests with the essence of the orchards as I, clad in my spiffy silver panne velvet palazzo pants and tunic, whisked them from the oven.

With a large silver spoon I would place each sizzling apple into the waiting bowl of white wine and frothy eggs beaten with cream. "A culinary triumph, a Medieval masterpiece!" the guests would say. I was creating a Classic Wassail. How could it fail? (Would you like the ways alphabetically or numerically?)

In the daydream, I turn and bow slightly, smiling the smile of a woman who knows she need not spike the ball when she's scored a touchdown. I offer the first cup to Jon, my late first husband. He lifts the cup to me, to our guests, and exclaims looking into it, "What in the hail ails the wassail?"

Oh, no! It isn't a dream! It's real life! This huge crystal (oh, all right, pressed glass) bowl of eggs, apples, and wine has curdled solid, apples rising to the top like some many-eyed monster. Now it no longer matters that my ensemble is silver, soft and sensuous; that the countless crystals, mirrors, snowflakes, and icicles suspended from transparent fishing line and white thumbtacks from our condo ceiling are spinning in the warmth of dozens of white candles, and that the room is sparkling with light like crystal confetti.

Our old round oak table has been transformed into a Cinderella oval, swathed in overlapping remnants of white and silver fabrics—lace, satin, tulle, tucked, pleated and gathered with ribbons, pearls and crystal garlands for this White Night. The buffet is indeed blanc.

The pale pâtés, the egg-white- and sugar-frosted white grape centerpiece, the magnificent galantine of turkey, veal, pork, and beef centered with pistachio nuts and chaudfroid, frosted with a white glaze and trimmed with silver eatable beads—now all for nothing. "What ails the wassail?" becomes the universal chant.

All for nothing now the delicate peeled and poached pears, the selection of cheeses—the Camembert, the huge Gourmandise, the melting Brie with slivered almonds. Alpine stacks of white plates and napkins flank avalanches of Swedish wedding cookies—all so white, so pure—all for nothing. What does ail that damn wassail? It seems to be moving with a life of its own.

You probably think I'm making this up. I'm not. Somewhere out there are about 150 people who were present when this actually happened. They may remember it. I know I do.

Classic Wassail was all that I had planned for drinks—I was inexperienced. Sympathetic guests soon took care of that problem. Actors and some of my more daring Household Finance Company co-workers skimmed the concrete curd from the wassail and proclaimed the drink which seethed beneath to be truly "classic."

Meanwhile on the other side of our cul-de-sac a very small kitchen fire had broken out. The Hazelwood fire brigade responded quickly, only to find that they could not get around the circle because of our guests' cars. This was "not good," explained the firemen.

An extinguisher squelched the little fire, but in expectation of a larger operation the firemen had tapped the hydrant. Rising winds swirled through the circle picking up a fine mist and turned our circle into an Olympic-sized skating rink, an automotive buffet blanc.

The January Thaw was working, in such crowded quarters instant friendships ignited, and soon three Vietnam vets were executing close-order drill on the winter wonderland of our lawn. Meanwhile back in the kitchen my husband was preparing to demonstrate the proper manner of serving a Blue Blazer, yet another "classic." This flaming concoction of spices and hot water also contains high-test bourbon. Jon, working at our kitchen island counter heated the water by candle-light, he lighted the bourbon.

Lifting his arms like a benevolent bishop, Jon began to pour the two liquids back and forth, a shining arc of blue flame linked by two silver mint julep cups at each end, a river of living fire. It was splendid, wild applause broke out.

It would have taken a man with more imagination than Jon to ignore the adulation. He bowed slightly and as he did, the entire Blue Blazer cascaded over his left arm. What a finish!

We put him out quickly, and though he smelled like ten nights in a barroom, he was none the worse for the experience. At this point someone should have taken away our matches, but we were so determined to be trendy that we proceeded with our January Thaw.

At 1:30 A.M. we whipped out the baked and sliced ham, pans of sautéed onions and mushrooms, the inevitable fondue pot filled now with Hollandaise sauce, and oven-toasted English muffins. In the biggest bowl we had, we whipped five dozen eggs into a feeding frenzy and poured it into a pound of melted butter in a huge camping skillet balanced over two alcohol burners.

Jon moved the spume (spatula with a hole in the center) through the creamy eggs, making mounds of gold.

Our friend who was documenting this event insisted that Jon move the operation slightly so he could get a better camera angle. Jon obliged and as the chafing-dish burners were shifted, grain alcohol splashed on the counter and ignited. For about three seconds the entire counter was on fire and then, just as instantly, it was all over. The flash on the camera didn't work, but it wouldn't have mattered because the friend forgot to load the film. So much for documentation. I think I'd better do it all again.

⇀ *Starvation Parties: It Is More* ⇀ *Blessed to Give*

Edward M. Alfriend

It takes a special sort of person to turn tribulations into triumphs. When writing Southern Hospitality, *I read in amazement how, during the bleak days of the Civil War, one family would "read" the dessert receipts—or receipts, as they were called then—after dinner in place of the succulent treats they had had during better times.*

That sad time in our nation's history also created a tradition that, thank goodness, we have no need to carry forth today—starvation parties. Or do we? Read the firsthand account of those events and ask yourself, might this not be a tradition worth re-creating for your favorite charity—a local food bank, the underprivileged, or to raise money for the hungry in warring countries? Think about it. And do notice the last paragraph of the selection: love can always bloom.

For many months after the beginning of the war between the states, Richmond was an extremely gay, bright, and happy city. Except that its streets were filled with handsomely attired officers and that troops were constantly passing through it, there was nothing to indicate the horrors or sorrows of war or the fearful deprivations that subsequently befell it. As the war progressed its miseries tightened their bloody grasp upon the city happiness was nearly destroyed and the hearts of the people were made to bleed. During the time of McClellan's investment of Richmond and the seven days' fighting between Lee's army and his own every cannon that was fired could be heard in every home in Richmond, and as every home had its son or sons at the front in Lee's army it can be easily understood how great was the anguish in every mother's heart in the Confederate capital. These mothers had cheerfully given their sons to the southern cause, illustrating as they sent them forth to battle the heroism of the Spartan mother who, when she gave her son his shield, told him to return with or on it.

And yet during the entire war Richmond had happy phases to its social life. Entertainments were given very freely and very liberally the first year of the war, and at them the wine and suppers were generously furnished, but as the war progressed all this was of necessity given up, and we had instead what were called "starvation parties."

The young ladies of the city, accompanied by their male escorts (generally Confederate officers on leave) would assemble at a fashionable residence that before the war had been the abode of wealth, and have music and plenty of dancing, but not a morsel of food or a drop of drink was seen. And this form of entertainment became the popular and universal one in Richmond. Of course no food or wine was served simply because the host could not get it or could not afford it. And at these starvation parties the young people of Richmond and the young army officers assembled and danced as brightly and happily as though a supper worthy of Lucullus awaited them. The ladies were simply dressed, many of them without jewellery, because the women of the South had given their jewels to the Confederate cause. Often, on the occasion of these starvation parties, some young southern girl would appear in an old gown belonging to her mother or grandmother, or possibly a still more remote ancestor, and the effect of the antique garment was very peculiar; but no matter how limited the host's or hostess's ability to entertain, everybody laughed, danced, and was happy, although the reports of the cannon often boomed in their ears, and all deprivation, all deficiencies were looked on as a sacrifice to the southern cause.

I remember going to a starvation party during the war with a Miss M., a sister of Amelie Rives's mother. She wore a dress belonging to her great-grandmother or grandmother, and she looked regally handsome in it. She was a young lady of rare beauty, and as thoroughbred in every feature of her face and pose and line of her body as a reindeer, and with this old dress on she looked as though the portrait of some ancestor had stepped out of its frame.

Such spectacles were very common at out starvation parties. On one occasion I attended a starvation party at the residence of Mr. John Enders, an old and honored citizen of Richmond, and of course there was no supper. Among those present was Willie Allan, the second son of the gentleman, Mr. John Allan, who adopted Edgar Allan Poe, and gave him his middle name. About one o'clock in the morning he came to one of the other gentlemen and myself and asked us to go to his home just across the street saying that he thought he could give us some supper. Of course we eagerly accepted his invitation and accompanied him to his house. He brought out a half dozen cold mutton chops and some bread, and we had what was to us a royal supper. I spent the night at the Allan home, and slept in the same room with Willie Allan. The next morning there was a tap on the door, and I heard his mother's gentle voice calling, "Willie, Willie." He answered, "Yes, mother, what is it?" And she replied, "Did you eat the mutton chops last night?" He answered "Yes," when she said, "Well, then, we haven't any breakfast."

The condition of the Allan household was that of all Richmond. Sometimes the contrasts that occurred in these social gayeties in Richmond were frightful, ghastly. A brilliant, handsome, happy young officer, full of hope and promise, would dance with a lovely girl, return to his command; a few days would elapse, another starvation party would occur; the officer would be missed, he would be asked for, and the reply came, "Killed in battle," and frequently the same girls with whom he had danced a few nights before would attend his funeral at one of the churches of Richmond. Can life have any more terrible antithesis than this? . . .

On one occasion when I was attending a starvation party in Richmond the dancing was at its height and everybody was bright and happy when the hostess, who was a widow, was suddenly called out of the room. A hush fell on everything, the dancing stopped, and everyone became sad, all having a premonition in those troublous times that something fearful had happened. We were soon told that her son had been killed late that evening in a skirmish in front of Richmond, a few miles from his home.

Wounded and sick men and officers were constantly brought into the homes of the people of Richmond to be taken care of and every home had in it a sick or wounded confederate soldier. From the association thus brought about many a love affair occurred and many a marriage resulted.

⌁ The Indelicate Art of ⌁
Procuring a Delicacy

Back in the 1960s and 1970s those of us who love food (I won't go so far as to call myself an epicure or a gourmet) longingly remembered the old-fashioned butcher shop, the smelly fish market, the cozy bakery, the irresistible candy shop, the seasonally colorful farmers market before, one by one, those mom-and-pop corner businesses began disappearing. Gone were the familiar faces, the alluring aromas, and individual service that had been part of our daily lives. They were replaced by impersonal, hermetically sealed grocery store chains.

I have to admit that one of the real benefits of the 1990s has been the rebirth of the specialty shops within some of the more upscale supermarkets. One that can't be beat is Atlanta's Harry's Farmers Market where every gastronomical pleasure can be fulfilled. But when I'm stuck at the beach or visiting a friend in a medium-size town where strip malls anchored by a Super Fresh or Food Lion dominate, and I have a craving for homemade soup or risotto that must *be started from scratch with a mess of bones, I'm miserable. No canned broth will do.*

Which brings me to something my mother told me when I was a child living in Robbins, North Carolina, a community where anyone who did not work in the textile mill farmed for a living. And some did both. Two strapping teenage boys came walking down the street with a tree branch stretched between their ample shoulders. Suspended from the middle of the limb was a possum. Mother, in her always no-nonsense, un-sugarcoated way, said, "There's nothing delicate about food."

Those of you with strong stomachs and hearty palates will enjoy Whit Joyner's delightful account of the artful gathering of food long before steroids and hormone-laced chicken feed had been heard of.

The Art of Dispatching a Chicken
WHIT JOYNER

Go around and ask people what their favorite bird is, and try to figure why they never give what's most often the true answer. Robins, tufted tits, hummers, oh sure.

When the delivery truck from Wyche's Grocery pulled up at our house, and a fryer was one of the items brought, word of mouth would flash around the neighborhood kids: *Mabel was going to kill a chicken today.* We adjusted our plans to be in the Joyner backyard when it happened. Plain chicken killings were boring, but Mabel's show was a pageant, with little parts for us in it. We were bit players and loyal fans. Generations attended, from toddlerhood until somewhere around puberty, when we got just too cool to deign.

Buying cold chickens at the store is still a somewhat new thing. Folks got a live bird, so they knew it was fresh. With ordinary killings, the send-off was with a good neck grip and just cranking him around, whereas the tonier might use an ax on a chopping block. (Peg Leg Bill Savage was the best firewood splitter in town, but I never saw him do a chicken. Maybe all the flapping threw him off-balance, or maybe he just couldn't dance away on that leg fast enough. Both methods tend to leave the doer splattered.)

As Wyche's truck pulled off, Mabel tied the hapless fowl to the lattice wood around the back of the house. Right behind him, her special chicken stick leaned just up under the house. Maybe a dozen kids now would begin wandering in and out of the backyard, guessing at when she was going to do it. She never would say. The object of our concern, standing with the string around his neck, gave leery, jerky scrutiny to our milling about.

When, and only when, she was ready, Mabel popped out the back door businesslike, with a stern face, and strode over to the chicken. Both serious and chattering, we fidgeted into a rough arc between her and the open yard, then fell quiet as she declaimed, "Don't get too close, I already washed this week. You know he's comin' after one of you." We moved and squeaked as courage rose and fell, jockeying close, strutting, darting away. All honor would be lost by anybody who ran out of the yard. With practiced economy, Mabel swiftly put one hand on her chicken stick, and the other grabbed the bird's feet. In a neat bend forward, she flopped the chicken down to look backwards through her legs, laid the stick across his neck, and stepped on each end of it. We all sucked breath and went taut as sea rope, and her transitory performance took place. All in an instant, her body became mobile grace, flowing upward in a seamless sweep and raising her arms out heavenward with all of that chicken but his neck and head. Her face now wore a big, bright grin as her hands opened and launched him out and away toward us, and we lit a shuck all over. We leapt, hollered, bumped, tripped, slid on the grass, all to escape that flying, spurting thing, eyeless but looking for revenge. And we accelerated it all when he hit the ground and ran about, his blood running away. Only as the bird wound through staggering, to twitching, then to stillness, did we regain our composure. There was calm discussion and reckoning for a time. Reflecting on how far and long he had flown, we looked the head over and sometimes swore we saw his eyes move. I began to think of drumsticks for my brother and me, and the gizzard for my father. As Mabel sat down and started plucking businesslike, she would designate one of us to put her chicken stick back in its place.

A Dense and Suetty Christmas Pie

SHARON PARQUETTE NIMTZ

Back in the Fifties, out in Midwest farming country, it was said of a particularly substantial or feisty man or woman, that they were full of suet. Being full of suet did not prevent you from feeling your oats, nor from sowing them either, so long as you did it responsibly, in a way that others could not help but respect.

But then, oats and suet have never been strangers to each other, not since human first tasted animal and knew how to build a fire over which to cook his gruel. Oatmeal with suet? Well no, the modern . . . if not palate then intellect has become tame, and partial to more delicate foodstuffs. But butter went into the bowl before the oatmeal in my benighted childhood (runnels of gold to appear haphazardly in spoonfuls of the cereal) and sugar on top to melt to a crisp, with a sprinkling of cinnamon, then creamy milk poured over, not so very divorced, after all, from a peasant's boiled porridge of grains, into which the available lump of suet, sweet dried fruit, and spices were tossed. Put this in a pudding cloth or a length of animal intestine, boil it, and you have a pudding, or a form of sausage. Wrap it in pastry, bake it, you have pie.

Scarce animal flesh, coveted, when captured required eating pronto, before spoilage set in. And so was tossed into every pot, no matter what the contents, and eaten for breakfast, lunch and dinner hors d'oeuvre to fruitplate, until it was gone, and desire for it built again.

Suet is a cold-weather fat, to line the innards of hard-working people, to keep them warm, and soothe them to replete sleep the long nights. Flayed from the kidneys of an animal butchered one dank, dark, chill Autumn dawn; the sheep, or the ox; rendered until molten, used to make candles, or soap, or as the mainstay in dishes such as the Suet Pudding and Mincemeat Pie that graced festive tables we gathered around with family and friends and neighbors against the coming of dead winter. . . .

But nothing signifies cold winter holidays as succinctly as the earthy yet majestic Mincemeat Pie, the Northerner's most brilliant dare to the encroaching dark—two succulent inches of chopped meat, apples, and raisins enclosed in pale, pricked, lardy crusts. It's a study in satisfying contrasts—fruit and meat, fat and sweet, crisp crust and mellow filling—and a study in irony, as it elevates these practical and basic ingredients, for ancient reasons and now with contemporary ease, to suetty, clove-and-spicy heights. Mincemeat climbs up out of that abyss to which we consign food that is not shrink-wrapped or fed

hormones. It is that rare example in which it is possible to turn the sow's ear into a silk purse, where ingredient plus technique renders, as in the French comfit, a glorious whole that is more than the sum of its parts.

It's a rustic, old-country food that never laid claim to easy accessibility, a food that calls for a passionate palate, a hunger, an appreciation of tradition and historic practicality; and it helps very much, to love it, if you have grown up with it and it has come to stand for the special days on which it is served. . . .

Granddad, who grew up with the tradition of Mincemeat Pie, did not care for Suet Pudding; my husband is indifferent to both—his father demanded old-country foods and the rest of the family submitted reluctantly; for my son they symbolize the invariably difficult twist my side of the family puts on life—down to and including holiday desserts, while to my young daughter, bless her little suet-loving heart, they are me chopping suet, and she loves her mincemeat. Then there is my brother-in-law, who grew up on easy American food but can eat, I believe *has* eaten, most of a whole mincemeat pie by himself before someone knew to smack his paddies, snatch that pie; and Dad, orphaned at an early age, came into the family and adopted Mincemeat and Suet Pudding with all of his heart. Perhaps they meant family to him.

Last year I wailed—just as Grandma always did—of my need of "some good venison neck for mincemeat." My plaint bore fruit, as the friend to whom I'd kvetched showed up shyly victorious on my doorstep clutching a bag full of the venison neck he'd procured and boned out for me. It took hours for two of us, taking turns, to chop it by hand. But when it was done, and aged in its rum, it was an unusually splendid mincemeat, in whose honor I made a suet pastry to wrap its whole meaty mélange, bringing the term *integrity of ingredients* to a particularly graceful fruition.

⟿ The Ubiquitous Fruitcake ⟿

If you are on the giving or receiving end of the traditional Christmas fruitcake, this is the poem for you!

⟿ The Meek Shall Inherit the Fruit Cake ⟿ Recipe That Has Passed Down, from as Far Back as Anyone Can Remember, On My Mother's Side of the Family

LYNN VEACH SADLER

This *fruit cake isn't just tradition—but* THE PAST.
I lacked wash pan/dish to cook it; wash pot, *saints be praised, was struck through.*
    *(Two soufflé dishes, two bundt pans—*this *fruit cake runneth over.)*
I lacked "clean homespun" to wrap it and lard stand to pyx it.
    (I used cheesecloth for swaddling clothes, mangered à la française.*)*
Lacking "scuppernong wine" to baptize it, I anointed with sherry and brandy. One of the nuts wasn't politically correct. (I had to raise it from the bad.)
I didn't bake in time for celebration—a minimum month before a Christmas resurrection.

Still this "Nutty Pineapple White Fruit Cake" is Deming's Total Quality Management.
No citron and lemon peel. (No hyssop?)
    (Its only bittersweet's my sin of omission—
    inadvertent excommunication of lemon juice and vanilla!)
Candied green and red cherries, candied red and green pineapple;
    three slices for every cherry, four for every wedge of pineapple.
And the nuts? Not just the expense—try picking out Brazil nuts!
    (The only way to buy them nude is to pick them out of a mix.)

Fruit cake—harmless ideé fixe*?*
It made this cook meek.

⟶ Worth the Planning ⟵

M. F. K. FISHER

M. F. K. Fisher is not just one of the great food writers of the twentieth century, she is one of the great writers. In this selection, "F is for Family," we see Fisher's famous quote, "There is a communion of more than bodies when bread is broken and wine is drunk" come to life as she determinedly breaks with obligatory tradition only to find a magical moment, worth the planning.

F is for Family . . . And the depths and height of gastronomical enjoyment to be found at the family board.

It is possible, indeed almost too easy, to be eloquently sentimental about large groups of assorted relatives who gather for Christmas or Thanksgiving or some such festival, and eat and drink and gossip and laugh together. They always laugh: in Norman Rockwell magazine covers and in Iowa novels and in any currently popular variation of "I Remember Mustache Cups" there is Gargantuan laughter, from toothless babe to equally toothless Gramp. Great quantities of home-cooked goodies are consumed, great pitchers of Uncle Nub's hard cider are quaffed, and great gusts of earthy merriment sweep like prairie fire around the cluttered table. The men folk bring out their whittling knives in postprandial digestive calm, the women (sometimes spelled wimmin to denote an inaudible provincialism) chatter and scrape and swab down in the kitchen, and the bulging children *bulge*.

The cold truth is that family dinners are more often than not an ordeal of nervous indigestion, preceded by hidden resentment and ennui and accompanied by psychosomatic jitters.

The best way to guarantee smooth sailing at one of them is to assemble the relatives only when a will must be read. This at least presupposes good manners during the meal, if the lawyer is not scheduled to appear until after it. Funeral baked meats have perhaps been more enjoyed than any christening cakes or wedding pottages, thanks largely to the spice of wishful thinking that subtly flavors them, as yet untouched by disappointment, dread, or hatred.

My own experience with family dinners has fallen somewhere between this facile irony and the bucolic lustiness of popular idealization. I remember that several times at Christmas there were perhaps twenty of us at the Ranch for a lengthy noon-dinner, to which none of us was accustomed. I always had fun, being young and healthy and amenable, but I do not recall, perhaps to my shame, that I had any *special* fun.

To be truthful, I was conscious by my eleventh or twelfth year that there was about the whole ceremony a kind of doggedness, a feeling that in spite of hell and high water we were duty-bound to go through with it, because my grandfather was very old and might not live another year, or because a cousin had just lost her abominable but very rich husband, or because another cousin was going to Stanford instead of Yale at Yale's request and so would be with us, or something like that. It was tacitly understood that the next day would find my sister Anne droopy and bilious, my mother overtired, and the cook crankily polishing glasses and eyeing the piles of the "best" Irish linen that had to be laundered. My father, on the other hand, would still be glowing: he loved any kind of party in the world, even a family one.

I seem, and I am thankful for it, to have inherited some of his capacity for enjoying such intramural sport, combined, fortunately, with my mother's ability to cope with it. In spite of my conviction that a group of deliberately assembled relatives can be one of the dullest, if not most dangerous, gatherings in the world, I am smugly foolhardy enough to have invited all my available family, more than once, to dine with me.

The last time was perhaps the most daring, and it went off with a dash and smoothness that will always bulwark my self-esteem, for it was the happy result of many days of thought and preparation.

Parents, cousins, new generation—all came. It meant hotel reservations in the near-by town, and great supplies of food and drink for a long holiday during which the stores were closed. It meant wood stored under cover for the fireplace in case of rain (it poured), and Band-Aids and liniment (my nephew and my two-year-old daughter fell off a boulder into the pond), and considerable self-control (my favorite male shot several of my favorite quail).

It meant a lot of work: I was cook, and before the festival I had food prepared or at least in line for an average of twelve persons a meal, three meals a day, for three days. And the right good wines. And the other potables, right, good, and copious. That, I say smugly, is no mean feat.

It was exciting and rewarding and completely deliberate. Nothing, to my knowledge at least, went wrong. There was an aura of gaiety and affection all about us—and that too, with people of different ages and sexes and beliefs, political and religious and social, is also something of a feat to attain and to maintain. The whole thing, for a miracle to bless me, went off well.

This is most often the case in planned celebrations, I think. Now and then there is a happy accident in families, and brothers and cousins and grandparents who may have been cold or even warlike suddenly find themselves in some stuffy booth in a chophouse, eating together with forgotten warmth and amity. But it is rare. Most often it must be prearranged with care and caution.

It must not simply be taken for granted that a given set of ill-assorted people, for no other reason than because it is Christmas, will be joyful to be reunited and to break bread together. They must be jolted, even shocked, into excitement and surprise and subsequent delight. All the old routine patterns of food and flowers and cups must be redistributed, to break up that mortal ignominy of the family dinner, when what has too often been said and felt and thought is once more said, felt, and thought: slow poison in every mouthful, old grudges, new hateful boredom, nascent antagonism and resentment— why in God's name does Mother always put her arm that way on the chair, and why does Helen's girdle always pop as she lifts the denuded meat platter up and away from Father, and why does Sis always tap her fingers thus tinnily against the rim of her wine glass? Poison, indeed, and most deeply to be shunned!

It takes courage to give a family party, and at least once I had enough to do it, being mightier in my youth than I am now. I was almost stony broke, unable to take no matter how judicious a collection of relatives to a decent restaurant. So . . .

I summoned my father, mother, brother, and sisters to a supper in the Ranch dining-room, to celebrate nothing at all. I managed to pay for it, almost to the least grain of salt: silly, but a sop to my proud young soul. I set the table with the family's best silver and china and crystal (especially the iridescent and incredibly thin wine goblets we have always had for "party").

I went to Bernstein's on the Park in Los Angeles and bought beautiful fresh shellfish: tiny bay shrimp in their shells, crab cooked while I waited, and lobster claws too, pink prawns, little mussels in their purple shells. I went down behind the Plaza and bought flat round loaves of sourdough bread and good spaghetti and sweet butter. I bought some real cheese, not the kind that is made of by-products and melted into tinfoil blocks. I bought Wente Brothers' Grey Riesling and Italian-Swiss Colony Tipo Red, and some over-roasted coffee blended on Piuma's drugstore counter for me. There, in short, was the skeleton of the feast.

The flesh upon this bony structure was a more artful thing, compounded of my prejudices and my enthusiastic beliefs. It is true that my comparative youngness made me more eager to do battle than I would be now, but I still think I was right to rebel against some of the inevitable boredom of dining *en famille.*

To begin with, I reseated everyone. I was tired of seeing my father looming against the massive ugliness of the sideboard, with that damned square mirror always a little crooked behind his right ear. I assumed, somewhat grandly, that he was equally tired of looking down the table toward my mother, forever masked behind a collection of cigarette boxes, ash trays, sugar shakers left there whether needed or not, a Louis Quinze snuff box full of saccharin, several salt shakers, a battered wooden pepper-mill, and an eternal bouquet, fresh but uninspired, of whatever could be gleaned from the garden. With never a yea or nay to guide me I eliminated this clutter from the center of the table—it had been on my nerves for at least fifteen years—and in a low bowl I arranged "bought" camellias instead of a "grown" bunch of this-or-that from the side yard.

My parents were rocked on their bases, to put it mildly, and only innate good manners kept them from shying away from my crazy plan like startled and resentful deer whose drinking place has been transferred.

Those were my first and most drastic attempts, clumsy enough I admit, but very successful in the end, to break up what seemed to me a deadly dull pattern. Then I used the sideboard as a buffet, which had never been done before in our memory. I tipped off my siblings beforehand, and we forced my father to get up and get his own first course of shellfish, which he enjoyed enormously after he recovered from the first shock of not having someone wait on him. He poked and sniffed and puttered happily over the beautiful platters of shrimp and suchlike and made a fine plate of things for my mother, who sat with an almost shy smile, letting the newness of this flood gently, unforgettably, into her sensitive mind and heart.

My brother poured the cold Grey Riesling with a flourish, assuming what had always been Father's prerogative. Later I served the casserole of spaghetti, without its eternal family accompaniment of rich sauce, and it was doubly delicious for that flouting of tradition.

The Tipo was good. The Tipo flowed. So, happy magic, did our talk. There we were, solidly one for those moments at least, leaning our arms easily along the cool wood, reaching without thought for our little cups of hot bitter coffee or our glasses, not laughing perhaps as the families do in the pictures and the stories, but with our eyes loving and deep, one to another. It was good, worth the planning. It made the other necessary mass meals more endurable, more a part of being that undeniable rock, the Family.

➤ The Tradition Continues ➤

If you ever find yourself around Austin, Texas, just as sunset approaches, drop by The Oasis, a huge restaurant on a cliff 450 feet above Lake Travis. The Oasis has a cascade of twenty-eight decks overhanging the west cliffside. Needless to say, there's an incredible view of the sun as it sets behind the distant hills. Now, don't ask where or when this tradition began, but at that moment when the sun slips behind the horizon, all eating and drinking stops while everyone applauds and The Oasis bell is rung in appreciation of another day, and another night. If you drop by and it happens to be your birthday or anniversary, or you're there from far away, let them know. You may be the bell-ringer.

We Love Ice Cream

MONA EVANS

Who doesn't love ice cream? Mona Evans, a writer in Jackson, Mississippi, finds this all-American favorite is a psychological panacea for many of life's traumas.

As a little girl growing up in Memphis, I developed a healthy fear of tooth extractions and shots. After several rather dysfunctional episodes in pediatric and pedodontic offices all across town, my mother refused to tell my younger sister, Paula, and me about our impending medical appointments. We would unsuspectingly pile into the old black Buick Special, and Mama would announce our destination when we were nearly there.

I remember one particularly difficult dental experience, during which my mother desperately tried to divert me by chanting repeatedly, "Just think about your pretty new blue bike." Mama soon shifted into an even more compensatory mode. After any dreaded appointment was over, we would emerge, red-eyed and heaving, to be whisked away to a soothing reward—ice cream.

Both of my children—Jay, now fifteen, and Whitney, eleven—temporarily inherited my fears of all things medical. When they were little, I handed down the ice cream tradition and it has continued, whether the visit is unpleasant or not. They, in turn, have insisted that we pass the tradition down yet another "generation"—to the family pets.

I have to confess that, after traumatic trips to the veterinarian, I have actually been to the drive-through at Dairy Queen for Rascal, the family schnauzer, and Raptor, the cat.

Soft swirl has become the panacea of choice for us all. Maybe our unusual family ritual will ease post-medical trauma for another family somewhere out there.

It Is Pleasant to Labor for Those We Love

Untold numbers of the children's essays on traditions involved food, dinnertime, and family reunions, spanning the generations and the seasons. As I read each one, I remembered the simple words on a nineteenth-century pressed-glass plate that is used for special meals at our home: "It is pleasant to labor for those we love." Yes, Poppin' Fresh does have it right: "Nothing says lovin' like something from the oven"—or at least from the kitchen.

I can't even count the numerous times that I have had a huge Saturday breakfast at my grandparents' house. My grandmother wakes up really early every Saturday morning, before the sun rises, and cooks and cooks. Everyone wakes up to the wonderful smell of the feast my grandmother has prepared. She spends the morning cooking home-made biscuits, sausage, bacon, country ham, eggs, and her homemade apples.

My grandfather has made up special names for some of his favorite foods. If you were to sit down at breakfast with us, you would surely hear my grandfather say things such as "Pass me some of that paste" (gravy), or "Aren't you going to eat any cat heads?" (biscuits). My cousin Alan has been known to down at least a dozen homemade biscuits piled high with gravy, crushed bacon, and bits of sausage. My grandfather calls this concoction a "masterpiece." These names may sound odd to you, but after visiting my grandparents a couple of times they will seem perfectly normal.

No matter what you call it, there is no doubt the food is absolutely delicious. You will always leave the table weighing more than you weighed when you sat down. Though my grandmother's breakfast is loaded with calories, it is also filled with the tradition of love that keeps families together.

Olivia Gray, middle school

◂ ▸

"Wake up and come help me bake, Brandon!" This is an obvious sign that Christmas is around the corner: traditional Christmas baking at my grandparents'. Every year since I can remember, we have baked delicious concoctions and then eaten them during the Christmas season. These wonderful treats include gingerbread men, gingersnaps, and sugar cookies. Let me tell you how this scrumptious day of baking with my grandmother went.

We woke up to the sensation of a wet dog's tongue licking our faces. Then, with extreme laziness, we got up and slowly drug our feet into the kitchen. After our arrival in the kitchen, the coffee was brewed and we sat at the table like lifeless blobs drinking coffee. After our momentary caffeine burst, we got up, showered, and started baking. While the cookies were in the oven, we watched the timer tick-tock away like men possessed. *Ding!*

After that sound, we were up from our seats like bullets. We pulled the cookies from the oven and let their sweet aroma fill the air. The cooled delectables were arranged on a platter, and were ready to be served.

This is one of my favorite family traditions, not only because I get to eat the cookies, but also because of the memories I hold in my heart.

Brandon Miller, middle school

As American as Apple Pie, Pasta, and Molasses

My family tradition lasts all year long and it involves making apple pies.

At the beginning of September every year, my mom buys a bushel of mountain-grown apples. We meet at my grandparents' house and set up an assembly line to make pies. At the start, my grandfather washes and peels all the apples. At the same time, my grandmother is busy making and shaping the dough for the piecrusts. My mom then puts the pie together and adds cinnamon, butter, and sugar. My grandmother adds a fancy shape or name and puts it on top. The pies are then wrapped in aluminum foil and put in the freezer to wait their turn to be baked. We make at least fifteen pies. My sister and I wait for the "stickies" made from leftover dough and eat them as soon as they come from the oven.

We eat apple pies all year long and always at Thanksgiving, Christmas, and Easter. The very special pie is the one that's baked for my birthday and has the name "Emily" on the top.

Emily Carter, middle school

This has been a wonderful day! Each year in October our family gets together and makes apple butter. My Paw-Paw has a copper-lined apple-butter kettle with a big wooden paddle to stir the apples with.

On a Friday night we got together like always and cut up three bushels of apples. Bright and early the next morning, Paw-Paw started a fire outside under the kettle. We put the apples in and added water and cooked them until they were smooth. Then we added about forty pounds of sugar and about eight small bottles of cinnamon flavoring.

After we have taken turns stirring all day, the apple butter was ready. We then took the kettle off the fire and dipped the apple butter out and put it in jars. After it cooled, we stored it in the basement to be used by my family and given to our friends.

We have done this for several years, and I really enjoy being with all my family, working and having fun making apple butter.

Staci J. Mills, elementary school

━ ━

My family has a special tradition that was brought over by the Wiel-pyszewski family in 1908. They arrived on a ship called the *Searatan.* With them, they brought the tradition of a Polish Christmas Eve dinner.

The Christmas dinner starts with everyone on my mom's side gathering at my mother's parents' house in Wilkes-Barre, Pennsylvania. The dinner begins with everyone taking a piece of wafer bread and going up to everyone else, giving them a little piece of their wafer bread and hugging them. Once we finally sit down, we eat a Polish dinner that consists of baked fish and pierogies, a dish kind of like ravioli, only filled with cheese or potatoes instead of meat. Also, we have sauerkraut and lima beans, cold red beet soup, rice and raisins or rice and plums, and a plate of fried mushrooms.

Now it is my grandmother who keeps this tradition alive in our life. Every year I look forward to seeing all my relatives and enjoying a home-cooked Polish Christmas Eve dinner.

Janet Chriscoe, middle school

━ ━

Each Sunday after church, we go to my grandma and my grandpa's to eat Sunday dinner. I like to find out what they are cooking. One grandma I call Nanny lives in the country. She cooks "real" homemade biscuits, collards, cabbage, candied yams, and fried chicken. My sister and I like for my grandma to mash up potatoes in collards, and we call it a mash-up.

My other grandma, Mother Peg, lives in Bath and cooks spaghetti, casseroles, pot roast, and seafood. Even though they cook very different food, they are both very good cooks.

Sunday afternoons are spent with family playing games, watching TV, and talking and laughing together. I will always remember Sunday afternoons at my grandparents'.

Blane Woolard, elementary school

Sunday is my favorite day because it is Pasta Day, an Italian family tradition. Grandma and my mother begin cooking the sauce around 9:00 A.M. and sometimes I help. It smells so good that I can hardly wait for dinner.

At 6:00 when Mom says "Dinner," everyone hurries from wherever he or she is. We all run to the table before Dad gets to the spaghetti bowl. We all grab the cheese and put loads of it on our spaghetti. Meanwhile, Mom still has the fluffy rolls in the oven, all toasty and golden. When Mom puts the rolls on the table, we all grab one while they're still hot. I feel warm as soon as I take that first bite of one of those soft delicious rolls.

As soon as we sit, everyone is quiet for a moment while we say grace. Then we begin talking about our day and what we did that week. Sometimes we see who can slurp up the spaghetti the fastest. Of course, Dad looks the funniest when he tries.

When dinner is over, we are so full that we can't eat another bite. Everyone enjoys Pasta Day, and it has been in the family for three generations.

Andrea Leone, elementary school

When I was little, I would go to my grandmother's house on the weekend. Early on Saturday morning I would get up before anyone else and make pancakes with my grandmother. It became our tradition.

My grandmother would put me on the counter and tell me to be careful so I wouldn't fall. Then she'd get out the milk, eggs, and pancake mix to make the batter. Grandmother would always let me crack the eggs. Sometimes I would crack them and they would spill on the counter. Grandmother didn't get mad if I made a mess.

We would put the batter on the griddle. She taught me to look for bubbles in the pancakes as they sizzled. I had the best time making them.

Then one day Grandmother became sick and we couldn't make pancakes anymore. Grandfather tried, but he just couldn't make them like Grandmother and I did.

My grandmother died, and now I don't get to make pancakes with her anymore. My new tradition is making pancakes with my dad. Our pancakes taste perfect. I still wish Grandmother could make them with me, though, just like when I was little.

Meredith L. Sheetz, elementary school

When we feel the first frost or see the first leaf fall, our family knows it's molasses-making time. We head out to the field and start cutting cane. We load it on a truck and haul it to a mill, where a skinner cuts off the skin. We take it down to the squeezer to get the juice out. We collect the juice in buckets placed on a huge pan. We take the pan and put it over a cinder-block oven. We put maple logs (burned for their sweetness) under the pan. Flat ladles are used to skim the top to get any excess cane. We have to constantly wet the sides so the molasses won't stick.

After we eat supper, the molasses is usually done. We take the pan off, put one side in an upright position, use a huge ladle to take the molasses out, and pour it in a skimmer. The good part falls in a huge bucket.

We get cut-up cane and sop the pan, which means we dip it in there and taste the molasses.

There's eating, singing, and dancing. This is our Gambill family tradition every year.

William Walter Gambill II, middle school

Supper to Go!

Though we admit that home cooking can't be beat, too often we get hung up on that word "homemade," especially in these days of dual careers and too many demands on our time. There are times when "homemade" just has to take a backseat. One particularly busy day when the kids were young, I remember throwing my hands up in frustration and asking the air, "Okay, Emyl, which are you going to do, take the kids to soccer practice or cook supper?" Obviously soccer practice won out. Jonathan Grieme's busy family puts a spin on the family meal, and the result is a new tradition that he really likes.

My family has a very different tradition that started six or seven years ago when I was about six years old. Every Friday, without fail, our family orders pizza. My mom will pick me up about 6:00 P.M. and take me to my parents' shop. At about 6:15, my mom or dad will order the pizza. My mom might pick it up if they don't deliver. Then, right when the pizza gets to our shop, I'll have to get the table and set it up in my dad's office. There we will watch TV or we might rent a video. After we are finished with our pizza, I have to clean up and put the table back. When I'm done, I ask Mom to make a banana milk shake for me. When I get it, I sit back in a chair, sip on my milk shake, and watch *TGIF Friday*.

So this is my family tradition. It sounds pretty weird, but I really like it because I just totally love pizza.

Jonathan Grieme, middle school

B-e-a-n-s

BEA COLE

When it comes right down to it, there's a reason why the tradition of gathering family together for food and celebrations will never die. As Bea Cole, a budding writer from South Royalton, Vermont, shows us, you can spell love "b-e-a-n-s."

Summer is over and the upcoming holidays are approaching fast. These festive occasions bring people together who might rarely see one another. Some families hold a yearly reunion. I've been brought up to believe that sharing is a very important part of the family structure. My family tries to spend many occasions together throughout the year to share our lives.

I guess we just like to party. We congregate for birthdays, Mother's and Father's Day, and anniversaries as well as the major holidays. We've even been known to gather for no reason at all except that it has been a while since we've seen each other.

These gatherings are usually a potluck deal. Everyone contributes what they can. We have meat, breads, casseroles, chips, pickles, and the like. The center of the meal is always a steaming pot of homemade baked beans. My mom is in charge of the beans. With some fifty-odd years of experience under her belt, she is the best candidate for the job.

If you aren't a real fan of baked beans, you would like Mom's anyway. Even my finickiest brother has come around and decided he likes them. It really isn't the maple sugar flavor or the enticing aroma that makes them special. It is the texture of the beans. When you put them into your mouth they melt on your tongue. You can chew them if you like, but it is not really necessary. Naturally, another spoonful must follow, because your taste buds are left wondering if that was as delicious as it seemed.

Making these beans is no small task. I know from experience that the end result can be very disappointing sometimes. Mom assures me that it is all in the parboiling. Boil them too long and you end up with mush. Don't boil them long enough and you will be eating brown bullets.

Then it comes time to add the remaining ingredients. A "dab" of this and a "little" of that. Nowhere in my cookbooks do I find a "dab" defined, and is a "little" considered the same as a pinch? If so, do I put more in if your pinch is bigger than mine? Most of my attempts at making baked beans have resulted in my husband commenting that they "aren't bad," which—translated from loving-husband lingo to reality—means that they aren't good, either.

Mom's beans are always great. They are the first thing put on plates as everyone circles the table, filling up for the first round. I have one brother who is known to fast before one of these parties. He's usually first in line.

In an amazing amount of time the food is eaten. Then we settle in and bring each other up to date on our lives. We watch as my baby teeters on unsteady legs and preteen girls, who were only babies yesterday, leap about. We talk about the things we do, the things we've done, and what we hope to be doing. Then maybe we "kids" (the youngest of whom is now approaching his thirtieth year) will engage in a game or a hand of cards.

Soon the shadows begin to grow long as the afternoon has crept away. Mom is getting tired, and it's time to get ready for tomorrow. Everyone collects their dishes and children and make for the cars. After a little more driveway conversation we head down our different roads, back to our own homes, feeling good to know that we've shared with the ones we love. Content for the time being, until the next time we get together over a great pot of beans.

A CIRCLE OF CHAIRS IS NEVER PROVOCATIVE OF GOOD
TALK UNLESS THERE IS A TABLE IN THE MIDDLE.
Louise Hale

CHAPTER 19

Letter Writing

WITH PEN IN HAND

~ Style and Grace ~

* EMYL JENKINS

I remember learning to master a fountain pen. Under Miss Neal's watchful eye, while trails of blue-black ink stained the page, I practiced making big circles. Eventually I could make the loops smaller, and ink blobs no longer marred my schoolgirl attempts at third grade calligraphy.

In those days handwriting had personality. Johnny's homework papers were always a little out of control. His letters ran across the blue lines and out into the margins. Anne's papers always had a big A+ written in red crayon across the top of the page. Her desk was always neat. My own B— handwriting expressed an unspoken restlessness. My desk was never neat.

Not so my mother's. At home she kept a diary. I can see her now in her straight-back Windsor chair making entries in the tapestry-covered combination diary-calendar always present on her desk.

Flipping through its pages now, I find many of her notations were casual, some little more than hastily entered scrawls. But for those events she really looked forward to—a garden club meeting or an evening concert—the entries were neatly written in a graceful, flowing script, each one entered with the marbled fountain pen she kept next to her diary.

Mother always dissuaded me from using her pen, telling me, "A pen point wears down into just the right shape for the owner. It won't write as well for anyone else." Yet many, many years later she gave me that subtly hued pen. By then her writing needs had dwindled to a trickle, her once busy life now passing day by day rather than year by year.

She meant for me to have the pen as a memento. But I keep it on my still strewn desk as a living, vivid reminder of her. And I use it frequently. Over time I have often wondered if perhaps writing angles might be hereditary, for her pen writes beautifully for me, even after all those years as her constant servant.

Until she gave me her pen, I picked up whatever utilitarian plastic writing tool I found lying around, heedlessly discarding it when it wore out. Then, a few years ago, I entered the age of technology, and for my professional writing I now use a word processor. How I appreciate the ease with which I can relocate a paragraph or experiment with various word choices. How I marvel at its speed.

But when the time comes to write a loving thank-you note, to compose a heartfelt letter of congratulations, or even to mark a special date on my calendar, I still reach for Mother's fountain pen, which waits patiently on my desk. As I begin to write, I feel a sense of graciousness and leisure that modern conveniences cannot provide.

Watching the point lay the glistening ink onto the paper, I feel compelled to do my best to make each circle perfectly looped, each letter permanently linked. Mysteriously, my usually scribbled hand-writing becomes more like my mother's graceful script.

Not long ago, when I wanted to select a special present for my daughter, who was at college, I chose a fountain pen. Then, as I was about to sign the sales slip with the clerk's eighty-nine-cent ballpoint pen, I hesitated.

Would Joslin really enjoy this? Would she even take the time to savor the pleasures of writing carefully and thoughtfully to make her feelings known? Would she learn, as I had, when to use the ever-ready ballpoint pen for jotting down everyday notes and quick reminders, and when to enjoy the pleasure of writing in her own individual style with a familiar and highly personal pen?

No, style and grace aren't hereditary. We must take the time to introduce our children to the finer pleasures of life. So when I received Joslin's thank-you note, written with her newly opened present, I not only read her words, I also looked at the page.

There were irregular spaces between her letters. An extra ink stain or two dotted her stationery. At present, she doesn't have her grandmother's easy-flowing hand. But her writing does have personality, and years from now, when she has worn the point down to just the right angle, grace and style will follow.

～ *Paper Pleasures* ～

MARY ALICE KELLOGG

Ironically, in this keyboard and voice-mail world of ours new attention is being paid to the art of letter writing. Yes, the kind of letter you write—*not dictate or thump out. It's time to bring back this nearly lost tradition, I am told in countless articles intended to instruct me how to write letters, tell me the importance of taking the time to put down my thoughts, and even meticulously explain the etiquette of letter writing in today's business world. The words jump off the pages of today's computer-generated magazines and newspapers. Reading them, I sometimes feel as if I've mistakenly picked up a turn-of-the-century ladies' magazine rather than an end-of-the-century cutting-edge unisex publication.*

But the time is well spent. Letters hold an important place in our personal lives and in history, as you will see. First Mary Alice Kellogg explains the importance of letters from her high-tech but deeply sentimental point of view, then Alexandra Stoddard gently persuades us that letters and letter writing aren't just good for the receiver; they are good for the one who writes them.

Right next to my state-of-the-art computer, printer, fax, and a telephone that does everything but chill beer sits a flowered hatbox that has as much to do with my work and my life as my hightech electronic helpers do. Inside the box are letters from my aunt, Marie Sawyer. For the 35 years of our correspondence, I saved every letter, postcard and note from her; it turned out she saved all of mine, too. When she died last year at 90, my letters to her were returned to me, and now they too snuggle in the hatbox, tied with ribbon.

I realize now what a gift we gave one another. The thoughtful handwritten or typed words on paper of our family history, personal dreams and details of everyday life united us as nothing else could. Aunt Marie didn't own a computer or believe in the fax machine and didn't even use the telephone much. I can now see her point. Our correspondence taught me the value of writing real letters to one another, taking pen in hand and thinking through what we wanted to express. When I untie the ribbons and leaf through the letters, I can hear her voice. When I read mine, I experience the diary I was always too busy to keep: anger at boyfriends, excitement over career, moves to different cities, changing my outlook through different stages of life. It's all in there, and I don't need batteries or electricity to read them whenever I want.

Also in my hatbox are letters from someone who has taught me that writing letters not only cements relationships, but can also create them. For the last 20 years I've been writing to Blake, a University of Wisconsin journalism professor who is one of my dearest friends. Blake and I have shared ups and downs, career changes, his retirement, family gossip, politics, philosophies. Unlike Aunt Marie, though, Blake is a high-tech pioneer, having embraced PCs, desktop publishing, e-mail and other communication advances long before everyone else.

But, like Aunt Marie, he values good "old fashioned" correspondence. We've never e-mailed, faxed or even Fed-Exed one another, but although he lives in Wisconsin and I in New York, I feel as much part of his family as if he lived next door. This comes as a surprise to those who know that Blake and I vowed early on never to speak on the telephone.

Indeed, we've never even met. Our friendship developed, strengthened, and deepened solely on the wings of thought and a postage stamp.

Especially in today's "I-need-it-in-a-nanosecond" world, there is something special about a letter sent, the treasures within. When we can fire off a memo into cyberspace without thinking, the act of writing a letter to someone is almost an occasion in itself. Indeed, the idea of "snail mail" as a way to bring us closer together is so quaint it's . . . well, downright *trendy.* Do I hear a chorus of "Everything old is new again"? I hope so.

Just think of what would happen if letter-writing were to die out: "Dear John" faxes adding insult to injury. E-mailed love letters, difficult to scent and unlikely to endure. Curling faxes of condolence. Stamp collectors becoming an endangered species. There are times when we want to receive a message that took some time to write or to live that moment of mystery when we open the hand-addressed envelope to see what's there and find something to hold and save should we choose. Decades-long correspondences are rare in any age, but a handwritten thank you or sympathy note means something and takes little time. When we commit things to paper, we're forced to focus on what's important, to think through what we truly want to say. Anger is tempered, affection deepens and thoughts are organized better when we don't shoot from the keypad.

Typing a letter is OK; sometimes it's a downright and considerate necessity. My friend Helga once said that receiving a handwritten letter from me was like receiving the Rosetta stone, a not-so-veiled reference to my lifelong losing battle to master Mr. Palmer's penmanship method. (And some clichés are true: I have a handwritten thank you note from my dermatologist that I have been trying to decipher for going on six months now. Nonetheless, I appreciated the thought.) Nor is it necessary to make like Martha Stewart and spend the weekend making homemade heavy paper from scratch with herbs imbedded in it upon which to send your greetings. Some of my favorite notes from Aunt Marie were dashed off on the unused parts of old Christmas cards she had received. Aunt Marie was into recycling long before it was fashionable, one of her endearing traits that comes alive whenever I go through her letters.

Mind you, technology is not the enemy of the thoughtful letter. While e-mail may lack a certain intimacy, it's still a miracle that allows us to be in touch like never before. Thanks to computers, mostly everyone from kindergarten on up knows how to type, something that must make Mr. Palmer's heirs shudder.

The trick is to use those skills for something more, something lasting and important. If current and future technology brings us into the tent of communication, the more tools the merrier. But what better way to stand out from the plugged-in pack than with your message put on a piece of real paper, sent in a real envelope bearing a real stamp? Marilyn? Elvis? Satchmo? Richard Nixon? If you think of it, even stamps provide an overlooked means of self-expression these days. I, for one, refuse to use the "Love" stamp when paying a bill.

It's the little things that do mean a lot. A love letter you can hold. The postcard that stands out not so much for the exotic picture on the front or the strange stamp, but for the message you send. A friend of mine, a well-traveled and busy executive, uses her computer to print out pre-addressed labels, then puts them on postcards to send to loved ones. The messages are handwritten, taking into consideration the person they're addressed to. They're always keepers.

I've been to 70 countries to date and sent Aunt Marie a postcard from every one. I know now how much she treasured those tiny messages, sent from places she would never see. And when I journey through my correspondence hatbox, I know that nothing can replace the treasures within. Poised as we are at the beginning of a new millennium, it will always be the thought sent and saved that counts the most in the heart.

~ The New Letter Writer ~

Helen Bevington

COMPLETE AUTOMATION COMES TO LETTER
WRITING. NOW YOU CAN WRITE, ADDRESS, AND
SIGN AS MANY AS 3,000 LETTERS PER HOUR.
From an advertisement

> *The trouble is, I hardly know*
> *Intimately, 3,000 people.*
> *At most I've counted 6 or 8,*
> *Which seems a lot, a gracious number,*
> *To whom in letters I might owe*
> *I might with love communicate.*
>
> *And yet it being in my power*
> *To send at random now epistles*
> *To 30,000? by the day,*
> *To everybody, by the hour,*
> *Vowing my love by automation—*
> *Sweet automatic words to say—*
>
> *I need but learn the gentle art*
> *Of meaning, 50 times per minute,*
> *The same love letter from my heart*
> *With the same protestation in it*
> *That I am yours, collectively.*
> *So far, the thought depresses me.*

The Virtues of Letter Writing

Alexandra Stoddard

One of writing's greatest virtues is the real ability to communicate deep truths and loving thoughts, but some people are willing, yet unconsciously inhibited. My dear Aunt Susie, who was raised in the Midwest in an era of great formality, said to me at lunch, "I hope you know how special you really are to me. I can't seem to express my love of you on paper very easily. It seems so permanent."

Many people do think their written replies will reveal the vulnerability of their souls. And, of course, they do. That is why letters are such a powerful form of self-expression. . . .

Noted author E.B. White observed that a reputation as a letter writer is an entirely different kind of exposure from what he was used to as a writer of prose. "A man who publishes his letters becomes a nudist—nothing shields him from the world's gaze except his bare skin," White said. "A writer, writing away, can always fix things up to make himself more presentable, but a man who has written a letter is stuck with it for all time." Little secrets and innuendos are revealed in private correspondance. . . .

Letters have a way of pinpointing the moment. We tend to describe the setting, what we are wearing, the weather, what we ate for lunch, what music we're listening to, our reaction to the current political situation. Rereading old letters can remind us where we once were physically and emotionally at one very specific time in our lives. When my mother died, I discovered she had saved most of the letters I had sent her, beginning when I was nine at camp in Maine.

. . . I scan the mail for a hand-addressed envelope with an attractive stamp rather than an impersonal computer sticker on an envelope run through a postage machine. I crave letters from someone who knows me personally rather than someone to whom I am merely "Dear Madam or Sir," or "Dear Friend," a name on a mailing list or the person who pays the grocery bill.

. . . I can never receive enough *real* letters, no strings. I gobble them up, knowing full well that in time I will respond to each and every letter I receive.

. . . As an adult in a committed marriage, I realize I will never be able to explore fully all the relationships in my brief life. I've discovered, however, that it is always a joyful, wondrous and mysterious delight to receive a letter from one for whom you genuinely care who lets you know they care, too. . . .

. . . A letter never written or mailed has deeper significance than our merely being too busy. No one is too busy to tip a hat to someone he admires. We have to ask: "Busy doing what?" Whether it be a note to a friend whose son has been hospitalized, a woman who has just lost her husband, an eighth-grade English teacher who helped you improve your writing, a friend of your daughter's who is homesick on her exchange program from college—pick up your pen out of caring, appreciation, and love. It is never a burden to lift someone's else's spirits.

⌁ The Legacy in a Letter ⌁

Though we can write about the lost art of letter writing, letters themselves speak most poignantly. How much the world would have lost had these next three letters not been written.

This letter I copied years ago from papers found in my former husband's ancestral home in tiny Ridge Spring, South Carolina. It is a long letter written by Angelica Kauffman Peale Godman who was the daughter of Charles Wilson Peale, the portrait painter, and the sister of Rembrandt Peale. She writes to her sister to tell her about the marriage of her son, Dr. Harry Robinson Godman, to Emeline Ward. The wedding took place on January 27, 1853. She wrote the letter ten days later, on February 6. It tells us volumes about the people, the place, the customs, the fashions, and the times. It is historically important. It is part of my children's legacy from their father's family.

My very dear Sister:

My pleasure was much increased by the receipt of your letter the evening I returned from the wedding after an absence of 10 days, quite a *long* visit for me, who has grown so very domestic. I quite dreaded paying so long a visit to a totally strange family where all was new and unfamiliar; the bride-elect I had seen twice, but only in full dress. It was not my intention to go until the day before, but as the carriage was to take down Miss Vic., the youngest daughter, who is at boarding school, it was the best opportunity for us to go, as it is a long ride of 40 miles, so, with a basket of good lunch, as there is no very inviting place on the road, we made an early start to get there in good time. Tom had the front seat all to himself and weary enough he was at the confinement. [Tom was the writer's grandson.] At two in the afternoon we arrived at a fine large house on one of the neatest plantations I have ever seen here [the home of the bride, purchased shortly thereafter by the Nicholsons, my children's direct ancestors on their father's side]; it is a very cold spell and could you have seen the welcome fires, it would have done you good. Augusta can tell you the beauty of light wood stuck through a great hickory fire in a fine granite fireplace. Capt. Ward's house is an unusually well built house with many improvements on the old southern style. By birth he is an Englishman, tho a resident of this state for 30 years. I thought many times of dear Mr. R. We did have a fine time truly, and if I never see a real southern plantation wedding again, I shall ever remember the one I did see. When I arrived all the preparations were going on; an old lady was there who superintends all the parties and weddings for 20 miles around, and the preparation for a wedding where all must be made at home, and many of the guests stay several days, etc.

I thought of the good old Saxon time, when I saw all those ovens on the hearth in front of a fire where the wood was seven feet long and the shovel was a spade, and andirons two good sized rocks; a whole sheep was roasted and a fat little pig lay snug in the oven for a half day's cooking, hams boiled and baked, turkeys, chickens, with a large bowl of chicken salad, 3 loaves of light bread as big as the top of a barrel and biscuits without number, that was the side table. For the cake, jelly whip and custard they used a barrel of sugar and 100 dozen eggs; now just imagine all that to be beaten up, sifted, citrun cut to decorate cake, citrun pudding and cocoanut, and you may suppose we were a busy house. Vic (sister of the bride and later wife of Dr. Augustus Fitch of Charleston) cut paper all day to dress the stands for the long table and what with apples, oranges, almonds and raisins enough for a hundred, it looked truly hospitable; wine and brandy aplenty; everybody merry, but "Pa" who seemed very sober; could he have chosen, he would rather that his daughter never married, or if she did to a rich man, but young ladies who have had their will about everything they fancy, generally take it when a good looking fellow like Dr. Godman comes along, whether Pa likes it or no; but I must tell you how nicely I was fixed. I did so dislike the thought of the Curious eye investigating my braid and the style of the night cap, etc., as I feared I should share a room with some other visitor, but to my joy, in honor of being the Lady-Mother, I had a nice room all to myself, and Tom, with a servant woman to wait on me always at sound of my bell, and to Tom's great delight, two nice little boys to play or wait on him, during our whole visit; he was too happy.

Mrs. Ward had the nicest little lap dog I ever saw, the spotted coach dog on the step, the terrier and watch dog, the peacocks, chickens of all kinds and color, ducks, geese, pea fowls, made the yard look beautiful. The whole affair must have cost the old gentleman a pretty penny. The bridesmaid came from Charleston and they had to send 25 miles to meet her where the cars stop; she arrived the same evening I did and we all enjoyed a good supper and when I went to my room, so delightful did the fire seem to me with the one big stone for the hearth, that, tired as I was, I took a book and sat down to read by the light of its broad blaze, finer than gas light. I cannot tell you how I enjoyed those fires and my maid, she kept me a fire all the day and lighted it by six, and though we did not breakfast until ten, my room was so lighted with the fire that I never opened my shutters nor raised the curtain. Thursday was the coldest day we have had this winter, 5 o'clock brought a merry group, Harry and 8 young men from Columbia, each pair in a buggy and a span of horses. They all went to a cottage, a pretty little building about 100 yards from the house where a good fire and servants awaited them, there they were at home when they got their trunks and a merry time they had dressing, making ties of white neck cloths. I never did see so many rich white silk vests and cravats. These southern boys go it strong, a merry set they were. The bride had had a fire in the big room two days to get it warm and all day she had been arranging her clothes and finery; there on the bed lay the spotless linen all crimped, the drawers with the fine little tucks and insertions, the white silk stockings and the little white Satin slippers, the white satin dress and the plain lace over the long bridal veil and wreath of white flowers; the short kid gloves with the deep lace frill, a diamond pin, a pair of gold earrings, and bracelets, completed the toilet. Now if I could only say that the bride was pretty, you would be delighted with the picture, but, alas, to my taste, she is not; a pretty foot, and hand, and commanding figure, has Mrs. Harry Godman, fine teeth, and a large mouth, light hair and blue eyes; no hopes for dark eyed grandchildren unless they take after their grand-sires like Tom; he has blue eyes, both father and mother dark. I think S's wife the best looking, tho Emeline is the most showy. Old Mrs. Godman (the writer herself) was quite the evening star and the gentlemen took her for the Dr.'s sister. My hair was so admired and my teeth, the envy of the room, a wonderful old lady and such a figure. I laugh even now as I sit alone when I think of the compliments, such an eloquent Lady to never have been called a great talker, or "emphatic" but eloquent. Quite captivated, Mr. Ward wanted me badly to go back with him yesterday. If I were to give you an account of the individuals that either amused or interested me, I should need to put it in a pamphlet form, of the rejected lover who sat gazing on the "happy man" but could see nothing wonderful in him; a peep at the bride's fair shoulders and heavy sigh, the echo of which came floating to me; the queer old Ma, who came with dear Arrabella, being an heiress of 70,000., a carriage and pair with her dressing maid on horse back, 3 horses and 2 drivers, with these 2 visitors for 3 days. The breakfast was quite à la fourchette at 10. The ladies in full dress, all lavendar silk of various kinds and shades, the brides maids with 4 frounces, they changed for dinner and then for the dance in the evening given on the next plantation by her brother Clinton Ward (later the C. W. Satcher home in Ward). There again were the same side tables and inviting viands, the finest syllabubs I ever tasted. Surely I ought not to forget the Hon. Bull Punch, for I had a glass of it spilt on my light grey dress and ruined it, to the deep regret of the gentleman to say nothing of my private sentiments.

The night of the wedding we got to bed at 3, the next at nearly the same hour. How different from a city dance as we approached the house to see the fires built near the house, looking so bright. Everybody had to come in carriages, to see the horses and the rigs, folks alighting was a pretty sight. The gentlemen behaved remarkably well, considering the amount of wine drunk. Saturday morning we had quite a lively scene when the 4 buggies were drawn up to the gate for eight of the gentlemen to go. Mrs. Ward had a lunch put up for each of them with a flask of brandy. A merrier departure you never saw, such adieus to the little heiress, lamentations and laughing, all in a breath. Most earnestly did Mr. Ward try to persuade them to stay until Monday, but a week had been lost and business must commence for they had stopped a night and a day on the road at some friends who came with them. Saturday the weather moderated and Mr. Ward drove me over some of his land and showed me the fine trees he was cutting down. They had 200 cords of wood in the wood yard. Mr. Ward is fond of reading and has a good number of books and a tree of exquisite elegance, an English holly, in the center of a cotton field.

Your letter, dear sister, was very interesting. We had heard of the sickness at John's with deep regret, poor Basingher, her trials are over. What can E. do with the children? How pleasant it would truly be could we all meet together. For myself, I cannot answer yet.

What time in April do you expect to be drawn together, the first or last of the month? How difficult to act when under conflicting feelings—the desire to see you all and the knowledge how much I shall be missed at home. Mary has never had the care of Tom, and Johnny is a handful. Truly he is the liveliest child I ever saw. We are so proud of him and Tom behaved so well at the wedding, was thought both pretty and smart, he has a very reflective mind and merry too.

If you thought the violets sweet, how much more would you our hyacinths, and daffodils, crocus showing their bright faces in the beds. My room without fire has been 75 for three days, such is the climate, at this moment it rains. I have my nightcap on for it seems between the housekeeping, sewing and children that Grandma can't get time in the day to write. If S has a leisure moment, I must find time to listen to him. Fortunately our house is in a pleasant place as I seldom leave it. I have not told you all that is floating in my head, or round my heart, but my eyes give out, so good night, dear sister, with much love to all.

I had a letter from Cousin Margretta and one from E. and I grieve to say, to her labor she has added a small school. What can her husband think her made of?

Your own sister,
Angelica

A Father's Letter to His Daughter

Next is another family letter, this one written by the Union leader who wrought destruction during his famed March to the Sea. General William T. Sherman was a despised man in the South, but as this gentle letter to his daughter, Maria Ewing Sherman, shows, he was a kind and thoughtful father and a general who was fighting for that which he believed. To me, this letter is as lovely and loving as any written in history. It gives us insight into another side of the human character of one of history's important players, all the while reminding us of the nineteenth-century tradition of May Day.

Written from Nashville, Tennessee, May 1st, 1864

Dearest Minnie:

This is Sunday, May 1st, and a beautiful day it is. I have just come from a long ride over my old battlefield of November 25th, which is on a high ridge about four or five miles from Chattanooga. The leaves are now coming out and the young flowers have begun to bloom. I have gathered a few, which I send in token of my love and to tell you I gathered them on the very spot where many a brave man died for you, and such as you. I have made up a similar bouquet for Lizzie, which I will send her in a letter today, so that both of you will have a present to commemorate this bright opening of spring. You can keep this bouquet in some of your books and though it may fade away entirely it will in after years remind you of this year, whose history for good or evil is most important, and may either raise our country's fame to the highest standard, or sink it to that of Mexico. . . .

ALWAYS YOUR AFFECTIONATE FATHER

Remembering a Great Man's Gentleness

We know that Thomas Jefferson was an inveterate letter writer. In his correspondence he discussed politics, religion, education, and farming. President John Adams wrote of him, "While you live, I seem to have a Bank at Montecello {sic} on which I can draw for a Letter of Friendship and entertainment when I please." Jefferson was a devoted grandfather to "his little playmates," as he called the four little girls of his daughter, Martha Jefferson Randolph. We learn this not from one of Jefferson's letters, but from one written a generation later by his granddaughter. Ellen, one of the Randolph girls, touchingly wrote:

My Bible came from him, my Shakespeare, my first writing-table, my first handsome writing-desk, my first Leghorn hat, my first silk dress. . . . Our grandfather seemed to read our hearts, to see our invisible wishes, to be our good genius, to wave the fairy wand, to brighten our young lives by his goodness and his gifts.

Pen Pals

While reading and reflecting upon those letters that tell us so much about history and the people, both famous and everyday, who shape the world while they are in it and leave a legacy behind, I became saddened, thinking that there is so much about us today that future generations will never know. None of those three letters can be found in history textbooks. Human emotions and kind deeds are seldom written about. Conflicts and tribulations are much more interesting to historians. As Tolstoi wrote, "All happy families resemble one another; every unhappy family is unhappy in its own fashion." It takes traditions handed down from one generation to the next to pass on the joy, the cheer, the merriment of life.

Which is exactly what happened when I received a handwritten letter from my childhood friend Jane Tucker Pullen. It was written on lovely stationery in a flowing, full hand. I'm sure Jane used to get an A + in penmanship. I knew as I opened the letter and a wisp of rosemary filled the air something special awaited me.

Dear Emyl,

I hope you will think this tradition is as special as I do. My grandmother Harris would tie a ribbon with a sprig of rosemary in it on all of her presents. Mother and my sister, Vickie, and I do this too—for rosemary is for remembrance.

Love, Jane

CHAPTER 20

Church and Religion

IN GOD WE TRUST

⸺ *Fundamental to Us All* ⸺

* EMYL JENKINS

My father tells me we were driving along Ebenezer Church Road.

That sounds like a pretty safe guess to me. Any seasoned traveler of
Southern country roads will tell you that every county in every state
south of the Mason-Dixon line seems to have at least one Ebenezer
Church Road, along with a Calvary Church Road, a Mount Pleasant
Church Road, and a Mount Zion Church Road.

We were coming home from church. It was a summer Sunday
afternoon in the late 1940s that day when strains of beautiful music

filled the air as we came around the bend in the road. Had it been wintertime I surely would have thought I was hearing angels from the realms of glory.

Daddy slowed the Studebaker to a crawl. Mother opened her window, for once not caring about her hairdo of tight finger waves. I stayed put.

From the car we saw a parade of white-robed bodies moving toward the rocky creek bed beneath the one-lane bridge we were approaching. As one body they trudged down the gently sloping incline, never missing a word. "Take me to the water, take me to the water, take me to the water . . . to be baptized."

"Stop! Stop!" Mother exclaimed. "It's a colored baptism."

Daddy pulled off the asphalt onto the grass. Country roads didn't have shoulders in those days.

We piled out of the car, but we didn't draw too close. That would have been disrespectful. I don't know if we were even noticed.

For the next several minutes I watched with amazement and not a little fright, as one person after the other, some big and some small—we were too far away to discern much more than their size—moved forward to be dunked into the water. I remember some had to go down more than once. Mother told me that was because the devil was still in them.

"When Virginia got baptized, she told me that she looked down in that pool of water and saw the devil's face. He told her to go back. Then . . ." Mother paused, slowly painting the scene of our maid's baptism. "Ginny said she looked up at her pastor. 'He was such a huge man I knew he could hold me under,' she said. And he did. Almost too long," Mother nodded knowingly.

I trembled at the thought of my beloved Virginia, the devil, the pastor, and the cold water in the rocky creek. It was all bigger than life and certainly nothing this properly reared Episcopal child could comprehend.

But I could capture the magic of the moment. I've never forgotten it.

After each baptism great shouts went up. Voices burst into song. The air was electrified with mystery and majesty.

No theatrical production could have moved me more. To my young, impressionable mind, the stirring music was sweet at the same time it was powerful. The flowing white robes added mystery. Mother's editorializing certainly heightened the drama. The sense that we were spying added tension and intrigue in my overactive imagination. It was thrilling.

I remembered this scene not long ago.

Thirty years later, it was another Sunday afternoon. The steaming

August heat rising from the New Orleans sidewalk was equaled only by the rapture I felt as I entered the restored brick warehouse. I was inside the House of Blues ready to lose myself in the Gospel brunch.

This time the robes were red and there was no creek for a baptism. This time, instead of standing close to my parents, I sat at a table for which I had tipped the waiter more generously than I should have. It was worth it, though, to drink in the joy and spirit of the singers close up. The music was sweet and powerful, just as it had been almost fifty years earlier.

As one, the choir on the stage swayed to and fro. In the front row freshly scrubbed, shiny-faced children huddled close, nervously glancing at one another to catch the rhythm and an occasionally forgotten refrain. Behind them, ample-bodied women gleefully clapped their hands in unison and praise. Across the back, tall, deep-voiced men, filled with zeal, whirled their handkerchiefs high in the air. Together, their powerful sounds rocked the rafters. "Amazing grace, how great thou art."

It was a glorious sight. One that filled my heart with music and high spirits. I wouldn't have missed it for anything.

But I'm awfully glad I saw the real thing on that long-ago Sunday afternoon.

And I'm glad my redheaded, freckled Scotch-Irish mother sang at Temple Beth Sholum on Green Street in Danville, Virginia, for the high holy days.

Mother had a beautiful, trained voice. She had learned the Hebrew music while living in New York in the late 1920s. When we moved to Danville and she learned that the synagogue had no choir, mother rounded up a quartet and taught the music to them. Single-handed, this devout gentile brought the soulful, poignant traditional music to the Jewish congregation. Throughout my youth I went to Beth Sholum for Yom Kippur and to Epiphany Episcopal for Christmas.

I know of no richer sound than the teki'ah gedolah blown at the end of Rosh Hashanah and Yom Kippur. I know of no carol more moving than "Away in a Manger." I know of no lyrics more stirring than "I once was lost, but now am found, was blind, but now can see." I am glad that I have known them all.

And I'm glad that my New England father took my children, his grandchildren, to visit the family grave sites in Webster, Massachusetts, many years ago.

We sat on hard benches while the children, Joslin and Langdon, played among the graves and headstones.

"Generations. That's what it's all about," Daddy said in his usual taciturn way that speaks volumes.

So maybe it's natural that one Sunday morning when I was visiting my recently married daughter, Joslin, and her husband, Mike, in Richmond, Virginia, they said, "How about let's take a couple of hours and go walk around Hollywood cemetery. It's really neat." The couple of hours turned into an all-day excursion.

We were not alone.

Bicyclers and joggers trod along the narrow, winding paths. A car filled with out-of-towners looking for a family grave site crept slowly by. An Asian family lighted the kerosene flame on the headstone of their departed and then spread a picnic lunch. A genealogist copiously jotted down names, dates, and places listed on the monument to the Confederate dead in her thick notebook. My own newlyweds strolled hand-in-hand in front of me.

These activities had nothing to do with sorrowful mourning. They had everything to do with quiet contemplation, beauty, remembrance, history, and the celebration of life.

You see, years ago, before movies and automobiles, whole families and their friends spent their Sunday afternoons picnicking and lounging in beautiful bucolic churchyards and cemeteries.

In those days lovers meandered under towering oak trees and stole kisses behind evergreen shrubs. Children frolicked in the open spaces and played hide-and-seek among the tombstones. And the melancholy could contemplate their own mortality in these settings made all the more beautiful by nature's uplifting gifts of lovely flowers and cheerful birds.

It was a rich and wonderful tradition.

These days it is easier to go to a Gospel brunch than to find a country baptism. It is easier not to go to church at all than to sing in the choir. It is easier to watch the Sunday afternoon ball game on TV than to make the effort to take a leisurely walk through the cemetery.

We can't turn back the clock. But we can be glad of our memories, for they bring us thoughts that feed our souls, even if we won't take the time to do so ourselves.

⌁ *Old-Time Religion* ⌁

HARTZELL SPENCE

White robes and gleaming faces. Picnic suppers and joyful voices. Hot nights and hell's furnace. The old-fashioned revival meeting was a combination religious and social event. Throw in rhetoric, bigger-than-life characters, and unswerving convictions and this celebration of faith was a rich part of America's cultural heritage. It still exists, but in a different setting.

The sandy brown canvas tents have given way to whitewashed stone tabernacles. Crimson red carpets have replaced the mud-and-grass ground floors. And fold-up slat-back chairs are used only when the padded pews are filled to overflowing. While amplified music plays, TV cameras zoom in on the saved and unsaved alike. Times may have changed, but the players are the same. The tradition of coming together in faith and hope came over with our forefathers.

The revival meeting has undergone many changes since its early days. There was a time when the followers of John Wesley were known as "the shouting Methodists" because of their vocal response to religious exhortation.

Even when I was a boy certain preachers had standard phrases they relied on to provoke cries of "Amen," and any evangelist who didn't "raise the roof" was not invited back another year. The old-time revivalists loved spontaneous encouragement. Today a minister would feel heckled if his congregation interpolated loud shouts of agreement during his discourse.

I remember an elderly Methodist bishop who worked for an hour and a half to thaw out a prewar congregation. He tried all his tricks but met only stony silence. Exasperated, finally, he interrupted his sermon to ask, "Are those bald heads I see down there or tombstones?"

No one answered.

"You, brother," he said, pointing to a man in an aisle seat, "have you a voice?"

The man nodded but did not speak.

"Then use it, man, use it," the bishop begged. "How does the Lord know you are a Christian unless you shout out the glory?"

His listener merely looked uncomfortable.

"Praise the Lord!" shouted the bishop. Even that drew no reaction. Again he pointed down the aisle.

"Can you say 'Praise the Lord?' "

"Why, of course."

"Then say it man, say it."

The man said it.

"You whisper!" the bishop roared. "Is that all you think of the Lord? Can't you shout? Come, now, follow me. Praise the Lord!"

This time there was a faint echo.

"That's better. Shout it now, louder."

The man shouted.

"Hallelujah!" cried the bishop. "Everyone in the auditorium, now, repeat after me, and use your lungs! Hallelujah!"

The reaction was half-hearted but promising.

"That's the spirit. Again, with all your might. Hallelujah!"

"Hallelujah!" came the answer.

"Now, after me: Praise the Lord!"

"Praise the Lord!"

"Now once more: Amen!"

"Amen!" This time the answer was tumultuous.

The bishop mopped his brow and smiled. "That's better," he said. "I was afraid for a moment I was addressing heathen."

There is a story told of a circuit evangelist in the early days of Indiana Methodism who spent two solid hours exhorting his backwoods audience to repent. At the altar call only a few timid women came forward. Angered at this lack of faith, the preacher glared about the church, then shouted, "I have a deep impression that some young man or woman in this house will be tramping the streets of Hell before I come again." The penitents' rail filled quickly.

Father was as much responsible as anyone in Methodism for a change in revival technique. He never exhorted anyone to be good lest he roast in Hell. Rather, he made the avenue of Christ so tempting that his congregation wanted to walk it with him.

In his regular sermons father usually chose a New Testament text: one in which the Christian way of life was a thrilling experience. During a revival father continued along this tack, though in his early ministry he usually brought in a professional evangelist to exhort those parishioners who responded only to the threat of brimstone, as had their fathers, when Hell-fire was needed to compete against the worldly excitement of free land and Indian murder.

Father's revival-meeting strategy always was the same on the first night. He worked on his regular church congregation. Graphically he recalled all the sins, both of commission and omission, of which his flock was guilty.

So profound was his understanding of human frailties, needs, and longings that every sermon he preached was personal. He never referred to an actual case, of course. But many in the congregation thought he did, and, as he was preaching, people would look furtively about to discover how many persons besides the pastor had discovered their secret sin. Sometimes half a dozen members would take personally the same remark and hasten to repent.

"I could tell whom I was hitting by the way they looked over their shoulders to see if the family skeletons were sitting behind them," father said years later. "And sometimes members would become angry and stay away, believing my sermon was aimed directly at them."

At the first revival meeting in the new tabernacle, father empha-
sized the need for an annual renewal, just as the housekeeper puts her
home in order and the businessman takes inventory. Then he hit his
parish amidships.

"How many of you," he asked, leaning across his pulpit intimately,
"have been uncharitable toward a neighbor or have not settled a quarrel? How many of you have neglected your children's religious training
because you were too lazy to get up in time for Sunday school? Do
you harbor a grudge against a business competitor? Have you overworked your employees or your hired girl? Can you come to the altar
of Christ with a pure heart? Or is your soul so crowded with little sins
that there is no room for Christ?"

He let that message sink in while the choir, always augmented for
revivals, chanted softly:

> *Just as I am*
> *Without one plea,*
> *But that Thy blood*
> *Was shed for me*
> *And that Thou bidd'st me*
> *Come to Thee,*
> *O Lamb of God, I come, I come!*

Father held up his hand. The singing stopped, but the organ continued the hymn. To its accompaniment father spoke: "There probably is
no one here tonight who is not trying to live as Jesus would have us
all live. But we are human, and we have sinned. Forgive us, O Lord."

From the retired-ministers' corner came a loud "Amen."

Responding to this reaction, father lifted his voice slightly. " 'There
is probably no one here tonight who deep in his heart doesn't want to
let Christ in. Open our hearts, O God."

Again came the "Amen" from several directions.

Father stepped from his pulpit to the altar rail.

"I ask all those who earnestly want to follow Christ to join me here
at the altar. Let God and your neighbors know that you humbly repent
your sins and that you earnestly desire to live the Christian life. Come!"

The choir sang the hymn again.

> *Just as I am, and waiting not*
> *To rid my soul of one dark blot,*
> *To Thee, whose blood can cleanse each spot,*
> *O Lamb of God, I come, I come!*

Nobody moved. But father knew the courage such a declaration required. He was in no hurry.

"We are assembled here," he resumed, "in a new tabernacle. Before us lies a year that will test our faith. Give us courage, O God."

"Amen!"

"We will need greater faith, greater love than ever before. Give us that faith, O God."

"Amen. Amen."

The congregation was a little restless now under the enchantment of the minister's voice and the repetition of the hymn.

Father walked up and down before the altar, then spoke again.

"I remember a man who once said to me: 'Brother Spence, why should I be saved? I am already saved.' My answer was: 'Brother, conversion redeems a man from the sins he has committed. But many a man thinks that because he is saved he can do no wrong and, thus encouraged, he develops new sins.' I have no doubt that many of you here tonight believe that because once you were saved you will forever remain in grace. That is not true. Salvation must be renewed. You need to cleanse your hearts anew. Your pastor needs to cleanse his own heart. Who will join me as I confess my own weakness?"

Father knelt at the penitents' rail, and again the choir sang. Three retired preachers came forward and knelt beside their pastor. Emboldened, a few church members slipped from their pews. Soon a score or more were kneeling.

The visiting evangelist then stopped directing the choir and stepped to the pulpit. That year he was Wilson Keeler, a famous exhorter who brought his wife as organist and his son as tenor and trombonist.

" 'Come unto Me,' " he said softly, " 'all ye who are weary and heavy laden, and I will give you rest.' How often you have heard those words. Yet how many of you actually come to Christ? How many of you are so proud of your Heavenly Father that you will publicly declare your desire to renew your Christian faith? Will you come?"

They came. The organ played. Father arose and went in turn to each penitent to whisper a few words. Mr. Keeler continued his persuasion.

"There may be many here tonight who have always tried to live the Christian life but have never publicly declared their Christianity. How often have we heard the words? 'I am not ready yet. Wait a little while.' When I was in Michigan last year a beautiful young mother attended many of our meetings, but she would not come forward. 'I am not ready yet,' she said. This year I returned to her town and asked for her. She was dead. And I was deeply touched. Once too often she had said, 'I am not ready yet.' Now it is too late. We never know when our turn may come. I may be next. You may be next. God grant that we may be ready. Come! Do it now, while the Hand is upon you! Do it now, that your heart may be at peace. Don't let the Devil struggle with your soul. Wrest him out and come to Jesus. Come and see how serene your life will be with God in your heart. Don't put it off. Don't say you are not ready. Come!"

They came.

The choir sang other hymns: "Rock of Ages," "Amazing Grace, how sweet the sound that saved a wretch like me," "My Faith looks up to Thee, Thou Lamb of Calvary," and "O Jesus, I have promised, to serve Thee to the end."

Father and Mr. Keeler alternated at the exhortation, with little anecdotes out of their own experience, simple emotional pleas that touched every kind of sinner. In half an hour, when all the church stalwarts had renewed their faith, father dismissed the congregation with a stirring prayer in which he begged God to lay his hand during the revival on all who needed salvation. Then he kept the penitents a little longer for another prayer, and the three retired preachers saw that all filled out a card detailing their names, addresses, and church affiliation, if any.

Rarely was the first night anything but a renewal of faith for regular church members, although a few stray sheep were rounded up. Father would use those saved on the opening night as an inspirational group that sifted through the audience in the course of the following meetings. During altar calls thenceforth little scenes occurred all over the tabernacle.

Mrs. Welch, who had been fighting with her neighbor over a boundary dispute, but could not sue her because the Discipline forbade Methodists from suing each other, slipped into the pew beside her adversary one night and put an arm around her. The two wept quietly for a minute; then Mrs. Welch led her neighbor to the rail and knelt with her.

Mr. Cambridge, angry for weeks at a parishioner who had bought a piano from a competitor, went to his enemy and shook his hand. The two talked for a moment, then went to the rail.

One night Mrs. Baker saw, sitting alone, a young woman who had applied at her millinery store for a job. Mrs. Baker went to her.

"You are Mrs. Salverson, aren't you?"

She nodded.

"May I help you?" Mrs. Baker whispered. "Perhaps if you tell me what's troubling you, it might help."

Wrought to an intense emotionalism by the repeated altar calls and music, Mrs. Salverson cried bitterly. "I can't do it any longer," she sobbed. "Night after night I have come here, but it does no good. I think of my two little children hungry at home. If God was as kind as these men say, wouldn't He keep my babies from starving?"

Mrs. Baker tried to put an arm around her, but Mrs. Salverson drew away.

"I have tried desperately to get a job," she said. "But nobody needs me.

"Have you no husband?" Mrs. Baker asked.

Mrs. Salverson shook her head. "He died a year ago and left nothing."

Tears filled Mrs. Baker's eyes.

"God bless you," she said. "I am a widow, too, and I have very little, but you are welcome to share it. I will find work for you."

A moment later Mrs. Baker led Mrs. Salverson to the altar.

One night, when the hammering of rain on the tabernacle's wooden roof echoed across many empty seats, Major Cooper spied a vaguely familiar face in the congregation. He finally placed it as that of Reuben Wright, once a regular churchgoer but now never seen. The major hobbled up the aisle and slid into Wright's pew.

"I haven't seen you in some time."

"I haven't been here." Reuben Wright scowled.

"Have you been out of town?"

"No."

"Have you been sick?"

"Let me alone," Wright said.

The major sat silently beside him for a long time. The altar call continued. The music swelled. Mr. Keeler's son played softly on his trombone an old hymn: "Jesus is tenderly calling, today. Calling oh, sinner, come home."

Wright stirred. "I haven't heard that for a long time," he said.

The major nodded.

"I was just thinking that, too."

"Do you remember," Wright asked, "how Wesley Carmichael used to play it on the cornet in Sunday school?"

"So he did," the major recalled. "Why, that's fifteen years ago!"

"Yes," Wright replied, "it's been a long time."

"But it would be good to hear him again," the major said. "I wonder if we could get him to play it Sunday? If we could, would you come?"

Wright hesitated. "The church has outgrown me. It doesn't want me around any more."

The major remembered now. Wright had stopped attending church when the choir had been reorganized eight years before. Wright's voice was gone, they had said. A flicker of sympathy came into the major's eyes.

"They don't need me, either," he said, humbly. "I no longer do anything except attend the Sunday service. And I get mighty lonely, sitting there by myself. Why don't you come out next Sunday and join me? It would help. Maybe we could organize an old duffers' Bible class, and you could teach. You used to discuss the Scriptures wonderfully, I remember."

Reuben Wright looked at the major for the first time. "Do you think we could?"

"Why not?" the major asked. "There must be others, like us, who have grown away."

"There's the Widow Jordan," Wright said. "She hasn't been to church since Albert died. There's Harry Gray—you remember him—"

"And Lizzie Carson," the major added, "whatever happened to Lizzie Carson?"

"We ought to find out," Wright suggested.

"Let's do it."

It was Wright now who sought the major's hand.

"You know," he said, "I've been hoping for years that I could get back to my church. I've missed it."

A moment later they walked up the aisle together. Father knew from their faces that something extraordinary had happened and gave them a special blessing.

— ◆ —

Another rainy night brought an entirely different scene. Forester Ross, entering by a side door, hung his wet coat on the end post that supported the altar. The corner was dark, since gas lamps in the tabernacle were centered as much as possible. After the sermon father, as usual, filled the rail with penitents and at the end of the service sent them to their seats. As usual, too, before his benediction he glanced up and down the rail, for sometimes a sinner, wrestling with a particularly heavy sin, remained at prayer after everyone else had gone. This night, in the dim corner by the door, he saw a figure hunched into a coat, head bowed so low it was out of sight.

Quietly father addressed the meeting. "We still have one soul at the altar. If upon his conscience there is a grievous burden, he needs our help. Let us all pray silently that he may recover his faith."

The organ played softly one verse of a hymn.

"Amen," father said, but the penitent did not rise.

Father waited a moment, then prayed aloud for mercy on the sinner. Still there was no response. Again father waited, then gave a broad hint. "Go in peace," he said, "and may the Lord go with thee."

Still nothing happened.

Thinking perhaps the man had fainted, father walked over to the dim corner. He put his hand on what should have been a shoulder and touched a post.

Unabashed, he turned to his flock, which by then realized what had happened.

"Let us not be dismayed," he said quietly, "that we have lifted up our prayers for an empty coat. Now you know how I feel, night after night, praying for living, breathing souls in this tabernacle who could respond and will not."

The Old Camp Meeting

*JOYCE SQUIBB, WITH THE HELP OF
HOUSTON CARDER AND AUBREY KEYES

To the best of my knowledge, the Sulphur Springs Camp Meeting in Jonesborough, Tennessee, is America's oldest continuous revival. Based on a rural eighteenth-century custom of getting together for religion and social fellowship, during the nineteenth century the camp meeting, as it was called, grew in popularity along with the increasing population of the countryside.

Today the tradition of the camp meeting is more viable than the meeting itself. The once-overflowing meeting day attendance has dwindled down to only a handful of faithful attendees. The newly erected marker citing the campground's inclusion on the National Register of Historic Places seems to tell us that the meeting place's past is more important than its future. Still, the tried and faithful devotees of the Sulphur Springs Camp Meeting have vowed that the meeting "shall not die." And so they pray: "O Lord, save us as a living part of this heritage in order that we may continue to praise Thee day by day in our life, to the honor and glory of Thy holy name, world without end. Amen."

The Sulphur Springs Camp Meeting had its beginning sometime between the years 1820 and 1823, although the first meetings might have occurred as early as 1815, being held under brush arbors. But its real beginning as a camp meeting began in 1845 when the Reverend William Milburn had the idea to build a shed to protect people from the weather. Payne Squibb donated the land, and a small shed was constructed in which to hold services.

Before the building of the shed, camp meetings were held all over Holston Conference. Time was set aside toward the latter part of the summer for the occasion. People came from as far as fifty to a hundred miles away to attend a two- to three-week revival. They came in wagons and in horsedrawn buggies equipped with necessary provisions: a coop full of chickens, freshly baked pies, and perhaps a cow to milk. A communal pot set on rocks above hot coals was used to cook the meat for all to share.

Horses were hitched under big oak trees by a creek, and the land to the right of the campground—it is now a cemetery—provided pasture for all the livestock. There were so many wagons coming in and so many animals grazing or tethered below the camp that dust would sometimes be an inch thick. It wasn't unusual for some horse trading to be going on.

One time some "fellers" from Chimney Top Mountain came galloping their horses up and down in the dust. According to Mr. Aubrey Keyes, who remembers the incident, one of the men said he was the biggest "tater" in the hills. John Sherfey, who was then sheriff, arrested him and fined him five dollars for disturbing the peace.

In the very early days of camp meeting, women wore bonnets instead of hats because hats were the style. Anyway, hats called attention to one's self. But, as camp meeting grew in size and popularity, clothes became important, for it was here that a person intermingled with more people than he might see all year long. Mothers began sewing weeks before the big event. Perhaps a new suit was purchased or even a new pair of overalls, but whatever the apparel, everyone wore his finest.

By the middle of the century these meetings were so popular that camps, or temporary living quarters, often two stories high, were constructed on the grounds not far from the church shed. In these, the families who came from a long distance would cook and sleep. In addition to the kitchen, the camp was outfitted with shelf-like beds long enough to accommodate all the women or all the men. Everyone slept crosswise in the wooden, strawfilled bunks, often five to six people deep. In some of the fancier camps, a white curtain hung around the downstairs bed and a ladder led to the upper loft or "upstairs" bed. The preachers had their own camp, or sometimes found lodging at a neighbor's home in the community.

In the early days, many "jack leg" preachers and circuit riders came into camp by wagon, horse, or some other means of conveyance. But with the coming of the automobile, the church sent a taxi to Johnson City to meet the Southern Railroad train and take the preachers out to the campsite.

The first water supply was a hand-dug well beside what is now Ray's Grocery Store. However, in 1903 a cemetery was opened above it and people didn't want to drink water that had flowed under the graves, so George Price hauled water on an ox-drawn wagon in wooden barrels. In 1910 a line was run from a spring to two adjoining concrete tanks. Ice covered with sawdust was hauled from Jonesboroughs. The sawdust was washed off of the ice in a small tank between the two larger ones. It was then dropped into the water in the two large tanks, which had several spigots. A tin cup attached by a chain to the tanks was used to drink from.

There were usually three services each day: morning, midafternoon, and evening. A ram's horn summoned everyone to the nine-o'clock morning service, at which time people would leave their camps and congregate in the shed. Sunday was the biggest day of the week, and for many years it was also the day of the Lovefeast. Bread and water were passed around and people would make their testimonials. During the evening service there would inevitably be an altar call, often accompanied by a lot of shouting.

It has been said that the women were more fond of shouting than men; however, Mr. Keyes tells a story of his uncle, Barney McCraw, veteran of the War of 1812, who one night got the spirit. He had never been a shouter even though his wife was frequently filled with the Holy Ghost. On this particular evening people were running up and down the aisles clasping their hands and shouting, when the spirit moved Uncle Barney, who all of a sudden got "happy." He ran through the middle of the crowd handing his hat to his wife, and in a loud voice he yelled, "Whoooppeee, they've got the devil rousted." You could hear him for a mile. This was called spasmodic religion, when people were just runnin' over.

One night Uncle Barney was leaned up against his camp in a chair watching a pot of beef cook when out of the darkness a rogue sow appeared. A service was in progress, after which people would be wanting to eat, and the sow, busily rooting in the "skinnings," was getting dangerously near the pot. So Uncle Barney, wishing to prevent the pot being overturned, filled a shovel full of ashes and threw them at the hind end of the pig who immediately took off with a tremendous squeal right toward the shed where worship was going on. It caused a great disturbance.

In 1900 the original shed was torn down and a larger one, which is the present shed, was constructed on the spot using many of the old beams that had been hand-hewn with a broadax. The new shed was estimated to hold over six hundred people.

In 1907 Mr. R. A. N. Walker built a dormitory above the shed that housed students during the school months and doubled as a hotel for those attending camp meeting during the summer. The dormitory was managed by Mr. "Cooper" John Keyes—the "Cooper" was affixed to his name because he bought land from the Coopers—who would bring six 1,000-pound beef cattle every two weeks and kill over two hundred chickens. It took a lot of meat to feed the ever-growing number of people who attended the meeting.

The toilet facilities which were provided for the people would be enough to deter the staunchest modern-day churchgoer from ever attending such a camp. An outhouse, set a little way above the ground but with no hole under it, was built for the women. The men had to go to the fields for their bathroom facilities. One doctor theorized that it was always after camp meeting that people were stricken with typhoid fever, perhaps because of the unsanitary conditions.

Although the first camp meeting had been conceived in a religious spirit, even requiring one day of fasting a week, the tone of the event had begun to change. Candy shacks and watermelon wagons had begun to appear on the periphery of the grounds, which were later enclosed by a picket fence. In order to help with the upkeep of the grounds, a ten cents admission was charged. Some people grumbled about the idea of paying to go to church, and others waited outside the fence until evening when everyone was admitted free. But, most paid the price. After all, it had become the big social event of the year.

With so many children attending, there were, of course, a few rules of conduct. No running was allowed, quiet times had to be observed, and there could be no "antney over" behind the corn crib. In later times, Hoopie Hide was a favorite game after the services were over, but looking for doodlebugs in the sawdust which covered the floor of the big shed offered much entertainment during the sermon. Looking in the little holes into which the doodlebugs had burrowed, the children would call softly, "Doodlebug, doodlebug, come on out of there."

"To everything there is a season and a time to every purpose under the heaven." It finally became apparent with the advent of air travel, television, the panoramic cinema, and the other myriad things that vie for the average American's time, that the time of the old fashioned camp meeting had passed. True, it is still attended today, but only a token number of people sit on the wooden benches under the hand-hewn beams singing the hymns that once carried over the hills the news that camp meeting was in session.

❧ The Retreat ❧

MARY JANE FRANCES CAVOLINA MEARA,
JEFFREY ALLEN JOSEPH STONE, MAUREEN ANNE TERESA KELLY,
RICHARD GLEN MICHAEL DAVIE

Call it a camp meeting or a retreat—the purpose is the same. Yet this well-intended religious gathering epitomizes the ongoing tug-of-war between past and present ways of doing things. To keep the tradition alive, most churches try to accommodate everyone—in good faith, so to speak. From the humorous, multi-author book Growing Up Catholic *comes this account of two different types of the obligatory "retreat."*

There are two basic kinds of retreats, the old-style contemplative retreat and the modern interpersonal retreat. The old-style retreat, which is favored by most of the religious and the exceptionally devout, usually lasts anywhere from a weekend to a week. Any longer than that and the retreat is no longer a retreat. You have become a hermit.

The old-style retreat takes place at a wooded, secluded abbey or convent and the days are spent walking in natural beauty while busily fingering a rosary. It is better not to speak to anyone, with the exception of small animals one meets in the woods, in order to maintain a reflective state of mind. Meals are taken in spartan surroundings. They are bland and not particularly filling, but this isn't The Four Seasons. It is a place where you can think about what a terrible person you are and, one hopes, get your act together enough to be a better person when you leave. While on the old-style retreat you will see some terribly religious people wandering aimlessly (sometimes into trees or small streams) with a look of perfect contentment on their faces. Try to be like them.

The modern retreat is for the more worldly, yet involved, religious and for high school students who cannot be quiet for ten minutes, much less a week-end. Those retreats take place at a wooded, secluded brother house, tucked far enough away in the hills or wheat fields that there is no easy access to a liquor depot where a six pack (or worse) could be purchased. The purpose of the retreat for high school students is to try one more time—and in their own language—to get them to think about their role as Catholics in the modern world.

As soon as they arrive at the brother house, which is a large wooden building not unlike a ski lodge, even if it's in the middle of Iowa, the seniors begin plotting how they will get out that night without getting caught. They are unsure how much punishment they may receive if caught, but this makes it all the more exciting. They are then divided into two groups, boys and girls, and shown to their monk-like cells. They find it strange that they should be sequestered in these bare dorms since the rest of the house, with roaring fireplaces and redwood beams, look like Jerry Ford's condo in Vail.

After orientation, everyone gets together to listen to "Bridge over Troubled Water." Certain interpersonal games are then played. In one game everyone sits in a big room with a chair in the middle. Each person must take a turn sitting in the chair and anyone can say anything they want to the person in the chair. Usually it is pretty tame stuff: however, every once in a while someone lets loose with, "You know, you seem so stuck up, you don't let anyone get to know you." Whereupon the person in the chair is reduced to tears. Another game involves being forced to select the person in the class you like least and going into the woods or fields with her for an hour without speaking. This exercise is designed to encourage strong friendships.

After three days of mind-boggling and heart-wrenching, everyone gets together and listens to "Bridge over Trouble Water" again, then gets on the bus and sits with the same friends they sat with on the way in, better for the entire experience.

After a modern retreat of this nature one boy will decide to become a priest or brother, two girls who were going to become Sisters decide not to, one boy has a nervous breakdown and three get suspended for drinking beer.

∼ Welcome, New Neighbors ∼

Yanceyville, North Carolina, is a quiet town in a rural county that borders on the Virginia state line. Aristocratic old families and good middle-class farmers have lived there side-by-side for generations. Around the outskirts of town there is plenty of pretty, rolling land. Rich people from nearby Raleigh and Durham could buy it up and make the region a fashionable place to have a second home. But there is no beach. There are no mountains. There is just land and forest and the stars at night.

That's what drew the Amish to the region, not in the nineteenth century or even in the 1930s, but just a couple of years ago. Now eleven Amish families live in that seemingly unlikely Southern setting.

I had never seen any Amish outside of Pennsylvania, and had someone asked me, I would have said they are a dying breed. I would have been wrong.

These days I delight in seeing the horse-drawn buggy rocking along the shoulder of Route 86 taking the family to the Food Lion grocery store. Once there, they tie the horse to the hitching post that the manager put up for them. Why not? Yanceyville is a neighborly place that understands traditions, even if they are not homegrown. Those people respect these people, their beliefs, and their ways, for as William Schreiber wrote in Our Amish Neighbors, *"To sit among the bearded, vigorous men and the hooded, gentle-appearing women during their Christian worship service, in barn or house, and to share their meal at a communal table, gives one an opportunity to understand the purpose and direction of these Christian primitivists."*

To the outsider, the Amish appear to be as strong as their beliefs. Their dress is as austere as their behavior. Their inner strength seems as unrelenting as their work ethic. They ask little of the world and the rest of us. Their purpose is to live an honest life, assured that their way of life is the right way. This vignette from Rosanna of the Amish *vividly captures the Amish life and tradition, from the order of the hymns to the positioning of the silverware on the table for the "preaching meal."*

Early Education

JOSEPH W. YODER

That evening Cristal said, "Now, you women folks get everything ready this evening; we want to go to preaching in the morning. Preaching is over at Benjamin Byler's and it is close to ten miles, so we must start a little before seven in the morning."

They were off to a good start in the morning. The full-grown corn along the way seemed to cool the air, and the horses were in fine fettle. The new carriage ran so quietly and the horses were so spirited that Cristal and Elizabeth began to analyze their own feelings to see if there might be a little pride there. It was just eight-thirty when they drove into Benjamin Byler's well kept lane.

And they were not the first to arrive. Already many white and yellow carriages stood in straight rows in the sod field just outside the barnyard. Mixed in with these were the buggies driven by the young unmarried men. Elizabeth and Rosanna alighted from the carriage and went into the house. One of the Byler boys came quickly to unhitch the horses and put them in the stable.

Cristal joined a good-sized group of men who had gathered under the "overshot" waiting until it was time to go into the house and begin the services. Cristal shook hands all around, whether he knew the men or not. Then seeing his relative, Joseph Yoder, he approached him, shook hands, and joined in the conversation. Just then Bishop Shem arrived. Two of the ministers and the deacon were already there. The bishop saluted the ministers and the deacon with the Holy Kiss and then shook hands with all the others.

In a moment the bishop said, "Well, I guess it's about time to go into the house," meaning that it was time to begin the preaching services. As Bishop Shem started for the house most of the old men followed. Soon one of the middle-aged men said, "I guess it's about time to go in," and that group went to the house. Soon all the younger men and boys followed and the house was full. While the men were taking their places, the women and girls came in and occupied the seats reserved for them.

The Amish people hold their preaching services in their houses or in the barn if the house is not large enough to accommodate the congregation, but they never hold services under trees or out in the open. The members share in turn at "taking preaching," which usually comes around about once a year. To accommodate these preaching services the Amish build their houses with movable partitions on the first floor. On preaching day all partitions can be removed and the lower part of the house becomes one big room. This makes it possible for almost everybody in the house to see and hear the preacher.

Each member provides himself with a set of benches that fit his house exactly. On preaching day these are placed properly and provide seats for the whole congregation. In one corner of this large room a table is placed and on it the hymnbooks are stacked. The hymns are all in German and the books are called *die dücke schnalle Bücher* (the thick buckle books—so called because the books are held closed by a buckle or clasp). These books contain about four hundred pages and are bound in leather.

Around this table the men singers are seated. The benches next to the table and running parallel the full length of the room are filled with other men as they come in. Next to this table, near the center of the end of the room, a bench or a row of chairs are reserved for the bishop and the ministers. The ministers face the singers' table. About two rows back of the ministers the young unmarried women sit, occupying three or four benches, and back of them the middle-aged and older women, and farthest away the mothers with babies and small children.

While the congregation is gathering, not a word is spoken. The men sit in silence with their hats on. When the house is well filled and the proper time has arrived, about 8:30 or 8:45, the deacon rises, takes some of the hymnbooks and passes them to the unmarried young women sitting just back of the men. One of the leaders of singing then announces the number of a hymn, and the men remove their hats.

As the leader begins singing and others join in, the ministers rise and withdraw to a room prepared for them upstairs. Here they engage in a short devotional exercise, attend to any church business, determine which one will "make the beginning" (preach first) and which one will preach the main sermon *(Gemeh halde)*. If there is any business relative to the church or any member, it is discussed here and a course of action agreed upon. Sometimes a decision is reached to bring the matter before the whole membership.

While the bishop and the ministers are in the *Abroth* (council), the congregation continues singing hymns. The second hymn, by tradition, is always *Das Lob Sang* (Hymn of Praise). It is never announced. Amish hymns are sung in one part only and are difficult to sing. There is no written music for these hymns. Young men must learn them by note from older singers and it frequently takes a long time. For that reason a young singer usually tries to lead this *Lob Sang* as his first attempt. He has the assurance, however, that should he get off the tune, there are older men sitting at his elbow who will take up the melody and help him along.

A third hymn is announced, but if the ministers return from the upstairs room before it is finished, the song period concludes with whatever stanza is being sung. It is not considered appropriate to sing long after the ministers return from the *Abroth* (council). As the ministers take their places again, they shake hands with all in reach who may have come in since the service began.

When the hymn is finished, the minister "making the beginning" rises and speaks for about thirty minutes. At the close of his talk the congregation kneels in silent prayer. This prayer is terminated by the bishop who stands up to indicate the close of the prayer period and the congregation rises with him. When the congregation rises, each member stands facing the bench on which he sat, while the deacon reads a chapter from the New Testament (never from the Old Testament).

After the reading, the congregation is seated and the minister who will preach the sermon stands up. He frequently preaches for an hour and a half and on special occasions for two hours. All this time the people are seated on backless benches, demonstrating endurance as well as devotion. Soon after the main speaker has begun his discourse, the hostess comes in quietly carrying a platter filled with good-sized pieces of half-moon pies. She gives a piece to each child in the room, for by this time the children are getting a little hungry and restless.

When the main speaker has finished the first part of his sermon, he is seated. He then calls on each minister and deacon present for a testimony or an additional thought, if they wish to give it. If a respected visiting Amishman is present, the speaker may call on him for a testimony whether he is a minister or not.

After the testimonies the main speaker rises again and expresses gratitude that his discourse was considered orthodox. After a few brief remarks, the congregation again kneels in prayer while the preacher reads aloud from the prayerbook. The same prayer is always used (the Amish never offer original prayers anywhere). When this prayer is ended, they all stand again facing the bench on which they sat as before, while the minister pronounces the benediction. As he closes the benediction with the words, *"Durch Jesum Christum, Amen"* (Through Jesus Christ, Amen), the whole congregation bow perceptibly at the knee and are seated.

At this point the deacon makes all the announcements, publishes the names of those intending to marry soon, and then requests the members to remain seated if there is any church business (the others are excused). Following the other announcements, he names the home where preaching will be held in two weeks. When he is through, some man at the singers' table announces the number of a hymn. When the last note of the hymn has died away, the men rise slowly, put on their hats, and slowly pass out of the house. As the men file out, the young women begin leaving and then the older ones. The women either go outside or to some other part of the house.

As soon as the room is empty, the man of the house and his helpers remove all the benches except a few retained for tables and seats. Then at the most convenient place, usually through the longest part of the house, two tables are set up made of two benches set side by side— one table for men and one for women.

Girls who have volunteered to help the hostess come quickly, spread white table cloths over these bench tables and set them. First a knife, a spoon, a cup and saucer, and a drinking glass are placed along each side of the table about two feet apart. Then large plates of bread, half-moon pies (dried apple pies), green apple pies, butter, apple butter, cream, red beets, and pickles are placed on the table. To this are added large bowls of hot bean soup. This is the standard preaching meal, and it never varies.

When all is ready, the man of the house goes to the door and announces, "Dinner is ready." The bishop, the ministers, the deacon, and the old men go in first until the table is full. While the men are taking their places, the old and middle-aged women are being seated at their table. When both tables are filled, the host announces, "The tables are full," whereupon the bishop says, "Let us pray." All bow their heads and engage in silent prayer. No audible blessing is ever uttered. When grace is over, the girls who set the tables come with large pots of hot coffee, offering coffee to all who wish it. These girls then wait on the tables, replenishing bread plates and pie plates and offering second helpings of coffee to all.

When everyone has finished eating, a brief pause is observed and then the bishop says, "If we are all through, let us give thanks," and a silent prayer of thanksgiving follows. When this prayer is over, both men and women arise from the tables and leave the room. The waitresses come and reset the tables, but they do not wash the dishes.

When the tables are ready the second time, the man of the house again goes to the door and announces that dinner is ready. The older men who have not eaten yet and the middle-aged men fill the one table, and the older women and the middle-aged women fill the table for the women. When the places are all taken, the man of the house announces again that the table is full, and without any word from the bishop or anyone else, they all bow their heads in silent grace. In the same way table after table is served and replenished, being filled each time with younger persons, until finally the little boys and girls who can care for themselves fill the table. Younger children go to the table with their parents. Finally when all have eaten, everything is cleared away.

The house wife never needs to worry about what she will serve for dinner; the meal is always the same. And there is a regular form of preparation. On the Wednesday prior to preaching services a half dozen women of the same church come and help polish the tinware. On Friday three or four come to help bake the bread, as many as forty big loaves. On Saturday a dozen women come to help bake about sixty green apple pies and four or five hundred half-moon pies. The latter are made of dried apples cooked to about the consistency of apple sauce. A piece of pie dough is then rolled out to the thickness of pie crust, circular in shape. The dried apples are spread on one half of it and the other half is brought over the apples and pinched tight at the edges making a pie the form of a half circle or half moon. These are laid on tin pie plates and baked. Since they are all of one piece with the edges tightly pinched together, they are easily served.

It usually takes from about one o'clock to three to serve a Sunday dinner. While one group is eating, the other men stand around the barn or in the yard and visit. The topic of conversation is usually crops, weather, markets, cattle, and sometimes religion. While the men chat outside, the women visit in the house. They generally talk about gardens, housecleaning, chickens, butter making, or some moral question. Sometimes a little gossip slips in. In this way Amish preaching serves two purposes, religious guidance and a social occasion.

About three o'clock, or sooner, if the family has all had dinner, the husband goes to the house or sends a little boy to see whether mother is ready to go home. From about 2:30 on, long rows of white and yellow carriages move silently out the lane, until the field where they were parked is again empty and preaching is over.

Our Religious Heritage

DOROTHY CANFIELD FISHER

Having the choice. That is the root of America's religious freedom, from the earliest days. This short passage by the well-known author Dorothy Canfield Fisher illustrates the importance the early settlers in Vermont attached to their religious beliefs, which, incidentally, allowed them to celebrate the traditions of the Old World in the new country.

Although repeatedly fined [in Connecticut] for using the Book of Common Prayer . . . they [Vermonters] continued stubbornly to hold Anglican services to the stately decorum of which they were much devoted. They had not come to New England to be Puritans and, being British to the core, they saw no reason for giving up their ideas just because other people disapproved. They wanted to celebrate Christmas and Easter and May Day, to say old familiar prayers out of the Prayer Book, to go to dances, to sing Christmas Carols—and they were very tired of living among people who considered such petty practices as hedonism.

⇢ Feeding the Minister, His ⇠ Horse, and His Flock

MAUDE ZIMMER

In the days before United Way and Meals on Wheels, each community or neighborhood took care of its own. Back then the oldtime country preacher was called upon to be more than a preacher. He was a minister in the real sense of the word. Often he, himself, was the town's charitable institution, both in need of charity himself and the distributor of gifts to others. Maude Zimmer remembers those days at the turn of the century, the gifts they shared with their pastor, the unnamed minister who shared those gifts with others, and his faithful horse.

Our congregation was too small to support a resident minister, and we had to share our pastoral leader on alternate Sundays with his hometown church twelve miles away. It was customary for church members to volunteer to entertain the preacher from Saturday until Monday, so that he could devote a full weekend to calling on his flock and delivering two sermons on Sundays.

Often no one volunteered; and when he hitched his horse in front of my father's store, climbed out of the buggy and went inside to determine his lodging place, Father would tell him tactfully that we would like for him to be our guest. The preacher would climb back into the buggy and jog along the street to our house. The wages man would unhitch the tired horse and supply him with food and drink; and Mother would do the same for the weary driver.

The preacher traveled in all kinds of weather. There were days when both he and his horse were covered with dust from the deeply rutted road. Sometimes they arrived in a rainstorm, and the water ran down their backs in little rivulets. Once the sleet was pelting them as they bowed their heads against a driving gale.

After the horse had rested awhile and the preacher had been fortified with a cup of coffee, they began their afternoon rounds. The preacher never walked. There was good reason for riding which anyone following on any particular day might soon discover.

Mrs. Powell, who lived just down the street from us, raised both chickens and children in large numbers. When the preacher called on her, she assembled the children to recite Bible verses for his entertainment. Then she presented him with a box full of fresh eggs which he placed on the buggy seat and jogged along to Mrs. Lerner's, the next house on his list.

Mrs. Lerner had left word with Mother to have the preacher call: not because she needed guidance or advice, but because she had baked that day. When he left her house he carried with him three loaves of fragrant warm bread.

After completing his calls in the village, he drove a mile or so to the home of Miss Lola and Mr. Zach Holton. Miss Lola was deeply religious, but Mr. Zach never attended church services. No one understood why, because Mr. Zach was a generous, good man.

After a few words with Miss Lola, the preacher set out to find Mr. Zach. The two men walked along together through the fields and the barnyard, talking; and no one ever knew what they talked about. When they returned to the house, their arms were loaded with roasting ears, or watermelons, or other products of the field and garden. In the winter Mr. Zach would take the preacher to the smokehouse and select the best ham and bacon and sausages to place in the back of the buggy.

Throughout the afternoon the preacher went from house to house. When he returned to our house at dusk, the old horse was almost spent from the long hours and the heavy load.

Sometimes there would be a bushel of shelled corn or a sack of meal from the grist mill. There were bales of hay for the horse and sacks of nuts and cookies for the preacher's children. Often there were live chickens or geese or ducks, which enjoyed the facilities of our fattening coops while their new owner partook of the hospitality of our home.

The preacher did not always get home with all the gifts which were bestowed upon him. Often he merely redistributed them. One day he left the luxurious house of Mrs. Broadhurst with a luscious cake packaged in a fancy box and tied with a satin ribbon bow. He next called on Mrs. Dorset, who lived in a shabby little cottage with a sagging roof.

Mrs. Dorset watched from her bed beside the window where she had lain for so long, suffering from a lingering illness. Her eyes, dark with pain, brightened when the visitor entered the creaking door and presented her with a luscious cake packaged in a fancy box and tied with a satin ribbon bow.

Much of the bounty of the buggy was given to those in need; and so the villagers vicariously shared their blessings through the wise and generous ministrations of the preacher.

While the calls were being made, the old horse waited, his head drooping with weariness as he patiently flicked away the flies. When at last he rested in our barn, his bare back bore the irremovable marks of too many long hours in the harness.

I am certain there is a special reward in the hereafter for the oldtime country preacher. I hope that somewhere in the great beyond there are green pastures and still waters for the preacher's assistant—his faithful horse.

~ A Painful Cleansing ~

*TAYLOR REESE

Every child's religious experience seems to include a little tomfoolery that eventually has to be reckoned with—usually by the parent who catches the delinquent. Whispering in church, smoking in the graveyard, or playing pool on Sunday—these were moral sins. But, as Taylor Reese discovered, worst of all could be fessing up during the minister's traditional neighborly house call.

Our small town church could seat about a hundred people if everybody sat close to one another.

The new preacher had a pretty wife, and neither was more than thirty. He was a conscientious messenger from above, and my relatives said he and his wife were good Christians. Mrs. Veale, however—she was one of the church's staunchest members—told my mother she had seen Pastor Duncan looking at Thelma Lou's legs longer than he needed to. But she qualified the statement with, "I suppose a man is a man, and no woman is going to change a man."

Now Thelma Lou played the piano for Sunday School and the organ for preaching services.

I liked Thelma Lou because she played hymns in a way they could be enjoyed, and always played them as they were written. Just before the preacher was ready to deliver his sermon, my father and Mr. Frank would pass the collection plate. It was at that time that Thelma Lou played beautiful classical religious selections. Some of the good people said that she had studied under a teacher who had been a student of Ignace Jan Paderewski. Few knew who he was, but Mama told me. Mama played, too, but not like Thelma Lou.

It was the tradition each Sunday, once the services were over, for a different family to invite the preacher to join them for the noon meal. Weekdays, the preacher dropped in to visit some of the parishioners. We were no exception.

It was a Wednesday. I distinctly remember that because Uncle Linwood had a chicken and egg route and he always stopped by our house on Wednesdays for the noon meal. We called it dinner, but the "fancy" people called it lunch.

As soon as Uncle Linwood left the house two of my brothers and I ran to the garage, got the hidden deck of cards, and the game began.

We played there not because it was raining or the sun was too hot, but because good people didn't play cards, at least out in the open. And although Mama and Daddy didn't pressure us about the issue, we knew they preferred that we play checkers. They just closed their eyes to the harmless card games we played in the garage, behind the barn, and in the woods.

We had been playing an hour or more when Pastor Duncan and Mrs. Duncan drove up. Daddy had already gone back to the field to plow. I stopped playing and ran out to see them.

"Won't you come in?" my mother said as they stepped from the car.

"Thank you," said the Pastor Duncan. "Mrs. Reese, how are you and Norbert?"

"We're fine, thank you."

"We just wanted to stop by and see how things are going and to have a little prayer. Where are the other children?"

"I don't know," said my mother. "They were out in the back yard playing just a minute ago."

"No, we weren't, Mama," I said. "We've been in the garage playing cards for over an hour."

There was no mistaking the look she gave me. Pastor Duncan helped allay her embarrassment by saying, "The Lord's youngsters will be youngsters, won't they, Mrs. Reese?"

"You're right," my mother said as the preacher began recounting their visit with Thelma Lou just before coming to our house.

My brothers never came out of the garage that day, and so the four of us—Pastor and Mrs. Duncan, Mother, and I—sat on the porch. Pastor Duncan told us about his sick aunt in Raleigh. She had cancer, he said. Mrs. Duncan said her mother was doing quite well after the operation for appendicitis.

They didn't stay as long as I wish they had.

As they were readying to leave, Pastor Duncan asked us to bow our heads for a prayer.

I remember it well. He prayed to the Lord that He would bless our family, and look after us. And then he thanked Him for the great cooks in the church, mentioning my mother specifically. I really thought he should have thanked my mother instead of Him.

He ended his prayer with these words—and to this day I've never forgotten them: "Lord, look down on this fine family, and grant each of them what they so rightly deserve."

As they drove out of our yard, Mama said to me, "Norbert, go to that oak tree over there and break me a switch. Don't get one too small, either."

I did. And as I walked toward her, she said, "The next time the preacher asks me a question, you let me answer."

And then she gave me what I rightly deserved.

～ An Inspired Gift ～

Feeding the underpaid minister is a tradition that I remember from my childhood. Two memories particularly stand out in my mind. Whenever a new pastor came to town, his family was given a "pounding party" to which the parishioners brought a pound of sugar, pound of butter, pound of flour, and so on.

The other was preparing a Scripture Cake anytime the minister was invited for dinner. These traditions seem to have known no regional bounds. I found this bare-bones Scripture Cake recipe written in my mother's script along with the note that she had copied it from my grandmother's Sturbridge, Massachusetts, cookbook.

2 1/4 cups 1 Kings 4:22
1/2 cup Judges 5:25 (3rd item)
1 cup Jeremiah 6:20
1 cup 1 Samuel 30:12 (2nd item)
1 cup Nahum 3:12
1 cup Numbers 17:8
1/4 cup Judges 4:19 (2nd item)
3 items Jeremiah 17:11
Add to taste, 2 Chronicles 9:9
a tablespoon baking power

ᛜ *The Village Church* ᛜ

WILLIAM BOHN

Is there a more familiar American scene than the Norman Rockwell–type white clapboard church nestled among primeval oak trees, its spire shining in the sunlight? That picturesque scene has long symbolized the freedom and spirit of our founding fathers. Even more powerful, though, wrote William Bohn in the 1950s, has been a quiet, unsung Protestant tradition many of us still remember and wish to keep alive. Together, the minister and the people of the village led lives of example. Bohn's essay reminds us that the occasional "black sheep" need be no reason to condemn the institution, for the good can far outweigh the bad.

In these days no one is inclined to give anything like due credit to the little Protestant churches that were scattered over the country during the nineteenth century. I am not thinking of the great official establishments with their seats in the few large cities. The Methodist Church had conferences, the Episcopalians had dioceses. But a boy in a country town saw little and heard little of these. What he did hear about was the little church on the public square and the saintly preacher living in his humble "parsonage." This church, guided and nurtured by this gentle shepherd, was not just an ecclesiastic institution that preached to people on Sunday and subsisted on the "offerings" they contributed. It entered deeply into the daily life and thoughts of most of the people—except, of course, the Catholics.

It is difficult to know whether to start with the people or the pastor. The whole institution was so deeply democratic that it is hard to decide which comes first. I lived in my lovely town of four hundred neighbors from 1886 onward. Fifty years before that, the circuit riders had been making their circuits, baptizing, burying the dead, and preaching to the living. There were no salaries and hardly any churches. No one expected organization, honors, or ease. It was a tough life with everything to give and little to get. But that's the way the new country was built—and it proved to be a first-class method.

The preachers had never attended any famous theological seminaries, but for their work they had just about the best sort of training you can imagine. They went straight back to John Wesley—and through him to Martin Luther and the Holy Bible. Their doctrines might sound a bit old-fashioned and overorthodox now, but those men believed in them completely and lived up to them with a devotion that was convincing. I knew some of these men intimately—so intimately that I would have discovered any traces of dross in their make-up. No matter how little they received or how disappointing life might be, their saintly calm was never disturbed.

Among all of those whom I knew, there was only one who furnished such a variation as might have furnished forth a story by Mark Twain or James Thurber. There came to our hamlet a man named Eastman. He differed from his fellows in several ways. In the first place, he was not content with the black and rather shiny garments that served as uniforms for his profession. His rather plump middle was covered by an emphatically gay waistcoat. And he was not content with the modest accretions to the church that were brought about by the regular increases in the population. No, by cracky! He wanted action. Whether we liked it or not, we should have revival services and crowds. And we did have them, but the treatment was not very successful.

All preachers, in those days, had horses. Without such an animal as assistant, you were stuck. And this man Eastman had an extra fine and shiny one. One bright sunny day my brother and I were on a hike far out among the farms, and suddenly we heard behind us a great swish and clatter. From the roadside where we sought safety we quickly viewed in a cloud of dust the pious preacher in jockey's uniform and on a racing sulky going down the road with his son on horseback beside him. The terrible truth flashed over us: The holy disciple was a racing man doubling as pastor. As soon as the news became common property, the oh's and ah's blew the fellow right out of the pulpit. Think of it! The wickedness of it! To drive a racehorse! A few of the sporting men who frequented the mysterious and shadowy saloons endeavored to defend him, but failed to get much of a hearing.

But this was the one exception. All the other pastors I knew were really saintly men. Even if now and then one came along who could not preach very persuasively, the old ladies would say, "He lives such a good life, no one would complain." But even if these men were not distinguished by learning, if they did not pretend to turn men to virtue and church membership by their eloquence, their lives were a constant and effective sermon. Especially was this true in relation to the young people of the village. It could be taken for granted that "the preacher" knew every growing boy and girl in or near the village. He followed with special interest each young hopeful who showed any promise of scholastic talent. In those Midwest states we had a little college in nearly every county, and it was part of the duty of the pastor to see to it it was filled with ambitious and promising youngsters. As soon as a youth showed the least sign of brains, the preacher would get busy discovering to what college the boy would prefer to go and how the necessary funds could be raised. Many a man who played a part in the development of that great agricultural section owes his education to the interest of a devoted five-hundred-dollar parson.

The influence of the country church and its educational value depended far more upon its democratic activities than upon its preaching or its doctrinal teaching. All the members took part in something. The young people who had any intelligence or energy took part in many sorts of organization. Some joined the choir and helped to select and rehearse the music. Others formed a young people's society and set programs for its meetings. Those who were interested in study or made more pretensions to learning would become teachers of Sunday school classes and arrange for the study of the Bible. It is characteristic of the time and place that all these things were arranged, and carried through by the members of the church, young and old, and not by the clergy. The growing youth had more experience in organization—in life in general—in connection with the church and Sunday school than in any official educational institution.

⇀ Prayer Is Power ↽

ALEXIS CARREL

In these waning days of the twentieth century more is being written about man's spirituality than ever before. It's only natural. Life is frantic and startling. Change is frightening. The unknown is bewildering. We are on the threshold of not just a new century, but a new millennium.

Ironically, in the midst of this reawakening of individual spirituality (New Age, some people call it), both new and old wars break out daily in neighborhoods and countries alike. In light of the complex state of the world today, personally I become downhearted when I listen to debates and arguments pitting various denominations, ideologies, and religious doctrines against one another. I despair that the religious wars of ancient and medieval times continue today, but under a new, whitewashed term to disassociate them from any religious connotation: ethnic cleansing. In my simplistic way I wish I could wave a magic wand and have peace on earth. But I am not alone. What answer is given most often when the question is posed, "If you had just one wish . . ." World peace.

As long as there are isms, disagreements over creation and evolution, tenets and philosophies, doctrines and dogmas will continue. The one aspect of religion almost everyone seems to believe in is prayer. Today the healing power of prayer is grabbing headlines. There's nothing new about that. The tradition goes back to pagan times. But when a learned scientist speaks out on the subject, we listen. Dr. Alexis Carrel received the Nordhoff-Jung medal for cancer research and the Nobel Prize for success in suturing blood vessels. His Man, the Unknown *was a best-seller in 1935. He wrote this piece in 1941.*

Prayer is not only worship; it is also an invisible emanation of man's worshiping spirit—the most powerful form of energy that one can generate. The influence of prayer on the human mind and body is as demonstrable as that of secreting glands. Its results can be measured in terms of increased physical buoyancy, greater intellectual vigor, moral stamina, and a deeper understanding of the realities underlying human relationships.

If you make a habit of sincere prayer, your life will be very noticeably and profoundly altered. Prayer stamps with its indelible mark our actions and demeanor. A tranquility of bearing, a facial and bodily repose, are observed in those whose inner lives are thus enriched. Within the depths of consciousness a flame kindles. And man sees himself. He discovers his selfishness, his silly pride, his fears, his greeds, his blunders. He develops a sense of moral obligation, intellectual humility. Thus begins a journey of the soul toward the realm of grace.

Prayer is a force as real as terrestrial gravity. As a physician, I have seen men, after all other therapy had failed, lifted out of disease and melancholy by the serene effort of prayer. It is the only power in the world that seems to overcome the so-called "laws of nature"; the occasions on which prayer has dramatically done this have been termed "miracles." But a constant, quieter miracle takes place hourly in the hearts of men and women who have discovered that prayer supplies them with a steady flow of sustaining power in their daily lives.

Too many people regard prayer as a formalized routine of words, a refuge for weaklings, or a childish petition for material things. We sadly undervalue prayer when we conceive it in these terms, just as we should underestimate rain by describing it as something that fills the birdbath in our garden. Properly understood, prayer is a mature activity indispensable to the fullest development of personality—the ultimate integration of man's highest faculties. Only in prayer do we achieve that complete and harmonious assembly of body, mind and spirit which gives the frail human reed its unshakable strength.

The words, "Ask and it shall be given to you," have been verified by the experience of humanity. True, prayer may not restore the dead child to life or bring relief from physical pain. But prayer, like radium, is a source of luminous, self-generating energy.

How does prayer fortify us with so much dynamic power? To answer this question (admittedly outside the jurisdiction of science) I must point out that all prayers have one thing in common. The triumphant hosannas of a great oratorio, or the humble supplication of an Iroquois hunter begging for luck in the chase, demonstrate the same truth: that human beings seek to augment their finite energy by addressing themselves to the Infinite source of all energy. When we pray, we link ourselves with the inexhaustible motive power that spins the universe. We ask that a part of this power be apportioned to our needs. Even in asking, our human deficiencies are filled and we arise strengthened and repaired.

But we must never summon God merely for the gratification of our whims. We derive most power from prayer when we use it, not as a petition, but as a supplication that we may become more like Him. Prayer should be regarded as practice of the Presence of God. An old peasant was seated alone in the last pew of the village church. "What are you waiting for?" he was asked; and he answered, "I am looking at Him and He is looking at me." Man prays not only that God should remember him, but also that he should remember God.

How can prayer be defined? Prayer is the effort of man to reach God, to commune with an invisible being, creator of all things, supreme wisdom, truth, beauty, and strength, father and redeemer of each man. This goal of prayer always remains hidden to intelligence. For both language and thought fail when we attempt to describe God.

We do know, however, that whenever we address God in fervent prayer we change both soul and body for the better. It could not happen that any man or woman could pray for a single moment without some good result. "No man ever prayed," said Emerson, "without learning something."

One can pray everywhere. In the streets, the subway, the office, the shop, the school, as well as in the solitude of one's own room or among the crowd in a church. There is no prescribed posture, time or place.

"Think of God more often than you breathe," said Epictetus the Stoic. In order really to mold personality, prayer must become a habit. It is meaningless to pray in the morning and to live like a barbarian the remainder of the day. True prayer is a way of life; the truest life is literally a way of prayer.

The best prayers are like the improvisations of gifted lovers, always about the same thing yet never twice the same. We cannot all be as creative in prayer as Saint Theresa or Bernard of Clairvaux, both of whom poured their adoration into words of mystical beauty. Fortunately, we do not need their eloquence; our slightest impulse to prayer is recognized by God. Even if we are pitifully dumb, or if our tongues are overlaid with vanity or deceit, our meager syllables of praise are acceptable to Him, and He showers us with strengthening manifestations of His love.

Today, as never before, prayer is a binding necessity in the lives of men and nations. The lack of emphasis on the religious sense has brought the world to the edge of destruction. Our deepest source of power and perfection has been left miserably undeveloped. Prayer, the basic exercise of the spirit, must be actively practiced in our private lives. The neglected soul of man must be made strong enough to assert itself once more. For if the power of prayer is again released and used in the lives of common men and women; if the spirit declares its aims clearly and boldly, there is yet hope that our prayers for a better world will be answered.

⁓ *"Prayer for This House"* ⁓

LOUIS UNTERMEYER

May nothing evil cross this door,
  And may ill-fortune never pry
About these windows; may the roar
  And rains go by.

Strengthened by faith, the rafters will
  Withstand the battering of the storm.
This hearth, though all the world grow chill,
  Will keep you warm.

Peace shall walk softly through these rooms,
  Touching your lips with holy wine,
Till every casual corner blooms
  Into a shrine.

Laughter shall drown the raucous shout
  And, though the sheltering walls are thin,
May they be strong to keep hate out
  And hold love in.

⤳ With Straight Eyes ⤳

Despite the great power of prayer, still, praying in public can be embarrassing and, at times, seemingly inappropriate. This is why my friend Margie Pipkin suggests that the tradition of the open-eye prayer is one everyone can be comfortable with. There is no need to bow your head. Just take the moment to give thanks, either aloud or silently. After all, in the tradition of this beautiful nineteenth-century Sioux prayer to the Great Spirit, translated into English by Chief Yellow Lark, we each should keep straight eyes and remember, as the Rev. Hill Riddle of Trinity Episcopal Church, New Orleans, tells us, prayer is a gift.

Oh, Great Spirit, whose voice I hear in the winds,
Whose breath gives life to the world,
   hear me. . . .
I come to you as one of your many children.
I am small and weak.
I need your strength and your wisdom.
May I walk in beauty.
Make my eyes ever behold the red and purple sunset.
Make my hands respect the things you have made,
And my ears sharp to your voice.
Make me wise so that I may know the things you have taught your children,
The lessons you have written in every leaf and rock.
Make me strong,
Not to be superior to my brothers, but to fight my greatest enemy—
   Myself. . . .
Make me ever ready to come to you with straight eyes
   So that when life fades as the fading sunset
   My spirit may come to you without shame.

The Gift of Prayer

The Rev. Hill C. Riddle, Trinity Episcopal Church, New Orleans

Prayer is a gift. Still, people have great difficulty with prayer. How often do I, a minister, have people say to me, "I don't know how to pray. When I pray, I don't know what to say. I feel like my thoughts are shallow, or when I start to pray, my mind begins to wander and I don't know what I am doing. I wonder if God's there. I wonder if my prayers are answered. And then sometimes I pray for things and I don't seem to get an answer."

All of these questions are things that human beings struggle with. It is a part of our spiritual journey. We struggle with prayer. But know that it does not matter what you say once you place yourself in God's presence.

Everyone is a prayer whether he knows it or not. Sometimes we are so out of touch with the spiritual dimensions in our lives that we don't know what we are doing. That is when the expressive statement that suddenly comes out of us in frustration and anger is itself a cry to God for help. It is a prayer.

For those going through the difficulty of being able to pray, remember, when you see a beautiful sight—a sunset, a flower, a mountain, the sea, a baby's smile—and you are moved by God's creation, it is the seeds of prayer that are in you.

Prayer is a gift, a gift to be used. The more we use the gift, the more we will discover the prayer and the power and the presence of God that is already in the midst of us.

～ *"Grace at Table"* ～

EDGAR A. GUEST

When I was but a little lad, not more than eight or nine,
The mother had a table prayer she taught us line by line.
With all the family gathered round, heads bowed and hands in place
We'd sit in solemn silence until one of us said grace.

"Be present at our table, Lord," her favorite grace began.
"Be here and everywhere adored," the little couplet ran.
"These creatures bless and grant that we"—I hear it now as then—
"May feast in Paradise with Thee!" and all would say, "Amen."

Day in and out through weal and woe, high gain or commonplace.
At every meal our heads we bowed throughout this simple grace.
"Be present at our table, Lord!" From all that has occurred
And all the joy that we have known—I'm sure He must have
heard.

~ An Uncommon Grace ~

John Steinbeck

Anyone who has read John Steinbeck's powerful and hope-filled novel, The
Grapes of Wrath, *has forever remembered this powerful scene where, at
Granma's insistence, grace is said. This is not the usual picture-perfect Ameri-
can family scene. It is a pure Steinbeck portrait of an earthy, rough-hewn
family trying to eke out an existence as they head for the promised land of
California.*

"Grace fust," Granma clamored. "Grace fust."

Grampa focused his eyes fiercely until he recognized Casy. "Oh, that
preacher," he said. "Oh he's all right. I always liked him since I seen
him—" he winked so lecherously that Granma thought he had spoken
and retorted, "Shut up, you sinful ol' goat."

Casy ran his fingers through his hair nervously. "I got to tell you, I
ain't a preacher no more. If me jus' bin' glad to be here an' bein'
thankful for people that's kind and generous, if that's enough—why,
I'll say that kinda grace. But I ain't a preacher no more."

"Say her," said Granma. "An' get in a word about us goin' to
California." The preacher bowed his head, and the others bowed their
heads. Ma folded her hands over her stomach and bowed her head.
Granma bowed so low that her nose was nearly in her plate of biscuit
and gray. Tom, leaning against the wall, a plate in his hand, bowed
stiffly, and Grampa bowed his head sidewise, so that he could keep
one mean and merry eye on the preacher. And on the preacher's face
there was a look not of prayer, but of thought; and in his tone not
supplication, but conjecture.

"I been thinkin'," he said. "I been in the hills, thinkin', almost you
might say like Jesus went into the wilderness to think His way out of
a mess of troubles."

"Pu-raise Gawd!" Granma said, and the preacher glanced over at
her in surprise.

"Seems like Jesus got all messed up with troubles, and He couldn't
figure nothin' out, an' He got to feelin' what the hell good is it all,
an' what's the use fightin' an' figurin'. Got tired, got good an' tired,
an' His sperit all wore out. Jus' about come to the conclusion, the hell
with it. An' so He went off into the wilderness."

"A—men," Granma bleated. So many years she had timed her
responses to the pauses. And it was so many years since she had
listened to or wondered at the words used.

"I ain't sayin' I'm like Jesus," the preacher went on. "But I got tired like Him, an' I got mixed up like Him, an' I went into the wilderness like Him, without no campin' stuff. Nighttime I'd lay on my back an' look up at the stars; morning I'd set an' watch the sun come up; midday I'd look out from a hill at the rollin' dry country; evenin' I'd foller the sun down. Sometimes I'd pray like I always done. On'y I couldn' figure what I was prayin' to or for. There was the hills, an' there was me, an' we wasn't separate no more. We was one thing. An' that one thing was holy."

"Hallelujah," said Granma, and she rocked a little, back and forth, trying to catch hold of an ecstasy.

"An' I got thinkin', on'y it wasn't thinkin', it was deeper down than thinkin'. I got thinkin' how we was holy when we was one thing, an' mankin' was holy when it was one thing. An' it on'y got unholy when one mis'able little fella got the bit in his teeth an' run off his own way, kickin' an' draggin' an' fightin'. Fella like that bust the holiness. But when they're all workin' together, not one fella for another fella, but one fella kind of harnessed to the whole shebang—that's right, that's holy. An' then I got thinkin' I don't even know what I mean by holy." He paused, but the bowed heads stayed down, for they had been trained like dogs to rise at the "amen" signal. "I can't say no grace like I use' ta say. I'm glad of the holiness of breakfast. I'm glad there's love here. That's all." The heads stayed down. The preacher looked around. "I've got your breakfast cold," he said; and then he remembered. "Amen," he said, and all the heads rose up.

"A—men," said Granma, and she fell to her breakfast.

— For Every Lady, A Fan —

MAUDE ZIMMER

In addition to the prayer books, hymnals, and Bibles tucked into the pockets nailed to the back of every old-timey church pew there was a stash of paper fans. Vivid, bold scenes depicting the Good Shepherd, the Last Supper, and the rolling away of the rock at Gethsemane were printed on them. These fans were more than utilitarian objects. They were inspirational and educational. I always thought church fans were unique to our sweltering Southern clime. But the church names printed on the fans I see being sold for preposterous prices in the antique malls these days confirm that fans were a church staple in Michigan and Minnesota as well as Mississippi. Modern air-conditioning may have made them unnecessary for cooling, but Maude Zimmer reminds us that fans are multipurpose. Even today they could still come in handy for these other uses.

In our little village church there were . . . indispensable articles which are seldom seen today in any places of worship—the ladies' fans.

In each pew were pasteboard fans donated by the proprietor of the village butcher shop, and they advertised his wares in bold black lettering. Most of the ladies, however, brought their own fans.

Some were made of palmetto, carefully cut and pressed flat while drying. They were finished around the edges with colored binding, except for the ones bound in black and used by those in mourning.

There were circular fans made of gaily printed Chinese silk mounted on lacquered sticks. There were folding fans made of printed paper or silk or even lace, with sticks of delicately carved ivory. In contrast to such elegance was the fan of old Aunt Lucy, who stirred the air vigorously with a fan made from the outspread wing of last Thanksgiving's turkey.

Without hearing a word the preacher said, a spectator could surmise the gist of his sermon by the movement of the fans in the congregation. If the preacher spoke gently of love and forgiveness, the fans moved back and forth with somnolent serenity. If he threatened his listeners with hellfire and damnation, the fans fluttered with agitation.

During one revival meeting the preacher ranted daily on so many aspects of sin that by the time the week and the meeting came to a close, many of the more delicate fans were reduced to shreds.

Besides cooling the atmosphere, a fan also served to stifle a cough or sneeze. They provided screens for brief whispered conversations. Sometimes they were used as implements of discipline when noisy children required a gentle rap to maintain quiet.

⇁ The Tolling Bells ⇀

E. W. HOWE

If every lady had a fan, every church had bells—sometimes joyful, other times sad—but always silvery bells.

High up in a steeple which rocked with every wind was a great bell, the gift of a missionary society, and when there was a storm this tolled with fitful and uncertain strokes, as if the ghosts from the grave lot had crawled up there and were counting the number to be buried the coming year, keeping the people awake for miles around. Sometimes, when the wind was particularly high, there were a great number of strokes on the bell in quick succession, which the pious said was an alarm to the wicked, sounded by the devil, a warning relating to the conflagration which could never be put out, else Fairview would never have been built.

When anyone died it was the custom to toll the bell once for every year of the deceased's age, and as deaths usually occur at night, we were frequently wakened from sleep by its deep and solemn tones. When I was yet a very little boy I occasionally went with my father to toll the bell when news came that someone was dead, for we lived nearer the place than any of the others, and when the strokes ran up to forty and fifty it was very dreary work, and I sat alone in the church wondering who would ring for me, and how many strokes could be counted by those who were shivering at home in their beds.

⟿ The Wisdom of Past Times ⟿

EMIL BRUNNER

The great Swiss theologian Emil Brunner, when addressing the topic of Christianity and civilization at the University of Saint Andrews in 1947, cited the important role of tradition in a world emerging from the horrors of World War II. Note carefully his discussion of the delicate balance between traditional and new ideas that come with every generation. Within this passage, his reference to the American system of checks and balances created in our Constitution is important to the thoughtful person's concept of the role tradition plays not only in religion but in world politics.

It has been observed by many that in England, as well as in Switzerland, the deep-rooted liberalism and individualism of the people has not produced the same dangerous quasi-anarchical effects which can be seen in other democratic countries, as, for instance, France; and it was often pointed out that this difference is accounted for by the strong sense of tradition in the first, which is lacking in so many other countries. But, so far as I know, the inherent relation between egalitarianism and the lack of tradition has never been made quite clear.

Rationalistic egalitarianism is necessarily anti-traditional because it claims equal right for any present decision with anything that has been decided previously. An existing parliament, elected by the people yesterday, has the right to upset to-day what has been decided in previous times by previous parliaments, kings, or similar powers. Egalitarianism tends to the atomisation of time, as it tends to the atomisation of communal society. It is, so to speak, an individualism of the time elements on the basis of the equal right of any given time.

Why should that which previous generations have decided be binding for me, for us, at this moment? Tradition—the assertion of continuity —is a non-rational principle, sometimes irrational, sometimes supra-rational, but, in any case, not to be accounted for in rational terms. Behind the emphasis on tradition stands a conception of man which is anti-individualistic, giving preponderance to the continuum of the generations over against the isolated present generation. It is the conviction of the traditionalist that the wisdom of past times, embedded in tradition, is greater than the wisdom of the present generation, taken by itself.

A similar idea is expressed in that system of checks and balances which is the basic idea of that marvelous piece of political wisdom known to us as the constitution of the United States, and—still more so—of the constitution of Switzerland, which is only partly modelled on the American. In both cases the egalitarian, rational element is counterbalanced by elements which allow past decisions to limit the freedom of decision of the present, and upon which rests the stability of the whole political structure. The interplay of the rational and individualistic principle of equality with the non-rational and non-individualistic principle of tradition, or of checks and balances by past decisions, is the clue to the mystery of the comparative stability of these three democracies in comparison with those which are based entirely on the rational principle of equality. If we ask where this difference comes from, I think the answer cannot be in doubt. It is the strength of the Christian tradition in all these countries—at the time when their present structure was formed—which accounts for this curious check on the egalitarian principle.

➤ The Meditation of My Heart ➤

*EMYL JENKINS

Few settings could be less like one another than the Southern Protestant church and the Jewish synagogue. Yet they both are part of the rich religious heritage that has made America the envy of people and countries throughout the world.

To that end, I will always remember the day my father and I took one of mother's prizewinning arrangements to the regional flower show being held in the parlor of the First Presbyterian Church in Danville, Virginia. Mother had choir practice at the synagogue, and since both houses of worship were only a block apart, after dropping her off, we took the arrangement to the flower show. Daddy found where the flowers belonged and then we began making the rounds to see the other arrangements. There was Mrs. Herman talking to Mrs. Tucker. The Vincents were chatting with Mrs. Johnson. I never gave it a second thought. These were neighbors and friends, all brought together by a common interest, flowers. Just as we were leaving, Daddy seized the moment, not to lecture me on peace and harmony or religion, but to observe: "The wonderful thing about a worthwhile activity is that it brings everyone together. Remember that."

I always have.

When walking in Audubon Park in New Orleans and I see tourists from around the world strolling, jogging, and Rollerblading side-by-side with the neighborhood regulars, I remember. When waiting for a taxi at L.A.'s Bonaventure Hotel and eavesdropping on the Oriental and Occidental businessmen talking to one another, I remember. When I'm at the symphony in Raleigh, and I notice the Catholic priest seated a couple of rows down from my die-hard Southern Baptist friends, and the physics professor newly arrived from India sitting across from the Jewish couple who own one of the region's oldest stores, I remember. And on those occasions I often hear Mother's sweet soprano voice practicing one of her favorite Jewish hymns, whose words we should all live by: "Let the words of my mouth, and the meditation of my heart, be acceptable in Thy sight, O Lord, my strength, and my redeemer."

What the Jews Believe

RABBI PHILIP S. BERNSTEIN

We don't have to believe what other people believe. But if we know why they believe what they do and the traditions behind them, how much more understanding of one another we would have. We might even see a little of ourselves in others.

The Jew has no single organized church. He has no priests. The concept of salvation by faith is alien to his mind. Yet he has deep religious convictions which run like golden threads through all Jewish history. For him Judaism is a way of life, here and now. He does not serve his God for the sake of reward, for the fruit of the good life is the good life. Thus his answers about the nature of his religious beliefs are profoundly different from the answers made by Christians.

Judaism around the world is marked by diversity of practice and latitude of faith. But for all the degrees of divergence on detail, a great common denominator of faith unites most American Jews. This unique agreement is not imposed from the top down upon the congregations, because the Jew acknowledges no supreme ecclesiastical authority, but rather it wells up from the depth of the Jewish heart, nourished in the long history of an ancient people.

In the days of ancient Israel the priesthood at Jerusalem laid down the law for all Jews. Then, in 586 B.C., Nebuchadnezzar besieged Jerusalem, demolished Solomon's Temple, and carried the Jews into exile in Babylon. With their Temple and their priesthood gone, the Jews in the strange new communities where they found themselves formed voluntary assemblages for common worship and study of the law. These congregations were called synagogues, quite free and independent of one another. This institution proved so valuable that it has been continued to this day as the method of Jewish worship. It also provided the basic pattern for the churches which, after Paul, the Christians set up and developed along more unified lines. Among the Jews, however, the synagogue has survived in its pristine form. Any ten adult male Jews today can establish a congregation.

In the central fortress of Jewish spirituality, the Torah is the repository for the Law of Judaism. Torah embraces a triple meaning. Primarily it is the Sacred Scrolls found in every synagogue. These are contained in an ornamental ark which, whenever possible, is built into the wall of the structure so that when the congregation faces it they look toward Jerusalem's Holy Temple. This is an abiding reminder of the Biblical Ark of the Covenant in which the Tablets of the Law were carried. The Torah scrolls are written by hand on parchment, fastidiously and often beautifully done by one who is usually a descendant of generations of scribes. In 1908 when the synagogue of which this writer is now minister burned down, an Irish policeman dashed to the ark and seized the Torah. He handed it to the rabbi, who was rushing up to the building. "Here," he said, "I saved your crucifix." Well, the Jews have no crucifix, but the policeman had the right idea: the scrolls are the most sacred symbols of Judaism.

Torah has a second meaning: the Pentateuch, the first five books of the Bible: Genesis, Exodus, Leviticus, Numbers, Deuteronomy. These books are the acknowledged foundation of Judaism, containing the principles of the faith, the Ten Commandments, the golden rule, the laws of holiness. The Pentateuch is at once the biography of the greatest Jew of all time—Moses—and the history of the formation of the Jewish nation and the development of its faith. It runs the whole gamut of Jewish spiritual experience from the sublime poetry of the creation narrative to the minutiae of the dietary laws. So precious is the Pentateuch to the Jews that they divide it into fixed weekly portions and read them on every Sabbath and holy day in the year.

When the sacred round is completed, there is the gay festival of Simchas Torah ("rejoicing in the law") at which the last verses of Deuteronomy are followed by the first verses of Genesis, symbolizing the eternal cycle of the law.

Finally, Torah means teaching, learning, doctrine. If a Jew says, "Let us study Torah," he might be referring to the Pentateuch or to the Prophets or to the Talmud or any of the sacred writings. He is certainly referring to the first obligation of the Jew to study God's ways and requirements as revealed in Holy Writ.

For a Jew the educational process begins at the age of five. According to tradition, a drop of honey is placed on the first page the child is to learn to read; he kisses it, thus beginning an association of pleasantness which is expected to last through life. When most of the world was illiterate, every Jewish boy could read and by thirteen was advanced in the study of a complex literature. Thus arose the love of learning, the keenness of intellect, to be found among so many Jews.

For all his love of learning for its own sake, the religious Jew finds much more in the Torah than burdensome legalism. It is an unending source of inspiration and practical help to him. He begins and ends the day with prayers. He thanks God before and after every meal, even when he washes his hands. All his waking day the traditional Jew wears a ritual scarf beneath his outer garments as a reminder of God's nearness and love. There are prescribed prayers for birth, circumcision, marriage, illness, death. Even the appearance of a rainbow evokes an ancient psalm of praise. In effect, law means the sanctification of life.

Jews never regarded the codification of law as a strait jacket. One basic device keeps it fluid: the oral law which supplemented the written law and was subject to emendation, interpretation, adaptation. For example, the ancient Torah says, "An eye for an eye." In itself this was an advance over the laws of the surrounding tribes, which usually prescribed death for the taking of an eye. Nevertheless the sages were not content to let this law stand. They said that the intent of the law was to compel the offender to pay in damages the accepted equivalent for the loss of an eye. Thus the written law was not repudiated but became the basis of a sensible adaptation to the realities of human society. As another example, the Torah proclaimed, "Remember the Sabbath day to keep it holy." Jews observed this commandment with the greatest seriousness, but in the oral law the rabbis evolved a whole series of necessary exceptions. They said the Sabbath could be violated to bring help to the sick or to defend oneself against attack. They formulated it into a principle, stating long before Jesus was born that the Sabbath was made for man, not man for the Sabbath.

The central prayer of Judaism is the Shema: "Hear, O Israel, the

Lord our God, the Lord is One." This is the heart of every Jewish service. More, it is recited by the Jew when he believes death is approaching. Together with "Thou shalt love the Lord thy God with all thy heart," it is to be found in printed form in the Mezuzah, the little tubed case placed on the doorposts of the homes of observant Jews, a constant reminder of God's presence and a sign of the Jewishness of the inhabitants.

Following Paul, the Shema took on a new significance. Although Jews are able, if they wish, to understand Jesus, the Jew of Nazareth, they have never been able to understand or accept the idea of the Trinity. Thus from the beginning of the Christian era to this day, the Shema has been the rallying point of Jewish loyalty confronting the persecution or the blandishments of a daughter religion.

For the modern American Jew two meanings have emerged which, while not new, are current in their emphasis. The first, suggested by the writings of Albert Einstein, is, in effect, the scientific confirmation of the unity of God which binds the atom to the stars in universal law. The advances in human knowledge, always welcomed by the Jew, seem to vindicate his basic belief in the oneness of the universe.

From God to man, from His Fatherhood to our brotherhood—this is the second meaning of the Shema to modern Jews. The concept of human oneness has always been an integral element in the Jewish religious outlook. Frequently this has been misunderstood because of the Jews' insistence on remaining a distinctive group. The Jew has never believed that brotherhood means regimentation, the elimination of differences, or the stifling of minorities. Loving your neighbor as yourself, he believes, requires respect for differences. One of the great rabbis who lived more than two thousand years ago said that the most important statement in the Bible was not the Ten Commandments nor the golden rule but "This is the book of the generations of man." To the Jews themselves the Scriptures were not the heritage of a single people but of all humanity.

The prayer which after the Shema has the deepest hold on all Jews is the Kaddish. In actual practice it is the prayer honoring the dead, recited for a year after the death of a loved one and on the anniversaries thereafter. Its solemn phrases exalt the name of God and pray for the coming of His Kingdom. "Exalted and hallowed be the name of God throughout the world. . . . May His Kingdom come, His will be done." There is no doubt that Jesus spoke this ancient prayer in the synagogue and that it became the basis for the Lord's Prayer.

Though honoring the dead, the Kaddish does not make specific the Jewish attitude toward immortality. For the Jews have never agreed on what happens after death. Most Jews of recent centuries have recited the Credo of Maimonides, the twelfth-century physician-philosopher who affirmed the physical resurrection of the dead. But the hearts of many stricken Jews have also echoed the lament of Job: "As the cloud is consumed and vanisheth away, so he that goeth down to the grave shall come up no more." Modern Jews have tended increasingly less to believe in physical resurrection. This probably accounts for the increasing trend toward cremation which is found among non-Orthodox Jews. Among American Jews the Kaddish is returning more to its original meaning, our acknowledgment of God's rule and readiness to leave our ultimate fate in His hands.

"The catechism of the Jew is his calendar," said Samson Raphael Hirsch, nineteenth-century German rabbi. One can learn more about the mainsprings of the Jew's spirituality from the cycle of year-round observances than from any formal statement of faith. In these are revealed his habits of thought and feeling, his historic memories and patterns of religious conduct.

In the annual cycle of religious observances followed by American Jews, the new year begins in the early fall—this year [1950] on September 12. According to traditional Biblical chronology, this week begins the 5711th year since creation. The advent of the new year is greeted in a spirit far removed from the festivities of January 1. It ushers in a ten-day period of penitence, culminating in the fast of Yom Kippur and dedicated to spiritual stock-taking. What is man? What is our life? What will be our fate? Some Jews have believed literally, others metaphorically, that on the new year the books of life are spread open before the Great Judge. In this period of judgment it is determined "who shall live and who shall die, who shall be at rest and who shall wander, who shall be tranquil and who shall be harassed, who shall become poor and who shall wax rich, who shall be brought low and who shall be exalted."

This holy-day period is pervaded with a solemn appraisal of the facts of our frail human existence. No attempt is made to gloss over the evils of life. God's ways may be inscrutable, but ultimately they are accepted as just. Therefore the fear of the Lord is the beginning of wisdom. Judaism offers no easy way to God. No son has been sent down to lead us to Him. No mediator intercedes for us. In the final accounting there is a purely personal relationship between the individual and his God. This is an awesome responsibility. Need we wonder, then, that this penitential period is known as the Days of Awe? Even the blowing of the Shofar, the ram's horn, which from Biblical times has announced the New Year, penetrates into the heart of the modern Jew and causes it to tremble.

The climax is reached on Yom Kippur. Like all Jewish holidays it begins at sundown, for Jews follow the Biblical pattern of creation: "There was evening, and there was morning, one day." The service opens with the Kol Nidre chant. This is the most stirring, the most haunting melody in the entire religious experience of Jews. The words are a plea for the absolution of vows made under duress the preceding year—a plea that was poignantly meaningful at the time of forced conversions of Jews to Christianity during the Middle Ages.

The spiritual concern of Yom Kippur is with our human sinfulness —but what is sin? To answer this question we must go back to Judaism's balanced interpretations of the nature of man. On the one hand there are no perfect saints in the Jewish tradition. Even Moses, the greatest Jew of all time, was denied admittance to the promised land because he disobeyed God. But Judaism, on the other hand, does not regard man as inherently sinful or depraved. Our instinctive drives are considered good because God gave them to us. There is no asceticism in Judaism, no retreat to monasteries. Celibacy is not required of the rabbis. The rabbis of the Talmud maintain that much good has come from our so-called "evil desires." They say that our sex drive has produced love, marriage, the family, the perpetuation of the race. Without the acquisitive instinct, they claim, homes would not be built, fields would not be tilled.

In its Hebrew origin the most commonly used word for sin means "missing the mark"—the repudiation of God's commandments. There are, it must be added, various formulations of God's requirements. While the Torah lists 613 commands, Micah reduced them to three: "To do justly, to love mercy and to walk humbly before God." How do we walk in God's way? The answer is given in the climactic moment of the Yom Kippur morning service, when the rabbi stands before the ark and, about to remove the scrolls, prays in words proclaimed of old to Moses: "God, merciful, gracious, long-suffering, abundant in goodness and ever true." Such are God's ways, and such must be ours. Atonement must include not only rapprochement with God but also expiation toward our fellow men.

On Yom Kippur, God forgives our sins against Him but not the wrongs we have done our fellow men. Only the penance of restitution can clear the way for God's grace. The rabbis go beyond this and say "Whoever has a sin to confess and is ashamed to do so, let him go and do a good deed and he will find forgiveness."

Jews, like other religionists, have been troubled by the paradox of man's sinfulness. Why, if we were created by a good and omnipotent God, do we have and use the capacity to do evil? Judaism has no general theological explanation of "sin" such as Christianity offers in the doctrine of man's fall. In the Jewish religion sinning is simply a wrong which the individual may or may not commit, depending upon his character and free choice. As the rabbis say, everything is in the hands of God but the fear of God. To free men and women, then, the Yom Kippur service brings this great challenge: "Behold, I set before thee this day life and good, death and evil . . . therefore choose life that ye may live."

In the atonement process there is a profound mystical element. God meets us halfway. First, we must acknowledge our waywardness. He who recognizes his sin has already begun to loosen its hold on him. Then, where possible, there must be expiation, restitution. Now the Jew is ready for penitent prayers. Many of them are in the plural form, "*We* have sinned, *we* have done perversely." Thus it is recognized how deeply we are involved in one another's weaknesses and failures. Then, worn with fasting and humble in penitence, the worshiper may be ready for God's forgiveness. But God's forgiveness does not come easily. He searches the innermost recesses of the heart; no secrets are hidden from Him. His probings make His task of forgiveness even more difficult. So on Yom Kippur, say the rabbis, even God Himself must pray:

> *May my mercy conquer my wrath*
> *So that I may treat my children with love.*

Jews leave Yom Kippur with a great sense of exaltation. This is tempered by a sense of relief, for no one can live continuously on that high and exacting level. Again the sense of balance asserts itself. After a lapse of only four days the Festival of Tabernacles begins. This is a happy fall holiday of thanksgiving.

With winter come two holidays which dramatize a distinctive feature of Jewish experience. Chanukah and Purim tell with colorful ceremony of attempts to destroy the Jewish people and of the defeat of the persecutors. This recurring emphasis on oppression and its overthrow represents a people's choice of what it wishes to remember. In this sense, as Thomas Mann has said, character is fate. The inner nature of the people leads it to select from its past that which is necessary for survival and for the perpetuation of its specific values. Thus memory shapes its destiny. So Jews have chosen to remember that always their faith and God's justice have prevailed against oppressors—from the age of the pyramids of ancient Egypt to the gutted Reichschancellery in Berlin.

Chanukah, which comes in December, is historical and deeply spiritual, commemorating the Jewish people's successful struggle against the persecution of Antiochus IV, less than two centuries before the birth of Jesus. Antiochus desecrated the Jews' sacred Temple in the year 168 B.C., by the erection of Greek idols, before which he ordered the Jews to bow down. Old Mattathias, the priest, aroused his people. Shouting "Whosoever is zealous of the Law, let him follow me," he and his son, Judah the Maccabee, led the outnumbered and ill-equipped Jews to victory—and to the rededication (Chanukah) of their Temple. They found a cruse of oil which, according to the account in the First Book of Maccabees, lasted eight days. Ever since, the Jews have lit candles in their homes for eight days, one the first night, two the second, etc.

Purim, which usually falls in March, is a folk tale almost devoid of religious meaning. In ancient Persia a vizier named Haman sought to exterminate the Jews for being "different." His wicked designs were thwarted by Queen Esther and her uncle, Mordecai. He who plotted to kill the Jews was himself hanged.

Perhaps even more than Chanukah and Purim, Passover is a festival of freedom, celebrating the liberation of the ancient Hebrews from Egyptian bondage. This first great mass emancipation in recorded history has always inspired not only the reverent memory of Jews but the imagination of all free mankind. On the American Liberty Bell are words not of Washington but of Moses: "Proclaim liberty throughout the land to all the inhabitants thereof." It may be safely said that after this first great liberation men were never content again to be in chains.

Each Jew is taught to feel as if he personally had been liberated from Egypt. This feeling is imparted chiefly through the Seder, the loveliest and most moving of all Jewish ceremonies. For this home observance of the first two evenings of Passover, the families gather from near and far. The atmosphere is festive. The service includes ancient gay songs and games for the children. At a dramatic moment during it, the door of the house is thrown open for the return of Elijah, the prophet, to bring news of the coming of the Messiah.

The profoundest meaning of Passover is something which sets Judaism apart from all other religions, for it marks the birth of a nation. Out of a mass of slaves Moses fashioned a nation and gave them a faith. From that day, Jews have never ceased to be a people. They have not been a sect or denomination.

Nationhood was the natural state of the ancient Hebrews in their own land. But what held them together as a people through the nineteen centuries from the time Titus drove them out until their return to Israel in 1948? Certainly their faith was the principal binding force. By the time of the dispersion their faith was surrounded by a whole rubric of laws and customs which set them apart—and was afflicted with a persecution only strengthening their sense of solidarity. Beyond this was the sense of mission: Jews believed they were the chosen people.

This doctrine has lent itself to much misunderstanding. It has been compared with the German Nazi or the Russian Communist sense of mission. But it has nothing to do with conquest, power, glory. Its classic definition was that of the prophet Isaiah, a "suffering servant." When the Jews were chosen, they received not a crown but a yoke. "You alone have I known; therefore will I punish you for your iniquities." Their burden was the acceptance of exacting responsibility, their goal the realization of God's justice—first in their own nation and then in the life of all humanity. A people that is so chosen (or, as some Jewish modernists believe, so chose) to be witnesses of the living God must live with a sense of special mission that sets them apart. They discourage intermarriage; by belief and custom they remain a distinctive group. This exacts a price, often a terrible one, for many men do not understand those who seem determinedly different. What they do not understand, they fear; what they fear, they hate. Out of this fear and hate have ever come persecution and pogroms—ever making service and suffering one for the Jews.

Why did the Jews reject Jesus? The answer is that they have never done so. We do not know from any contemporary Jewish sources what the Jews thought about the young carpenter from Galilee who died on a hill overlooking Jerusalem. There is not a single reference to him in any existing Jewish document of that period.

Only later when Paul fashioned a new religion around Jesus, the Christ, did Jews take cognizance of him. Then they rejected not Jesus, the Jewish teacher, but Christ, the Messiah. There were, for them, definite criteria for the advent of the Messiah. He was to usher in the Messianic Kingdom of justice, truth, and peace—but after Jesus wars, oppression, corruption continued as before. The Jews were also especially repelled by the claim that Jesus had fulfilled the law, which thenceforth could be disregarded.

Finally, Jews have rejected Christianity because of the concepts with which the Church fathers buttressed and embellished the new faith as they spread it through the pagan Roman world. Completely alien to Jewish thought were such ideas as Immaculate Conception, virgin birth, the Trinity, the Holy Ghost, vicarious atonement, the "fall." The religion *of* Jesus was understandable to them; it was Jewish. The religion *about* Jesus was beyond their recognition.

Over the centuries the Jewish attitude toward Jesus has been conditioned by another factor: Christian persecution. The stubborn intransigence of the Jews in their faith has always seemed to many Christians a challenge crying for some kind of retaliation or at least retort. But, as anti-Semitism in recent times has become less religious than political, Jews in turn have felt more able to accept Jesus' role in their own history. Jesus' basic teachings have been found to be Jewish. His stature is that of the Hebrew prophet, fearless fighter for righteousness. As with Isaiah and Amos before him, he did not merely echo his people's convictions. Passing through the alchemy of his sensitive soul, the ancient beliefs found a new emphasis; they received the immortal impress of his luminous, loving personality.

None of this, however, reflects any readiness of Jews to accept Jesus as Christ—for, by history and conviction, the Jews have their own concepts revolving around the Messianic idea. Here one must distinguish between traditional and modernist Jews. The Orthodox still believe in the coming of a personal Messiah and pray each day for his advent. A large segment of the liberal Jewish community has discarded the notion of a single Messianic Personality who is to save mankind. In its place they affirm their faith in a Messianic Era to be achieved by the co-operative work of good men of all nations, races, and religions. With few exceptions religious Jews today believe in the restoration of Israel and the ultimate redemption of mankind. To most liberal Jews the solution of the historic Jewish problem through the founding of the commonwealth of Israel is a step toward the fulfillment of the democratic and Messianic aspirations of prophetic Judaism. This return to Zion is essentially religious in its motivation, for it is charged with a profound mystic conviction that thus will the Jews again make a contribution to mankind. Nearly four thousand years ago a tribe emerged from the desert and attached itself to the soil of Palestine. This union of land and people received a divine blessing. From it came Moses and Jesus, Judaism and Christianity, the Ten Commandments and the Sermon on the Mount. Is it too much to hope that the return of this courageous people to that sacred soil may again yield new insights, new healing and hope, to the troubled children of men?

The Jews are, in the prophet's arresting phrase, "Prisoners of Hope." The Jewish outlook is deeply and abidingly optimistic, progressive, forward-looking. A people that has endured so much knows that it can survive more. Hope wells from faith in a good God whose ways may sometimes be obscure but whose justice and goodness are ultimately triumphant. It inspires Jews constantly to strive for a better world, to be in the thick of movements for social reform. Even the nonreligious Jewish radical, who may ignore his Jewishness, is the product of its Messianic fervor.

Until the modern world emancipated the Jew from the ghetto, the

Torah was the established basis of his life. He lived in a world of his own where the law could be observed without complications. Once he emerged into modern society, however, the whole foundation of His life was shaken, and the observances of his beliefs seemed in ever sharper conflict with the world about him. Some Jews accordingly became indifferent to the demands of their faith, and this process was abetted by the steady secularization of life in America. Some have outspokenly repudiated it; others sought to disappear as Jews, simply to melt into the general environment. Still others, a small number, chose to go to Palestine, where one can live, they believe, a completely uncomplicated life as a Jew. But the great majority of the American Jews continue to be loyal to Judaism in principle, see no reason for surrendering their distinctive beliefs and observances, and plan to live their lives out in this land which they love and where their roots are deep. What about them?

They give a threefold answer—Orthodox, Reform and Conservative. Orthodox Jewry still maintains in principle the absolute authority of the revealed Torah. Adaptation there may be, but the basic law is unchangeable and inviolable. Nevertheless Orthodox Jews face the same problems in the modern world as do the others.

Reform Jews follow an entirely different line. They maintain that Judaism is the sum of the evolving religious experience of the Jewish people. It is and always has been subject to change. By their views, for example, the observance of ancient dietary laws is optional. The Reformers permit men and women to sit together in the synagogues; men may shave their faces; the New Year is observed for one day, not two.

Conservative Judaism is a midway house. Arriving later on the American scene, it sought to avoid the extremes of the Reformers, reconciling tradition to American conditions without compromising its integrity. Of late the difference in observance between many Conservative and Reform Jews has narrowed very much, and there have been proposals advanced for merging the two groups.

All the modern debate concerning Jewish law and its application is related to the final holiday, Shavuos, the Feast of Weeks. Observed in the late spring, it was originally a festival celebrating the gathering in of the first harvest. In the course of time, like most Jewish holidays, it came to be associated with an historic event—in this case the giving of the Torah on Mount Sinai. The poetic imagination of the Jew has embroidered this scene with haunting beauty and with universal meaning.

For Reform Jews, Shavuos has become the logical occasion for confirming Jewish youth in the faith of their forefathers when, after eight to ten years of study, they are deemed worthy of standing before the sacred ark and being accepted into the company of adult Jews. With the traditional Bar Mitzvah ceremony the boy is henceforth to be held responsible for living a Jewish life.

At this ceremony of confirmation the whole great heritage of Judaism is summoned to mind, with a poignant sense of immediacy evoked by the Jews' ever keen sense of history and memory of suffering. It is, for both the old and the young generations, a moment at once of sorrowful reflection and sober dedication.

For my son Stephen and myself, this moment and ceremony came January 25, 1947, in Frankfurt, Germany. It was a singularly provocative place for such a ceremony—the ruins of one of the most battered cities of Germany, but a city whose centuries, long before the Nazis, were enriched by the traditions of a great Jewish community, bright with names like Rothschild, Speyer, and Ehrlich. Here, in the charge which I delivered to my son, I summed up the spirit which animates my beliefs:

". . . The oppressor may triumph for a moment, but his house is built on sand. It cannot withstand the irresistible moral laws of history. And Israel survives.

"The Lord says: Fear not, for I am with thee. That is a magnificent promise and an imperishable source of hope. It makes me proud I am a Jew. Despite the misfortunes of my people, I would not exchange that heritage for anything in the world.

"It is this heritage which we formally transmit to you today, Stephen. When I place my hands upon your head in benediction, I will be the humble instrument through which will flow the stream of history and memories of the great and the good in Israel, the ideals and the aspirations of our people, the strength and the lift of our faith. It is something which places upon you a solemn responsibility to be worthy of its precepts, to be loyal to its ideals, and to express them in a life of service.

" 'So be the Lord with you as I will let you go.' "

— *The Tradition Continues* —

FUNDAMENTAL TO US ALL

Religious convictions are the deepest and most fundamental of all of our personal beliefs. To my way of thinking, every person should seek out meaningful ways to enhance his spiritualism, rather than have another's ways imposed upon him. This has nothing to do with political correctness. It has everything to do with respect for all living individuals and their heritage. Yet, to ignore the place of religious traditions in a child's life is to deny that child a rich and lasting experience, as these firsthand accounts confirm.

Diary! Diary! Do you know what that man did again this year?

Well, of course you don't. He, Granddaddy "Snook," recited that same old tired blessing: *"And God bless us all and abide in our hearts hence forth now and forever more, Amen."*

He has used this same prayer for over ten years. I think that if Granddaddy Snook is going to use this prayer that he should at least make it classy.

For example, what is "hence"? Is it in the present or past tense? Does it mean this or that? And what does he mean by "now and forever more"? What "more comes" after forever? I think he is just an old man trying to hold on to a family tradition.

Granddaddy Snook told me once that his grandfather Oscar started this blessing. Since his grandpa Oscar was not educated, the fancy words he wanted to use were not in his vocabulary. He asked the white man he worked for, Tom Bunkhanna, for some help. Bunkhanna found it rather strange for a Negro to want to use white people's words. He ridiculed Grandpa Oscar and told him to say, "Lord, bend us over the commode. We'll well appreciate it." Grandpa Oscar proudly gave thanks using this blessing and so did his two sons after him.

Granddaddy Snook had more education than his father and grandfather so when he gave the blessing, he said what Grandpa Oscar couldn't: "Lord with our heads bowed toward Earth's dust, I feel the need to say thank you. And God bless us all, and abide in our hearts hence forth now and forever more."

You know, Diary, I feel different now. Suddenly Granddaddy Snook's blessing seems necessary. The blessing is almost symbolic of our family. The blessing started in shame as Grandpa Oscar's blessing when he was poor and dependent on others. Now that blessing has overcome laughter and mocking. Today we laugh at Granddaddy Snook's blessing and I want to change it, make it make sense and be more classy.

When my turn comes to bless the dinner table, mine will be one of victory, for now the only person our family is dependent on is God.

Nikita Sharron Adams, high school

Many families have different traditions. Our family, for example, has a certain tradition that is special to us. We always hold hands when we say the blessing and pray to God. At every meal when we say the blessing, it is a wonderful feeling to hold the hand of the person beside you.

Since both my mother and father work, the only time that we can really sit down together is at the table at suppertime. Holding hands at the table shows our love and admiration for one another.

Holding hands at the table helps us concentrate on the prayer which we are praying. Sometimes it even keeps our hands out of our plates when we are very hungry. Holding hands also calms you down so that you can think clearly.

Holding hands at the table also helps us show our feelings for one another. It shows how we care about you and your families. Also, in a special way, it shows that we care for God.

My tradition shows all the special feeling that our family has for each other. Sometimes at the end our blessing, we give a little squeeze as if to say, "I love you!"

Melanie Katherine Tatum, elementary school

One family tradition is lighting the Sabbath candles. It is really one of my favorite traditions. We wait until sundown on Friday night, since the Jewish day starts at sunset. When it is sundown, we light the candles and say a prayer and the prayer starts like this, "Ba-ruch ah-tah Ah-do-nal El-lo-hay-nu Mel-lech ha-o-lam, a-sher kl-d' shah-nu b'mitz-vo-tav v'tzl-van-ny L'HA-D'LICK NAIR SHEL (SHABBAT) V'YOM TOV."

After this prayer, we light the candles.

My brother and sister go outside to play while Dad makes a special dinner. When he is finished, he calls us in and we eat a family dinner, then we help Dad with the dishes. After that, we either go to the synagogue, or play a game, or a sport. Then we go to bed, or watch a movie. When we get tired, we go to bed and wait till next Friday to do it again. People have been doing this for thousands of years, and our family keeps the tradition alive so people will probably be doing this for a long time to come.

Ariel Kowalick, elementary school

It is a typical Wednesday night. My family and I are sitting in the living room waiting for my brother, Tim. It is his night to give the starting prayer. We have this family tradition where we sit down for an hour every Wednesday night and read the Bible.

When my mother was younger, her mother made her and her five brothers sit down every Monday, Wednesday, and Sunday night to read the Bible. They would read for an hour. They each had to read one column apiece, starting with the oldest. At the end, there would be a finishing prayer.

If I ever have children we will have a family night. First, we will say a starting prayer and then we will read the Bible for an hour. I have not decided if we will read one column apiece or two columns apiece. When we get to the finishing prayer part, each of us will get to say a part of the prayer.

It is about time for my brother to come in. Ah, here he is now. So we must start.

Cynthia Eubanks, high school

On my Dad's side of the family, it is a tradition to learn Hebrew in order to have your Bar or Bat Mitzvah. In this ceremony you are becoming an adult. You read from the Torah, which is like the Bible, but older and is written in Hebrew. Hebrew is very difficult and a lot different from English. I'd say I'm doing pretty well. I'm nine now, so I only have a few years to go until my Bat Mitzvah. To tell you the truth, I'm kind of scared, with only five years remaining. I don't know if I can learn to read the Torah in time.

I like this tradition, since it gives me a chance to be unique in a special way. I'm proud to be Jewish and study Hebrew because my ancestors have been Jewish for a long time. Judaism has existed for thousands of years. Being part of an old tradition is interesting and also serious. I want to pass this tradition on forever.

Perry E. Cooper, elementary school

A year ago, my dad started a new family tradition. After the blessing before our meal, we read a passage from the Bible. My sister, brother, and I take a turn each night. We are reading the New Testament from beginning to end. Then we will read from the Old Testament. My mom or dad explains what we read. It has helped us to learn about the Bible and the morals our country was founded on. My younger brother's reading has improved greatly since we began this tradition. My parents are passing their values to us through this tradition. I hope to continue this tradition with my own family someday, and so do my brother and sister.

Christ Pero, elementary school

Desiderata

Go placidly amid the noise & haste, & remember what peace there may be in silence. As far as possible without surrender be on good terms with all persons. Speak your truth quietly & clearly; and listen to others, even the dull & ignorant; they too have their story.

Avoid loud & aggressive persons, they are vexations to the spirit. If you compare yourself with others, you may become vain & bitter; for always there will be greater & lesser persons than yourself. Enjoy your achievements as well as your plans.

Keep interested in your own career, however humble; it is a real possession in the changing fortunes of time. Exercise caution in your business affairs; for the world is full of trickery. But let this not blind you to what virtue there is; many persons strive for high ideals; and everywhere life is full of heroism.

Be yourself. Especially, do not feign affection. Neither be cynical about love; for in the face of all aridity & disenchantment it is perennial as the grass.

Take kindly the counsel of the years, gracefully surrendering the things of youth. Nurture strength of spirit to shield you in sudden misfortune. But do not distress yourself with imaginings. Many fears are born of fatigue & loneliness. Beyond a wholesome discipline, be gentle with yourself.

You are a child of the universe, no less than the trees & the stars; you have a right to be here. And whether or not it is clear to you, no doubt the universe is unfolding as it should.

Therefore be at peace with God, whatever you conceive Him to be, and whatever your labors & aspirations, in the noisy confusion of life keep peace with your soul.

With all its sham, drudgery, & broken dreams, it is still a beautiful world. Be careful. Strive to be happy.

Found in Old Saint Paul's Church, Baltimore, dated 1692

CHAPTER 21

The Sharing Traditions: America's Diary

THE PASTIMES OF PAST TIMES

~ A Potpourri of Memories ~

The Saturday night dance, the coming together of a company's retired employees, the fellows' poker game, granddad and the neighborhood kids playing baseball, getting together for a quilting party, gathering with friends in New Orleans for a Sunday afternoon soiree, flying a kite with your friends, looking at the painted barns of Pennsylvania . . .

Traditions are pivotal in our lives. While our varied and different traditions may distinguish us one from another, at the same time, traditions bring us together in laughter and friendship. Most important, they show us that more often than not, we are very much alike. Traditions are, in the richest sense, shared experiences.

The Salon Story

* MARDA BURTON

For years you could tell when Marda Burton was welcoming guests for that once essential, but now seldom enjoyed tradition—the soiree. She hung out a welcoming flag from her second-floor balcony in the French Quarter of New Orleans. Actually this old tradition is now gathering new life. These days Marda's soiree is held at Le Petit Theatre in the French Quarter the first Sunday of each month and is open to the public. There are several such groups in other cities across the country as well.

The nicest thing about tradition is that mostly fun things get carried forward. Take my Sunday afternoon soirees, for example. Based on the old custom of holding open house to receive friends and offer them hospitality, my parties in the French Quarter were specifically inspired by the legendary salons of Paris where artists and writers came to see and be seen, to talk and sometimes to listen.

As a young girl living in Laurel, Mississippi, reading about Madame de Staël and Gertrude Stein, I dreamed of someday holding my own elegant salon. But it was not until many years later when I moved into the perfect French Quarter setting for such an affair—huge rooms, wide balcony, many floor-to-high-ceiling windows—that I began to set my plans in motion.

While de Staël's concerns were primarily literary and Stein was a patron of artists, my own interests encompass all the arts. In my first printed invitations I tried for an acronym. But Marda Burton's Sunday Afternoon Literary, Artistic, Musical, and Drinking Salon didn't quite work. Everything else did. Almost too well.

I've always regretted abandoning the piano immediately following my dreaded senior recital, which consisted of no-talent, robot-like renditions of "Maleguena" and "Claire de Lune." So my first salon-related purchase was a restored Fischer baby grand for talented friends to play. It had to be lifted over the balcony by crane. The next acquisitions were dozens of champagne glasses, which require constant replacement. At more than fifty parties endless glasses have been trashed, but so what? I don't drink out of plastic, nor do my guests, even when a hundred or two pass through the door.

Numbers would perhaps never have become a problem had I not had a bright idea I thought would save time and effort. It involved, in lieu of personal invitations, flying a colorful flag from the balcony the week before each party. Anyone who has ever been invited (I can hardly take a step in the French Quarter without running into someone I know) can attend with a friend. Then that friend, in turn, can come to the next salon and bring a friend. Often guests bring interesting visitors from out of town. Strangers appear, having been told about the salon by those out-of-towners. It was even mentioned in a *National Geographic* story about New Orleans. Understandably, an overflow crowd is the result, and it's getting bigger. Now I don't put out the flag, but the word still goes out, perhaps by jungle drums.

Less predictable are the intriguing and deeply felt offerings of countless musical performers, authors and poets reading from their current works, actors performing both comedy and drama, and artists who show and explain their creations. None are paid, although if street musicians come upstairs to entertain, I pass the hat. Until I began the salon, I never dreamed New Orleans was so crammed with talent and those eager to share it. It makes me wonder what exceptional abilities would surface, given the chance, in even the smallest town.

On purpose, I keep the event extremely informal, with presentations scattered intermittently over the afternoon, usually not knowing in advance of the day what will transpire. I like the idea of individuals showing up unexpectedly to enchant and amaze. Wonderful performances and readings happen as if by magic, as well as some not so wonderful, and some absolutely hilarious. I adore the spontaneity of it all.

Of course, when celebrities are in town, their hosts like to introduce them to the salon. Among the most memorable were Tennessee Williams' brother, Dakin, who declaimed his brother's poetry, and Rex Reed, Dick Cavett, and Carrie Nye who threw Mardi Gras beads from the balcony. The Dixie Cups sang, as did the Phantom of the Opera. For my birthday, a local playwright wrote and produced an amusing skit about me, later expanding it into a full-length play he called "The Salon Story."

Celebrities are always fun, but providing a stage for unknowns is dearest to my heart. I remember the tenor who with tears running down his face sang his mother's favorite song the week she died, the youthful symphony conductor who played piano exquisitely, the writer who read a short story the week after her book was published, the humorist who writes about her now-dead ex-husband (she says she didn't kill him, although she kept thinking of untraceable ways to do so), the poet whose "Bugs Bunny" reading is always in demand, the pianists and groups who found jobs as a result of performing at the salon.

As if all that weren't enough, much networking goes on among the lively mix of people, often unbeknownst to me. When I'm telephoned the next day by gents who've lost their paper napkins with phone numbers jotted down, I'm prompted to point out that my salon is not a singles bar. But I'm happy to say that more than one couple has met and fallen in love over my at-risk champagne glasses.

So, okay, this is not a short party. It begins at three o'clock and, on occasion, lasts past midnight with night owls sending out for pizza. Most drift off around eight or nine o'clock when hunger strikes. Sometimes I go with them. Once in a while I'm forced to recite Prospero's speech from *The Tempest,* the one that begins "Our revels now are ended."

Besides fruit and cheese, I put out cases of champagne and wine, set up the bar, and let people help themselves. No bartender to slow things down and add to the expense, but, consequently, my tiny train-style kitchen is a madhouse. Two friends who help with the chaos had aprons made saying "Marda's Little Helpers."

Some guests bring contributions of food or drink, but no matter what or how much, it all gets consumed. I loathe BYOB parties where everyone has to keep up with his own bottle, so whatever is brought gets put into the fridge or the wine buckets for the entire crowd. There's seldom anything left over, except a messy apartment, and fifty to a hundred empty bottles. To get rid of the latter, I insist the last twenty or so guests each take away three or four empties, which they dispose of in trash bins along the street.

To alleviate crowding, I could move the entire party, in good weather, to my building's spacious back deck, but that would mean complicated arrangements involving piano, bar, and seating. As it is, the soiree is fairly effortless; and I refuse to let it become too much trouble. A basically lazy hostess, I hate having to balance guest lists, invite people each time, plan programs, set up an outside venue, and then worry about the weather. My ideas about entertaining derive from a long tradition in my own family: the hostess is required to have as much fun as the guests.

In light of this requirement, those exquisite Parisian salons and my desire to emulate their elegance must bow to today's reality. I believe it happened when the first prized crystal champagne flute "fell" off the piano and shattered on the floor. I decided right then and there that what matters most at the salon—my updated tradition, if you will— is not elegance at all, but sharing the uncommon enthusiasm of my guests.

To Help Them Quilt

Laurel Thatcher Ulrich

"I'd love to talk," my college roommate, Emily Riker Seaver, began, "but my quilting group's here." Gathering to quilt is as old a tradition as the American colonies, as we read in this excerpt from The Midwife's Tale *set in the eighteenth century. Happily, quilting and quilting parties show no sign of fading away.*

"The girls had the Ladies to help them quilt," Martha wrote on November 1, four days after Hannah's wedding. Quilting was the most insistent of the matrimonial preparation. The first round brought the neighbors, the women coming by turns, Sally Cox and Sarah Densmore on October 30, Polly Pollard, Mrs. Damrin, and Mrs. Livermore on October 31, and the unnamed group of "Ladies" on November 1. Whether Parthenia's was the first or the only quilt to go into the frame during the three-day period we do not know.

A different kind of stitching, less social, more intense, consuming the total attention of the two brides for a full day or more, began later that month. Hannah had begun "piecing a Bedquilt" on November 20 (two days after Parthenia's wedding), but had interrupted her work to weave a tow and woolen blanket. On November 26, she put the quilt "into the Fraim" and with the help of Parthenia and Dolly "quilted it out before shee slept." Parthenia's "Callico Bed quilt" came next. This time Martha as well as the girls helped with the quilting. Parthenia finished it the next day.

These quilts probably combined a top made of imported fabric, a filler of combed wool, and a homespun lining, the three layers being stretched tightly on a wooden frame, marked with chalk, then quilted together. (In the fanciest quilts, the stitching formed an intricate maze of feathers, fans, and scrolls.) One of the oldest pieced quilts known to have been in America is a Maine coverlet, long identified as a "wedding quilt" because of the appliquéd hearts in the center. Hearts or no hearts, the quilts made in the Ballard house in November of 1792 were clearly associated with the transition from girlhood to marriage. In this sense, quilting, too, was one of the rites of marriage. . . .

In each of the two autumns before Hannah's marriage, there were quiltings at the Ballard house, each involving several days of individual and group work before the men arrived for a dance. On November 8, 1790, "The girls quilted a Bed quillt & went to Mr Craggs spent Evng." The next day, "The girls quilted two quilts. Hannah Rockwood & Mrs Benjamin helpt the Evening. We Bakt mins and pumpkin pies. Mrs Porter here." Then on November 10, "My girls had some neighbours to help them quilt a bed quilt, 15 ladies. They began to quilt at 3 hour pm. Finisht and took it out at 7 evening. There were 12 gentlemen to tea. They danced a little while after supper. Behaved exceeding cleverly. . . . Were all returned home before the 11th hour."

The next year, on September 19, Martha wrote that her girls had spent part of the day "peecing Bed quillts." This can hardly have been the intricate patchwork common to the next century, however, for they also managed to do the family wash that day and then to go to a neighbor's house with Moses Pollard at night. The next day they "put a Bed quillt into the fraim" and "Bakt cakes & pies." On September 21, they "had a quilting, got out one & partly quilted another," before the gentlemen arrived for refreshments and a dance.

Young men helped to celebrate the completion of quilts just as young women celebrated a house- or barn-raising by gathering for a dance.

Choir Practice in Dallas, Texas

*EVELYN PONDER

What's in a name? Sometimes a "white lie." But it's a great way of sharing and carrying on a tradition.

The once-a-month poker club is made up of seven longtime friends, three of them going back to first grade, and the others at least a twenty-year friendship. It all started with these good friends gathering for a nickle-dime poker game once a month at one of the member's home.

The host couple (the wife, of course) prepares a typically Southern dinner. Bar-b-que, chicken pie, and, yes, occasionally fried green tomatoes or fried okra, are favorite fare. Whatever, it is always cooked and served superbly, which keeps us on our toes! Not that we're exactly competitive, but we do all try to create something special when it is our turn. Most often I'm asked to fix my seafood gumbo. Because of the time inolved in the preparation—a full day of cooking, another day for the seasoning to set up, and then the serving of it—this truly is a labor of love. I only prepare it for special friends, but for the "choir," I'll do it.

Choir? This is a poker club.

You see, we teasingly refer to poker night as choir practice, just in case you are asked where your husband is that evening. It just didn't sound proper to say, "He's playing poker." It sounds so much better to say, "He's at choir practice," and hope you're not asked how long he's sung in the choir and asked if he sings tenor or bass—and keep a straight face all the while! (Incidentally, all these men really are active in their community, business, civic, and, yes, church activities, and, believe it or not, not only can these poker-playing friends carry a tune but they're actually quite good!)

At Christmas, the "choir" treats their patient and hardworking wives to a festive dinner, complete with place cards in the shape of fully robed choirboys. Often they even have real carolers entertain us. This is all done with good cheer and great festivity.

Truthfully, though, the best part of this on-going tradition isn't the poker game. It is the affection, support and friendship that has grown strong among the couples. We have suffered though good times and bad, even the loss of children and parents.

In the end, that poker-playing night is worthy of any choir practice.

Baseball in Mumford's Pasture Lot

Samuel Adams

Ever hear someone, maybe your grandfather, complain that baseball is not the same sport that it used to be? Thanks to TV, instant replays, and players' strikes, it isn't. Still, baseball manages to thrill youngsters, no matter what the rules may be. To take you back to an earlier time, here is an 1880s reminiscence of America's favorite sharing pastime—a pickup game of baseball, the way it used to be. Incidentally, this essay is my twenty-eight-year-old son, Langdon's, favorite piece in this book. "It's timeless," he says.

A smart single rig drew up to the hitching post of No. 52 South Union Street as we three boys approached. Out of it stepped a short, red-faced, dapper man who secured his horse and then addressed us.

"Does Mr. Myron Adams live here?"

"Yes, sir," John said.

"We're just going in to see him," Sireno added. "He's our grandfather."

"Well, you can wait," the stranger said. "I've got private business with him."

"If you're trying to sell him a colored enlargement of a photograph—" John began but got no further.

"I ain't," the caller interrupted. "My name is Phillips and I represent the Rochester Baseball Club."

"There isn't any," I said glumly.

It was cause for humiliation to every right-thinking inhabitant of the city, young and old, that in the spring of the baseball-mad year of 1879, Rochester was represented by no professional team whatever.

"There will be if I can sell fifty of these here tickets, good for the whole season and only ten dollars," Mr. Phillips said. "D'you think he'll pony up? How's he on baseball?"

"He wouldn't know a Dollar Dead from a Young America if it hit him in the snoot," Reno answered. The Dollar Dead was the standard amateur ball, the Young America the twenty-five-cent junior favorite.

"I'll have a crack at him anyway," Mr. Phillips decided. He vanished into the cottage, and in a few minutes we heard Grandfather, in his deep and resonant voice, putting an end to the interview. "What?" he cried. "Money? To witness what should be a *gentleman's* pastime? Nonsense! Fustian! Good day to you!"

The crestfallen visitor came out, silently climbed into his buggy, and drove away. We went in to pay our duty call.

A week later, the three of us ran upon Mr. Phillips again, this time in Livingston Park, and heard from him tidings of great joy. In spite of Grandfather's recalcitrance, Rochester was to have its team. Mr. Asa T. Soule, the patent-medicine magnate, had just come forward with an offer to finance a club out of his private pocket, provided it should bear the name of Hop Bitters, the cure-all he manufactured.

The news spread fast and, as the opening of the season drew near, Rochester glowed with restored pride. In its first game the new club swamped an amateur nine, fourteen to six.

Next, an exhibition game was scheduled against Rochester's ancient and bitter rival, the Buffaloes, who were in the National League and therefore supposedly a cut above us. It was to be the event of the year, and the admission was fifty cents. John, being ten years old and our senior member, put the painful question to Reno and me.

"Where are we going to get half a dollar apiece?"

"Grandpa Adams," I suggested doubtfully.

"In your mind, baby mine!" Reno said, using the most emphatic negation of the time.

"What other chance have we got?" I asked. Nobody had an answer. Fifty cents was unthinkably hard for a small boy to come by in those days. Grandfather was our only hope.

In preparation for the desperate attempt upon his purse, we all three devoted the next week or so to attending him with great assiduity. We mowed his lawn. We weeded the vegetable patch. We suffered errands gladly. When but two days remained before the game, we decided the time had come. We washed our hands and brushed our hair, and since none of us coveted the honor of putting the momentous question, I plucked three timothy heads for the purpose of drawing lots.

"Shortest straw pulls the skunk's tail," I said. This was formula; no disrespect was intended.

John drew the short one, and, led by him, we went to face our grandfather. John opened cautiously, speaking of the importance of the coming event to Rochester and the Hop Bitters Club. "You know, Grandpa, our team's named for the medicine," he said brightly.

The old gentleman glanced at the mantel, where stood a dark amber bottle containing the spirituous and inspiriting "Invalid's Friend & Hope."

"Why, yes," he said. "A superior restorative. Very comforting to the system," a sentiment shared by thousands of the old gentleman's fellow-teetotalers.

"It's a dandy ball team," Reno gloated.

"I assume that you refer to its costume?" Grandfather said coldly. He did not countenance slang on our lips.

"Yes, sir," Reno agreed hastily. "You ought to see their uniforms."

"I am willing to believe that they present a macaroni appearance," the old gentleman said. "But what is the precise connection between this remedy and the projected contest?"

"Mr. Soule is giving the money for the club," John explained.

"Mr. Asa T. Soule? I was not aware that he had sportive proclivities."

"Oh, he's not really a sporting man," John hastened to disclaim. "No, sir! He—he's quite religious. Why, he won't have a player on his team who ever played on Sunday."

I saw that Grandfather, a strict Sabbatarian, was impressed. "They've got a rule against Sunday games in the National League," I said, opportunely recalling an item in the *Democrat & Chronicle.*

"Baseball is a very Christian game, sir," John added.

"I daresay, I daresay," the old gentleman conceded. "But it is not, by all accounts, what it was in my day. When I first came here, the Rochester Baseball Club met four afternoons a week. We had fifty members. That was in 1827."

"I play first base on the Livonia Young Eagles," Reno said eagerly. "Where did you play, sir?"

"In Mumford's pasture lot, off Lake Avenue."

"Reno means what position, Grandpa," I explained.

"Batter, for choice," said the old gentleman.

"You couldn't bat all the time," Reno demurred.

"No," Grandfather said. "But I preferred to. I frequently hit the ball over the fence."

"When your side was in the field, where did you play?" John asked.

"Wherever I thought the ball most likely to be batted, naturally," the alumnus of Mumford's pasture lot replied, manifestly annoyed at the stupidity of the question.

"That's a funny kind of a game," Reno muttered.

"I see nothing humorous in it," Grandfather retorted. "The cream of Rochester's Third Ward ruffleshirts participated in the pastime."

"Lots of the nicest boys in town go to baseball games now," I said hopefully.

"Well, well." Our grandfather's deep accents were benevolent. "I see no reason why you should not attend. You are old enough to go by yourselves, I suppose."

"It isn't that exactly, Grandpa," John said. "You see, sir—"

"It costs money to get in," Reno blurted.

"So I was informed by the person with the inflamed nose," said Grandfather dryly.

"Only fifty cents," John said with admirable casualness; then he added, "We thought, sir, that perhaps you would like to come along with us and see how they play it now, just for once."

There was a breathless pause. Then Grandfather said, "Fetch me the emergency cashbox from the desk."

Hardly able to believe our ears, we fell over one another to obey.

During the next forty-eight hours, John, Reno, and I debated long and seriously as to whether we should brief Grandfather on modern baseball, which he was about to see for the first time. All of us were, of course, experts, although we had never seen a professional game. We knew the rules and the etiquette of the diamond and could have passed perfect examinations on the quality and record of every wearer of a Hop Bitters uniform. Reno and I were for giving Grandfather the benefit of our erudition, but John outargued us. Older generations, he pointed out, did not take kindly to instruction from younger.

"He'd just tell us that he played the game before we were born," he said.

On the great day, Grandfather and the three of us arrived early at Hop Bitters Park and found good places in the fifth row directly back of the plate. Before our enchanted eyes there stretched the greensward of the diamond, bounded by the base paths. It was close-cut, but the outfield was practically in a state of nature, its grasses waving gently in the breeze. We had heard that the Buffalo manager had entered a protest against the outfield's unmown state, complaining that he had not brought his players all the way to Rochester to have them turned out to pasture.

The stand filled up promptly. There must have been as many as three hundred people present, mostly of the prosperous classes. Mr. Mudge, the undertaker, and Mr. Whittlesey, the Assistant Postmaster, took seats in front of us and were presently joined by Mr. Toogood, the Troup Street livery-stable man. Two clerks from Clenny's China Emporium crowded past us, while on the aisle side the manager of Reynolds Arcade took his place, accompanied by Professor Cook, the principal and terror of No. 3 School. Back of us sat a red-necked, hoarse-voiced canalman. Mr. Mudge addressed our grandfather.

"A pleasure and a surprise to see you here, Mr. Adams."

"The young must have their day," Grandfather replied amiably. "*Maxima debetur puero reverentia,* you know."

"Yes, sir; I don't doubt it for a minute," the liveryman said earnestly. "I hear those Buffaloes are tough."

"We can lick 'em," I said loyally.

"Rochester boasted a superior club in my day, also," Grandfather said.

"Did you play on it, Mr. Adams?" inquired Professor Cook.

"I did, sir, for two seasons."

"I assume that the game as then played differs from the present form."

"You are justified in your assumption, sir," said Grandfather, who then entered upon an informative discourse regarding the baseball of 1827.

The play at Mumford's pasture lot, he set forth, was open to all fifty active members of the club. The pitchers, who were ex officio the captains, chose up sides. Twelve to a team was considered a convenient number, but there might be as many as fifteen. A full turnout of members would sometimes put three teams in the field. Mr. Mudge expressed the belief that this must result in overcrowding. Where did they all play?

Pitcher, catcher and basemen, Grandfather said, remained in their positions. The basemen stood touching their bases with at least one foot until the ball was hit. The remainder of the out team formed a mobile defense, each man stationing himself where he foresaw the best opportunity of making catches. Mr. Toogood wished to know what the third team did while two were in the field. It waited, the veteran explained. At the close of each inning, when three batters had been put out—whether on flies, fouls, or by being touched or hit with the ball—the runs were totted up and the side with the lower score was supplanted by the third team. This continued until the hour agreed upon for stopping, which was usually sunset. Then the team with the largest total was adjudged the winner.

"Sounds like three-old-cat gone crazy," Reno muttered in my ear.

Further elucidation of the baseball of Grandfather's day was cut short by a shout of "Here they come!," as, amidst loyal clamor, the home team strode forth in neat gray uniforms, the name of the sponsoring nostrum scarlet across their breasts. They were a terrifically masculine lot, with bulging muscles and heavy whiskers. Eagerly we boys identified our special heroes, having often trailed them through the streets to the ballpark entrance. "That's Meyerle, the first base," John said. "He can jump six feet in the air and catch the ball with his left hand."

"The little, dumpy one is Burke," said Mr. Toogood. "He's shortstop. You oughta see him handle daisy-cutters! Oh, my!"

"McGunnigle, our right fielder, batted pretty near three hundred with Buffalo last year," Mr. Mudge told Grandfather proudly.

"Three hundred runs?" Grandfather asked with evident skepticism.

The reply was drowned by the loudest shout of all. "There he comes! Tinker! Tinker!" A hundred voices chorused, "What's the matter with Tinker!" and three hundred antiphonal howls responded, "HE'S ALL RIGHT!"

The canaller leaned over and spoke confidentially in Grandfather's ear. "You watch that fellow Tinker, Mister. If a high fly goes out to left field, he'll git under it and do the prettiest back flip ever you seen before he catches it. You wouldn't see nothing like that in the League. Used to be a circus man."

"I shall make it a point to observe him," Grandfather said.

Out came the enemy at a carefree trot. They were even more muscular-looking than our heroes and sported whiskers at least as luxuriant. They lined up near the plate, faced the stand, and saluted the crowd grimly, fingers to the peaks of their green caps. We boys joined lustily in the chorus of opprobrious hoots that was the response. A man in street clothes appeared and took a stand a yard behind the catcher, who stood five yards back of the plate.

"On which side does that person play?" Grandfather asked.

"He doesn't play," Mr. Mudge answered. "He's the umpire. He makes the decisions."

"In our game, we had no need of such intervention," Grandfather said. "If a point of dispute arose, the captains consulted and came to a composition."

"Suppose they disagreed?" Professor Cook suggested.

"Then, sir, they skied a copper for heads or tails and abode by arbitrament of the coin, like gentlemen and Corinthians," Grandfather replied. He turned his attention to the scene below. "Why is the tall man throwing the ball at the short man?" he inquired.

"That's our pitcher, Critchley, sooppling his arm up," Mr. Toogood said.

Grandfather frowned. "That is throwing, not pitching," he said. "He should keep his arm down."

"He's only got to keep it as low as his waist," Reno said.

The old gentleman shook his head obstinately. "Knuckles should be below the knee, not the waist. A highly improper procedure."

The Hop Bitters team had now taken their positions and were standing, crouched forward, hands upon knees, in the classic posture. A burly Buffalo player stalked to the plate, rang his bat upon it, and described threatening arcs in the air.

"High ball," he barked at the umpire.

The umpire shouted to the pitcher, "The batsman calls for a high ball."

Grandfather addressed the universe. "What in Tophet is this?"

We boys were glad to enlighten him. "He wants a pitch between his shoulder and his belt," John said.

"If he'd called for a low ball, it'd have to be between his belt and his knee," Reno added.

"Do you mean to say that he can choose where the pitch is to come?" Grandfather asked incredulously.

"Yes, sir. And if it doesn't come there, it's a ball, and if he gets eight balls, he can take his base," I said.

"I should admire to bat in such circumstances," said Grandfather.

"Maybe it wouldn't be so easy," Reno said. "Critchley's got a jim-dandy curve."

"Curve?" asked the old gentleman. "What may that be?"

"Outcurve or incurve," Reno told him. "It starts like this, then it goes like this or like this—sorta bends in the air—and whiff! One strike!"

"Bends in the air!" An indulgent smile appeared on Grandfather's visage. "These young folk will accept any absurdity," he said to Professor Cook.

"Some do hold it to be an optical illusion," the principal said diplomatically.

"Certainly," Grandfather said. "Anything else would be contrary to the laws of God and nature. Let me hear no more of such fahdoodle," he concluded sternly, turning his back upon Reno.

The first inning was uneventful, as were the second and third. Pitcher Critchley's optical illusions and those of the opposing pitcher were uniformly and dully successful. Grandfather fidgeted and commented sharply upon the torpor of the proceedings.

"Lackadaisy-dido!" he said. "Why does not someone hit the ball?"

"A couple of goose eggs is nothing, Grandpa," John said. "Just let our team once get a start and you'll see."

The last of the fourth inning supplied a momentary stir. A high foul came down just in front of us, and the Buffalo catcher raced after it. The ball slithered from his outstretched fingers. We boys shrieked with delight. He glared at us and Grandfather addressed him kindly.

"Young man, that was ill-judged. You would have been well-advised to wait and take it on the first bounce."

We held our collective breaths, but the wrath died out of the upturned face.

"Look, Mister," the catcher said, earnestly argumentative, "that ball was a twister. How'd I know where it would bound?"

The canaller back of us raised a jeering voice. "Butterfingers! Whyncha catch it in your cap?"

"You can't catch a ball in your cap any more," John said to the canaller. "It's in this year's rules."

"Back to the berm, fathead!" the catcher added.

The umpire walked up, lifting an authoritative hand. "No conversation between players and spectators," he snapped, and the game was resumed.

Later there was a considerable delay when a foul sailed over the fence. Both teams went outside to search for the ball, and Grandfather took the occasion to expatiate upon the superiority of the old-time game.

"Our Saturdays," he said, "were very gala affairs. Ladies frequently attended, and refreshments were served."

"Did you have uniforms, Grandpa?" I asked.

"Uniforms? We had no need of them. We removed our broadcoats, hitched our braces, and were prepared."

John said, "Our nine has militia caps with brass buttons."

"Fabricius Reynolds played catcher in a canaller's tall castor," Grandfather recalled. "It was of silky beaver, gray, with a picture of the *Myron Holley* passing through Lock Twenty-three painted on the front. Very bunkum."

"I've got a fifteen-cent Willow Wand with 'Home Run' on it in red letters," Reno said proudly.

"Hamlet Scrantom's bat was of polished black walnut with his initials on a silver plate," the old gentleman went on. "He was a notorious batsman."

— ·· —

The quest for the lost ball was eventually abandoned, Mr. Soule reluctantly tossed out a new one, the umpire called "Play ball, gents!," and the dull succession of runless innings continued. Then in the opening half of the sixth, with two Buffaloes out and two on base, a break came. A towering fly to left field brought a yelp of anticipatory delight from the admirers of the accomplished Tinker. Fleet of foot, he got beneath the ball while it was still high in air. His back flip was a model of grace and exactitude. Down came the ball into his cupped and ready hands—and broke through. Amid howls of dismay, he chased it, scooped it up, and threw it home. It went four feet above the catcher's reach, and the Buffalo runners galloped merrily in.

"Boggle-de-botch!" Grandfather exclaimed.

John plucked at his sleeve. "I want to go home," he said brokenly.

"Do not show yourself such a milksop," the old gentleman said. "How far is our own club behind?"

"Three runs," John groaned.

"And there's another," I added, almost in tears, as the Buffalo shortstop sent the ball over the left-field fence.

"Pooh!" said Grandfather. "Four runs is not an insuperable advantage. Why, I once saw Hamlet Scrantom bat in more than that at one stroke."

We stared at him. "How could he, Grandpa?" John asked. "Even if there were three men on base—"

"There were. I was one of them."

"—that would be only four runs."

"Seven, in this instance," the old gentleman said cheerfully. "Hamlet knocked the ball into a sumac thicket, and we continued to run the bases until it was found and returned."

From then on, the Hop Bitters were a sad spectacle. They stumbled and bumbled in the field, and at bat, as the embittered Reno said, they couldn't have hit a rotten punkin with the thrill of a four-horse bob. On their side, the enemy fell upon Pitcher Critchley's offerings with dire effect. They dropped short flies over the basemen's heads. They slashed swift daisy-cutters through the impotent infield. They whacked out two-baggers and three-baggers with the nonchalance of assured victory. Grandfather assayed the situation.

"The Buffaloes appear to have the faculty of placing their strokes where the Rochesters are not," he said sagely, a comment later paralleled by Willie Keeler's classic recipe, "Hit 'em where they ain't."

We boys and the Rochester rooters around us became silent with gloom. Only Grandfather maintained any show of interest in the proceedings. He produced a notebook from the pocket of his ceremonial Prince Albert coat and, during what was left of the game, wrote in it busily. We were too depressed even to be curious. It was a relief when the agony ended, with a pop fly to the pitcher.

"Three out, all out," the umpire announced. "The score is Buffaloes eleven, Hop Bitters nothing. A game will be played in this park . . ."

But we had no heart in us to listen.

We went back to Grandfather's cottage, and over a consolatory pitcher of raspberry shrub in the sitting room he delivered his verdict.

"The game is not without merit," he said thoughtfully, "but I believe it to be susceptible of improvement."

Surprisingly, the Hop Bitters nine beat both Worcester and Washington in the following fortnight. On the strength of their improvement, a return game with Buffalo was scheduled for August, and we boys resumed what Grandfather would have called our "officiousness" at Union Street; we were sedulous in offers to mow, to weed, to fetch and carry. On the last Saturday in July, when a less important game, with Syracuse, was on the card, we found the front door locked and our step-grandmother out back, tending her hollyhocks. "Where's Grandpa?" I asked.

"You'd never guess," the old lady said with a twinkle.

"Gone canalling," John surmised.

"Mr. Adams is attending the baseball game, if you please," his wife said, "and no more thought of the fifty cents expense than if it was so many peppercorns. This is the second time since he took you boys. I do believe he has ideas."

Grandfather did, indeed, have ideas. We learned of them later. The notes made while the Buffaloes were swamping the wretched Hop Bitters were the groundwork of a comprehensive plan which turned up among his papers after his death. It was a design for the betterment of baseball and was addressed to Mr. Soule, the Hop Bitters Baseball Club and the Citizens of Rochester, New York. A prologue, which still seems to me to have its points, introduced it.

The purport and intent of the game of baseball, as I apprehend, is to afford healthful exercise to the participants and harmless entertainment to the spectators. In its present apathetic and supine form it fulfills neither desideratum. A scant dozen runs for an afternoon's effort is a paltry result, indeed. I have seen twice that number achieved in a single inning when the game was in its prime. I therefore have the honor, sir, to lay before you a prospectus for the rejuvenescence of the pastime and its reclamation from the slough of inertia and monotony wherein it is engulfed as practiced in your ballpark.

The plan provided for an extra shortstop between first and second bases and two additional outfielders to take care of long flies. But the really revolutionary proposal dealt with the pitching. The expert of Mumford's pasture lot approved of one innovation he had witnessed, the right of the batter to call his ball. But this did not go far enough. Grandfather's rule proscribed the pitcher from "any motion or pretense delusive of or intended to delude the eye of the batter."

"Such practice," he wrote, "savors of chicanery and is subversive of true, Corinthian sportsmanship." So much for curves!

Whether Mr. Soule ever received the memorial I don't know. Certainly he did not act upon it. A Rochester team took the field in the following spring with the usual complement of nine players and Grandfather never went to another ball game.

— *The Day We Flew the Kites* —

Frances Fowler

Ask an adult, "What is your favorite tradition?" More than likely the answer will be a tradition remembered from childhood, one that holds memories of pleasant times and laughter. This touching story of that timeless spring tradition—kite flying—is a reminder that heartwarming memories of sharing times can sustain us when we are faced with life's bitter tragedies.

"String!" shouted Brother, bursting into the kitchen. "We need lots more string."

It was Saturday. As always, it was a busy one, for "Six days shalt you labor and do all thy work" was taken seriously then. Outside, Father and Mr. Patrick next door were doing chores.

Inside the two houses, Mother and Mrs. Patrick were engaged in spring cleaning. Such a windy March day was ideal for "turning out" clothes closets. Already woolens flapped on back-yard clotheslines.

Somehow the boys had slipped away to the back lot with their kites. Now, even at the risk of having Brother impounded to beat carpets, they had sent him for more string. Apparently there was no limit to the heights to which kites would soar today.

My mother looked out the window. The sky was piercingly blue, the breeze fresh and exciting. Up in all that blueness sailed great puffy billows of clouds. It had been a long, hard winter, but today was Spring.

Mother looked at the sitting room, its furniture disordered for a Spartan sweeping. Again her eyes wavered toward the window. "Come on, girls! Let's take string to the boys and watch them fly the kites a minute." On the way we met Mrs. Patrick, laughing gingerly, escorted by her girls.

There never was such a day for flying kites! God doesn't make two such days in a century. We played all our fresh twine into the boys' kites and still they soared. We could hardly distinguish the tiny, orange colored specks. Now and then we slowly reeled one in, finally bringing it dipping and tugging to earth, for the sheer joy of sending it up again. What a thrill to run with them, to the right, to the left, and see our poor, earth-bound movements reflected minutes later in the majestic sky-dance of the kites! We wrote wishes on slips of paper and slipped them over the string. Slowly, irresistibly, they climbed up until they reached the kites. Surely all such wishes would be granted!

Even our fathers dropped hoe and hammer and joined us. Our mothers took their turn, laughing like schoolgirls. Their hair blew out of their pompadours and curled loose about their cheeks; their gingham aprons whipped about their legs. Mingled with our fun was something akin to awe. The grownups were really playing with us! Once I looked at Mother and thought she looked actually pretty. And her over forty!

We never knew where the hours went on that hilltop day. There were no hours, just a golden, breezy Now. I think we were all a little beyond ourselves. Parents forgot their duty and their dignity; children forgot their combativeness and small spites. "Perhaps it's like this in the Kingdom of Heaven," I thought confusedly.

It was growing dark before, drunk with sun and air, we all stumbled sleepily back to the houses. I suppose we had some sort of supper. I suppose there must have been a surface tidying-up, for the house on Sunday looked decorous enough.

The strange thing was, we didn't mention that day afterward. I felt a little embarrassed. Surely none of the others had thrilled to it as deeply as I. I locked the memory up in that deepest part of me where we keep "the things that cannot be and yet are."

The years went on, then one day I was scurrying about my own kitchen in a city apartment, trying to get some work out of the way while my three-year-old insistently cried her desire to "go park and see ducks."

"*I can't* go!" I said. "I have this and this to do, and when I'm through I'll be too tired to walk that far."

My mother, who was visiting us, looked up from the peas she was shelling. "It's a wonderful day," she offered, "really warm, yet there's a fine, fresh breeze. It reminds me of that day we flew the kites."

I stopped in my dash between stove and sink. The locked door flew open, and with it a gush of memories. I pulled off my apron. "Come on," I told my little girl. "You're right, it's too good a day to miss."

Another decade passed. We were in the aftermath of a great war. All evening we had been asking our returned soldier, the youngest Patrick boy, about his experiences as a prisoner of war. He had talked freely, but now for a long time he had been silent. What was he thinking of—what dark and dreadful things?

"Say!" A smile twitched his lips. "Do you remember . . . no, of course you wouldn't. It probably didn't make the impression on you it did on me."

I hardly dared speak. "Remember what?"

"I used to think of that day a lot in PW camp, when things weren't too good. Do you remember the day we flew the kites?"

Winter came, and the sad duty of a call of condolence on Mrs. Patrick, recently widowed. I dreaded the call. I couldn't imagine how Mrs. Patrick would face life alone.

We talked a little of my family and her grandchildren and the changes in the town. Then she was silent, looking down at her lap. I cleared my throat. Now I must say something about her loss, and she would begin to cry.

When she looked up, Mrs. Patrick was smiling. "I was just sitting here thinking," she said. "Henry had such fun that day. Frances, do you remember the day we flew the kites?"

~ Saturday Night in the ~ Georgia Countryside

J. L. HERRING

We talk about the three-day weekend and the thirty-hour workweek these days. Home offices are growing at a rapid rate. But one thing never seems to change—Saturday night. Or has it? Whatever happened to Saturday night as a family night? It seems to have become a past tradition, as this 1918 memory of Saturday nights in the country of over a century ago recalls.

Forty years ago, and Saturday night.

The work for the week is done, supper is over, and the family is grouped around the blazing fire of resinous pine.

During the afternoon, the Boy has "knocked off" to walk the mile to the village post office and bring the weekly paper, arrived that morning by horseback carrier from the town twenty miles away.

In the rocking-chair in the chimney corner the Father sits, where the firelight falls on the paper to best advantage. He reads aloud, thus all sharing alike in the treasured store.

In front, the Mother with busy fingers, improves the time while listening to the news, for knitting neither interferes with hearing, comment nor conversation.

At the other chimney corner the Boy lazily reclines. His task is to keep the fire going, and as each stick of wood is the product of his own hard labor, none is wasted.

The newspaper is a treasure chest of eight compartments, each filled with nuggets or jewels that come to light as the page is turned. There was the serial story of absorbing interest; we could with difficulty wait for the week to pass to hear it slowly unfold plot and counterplot and breath-stifling event. Then the news of the week; not so much news as we have now, for there were no great news-gathering organizations and the telegraph was still one of the world's wonders, but a little politics, a few murders, very little sensation and no yellow journalism. Papers were better edited then, we think; gave more space and time to literary efforts, and little to wire news. Perhaps they were better; we do not know; certainly they were then, as they are now, and will be tomorrow, mirrors reflecting the communities and the world in which they were published.

How well is remembered the scent of the fresh ink as the wrapper was torn off and the paper unfolded! Perhaps there the Boy got the taste for the newspaper in his blood, which later developed into an incurable disease—or affliction, according to the viewpoint.

From time to time the Reader paused, as some item of more than usual interest was read, and the family joined in discussing it. The family group broke up only when there was no more paper to read and the hour was so late that we were glad the next day was Sunday and early rising not compulsory.

The days are gone, the pine is gone, there is no vestige left of the home that sheltered the three. The Mother's busy hands are folded and at rest; the eyes of the Reader grew dim and sightless, the voice now is only a memory; of the group the Boy alone is left and much that was with him then is forever gone.

But green as the hillsides of the days of youth; sacred as the memories of the hallowed dead; treasured as jewels in the storehouse of life, is the recollection of the Saturday night of long ago; for to the eyes of the mind it is as close as yesterday.

If you are near fifty, what did the Saturday night of forty years ago bring you?

⁓ *Bringing Back the Fun* ⁓

Beth Tolman and Ralph Page

Still, people do remember those times and seem unwilling to let the memory of them go. This piece was written in the late 1940s. I think about it every time I turn on TV and pause on the Nashville Network and smile (and shuffle my feet) while watching everyone do the Texas two-step.

Country dances are just mere names now, along with the old-time tin peddler, red flannel ankle-lengths, and dried apples in the attic. However, in a few isolated "islands" dotted over the country the dances have been actually fanned back into life. And in the remoter hillbilly sections the dances are probably still being done to the tune of a sawing fiddle or two for want of anything more available. In still other places is found a merging of a town and country, young and old, modern and antique—examples of true democracy. For over the thresholds of these town halls you are always the equal of you. For instance, old Mrs. Velvet Bustle of New York City and Palm Beach trips lightly with Ben Bumpkin and loves it. Old man Hayseed never fails to date with Deborah Deb from the city in a lithesome basket quadrille. Of course, when imported people first began to sprinkle the sets with their untutored selves, there was resentment. But as old-timers realized that the jigs were changing to fall in with the more speedy times, they opened up their attitudes and thankfully realized the country dance was being carried along by coming generations— and not being hurtled to an undeserving grave.

Back Road Beauty

Part of the fun of getting off the interstate and pulling onto the two-lane roads that take you along mountain streets, along railroad tracks, and up to a country store in every state are those unique, all-American landmarks that vary from region to region. Wallace Nutting, the turn-of-the-century Congregationalist minister turned writer, photographer, and antiques expert, was so taken by the beauty of our land and the specialness of the people that he wrote a series of books about the states—Virginia Beautiful, Vermont Beautiful, *and so on. In* Pennsylvania Beautiful *he called our attention to the "barn art"—the tradition of decorating farm building to liven up the countryside. Nutting and others have tried to associate these symbols with various superstitions, but this is all circumspect. If you insist upon making a connection between the designs, try these furnished by Linda Banis of the Reading and Berks County {Pennsylvania} Visitors Bureau.*

Scallop border	Tranquillity, smooth sailing
Closed circle border	Eternity
Triangle	Trinity
Four-pointed star	Good luck
Five pointed star	Star of Bethlehem, Epiphany, protection from evil, the five senses, good luck
Double five-pointed star	Morning star, sun, and light
Six-lobed petals (open tulip)	Faith, fertility, safety
Six-pointed star	Good luck, good fortune, love star, perfect marriage, protection from lightning
Eight-pointed star	Perseverance
Twelve-pointed star	Rationalism and justice
Four raindrops	Adequate rain throughout the four seasons
Wagon-spoke design	Wheel of fortune

～ You've Got a History Behind You ～

*BETTY HODGES

Why traditions? Because, as journalist Betty Hodges discovered, we won't let them die. They bring us together for laughter, food, memories, company, and sharing.

For years the retirees of the Stemming Department of the American Tobacco Company in Durham, North Carolina, largely female, though a few males were hired to operate the machinery, held an annual reunion in the dining hall of Oldham Towers, a housing facility where many of them lived. They'd raise their voices in the old songs they'd used to lighten the load of their toil, read a little Scripture, share a poem or two mocking their state as senior citizens, and eventually they'd spread a feast they'd brought to share. But mostly, they remembered.

" 'Sing while I'm here,' " the soloist sang out, and the group seated around the tables took up the refrain.

" 'Sing while I'm here, in Jesus' name, hallelujah,' " they chimed in.

"Once again," urged the soloist, and when the song was over, Mrs. Roxie McCullough took to the podium in the Memorial Center at Oldham Towers.

"It was a long time ago when we heard that at the stemmery," she said.

"Yes, yes," those in the crowd answered.

Former workers in the Stemming Department of the old American Tobacco Company, they'd gathered at Oldham for a reunion.

First there was the program Mrs. McCullough had arranged and at its end there would be a feast. A long table at one end of the room was already laden with dishes participants had brought—fried chicken, potato salad, bowls of turnip greens, and cakes of all descriptions. From the adjacent kitchen there was the promising odor of frying fish, and several women were filling plastic cups with ice, setting them by the big three-liter bottles of soft drinks.

"You come eat with us," Mrs. McCullough had told a guest. "I've cooked up a lot of food and I want you to help eat it."

After that first song Mrs. Betty Durham read the Scripture, the ageless verses from Ecclesiastes. " 'To everything there is a season and a time to every purpose under the heaven: A time to be born, and a time to die. . . .' "

Mrs. Colleen Chambers, summoned for a prayer, gave thanks for blessing after blessing, a low, rhythmic murmur of affirmation rising like a Greek chorus from the bowed heads all around her.

There were more songs, "Leaning on the Everlasting Arm," "When I Hear I Will Answer," "Just for a Little Talk with Jesus," "Love Lifted Me," "The Little Wooden Church on the Hill," "May the Work I've Done Speak For Me."

Mrs. Helen Mitchell brought her group. Earl Artis and Mrs. Lucille Norris both sang solos.

When Mrs. Alice Williams raised her voice to the tune of "I'm So Glad That Jesus Knows," the group chimed in in full force. Mrs. McCullough called out her approval: "We're getting there now! Doesn't that take you back? That's the kind of thing we did back then."

And there were some poems, some funny rhymes laughing at the aches and pains of aging from Mrs. Lucille Walker, some homespun verses of encouragement and hope from Mrs. DeNina Austin.

Then it was time to eat and Mrs. Ora McDaniels asked the blessing, adhering to Mrs. McCullough's admonishment not to give "any long prayer."

After that the line formed at the foot of the long table, with diabetics urged to go first.

Over the fried fish and chicken, the potato salad, turnip greens, and fried corn bread patties, they talked about the old days at the stemmery.

Mrs. McCullough recalled the days when, as a teenager, she'd gotten her first job at the stemmery.

"It was the first little money I made," she said. "The eight years I spent at the American Tobacco Company are the years I grew up. There were people I worked with that helped me, and I'll never forget them."

"You got a history behind you," said W. P. Edwards. "Think about those people who worked in the stemmery and what you did with your money that helped this city grow."

"He was a union man," Mrs. McCullough said. "Mr. Edwards helped make our working conditions better. It was so hot in the stemmery, but he got us fans and a cafeteria to eat in. The union helped us out."

Bobby Lipscomb, one of the vocalists, couldn't stay for lunch, but he took time to identify himself.

"My daddy was Haywood Lipscomb," was the answer.

Through it all, Mrs. McCullough moved from table to table, sharing a picture she said, "Mr. Penn, a foreman, had taken in the '30s," a snapshot she'd had enlarged. "That man," she said, "he'd jump from machine to machine; it was something to see." "That's Lily Mae Harris, there in the front," she said. "And that's my back right there, see?"

The picture passed from hand to hand, and one after another they'd nod their heads, looking into the past on the three-by-five piece of paper in front of them.

"Yes, yes, that's it," they murmured, and passed the picture on.

"I want it back, now," Mrs. McCullough reminded them. "Mr. Penn took that picture. I can see him now, jumping from machine to machine. That was a long time ago."

～ ～

This reunion was held in 1993, and the numbers were already dwindling. Mrs. McCullough, the group's traditional organizer, reports that after the 1995 gathering, when the guests outnumbered the original stemmery workers, she'd decided that would be their swan song.

"But I don't know," she added after a moment's thought. "Some of them are asking me to have another one, that the people here at Oldham enjoy it and want us to keep on doing it. We'll see; you can't ever tell."

The tradition continues . . .

PART FOUR

AN AMERICAN TRADITION: REMEMBERING OUR HERITAGE

CHAPTER 22

Americans All

TO REMEMBER OUR FOREFATHERS

~ *Great Men* ~

RALPH WALDO EMERSON

Not gold, but only man can make
A people great and strong;
Men who, for truth and honor's sake,
Stand fast and suffer long.

Brave men who work while others sleep,
Who dare while others fly—
They build a nation's pillars deep
And lift them to the sky.

America, the world's melting pot, is truly the greatest country in history. Here, as in no other land, men and women of all faiths, cultures, races, beliefs, and economic and social backgrounds have lived, worked, worshiped, and raised families since the sixteenth century. Few people seem to realize that the very first settlers came here just as the medieval era in history was coming to an end. The conquistadores who settled Florida still wore helmets and breastplates of metal. The Puritans in New England and the Cavaliers in Virginia lived in thatch-roofed huts. Over the years, separately at first, and then together, these pioneers and founding fathers, who'd had so many differences in Europe, formed the foundation for the country we have become. Now, as we approach yet another century, the twenty-first century, America is still looked upon by the world as the land of the free and the home of the brave.

As this book comes to a close, it is good to take a last look at the very character of the people who have brought us to this place in time. These closing words, strong and clear, come from the great and the small alike, from poets and leaders, everyday citizens and children. Many of these traditions come from holiday seasons and religious celebrations. Many of them are newly brought to America by immigrating families. They all celebrate life, laughter, and sharing. They remind us that if we will take the time to remember the best of the past, we will continue to be the hope of the future.

⤙ The Tradition of Democracy ⤙

MARGARET THATCHER

It may seem strange to include in these pages remarks made by Margaret Thatcher, the former British prime minister, excerpted from an address she gave in Michigan at Hillsdale College's Center for Constructive Alternatives in the fall of 1994. Although we chose to break away from Great Britain in 1776 and fought them in the Revolutionary War, the British people are now our most loyal ally. Margaret Thatcher explains in this wonderful speech why the course that led America away from Great Britain is now the guiding course for the rest of the free world. If you need some inspiration, or if you wonder why it's great to be an American, look no further and read on!

History has taught us that freedom cannot long survive unless it is based on moral foundations. The American founding bears ample witness to this fact. America has become the most powerful nation in history, yet she uses her power not for territorial expansion but to perpetuate freedom and justice throughout the world.

For over two centuries, Americans have held fast to their belief in freedom for all men—a belief that springs from their spiritual heritage. John Adams, second president of the United States, wrote in 1789, "Our Constitution was designed only for a moral and religious people. It is wholly inadequate for the government of any other." That was an astonishing thing to say, but it was true.

What kind of people built America and thus prompted Adams to make such a statement? Sadly, too many people, especially young people, have a hard time answering that question. They know little of their own history. (This is also true in Great Britain.) But America's is a very distinguished history, nonetheless, and it has important lessons to teach us regarding the necessity of moral foundations.

John Winthrop, who led the Great Migration to America in the early 17th century and who helped found the Massachusetts Bay Colony, declared, "We shall be a City upon a Hill." On the voyage to the New World, he told the members of his company that they must rise to their responsibilities and learn to live as God intended men should live: in charity, love, and cooperation with one another. Most of the early colonists were infused with the same spirit, and they tried to live in accord with a Biblical ethic. They felt they weren't able to do so in Great Britain or elsewhere in Europe. Some of them were Protestant, and some were Catholic; it didn't matter. What mattered was that they did not feel they had the liberty to worship freely and, therefore, to live freely, at home. With enormous courage, the first American colonists set out on a perilous journey to an unknown land—without government subsidies and not in order to amass fortunes but to fulfill their faith.

Christianity is based on the belief in a single God as evolved from Judaism. Most important of all, the faith of America's founders affirmed the sanctity of each individual. Every human life—man or woman, child or adult, commoner or aristocrat, rich or poor—was equal in the eyes of the Lord. It also affirmed the responsibility of each individual.

This was not a faith that allowed people to do whatever they wished, regardless of the consequences. The Ten Commandments, the injunction of Moses ("Look after your neighbor as yourself"), the Sermon on the Mount, and the Golden Rule made Americans feel precious—and also accountable—for the way in which they used their God-given talents. Thus they shared a deep sense of obligation to one another. And, as the years passed, they not only formed strong communities but also devised laws that would protect individual freedom—laws that would eventually be enshrined in the Declaration of Independence and the U.S. Constitution. . . .

Sir Edward Gibbon (1737–1794), author of *The Decline and Fall of the Roman Empire*, wrote tellingly of the collapse of Athens, which was the birthplace of democracy. He judged that, in the end, more than they wanted freedom, the Athenians wanted security. Yet they lost everything—security, comfort, and freedom. This was because they wanted not to give to society, but for society to give to them. The freedom they were seeking was freedom *from* responsibility. It is no wonder, then, that they ceased to be free. In the modern world, we should recall the Athenians' dire fate whenever we confront demands for increased state paternalism. . . .

So long as freedom, that is, freedom *with* responsibility, is grounded in morality and religion, it will last far longer than the kind that is grounded only in abstract, philosophical notions. Of course, many foes of morality and religion have attempted to argue that new scientific discoveries make belief in God obsolete, but what they actually demonstrate is the remarkable and unique nature of man and the universe. It is not hard to believe that these gifts were given by a divine Creator, who alone can unlock the secrets of existence.

The most important problems we have to tackle today are the problems, ultimately, having to do with the moral foundations of society. There are people who eagerly accept their own freedom but do not respect the freedom of others—they, like the Athenians, want freedom from responsibility. But if they accept freedom for themselves, they must respect the freedom of others. If they expect to go about their business unhindered and to be protected from violence, they must not hinder the business of or do violence to others.

They would do well to look at what has happened to societies without moral foundations. Accepting no laws but the laws of force, these societies have been ruled by totalitarian ideologies like Nazism, fascism, and communism, which do not spring from the general populace, but are imposed on it by intellectual elites.

It was two members of such an elite, Marx and Lenin, who conceived of "dialectical materialism," the basic doctrine of communism. It robs people of all freedom, from freedom of worship to freedom of ownership. Marx and Lenin desired to substitute their will not only for all individual will but for God's will. They wanted to plan *everything,* in short, they wanted to become gods. Theirs was a breathtakingly arrogant creed, and it denied above all else the sanctity of human life. . . .

Communism denied all that the Judeo-Christian tradition taught about individual worth, human dignity, and moral responsibility. It was not surprising that it collapsed after a relatively brief existence. It could not survive more than a few generations because it denied human nature, which is fundamentally moral and spiritual.

The West began to fight the moral battle against communism in earnest in the 1980s, and it was our resolve—combined with the spiritual strength of the people suffering under the system who finally said, "Enough!"—that helped restore freedom in Eastern Europe and the Soviet Union—the freedom to worship, speak, associate, vote, establish political parties, start businesses, own property, and much more. If communism had been a creed with moral foundations, it might have survived, but it was not, and it simply could not sustain itself in a world that had such shining examples of freedom, namely, America and Great Britain.

It is important to understand that the moral foundations of a society do not extend only to its political system; they must extend to its economic system as well. America's commitment to capitalism is unquestionably the best example of this principle. Capitalism is not, contrary to what those on the Left have tried to argue, an amoral system based on selfishness, greed, and exploitation. It is a moral system based on a Biblical ethic. There is no other comparable system that has raised the standard of living for millions of people, created vast new wealth and resources, or inspired so many beneficial innovations and technologies.

The wonderful thing about capitalism is that it does not discriminate against the poor, as has been so often charged; indeed, it is the only economic system that raises the poor out of poverty. Capitalism also allows nations that are not rich in natural resources to prosper. If resources were the key to wealth, the richest country in the world would be Russia, because it has abundant supplies of everything from oil, gas, platinum, gold, silver, aluminum, and copper to timber, water, wildlife, and fertile soil.

Why isn't Russia the wealthiest country in the world? Why aren't other resource-rich countries in the Third World at the top of the list? It is because their governments deny citizens the liberty to use their God-given talents. Man's greatest resource is himself, but he must be free to use that resource.

Democracy is never mentioned in the Bible. When people are gathered together, whether as families, communities, or nations, their purpose is not to ascertain the will of the majority, but the will of the Holy Spirit. Nevertheless, I am an enthusiast of democracy because it is about more than the will of the majority. If it were only about the will of the majority, it would be the right of the majority to oppress the minority. The American Declaration of Independence and the Constitution make it clear that this is not the case. There are certain rights that are human rights and which no government can displace. And when it comes to how you Americans exercise your rights under democracy, your hearts seem to be touched by something greater than yourselves. Your role in democracy does not end when you cast your vote in an election. It applies daily; the standards and values that are the moral foundations of society are also the foundations of your lives.

Democracy is essential to preserving freedom. As Lord Acton reminded us, "Power tends to corrupt, and absolute power corrupts absolutely." If no individual can be trusted with power indefinitely, it is even more true that no government can be. It has to be checked, and the best way of doing so is through the will of the majority, bearing in mind that this will can never be a substitute for individual human rights. . . .

Free societies demand more care and devotion than any others. They are, moreover, the only societies with moral foundations, and those foundations are evident in their political, economic, legal, cultural, and, most importantly, spiritual life.

We who are living in the West today are fortunate. Freedom has been bequeathed to us. We have not had to carve it out of nothing; we have not had to pay for it with our lives. Others before us have done so. But it would be a grave mistake to think that freedom requires nothing of us. Each of us has to earn freedom anew in order to possess it. We do so not just for our own sake, but for the sake of our children, so that they may build a better future that will sustain over the wider world the responsibilities and blessings of freedom.

The Children Speak

Today I would like to express something that is very dear to me. It is a tradition that my family and our culture celebrate. The name of my culture is Islam, and the Islamic name for this tradition is Eid. It is similar to the Christian celebration of Christmas. We celebrate Eid on the full moon of April. On Eid we wake up at five o'clock in the morning to attend an Islamic church and to pray to Allah. Afterward, we eat a light breakfast and exchange gifts. At lunchtime, my family eats foods that originated from our home country of Bangladesh. Finally, around six in the evening, we go outside and pray to Allah again and observe the full moon. This day has always been and will forever be special to my family and me.

Ahmed M. Khan, elementary school

Id ul-Fitr is a religious holiday that our Muslim family celebrates at the end of month of Ramadan based on the lunar year. Ramadan is the ninth month of the Muslim year and is a period when devout Muslims fast. Fasting begins at daybreak and ends at sunset. We fast because we are told to realize the hardship of needy and poor people. We also read the Qur'an [Koran], a sacred book that we live by. Muslims are happy and thankful at Id, which is similar to the feeling Christians have at Easter. Because of the large gathering, Id prayers are offered in a large mosque. All of our family goes to Raleigh, North Carolina, to pray, since there is no mosque in Burlington. After prayer and a sermon, we greet each other with *"Eid Mubarak,"* which means "Happy Eid." We then go to the homes of friends and relatives to visit, eat lunch, and exchange gifts, which makes it a little like Christmas for Muslim children. Going to Raleigh for Id-ul-Fitr is a family tradition that I always enjoy.

Ali Nasir Chhotani, elementary school

One of the most treasured family traditions for my family is the Italian Christmas. It is celebrated on Christmas Eve. All the family gathers together for good food and fun. This tradition is very special to my family.

This tradition goes back to my great-grandmother Riccardo from Italy. When she came over to the United States, she lived in northeastern Pennsylvania. She had a very large family of eight children—seven girls, one boy. They were a very close family.

The dinner was very religious. Being Catholic, no meat was served, they would only eat seven fishes. They are: bacula, catfish, anchovy (sauce), shrimp, smelts, squid and eel. Also, they ate assorted kinds of pasta, fruits and roasted chestnuts.

After dinner, the family would exchange presents. A "Santa Claus" would come and give out candy for the children. It was always fun for the children.

This tradition is very important to our family today and one day I hope I will be able to pass it on to my children. It is a great way to get the family together once a year.

Matthew Paul Schmidt, elementary school

Vietnamese New Year is special. On New Year's Day, everyone in my family dresses up in new clothes and wears new shoes. Then my brother and I bow to our parents and wish them lots of luck and lots of money in the New Year. Our parents give us a red envelope with money inside. My brother and I also wish our grandma, grandpa, aunts and uncles a good new year.

After that we go to the New Year's fair. At the fair, we watch the dragon dance. We also watch the firecrackers exploding. At night, we have a New Year's party at our grandma's house. We eat a lot of good food. Then we play with our cousins. When it is getting late, we go back home and go to sleep. I like New Year's because it is fun and special.

Jimmy Nguyen, elementary school

— ◆ —

Hooray! It is the Chinese New Year. I am always the only one to get up first and go to the bathroom. When everyone is ready, we set off to my grandpa's house for a traditional morning gathering. All my uncles and aunties were there, too, with us eating a vegetarian meal, then the lion dancer comes. It is believed that a long, long, time ago, a lion named "Nei" would come and ruin the village during New Year, but it was afraid of anything red and deafening noise.

When people in ancient China knew this, they immediately wore red clothes, decorated all the surroundings red, and prepared a lot of thunderous firecrackers. At the moment, the lion came and was defeated by the villagers. Therewith, everyone wore red and played with firecrackers.

While the lion-dancers were dancing in front of my grandpa's house, the lion-dancer would take the lettuce tied with a red packet called "Huang Boa" that contained money in it which were hooked on the doorway. Every elder gave the children "Huang Boa," too.

This tradition is exciting, delighting and important to the Asian-Chinese people for centuries. I am looking forward for another Chinese New Year.

Wee Guan Goh, middle school

— ◆ —

Chinese New Year is in February and is celebrated for three days.

Aunts, uncles, cousins and my family go to Grandma's house. Everyone greets one another and talks. My aunts and mom go into the kitchen and start cooking.

We eat different kinds of delicious Chinese foods: pork, chicken, sea cucumbers, black mushrooms, seafood and fish. Each food has a different meaning. Fish means a successful year. Adults usually drink wine, champagne, or hot tea. Dessert is Chinese egg cakes, oranges, and sweet rice cakes. Oranges mean having a good year.

After dinner is my favorite part. Kids start exchanging red envelopes which contain money.

No one sleeps. Men stay up all night playing different card games such as Chinese poker. Women drink tea and chat. Smaller kids run around and play games, screaming and yelling. Grandma's house sounds like a madhouse. Smaller kids don't have the stamina to stay up all night.

On New Year's, everybody awakes early, the women wear dresses, this part I don't like because it makes me feel uncomfortable.

Breakfast is simple, like rice soup.

After breakfast, friends come and we exchange little red envelopes. The whole house sounds like a mall. Everybody talks at once. My cousins run around acting like idiots.

For dinner, we have what we had last night. Adults eat first. Then kids eat.

The day is over. Everyone leaves happy and hopes for a great year.

Chonly Wang, middle school

⁃ ⁃

My family tradition is that we have to learn to speak my native language, which is Greek. We start by learning simple words like "no," "yes," "earth," "restaurant," and "salad." These words are easy to pronounce—for example, "yes" is *"ne,"* and "earth" is *"gey."*

At home when my dad and grandpa speak Greek, we come in and talk with them. If I did not learn to speak Greek, I could not understand my dad and grandpa talk. When the Greek festival comes, we have to do a Greek dance on the stage. Understanding Greek helps us follow directions and know what the audience is saying and to encourage us. When we get a little older, we will start going to Greek school two afternoons a week and learn more Greek, including writing and reading Greek, and about Greek traditions that we are trying to keep alive.

Tommy Pistolis, Jr., middle school

⁃ ⁃

As I think of all my family's traditions, the corny, the sentimental, and even the ridiculous ones, all of the memories come flooding back into my mind. Although the Benavidez family has many traditions, one just seems to stand out, the annual tamale making. For as long as I can remember, the Benavidez family has always started their Christmas season with the traditional tamale making. The tree may have been trimmed, the lights could have been on the house, and the Christmas shopping could have been completed, but it never felt like Christmas until those 50 dozen little spicy tamales were made. Each year at least 50 people would gather at my grandparents' house to make the main part of our Christmas dinner. Aunts, uncles, cousins, great-grandparents, grandchildren, young and old would all take part. They would make an assembly line around the long tables filled with 50 pounds of masa (cornmeal), roast beef, roast pork, roast chicken, and red chilies for the sauce. My grandmother would supervise each creator to make sure each tamale was perfect.

Families all have their own traditions, but I like to think that our Christmas tradition takes on a look all of its own. It is such a heart-warming feeling to know that each member of our large family cares and honors this tamale making so much that they have each made it a timeless tradition.

Elizabeth Benavidez, high school

One of the most influential traditions in my family has been carried on for generations. This is a Christmas Eve dinner, which is a very unique and special time for us all. Because my father's family is of Swedish descent, it is customary for my family to prepare a Smorgasbord, which is a Swedish feast with a large variety of dishes. This meal is always eaten in my family's dining room, which these days is rare because of lack of time. There are also traditions within this feast, such as the type of food prepared. Some of the dishes are rather ordinary, while some are definitely not foods that you would find in the frozen food section at the supermarket. A few examples are Swedish meatballs (which are made according to a recipe centuries old) and Swedish Limpa Bread, which happen to be two of my favorites. This tradition was carried out by my great-grandmother and still is carried out by my grandparents. Also, an antique tablecloth is always placed on the dining room table. This tablecloth was made by my great-grandmother while she was coming from Sweden to America on a ship much like the *Mayflower.*

Curtis Ostrom, middle school

Doughnut Day is a special, unique day for my family. Doughnut Day is always the day before Ash Wednesday.

It starts the night before Doughnut Day. My mother prepares the dough from a special recipe containing mashed potatoes that has been handed down from generation to generation. Every member of my family receives a strip of rolled-out dough. First the dough is sliced out into three sections. We then braid the dough, similar to braiding hair. My family also makes traditional doughnuts. Overnight the dough shapes rise. When I wake up in the morning, I smell the aroma of the mouthwatering dough. When I rush downstairs and into the kitchen, I see what looks like a Santa's Workshop. Instead of elves constructing toys, it's my mother immersing the homemade doughnuts in the sizzling oil. I select my braid and place it in the bag full of snow white powdered sugar. I then devour the scrumptious pastry.

I believe Doughnut Day was brought to America by the Germans immigrating to Pennsylvania. Their holiday of Faschnacht is when they eat all of their sweet foods before the fast of Lent.

JoAnn Bower, elementary school

My father is Puerto Rican. His family customs and those of my mother, an Anglo, have merged for some rather unusual holiday traditions.

One of my favorite traditions occurs on New Year's Day. In Puerto Rico, January 1 is equivalent to the American April Fool's Day. It is called Año "Viejo." The day begins with a series of outrageous lies that you plan all year long. For instance, an elderly maiden aunt may say that she has just learned that she is expecting a child. Telephone calls are placed to family members trying to convince them that the tall tales are true. The calls always end with wishes for a *feliz año nuevo.*

At dinner the night of January 1st, my mother's family tradition, one which she says has been done for generations, takes place at the table. Everyone must tell something good that the old year brought them. Then they must make a wish for the new year, not for themselves but for everyone seated at the table. This continues until everyone has had a turn.

After grace, the oldest family member present calls the names of all loved ones and friends who died during the old year.

The best part comes now—the food. Every year black-eyed peas are on the menu. In the serving bowl with the peas my mother puts a shiny new penny and covers it with the peas. The person who serves himself the penny will receive "luck" in the new year.

My New Year's Day is a combination of frivolity, somber memories, and hopes for the New Year.

Joshua H. Rivera, middle school

Family traditions, whether everyday ones or once-a-year, are what makes families unique and special. Since my father is from Greece, we have one special tradition which we observe each Easter in honor of the resurrection of Jesus. On Easter Sunday, all of my family gathers at our house. The children play outside, and the adults converse among themselves while the lamb is roasting over the charcoal. When it is time to eat, we all wash up carefully and sit at our special tables—one

An American Tradition: Remembering Our Heritage 625

for the children and one for the adults. Then we all bow our heads and say a blessing, first in Greek and then in English. Everyone enjoys a grand meal! Following the dinner is a very unusual tradition—the breaking of the eggs. My grandmother has dyed many colorful eggs for the occasion. Everyone takes an egg and then selects another person. Each person hits the other's egg with his own, but not too hard. The person whose egg cracks, loses. I'm not really sure why we do this, but it's fun anyway. When all of the food is eaten and all of the eggs are broken, people gradually leave. Easter is a fun holiday and a great tradition for my family.

Nicholas Bakatsias, middle school

La Befana Day [Epiphany] is always a special day at my house. It is a family time for us. In case you're wondering, La Befana Day is a holiday that comes from Italy, like my dad. It is in January and it's sort of like Christmas. La Befana, a nice old lady, brings gifts (like Santa) on January 6.

La Befana Day really begins at night. My sister and I put out our shoes and leave a note and something tasty for La Befana to eat. Then we scurry off to bed. In the morning our shoes are stuffed with nuts, hard candy, and toys.

I like La Befana Day because it makes me feel close to my family. I get a warm feeling around me, even though it is really very cold. I feel lucky to be able to celebrate La Befana Day because it makes the spirit of Christmas last that much longer.

Kathryn Pezzi, elementary school

There are many family traditions that I take part in each year. My favorite out of all these traditions is Raksha Bandhan.

Raksha Bandhan is a tradition from the Hindu religion. Raksha Bandhan takes place every year in August. Raksha Bandhan means protection of relationship between brother and sister. This tradition only happens if there is at least one brother and one sister. On this day the brother and sister pray for strong relationships, and that their love will always flourish. The sister usually covers her head for good luck and the brother wears white clothing.

Last year in August, I participated in Raksha Bandhan. I woke in the morning, took a shower and got dressed in my best clothes. Then, my sister and I prayed for two hours. After that, my sister tied a string around my right wrist to symbolize our love. She also put some Indian sweetdish in my mouth. The sweetdish is for good luck. In return I gave my sister a gift and took her out to eat for lunch. This tradition helps us keep our bond strong and our brother and sister love eternal.

Anuj Jaggi, high school

If my family could not come to an agreement, Christmastime could be very confusing, because my mom is German, my dad Italian, and all of us kids were born in the United States. Since, in each country, Christmas is celebrated differently we have to compromise a lot.

In Italy, or at least in Sicily, the part of Italy where my dad comes from, Christmas is not the biggest holiday of the year the way it is here. Instead, on the sixth of January, the day of the Three Holy Kings, children go from door to door and collect candy, almost like we do on Halloween. They have to sing a song, and then they are given candy.

In Germany, Nikolaus-day is on December 6th. On this day, Santa Claus visits children in their homes. When Nikolaus comes in, the children have to say a poem for him, and then he looks in his big book whether they have been good or bad throughout the year.

On Christmas Eve, the Christkind comes. On that evening, everyone has to stay out of the living room until they hear a little bell ring. Then they are allowed to go in and find a lit Christmas tree with presents underneath, which they can open right away.

It is difficult to combine these customs, so we have decided on our own special blend of Christmas. We usually get an Advent calendar, on which a door has to be opened every day, starting December 1st and ending on Christmas Eve. It is hard not to open all the doors at once, but that would take away from the anticipation which makes Christmas even more special.

We decorate our house just like all American families, but we don't start quite as early. Since in Germany the tree does not go up until December 24th, my mom always makes a compromise with us, when we don't want to be different from everybody else. So we usually put up the tree about two weeks before Christmas.

At our house Nikolaus does not come on December 6th. Since we live in the United States, he comes on the night before Christmas, and we leave cookies and milk for him just like all the other children in this country. My brothers always make sure that we don't have a fire burning in the wood stove, even if it is real cold.

When we wake up on Christmas morning, we usually wake up our parents and then go and open the presents. Only one year we opened all the presents before my parents were even up, and that's why we have no good photos of that year.

On Christmas Day we either invite friends to our house or we go to their house. All of our grandparents and uncles and aunts are in Europe, so we can't be with any of our family. Sometimes that's sad, but it is good to have friends who are in the same situation.

Although the customs of our house are a little mixed up, I think that this way we can have the best of all. We can have a little bit of Europe and a little bit of America.

Mariangela Mascali, middle school

Although I was born and raised in the United Kingdom and United States, my family origins are in the Gujarat Province of the country India. In India there are more than fifty languages. In Indian my mother's tongue is Gujarati. We celebrate so many festivals during this whole year, like holi, Dewali, navratre.

On Dewali, we cook good food, sweets and sit together, and eat, buy presents for children, and make fireworks. Our New Year starts from the next day. Dewali is very special in all Hindus' lives. That day, the god Rama came back from serving fourteen years in a forest and the whole town was very happy. They welcome Rama, his wife Sita and his brother Laeman. Since then we celebrate Dewali.

All our festivals have religious stories. And we enjoy them all.

Jayraj Sisodia, middle school

One of my family traditions is that when someone graduates from school or college, we cook a pig. The way we cook the pig is that we dig a hole in the ground in the shape of a rectangle big enough for the pig. Then we start a fire. After the fire is good and hot we put special rocks that are like charcoal and take in heat on the fire. Then after all the rocks that are lava rocks turn white, we make the rocks flat and let them get hotter. While the rocks are getting hotter, we wrap the pig—or in the way we say it in the Samoan Polynesian language, in "umu"—in wire, and we cover it with banana leaves. Next, we put it on the rocks and cover it with more rocks and then more leaves. Finally, we cover the pig with blankets to keep it very hot. To cook the pig, it takes about three to four hours and it tastes really good. That's the roasting of a "po'ua'a" for the graduate.

Daniel Brock To'oto'o, middle school

My family tradition involves the girls in my family. When you turn thirteen, you get a special Indian wrist band. The wrist band is blue with green, orange, and yellow triangles on it. It started with my great-great-grandma. She was a full-blooded Blackhawk Indian. She gave it to my great-grandma. Then it got passed down to my grandma and then to my mom. When I turn thirteen, she'll pass it down to me.

I like this tradition. When it gets passed to me, it will make me feel like a full-blooded Blackhawk Indian. When I get it, I will wear it all the time. When I get older and get married with kids, I will pass it down to them when they turn thirteen.

LaTisha T. Lewis, elementary school

I am a Meherrin Indian. Each year my tribe has a Pow-Wow. My mama, my sister, and I dress up in our native costumes. My daddy doesn't dress up but I don't know why! Sometimes we sell spider plants and candy to people who come to the Pow-Wow. My favorite thing to eat there is Indian Tacos. My mama reads to me about Indian life so I can understand the things we do and see at the Pow-Wow. When I grow up, I'm going to take my children to the Pow-Wow and read to them about Indian life. I'll teach them how to dance like Indians and other Indian things, just like I've been taught.

Ashley Mountain, elementary school

Have you ever wondered what Christmas in the jungle is like? I spent eight years living there, so I would know.

Since we spent eight Christmas seasons in Peru, South America, our family developed many special jungle traditions. Christmas trees don't grow in the jungle, so we had an artificial one. We set it up on the eighth of December, the last single holiday before Christmas break. On that day, we also decorated the house and yard.

Another Christmas tradition was to go swimming in the nearby lake on Christmas Day. This was so different from what you could do in the United States. It felt cool in the hot climate, and I enjoyed it.

One more Christmas tradition was to read the story of Jesus' birth out of the Book of Luke in the Bible. This helps us remember the true meaning of Christmas. We did this on Christmas morning before opening our presents.

Here in the U.S., I sincerely doubt that we will go swimming on Christmas, but we may develop new traditions much like yours. I hope we will continue all the other traditions we started in Peru, because I want to be reminded of what I call home.

Alex Lockhart, middle school

An American Tradition: Remembering Our Heritage 629

Today I celebrated Three Kings Day with my family. Three Kings Day is my favorite Puerto Rican tradition. Yesterday my family and I went to a field and gathered wet, moist grass and filled our shoe boxes halfway. When we got home we had a special dinner of pig, rice and beans, ham, corn, plantains and homemade buns. At bedtime, we put the shoe boxes next to our beds, said our prayers and fell asleep.

This morning I awoke first and looked at my shoe box. Most of the grass was gone. All of our boxes had lots of pennies, candies, and presents in them.

The reason we put grass in our boxes is so that the Three Kings' camels can eat something in their long travels to all the Puerto Rican families in the world. After the camels eat the grass, the Three Kings put presents in the boxes. Mom and Dad said to never, ever ask the Three Kings for certain presents. They know what to give us and always will. The good thing about not asking for certain presents is that I always get the best!

Erika Lynette Hernandez, middle school

I am trying hard to adjust to life in the United States, but being a foreign exchange student is not easy. As I reflect back, I think of my family in the northern part of Norway, near the Arctic Circle, where I lived for sixteen years.

In northern Norway there is no sun for months and it snows continuously. All people need light to survive. If they do not have light, they try to make light. As long as I can remember, my mom and I have tried to make this dark and awful time into something nice.

During winter we made big snowcastles, snowmen and igloos. What I remember most are my mom's small snowcastles, made of snowballs stacked on top of each other until they almost look like altars. Inside these small snowcastles, we put candles. They light up the night!

In my mind, this is a cherished and beautiful sight. It has also delighted our neighbors each year. Mom and I, in a dark and dreadful time, made light for our family and neighbors.

This is the tradition in my family I remember most. My mom and two sisters are still keeping this beautiful tradition alive, while I am here. I know when I am grown and have children, I will continue this tradition because it means so much to me.

Kristin Mörch, high school

My family is from Colombia, South America. We have a very special family tradition that we do on Christmas Eve.

On Christmas Eve, each person gets a glass jar filled with water in which to crack an egg. We keep the jar in the kitchen. The next morning we open our presents. We go into the kitchen to see what our egg looks like. The South American tradition is that what you see in the jar is what you'll see sometime in the future.

Last year the egg that was in my jar had formed into what looked like a bridge. I'm hoping that perhaps the bridge in the jar will be the Golden Gate Bridge in San Francisco. I would like to visit sunny California.

My mother also cracked an egg in the jar on Christmas Eve. Her egg took the shape of a palm tree. She went to beautiful Puerto Rico on her vacation.

My family tradition is fun for both children and adults. Why don't you try cracking an egg into a jar with water on Christmas Eve? Maybe you can see your future on Christmas morning.

Jaime Angarita, elementary school

~ *What Is an American?* ~

ST. JEAN DE CRÈVECOEUR, 1782

St. Jean de Crèvecœur, a Frenchman traveling in eighteenth-century America, was so impressed with this country's democracy that he became our most enthusiastic proponent. Were he traveling here today, Crèvecoeur would find more diversity, but hopefully he would recognize the same spirit and pride in America's people, be they Mayflower *descendants or recent arrivals to our shore.*

What attachment can a poor European emigrant have for a country where he had nothing? The knowledge of the language, the love of a few kindred as poor as himself, were the only cords that tied him: his country is now that which gives him land, bread, protection, and consequence. *Ubi panis ibi patria* [where there is bread, there is one's fatherland], is the motto of all emigrants. What then is the American, this new man? He is either an European, or the descendant of an European, hence that strange mixture of blood, which you'll find in no other country. I could point out to you a family whose grandfather was an Englishman, whose wife was Dutch, whose son married a French woman, and whose present four sons have now four wives of different nations. *He* is an American, who, leaving behind him all his ancient prejudices and manners, receives new ones from the new mode of life be has embraced, the new government he obeys, and the new rank he holds. He becomes an American by being received in the broad lap of our great *Alma Mater.* Here individuals of all nations are melted into a new race of men, whose labours and posterity will one day cause great changes in the world. Americans are the western pilgrims, who are carrying along with them that great mass of arts, sciences, vigour, and industry which began long since in the east; they will finish the great circle. The Americans were once scattered all over Europe; here they are incorporated into one of the finest systems of population which has ever appeared, and which will hereafter become distinct by the power of the different climates they inhabit. The American ought therefore to love this country much better than that wherein either he or his forefathers were born. Here the rewards of his industry follow with equal steps the progress of his labour; his labour is founded on the basis of nature, *self-interest;* can it want a stronger allurement? Wives and children, who before in vain demanded of him a morsel of bread, now, fat and frolicsome, gladly help their father to clear those fields whence exuberant crops are to arise to feed and to clothe them all; without any part being claimed, either by a despotic prince, a rich abbot, or a mighty lord. Here religion demands but little of him; a small voluntary salary to the minister, and gratitude to God; can he refuse these? The American is a new man, who acts upon new principles; he must therefore entertain new ideas, and form new opinions. From involuntary idleness, servile dependence, penury, and useless labour, he has passed to toils of a very different nature, re-warded by ample subsistence.—This is an American.

⸺ *I Am an American* ⸺

ELIAS LIEBERMAN

I am an American.
My father belongs to the Sons of the Revolution;
My mother, to the Colonial Dames.
One of my ancestors pitched tea overboard in Boston Harbor;
Another stood his ground with Warren;
Another hungered with Washington at Valley Forge.

My forefathers were America in the making:
They spoke in her council halls;
They died on her battle-fields;
They commanded her ships;
They cleared her forests.
Dawns reddened and paled.
Staunch hearts of mine beat fast at each new star
In the nation's flag.
Keen eyes of mine foresaw her greater glory:
The sweep of her seas,
The plenty of her plains,
The man-hives in her billion-wired cities.
Every drop of blood in me holds a heritage of patriotism.
I am proud of my past.
I am an AMERICAN.

I am an American.
My father was an atom of dust,
My mother a straw in the wind,
To His Serene Majesty.
One of my ancestors died in the mines of Siberia;
Another was crippled for life by twenty blows of the knout.
Another was killed defending his home during the massacres.
The history of my ancestors is a trail of blood
To the palace-gate of the Great White Czar.
But then the dream came—
The dream of America.
In the light of the Liberty torch
The atom of dust became a man
And the straw in the wind became a woman
For the first time.
"See," said my father, pointing to the flag that fluttered near,
"That flag of stars and stripes is yours;
It is the emblem of the promised land.
It means, my son, the hope of humanity.
Live for it—die for it!"
Under the open sky of my new country I swore to do so;
And every drop of blood in me will keep that vow.
I am proud of my future.
I am an AMERICAN.

The Tradition Continues

"Dear Emyl," my friend and author Margaret Maron wrote, "I know your book of traditions has probably gone to press, but when I was describing it to a friend, she said, 'You did tell her about your clothes-pins, didn't you?'"

That's what happened. Friends told friends, and people began to remember traditions they had forgotten. Though I've received and gathered enough traditions to last a lifetime, I know there are more. And I know other people are as curious and eager to learn about these traditions as I am. So I invite you to send your traditions on for me to share with others to

Emyl Jenkins
The Book of American Traditions
P.O. Box 2580
Danville, Virginia 24541-2580

About Margaret's clothespins . . . Her letter continues:

"Well, I didn't, and now it may be too late, but this might amuse you anyhow. It's our traditional icebreaker at large parties where lots of the people know us, but may not know each other. This is not for a formal party, mind you, but an outdoor reception, pig-picking, picnic, family reunion of distant cousins, et cetera. (Although . . . I was once at a pre-wedding patio party that was thrown to introduce the two families to each other and everyone was so stiff and ill-at-ease that I went and found my hostess's clothespin bag and commandeered a couple of mischievous kids.)

What you do is secretly give two or three kids a pocketful of spring-type clothespins and tell them to follow your lead. You pause to speak to someone and while patting him on the shoulder, you clip a clothespin to his jacket without his noticing. You do this to the hem of Aunt Maude's skirt, to Uncle Ed's collar, to the ribbons in Cousin Tiffany's hair. The kids quickly get the idea and think it's hysterically funny. Soon, a fourth of the unsuspecting guests are walking around with clothespins attached to various parts of their clothing and wondering why everyone else is laughing. The other three-quarters have caught on now and when someone approaches, they start laughing and back away and declare that no one will surprise *them*—and at that very instant, an opportunist behind them gently clips one on. Soon everyone's slapping at his back trying to see if there's a clothespin. Children are wide-eyed when they see stuffy old Aunt Maude impishly sneaking a clothespin onto their dad's shirtsleeve.

It's such a silly, harmless game that all stiffness melts away into laughter. (The two new families I mentioned above thought it was the best party they'd ever attended. Sharing laughter creates an immediate bond.)

And, I would add, sharing laughter is what traditions are all about.

SCIENCE AND TECHNOLOGY REVOLUTIONIZE OUR
LIVES, BUT MEMORY, TRADITION, AND MYTH FRAME
OUR RESPONSE.

Arthur M. Schlesinger, Jr.

Acknowledgments

Special thanks go out to libraries and used book stores across America for keeping the books of the past close at hand. Particular thanks are due to the researchers at the Wake County Public Library in Raleigh, North Carolina, who were so extraordinarily helpful and patient. Thank-you to my parents, Louise and Langdon Joslin, for passing along to me the tradition of a love of books and reading. A vast number of selections included in these pages I first read as a young girl and I never forgot them. Thank-you, Susan Urstadt, for your professional guidance and personal enthusiasm, but most of all, for good times—an unbeatable tradition. Annique Dunning, once again, you proved to be an invaluable researcher. To Sharon Squibb and my many friends at Crown, Chip Gibson, Amy Zelvin, Gail Shanks, Andy Martin, Ann Patty, Lara Webb, Patty Flynn, Kim Hertlein, Laurie Stark, and Betty Prashker, thank-you. Ken Sansone, how I miss you; I know you would have loved this book. Thank-you, also, each and every person who told me his or her favorite tradition through written and spoken words. How I wish I could have included each tradition —especially every child's tradition supplied so graciously by the International Reading Association and Mary Ellen Skidmore. Thank-you everyone—friends, strangers, laymen, and especially the talented editors and endearing writers of nonfiction and fiction who took the time to recount his or her own and others' turn-of-the-century memories and traditions, thereby preserving for us a rich heritage on which we can build the future, especially Robert P. Tristram Coffin, Edwin Mitchell, Francis Parkinson Keyes, Aileen Fisher, James J. Metcalfe, Edgar Guest, Dorothy Canfield Fisher, Gladys Taber, Maymie Krythe, Charles J. O'Fahery, Robert H. Schauffler, Douglas Malloch, Bertha L. Heilbron, James S. Tippett, Helen Ferris, Russell McLauchlin, Marjorie Kinnan Rawlings, Emma Gray Trigg, W. H. Davies, Kahlil Gibran, Bess Streeter Aldrich, Nancy Byrd Turner, Hartzell Spence, Eleanor Hammond, Nell Athern, Langston Hughes, Cecilia G. Gerson, Mary L. Curtis, James Coleman Harwood, Barry Lopez, Robert Malloy, Louis Untermeyer, Rabbi Philip S. Bernstein, Jadah Halevi, Samuel Adams, Ogden Nash, Elias Libermann, Dorothy Brown Thompson, David Grayson, and Sadie Rose Weilerstein. How difficult it was to select from their many writings to give a new generation just one sampling of their works, their words, and their wisdom. Thank-you to the busy and popular writers of today who took the time to pen new pieces, or gather from their earlier writings, the special selections included here, especially Margaret Maron, Jan Karon, Claire Whitcomb, Dee Hardie, Gerry Davis, Bea Cole, Betsy Mullen, Lynn Veacj Sandler, Nancy Ruhling, Clark Morphew, Liz Seymour, Hampton Sides, John Pierson, Susan Williams, Sharon Parquette Nimtz, Sharyn McCrumb, Lee Smith, Alexandra Stoddard, Susan Newman, Diane Mott Davidson, MariJo Moore, Elizabeth Daniels Squire, Susan Rose, Catherine Hamrick, Mary Alice Kellogg, Marda Burton, Betty Hodges, and thank-you, Dr. Maulana Karenga, for the creation of Kwanzaa, and Mary Landrum of Dallas, Texas, for bringing back the tradition of the cake pulls. Thank-you to the editors of *Victoria* magazine for first publishing my essays "Lessons My Mother Taught Me," "I Never Knew My Grandfather," and "Style and Grace," which led me to explore other traditions more fully.

Permissions

❧ ❧

Persistent and prudent care has been taken to receive permission to reprint the selections included in these pages and I gratefully acknowledge those who helped in the search and those who granted permission. I apologize for any oversights. In some cases where selections are not acknowledged the author has searched diligently to find sources and/or get permission to use them, but without success. Authors and sources included in these pages follow.

❧ ❧

"It's Thanksgiving Because It's Homecoming," Edith Blake and the estate of Henry Beetle Hough; "A Tradition Transplanted," Vincent B. Boris and *Vytis;* "Christmas Tree" by Aileen Fisher. Reprinted from *Christmas Plays and Programs* by Aileen Fisher. Copyright © 1959 by Aileen Fisher. Publisher: Plays, Inc.: Boston, Mass.; "The Irresistible Charm of Advent Cards," Shelia Stroup and the *Times Picayune;* "That Hardy Perennial, Christmas" and "Abenaki Clambake," from *Mainstays of Maine,* Jane M. Coffin and the estate of Robert P. Tristram Coffin; "The Christmas Pageant" and other selections by Maude Files Zimmer, Robert Speller & Sons, Publishers, Inc.; "My Library Fireplace" and other Frances Parkinson Keyes selections, Marion S. Chambon and the Beauregard-Keyes House, New Orleans, La.; "Up the Chimney," Ted Mitchell, the Thomas Wolfe Memorial, Asheville,

REMEMBERED JOYS ARE NEVER PAST.

James Montgomery